Lynda Page was born and brought up in ~~~~~~ eldest of four daughters, she left home at seventeen and has had a wide variety of office jobs. She lives in a village near Leicester. Her previous novels are also available from Headline, and have been highly praised:

'You'll be hooked from page one' *Woman's Realm*

'Cookson/Cox aficionados who've missed her should grab this. Romantic and gripping' *Peterborough Evening Telegraph*

'Filled with lively characters and compelling action' *Books*

'As always with Page, the text is rich in Leicester dialogue, there's a wealth of well-drawn characters and a happy ending' *Leicester Mercury*

'It's a story to grip you from the first page to the last' *Coventry Evening Telegraph*

# Now Or Never

## and

# In For A Penny

Lynda Page

**headline**

NOW OR NEVER first published in Great Britain in 1999
by HEADLINE BOOK PUBLISHING

IN FOR A PENNY first published in Great Britain in 2000
by HEADLINE BOOK PUBLISHING

First published in this omnibus edition in 2005
by HEADLINE BOOK PUBLISHING

A HEADLINE paperback

10 9 8 7 6 5 4 3 2 1

ISBN 0 7553 2666 0

Typeset in Times

Printed and bound in Great Britain by
Mackays of Chatham plc, Chatham, Kent

Headline's policy is to use papers that are natural, renewable and
recyclable products and made from wood grown in sustainable
forests. The logging and manufacturing processes are expected to
conform to the environmental regulations of the country of origin.

HEADLINE BOOK PUBLISHING
A division of Hodder Headline
338 Euston Road
London NW1 3BH

www.headline.co.uk
www.hodderheadline.com

# Now Or Never

For Karen and Jim Green

This book is dedicated to you both with my deep gratitude.
Someone was indeed looking after me the day we met.
Without you both, I would never have got through
such a traumatic time. Thank you.

Many thanks to Frank Gutteridge for his invaluable information on the life of a funeral director, and for a good night spent in the pub!

# Part One

# Chapter One

'It's not true . . . it can't be. You wouldn't do that. Tell me it's not true? Mother, *please*?'

Piercing steel-grey eyes glared coldly into the terror-stricken ones staring wildly up at her. Prising away the hands gripping the front of her coat, Harriet Ashman swung back her arm and smacked her daughter hard across the face. The sharp slap resounded loudly around the tiny, sparsely furnished bedroom. 'Control yourself, Maude. What must Mrs Baldicott be thinking? Get dressed and put your things together, we have a long journey to make.'

But the journey, or rather what awaited her at the end of it, was of no importance to Maddie Ashman. All that dwelt in her mind was the devastating news her mother had just so matter-of-factly delivered. Spinning on her bare feet, thick calico nightdress billowing, she fled from the bedroom.

Downstairs in the inviting kitchen of the shabby but cosy village cottage, elderly Mrs Baldicott, the woman who had taken Maddie into her home and cared for her for the last seven months, was sitting at a well-scrubbed pine table, hands clasped tightly, looking grave instead of her usual kindly, rosy-cheeked self.

As her guest burst into the room, Nancy Baldicott's head jerked up. Maddie had only to witness that grim expression to have the truth of her mother's announcement confirmed.

'Maddie, I'm . . . I'm so sorry,' Nancy stammered, half rising. 'Believe me, I'd no idea what yer mother had planned.'

'You could have stopped her!' shrieked Maddie. 'She's

*my* baby. Mine. Not my mother's.' Picking up her nightdress, exposing bare legs, she dashed to the door, wrenched up the latch and ran down the ash path, screaming. 'Where is she? Where's my baby?'

Panting hard, Nancy caught up with Maddie at the gate, managing to stop the hysterical young woman from charging through by forcing her plump body in front of it. 'Come back inside,' she pleaded, grabbing hold of Maddie's arm. 'Yer'll catch yer death.'

'I don't care,' she cried, wrenching herself free. 'I want my baby. Where is she?' She grabbed hold of Nancy's shoulders, gripping hard. 'You must know. You must.'

The old lady's conscience stabbed her painfully but it was more than her reputation was worth to divulge what she knew. Vigorously she shook her head. 'I don't, me duck.' She hated telling the lie but had no choice. 'All I know is that yer mam took her out in the garden. Bit of fresh air, she said, while you got yerself ready for the journey home. When she came back alone all she said was: "A woman with money's taken her. She'll be looked after proper." That's all she told me.'

Maddie was devastated. Her whole body shook, face crumpling as a torrent of tears gushed down her cheeks. Releasing her hold on the elderly woman, she gripped herself tight around her stomach, swaying backwards and forwards in distress. 'How could my mother do this, Mrs Baldicott? How could she?'

Nancy gnawed her bottom lip anxiously, unable to find any words of comfort. 'Maybe . . . maybe she felt it were best, in the circumstances.' Her voice was kind. Forcing a smile, she tenderly placed one fleshy arm around the young woman's shoulders, drawing her close. 'Maybe it is, Maddie love. It's no picnic bringing up a . . . a . . .'

Maddie stiffened, lifting her head to look Mrs Baldicott straight in the eye. 'Bastard,' she erupted. 'Awful word, isn't it, for a baby without a father?'

4

'I was going ter say, it ain't easy bringing up a baby on yer own.'

'But that's just it – I wasn't going to be on my own. My baby has a father. It was the truth I told when I said Josh was thrilled about it. He knows all about my mother and how she is, and although he didn't feel it right, he said it would be best for us to run away and get married and face whatever we had to after. He said his mother would find room for us until we got a place of our own. But I couldn't do it Josh's way. I felt my mother didn't deserve that. I tried to break the news to her, I did really, but she challenged me before I could gather the courage.'

Maddie's face, already ashen, paled even more at the memory. 'It was awful, Mrs Baldicott. I thought she'd be angry. I thought she'd throw me out, want nothing more to do with me.' She shook her head in bewilderment. 'But not this. Never did I think she'd do anything like this. She got me here under false pretences, Mrs Baldicott. It never crossed my mind that her intention was to leave me here without a penny to my name until after the baby was born. I never had a chance to see Josh and explain in person. To do anything. I can't understand why he hasn't answered my letters.' She wrung her hands so tight her knuckles shone white. 'Oh, Mrs Baldicott, what's he going to say when he finds out what my mother's done? That she's given our baby away.'

From the corner of her eye Nancy spotted two village women approaching on their way to the shops. Wanting to avoid being drawn into conversation, she nodded a quick greeting then turned her back to them, steering Maddie down the path. 'I . . . Look, lovey, I know what you told me about Josh. He sounds a fine young man, but . . . well . . . I didn't want to speak me mind while you were expecting, didn't want to upset yer like. But I do think it's odd he's never bin in touch at all while yer've bin here.'

Maddie stared at her in confusion. Mrs Baldicott was

5

only voicing what she herself had agonised over for the last seven months while their baby had grown within her. She could excuse Josh's failure to visit, the journey being a long one and fares hard to find once dues from his wage had been paid out. Despite all the reasons she had come up with for his failure to appear, though, even *she* couldn't excuse him for not replying to her letters. But at the moment it was not her chief worry. Her missing child was.

'I can't think about that now. I need to find my baby, then I can worry about Josh.' Maddie eyed the older woman beseechingly. 'You must have seen something, Mrs Baldicott? Who she handed my baby to?'

The other woman shrugged helplessly. 'I didn't.' And she was telling the truth. 'I watched for a minute from the window as yer mother walked down the path . . .' Her voice trailed off. She wanted to say what a lovely sight she had witnessed, seeing grandmother and granddaughter becoming acquainted. But she couldn't. It had upset her greatly to see the way Harriet Ashman was holding her grandchild. If she hadn't known better she would have thought the woman was carrying a dead dog. Harriet had held the child stiffly away from her, her long thin nose in the air, as if there was a nasty smell wafting up it.

Mortified, Mrs Baldicott had turned away and busied herself mashing a pot of tea to fortify her guests before their journey home. 'She told me she was teking the baby for a breath of fresh air. I didn't suspect nothing amiss, Maddie, nor have a clue what she was up to. This state of affairs is as much a shock to me as it is to you. Usually I'm told beforehand what's gonna happen, so I can help prepare the likes of yerself whilst yer with me, soften the blow, but yer mam kept her own counsel. She never said a word. Maddie love, the job I'm paid ter do is to care for the mothers during their confinement. Even if I'd known yer mam's intentions, I'd have had no right to interfere.'

'And it seems I've no rights either, doesn't it?' sobbed

Maddie. Her face clouded angrily. 'But my mother's not going to get away with this,' she whispered fiercely. 'She's not, Mrs Baldicott. All my life I've had to go along with her wishes. But this time I'm not going to. This time she's gone too far. I want my baby back and I'm going to get her.'

Moments later, teeth gritted in determination, fists clenched, Maddie was back in her bedroom.

Blandly ignoring her precipitate dash from the room, Harriet clipped shut a faded tapestry carpet bag and said matter-of-factly, 'You should have had all your packing done, Maude. It's not as though you didn't know I was coming to collect you today.' After buttoning up her black coat, she repositioned the black felt hat over the tightly pinned iron-grey bun on the top of her head. 'Now get a move on. I'll not be happy if we miss that train. I want to be back before tea-time.'

Momentarily, Maddie froze, taken off guard by her mother's seemingly complete disregard for this dreadful situation, one she herself had masterminded and executed without any regard at all for her daughter's feelings. A vision of her baby gave Maddie the strength to resist. 'Stop it, Mother! Stop acting like there's nothing wrong. I want to know what you've done with my baby? I want her back and I'll not leave this room until you tell me where she is.'

Setting her jaw, Harriet glared at her stonily. 'I will not have you addressing me in that tone of voice. I will not tolerate it. Neither will I put up with hysterical behaviour.'

Maddie stared at her, eyes ablaze. 'Hysterical behaviour? Mother, you calmly announce that you've *given my baby away.* How do you expect me to react? Do you expect me to be grateful?'

Harriet seemed momentarily shocked. This was the first time her usually even-tempered, easily manipulated daughter had ever stood up to her. Her assumption that Maddie would accept this situation without a fuss had been very wrong and Harriet wasn't prepared for it.

Abruptly turning away, she walked to the window and stared blindly out, anger swelling within her. If she wasn't careful Maude's stupidity could jeopardise all she herself had worked hard for, and Harriet wasn't about to permit that. She hadn't worked hard all these years, clawing her way out of poverty, to have her hard-won position snatched away from her. Especially not by her daughter.

Her mind drifted back in time and she saw herself as a child of seven, just days after her father had been killed in an accident on the farm where he worked. Straight after the funeral came the humiliating eviction from the dilapidated tied cottage where she had lived all her short life. No remorse had been expressed, no sympathy shown, except for a few kind words from fellow workers as her mother had struggled with the borrowed handcart in which were piled their few worldly possessions. The dispirited mother and child trudged the mud-rutted lanes to the nearest town of Market Harborough, a thriving place twenty or so miles from the far larger city of Leicester, not having a clue what would happen to them there.

Sitting on a grassy hill overlooking the town, Harriet's grieving mother, Hilda Grimble, had stared down silently for what seemed like hours. Eventually she turned to Harriet, a steely glint in her eyes. 'We ain't gonna be beaten, 'arriet. You'll see we ain't. Me and you, we'll show 'em, so we will. I don't care how we earn our livin' but we ain't never gonna be chucked out of our 'ome again. Never, you 'ear? Now come on,' she'd said, rising. 'We've a lot to do before we sleep ternight.'

An excited Harriet had jumped up eagerly to help her mother push the cart towards town, visions of grandeur crowding through her mind. For as long as she could remember she had hated life on the farm. The conditions they had lived in there had been dire: the cottage damp and cold even in summer; the food they ate no better than pig swill; the clothes on their backs threadbare. She couldn't even remember receiving a present at Christmas, except for a ragged doll salvaged by her mother from the farmer's dustbin, without his knowledge. It had had no hair and had lost one of its legs. For that Harriet had been expected to be grateful. Even at a tender age she'd inwardly questioned why she should be. The farmer's children had all they could ever want and she nothing, all because of who had parented them. It wasn't fair. Why couldn't she have been born to people who could provide better for her?

She'd shed no tears when her father died. Neither of her parents was the demonstrative kind. They hadn't had the time. All their efforts were channelled into keeping body and soul together, and from the moment she could walk Harriet was encouraged to do her bit. On her father's death she'd realised they would have to leave their home, but all that had meant to her was that life must surely now take a turn for the better. Hilda's declaration that morning on the hillside happily confirmed Harriet's belief and for the rest of the journey she indulged in wonderful fantasies.

Her mother would get a good job earning lots of money, and they would live in a nice house; Harriet would attend a good school wearing pretty clothes, with a special dress for Sundays. Just like the farmer's children.

But she was to be cruelly disappointed.

On reaching town, Hilda set about selling everything she possessed, including her thin gold wedding ring. Using a good portion of the money she paid a month's rent on a crumbling, filthy three-storey property up a side street, just off the town centre, on the poorest side of town. The day following, working all hours, Hilda and a by now sullen Harriet cleaned all the rooms, salvaging anything that could be of use, then distempered the walls.

The small front room was turned into a makeshift shop selling anything that would make a few pennies' profit. Nothing, whatever state it was in, was overlooked. A handleless chipped cup, a chair minus one leg, a book with pages missing . . . in Hilda's view anything might be of use to someone at a reasonable price. The two attic rooms, sparsely furnished, afforded a cheap night's lodging to a succession of rough working men.

Nothing was as Harriet had expected. Life now was worse than before, if that was possible. The shop was filled with stinking junk, the attics with stinking foul-mouthed drunks. Her mother was contented with the way she made her frugal living, for the first time in her life independent, not reliant on anyone else, and that was the way she intended to stay. So happy was Hilda that she remained oblivious to the bitter resentment seething within her daughter.

Harriet made no attempt to make friends with the neighbouring children, preferring her own company to playing childish games or becoming involved in petty squabbling. When she wasn't dragooned into helping her mother run the business, she took to filling her solitary hours by reading the piles of musty, dog-eared books that came through the shop. Reading opened up a new world to her and it did not take long for her quick mind to realise that in this way she could educate herself in more subjects than the basic 3 Rs she learned at school.

Over the years the mildewed pages taught her much and by the time she reached adulthood anyone who did not know Harriet's origins would never have guessed from her practised deportment, elocution, and carefully chosen good quality second-hand clothes, her lowly beginnings and humble home.

The bitterness of her life had hardened Harriet to such an extent that by the time her mother passed away from pneumonia at the age of forty-two, weakened by her years of toil and poor standard of living, she did not shed a tear, just stared around bitterly at her meagre legacy. Crumbling rented premises housing her own poor, sparsely furnished living accommodation; one room used as a shop which overflowed with what she felt amounted to no more than rubbish; two small attic bedrooms offering a night's lodging hardly one step up from the workhouse to a bedraggled clientele barely able to afford the pittance charged.

Harriet was then seventeen years of age. Like her mother years before, she sat and contemplated her position. The conclusion she came to was that she could either shut the shop and carry on with her job, hoping that she might eventually acquire a husband and live the hand-to-mouth existence of her neighbours, or else put her years of self-education to good use and improve on what her mother had left her.

She chose the latter course, taking time to plan her future down to the smallest detail. At last she was satisfied it was a sound scheme, one formulated to ensure she never again tasted poverty. It would take skill, cunning and an iron will. She knew she possessed all three.

To finance her plan she kept on at her job for the time being. In her spare time, cutting her outgoings to the bone, she set about transforming the shop into a haberdasher's – haberdashery being as far removed as possible from what had been sold here previously. The attic rooms were cleared and given a fresh coat of paint, cheap but sturdy furniture installed, and the coarse workmen replaced with far more suitable lodgers for what she had in mind: travelling salesmen. To Harriet's delight, all this coincided with an upturn in the rundown area's fortunes and it became much more desirable.

The shop slowly began to pay its way and her two rooms were regularly occupied. Two years from the day Harriet had formulated her plan, all that remained for her to achieve was to find herself a suitable husband.

He came in the shape of twenty-three-year-old George Ashman, an insurance agent working from a large office in Leicester, who had been drafted to Market Harborough and had taken one of her rooms.

George was not at all good-looking, indeed had a severe limp caused by a club foot, but that did not matter as Harriet knew her own lack of physical attributes meant she would never ensnare a handsome man. George with his own affliction, would more than likely be grateful someone was showing an interest in him. He was quiet, polite, and seemed eager to please his 'amenable' landlady. Insurance agents were respectable men with high principles and were, she guessed, reasonably paid in comparison to many other trades. He was an orphaned only child, so there would be no family interference. George was near perfect for what she was looking for. They were married four months later. Maude was to be their only child.

And nowadays Harriet was looked upon as a respectable widow, whose sadly deceased husband had held a good position in life. Looking back, she felt she could not have achieved more considering her poor beginnings.

But all that was in jeopardy. All she had striven to gain could yet be lost, and all because of the thoughtless, selfish actions of her own daughter. Harriet wasn't about to let that happen.

Her cold grey eyes narrowed. The man had been dealt with. The result of that sordid liaison also. Maude's sudden unexpected show of rebellion had momentarily taken Harriet off her guard but it was nothing she could not handle. Hadn't she handled everything else most satisfactorily? But one thing she felt she must do this time was to make sure Maddie never again jeopardised her mother's respectability.

Harriet took a deep breath and slowly turned to face her daughter who anxiously awaited her response. Head raised, back ramrod stiff, face stony, she spoke. 'I'll make allowances for your outburst this time, Maude. I suppose some sort of emotional display is to be expected in the circumstances. But never again. I will hear no more of your blatant lies or excuses for your own wanton behaviour which,' she hissed, 'I've taken great pains to cover up – something, I might add, that did not come cheap. No one has any idea about your shame. People think you've been nursing an old friend of mine through a difficult illness. And that's the way it's going to stay.'

She clasped her hands and pursed her thin lips. 'I don't suppose for one minute you stopped to consider what this would do to my reputation, or to your father's memory. I never thought you could be so selfish, Maude.'

She paused momentarily to draw breath. 'How could you?' she pressed on. 'How could you sink so low as to associate yourself with the likes of people living in such . . . such squalor! And to think that you seriously intended to marry him. Huh!' She shuddered and shook her head vigorously. 'Never, never would I have believed this could happen. I don't care what you say about the man. I don't care how wonderful you think him or what promises he's made you. I know without a shadow of a doubt that if I'd allowed you to marry, within months you'd have been reduced to his level.' Her eyes glinted maliciously. 'Is that what you want for yourself, Maude? A damp, infested hovel full of a horde of screaming offspring, and you forever wondering how you're going to feed them because that wonderful man of yours has drunk his wage at the pub?'

Maddie gazed at her, round-eyed. 'No, Mother, you have it all wrong!' she exclaimed. 'If only you'd listened to me, let me explain properly, agreed to meet Josh before you made me come here. He isn't like that, and neither is his family. Yes, they're poor but they're good people, Mother. They work hard like we do, they do their best. They . . .'

Harriet raised a hand in warning. 'Stop this nonsense! You've been blinded, Maude, blinded by what you thought was love.' Her face darkened. 'I did what any decent mother would do, and in time you will see that. When will you realise I've saved you, Maude? Saved you from a fate worse than death. I did the only thing I could, and that was to get you away from him and hope you would come to your senses.'

She thrust out her skinny chest. 'What you did was unforgivable. You committed the very worst sin and you're going to pay dearly for that. Your whole relationship with this man was built around deceit. You lied and connived your way through it. I thought I had raised you better than that. Raised you to respect yourself. I see now I was wrong.' Harriet snorted in disgust. 'You gave yourself to the first man who showed interest, never looking for the reason why. After all, Maude, you're approaching twenty-five, well past marriageable age, and hardly what would be classed as a beauty. No, far from it.'

Ignoring her daughter's gasp of horror, she continued, 'The man fooled you, Maude! He fooled you good and proper. I don't care what cock and bull tale you've told me about your plans for your future. If he'd been a decent type, he'd have called to introduce himself properly the very first time he courted you. Or at the very least, when you told him you were pregnant, he should have insisted you told me together instead of planning to sneak away like thieves in the night. Any decent man would never have thought of it. But then, he's not decent, is he? He did nothing to endear himself to me at all. Which was why I got you away. I thought if this man was as worthy as you declared him to be, then he'd come and show it. But did he? No, he did not!

'He's had plenty of time to prove his worth. I know you've written to him. Well, you have, haven't you?' she challenged. 'So knowing where you were, why didn't he board the first train heading this way? Or at the very least have the courtesy to reply to your letters. But you've heard nothing, have you? Not a peep. I know,' she said smugly, 'because I asked Mrs Baldicott. But I didn't need to ask, I knew it already. Made it my business to find out. He fled from Market Harborough only days after I brought you here.'

Face contorted in disbelief, Maddie cried. 'What? No, Mother! I don't believe you. Josh wouldn't do that to me. There's another reason why he's not contacted me, there has to be.'

Harriet's lips tightened indignantly. 'Don't brand me a

liar like you, Maude,' she hissed. 'He's gone, I tell you. Abandoned you without a by your leave. Now sit down,' she ordered, 'and if you interrupt again, you'll wish you hadn't.' She waited while her heartbroken daughter slumped into a chair. 'Admit it, Maude, you've been used. You can think what you like but I believe he saw you as his chance of bettering himself, getting out of that hell-hole he lived in and his lowly paid job. I expect his family thought the same and encouraged his relationship with you. After all, I have a business. It might not be much in some eyes, but it's a damned sight more than they have. Well, their plan backfired, didn't it?' She shook her head triumphantly. 'I *knew*. I saw it all the moment I forced you to tell me about your sordid affair. It was all as clear as daylight to me. And, as a matter of interest, if I hadn't have confronted you that night, when would you have told me?'

Maddie hung her head.

'Oh, Maude, how could you have allowed yourself to be taken in so easily? Were you that desperate for a man?' Harriet tutted in disdain. 'And I thought my daughter was a respectable woman. You do realise, don't you, that you've ruined any chance you ever had of getting married to anyone decent? Of course, with so many men losing their lives in the war, your chances were already severely reduced. The ones who are left have their pick, which doesn't leave much hope for you. The most you can hope for now is that some elderly widower will take you, but even that possibility seems remote now you've been soiled.'

Her nostrils flared. 'Now, I've said all that is ever going to be said on the matter. I won't hear that man's name mentioned again. And, before we leave this room, I want a solemn promise you'll go nowhere near his family enquiring after him – unless you want to be humiliated even more than you already have been. As for the child, it never happened. Is that clear? Maude, I asked you a question. I expect an answer.'

She raised her head slowly, face filled with horror. 'I can't, Mother. I can't just forget about my baby. Please don't expect me to do that. Just tell me where she is, please? I'll go away with her. I won't cause you any . . .'

'And how will you provide for yourself and the child?' Harriet erupted. 'You have no money to speak of, and don't expect any help from me. Within a matter of weeks you'd be facing the workhouse. Would that be fair to the child? Well, would it? Or to go through life branded a bastard? Think about *that*, Maude. She's been given to people who can care and provide for her. Be realistic. You cannot give your child what it needs. You were selfish enough to bring it into the world – don't selfishly deprive it of the right to a proper upbringing.'

Harriet paused momentarily to pick up her handbag. 'Anyway, none of this matters. The child is gone. You'll get over it.' She walked towards the door and pulled it open. 'Now I'm going to settle up with Mrs Baldicott. I expect you to be ready in ten minutes.'

Numb with shock, Maddie stared at the closed door for several seconds. Then the full realisation of her situation and its hopelessness struck her like a blow. So violent was the pain of it that she moaned in agony and slid to her knees. In her mind's eye she saw again the events leading up to this dreadful betrayal.

# Chapter Two

She saw Josh: tall, handsome, a merry twinkle in his blue eyes, light brown hair cut tidily, shabby clothes covering his broad frame, but worn proudly. He had been the first person to awake within Maddie feelings she had not known existed. He had taught her to love.

For Maddie Ashman, before she met Joshua Jenks, life had been lonely. A naturally warm, bright and inquisitive child, from a very early age Maddie had learned not to expect emotional warmth from her cold, austere mother, and had received none. Of her father she had few memories; he had died when she was two years old. She knew little about him, practically nothing in fact, and had long ago stopped asking, knowing her questions would only receive a silent rebuff from her grieving mother.

She made few friends or close acquaintances as she grew up. At school the other girls – the ones who did not already ridicule and ostracise her for the way Harriet forced her to pronounce her vowels and be ladylike – stopped being friendly, fed up with the excuses constantly made to their well-meant overtures, despite knowing that Maddie's mother was behind them. Harriet made it blindingly obvious she thought nobody good enough to associate with her daughter. Maddie herself knew that to question or rebel against her mother's decisions was futile; the resulting punishment would be harsh and nothing would change her mother's bigoted point of view.

After school and at weekends, when her allotted chores

had been done, Maddie would sit and practise her sewing and knitting skills. These had not come easily but her mother had insisted on her acquiring them nevertheless.

At fourteen years of age, Maddie's stated wish to go out to work went unheeded. Her skills were to be put to the use her mother intended. A small windowless room under the shop stairs was cleared. A treadle Singer sewing machine, the one she'd over the years painstakingly practised on, was installed, along with a table, lamp, and drawers in which to hold her equipment and materials. There, from early morning until closing time, Maddie would sit carrying out alterations and repairs to customers' garments, emerging only for her lunch.

Occasionally, the pinning of a hem or tuck at the waist would bring her into contact with a customer. These intrusions into her solitary day were welcomed. For her work she received five shillings a week from which she was expected to purchase all her personal needs.

Outings were few. On Saturday afternoon she accompanied Harriet on their weekly shopping trip, on Sunday morning to church. Maddie's only luxury was her solitary walk on a Wednesday afternoon, and occasionally on a warm summer evening if all her work was finished.

So accustomed was she to this rigid routine and the years of having it instilled in her by Harriet that her chance of marriage was extremely limited, that Maddie had no expectations and, to save herself unwarranted pain, never allowed her thoughts to stray as far as sweethearts and marriage. She felt it was pointless. Her chance of ever meeting a member of the opposite sex in social circumstances was non-existent. Besides, suppose she should ever be fortunate enough to do so she would be terrified of making a fool of herself.

Having long ago accepted her lot in life, meeting a man she could love and having her feelings returned was totally unexpected.

One cold Wednesday afternoon in March, forgetting the lateness of the hour as she was enjoying her freedom, Maddie was wandering down her favourite stretch of the tow path beside the canal. Engrossed in watching a pair of elegant swans gliding silently by, she did not see an icy puddle, slipped and lost her balance. From the opposite direction, pedalling hard on a rusting bicycle, thinking only of his desire to get home after his long day as an apprentice machine mechanic in the local corset factory, twenty-year-old Joshua Jenks did not see the prostrate figure on the ground until he was almost upon it.

Shocked, he steered sharply away to avoid a collision. His front tyre met a protruding boulder and Josh tumbled over the handlebars to land in the canal. Screaming in shock, beside herself for having been the cause of the accident, instantly forgetting the pain of her own bruised backside and pride, Maddie jumped up and rushed to aid the sodden man emerging from the icy water.

'I'm so sorry,' she blurted, grabbing the dripping sleeve of his jacket to help him out. 'I slipped on some ice. I couldn't warn you, I didn't see you coming. I really am so dreadfully sorry.'

Standing on the canal bank, water draining from him, Josh shivered violently. 'If it's anyone's fault, it's mine. I was pedalling too fast and wasn't looking where I was going.' A twinkle of amusement lit his eyes. 'Anyway, there's no damage a good wash won't put right.' He glanced quickly at his bicycle. 'That's still in one piece thank God, 'cos it's me brother's and if 'ote 'appened to his precious bike he'd skin me alive.' He brought his eyes back to her. 'What about you?'

'Me? Oh, I'm fine,' Maddie insisted. 'It's you I'm concerned with. You're sure you're all right?'

'I'm sure.' He stared down at himself. 'But that won't be the story when I get home 'cos me mam's going to batter me senseless when she sees the state I'm in.'

Maddie's face clouded over in alarm. 'Oh, will she be terribly angry? Would you like me to call and explain . . .' Her voice trailed off when she saw the corners of his mouth twitch. 'You're having fun with me, aren't you?'

'My mother's always threatening to batter all of us senseless but she won't. I know her. She'll laugh when I tell her what happened then fuss all over me – but not before reminding me she always said that one day I'd fall hard for a pretty lady.' Josh quickly realised he had embarrassed the young woman before him and hurriedly added, 'I'd better get off before I freeze ter death.' He picked up his bicycle and sat astride it, making to set off, then he paused. 'Do you walk down here often?'

'Oh, er . . . yes, I do. Most Wednesday afternoons. Not usually quite so late as this, though.'

'Well, I'll just have to hope you're late again then, won't I? Tarra.'

She stared after him bemused as, still dripping water, he pedalled off. 'Tarra,' she said absently. 'Oh, I mean, goodbye.'

As Maddie made her way home she tried to work out just what these parting words had meant. It never entered her head that he was hoping to see her again.

During the following months, depending how she managed to time her Wednesday walks and when Josh finished work, they would occasionally encounter each other. Maddie found herself looking forward more and more to these weekly encounters which brightened her mundane life considerably, and becoming more and more disappointed when their paths did not cross.

As time passed their general polite chit-chat gradually progressed to including details about themselves, although it was Josh who did most of the talking as he had so many tales of his large, close-knit family to impart.

It took six months before he formally asked her out. They were walking along the tow path together, happily chatting, when suddenly he drew to a halt and stared at her nervously.

20

'Maddie . . .' he began, mindful of the red tide of embarrassment creeping up his neck '. . . I, er . . . thought I'd go for a walk in the park on Sunday. Thought I might listen to the band – I've heard they're not bad. Would, er . . . well, yer could if yer wanted?'

Perplexed, she frowned. 'Could what, Josh?'

'Come too. I could call for yer. Square it with yer mother. That's if yer'd like to, that is?'

Eyes wide, she stared at him dumbstruck. Was this handsome man really asking for her company? At twenty-one years old she suddenly felt unworldly, with not a clue how to respond to such an invitation, never having believed she would receive one. And she could not decide if he was asking to escort her or just asking if she was doing nothing better and wanted to tag along? To get it wrong would be so embarrassing for both of them.

A wave of acute self-consciousness flooded through her and she felt her cheeks glow. She knew how dowdy and old-fashioned she looked, the style chosen as always by her mother: unbecoming plain calf-length buttoned dress, hand-knitted cardigan, serviceable brown boots. Her long mane of chestnut hair was pulled severely back and tied by a piece of brown ribbon at the base of her neck.

In all the time she had been acquainted with Josh, despite being fully aware of her own growing attraction towards him, Maddie had never dared allow herself to hope he would be interested in anything more than friendship with her. A man as good-looking as Joshua Jenks could have his pick of the girls, of that she had no doubt. But now he was looking at her eagerly. Oh, it was all so confusing. Suddenly she realised he was speaking.

'Look, Maddie, I didn't mean to offend yer. I just thought you might like an afternoon out, 'cos from what I gather you don't get out much. Well, not at all, do yer?'

It's as I should have guessed, she thought, dispirited. Josh had only asked because he felt sorry for her. She raised her head, forcing a smile to her face. 'I don't go out much because I'm so busy, what with my work and helping my mother. I get hardly any free time. In fact, I was thinking I'd have to stop my Wednesday walks for a while,' she lied to save face. 'Thank you for your offer,' she added lightly, 'but I'll have to decline, I'm afraid.'

His unmistakable disappointment shocked her.

'Yer don't have to make excuses, Maddie,' he muttered, shuffling his feet. 'I shouldn't have asked yer. I'd no right. I'm sorry, really I am.'

Tilting her head, she frowned quizzically. 'Right? What do you mean by that, Josh?'

'Well, I ain't, have I? I mean, your mam owns a shop. Me and my family . . . well, we work in factories. Me dad takes whatever he can get but he's outta work more often than he's in. That's what I mean. I ain't in your class, Maddie, and I shouldn't have embarrassed yer.'

Anger welled within her and before she could check herself she blurted out, 'How people earn their living is of no consequence to me, Josh, and I'm surprised to hear it is to you. May I remind you that it is my mother that owns the shop, not me, and as such I work for someone to earn my living, the same as you.' Although, she thought, my mother certainly wouldn't voice the same opinion.

He grimaced. 'Well, that's told me, ain't it? I'm sorry I offended yer.' His face fell. 'It doesn't matter to me neither, honest it doesn't. I like yer, Maddie. I don't care what yer mother's got. I just thought she might object to me, that's all. Look, I'd really like to take yer for a walk. I'd be honoured. I've been trying to summon up the courage to ask yer for ages.'

She gasped in surprise. 'You have?'

He nodded solemnly.

Her face lit up, her delight obvious. 'Then I'd like that very much too.'

His grin was eager. 'Sunday then? I'll call for yer, will I?'

'Call for me? Oh!'

He frowned. 'What is it?'

Her thoughts whirled, knowing instinctively from past experience that should she tell her mother about her outing Harriet would want to know all the details and when she did her disapproval would be voiced and the outing stopped. Maddie couldn't bear to risk that. She wanted so much to accompany this man. Besides, she doubted there'd be another invitation after Sunday so what was the point of causing unnecessary affront? Her decision, rightly or wrongly, was made quickly. 'My mother doesn't like to be disturbed on a Sunday afternoon so it might be best if I met you somewhere.'

Josh nodded in understanding. 'My folks like to take a nap after dinner. With all us lot in the house, they reckon it's the only time they get any peace to . . . to . . .' He cleared his throat in embarrassment. 'Well, if yer sure yer mam won't mind me not introducing meself, I'll meet you at the park gates. Will two suit yer?'

She smiled and nodded.

Over the three days that followed, Maddie fought to keep check of her excitement, wishing with all her heart she had someone in whom to confide. It took all her strength to keep her emotions in check so as not to arouse any suspicions within her mother. But as nervous anticipation mounted she wished wholeheartedly she had refused the invitation; the build up to it was making her feel ill.

To her relief Sunday finally dawned.

The morning dragged slowly. All the usual routine tasks seemed to take longer than normal. Finally she managed to escape to her room to tidy herself and hopefully calm her nerves.

Taking a last look in the mirror, she smiled, pleased with her reflection. Her hair was tied in its usual style but several tendrils had been freed to frame the sides of her face. She felt that the slight alteration softened her features.

On her plain Sunday blue dress she pinned a brooch, the first piece of jewellery she had ever owned. It was only costume jewellery, costing one shilling and sixpence, and in order to fund it she had gone without purchasing several weekly necessities, deciding she could make do until the following payday. She felt her decision had been right as the brooch's presence helped to alleviate the plainness of her attire. She would have liked to wear some lipstick but makeup of any description was forbidden by her mother and besides she did not own any, so Maddie pinched her cheeks and rubbed her lips until both glowed pink. Finally, taking a deep breath, she slipped her coat over her arm and made her way down the stairs.

Standing in the backroom doorway, heart beating painfully, she addressed her mother, praying that nothing would happen to put a stop to her outing. 'It's . . . it's such a lovely afternoon, I thought I'd go for a walk. Leave you in peace to have your nap.'

Her mother's beady eyes missed nothing and as she eyed her daughter shrewdly, Maddie was suddenly afraid that somehow Harriet had guessed what she was up to. Her heart beat so loudly she was terrified it would be audible. 'I've nothing else to do, Mother. I've no sewing outstanding. The tea things are ready. I forgot to renew my books at the library so I've nothing to read. I thought I might go to the park and listen to the band.'

Harriet looked at her for several long moments before sniffing dismissively. 'Well, go if you're going. And don't be late. Tea's at five, not a minute after.' She glared at Maddie. 'And no talking to strange men, you heed?'

She nodded.

She made to depart but her mother's voice stopped her. 'What have you done to your hair? It looks stupid. Go back upstairs and do it properly. And what's that on your dress?'

Maddie's hand flew to the brooch. 'Just something I bought. I . . . I thought it was nice.'

24

'Nice!' Harriet snorted in disgust. 'It's trash. Take it off.'

'But, Mother, I . . .'

'I said, take it off and throw it away. No daughter of mine is cheapening herself by wearing gaudy trinkets like that. And another thing, my girl. If you can afford to waste good money on such things then I'm paying you too much.'

Resigned, Maddie did as was told, realising she should have known better. She threw the offending article in the waste basket by the fireplace then returned to her bedroom to redo her hair.

Back in the doorway she addressed her mother again. 'Can I go now, Mother?'

A dozing Harriet opened her eyes and studied her daughter hard. Her mean mouth tight, she nodded grudgingly.

Maddie did not dare allow herself a sigh of relief until she had closed the front door securely behind her and was halfway down the street.

The outing went much better than she had dared to expect. Despite her nervousness, within minutes of meeting Josh she began to relax. Her escort was attentive, entertaining, a pleasure to be with, but what came as the greatest surprise to Maddie was that he made no effort to hide his own obvious delight to be in her company and took great pains to ensure she was enjoying herself. He need not have worried.

Never in her life had Maddie been so happy. Mingling amongst the crowds, they licked ice cream from cones bought from the vendor, drank tea from the pavilion, strolled around the ornamental lake and listened to the band. The afternoon passed far too quickly for both. Reluctantly they parted but not before arranging to meet again.

On her way home, Maddie's thoughts returned over and over again to every minute detail of her lovely afternoon and she wondered how she was going to get through the days that followed until she saw Josh again. Suddenly she stopped walking as worry began to fill her. She stood deep in thought for several long moments, mulling over her dilemma, then smiled in relief. No, she hadn't lied to her mother. She *had* gone for a walk in the park and she hadn't spoken to any strange men. Josh wasn't a stranger at all. She'd known him for months. Her only crime, should her mother choose to see it that way, was that she had been economical with the truth. But the truth was still the truth.

Over the months that followed they would meet whenever possible. The winter months proved the most difficult. Making excuses to her mother for wanting to take walks in the bitter cold was hard and sometimes two or three weeks would pass when Maddie did not see Josh at all. These times proved purgatory for her as she missed his company dreadfully. She knew that he had trouble understanding the problems she faced over meeting him openly but gradually, as they got to know each other better and the truth of her closeted life slowly emerged, he began to appreciate her difficulties.

Getting out to meet him was not her only problem.

Forming a close relationship with Josh did not come without its setbacks for Maddie. As their feelings grew more serious she spent many a sleepless night worrying if she was handling matters right, feeling so unprepared and, worse, having no one to turn to for advice on these alien emotions. But she need not have worried. Josh, she was to learn, was a gentle and patient man with no intention of forcing her into anything with which she did not feel comfortable.

As their feelings intensified and Maddie began to understand and appreciate how it felt to be loved and needed, the truth of how starved of affection she had always been, of how truly cold and unemotional her mother was, became glaringly obvious. She began to pity Harriet, and to pity herself for what her mother and she could have shared had things between them been different. But Maddie knew it was no good wishing for any change in Harriet. Despite her great sadness for what might have been, she was happy in her love for Josh.

He was a man who was proud of his family and never tired of telling Maddie about them. She in turn never tired of listening to his tales of this close-knit family, and as time passed felt that through him she had come to know all the Jenkses. As her picture of them built, the one thing above all that became clear to her was that what they might lack in material wealth was more than compensated for by the love and respect they felt for each other. She could not help feeling a certain envy and sadness for what she herself had never had.

Their first embrace was a clumsy attempt brought about by Maddie stumbling as she slipped on a grassy incline. Josh automatically jumped to her aid. Despite springing from him in alarm, unused to being held in such an intimate manner by another human being, never would she forget first feeling his arms around her: the warmth, the comfort, the surge of excitement shooting through her, flaming through her whole being. Neither could she forget his first kiss, as he, unable to resist her anymore, momentarily forgot himself and clasped her in his arms, planting a quick, stolen, peck on her lips then immediately begging her forgiveness.

He did not need it. Maddie had liked the feel of his tender lips on hers and in truth wanted more.

It was a lovely summer's evening when Josh asked her to marry him. They had been seeing each other for nearly three years. Three years of secret meetings.

Sitting in a deserted field under a hedge, content in each other's company, they had watched in silence as the sun began to set, marvelling at the spectacle created by its wide golden rays spreading right across the darkening sky. She had been conscious of the time, that she really ought to be getting home, but her desire not to leave the man she had fallen deeply in love with proved too great and she prayed just a few minutes longer with him would cause no harm.

Turning to look at her, Josh took a deep breath, praying his nerve would not leave him, desperate to ask something he had wanted to for such a long time. This place would make the perfect setting. Conscious that he was staring at her, Maddie turned to smile at him. As she did so he cupped her chin gently in his large hand, looking deep into her lovely eyes.

'Maddie?'

'Mmmm?' she whispered.

Steeling himself, he took a deep breath. 'Marry me, Maddie? I've had enough of sneaking around and I know you have too. I know yer mam won't think I'm good enough, but I am. I work hard and I'm clean-living. I love yer, and I'll make yer happy. She won't be sorry she's got me as a son-in-law. I think she could do a lot worse in fact. When I get to meet her I'll do me best to get on with her, I promise.' His eyes clouded in anxiety. 'What d'yer say, Maddie?'

His proposal, something she had longed for but never thought to hear, came as a complete shock and she stared at him for several long moments before finally uttering, 'Oh, Josh, I love you too. Are you sure? Are you really sure it's me you want to marry?'

'Sure?' He laughed. 'Maddie darlin', Maddie, I wouldn't have asked yer if I weren't.' He eyed her gravely. 'Yer not still believing that nonsense about being ugly, are yer? 'Cos yer not, Maddie. How many times do I have to tell yer? Anyway, ugly or beautiful, it ain't yer looks I want to marry yer for, it's you.' Then he added, with a twinkle in his eye, 'But it does help that you're as pretty as a picture and I wish you'd believe me when I tell yer that.'

She gave a tight smile. She wanted to believe him, she had no reason not to believe anything he said, but after years of having her mother – the one person who was supposed to have her best interests at heart – instil in her that she was plain, despite what the mirror told her, that belief was deeply rooted within her.

For reassurance she looked deep into his eyes and would have had to be blind not to see the devotion there. However he judged her beauty, he did love her, there was no doubt of that in her mind.

'I want to marry you too, Josh,' she responded softly. 'I want that so much and feel so honoured you've asked me, but . . .'

'But what, Maddie?' he erupted anxiously. 'Yer not going ter turn me down? Please say yer not?'

She shook her head. 'No, I'm not. It's my mother who will.' She wrung her hands despairingly. 'I've not exaggerated what she's like – if anything I've played it down a little. She's never allowed me to have friends in any shape or form. We'll have a fight on our hands and I'm not relishing the prospect.'

He sighed in exasperation. 'Me mam says she's always been strange.' The words slipped out before he had had a chance to check himself.

Her eyes flashed a question. 'Pardon? Your mother? You've told your family about me?'

Frowning quizzically, he nodded. ''Course I have. We don't have secrets in our house, I've told yer that often enough. The only reason I ain't took yer round to meet 'em is that I didn't want to scare you off. They can be a rowdy lot. Me mother's chuffed about us because she knows how much you mean to me. She knows you're special. But it's no good me lying: she doesn't think much of yer mam. Said she can't for the life of her understand how she managed to get herself married in the first place.

'My mother and yorn were at school together. Me mother remembers Harriet well. Says she was different from all the other kids. Never had any friends and never made any effort to make any. Me mam's family was poor, Maddie, same as all the folks roundabout our streets. Your mam was dressed no better than the rest. Sometimes she never had no shoes on her feet nor arse in her britches.

'Me mam remembers the shop before it was altered. Said

all but rubbish was sold there and pennies were snatched at 'cos yer mam and grandma bloody well needed 'em. They were making a living, there ain't n'ote wrong in that. But yer mam's no right to feel she's above the likes of my family just 'cos she had the good fortune to make life a bit better for herself.' His face fell as he noticed the astonished expression on Maddie's. 'Didn't you know about that?'

She shook her head. 'No, I didn't. I thought we'd always had the haberdasher's. My mother's very sparing in what she tells me about the past.'

He grimaced remorsefully. 'I'm sorry, Maddie. Me and me big mouth.'

'It's all right,' she whispered, suddenly struck by how little she knew about her own family, something she had never dwelt on before because she hadn't thought there was anything to know. But now she wondered. 'You've a right to your own opinions,' she said distractedly.

'I've not met yer mam, so they ain't my opinions, Maddie, they're me mam's and she never hides what she thinks.' He paused, just stopping himself from telling Maddie that when he had first informed his mother about his sweetheart, she had asked him if it was wise to associate himself with the daughter of Harriet Ashman and had advised him to be careful. Advice he had chosen to ignore, thank goodness. 'Regardless of her mouth, you'll like me mam, Maddie,' Josh said with conviction. 'She's a good woman and her heart's in the right place. You'll like all me family. And they'll love you.'

She sighed. 'I do hope so. And if your family are anything like you, I shall have no trouble in liking them. But I can appreciate how your mother feels about mine. She's . . . well . . . she can be very difficult to get along with. But, regardless, she's my mother, Josh, and there's a part of me that admires the way she must have worked to improve her life after what you've told me.' Her face grew troubled. 'She won't give her consent to our marriage, you know.'

'You don't need her consent, Maddie, you're over twenty-one.'

'I know, but I can't get married without it. I wouldn't feel it was right. And there's the fact that I've been seeing you for such a long time without her knowledge. They'll be hell to pay when that comes out. Oh, Josh . . .'

He grabbed her in his arms, holding her protectively. 'Stop worrying over problems that ain't happened yet,' he soothed. 'We'll tackle her together. Once she sees how much we care about each other and how determined we are, I'm sure she'll be glad for us.'

Looking up into his eyes, Maddie smiled wanly, praying he was right but knowing deep down he wasn't.

'You'll arrange for me to come around to meet her soon then?'

'Er . . .' Maddie frowned. 'Give me a little time first, please. I'll . . . I'll try and break it gradually then it won't come as so much of a shock to her.'

He sighed. 'All right, but not too gradually, Maddie. I don't want to wait forever. I want to make yer me wife as soon as possible. Me wage ain't that great but I keep me head down in the hope I'll get promoted. I've worked things out and I can afford to rent us something small to start with, but me mam said in the meantime she'd find room for us. We'd be cramped but we'd be together, Maddie.' His grip tightened. 'Oh, Maddie, I love you so much. You were well worth landing up in the canal for. I know facing your mother ain't going to be easy but I'll be there with yer all the way.'

He released her, bent his head and kissed her with deep longing. She responded willingly and before they both realised what was happening all their pent-up emotions were released and in a deserted field, sheltered by a dense hawthorn hedge, they sealed their love.

When it was over Josh stared at her in utter remorse. 'Oh, Maddie, Maddie, I'm so sorry! I didn't mean that to happen. I just got carried away. I've wanted to love you like that, to feel you, be near you, for such a long time. Please forgive me?' he begged.

She reached up, running one hand tenderly down the side of his face. 'Hush,' she soothed. 'I should feel it was wrong but I don't, Josh. Loving you is right, I know it is. I'm as much to blame as you are. I wanted you too. But we mustn't do it again. Not until we're married.'

He nodded vigorously. 'The sooner you tell your mother, Maddie, the sooner we can stop this sneaking around.'

Maddie dreaded the confrontation and it was all she could think of. It filled her every waking moment and troubled her sleep. How did you approach your unapproachable mother and inform her you were going to marry a man she had never met, had never actually known existed? Hardly casually over a cup of tea.

Fully aware of Josh's growing impatience and of her own need finally to unburden herself, at the very last minute her nerve would always desert her. Over two months later Maddie was no further forward. But over that two months another, more serious reason for tackling her mother began to manifest itself and now she was sure. Since making love to Josh she hadn't had her monthly curse and that could mean only one thing. She was carrying his baby.

Any worries she'd had over Josh's reaction to her condition were quickly swept away. Grabbing her up in his arms, he swung her around, yelling out in delight. 'You'll have to tell her now! We'll get married straight away. If yer that scared, we'll run away. I mean to marry yer, Maddie, one way or another, and with the baby coming I'm even more determined. Me parents will be all right about it. They understand these things happen.' He pulled her tightly to him, crushing her protectively, trying in his rough way to alleviate her fears. 'Let me come with yer now? Let's go and tell her together. Let's go and get it over with.'

'No, no, Josh!' she cried, alarmed. 'It was bad enough thinking about facing her before. But to tell her I'm expecting . . .' She paused momentarily, the enormity of the task filling her with dread. Her voice faltered. 'I . . . I have to do this myself. To prepare her before she meets you, Josh. At the weekend. Sunday after church,' she assured him. 'I'll do it then, I promise.'

It was a Wednesday evening. She had three days to build up her courage. She had to do it now. She had no choice.

But she had bargained without her mother.

That night, as she was getting ready for bed, Harriet appeared unexpectedly in the doorway. Maddie knew instinctively by her whole manner that something was terribly wrong. In her mother's hand were several strips of padded linen which she was brandishing.

'Is there something you have to tell me, Maude?'

Her voice was hard and cold. Maddie flinched. Her eyes flew to the articles in her mother's hand and the horrifying truth dawned. In her worried state she had forgotten that someone else would notice she had not used them recently. Her mother knew she was pregnant.

Face draining of colour, she fought to stop her body from quaking. 'Mother,' she murmured, 'I . . . please let me explain. I've met a man. Josh . . . his name is Josh. I've known him nearly three years. We love each other, Mother, and we're going to be married. I've tried to tell you, I have really. He wants to meet you. You'll like him. I . . .'

'So you won't be needing these then?' Harriet cut in icily, flapping the strips of linen in a sarcastic gesture.

Maddie's whole body sagged. 'Oh, Mother, I'm so sorry. I didn't mean to hurt you. Please believe me, I didn't.'

'When's it due?' Harriet asked stonily.

'Due? Oh, I . . . I . . . haven't worked it out. March . . . no, sometime in April next year.'

Without another word or displaying any emotion, Harriet turned and left the room.

Maddie slept not a wink that night and rose the next morning, gritty-eyed and drained of energy, worried witless as to exactly how her mother was going to react. Several possibilities raced through her mind, none of which she relished. She had heard her mother's scathing opinions of fallen women before. At the least she would be disowned and thrown out on the streets, Maddie thought.

The response she did get totally confused her.

She arrived in the kitchen to find her mother donning her coat.

'I'll need you to manage the shop today. I've an errand to do,' Harriet announced matter-of-factly as she picked up her hat and pulled it on. 'Mrs Day is coming in to collect the dress you altered. Charge her a shilling.' Picking up her handbag, she headed for the door. 'I'm not sure what time I'll be back so keep me some dinner hot. Use the remains of the meat pie from yesterday.'

Maddie's thoughts raced. It was most unusual for her mother to be going out at such an early hour, and where on earth was she going? But she knew better than to ask. She was worried, though. Harriet had never allowed her behind the counter before. The shop was solely her domain. But Maddie supposed she could manage. Far more disconcerting was her mother's calm demeanour. It was as though the dreadful revelation of yesterday evening hadn't happened.

'You did hear what I said, Maude?'

Maddie jumped, startled. 'Pardon? Oh, yes, I did. But, Mother, I've never worked in the shop before. I don't know what to do.'

Passing by her as she headed for the door, Harriet eyed her blankly. 'I'm sure you'll manage,' she said tonelessly as she departed.

By the time she returned it was well after eight and Maddie's nerves were frayed.

As she heard the back door open and shut, she shot out of her chair, the sewing she had been trying to concentrate

34

on falling in a heap on the linoleum. 'Oh, Mother,' she exclaimed when Harriet appeared. 'I was worried about you being as it's so late. I . . .'

'No need to be,' she cut in sharply, taking off her outdoor clothes and hanging them up. 'My dinner in the oven, is it?'

'Er . . . yes. I'll get it for you and make a fresh pot of tea.'

Maddie rushed off to the kitchen and when she returned Harriet was seated at the table. Maddie put the plate in front of her. 'Be careful,' she warned. 'It's scalding.'

'One thing I am not, Maude, and that is stupid. Isn't it obvious that a plate taken out of the oven is bound to be hot?'

Maddie gulped. 'Yes, Mother,' she said quietly.

'How did you get on in the shop?'

'Very well, I think. The customers . . .' She paused, about to say that they had seemed happy with her service. Several had remarked that they hoped to be served by her again, but she thought better of repeating this. 'Asked after you, Mother. Mrs Day came in for her dress and I charged her a shilling as you instructed. Mrs Hardy asked if we could get her some special braiding for some cushions she's making. I told her I was sure you would try the next time the representative came in. The takings are in the bag on the sideboard along with the receipts for you to check. Did I do right, Mother?' she asked tentatively.

'Did you quote Mrs Hardy a price?'

'No. I couldn't, could I, as I have no idea of costings.'

A disgusted look on her face, Harriet pushed the plate away from her. 'I can't eat that, it's all dried up,' she said, rising. 'I'm going to bed, I've had a tiring day. Make sure you lock up properly before you come up.'

After Harriet had left, Maddie stood staring at the nearly full plate, her fraught nerves jangling. Apart from the fact that her mother's complaint about the food was totally unwarranted, the fact that she still had not mentioned a

35

word about her intentions regarding Maddie's condition was worrying in the extreme.

It was still two days before she could see Josh and they suddenly seemed endless.

By Saturday evening Harriet still had not commented on the subject and Maddie was reaching breaking point.

'That food cost good money, Maude, stop pushing it around your plate and eat it before it gets cold.'

'I'm not hungry, Mother,' she replied, laying down her knife and fork. 'I have a headache. If you don't mind, I'll clear the kitchen and go to bed.'

'I *do* mind. As you are fully aware, Maude, I abhor waste of any description but especially that of food. Now I'm sure your headache will not hinder you from eating what is on your plate.'

Maddie stared down at the two boiled potatoes, spoonful of Savoy cabbage and small helping of mutton stew growing cold on her plate. The sight of it made her feel sick, let alone the thought of forcing it down her throat. But she knew she must. Harriet would not allow her to leave the table until she had.

Not waiting for any response her mother snapped, 'Eat up, Maude.'

Maddie took a deep breath before replying quietly, 'Yes, Mother.'

It was nearly two hours later before she felt it safe to announce she was going to bed. Harriet was sitting stiffly in a worn leather armchair by the sparse fire, reading a book.

'Goodnight, Mother,' Maddie ventured tentatively.

Harriet's reply was curt. 'Goodnight.'

That night was much like all the others recently: restless, with sleep a long time coming. Maddie awoke the next morning feeling totally unrested, eyes gritty, wishing wholeheartedly she could stay in bed until it was time to ready herself for her meeting with Josh.

Arriving in the kitchen she was surprised to see her

mother had already prepared breakfast, something that was usually Maddie's task.

Without a word of greeting Harriet announced, 'We're not going to church today, Maude. You're to accompany me on a visit to an old friend of mine. She's not well. We need to set off shortly as it's quite a journey.'

As she stood rooted to the spot Maddie could not decide what had shocked her the most. The fact that for the first time in living memory they would not be attending Sunday service or the fact that her Mother had a friend, someone she had never mentioned before. And not only that but Harriet was concerned enough about her to pay a visit because she was sick. Maddie knew better than to ask any questions. Then, suddenly, another thought struck her and a sickening fear rose up inside her.

'What . . . er . . . what time d you expect we'll arrive back, Mother?'

Saucepan of porridge in hand, Harriet spun around. 'Late, I would have thought. Why?'

Maddie eyed her anxiously. She had arranged to see Josh at two-thirty down by the canal. He was expecting to hear what reception she had received on divulging her news and to make plans for their wedding. He would be worried if she did not show up and the thought of not seeing him filled her with dread. What could she do? Her mind raced frantically. 'I . . . I have some sewing to finish,' she lied, hoping she could find some.

'It can wait,' Harriet snapped dismissively, slapping a spoonful of porridge in a dish which she placed before Maddie. 'Eat up,' she ordered. 'I'm just off upstairs to collect a few things to take to my friend. A few clothes that are of no use to me anymore that I know she can make use of.'

Maddie was too distressed to listen to her mother. All she could think of was Josh and what he would be feeling and thinking should she not arrive back in time to meet him. How could she get a message to him?

The journey was a long and confusing one for Maddie, consisting of a three-hour rail journey, the train stopping at every station en route, then an age on an omnibus. They had been unceremoniously bumped up and down on the uncomfortable wooden seat for several miles down uneven narrow country lanes before Maddie dared venture to ask her mother where they were heading.

'Not far now,' she replied in a tone that warned Maddie against probing any further.

They alighted from the omnibus in the middle of a busy village which Maddie just caught the name of as the vehicle entered its boundaries: Ibstock. She had never heard of it.

Hurrying ahead of her, Harriet finally stopped by a garden gate, leading to an old miner's cottage in the middle of a row of eight identical houses. All the gardens were neat and the cinder paths running down to the front doors evenly edged by bricks.

Harriet faced her daughter. 'Take this bag,' she ordered, handing Maddie the heavy carpet bag of clothes she had insisted on carrying. As Maddie did as she was bade, Harriet snatched her handbag from her. 'You won't be needing this.'

Maddie eyed her in confusion but before she had time to query it, from the pocket of her coat Harriet produced an envelope which she thrust at Maddie. 'Give this to Mrs Baldicott. She's expecting you.'

Maddie eyed the envelope, bewildered. 'Mother, I don't understand. What's going on?'

'I'm sure it'll all become clear, Maude. I haven't time to explain, I have a bus to catch.'

'You're not staying to see your friend? What . . .'

Harriet grimaced. 'I said, Mrs Baldicott will explain.'

Open-mouthed, Maddie stared in mystification as her mother abruptly turned away and hurried off in the direction they had just come from. Her mind raced wildly, trying to fathom a reason for this bewildering behaviour, but nothing tangible emerged. And just how did her mother, she thought, expect her to get home without any money? Had she not realised what she was doing when she had taken her handbag from Maddie. Why had she done that?

Gnawing her bottom lip, extremely troubled as she wondered what best to do, she turned and stared at the cottage and as she did so the door opened and a small, tubby woman appeared, kindly face smiling, one outstretched arm beckoning her forward. She looked the picture of health, nothing like what Maddie had been expecting from the picture her mother had conjured up of her desperately ill friend. Despite her confusion Maddie had no alternative but to go and greet the old lady, but what excuse she could make for her mother's sudden departure was beyond her.

'You must be Maude, dear, come on through,' she said as Maddie reached her. 'I'm Mrs Baldicott. I thought yer mother would've stopped at least for a cuppa before she made her way back. Still, never mind, you're here now so let's get you settled. But tea first, I think, eh? It's a fair journey from Harborough. I've never been further than Coalville meself which is our nearest town. Put yer bag down, dear, I'll show you up later and then you can unpack,' she said, busying herself making the tea.

'Unpack?'

Nancy Baldicott stopped what she was doing and looked across at the bewildered young woman standing just inside the door. 'Well, yes, you'll want to put yer clothes away, won't yer? They'll be all creased in that bag. There's plenty of drawer space in the tallboy and I've lined the drawers 'specially for yer with fresh brown paper. There's a vase of wild flowers I collected this morning on the window sill. Wanted to make yer feel welcome 'cos . . .' she sighed heavily '. . . 't'int really nice circumstances that brings yer to stay with me, now is it? Still, we won't talk about that just now. But just to put yer mind at rest, I'll try and make yer stay as pleasant as possible and when the time comes Mrs Sims –

she's the woman that sees to all the deliveries in this village – will be on hand for yer.' The look of steadily growing horror on the young woman's face suddenly registered and she asked, 'You did know why yer were coming here, didn't yer? Yer mother has explained our arrangement?'

A sickening fear was rising within Maddie as slowly the kindly words struck home and the dreadful truth of her situation flooded through her. Her eyes flew to the bulky envelope she was still clutching in her hand and suddenly she knew what was in it. It wasn't a letter, it was money. Payment for her keep.

Her mother had lied to get her here and left her a virtual prisoner to hide her shame. And, equally as important, get her away from Josh.

And here she had been for the past seven months, fussed over by Nancy Baldicott. And if truth be told, if the situation had been different, Maddie would have been very happy. Nancy Baldicott was everything her mother was not and had been kindness itself during the whole of Maddie's confinement. But not once during that time, not while helping around the house, or going for walks, or when Mrs Baldicott had been allaying her fears and educating her on the life growing within her – nor even when she had been becoming increasingly anxious over the lack of any communication from Josh – did Maddie ever have a suspicion that her mother would plan something so terrible as taking her baby from her without a word of warning.

Suddenly a vision of her baby returned to haunt her. She had been beautiful, a fine coating of dark hair on a perfectly shaped head, violet-blue eyes staring knowingly from her tiny round face. Maddie had fallen instantly in love with her as soon as the elderly midwife had placed her in her arms. A great surge of love, joy and protectiveness had filled her very being, a feeling that was utterly indescribable. If only Josh could have been there to share these precious moments, her happiness would have been complete.

But Josh was not for whatever reason and the little being responsible for her momentary happiness had been taken from her. Her arms and heart were empty, aching excruciatingly. The loss of Josh she could possibly accept in the end, but not the loss of her child. That Maddie knew she could never do.

Her eyes alighted on a scrap of white linen that had fallen to the floor, a minute nightgown sewn with so much love and care that she had removed from her baby's tiny body only an hour or so ago after tenderly bathing her, ready, as she had innocently thought, for the journey home. With a choking sob, Maddie leaned over to scoop it up, burying her face in the softness of the fabric. She could smell the sweet odour of her child still lingering.

Her thoughts flashed to the woman who was holding her now. What was she like? Was she kind? Caring? Would she love and protect her baby to the exclusion of all else, as Maddie herself would have done?

A surge of great anger against her mother welled up in her. How could Harriet have done this? How could she have acted so cruelly and insensitively?

But despite the lust for revenge that swirled through her, Maddie knew that retaliation against her mother of any sort was futile. She could rant and rave and issue threats until she was blue in the face – Harriet would remain unyielding, of that Maddie had no doubt. Since she'd been a very young child she had known of her mother's inability to show any form of emotion, but not until now had she realised how cold and calculating Harriet truly was. The fact frightened her.

She raised her chin, eyes narrowed determinedly. Her mother might rule her life but one thing she could not do and that was crush her hopes. Maddie knew she would never be able to forgive her for what she had done. Returning home with her and carrying on with her old way of life as though nothing had happened was a challenge she did not know if she could rise to, but as matters stood now she had no choice. She had no money and nowhere to go, no relatives that she knew of, no friends to offer safe harbour while she got herself sorted. But, she silently vowed, one day, she didn't know when or how, she would be reunited with her child. That faint hope would have to be enough to keep her going. Give her a reason to carry on. Because as things stood now, she had nothing else. Her mother had made sure of that.

Rising awkwardly, she took a deep, ragged breath and began her packing.

'Young Maddie gone then? Pity I missed her, I wanted to say cheerio. Nice gel, Maddie. About the best one yer've had, Nancy. I will have a cuppa, thanks for asking. Oi, Nancy, you ain't heard a word I've said, 'ave yer? In fact, I don't think you even noticed I'd come in.' A disgruntled Betty Rumkin plonked her heavy body down on a chair opposite her neighbour at the table and eyed her in concern. Although unrelated, the two widow women, who had been neighbours for more years than either cared to admit, were like two peas in a pod and were often mistaken by strangers for sisters, much to their amusement.

But Betty could see Nancy was far from amused at the moment. By the look on her face, her neighbour was deeply troubled about something. 'Come on, old gel, what's ailing yer?' Betty asked helping herself to a cup of tea. She looked in disgust at the liquid as it spilled from the spout of the brown teapot. 'By God, Nancy, I like me tea brewed but this'd kill weeds! How many spoons did you put in the pot and how long has it been stewing?' She took a tentative sup and shuddered. 'Well?' she demanded. 'Sprouts gone watery? Forgotten to peel the spuds? I ain't leaving 'til yer tell me. And yer'd better hurry unless yer want me burnt dinner on yer conscience.'

Nancy sighed heavily. 'Oh, yer n'ote but a nosy busybody, Betty Rumkin,' she said good-naturedly. 'Well, if yer must know, I'm worried about Maddie. No matter which way I look at it, it i'nt right.'

'What ain't?'

'What the mother done, that's what.'

Betty pursed her lips. 'That thin, stuck-up-looking creature I saw coming up your path this morning?'

'That's 'er.'

'Come to collect Maddie, din't she? You did tell me it was today she was going home, din't yer? So didn't her ma take her then?'

'Oh, she took her all right. It's what she done with the baby and how she done it that's bothering me.'

'For God's sake, Nancy, will yer stop going round the 'ouses and tell me?' Betty erupted impatiently.

Nancy wrung her hands angrily. 'Got the little mite adopted without a word to young Maddie, not a peep, *that's* what she done. Maddie was beside herself. Before yer say it, I know that having the baby farmed out was probably best all round in the circumstances, but she could have discussed it with the girl first, prepared her like, or even told me so I could do it. But that's not the only reason I'm so het up.'

'It ain't?' Cradling her cup, Betty's eyes narrowed in interest.

'No, it ain't. Yer know yerself how thin these walls are, don't yer, Betty?'

'I do. Often I've heard the bones creak on yer corsets, Nancy, as yer've struggled to get 'em on.'

She was too upset to comment on her neighbour's flippancy. 'Well, Madam obviously didn't realise and I heard all she said to that poor gel.'

'And just what did she say?'

'Said Maddie was plain. *Plain*! Can yer credit it? And that young gel as pretty as a picture, and with a lovely nature too. Goodness me, most mothers'd be beside 'emselves to have a daughter like Maddie and want the best for her like we did for ours. But obviously not her. And that's not all.

43

She told Maddie she'd no chance of ever getting a husband now she was soiled. And what she said about that young man of Maddie's defies belief . . .' Nancy reeled off to Betty most of what she had overheard.

'Maddie really loved that young man. There was no need for it, Betty. No need for her to be . . . be . . . well, so nasty about it all, especially considering what she'd done with the baby. Maddie was upset enough about that without the rest on top.'

'This is Maddie's *mother* yer talking about? Her own mother?'

Nancy nodded. 'The very one who abandoned that poor gel with not a penny to her name and only condescended to visit her once in all the time she was here. Brought a woman with her then. Said she was a friend of 'ers. Said her name was . . . oh, I can't recall it now, but I'd know it again 'cos it was so posh-sounding. Hardly said a word the whole time she wa' here, but nice woman she wa'. I must say, I took to 'er. Lovely clothes she had on. I remember it crossing me mind that it were odd that a nice woman like that would be friendly with the likes of Harriet Ashman. Still . . . Oh!' Nancy suddenly exclaimed. 'So that's who she wa'. Well, I'll be blowed.'

'What is it, Nancy?' asked Betty, confused.

'It's obvious, ain't it? That woman were no friend, she wa' the woman who took the baby. Mrs Ashman had brought her along to give Maddie a look over, see what she was like before she made the final commitment. Fancy me not realising at the time. Too blooming trusting, that's what I am.' Her eyes blazed angrily. 'D'yer know summat, Betty? In all the time young Maddie was with me, not once did she ever say a word against her mother. Not once.' She paused for breath. 'We're both mothers, Betty. How can a real mother be like that, eh? You know I've come across some in my time doing this kinda work, and some of the things that have happened have made me weep. How many times have you comforted me, Betty? And I've vowed never to do it again, no matter how much I needed the money. But then I have, mainly because I feel in my way I'm helping these poor young gels. But this . . . this has to be the most terrible situation and she has to be the worst mother I've ever come across.' She sighed distractedly. 'It just seemed to me . . .'

'What? Seemed what ter yer, Nancy?'

'Maybe I'm imagining things, Betty, but I feel that Mrs Ashman wanted to . . .' She tutted. 'I don't know the right word for it . . . make young Maddie believe she was worthless, I suppose. That's what it seemed like to me. She just went on and on at her, never letting up. Oh, Betty, 't'aint right what that lovely young gel's got to put up with,' she muttered in distress.

'Eh, now, come on, gel,' Betty soothed, placing a comforting hand on top of her friend's. 'There's n'ote yer can do. There ain't no point in upsetting yerself needlessly.'

Nancy sniffed. 'I know. I'd give anything to have talked to Maddie before she left, tried to comfort her somehow, but I never got the chance. Oh, it grieves me, so it does.'

'I got to like Maddie very much meself but you were really fond of her, weren't yer, Nancy?' Betty said softly.

'Yes, and I still am.' She shrugged her shoulders helplessly. 'But yer right. What can I do, eh? I was paid to do a job. I ain't supposed to get involved. Anyway, what's done is done. Maddie's gone home and I don't expect I'll ever hear from her again. But I'll tell yer this, Betty,' she said, struggling to raise her weary body from off the chair, 'if ever I clap eyes on that woman again, I'll give her a piece of my mind!' She made a grab for the teapot. 'But then, d'yer know summat, Betty? I don't think whatever I said would make an 'aporth of difference to her.'

Her neighbour grinned, trying to lighten the situation. 'I dunno, Nancy, it might. You do have a way with words when yer dander's up.'

Her friend shook her head vigorously. 'No, Betty, not a

chance. Even with my tongue. That woman is selfish, and it's my opinion that what she done with that baby, and what she said to Maddie, and the way she treats her, is all done for her own ends and nothing more. Well, it's obvious, ain't it? She don't want her daughter to have a life, does she? And the worry is I don't think young Maddie knows what her mother's up to. Selfish bitch that she is.'

'Oh, Nancy, them's strong words for you.'

'The way I'm feeling at this moment, Betty, I could easily use stronger but . . .' A glimmer of amusement kindled in her eyes. 'I won't 'cos I don't want to make you blush. Now I'm gonna put the kettle on and try and put all this to the back of me mind.'

Nancy Baldicott knew they were brave words. Never in all her years remaining would she forget this day. All her thoughts were for the devastated young girl who had just left and the fear she felt for Maddie's future. Indeed, if there *was* much of a future for her with that woman as her mother.

# Chapter Three

'Ouch! Goodness me, watch what you're doing. You're supposed to be putting those pins in the hem of my skirt, not sticking them in me.' Mrs Green turned on Maddie in annoyance, then her face softened. 'You've been doing alterations for me for how long now? Must be getting on for ten years, and I've never known you to be so careless, Maddie. And you've hardly said a word since I arrived. Is something the matter?'

From her kneeling position on the floor, slowly removing dressmaking pins from her mouth, Maddie stared up at her client. Yes, something was the matter, she wanted to scream. It was her daughter's birthday today. Her first birthday. A day that should have been filled with celebration. A day for happiness. Instead she felt so wretched she was having trouble even thinking straight.

It was a year since that devastating day at Mrs Baldicott's, a year of pure living hell for Maddie as she'd fought to appear outwardly normal while inwardly fighting terrible emotions.

Josh's desertion of her she still could not fathom. Although it had been extremely difficult, out of respect for her mother she had kept her promise and stayed well away from anywhere she might bump into him. In fact she had hardly left the house at all except to accompany her mother to church and to help with the shopping. Secretly she had hoped that one day Josh would miraculously appear, his excuse for his disappearance something she couldn't imagine, but nevertheless something valid and believable. But as weeks then months passed she knew her hopes were futile and painfully began to accept her mother's interpretation of events as the truth despite her own terrible regret for feelings which would not die, no matter how hard she tried.

The loss of her child was another matter and no matter how hard she fought it was something she could not overcome. The ache in her heart, the emptiness of her arms, were still as acute as ever and she continually battled with frenzied worries as to how her baby was faring and terrible longings to gather the child to her and never let her go.

But how could she explain any of this to Mrs Green, when she, like all the others who knew her, had no idea of the true reason why Maddie had spent seven months away in the country?

'Let me fetch your mother,' she heard Mrs Green suggest.

'Oh, no, no,' Maddie interrupted, awkwardly rising. 'I'm all right, really I am. Just a bit of a headache, that's all.'

'Looks more than that to me. You're as white as a sheet.' The customer frowned, eyes narrowing thoughtfully. 'In fact, you haven't been the same since you came back from looking after your mother's sick friend. What illness was she suffering from? I know it's about a year ago but was it anything you could have picked up, do you think?'

Mrs Green placed a kindly hand on Maddie's arm and this small act shattered all the girl's self-control. She burst into tears.

'I'm so sorry,' she sobbed. 'Please forgive me,' she gasped, rushing from the room. She flew up the stairs and into her bedroom where she collapsed on her bed, sobbing hysterically.

Moments later her mother strode into the room, to loom over her. 'What on earth is going on?' she demanded impatiently.

She was the last person Maddie wanted to speak to at

48

this moment, the reason for all her misery. 'Please leave me alone, Mother.'

'I beg your pardon?' Harriet hissed indignantly. 'Just who do you think you are, addressing me in that tone of voice? I'm your mother. Now stop this nonsense and get up. You have a client waiting.'

Between choking sobs, Maddie struggled for breath. 'I . . . I can't.'

'Can't! You will. I haven't time for this. I've left the shop unattended. Now compose yourself, rinse your face and get back to Mrs Green.' Harriet leaned over, grabbed Maddie's arm and yanked her upright. '*Now*, I said.'

'I can't,' she wailed, chin buried in her chest. 'I can't face anyone. You know, don't you? You know what day . . .'

'Don't you dare!' Harriet warned. 'I told you a year ago that what happened was over and you were never to mention it again. I meant what I said, Maude. All that happened you brought on yourself.' Folding her skinny arms under her flat chest, she reared back her head. 'I told you you were going to suffer and you have, haven't you? Well, it's my opinion you're getting your just deserts, and wallowing in self-pity is only making matters worse for you. You've had more than enough time to put all this behind you.' Pulling a large handkerchief from the pocket of her black shop dress, she blew her nose noisily. 'If anyone deserves pity it's me, what with this dratted cold I can't shift. Now pull yourself together and get back to attending Mrs Green before we lose her custom.'

Her tone was hard and cold. Maddie flinched. Slowly she raised her head and looked straight at her mother. What she saw shocked and frightened her. The harsh lines of cruelty etched around those thin lips, the smug gleam in the hard grey eyes. But most alarming for Maddie was the gnawing suspicion that her mother appeared to be enjoying her misery and was deliberately adding to it by a refusal to show any sympathy towards her, even a show of compassion.

She shuddered, desperate to rid herself of these dreadful feelings. Dear God, she thought, please tell me I'm wrong. Her mother had told her that what she had done had been carried out in her own and the baby's best interests. She *had* to believe that. The alternative was just too terrible to contemplate.

'I'll tell Mrs Green you'll be down in a moment,' Harriet announced stonily as she turned and made her way out of the room.

# Chapter Four

'What about cottons, tapes and elastics? Need any of that stock replenishing this time round?'

'Oh, er . . .' Maddie frowned, feeling mortally inadequate, still taken aback by this salesman's unexpected appearance. Her mother had not informed her that the Coates Cottons and Haberdashery representative was due to call and she knew nothing of their stock levels. It was remiss of her, Maddie thought, to leave her so unprepared. But then, she supposed, Mother was ill, bad enough to have taken to her bed for the last three days, something that had never happened in living memory before, which left Maddie to cope with the care of her, the house, run the shop and keep the customers' alterations and repairs up to date. Regardless of how ill she might be, Harriet still wanted a blow by blow account of the events of the day and no matter how well Maddie felt she had done, her mother would always find something to grumble about.

For Maddie, although she did not like to see her mother suffer, this illness had afforded her some measure of freedom which she was enjoying immensely. Despite her mother's carping she felt she was handling it all very well, especially the shop, considering she had only once before been allowed behind the counter and that only for a day.

She decided it was best not to guess what stock to take and risk the inevitable reprimands but, rightly or wrongly, to trust the salesman. 'Well, actually, I've no idea how much stock Mrs Ashman usually holds. I presume you're more knowledgeable on that than me?'

As the words left her lips a rush of excitement raced through Gilbert Frisby, a tall, swarthy man, his dark hair plastered down with brilliantine. He flashed Maddie a brief winning smile as he set his trilby hat aside and turned around his large brown stock case, filling the counter, giving her a better view of the range he was carrying.

The owner of Ashman's was his least favourite on the list he'd inherited when he had taken over from old Harry Dolby on his retirement six months ago. As usual this visit to Ashman's was first on his daily agenda in order to get it over with. Harry Dolby, when handing over, had not had a good word to say about Harriet Ashman and Gilbert's own opinion seconded that. He too found her a humourless, austere woman, any salesman's skills wasted upon her, and never in all of Harry's or his fortnightly visits had she offered any kind of refreshment, unlike most of his other small outlet customers who enjoyed perusing his new lines and listening to his advice, whether good or not. Sales were always paramount in Gilbert Frisby's mind, no matter how they were acquired. Selling was his job and what paid his wage.

It had been a pleasurable surprise to breeze into the shop this morning, steeled to deal with Mrs Ashman, and then find this diffident assistant behind the counter. Visions of persuading her to place a large order tantalised Gilbert.

'I suppose that's understandable, you've obviously not worked here long,' he replied jauntily, concentrating on unearthing from his case several samples of new lines with which he hoped to tempt Mrs Ashman's new assistant. 'I carry all the basics so why don't you look over these samples while I check the drawers of stock and fill up? Then we can discuss what quantities of new lines you want and I'll take your order. The new braidings are particularly worth a look. Going down ever so well with my other customers they are. And we've extended the colour range of the mother-of-pearl sequins.'

Maddie accepted the sample pieces and glanced over them. The salesman was right, they were very attractive and of good quality and would enhance the plainest of outfits. But her mother did not stock anything like this for her regular customers. The most frivolous items in the shop were embroidered white handkerchiefs with a choice of a butterfly or flower in the corner or ones edged in white Nottingham lace.

'Yes, I think they're very nice,' said Maddie, putting the samples down next to his case, 'but we don't have any call for items like this.'

'If you don't mind my saying so that's the mistake your employer makes.' Gilbert lowered his voice confidentially. 'Of course, I've no idea how well this shop does but judging by the stock levels it can't do *that* well.'

A natural instinct to defend her mother rose up in Maddie. 'It's Mrs Ashman's shop and whether it does well or not is her business.'

'Yes, but . . .' Gilbert looked at her more closely, intending to inform this woman that what was sold paid her wages and so it was in her own interests to try and persuade Mrs Ashman to buck up her ideas. Instead, as his eyes met hers, he openly stared, realising with a sense of shock that his first impression of this woman had been very misleading. Admittedly the severe scraped back hairstyle did nothing at all for her but it still could not disguise a very attractive face. And those eyes! Arresting big violet-blue ones . . . he was finding it difficult to drag his own gaze away from them. And if he was not mistaken, beneath her unbecoming plain beige dress was a very shapely figure. With the right clothes and a change of hairstyle, she would be stunning. No woman would deliberately make themselves unattractive, so maybe it was a condition of her job she should dress like this for work. That would be typical of Mrs Ashman.

With growing unease Maddie wondered why he was staring at her so intently. 'Is anything the matter?' she asked, wondering if she had grown an extra head or worse.

Gilbert jumped. 'Eh? Oh . . . I was . . .' He suddenly realised he had completely forgotten what they had been talking about.

'You were about to tell me how Mrs Ashman should run her business?'

'I was?' He grinned suddenly and shrugged his shoulders. 'I was just trying to help, that's all. It's in my interest as well as yours if our goods sell well. But, to be honest, I know I'm wasting my time so far as Mrs Ashman's concerned. She's not the approachable type. I'll check your basics, will I?' And he added, as the bell on the door clanged, 'While you see to your customer. Er . . . what did you say your name was?'

'I didn't – but it's Maddie.'

She had to send the customer away empty-handed as she could not supply the style of replacement black suspenders wanted for her fashionable corselette and suddenly realised, with some concern, exactly what the salesman had been getting at.

Her mother's kind of shop was slowly dying out. Now the Great War was over, fashions were changing. 1926 saw the modern woman wearing shorter skirts and dresses which were made from much softer materials and in a wider variety of colours. Undergarments and accessories had not escaped the dictators of style either, and customers demanded the right to purchase the latest designs. Subsequently competition among retailers was fierce. Maddie had noticed as she had passed it on her way to church a display in the shop window of a close competitor a couple of streets away. Judging by the carefully thought out window, the owner stocked a wide range of lingerie for the younger woman, together with various accessories such as belts and scarves, while still catering for regular older customers. If Maddie had not been with her mother she would have liked to have stopped and looked more closely at a delicate ivory slip edged

54

with lace that had caught her eye.

Worried by the recollection, she tightened her lips. The salesman's warning was timely. Her mother's business would gradually grind to a halt as her loyal customers died off if she didn't modernise her ideas and bring in a new clientele. The trouble with Mother, Maddie thought, was that she was so set in her ways and unwilling to change, or even listen to informed suggestions, that she could not see she was heading for her own downfall.

'So I can't tempt you to try any of the new lines?' Gilbert said as, business concluded, he shut his case and handed Maddie an invoice for the replacement stock.

Settling up, she smiled. 'Not this time around. But I will speak to Mrs Ashman,' she tentatively volunteered. She felt she must at least try. It was against her nature to do otherwise.

'You will?' He laughed. 'Rather you than me!'

Slapping on his trilby, he picked up his case and headed for the door. 'Tarra, then. See you in a fortnight.' Pulling the door open, he hesitated before turning back to face her. 'I've been given complimentary tickets for the music hall next Wednesday evening. I deal with the wardrobe department there and sometimes they give me spares.' He pulled a wry face. 'Well, it's no fun going on your own, is it?'

'No, I suppose not,' she responded a mite uncomfortably, wondering where this conversation was heading.

Shutting the door again, he put down his case and returned to the counter. 'To tell you the truth, I don't half get lonely when I'm travelling. While I'm in Harborough I lodge with Ma Griffin on Wartnaby Street. It's cheap and cheerful and she's a nice old dear but not much company and the evenings drag.' He smiled at her encouragingly. 'Anyway,' he said, scanning her up and down, 'you look to me like you could do with a good night out. I don't expect you have much fun working here.' He frowned suddenly. 'You haven't already got a fella, have you?'

Maddie reddened. 'No, I haven't.'

The relief on his face was apparent. 'Well then, what do you say? I happen to know there's some good acts on.'

An array of thoughts raced frantically through her mind. Was this man really asking for her company? And would her mother let her go? Holding her breath, Maddie pressed her lips together. Although she was not particularly struck by Gilbert Frisby, he seemed a decent enough man and surely her mother couldn't object to her accompanying him to the music hall for one night. The thought of an evening out was appealing. Although she had always longed to, she had never been to the theatre. And he was right, she could do with a night out, and in return could give him the company he sought. Mother should be well on the mend by next Wednesday and it was half-day closing so Maddie had plenty of time to finish her chores and ready herself. She would just have to be very careful about when she chose to tell her mother.

'Yes, I would like to go. Thank you for asking me.'

'Right then,' said Gilbert, pleased. 'I'll call for you, shall I, about seven?'

Maddie smiled. 'Seven will be fine.'

'What's your address?'

'Pardon? Oh, here. Call for me here.'

'Here? You live in then, do you?'

She nodded. 'I do. Mrs Ashman's my mother only she's ill at the moment – that's why I'm in the shop. Usually I'm in the room at the back taking care of the alterations.'

The shock in his eyes was unmistakable and she knew it wasn't all down to the fact that Harriet Ashman was her mother; it was remorse for his plain speaking about her. 'I'll understand if you want to change your mind,' Maddie offered politely, as a get-out for him.

Common sense told Gilbert that he really should not get himself tangled up with anything to do with Harriet Ashman but he couldn't very well retract the invitation now. Anyway, it was only one night. He didn't need to ask her out again. Pity. From what little he'd seen of her, he felt he would have liked to have got to know Maddie Ashman better. 'No, I don't. I'll call for you at seven on Wednesday then.'

It wasn't until several minutes after he had left that Maddie discovered he'd left behind a box of three dozen cotton reels. She put them aside to give to him when he returned after discovering his loss.

Two days later Harriet had felt well enough to get out of her sick bed and was issuing orders from a chair by the fire. 'There's dust in here, Maude. You know very well I abhor filth. And what about Mrs Cotting's cushion repair? A ten-minute job. Why haven't you done it?'

'I hadn't the time,' she replied evenly as she placed cutlery on the table. 'I didn't finish until after eleven last night and by the time I'd prepared today's meal and tidied up, I didn't get to bed until well after twelve. Mrs Cotting did say she wasn't in a rush.'

'Mrs Cotting is a customer of long standing. No matter what she said you should still have got it done. It's obvious you can't cope, Maude.' Ignoring the hurt expression in her daughter's eyes she continued, 'I'll have to come back to work tomorrow, whether I'm well enough or not.' Harriet sniffed and blew noisily into her handkerchief. 'What have you prepared for lunch? Did you fetch that piece of haddock like I asked, and have you remembered to cook it slowly? My stomach is still very delicate.'

'I'm sorry, Mother, again I didn't have the time. The customers this morning seemed to take ages choosing what they wanted, and there were repair jobs coming into the shop too which I had to deal with. I didn't feel it right to shut up while I went out on an errand, I didn't want to lose the custom.'

Harriet grimaced, nostrils flaring. 'Oh, you didn't? The fishmonger is only a few doors down. You'd have been five minutes if that. The customers would have waited.' She exhaled sharply. 'Through no fault of my own I leave the running of the business to you for four days and that makes you an expert, does it?'

Maddie took a deep breath. 'No, Mother, of course it doesn't. I was just trying to do my best for you, that's all.' As she was speaking she thought how contradictory her mother was. First she was being reprimanded for being inconsiderate and not completing Mrs Cotting's work, despite the customer's saying she wasn't in a hurry: now she was being scolded for considering the customers by not shutting up shop while she went out on an errand. Whatever she did she could not win. Regardless, Maddie fixed a smile on her face. 'I've done you a nice piece of ox liver that I'd already arranged for the butcher's boy to deliver. I've stewed it slowly with vegetables. But I could do you a lightly boiled egg if you'd prefer?'

Harriet sniffed disdainfully. 'The liver will have to do, being's you've already done it,' she said grudgingly. Through narrowed eyes, she watched her daughter turn back to the kitchen and her mouth clamped tight as her thoughts returned to their previous conversation. Her daughter was right. Business had never been great and to lose even one customer could damage their meagre profits. Harriet cared very deeply about money but to achieve greater profits would be far too costly in other ways. Things were working out just the way she had planned many years before. To change the plan now could bring outside influences to bear and then she could lose control of everything she held dear. Harriet wasn't prepared to risk that. She realised Maddie was hovering by the door, eyeing her uncertainly.

'What?' she snapped.

Clasping her hands, her daughter stepped several paces forward. 'Well,' she began slowly, choosing her words carefully, trying to keep her enthusiasm from showing. 'When Mrs Green came in to collect her skirt she informed me she had recommended me to a Mrs Wilcox who's just moved to town with her husband from somewhere up north. I don't know how Mrs Green came across her but apparently Mr Wilcox is a solicitor and is going to be opening an office here. He has just bought a big house on the Kilby Road. Mrs Wilcox needs someone to make all her curtains and matching cushions. Wasn't it good of Mrs Green to suggest me? She said Mrs Wilcox would be in touch.'

'I can't spare you. You'll have to tell her to find someone else,' Harriet declared resolutely.

Taken aback, Maddie stared at her, wanting to question her reason for turning down such a lucrative offer, not to mention the further work it could generate. It didn't make sense. Why deliberately turn down work without even attempting to see if they could handle it? Maddie knew she could do it, but more importantly she would really have liked to have done it. Being inside that lovely big house, advising Mrs Wilcox on fabrics and designs . . . For a moment she pondered taking the job without her mother's knowledge. But she knew the thought to be an idle fantasy. Her mother felt it was her right to know exactly how Maddie's time was spent every minute of the day.

'Are you going to get my dinner or stand there gawping like an idiot while I starve? It'll soon be time to open the shop again.'

'What? Oh, yes, Mother, of course.'

A preoccupied Maddie made her way back to the kitchen. In view of Harriet's response she thought it best not to mention her conversation with Gilbert Frisby on considering new lines, nor did she relish the prospect of telling her of her trip to the theatre.

It was Wednesday by the time Maddie did pluck up the courage and then only because she dare not leave it any longer. She waited until her mother had laid down her knife and fork after their midday meal. Taking a deep breath, she opened her mouth to speak but Harriet beat her to it.

'That piece of chin beef was tough,' she complained. 'Or maybe it was your cooking, Maude. Did you sear it first in hot fat to seal in the juices, like I've instructed you?'

Maddie inwardly flinched. Why did her mother always have to address her as though she was a child? 'Yes,' she replied evenly. 'And I cooked it slowly in the oven.'

'Well, obviously not slowly enough. Why can't you do as you're told, Maude? I really can't be expected to run the shop as well as cook the midday meal, but I suppose I'll have to. I can't risk my teeth on tough meat again.' She eyed Maddie sharply. 'Have you something you want to tell me? You're acting like a scared rabbit.'

She gulped. 'Oh, well . . . yes, I do. I'm . . . well, I'm . . .'

'For goodness' sake, girl, out with it. I haven't all day!'

Maddie blurted out, 'I'm going to the music hall tonight.'

Harriet pursed her lips. 'Really?' she said matter-of-factly, rising to gather the dirty crockery. 'Well, if that's your idea of entertainment, I hope you enjoy yourself.' Maddie stared at her astonished, this response the very last she had expected. She took a deep breath. 'With Gilbert Frisby, the Coates Cottons salesman,' she added, hesitantly.

Still continuing her task, Harriet sniffed. 'As I said, enjoy yourself. Just make sure you're home before ten. You still have to get up for work in the morning.'

Shocked, Maddie muttered, 'I will. Thank you, Mother.'

Frowning, Maddie glanced at the clock above the jeweller's across the road, then up and down the street. It was a warm, pleasant June evening and plenty of people were about, either coming or going or just milling around talking with friends. Although she wasn't, she felt conspicuous standing outside the shop and the longer she waited the worse the feeling grew.

It was ten minutes past seven and there was no sign of Gilbert. For a moment she wondered whether she had mistaken their arrangement but she knew that she hadn't.

Seven o'clock, he had said. Well, it was now nearly a quarter past and if he didn't hurry they would be late. Maddie understood the show started at seven-thirty.

At a quarter to eight all her hopes had faded, there were no excuses left. Resigned, she made her way back inside.

Her mother looked up from her book as Maddie entered the sitting room. 'You're back early.'

She swallowed hard. 'Mr Frisby didn't come,' she said softly. 'Something must have happened and he couldn't let me know.'

'Or just didn't bother.'

'Pardon?'

Harriet snorted, glancing her daughter up and down. 'Well let's face it, Maude, the man felt sorry for you, that's why he asked you out in the first place. It's my opinion that as soon as he left he regretted his action. When will you learn? Men like him don't take out plain women like you unless there's good reason to.' She ignored the look of devastation on her daughter's face. 'Best advice I can give you, my girl, is not to accept any invitations in future, no matter how genuine you think they are. It'll save you the humiliation. Now why don't you get yourself a glass of warm milk and go to bed? A good night's sleep and you'll forget all about it come morning.'

Maddie was too dispirited to respond with any more than, 'Yes, Mother.'

Upstairs in her cold, sparsely furnished bedroom, a dejected Maddie caught sight of herself in the mirror just as she was about to get undressed. She stared at herself. She had made such an effort to look nice even if her skirt was not made of fancy material, her high-buttoned blouse just a sprig cotton print, and her hair tied back in a plain bow. If she'd done otherwise Harriet would have given her no choice but to revert to her original style. But she did look clean and neat.

She sighed. Men preferred good-looking, fashionably

dressed women on their arm. Her mother was right. Neat, clean and plain-faced only got a look in if nothing else was available. Maybe Gilbert had had a better offer but she herself preferred to think that as the busy man he was, work had waylaid him and he just had not found the time to let her know.

Slipping off her clothes, she folded them neatly, thinking this was another hard lesson she had learned. How many more must she be cruelly taught before her days ended?

But Gilbert's thoughtlessness was not the only matter that was troubling her – something far more worrying was.

Crossing to the window, she pulled aside the net curtain and peered out. The pleasant early-summer evening was drawing to a close. Voices and sounds drifted on the warm air. Mothers herded their offspring inside; men's boots clattered on the cobbles as they made their way home from work or off to the pub to wash the day's grime from their throats; groups gathered on corners. There was the clip-clop of horses' hooves pulling late delivery carts; a distant factory hooter sounding the beginning of the evening shift. Maddie heard little or none of this. All her thoughts were centred on her mother.

Lifting her eyes she focused them blankly on the bright crescent moon hanging low in the darkening sky, wispy clouds drifting across it. She frowned. Just why was Mother so caustic towards her? Why was it she appeared to go out of her way to add further pain or humiliation to any Maddie was already suffering? Were not mothers supposed to nurture their children, encourage them to do well, share in their happiness, be a comfort in physical or emotional pain? Why did hers show none of these traits? In fact, just the opposite.

Sighing, she tilted her head, eyes narrowing questioningly. But more importantly, why did she herself, no child any more but a grown woman of twenty-six, allow herself to be intimidated so blatantly, so much so that she was frightened to be herself or voice any opinion? She allowed her mother to rule her, going along with her wishes in order to live a peaceful life. Why couldn't she stand up for herself, put her own point across? What was it about Harriet that made her feel unable to do this? Or was it that she herself had acted this way for so long she didn't know how to do otherwise?

Her thoughts, as they had done many times in the past, strayed to the man who had fathered her and suddenly she wished her mother would unyield and talk to her about him, then maybe she would understand herself a little better. Maddie tried to picture her father but couldn't. She didn't know if he was tall or small, fat or thin, and of his features she had no idea. Did she take after him in any way at all? She sighed. Was his death the reason behind her mother's bitterness, her coldness, her unwillingness to administer any kind of warmth? Had his death affected her so much she had closed down her feelings by way of shielding herself from further hurt? If that was true then she must have loved him very much.

Maddie tried to picture her mother happy, the several brothers and sisters Maddie might have had clinging to her skirts. Tried to feel the family unity that could have reigned, had her father lived. She couldn't. She had never seen her mother smile, never witnessed her happy, and even visualising Harriet in different circumstances was impossible. She knew she was wasting her time trying.

People suffered greatly through their lives and dealt with grief in varying ways but their basic natures did not alter. If she was honest with herself Maddie knew her father must have been a man very much of her mother's nature or else there would have been nothing to have brought about a marriage between them in the first place. Maddie shuddered violently and suddenly felt a great need to get out of this house, away from the walls that had been her sanctuary for over a year while she had striven to heal herself. For a while she needed to be away from her mother's prying eyes and critical tongue, to be alone with her thoughts. She had once enjoyed solitary walks. Maybe she could do again. She would have to do something unless she wanted to become a total recluse.

Tomorrow night, she decided, she would go for a walk after all her chores were done. The fresh air might clear her head and help her to think straight, stiffen her resolve to face things as they were. She must get on with things. If she was honest with herself, her life could be much worse. She only had to poke her head out of the door to see the poverty that reigned locally, worry and deprivation etched on people's faces. In that respect at least she could consider herself lucky.

# Chapter Five

'I shan't be long, Mother.'

'Where are you going?'

Maddie shrugged her shoulders as she made to pick up her handbag then decided she wouldn't need it. 'Nowhere in particular – just for a walk.'

'It's too late to go walking by yourself. You are going to be by yourself, I trust? Nothing you're keeping back from me, is there?'

'No, Mother,' she replied evenly, trying to keep her irritation from showing. 'I'm going completely by myself. And it's only just gone eight, still plenty of light left.'

'Huh! Well, if you must. Just show some consideration and don't be long. I don't intend sitting here until all hours worrying on your behalf.'

Maddie looked across at her. Was Harriet showing genuine concern for her welfare or giving way to displeasure that her daughter was doing something that brought her into contact with the outside world, something Harriet couldn't control without insisting she accompany her? And Maddie knew she wouldn't relish that prospect, not after she had settled herself for the night. If she herself was honest, wasn't that why she had left it this late, to avoid the prospect of Mother insisting she came too?

'Well?'

'Pardon?'

'I thought you were going for a walk?' Harriet snapped.

'I am. I . . . I was just contemplating whether I would

need a cardigan. I don't think I'll take one.'

Harriet tutted. 'Well, at least you've made one decision. Just fill the kettle and swing it across the fire first. I'll have to make my own cocoa.' It was not a statement but an accusation.

'Oh!' Maddie's face filled with remorse. It fell to her to make the last drinks of the evening and in her haste to get out she had forgotten that task. 'I'll do it before I go.'

Harriet flapped her hand in irritation. 'No need. I'm sure I can do it myself . . . for one evening,' she emphasised.

Standing outside on the pavement, Maddie looked up and down the street, undecided as to what route to take. Left took her towards the canal, an area she hadn't been near for well over a year in order to avoid reviving memories she was trying hard to forget. Right took her to the town centre just past which was the park. In her frame of mind the park would be the ideal place for a stroll at this time of night; plenty of people would still be about on this warm summer evening, enough to stop her feeling any more conspicuous than normal.

She had just turned into the main high street when she noticed a figure approaching, head bowed, hands dug deep in his jacket pockets. Her heart thumped and her footsteps slowed. It was Gilbert Frisby. He was only a few feet away from her and a meeting was unavoidable. Maddie's thoughts raced frantically. She wasn't sure what to do. Despite the fact that he'd let her down, it wasn't in her nature blatantly to ignore him, though in the circumstances neither did she feel she could casually pass the time of day either.

Suddenly she frowned. There was something about him that wasn't right . . . then it dawned on her that his whole persona radiated unhappiness. Her immediate thought was that someone close to him had died. Her own concern as to how to handle this awkward situation was forgotten as her caring nature took over.

As he passed her, she waylaid him. 'Mr Frisby, are you

all right? Mr Frisby?' she repeated.

He stopped abruptly and eyed her, confused. 'What?' Then his eyes flashed recognition and his already frowning face filled with fury. 'You!' he spat. 'You've some brass neck, talking to me.'

Maddie gasped, shocked. She had been wrong. Gilbert Frisby was not upset – he was furious about something and all her instincts were screaming a warning that it was something to do with her. Though how was beyond her, she barely knew the man. 'I beg your pardon?'

'You can beg as much as you like but you'll get no pardon from me. Proud, are you?'

'Pardon?' gasped Maddie.

'Pardon,' he mimicked. 'Is that the only word you know? You heard me. I said, proud.' He pushed his face so close to hers she could smell his breath. He'd been drinking. 'How does it feel, eh, to lose a man his job? Makes you feel good, does it?'

Maddie recoiled in shock. 'I . . . I don't understand?'

He looked at her in disgust. 'Don't play the innocent with me. She told my boss I was hounding you. Wouldn't leave you alone. Is that what you told her? For God's sake, I only asked you out for the evening. You call that harassment, do you? You're mental, you are. You want locking up.' He pushed Maddie so hard she stumbled backwards. 'Get out of my way,' he spat, and strode off.

Recovering her senses after his attack, her mind raced, trying to fathom a reason for his behaviour. But she couldn't. Neither could she work out who this 'she' he referred to was. Regardless, she was innocent of his accusation and couldn't let him go without making him believe her. 'Mr Frisby, wait!' cried Maddie, running after him and grabbing his arm. 'Believe me, I don't know what you're talking about. Honestly,' she stressed. 'Will you please stop and listen to me? Please, Mr Frisby.'

The tone of her voice halted him and he studied her hard

for several long moments. 'You don't, do you?' he said finally, his harsh expression softening slightly. 'You haven't a clue what I'm talking about, have you?'

Maddie shook her head. 'No, I haven't.' She raised her hands in a helpless gesture. 'The only thing I do know is that we had an arrangement for Wednesday evening at seven. I waited for you but you never came. I thought . . . thought you were too busy to let me know. So I went home.'

He frowned, confused. 'Eh? And you didn't send her to see me?'

'No.' She eyed him, frowning in bewilderment. 'Just who is this person . . .' Her voice trailed off as slowly the truth dawned. 'Oh! You mean . . . my mother? That's who you're referring to?'

Flaring his nostrils, he nodded. 'She came to my digs. Demanded to see me. Told me how upset you were that I'd dared to proposition you in that way. That you had no intention of being seen out with the likes of me and I wasn't to humiliate you by asking you out again. In front of my landlady as well.'

'What?' Gasped Maddie, mortified. 'I can assure you, Mr Frisby, I never said any such thing.'

'You didn't?'

'No, I didn't.' Her confusion mounted. 'When was this? When did my mother come to see you exactly?'

'Tuesday evening.'

'Tuesday evening? Then it couldn't have been her. I didn't tell her I was going to the music hall with you until about an hour before we were to meet. You must be mistaken.'

His face darkened. 'Listen, it was Mrs Ashman, I tell you. I'd know that woman if it were pitch black. The sound of her voice is enough to set anyone's teeth on edge! She may be your mother, but she's been the bane of my life since I took over Harry Dolby's round. I can't pretend I'm fond of her and there's no way I'd ever mistake anyone else for her. There is no one else like her. So when I say she came on

Tuesday, she came on Tuesday.'

He was so adamant Maddie had to believe him. And thinking about it, her mother had popped out that night without saying where she was going. But all the same . . . 'It doesn't make sense. As I've already said, I didn't mention a word of our arrangement to her until an hour before. So it couldn't have been her who came to see you, could it?'

'Oh, but she did know.'

'She did? How?'

'I told her.'

'You?'

'Yes, I mentioned it when I dropped in for the box of cottons. I'd had a run on white cotton and it was my last box. I hadn't realised I'd left it behind at your shop until I needed them. Monday morning it was. I wouldn't normally have bothered, it was miles out of my way, but one of my customers was desperate and couldn't wait until my next visit. As I was leaving I just asked her to tell you I was looking forward to our night out and not to be late as the show started promptly. She asked where I was taking you. Seemed really interested. I told her and she said she hoped we had a nice time. Quite pleasant she was. Not like her normal self at all,' he snarled. 'So, you see, she did know.'

Maddie listened, stunned. This situation was dreadful. How could her mother do this to her? She felt so humiliated she wanted the ground to open and swallow her up. To die on the spot would be better. What must this man think of her. With an effort she raised her eyes to meet his. 'Look, I . . .'

'Don't bother,' Gilbert told her. 'Nothing you can say will put any of this right. I have nothing but pity for you. You can't have any life living with her.' A nasty smirk curled the corners of his mouth. 'But then, maybe you deserve each other. But one thing I'll never understand – why did she have to write to my boss and get me the sack? Why did she have to do that, eh? The evil bitch.'

69

Maddie gasped. 'She did what?'

'You heard. Sent the letter special delivery. Wrote that she was disgusted the company employed people like me and consequently didn't want any more to do with Coates Cottons. She hoped my conduct would be suitably addressed. *Suitably addressed,*' he hissed. 'Oh, they did that all right, didn't they? My boss came personally to do the deed. Wouldn't listen to my side of things but finished me on the spot. And without a good reference, I'll be lucky to get another job. I was so shocked by it all I had to have a few pints.' He glared at her. 'Yeah, I'm drunk, and who can blame me, eh?'

Totally horrified, Maddie clasped her hand to her mouth. 'Mr Frisby, I'm so sorry. I don't know what to say . . .'

'Then don't say anything,' he exclaimed, expression murderous. He jabbed her hard in the shoulder with his finger. 'Your family has done enough. I wish I'd never clapped eyes on either of you, especially her. I just hope she can sleep at night. Now I think I'd better collect my belongings from my digs before I do something I regret.' He raised his hat and said sarcastically, 'Good evening, Miss Ashman. What a pleasure it's been.'

Spinning on his heel, he clapped his hat back on his head and marched off down the street.

Maddie stared after him, unaware of passers-by taking an interest in her, wondering why she was standing in the middle of the pavement, her face white with astonishment.

It took someone accidentally bumping into her to get Maddie moving. Although it was not her fault, she apologised profusely then stepped back until she came up against a wall which she slumped against, mind fully occupied with her conversation with Gilbert Frisby. He just had to be lying, he had to be. It was too terrible to think that her mother would go to such lengths in order to deny her a night of pleasure. But why would he lie? What reason would Gilbert Frisby have for concocting such an elaborate tale?

Her jumbled thoughts whirled madly. It seemed they didn't quite fit together, but she knew they would if she allowed them to. It was only fear that held her back. Fear to face the truth about her mother.

Maddie's heart beat painfully. If her mother had done this terrible thing then an innocent man had lost his job and that wasn't right. Maybe it was too late to do anything about that dreadful situation, but regardless, she had to know the truth. The only way to get it was to do something she had never done before and that was to tackle Harriet. The thought petrified her.

Face ashen, a deeply burdened Maddie slowly made her way home. She stood for several minutes at the back door, summoning all her courage, before she took several deep breaths and let herself in.

Harriet was in the kitchen, bending over the sink washing the cup and saucer she had used for her nightcap. Without raising her head, she said, 'You didn't stay out long.'

Maddie's hands felt clammy and beads of sweat began to form on her brow but she was determined not to let her courage fail her. 'I . . .' she began faltering.

'For goodness' sake, Maude, stop stammering and say what you've got to say. I haven't all night.'

Her mother's sharp retort sent a wave of panic through her and Maddie felt her courage begin to ebb. But she knew that she must not let it. If she did not get to the bottom of her problem she knew she would never rest easy. Steeling herself, she took a deep breath. 'I only got as far as the main street when I met Gilbert Frisby. You know, Mother, the Coates Cottons salesman.'

Maddie watched her mother closely for any tell-tale signs but not a muscle on Harriet's face twitched as she reached over for a drying cloth and turned to face her daughter. 'I do know who Gilbert Frisby is,' she said tersely. 'Is there a point to this story, Maude?'

'Yes, there is.' She clasped her damp hands together

tightly. 'I . . . thought you'd be interested to know he's been sacked.'

Harriet sniffed disdainfully. 'Really? And what makes you think I'd be interested in that? He's nothing to me. Now I'm tired and I'm going to bed. The kettle is just off the boil if you want a cup of cocoa. Make sure you lock up properly before you come up.'

With that she headed out of the room, leaving Maddie none the wiser, listening to her footfall as she climbed the stairs.

Early the next evening Maddie stopped suddenly at the bend in the tow path and surveyed in delighted surprise the busy scene before her. She had had the most dreadful day, unanswered questions still whirling in her mind as she'd fought to carry out her daily duties as though nothing was amiss.

Sitting opposite her mother during mealtimes had been the hardest thing to do. She had found it difficult to look her in the eye without wondering if Harriet could possibly be the terrible person Maddie now strongly suspected she was.

Her announcing that she was going for another walk that evening had not pleased Harriet at all and several obstacles had been put in her way. But, much to her own surprise, Maddie had stood her ground, her need to get out of the house far outweighing the backlash for blatantly disobeying her mother's wishes.

So distracted was she, she hadn't realised her route had taken her down the canal tow path, let alone a mile or two along it, until the noises of the barge people going about their business only yards away suddenly broke in on her. For a moment her worries flew from her. Foxton Locks! She could not remember the last time she had come here and it was like seeing it for the very first time.

A series of canal locks, seven in number, had been cut

into a hillside, affording a never-ending succession of canal traffic passage on its journey to and from the Grand Canal that shipped goods from the Liverpool and Manchester docks right across the Midlands and beyond. It was an extremely pretty countryside setting between Market Harborough and Leicester, quite near the borders of Northamptonshire, and local people would come to spend their leisure time watching the antics of the canal folk as they went about their business.

Not far away from where Maddie stood a wide basin off the main artery of the canal afforded barges moorings for the night and in early evening it was a hive of activity.

As she wandered forward, Maddie could see several barges queuing to journey through the locks to the top of the hill. At the top other barges were lined up to make the journey down. She smiled to herself. The locks reminded her of steps, only these were water steps. How clever of the engineer who had managed to solve this problem when confronted with the hill during the construction of the canal.

Some of the barges were great rusting monsters, their long narrow cargo holds filled with coal and steel, the men in charge dirty rough-looking types, the horses pulling them, although looking reasonably well-fed, pitifully tired. Other barges were obviously used as dwellings and were brightly painted with intricate designs peculiar to the canal people. Tattered washing flapped from raised lines running the length of the barge roofs and chimneys smoked from ovens burning down below.

Bare-footed, grimy children skittered up and down the tow path, some doing their best to hinder the harassed lock master and his helper as they strove to open and close the huge wooden gates in order for water to fill or empty from the locks. Until all the barges had received safe passage there would be no rest for them.

On a barge nearby, sitting on a stool by the tiller, legs spread wide, sat an elderly woman, her skin weathered to a very dark brown and creased to such an extent it reminded Maddie of a piece of crumpled linen. She was contentedly smoking a clay pipe, eyes fixed on several small children whom Maddie assumed to be in her charge. She was probably their grandmother or maybe even their great-grandmother, her age being indeterminate.

Immersed in the activity around her, for once free from painful thoughts, Maddie did not at first see the child before her until the younger one that was perched on her hip made a sound. Maddie was startled at first, then smiled warmly at the owners of two pairs of large brown eyes set in two grubby faces, feeling sadness rise in her at their dirty, unkempt appearance.

'Hello,' she said softly.

Still staring, the child she guessed to be about five shifted the baby higher on to her hip. As she did so Maddie's attention was drawn and a great surge of sorrow washed through her. The baby was around the age her own child would be now and it took all her strength to fight a desire to grab it to her and wrap it in her arms, just for a minute.

Faced with a total stranger gazing so intently, the baby's face puckered and it let out a shrill wail.

Before Maddie knew what was happening several people were upon her and a bedraggled woman roughly caught her arm, pulling her back, while another grabbed up the baby in one hand and snatched the young girl's hand in the other.

A shabby man raced up. 'What's 'app'nin', Rosa?' he demanded, whipping off a stained red-spotted neckerchief to wipe his brow. He shot an accusing glance at Maddie.

'Gon' pinch baby, she wa',' the woman holding the children spat accusingly.

Astounded, Maddie struggled free from the other woman's grip. 'I was not!' she proclaimed. 'I was only . . .'

'Ged out of it,' Rosa hissed, clutching the baby protectively to her. 'Gon' pinch my baby you wa'. I saw the way you were lookin' at 'er.'

'Rosa!' a deep voice bellowed. 'Leave the woman alone. Wan't doin' no harm. Get children inside and be about yer business. And you too, Harry and Mary.'

All eyes turned to stare across at the old lady on the barge.

'But Gramma . . .' Rosa protested.

She wagged her pipe warningly.

Rosa's lips tightened and with a jerk of her head towards Harry and Mary, she turned and marched back down the tow path, the others following.

'You,' the old lady addressed Maddie. 'Come,' she beckoned. 'Come here.'

The terrible misunderstanding still fresh in her mind, Maddie hesitated.

The old lady beckoned again. 'Come, chile.' She smiled, her lined face creasing into folds, mouth revealing two rows of tobacco-blackened gums.

Maddie stared at her. A great desire to turn and flee from this situation filled her but there was something about this old lady, something that was drawing Maddie towards her. Not knowing why, she suddenly found herself negotiating the short narrow plank from the path on to the barge.

On board the old lady indicated a rickety wooden stool set to one side of her. 'Sit,' she ordered.

Maddie eyed the stool, then looked uncertainly at the old woman. 'Please believe me, I wasn't going to take the baby. I was only . . .'

The woman raised her hand to silence Maddie. 'Sit,' she ordered again.

Maddie obeyed.

Laying down her pipe on an upturned rusting pail nearby, the old lady took Maddie's hands in hers and as she did so shut her eyes, emitting low inaudible murmurs.

At the touch of her fingers a shiver shot down Maddie's spine, then she felt warmth spread right through her and sat transfixed.

Several long moments passed before the ancient woman's hooded eyes opened and she released Maddie's hands. She nodded several times.

'You've known deep pain, chile, but have faith,' she muttered in a deep throaty drawl. Rheumy eyes fixed on Maddie's, boring deep. 'What is lost can be found, you 'ear me? But you, chile, open your eyes. See what is there. Face it. Nothing'll begin for you 'til you do. Be strong. You're kind,' she said, one fist thumping her own chest. 'In 'ere where it matters. A good chile, you are.' She reached over and ran a gnarled hand down the side of Maddie's face. 'Pretty lady, you must believe that.' She took a deep breath and picked up her pipe which she placed in her mouth. 'Now go, and think on.'

The next thing Maddie knew she was on the tow path yards away from the barge, not able to remember how she had got there. For several moments she stood bewildered, staring around her. The barge people were going about their business just as they had been when she had first turned the corner minutes earlier, the children either playing or annoying the lock master. She looked across at the old lady on the barge who appeared to be asleep.

Maddie frowned. It was as though the whole episode had never happened, as though she'd imagined it somehow. But she knew she hadn't.

Deeply disturbed, she turned slowly and made her way back down the path, mind going over and over the words spoken by the old lady.

Presently she came to a small recess in the thick hedge and absently squatted down on a flattish boulder embedded in the ground, heedless of the scruffy young boy several yards downwater, fishing with a home-made rod, anxious to catch his family their supper.

What had the woman been trying to tell her? 'What was lost could be found . . .' What had Maddie lost? And what else had been said? 'Open your eyes.' What did that mean exactly? She pondered deeply but couldn't make sense of it.

Elbows on knees, she rested her chin in her hands, fixing her gaze on the ripples of the canal, and as she did so a vision of Josh appeared and her heart began pounding painfully. She saw him climbing out of the canal after the accident on their very first meeting and although he hadn't at the time, now he was smiling that special smile that was for her alone, eyes filled with love. Other scenes from the past followed swiftly.

Their first outing to the park, the first time he'd ventured to hold her hand, their very first clumsy kiss, then the memorable night they had celebrated their love under the stars. Despite her determination to lock away these memories, so strong were they still, so fresh, that she could feel the pressure of his arms around her.

Then her thoughts fixed on the man himself. The Josh she knew. The man who had taken the time to get to know her, showing patience, consideration and understanding towards her problems when she knew deep down they must have frustrated and annoyed him. He'd told her he loved her and wanted to marry her. And how willing he had been to confront her mother, despite knowing the reception he'd receive when Maddie had told him of her worrying condition.

She took a deep breath. Now she had allowed herself to reflect she knew without a doubt Josh had not set out to entrap her just to better his own position, and nor was he a man to abandon her without good reason. Her mother had been wrong. And, anyway, Harriet was in no position to judge him when she had never met him and taken the trouble to get to know him.

Suddenly the vision of Josh vanished and a picture of Gilbert Frisby appeared. An angry Gilbert Frisby, one who had just lost his job through . . .

Maddie gave a startled gasp, hand clamped against her

mouth, nails digging into the flesh. 'My God!' she groaned as it all suddenly became clear and she realised just what the old woman had been trying to tell her. See! Look! Not at everyday sights but at what was actually going on right under her nose. Important things, terrible things she did not want to acknowledge. But suddenly she was forced to because of an old woman's ramblings.

She knew she was being told to acknowledge that if her mother had gone to such trouble over a night out with Gilbert Frisby, what else had she been capable of? What else had she done to stop Maddie from straying? Was that why Josh had not replied to her letters, had seemed to desert her? Had her mother warned him off too?

Clasping her hands to the sides of her head, Maddie doubled over and rocked with agony. Every fibre of her being begged for these thoughts not to be true, while every ounce of her intelligence struggled to force her to acknowledge that they were.

She raised her head and stared blindly around. She needed answers. She could not go on any longer fighting her emotions, day in, day out, living with a woman she did not know if she could trust, mother or not.

Maddie knew what she had to do. The only thing she could do to have her suspicions allayed or confirmed. Something she should have done well over a year ago but which she had shied away from for fear of what she would find out.

She would have to go and see Mrs Jenks, Josh's mother. She would have to go now, it could not wait. The thought made her shudder violently and she bit her lip so hard she drew blood and wiped it away with the back of her hand.

She rose resolutely and almost ran back down the path, conscious that if she did not hurry, her courage might fail her.

She knew where Josh lived, he had never hidden the fact from her, and as she turned the corner of a street in a miserable over-populated area of dilapidated terraces on the west side of town, a fleeting worry that he might have returned and she would encounter him raised itself and was hurriedly rejected. Whether Josh was back in Market Harborough was not important at this moment. Getting to the truth was.

What she would do when armed with the information hadn't crossed Maddie's mind.

The door she arrived at, although badly in need of a coat of paint, was clean, as were the windows and old nets hanging inside. The step, although not Cardinal polished, had been recently swept and mopped. The same could not be said of the other houses she had rushed by. Maddie stood for a moment and stared at the tarnished iron numbers nailed to the door: 81. The number, Josh had once laughingly told her, reminded him of his parents. Eight for his mother as she was small and fat, and one for his father who was tall and thin.

As she raised her hand to knock, Maddie hesitated for a moment. But before she could think or do anything further the door suddenly shot open and a woman not far from her own age stood there. Maddie knew then she had come to the right house as this person was the image of Josh, only the features were finer and she was not so tall. She was dressed in a plum-coloured dress with a Peter Pan collar, obviously on her way out.

They both stared, startled to see each other.

'Oh!' the woman exclaimed, a smile on her pretty face. 'Yer gave me a shock. Who did yer want? Silly me. Me mother, in't it?'

There was no going back now and Maddie gulped. 'Yes, please, if she's in?'

'Mam!' the woman turned and called down the passage. 'Miss Bundy's 'ere to see yer about our Jeffrey.' She turned back to face Maddie. 'She's in a flap is me mam 'cos you're coming. But we've all said to 'er that if our Jeff is brainy enough to go to the grammar, then it's up to us to see that 'e does.' She cocked her head proudly. 'Right bright spark is our Jeffrey – but then, you know that, don't yer, Miss Bundy? You being his teacher. And it wouldn't be right to deny me brother this chance, now would it? Fancy our Jeff, eh? The first of the Jenkses to get the chance not to land up in the corset factory. Mam!' she called again as she stepped on to the cobbled pavement. 'Yer'll have to excuse me, Miss Bundy, I'm late. Always late I am. Still, never mind, if 'e doesn't wait for me then 'e ain't worth it, is 'e? Tarra,' she called, heading off down the street.

A small woman came bustling down the dark passage. She was wiping her hands on a stained floral wraparound apron. 'Oh, I am sorry, Miss Bundy,' she murmured apologetically as she arrived on the doorstep. 'I din't expect yer 'til about nine. Yer note did say you couldn't mek it before 'cos yer'd school things ter see to. Oh!' she said, taken aback. 'You ain't Miss Bundy.'

Maddie nervously cleared her throat. 'No, I'm not. I'm . . . Mrs Jenks, my name is Maddie Ashman. I've come to see you . . . come to ask you . . .'

As she was speaking Sadie Jenks's face turned white then red as her caller's identity registered. 'You!' she spat. 'You ain't got n'ote to ask of me. How dare yer? How dare yer stand like a brazen hussy on my doorstep after all you've done? Clear off, yer 'ear me? Clear off. And I ain't a violent woman but if you ever show yer face round 'ere again there'll be n'ote left of it, time I've finished.' She stepped back and grabbed the door, aiming to slam it.

'Please, Mrs Jenks, please listen to me,' Maddie pleaded, placing one hand on the door to stop it from shutting. 'It's not what you think.'

The door was pushed open again, hitting the passage wall. 'Not what I think? I don't 'ave ter think – I *know*. You ruined my son's life you did, wi' what you done. Scarpered, din't yer, without a word, wi' 'is child in yer belly? But yer

80

couldn't tell 'im yerself. Oh, no. Sent 'er down. She stood on my doorstep just like you are now. Told me 'ow you wanted n'ote more to do wi' my Josh after 'im forcing 'imself on yer like that and that the baby wa' gonna be adopted. That baby wa' our first grandchild, our own flesh and blood. But never a thought wa' given to our feelings, wa' there? My son,' she cried furiously, stabbing herself in her ample chest, 'wouldn't force 'imself on anybody, let alone the likes of you.

'I told 'er to fetch the coppers and we'd sort it out proper. Oh, she backed off then, din't she? 'Cos she wa' bloody lying about that and she knew I knew she wa'. I sent her scarpering then, I can tell yer. I weren't 'aving the likes of 'er standing on my doorstep telling me a pack of lies. I remember 'er when she had no shoes on 'er feet and 'oles in her knickers. I've better in my 'ouse than what 'er own mother sold in that shop and that's saying summat. She ain't got no right to try and mek me feel my son ain't good enough for 'er daughter. She should remember where she came from, she should.'

Without pausing for breath she continued, 'It broke my Josh's heart when I told 'im. Cried like I've never seen a man cry. Before I could stop 'im 'e rushed round to see yer mam, plead wi' 'er to tell 'im where you were so 'e could 'ear the truth of it from yer own lips. But would she? Would she 'ell tell 'im? She said to 'im you were frightened of 'im and had had to go away. And then she had the nerve ter say that 'e only struck up wi' you ter better 'imself. Who the 'ell does she think she is? My son wouldn't take up wi' bloody royalty itsel' just to do that. We Jenkses might not 'ave much but we do 'ave our pride.

Sadie's eyes blazed furiously. 'Anyway, missy, 'ow come if 'e forced 'imself on yer, he was thinking yer were getting married? Asked me and 'is dad if yer could both live 'ere for a while 'til yer got a place of yer own, 'e did. Answer me that, eh?' Without waiting for a reply she stabbed Maddie angrily in the chest with her finger. 'No, yer can't, can yer? Because yer *'ad* promised ter marry 'im. My Josh is not a liar. Not like you. Told yer mam that cock and bull when yer found you were expecting, did yer, to cover up what you'd done? Well, madam, yer needn't think yer can come round 'ere now for whatever it is yer want. I won't 'ave it. Yer've caused enough trouble in my 'ouse, you'll cause no more.

'My Josh is 'appy where 'e is. It took 'im long enough to get over you. I ain't 'aving it raked up again just for you to upset 'im.' Sadie puffed up her chest. 'For your information 'e don't live round 'ere no more and 'e's happily married wi' a kiddy on the way. And yer needn't think of writing any more letters 'cos they'll go the same way the others did. Unopened on the fire. It's my opinion he had a lucky escape, just like your father. I don't hold wi' men who walk out on their families but in yer dad's case I wanted to pat him on the back when I heard and congratulate him fer having the courage.

Maddie was gazing at her, stupefied. 'What do you mean?' she gasped. 'My father's dead. He didn't leave my mother.'

Sadie Jenks gave a loud bellow. 'Is that what she told yer? Dead indeed! He's no more dead than my old man and your mam's no more a widow than I am. The last I heard of yer dad he was very much alive and living in Leicester, still working for Amicable Refuge Insurance. Now, I've said all I'm gonna say to you and that were far more than I ever intended should I clap eyes on yer. So clear off.'

'What's goin' on, Sadie? What's all the shouting about?' a male voice called from inside.

'N'ote, Albert. Just a woman got the wrong 'ouse.' She glared at Maddie warningly. 'But I've put her straight. Told 'er where to go.' She leaned forward and pushed an open-mouthed Maddie hard in the chest again. 'Now, I said, clear off.'

With that she stepped back inside and slammed the door. Maddie stood rooted to the spot, eyes wild, mouth still open and mind running riot. Of all that she had expected to hear, this was the very last thing. She shut her eyes tightly. She had what she'd come for, hadn't she? She had heard the truth, no matter how shocking. But above all the words 'he's happily married with a kiddy on the way.'

Her Josh, the man she still loved more than life itself, now loved someone else and that someone was having his baby. It should have been Maddie having her second by now if her mother had not interfered. And then to learn that her father was not dead but very much alive and living in Leicester . . .

The pain building within her had only just begun to manifest itself but already it was unbearable.

It was then that Maddie knew she hated her mother. All these years she had suffered Harriet's harsh, unfeeling ways, her own continual fight to appease her, and then to find that Harriet had done all this to her for reasons she could not begin to fathom.

'No more, Mother,' Maddie uttered with conviction. 'No more.'

Filled with a rage so intense that she shook, she made for home.

There was no hesitating outside the door to gather her courage this time. On arriving, she almost wrenched the handle off in her haste to get inside.

Harriet was making herself a drink when the door burst open and Maddie charged in. The unexpected commotion made her drop the cup she was holding and she spun round to see what was happening.

'What the . . .' she cried.

Spotting her, Maddie stopped abruptly, eyes blazing, fists clenched. 'Why, Mother?' she erupted. 'Why?' Unable to control her fury she leaped at Harriet, grabbing her shoulders and shaking her hard, far too incensed to be shocked by her own uncharacteristic violence. 'Why? Tell me why?'

Placing both hands on Maddie's shoulders, with all her

strength Harriet pushed her away, glaring at her in a mixture of outrage and bewilderment. Maddie stumbled against the stone sink.

'What on earth has got into you?' Harriet demanded, straightening her rumpled blouse. 'How dare you manhandle me in such a way? Have you been drinking?'

'No, I have not,' Maddie cried, righting herself. 'You didn't think I'd find out, did you? But I have. I know it all now. Every last despicable detail. What have I ever done to you for you to treat me this way? Answer me! Tell me. Try and make me understand.'

Harriet's mouth was opening and closing as a terrible fear began to dawn on her. 'I don't know what you're talking about.'

'Yes, you do. My father! He's not dead, is he? Why did you lie to me?'

'He *is* dead,' Harriet snarled. 'To me he died the day he walked out on us.'

'But I had a right to know he was still alive. I . . .'

'Right?' her mother hissed. 'That man fathered you and nothing more. Where he's concerned you have no rights. I'm the one who raised you, your loyalties lie with me. So far as I'm concerned he's dead and I'll have no further mention of him, is that understood? Now go to your room.'

'No, I haven't finished yet, Mother. You sent Josh away. You did, didn't you? Admit it. You told the most terrible lies to him and his mother. You . . .'

'Against my orders you've been to see that man's mother?' Harriet erupted.

'Yes.'

Face purple with rage she slapped Maddie hard across the face. 'How dare you disobey me? Go to your room,' Harriet repeated.

Gasping for breath, Maddie clasped one hand to her smarting cheek. For several seconds, while she fought to regain her senses, the silence that engulfed the room was deafening. Then Maddie said firmly, 'I will not go to my room. I'm not a child, Mother. I'm an adult with a mind of my own and I wish to be treated as such. I'm not going anywhere until you give me some answers. I want to know why you've gone to such lengths to keep me tied to this house. You've done everything you can to stop me from having an outside life. You took my baby from me, got rid of the man I loved and who loved me back. You even got Gilbert Frisby the sack for daring to ask me out to the music hall. I want to know why. It's not as if you love me, Mother, is it? You've never said a kind word to me. In fact, I don't think you can stand the sight of me. So why have you gone to such trouble to keep me here?'

Open-mouthed, Harriet stared at her for a moment then her whole face contorted darkly. 'I have nothing to answer for.'

Maddie stared back, dumbfounded. 'Nothing, Mother? Nothing at all?'

'Nothing.'

Maddie stared at her for several long moments. 'Then I have my answer,' she said softly.

Calmly she turned and headed out of the room.

Upstairs in her bedroom she unearthed the canvas bag, the same one that had held her clothes for the journey to and from Mrs Baldicott's the year before, and pulling open the drawers of her tallboy, filled the bag with her clothes and personal belongings. Then she opened the tin containing her meagre savings, tipping the contents into her purse. Putting on her coat, she closed the bag, picked it up, and without a backward glance headed down the stairs.

Harriet, having swept up the smashed cup, was filling the kettle. She was shocked to see Maddie dressed for outdoors, eyed the bag then lifted her brows questioningly. 'Where do you think you're going?'

Hand on the back doorknob, Maddie turned to look at her. She paused, suddenly realising she hadn't given that a thought, just knowing she could not stay in this house with her mother a moment longer.

As Maddie looked back at her for the last time she realised that even hatred for her had gone. She felt nothing for the woman before her. But then, how could she be expected to? Harriet obviously didn't consider her worthy of so much as an explanation for her own dreadful misdeeds.

Maddie took a deep breath. 'I've no idea,' she said matter-of-factly. 'But I've nothing to stay for here so wherever I end up it has to be better.'

'Where you end up! You're leaving?' Harriet said incredulously.

'Yes, Mother, I am.' Maddie could hardly believe her own calmness.

Harriet smirked. 'You'll be back. You're incapable of fending for yourself. You'll soon realise what I did was just to protect you.'

'Protect me? From what, Mother?'

'Yourself,' came the harsh reply.

Maddie's face hardened. 'Oh, yes, Mother. Because I'm plain and easy prey for all those men out there who see me as a way to better themselves. Well, maybe I am plain, I have no choice but to believe that because you've constantly told me so, but you've never done me the courtesy of letting me make my own mistakes either. Allowed me to trust in my own judgement.' Her eyes narrowed and she stared at Harriet hard. 'I don't believe you've done all this just to protect me. This is to do with you, Mother. I don't know why, though, and as you're obviously not going to tell me then I'll never know, will I?'

The second brutal slap that Maddie received on her cheek sent her reeling back to slam against the wall. Hand on cheek, she froze momentarily. She had never before seen her mother in such a temper, such bitterness emanating from those icy grey eyes. She shuddered as old fears rose within her and for a fleeting moment an automatic instinct to appease her mother began to take hold. Then the words the old barge lady had spoken echoed in her mind. 'Face things. Nothing will begin for you until you do.' And she had faced up to things, had got to the hurtful truth. If she backed down now, even long enough to formulate some plans, she ran a grave risk of allowing her mother to regain control and then she would never get away. To run her own life, she had to strike out on her own. That would never happen while she stayed under this roof. It was now or never.

Righting herself, and with all the force she could muster, she retrieved the bag from Harriet's grasp, spun around and walked out of the door.

She had reached the park, put the heavy bag to one side of a bench and sat down before she dared allow her thoughts to dwell on just what she had done.

Maddie stared around her. It was growing dark and apart from a few people out walking their dogs, the park was deserted. Soon the gates would be shutting. She couldn't stay here.

She suddenly felt so alone. She had no idea where to go, no one she knew well enough from whom to seek sanctuary. Tears pricked her eyes as the enormity of her situation filled her. 'Oh, God,' she uttered. 'What am I going to do?'

She jumped as she felt a hand touch her shoulder. 'You all right, miss?'

Her head jerked up. 'Oh, yes,' she gulped to the park attendant who despite his kindly question appeared to Maddie to loom menacingly over her.

'Only I'm about to lock the gates.'

'Oh, yes, of course.' She rose hurriedly and retrieved her bag.

By the iron railings outside the park gate, she put down her bag again and stared around. She needed somewhere to rest for the night, somewhere she could gather her thoughts and make some sort of plan. Despite the lateness of the evening she supposed she could try and get a room in a lodging house. But its being such a small town, it was all so close to home and the thought of bumping into her mother, whom she couldn't be sure hadn't come out in search of her, terrified Maddie witless.

That question again. Where would she go?

She stood for several moments, deep in thought. Then the answer was revealed. She wasn't quite on her own, was she? There was one person she could turn to now, despite believing for the past twenty or so years that he was dead. In her hour of desperate need she had no alternative but to seek out her father.

# Chapter Six

Maddie woke with a start as, brakes applied, the early-morning train hissed and chugged on its approach to Leicester station, clouds of steam and white smoke billowing. She stifled a yawn, put her hands on her hips and stretched her aching back. She had just spent a most uncomfortable night on a hard wooden bench in a dark corner of the deserted, chilly waiting room of Market Harborough railway station. It had been somewhere to hide from her mother and, her finances being as they were, she'd felt it unwise to spend money on lodgings for the night.

Her racing thoughts had not allowed her to sleep until an hour before dawn, then she had slept so deeply that not even the comings and goings of the milk then mail trains, the loading and offloading of freight which had included cages of squealing piglets and squawking fowl off to various markets around the shires, had woken her.

The Station Master had, though, and Maddie had been mortally embarrassed. Now she was embarrassed again, having fallen asleep on the hard seat, the side of her head bumping rhythmically against the window of a third-class carriage. Her confusion this time was caused by a shabby young man sitting opposite, staring at her. Ignoring him, she turned her head to look out of the window.

They had just travelled under a soot-blackened iron bridge, then a canal. Now the view consisted of the backs of grimy rundown red brick terraces, well-worn washing on lines, barefoot grubby children sitting on crumbling back walls, waving at the train as it passed. The young man opposite waved back, which Maddie thought to be a kind gesture. They passed several factories, tall chimneys oozing black smoke, then a coal yard. On the embankment bordering the yard, Maddie caught sight of several women and children armed with sacks scouring the bank for lumps of coal that had tumbled from the heaps above, constantly on the lookout in case they should be spotted.

'Poor sods, I 'ope they don't get caught like I did once,' the young man said absently.

Maddie turned her attention to him. 'I beg your pardon?'

He pointed out of the window. 'I thought that kinda thing only 'appened in Ket'rin'. Thought the folks that lived 'ere 'ud be able to afford the coal man callin'.'

'Is that where you come from?' Maddie asked politely.

'Kettering. That's a few miles from Market Harborough where I li— used to live.'

He eyed her keenly. 'They're all rich there too, ain't they, in 'Arborough?' He ran his eyes over her. 'But you don't look rich,' he said bluntly. He didn't wait for a reply but continued, 'I'm gonna be rich one day. I've finished me 'prenticeship. Me mam worked her backside off to get me a trade but they didn't keep me on, the bastards! So I'm off to Leicester. Loads more factories in Leicester. I spent nearly all I've got on me train ticket so I 'ope I get set on quick. I'm gonna 'ave ter find cheap lodgings 'til me money starts rolling in but that should be easy enough 'cos I ain't gonna be fussy, then I'll get a place of me own and send for me mam and brothers. I'll keep 'em all, I will. Then me mam won't 'ave ter scrub floors no more or take in washing. She can rest, purra feet up while I tek care of 'er.'

As the young man relayed visions of his prosperous future, pity for him rose within Maddie. She had a terrible suspicion that very shortly he was going to have his dreams cruelly dashed but could not bring herself to comment. Far better he found out in his own way than from a stranger on a train.

She smiled at him. 'I bet your mother's very proud of you?'

'Oh, she is. Since me dad scarpered wi' that trollop from the factory I've bin 'ead of the 'ouse. Wouldn't 'ave managed wi'out me, wouldn't me mam. She cried buckets when I left. But I told 'er, she won't be crying when she sees the 'ouse I'm gonna get 'er or the balance in me bank book. A year, maybe two, I reckon it'll tek me. 'Cause in the meantime I'm gonna send 'er money each week.'

What plans this young man had, which Maddie did sincerely hope would come to fruition, but it was her guess that inside six months he'd be heading back on the train, wiser but no richer. But she hoped he was right about his job prospects because she needed to get a job herself and as quickly as he did. The only difference between them being that she only expected to earn a basic living. Becoming rich, if you were not born it, happened only to a chosen few.

''Ere we are,' he cried, jumping up. 'Wanna 'and wi' yer bag to the platform?'

'Yes, please,' Maddie replied gratefully.

After he had deposited her bag, she held out her hand to shake his. 'Thank you,' she said. 'And I wish you all the best.'

'Ta very much, but I won't need it.'

He touched his threadbare cloth cap and headed off.

Heaving her bag along, Maddie followed with the rest of the throng.

The tea was weak, leaves floating in it, and was only lukewarm; the bread, which could not be classed as the toast she'd asked for as it had hardly seen the inside of the grill, was dry whatever it was spread with – she had asked for butter, which this definitely was not. But Maddie was ravenous and at least what she had eaten had gone some way to stop her stomach from rumbling. She dare not order anything else on offer, mindful she had no idea how far her savings had to stretch.

As she had emerged from the station the hustle and bustle of the city hit her full force and immediately a dreadful fear of the unknown filled her. She suddenly felt so lost and alone. Market Harborough had been the town of her birth, the sights, sounds and smells of it familiar, and although her mother had seen to it she had no friends there, she had at least known people to pass the time of day with. She had no such luxury here.

Maddie had spotted the café just after leaving the station, its shabby exterior and what lay within not registering, and had hurried towards it, feeling an overwhelming need to sit for a while and gather her thoughts.

Staring down into her empty tea cup, frightening thoughts had flooded in. What if she couldn't find her father? And if she did, what if he demanded to know what had caused her to leave Market Harborough to seek him out? How could she explain to a man whom she had thought dead until hours ago all that had transpired, expect him to understand and show sympathy towards her? What if he turned her away in disgust? If only she knew what his character was and the reasons for his abandonment of herself and Harriet. Being armed with just a little knowledge would have helped her prepare her approach to him. But she had none and couldn't envisage what was going to happen.

Her worries mounted at the thought of being unable to secure work or anywhere to live. What would she do if she found she had no choice but to return to her mother? Oh, God, her mind screamed. That was one thing she *couldn't* do. After all that had transpired, whatever happened to her, whatever she was reduced to, that was one thing she couldn't do. Determination filled her then. She had come this far, there was no going back. She would have to face her father, then, whatever the consequences.

The lanky young waitress hovering nearby approached

her as she pushed away her empty plate. 'Can I get yer 'ote else, Madam?'

Distracted, Maddie raised her head. 'Pardon? Oh, just the bill, please. Oh, and maybe you can help me. Can you point me in the direction of the Amicable Refuge Insurance Company offices, please?'

The waitress stared vacantly. 'The what?' Grimacing she shook her head. 'Never heard of 'em,' she muttered as she wrote out Maddie's bill on a pad hanging by a chain from the belt around her waist. 'Me mam uses the Widows and Orphans for her funeral. Tenpence a week she pays to Reg Nunn who calls.' She tore off a copy of the bill and handed it to Maddie. ''Ope everythin' was all right for yer, madam.' The practised phrase was spoken insincerely. Without waiting for a reply she turned and was immediately summoned by the customers on the next table.

Reaching inside her handbag for her purse, Maddie glanced at the total due on the bill and her eyes widened in shock. A shilling for a cup of insipid tea and slice of thin dry toast! It was daylight robbery. Not that it had been a regular occurrence for her to visit a café but she did know that the bill was twice as much as it would have been in Market Harborough. She hoped everything else in Leicester wasn't as expensive. She remembered the young man on the train. Maybe her prophecy of six months' survival in this city should be cut to three.

She hurriedly slipped out of the café without leaving a tip. In her precarious financial state she felt she could not afford to be that generous.

Back on the main street, the bag containing her worldly belongings seeming to get heavier with each step she took, she headed off again in the direction of the town centre, feeling that was the best place to begin her search.

Under any other circumstances Maddie, whose solitary walks along the canal tow path had been the furthest she had ventured out of the small market town of her birth, would have taken the time to stroll along and savour the sights of this new and exciting place. She would have stopped to admire the fine Victorian redbrick buildings housing banks, hotels and the numerous businesses operating in this thriving city, and then, as she drew nearer the town centre, weaving her way through the crowds, taken time for a leisurely look in the windows of the shops selling everything the residents of the city and surrounding villages could ever want to buy. Even the amount of traffic, the trams and buses, horse-drawn drays and cabs and motor-powered trucks and automobiles congesting the road she was walking down, would have had her gazing in awe.

But she had no time for any of that at the moment.

On her way she stopped several people to ask for directions but their responses were all the same: a shrug of the shoulders and a shake of the head before hurrying on their way. Maddie began to wonder if the natives did not take kindly to strangers, even those from only twenty miles away.

She was at a crossroads now, where Granby Street ended and Gallowtree Gate began. The shops were dense hereabouts and she guessed this was about the centre of town. Spanning one corner of the crossroads was a large branch of Woolworth's, and across the road, through a wide gap between the buildings, she saw the entrance to the market place. It looked to be a large market from the part she could see, far bigger than the small Wednesday and Friday one held in Market Harborough where local farmers sold their produce. Opposite was a bank and across from that a building society. She glanced down Gallowtree Gate and looming in the distance could see the Clock Tower, the famous Leicester landmark. The hands on one of the four faces read twenty minutes past twelve. Time was marching on and she had nowhere to sleep tonight. Surely her father's place of business must be in the vicinity somewhere? Someone must be acquainted with it. She rubbed her cheek worriedly.

'Excuse me?'

Maddie jumped, spinning around to find a man of about her own age emerging from the gents' outfitters behind her.

'I've been watching you. You seem to be lost. Can I help at all?'

Her previous fear that the people of this city did not take kindly to newcomers was dispelled. 'Oh, I do hope you can,' said Maddie hopefully. She told him the name of the place her father worked. 'I haven't a clue where to begin to look so I'd be grateful for any help you can give me.'

'I can tell you exactly where that is. I used to work for a company next door until I got fed up with office work and decided to try my hand at selling. It's a few streets away but if you follow my directions you should find it easily enough.' He proceeded to explain to her. 'Now have you got that? Go back up this road, and turn left into Rutland Street. When you cross Charles Street you'll see the police station opposite. Go down it until you come to Queens Street. The Amicable is halfway down. You can't miss it.' He smiled. 'Leicester might not be the size of some cities in England but unless you're born and bred here, like me, it can be confusing to a visitor.'

'Yes, I'm beginning to realise that. Thank you so much for your help.'

Before responding he admired for a moment the tired-looking, plainly dressed but very pretty young woman before him. 'It was my pleasure, and if ever you get lost again, don't hesitate to come here and ask me for directions. I'd be only too happy to oblige.'

The suggestive tone of his voice made Maddie blush. 'I will,' she said, hurriedly making her departure.

His directions were very precise and ten minutes later she turned into Queens Street. The long street, other roads intermittently branching off it, contained an assortment of buildings, some, she deduced by their crumbling appearance, dating back maybe two hundred years. The one she was seeking was halfway down, of newer construction than the others. It was a narrow four-storey building which seemed to have been squashed in as an afterthought between two others housing coal and wine merchants. She checked the brass plate on the front of the building. AMICABLE REFUGE INSURANCE COMPANY, Established 1827. The company her father worked for was ninety-nine years old.

Heart pounding painfully, she took a very deep breath, steeling herself for what faced her, climbed the worn stone steps leading up to the imposing door and entered,

The narrow reception hall was panelled in dark oak the floor stone-flagged. Several doors off it, which were shut, led she presumed into offices. Halfway down the passage rose a steep narrow staircase. What lay beyond it was impossible to make out. From somewhere inside the building she could hear the muted rhythmical clacking of a typewriter. Apart from that indication of a human presence the place seemed deserted. She stared around, unsure what to do. Then she saw a door marked WAITING ROOM and thought this must be where visitors were supposed to go until someone came to attend to them. She made her way towards it.

The room, like the entrance hall, was dimly lit, the same oak panelling lining its walls, the only furniture five straight-backed chairs placed in a row, nothing covering the heavily varnished wooden floor. A huge round clock ticked loudly on one wall. It was a minute to one. Placing her cumbersome bag to the side of the chair at the end of the row, Maddie sat down and waited. And waited. The clock ticked slowly on. It now read ten minutes to two. Fifty minutes had passed and seemed to Maddie like so many hours.

Outside, Maddie heard people coming and going. A man entered the room and sat down. He didn't appear to notice her presence, but instead was preoccupied with a letter in his hand. A male face poked around the door and a pair of squinting eyes focused on the seated man who rose and left the room. Maddie frowned, it should have been her turn to be fetched as she had arrived first.

Then, too maiden-looking ladies came in and, moments later, the same male head poked around the door. 'Misses Jones, this way, please.' The women rose and departed.

'Just a minute,' called Maddie, but she was too late. The man had gone. Next time he appears I'll make sure I catch his attention, Maddie inwardly fumed, angry that she was being so blatantly ignored.

The room was stuffy and she found it increasingly difficult to stop her eyelids from closing.

The next thing she knew someone was shaking her arm.

'Oi, come on, wake up! Yer can't sleep 'ere.'

She woke with a start, staring straight into a grotesque face just inches from her own. Maddie yelled in shock. 'Where am I?'

The face receded as the body it belonged to straightened up. 'Why, yer 'ere, that's where yer are.'

'Here? Where . . . Oh!' she exclaimed as it all came back. Her eyes flew to the clock which now read twenty minutes past six then back to the shabby woman standing before her. She was old, very old, judging by the deeply lined skin covering her face which was heavily pitted with blackheads, especially on her nose. Her sparse, snow white hair was scraped up into a thin knot on the top of her head. She stooped due to a hump on her back. In one hand she was holding a scrubbing brush.

Another woman, equally as old, shuffled through the door. 'What's goin' on, Myrtle?'

'We've a trespasser,' she cackled gleefully. 'Better get the bobbies.'

Maddie jumped up, all traces of sleep flying from her. 'No, I'm no trespasser. I was waiting to see Mr Ashman. Only . . . well, I waited in here and no one came. I must have fallen asleep.

'Did yer report to the office?' Ethel asked.

Maddie shook her head. 'No. I didn't know I had to.'

Myrtle eyed her scornfully. 'If yer didn't announce yer presence, 'ow d'yer expect anyone ter fetch yer?' She gave a gleeful cackle. 'Mr Dibble, the Clerk, wouldn't 'ave spotted yer huddled in the corner, 'im being so short sighted. I've heard it said he won't wear spectacles 'cos he's afraid the young ladies won't take a fancy to him. Vain bugger, he is. I wouldn't mind, but he's as ugly as sin, so specs or not he's no chance wi' the ladies.' She chuckled again and so did Ethel.

Myrtle eventually composed herself and eyed Maddie sternly. 'Mr Ashman's gone 'ome. Said goodnight ter me a few minutes ago. They've all gone 'ome,' she announced. 'Yer'll 'ave ter come back termorra. We're ter lock up, see, once we've finished the cleaning. It's our responsibility, ain't it, Effel?'

'It is,' she agreed proudly. 'Responsible we are.'

Maddie's mind raced frantically. She had to see her father tonight. She had nowhere to sleep. 'But I need to see Mr Ashman tonight! It's really important. I need to find out where he lives. Do you know by any chance?'

'Can't tell private things like that to strangers. Anyway we don't know.'

'I do,' piped up Ethel.

Myrtle turned on her. 'Yer do? 'Ow?'

She just shrugged her shoulders. 'Yer don't work somewhere fer thirty years and not find out things.'

'Oh, pokin' around, was yer? You'll get shot one of these days, wi' yer pokin' and pryin'. By the way, did yer ever find out . . . Oh, never mind that now.' Myrtle turned back to address Maddie. 'You could be anyone. Yer'll 'ave ter wait 'til termorra.'

'But I can't!' Maddie's shoulders sagged despondently at the thought of trying to find lodgings for the night in this alien city then beginning this process all over again. Her whole sorry situation crowded in on her and before she could stop herself she burst into tears.

Both women stared at her.

Chores forgotten, Myrtle took charge. ''Ere, come on, me duck, sit yerself down,' she ordered, grabbing Maddie's arm. 'N'ote's that bad it's worth bawlin' over. Effel, go and mek the gel a cuppa. And mek sure yer tidy away just as yer found things. Don't want them knowin' we mash up. Be 'ell to pay. Oh, and Mr Partridge keeps 'alf a bottle of whisky behind the black box on the third shelf of 'is bookcase. Put a tot in the tea.' She addressed Maddie. 'Medicinal, me duck.'

''Ow d'yer know about the whisky?' asked Ethel.

'Same as you know where Mr Ashman lives. Now 'urry up afore this gel keels over.'

Ethel scuttled away.

'Now what's so important yer need ter see Mr Ashman ternight?' Myrtle asked, settling her aged bones on the chair next to Maddie, beady eyes glinting keenly.

Maddie reached inside the pocket of her coat and pulled out a handkerchief. She dabbed her eyes then blew her nose noisily. 'He's my father. I've travelled from Market Harborough to see him. Surprise him,' she added, feeling some sort of explanation was needed but not wanting to go into further details at present. 'Only I've mislaid his address.'

'Oh, well, why didn't yer say yer wa' 'is daughter? Oh, lovely man is Mr Ashman. Always teks the trouble to speak ter me an' Effel. Not like the rest. Stuck up they are. Ah 'ere's Effel now wi' the tea. Did yer find the bottle?'

'I did,' she replied, carrying the china cup carefully as she shuffled in, the large holey slippers on her feet flapping. One of her knitted stockings had slipped down and was bunched around her ankles, just visible beneath her threadbare black twill skirt. 'I put a good dollop in.' And had herself another good dollop while she was at it, probably would again in the future now she knew where the bottle was hidden. But she wasn't about to divulge that. 'Drink this while it's 'ot,' she ordered, handing the cup to Maddie.

She accepted gratefully. The tea had grown tepid during the time it had taken Ethel to journey from the kitchen to the waiting room and Maddie gulped it down, shuddering as the sharpness of the alcohol hit the back of her throat. Regardless, she instantly felt better as its effects began to seep into her blood. She handed the cup back to Ethel. 'That was much appreciated, thank you.'

Ethel gave a toothless beam. 'My pleasure, me duck. Famous for me tea I am.'

'This is Mr Ashman's daughter,' announced Myrtle. 'She's 'ere on a surprise visit all the way from Markit 'arbor and can't remember the address.'

Ethel scowled thoughtfully. 'Daughter, eh?' She scratched her neck worriedly. 'Yer did say daughter?'

'Fer God's sake, Effel, yer deaf or summat? Just give the gel the address. She needs to get on 'er way and we need to finish what we're paid fer.' Myrtle turned to Maddie, looking worried. 'Yer won't tell no one where yer got the address from, will yer, me duck? Only we'd get the sack.'

Maddie patted her arm reassuringly. 'Don't worry, I won't.'

Standing at the front door the two aged women watched Maddie, armed with directions, make her way down the street.

'Summat fishy goin' on,' muttered Ethel as they made their way back inside.

'Wadda yer mean?'

Ethel grimaced as she grasped hold of the broom she had propped against the door earlier and began to sweep the floor. 'She ain't 'is daughter. I've seen Mr Ashman wi' 'is daughter and that ain't 'er. 'Is daughter's younger for a start and 'er hair's fairish. That woman's much darker. I saw 'em, see, shopping in the market just before last Christmas.'

Down on her knees now, Myrtle dipped a scrubbing brush into a pail of water and began scrubbing the floor. 'Well, yer must be mistaken. Yer know what yer eyesight's like. I keep telling yer to get down to the Sally Army and get yerself some specs.'

'N'ote wrong wi me 'earing, though. The gel that was wi' 'im called 'im Dad. Anyway, when he saw me he said 'ello, introduced me to 'er. Said, "Ruth, this is Mrs Crump what does for us at the office." Now who but Mr Ashman would acknowledge the likes of us, eh?'

Myrtle paused thoughtfully for a moment, then looked up at Ethel knowingly. 'Well, yer daft 'a'porth, maybe 'e's *two* daughters. Never thought of that, did yer, eh?'

Ethel pursed her lips. 'Maybe 'e has. One living in Collins Court and the other in Markit 'arbor. Fishy, don't yer reckon?'

'Oh! Mmmm. Well . . . if she ain't his daughter, who d'yer reckon she wa' then?' Myrtle muttered worriedly. 'Fancy piece, d'yer reckon? And she seemed such a decent type.' Her lips tightened, eyes narrowed. 'Mind you, yer can't tell these days. No, yer can't. Teks all sorts, dunnit? Oh, I'm all intrigued now and we'll never find out 'cos it's not like we can ask Mr Ashman if she's 'is fancy piece, now can we?'

Ethel laughed, a dry cackling sound. 'Not likely!'

Myrtle grimaced as a worrying thought suddenly struck her. 'Listen, Effel. A' yer listenin'?'

'I said, there's n'ote wrong wi' me 'earin'.'

'Good, 'cos if 'ote should come of this, best say we've never seen that woman before, all right?'

'Whatever yer say, Myrtle. You seem ter think you're the boss.'

She frowned crossly. 'What were that?'

Ethel started brushing vigorously. 'N'ote, Myrtle, it were n'ote.'

# Chapter Seven

The small shabby courtyard had been hard to find and surprising to come across, seeming oddly out of place amongst the maze of back-to-back streets surrounding it. Maddie had got off the tram halfway down the Uppingham Road as the two old ladies had directed, then walked down several terraced streets, the last one up and down several times before she had found the narrow cobbled jitty that led to Collins Court. It was growing dark, the gas lamps yet to be lit, and although children were evident in the main streets, the courtyard was deserted.

The paintwork of all the surrounding houses was an identical dull brown, peeling in places, and the guttering on several roofs was loose in parts, but regardless Maddie could tell by the white nets at the windows and the clean steps that the residents of these houses looked after their homes as best they could.

Her father lodged in number 10, so Ethel had told her, and Maddie hoped the old lady's poking and prying had elicited the correct information.

She stood before number 10 and stared at it. What had happened in the last twenty-four hours and brought Maddie to this door had left her exhausted, mentally and physically. Should this address be wrong, or should she not be welcome here, offered help to begin her new life . . .

Shutting her eyes, she said a silent prayer then raised the metal knocker, letting it fall with a thud against the door.

After what seemed an eternity she heard the soft sound

of approaching footsteps and the door opened to reveal a pleasant-faced, middle-aged woman of medium height, her light brown hair parted down the middle and arranged in coils around her ears. Her clothes, a plain wrapround apron covering a dark skirt and white high-necked blouse, although far from new were clean and pressed. She radiated warmth and Maddie immediately took to her.

'Hello.' The woman's tone of voice was not refined but neither was it coarse. 'Can I help you?'

From inside the house Maddie could hear the sounds of people talking, laughing, the clattering of cutlery and china. Instantly she knew this to be a happy home and her hopes of being made welcome here soared.

'I do apologise for calling at this time,' she began. 'You're obviously in the middle of your meal . . .'

'That's all right, my dear, this door is always being knocked on for one thing or another,' the woman interrupted, smiling to put Maddie at ease.

Sarah scanned her eyes quickly over the woman on her doorstep. She looked worn out, ready to drop, the weight of the world pressing down on her slim shoulders. She was too old to be a friend of Sarah's daughter, though. She wondered what was in the large bulky bag by the caller's feet and frowned as a strange sensation washed over her. It was most peculiar but the young woman seemed familiar somehow though Sarah couldn't place what it was that would give her that feeling. She mentally shook herself. She was tired, had had a long day and the light must be playing tricks.

'What can I do for you?' she asked.

Maddie's reply made Sarah's blood run cold.

'I'm looking for my father, Mr Ashman. I've been told he lodges here.' Maddie watched with rapidly growing horror as the woman's face drained of colour. She had clasped her hands and was wringing them. Maddie frowned, bewildered. What on earth had she said to cause such a reaction? All she'd done was enquire after her father.

'Does he live here?' she asked tentatively.

Sarah stared at her blankly and Maddie repeated her question.

'Oh . . .' she gulped. 'Er . . . yes, yes. Mr Ashman lives here.'

Maddie sighed, relieved. 'Oh, I thought for a moment I'd got the wrong address. If it's not convenient I could call back?' It was the last thing she felt like doing, having to wile away an hour or so in strange streets, but she felt she must at least offer, having called, at such an inconvenient time.

Sarah's thoughts were racing frantically. Never had she envisaged this dreadful situation. Not given it the least consideration or prepared herself for it. What on earth was she to do now?

'Mam,' a voice called. 'Dad sez hurry up, your dinner's getting cold.'

Sarah turned her head. 'I'm . . . I'm just coming.' She looked back at Maddie. There was nothing she could do, this situation was beyond her control and had to be faced. There was no time for warnings. Taking a deep breath, she stood aside. 'Please, Maddie, come in.'

Leaving her heavy bag just inside the doorway, she followed her father's landlady down the dimly lit passageway. Despite her rapidly increasing apprehension of what lay in store, it did strike Maddie that the woman had addressed her by name, and the name she preferred at that. Her father had obviously spoken of her to his landlady which must be a good sign. But the question of how he had known her name, considering he had left when she was not much more than a toddler and hadn't started to call herself it then, also occurred to her.

Before she could think about it further they had arrived.

As they entered the room Maddie was instantly enveloped by a highly charged atmosphere of warmth and family unity. A well-stacked fire was burning in the grate of the black leaded range which practically filled the wall opposite and the dark oak furniture was lovingly cared for. Embroidered cloths on the back of the two worn but comfortable-looking fireside chairs to either side of the range, several cheerful prints and fluted glass bowls, plus various articles and personal bits and pieces left lying around by the room's occupants, enhanced its air of homeliness.

Maddie became aware of three people sitting around a table in the centre of the room: a good-looking young man of about eighteen, a very pretty girl a year or so older, and a middle-aged man at the head, all chattering as they ate their meal. The man was of medium height, thick-set, the strip of greying hair framing his balding pate trimmed neatly, features pleasant. He wore a pair of metal-framed glasses on his short nose. From Maddie's instant appraisal he looked a kindly sort. This was obviously the woman's family. Her own father must be in his room, thought Maddie.

'George,' Sarah addressed the man, and there was a tone in her voice that made his head jerk up. 'George dear, you have someone to see you.'

Maddie fixed her eyes on the man, thinking it a coincidence that her father also was called George.

Mouth curving in an automatic smile of welcome, he turned his attention to the visitor and as he did so the smile faded, the clatter of his knife and fork hitting his plate resounding loudly in the still room. Maddie frowned at him, bewildered, wondering why her presence had had such an effect but before she had time to think further the pretty young woman blurted out worriedly, 'What's the matter, Dad?'

'George,' Sarah urged. 'Why don't you take Maddie into the parlour? You need privacy to talk.'

Maddie flashed a bewildered glance at Sarah. There was something going on that she didn't quite understand.

'Yes, my dear, you're right,' he replied, rising.

As he came towards Maddie foreboding rose within her

and she wanted to pick up her bag and flee, but was unable to.

He was at her side now, smiling reassuringly, but his eyes were those of a deeply troubled man.

'Come, Maddie,' he urged, cupping her elbow.

Totally dumbfounded, she allowed him to guide her out of the room.

In the corridor she stopped and turned to him. 'Has something dreadful happened to my father? Is he dead? Is that what you have to tell me?' she whispered.

He shook his head, eyes filling with tenderness. 'Your father is very much alive, my dear,' he replied, voice thick with emotion. 'You're looking at him, in fact. I'm your father.'

Her shock was immediately apparent and George tightened his hold on her arm. 'Come through to the parlour, Maddie dear, we need to talk.'

Those left behind in the back room sat in silence for several long moments after George and Maddie had departed. It was the young man who spoke first. 'Mam, who was that woman?'

'Yeah, Mam,' echoed the girl. 'Who . . . ?' Then a possibility struck her and her hazel eyes widened excitedly. 'Mam, is that . . . is she . . . ?'

Sarah raised her hand. 'Not now, Ruth. Not now.' Sighing deeply, she shut her eyes, acutely aware that her own children needed to be spoken to as well. But at this moment all her thoughts and feelings were with the two people who had just left the room.

Standing with his back to the empty fireplace, George Ashman shifted nervously from foot to foot, acutely aware of Maddie's unblinking eyes fixed upon him. She was standing against the horsehair sofa, both hands clutching one arm for support, waiting for him to begin his explanations. But he didn't know how to. 'I'm . . . er . . . afraid it's a bit chilly in here,' he babbled uncomfortably.

'We don't use this room much. Hardly at all really.' His voice trailed off as he became conscious he was using unnecessary small talk as a stalling tactic.

A feeling of helplessness washed through him. Standing so near was the person whose very existence was the reason for this whole dreadful mess, a person he'd striven hard to protect, to the detriment of others yet no blame could be attached to her for their suffering. You couldn't blame anyone for the fact they'd been born.

At this moment she looked so lost, so vulnerable, far younger than her twenty-six years. A sudden great rush of deep love for her filled him. He fought a compulsion to rush across to her, crush her to him and beg her forgiveness for the pain he knew he was about to cause her. But he couldn't do that, he had no idea how she would react.

There were many questions he wanted to ask Maddie too, but all that would have to wait until a story had been told.

He realised she was speaking, her voice so low it was barely audible. 'Pardon?' he said.

She cleared her throat. 'They . . . they called you Father. Are you their father?'

He gnawed his bottom lip anxiously for what seemed an age. 'Yes, Maddie,' he answered finally, face grave, his low voice filled with emotion. 'Yes, I am. Please, sit down and let me explain. It's a long story. I knew one day it would have to be told, but not in these circumstances.'

He watched in concern as she sank down on the sofa, clutching the front of her coat as if for comfort.

'Are you cold, Maddie? I'll light the fire.'

'No, no,' she uttered. 'I'm just . . . just . . .'

'I know, my dear,' he interrupted. 'You must be very confused.'

She looked at him for a moment and suddenly her bottom lip started to quiver as tears pricked her eyes. 'You said I'm your daughter?'

'And you are. You're as much a part of me as Ruth and Roy.'

'So you divorced my mother? She just said she was a widow to cover that up?'

He looked astounded. 'Widow!' he exclaimed. 'Your mother told people that?' His eyes filled with horror as a terrible thought dawned on him. 'Maddie, did she tell you I was dead?'

She nodded. 'I thought so until I found out by accident yesterday that you weren't.'

'Oh, my God,' he groaned. 'How could she?' His eyes filled with tears. 'Maddie, have you never received the gifts I've sent you each birthday and at Christmas? Or any of my letters?'

She shook her head. 'I've received nothing. As I said, I thought you were dead.'

'Has Harriet told you anything about me at all?'

'No,' she uttered. 'She wouldn't speak of you.'

He sighed long and loud. 'Now I know why you've never contacted me. I always wondered . . .' His voice trailed off and he eyed her searchingly. 'I've watched you grow, Maddie. Several times a year I've travelled to Market Harborough and hidden, waiting until I could catch a glimpse of you. Sometimes it was for hours but as long as I saw you I didn't mind. As you grew older it became harder to see you but I made discreet enquiries to find out if you were faring all right. Times – oh, so many times,' he whispered sadly, 'I've wanted to approach you but knew it best not to. I knew, you see, that should your mother find out we'd had any contact, you'd incur her displeasure.'

Maddie was staring at him dumbstruck, these revelations the last she'd been expecting to hear. 'I wish you had though, Father,' she whispered.

He smiled sadly. 'So do I.'

She frowned at him, bewildered. 'If my mother is still your wife then that woman . . . Sarah . . .'

He squeezed her hands tightly. 'Maddie, please let me explain it all to you. Allow me to do that first, then you can ask anything you like and I'll answer as best I can. I have to warn you, though, it's not a pleasant story. It will be painful for both of us.'

A tap sounded on the door and Sarah entered carrying a tea tray which she put down on an occasional table to one side of George. She smiled hesitantly at Maddie. 'I've made you a sandwich for now. I hope cheese is all right for you?'

The last thing Maddie felt like was eating but she managed to say thank you.

Sarah glanced worriedly at George. 'If you need me . . .'

He smiled wanly. 'Thank you, my dear, I'll call if I do.'

She hovered uncertainly. 'Right, I'll leave you to it then,' she said, walking out of the door which she shut behind her.

Several moments of tense silence passed while George poured the tea and handed a cup and the plate of sandwiches to Maddie. He eased himself back on the sofa. The time had come, he could stall no more. He smiled weakly at his daughter before taking a deep breath and forcing his thoughts back over the years to when he was a young man of twenty-two and the fateful day it all began.

# Chapter Eight

'The first time I met your mother was one bitterly cold night when I was desperate for lodgings. It was my first visit to Market Harborough and I didn't know the town. I'd just been promoted and given my own area, covering the south of Leicestershire. Other agents in the firm weren't happy, felt I was too young and inexperienced for such responsibility, wouldn't have been sorry to see me fall flat on my face. In truth, they wanted the round for themselves.'

He paused thoughtfully for a moment. 'I've started at the wrong place, Maddie. I should tell you about myself first. Maybe then you'll understand things . . .' he sighed '. . . a little better. I was raised by an elderly great-aunt and uncle who welcomed me to their home after my parents died of cholera after it swept through the village of my birth, killing half the population. That was 1878. A terrible year. Many children were orphaned and parents left childless. I don't remember it. I was only two. They were a grand couple, Robert and Laura Hubble, with no children of their own. This . . .' he tapped the side of his foot, '. . . I was born with. A club foot. It stopped me doing many things. I couldn't play football or run very well. My biggest regret was that I couldn't fight in the war.' He shook his head sadly. 'All I could do was help the police as a voluntary night patrol man and a fire helper. Anyway not many people would have taken in a child with my deformity, family or not, but they did, bless them, and never made me feel any different from anyone else. Aunt Laura said it made me special.

'My aunt and uncle didn't have much themselves, actually they were quite poor, but they gave me a lot of love, Maddie.' He exhaled slowly. 'I wish you could have known them. You would have liked them and they would have loved you. I still miss them very much.' He looked at her, smiling distantly. 'I've always thought you have a look of your Great-great-aunt Laura about you. I have a photograph of both of them somewhere. I'll look it out and you can judge for yourself.

'I was quite a shy boy, liked to read and fish – the usual boy stuff. I had a friend named Nobby Clarke and we were usually to be found together.' He grinned. 'The tales I could tell you about some of the things we got up to! Just boyish fun, you understand, Maddie, nothing more than that. I helped Aunt Laura as much as I could around the house or by running errands for her.

'Uncle Robert worked for the Amicable Refuge, spent his entire life selling and collecting weekly payments for penny policies, winter and summer, whatever the weather. The old widow ladies loved him. Nine times out of ten he'd end up fetching their shopping or helping to get the washing in. In the school holidays I used to accompany him on his rounds and some evenings if I'd done my chores. That helped with my shyness. Those customers of his, especially the old ladies, didn't hold with shyness. If they asked a question they expected an answer.' He smiled. 'It did me good, helped bring me out of myself.

'That's the reason I grew up wanting to be an insurance man. I couldn't see myself doing anything else. By the time I left school at fourteen, Uncle Robert had retired, he was over seventy and his health not so good, but out of respect for him his old firm took me on as a clerk. Glorified tea boy was more like it to start with but I loved the work. I listened and learned and when I was eighteen I was put with a master of his trade.' George smiled at the memory. 'Archie Crabtree. What a character he was! Wouldn't have anything to do with penny policies, was into larger deals for companies and the well-to-do, and what he didn't know about the business wasn't worth knowing. He taught me well.

'I knew Archie was the main instigator of my promotion. Really stuck his neck out to persuade the bosses to give me the chance. I couldn't let him down. Didn't want to let myself down either. Chances like that didn't come along very often and certainly not at the age I was. I was determined to do well. That's what took me to Market Harborough late that night. Armed with no more than a list of old established customers and some possibles to try, I thought it best to start as I meant to go on. So instead of catching the train in the early morning to begin my round, I caught the last one the night before to get an early start.

'It was pitch dark when I arrived, it had just begun to snow and the town was deserted – not the best time to be looking for a place to stay. I nearly missed the Vacancy sign when I passed by the haberdasher's shop. It wasn't the usual kind of establishment offering a bed for the night. I can't honestly say I took a fancy to the place but I was relieved when I was told a room was available.'

George paused for a moment, realising that the story he was relating was going to be painful enough for Maddie to absorb and very aware it concerned her mother, therefore some details, although pertinent to himself, he felt it best to miss out. So he did not mention that on stepping into the house he was immediately transported to a place straight from Dickens. The rooms had the minimum of furniture and the whole place was icy cold, the small fire burning in the grate of the main room doing nothing to raise the temperature. No fuel lamps evident, just tallow candles, although when he did agree to take the room a lamp was produced with only enough oil for an hour or so's use.

Harriet's welcome to him, a paying customer, was sparingly given, as if she was doing him a great service by just letting him into her house, which wasn't done without searching questions being asked or until satisfactory credentials had been produced.

He also felt it best not to tell Maddie that his first impression of Harriet Grimble had not been favourable either. He had found not one endearing quality about her at all, from the severe style of dress covering her thin shapeless frame to her abrupt, cold manner.

'In the morning as I was leaving,' he continued, 'Harriet offered me a cheaper rate should I take the room for the rest of my stay. I accepted.' He missed out the fact that he had deliberated deeply before agreeing, finding the lure of a more comfortable abode and cheery landlady difficult to fight against. 'It seemed sensible at the time as every penny counted.' Those saved pennies, he thought, had cost him dearly in more ways than one.

'I left the Friday morning and to be truthful never expected to see Harriet again as I'd been told of another place I could stay when I was next in the town which . . .' he chose his words carefully '. . . sounded like it would suit me better.'

He stopped his narrative for a moment and eyed Maddie in concern. 'You're shivering. It'll only take me a moment to light the fire,' he said, attempting to rise.

'No, I'm fine, really I am,' she insisted, the chilliness of the room the last thing on her mind. 'Please, go on.'

George settled back again to take up the story.

'As I was saying, I never expected to see Harriet again and it came as a surprise to be told a few weeks later that she had written to the office and had asked for me to call personally on her and discuss her insurance needs. I never thought of anything other than possible new business.

'I wrote and arranged to call on her the following week when next I was in Harborough. A Wednesday night.' His lips tightened. 'I remember that night well,' he said coldly. How could he ever forget the night that had led to the sealing of his fate. 'I was quite taken aback when she opened the door. The change in her was marked. For a moment I thought I had the wrong house. Her hair had been styled, she wore a very nice blue velvet dress, old-fashioned but it suited her, and rouge.' And as he had done so many times in the past, he wondered how he could have been so naïve as not to have suspected what was in Harriet's mind.

'There was a large fire burning in the grate and a bottle of sherry and glasses on a small table by her chair. I've never been a drinker but felt obliged to have a glass. Being on the road can be lonely and it was nice to pass an hour or so in company, albeit on business too.' He leaned forward and clasped his hands. 'Harriet was talkative and very attentive and I have to admit the time passed very pleasantly. I was surprised to find that several hours had gone by when I came to take my leave. I arranged to call again as soon as I had the information she had asked for.

'It took several calls over a period of weeks before she instructed me to go ahead and have the documentation prepared.' He omitted to tell Maddie that it did strike him at the time that although her queries were very plausible, Harriet purposely delayed matters to keep him having to call. Despite her obvious efforts, Harriet held no appeal for him in any form but that of client and her attempts to charm, including the girlish giggle that constantly shrilled out, did nothing but grate on him. Nevertheless, to be truthful, he couldn't deny that although he gave her absolutely no encouragement, her blatant attentions towards him did much to bolster his ego.

'Each visit I was made comfortable before the fire with a glass of sherry, Harriet listening attentively to everything I had to say. When I arrived with the policies for her to sign I was taken aback to find she had a meal waiting, and whisky instead of sherry. She said it was the least she could do considering all the trouble she had put me to in organising her affairs. I had already eaten, but I couldn't hurt her feelings. The meal was very palatable and I found I had a taste for whisky . . .' His voice trailed off and he lowered his head. 'I realised how much when I woke the next morning.'

Her father was just staring at her and Maddie frowned back, confused, then the truth hit her. 'Oh!' she exclaimed, reddening. 'I see,' she muttered, averting her eyes in embarrassment.

No, you don't, Maddie, George thought ruefully. You automatically think that, plied with drink, I seduced Harriet that night. But that was not how it was at all. His mouth set in a grim line as he remembered just what had taken place.

It was still dark, he guessed it to be the early hours of the morning, when he had woken totally befuddled, to find Harriet slipping between the sheets beside him. She was naked.

The closest he had ever come to a naked woman before was a hurried glance at the black and white postcards of nudes the men at work slyly passed around. To be in such close proximity to one obviously very willing, and himself unaccustomedly mellowed with whisky, was too much for will power or common sense.

He cleared his throat uncomfortably before continuing. 'I make no excuses, Maddie. What happened, shouldn't have. I left before Harriet woke the next morning. I suppose I was too ashamed to face her.' He paused for a moment while he took a drink of tea. 'About two months later I got a summons to call upon her. I automatically assumed it was a matter of business.' He kept to himself that he would have done anything not to have made that visit, not particularly wanting to see Harriet again. But as he was the sole representative for Amicable Refuge in that area he had no choice.

'She welcomed me in, sat me down and we chatted for several minutes about . . .' he shrugged his shoulders '. . . the weather, this and that.' He paused, lips tightening grimly. 'Then she told me the real reason she had requested I call. It had nothing to do with insurance.'

He stopped abruptly and, shoulders slumping, ran a hand over his chin. What he had to tell Maddie next could not be prettied up to save her feelings. He hoped he had managed successfully to withhold the full extent of Harriet's guilt, letting Maddie assume the blame lay with him. But regardless of where blame lay, just how did you tell your daughter that a good measure of whisky was solely responsible for her existence?

Lowering his head, he took a deep breath but before he could say a word Maddie whispered. 'Mother was pregnant, wasn't she? With me.'

He stared at her for several long moments, then nodded. 'Yes.'

Maddie's whole being felt numb as she fought to comprehend just what her father was telling her. As realisation took hold her heart began to thump, its beat growing faster until it battered so painfully she thought it to be trying to break out of her chest.

No, she wanted to scream, please tell me this isn't true! After all she had learned in the last twenty-four hours, some of which she was still having difficulty trying to understand, let alone come to terms with, this news was just too terrible to take on board.

So that was why her mother had been so cold towards her! Her birth had been a dreadful mistake. A great burden of responsibility weighed her down. There were so many questions still unanswered, so much explaining still left undone, but at this moment Maddie was too distressed even to think further than the pain she had been the cause of. An overwhelming urge to get as far away as she could from the man who had accidentally fathered her filled her.

She leaped up from her seat. 'I'm so sorry,' she blurted out. 'Truly I am. However can you ever forgive me?'

The compulsion to leave grew and, spinning on her heel, Maddie fled from the house.

Hearing the commotion of doors opening and banging,

Sarah appeared in the parlour doorway. The haunted look on George's face sent fear racing through her. She rushed over to him and laid a hand on his arm. 'George dear, what's happened? Where's Maddie gone?'

'I couldn't stop her, Sarah. It's all gone wrong. She . . . Oh, God, from what she said . . .'

'What did she say?'

'She apologised. Asked my forgiveness. Oh, Sarah, I never got a chance to finish what I had to tell her. I only got as far as Harriet's summons to me on finding herself expecting. Maddie has got it into her head that it's all her fault.'

Sarah sighed heavily. 'That poor girl, she must be in a terrible state. And we still don't know what brought her to us in the first place, do we? Come on, we must find her. She can't have got far. Ruth and Roy will help.'

# Chapter Nine

Maddie had not known which way to turn when she bolted from the house. Not that the direction mattered to her. Getting away from somewhere she was obviously not wanted had. Her lungs were at bursting point, legs like lead, when the road she had run down ended at an iron gate. She had arrived at the side entrance to a small park. Panting heavily, she stared through the railings into the green area beyond. The tranquil scene spread before her, beckoning her in along with the empty wooden bench she could see beneath the branches of a huge oak. It offered sanctuary while she gathered her scattered thoughts. Maddie pushed open the gate and hurried through.

Sometime later night was rapidly falling, a half moon now visible and several stars twinkling in a cloudless sky. A chilly wind was rising, rustling eerily in the leaf-laden branches above. Maddie shivered, hugging her coat closer around her. A woman, fur collar turned up on her smart coat, heels clicking on the asphalt path, arrived abreast of her, a brown and tan cocker spaniel pulling on its lead. The dog stopped and sniffed at Maddie's leg. Stiffening, she watched it warily.

Seeming not to notice how uncomfortable her dog's actions were making Maddie, the woman smiled brightly. 'Good evening,' she said.

Maddie stared vacantly at her, finding it hard to give a reply. To her, there was nothing good about this evening whatsoever.

Indignant at receiving no reply, the woman give the lead a tug. 'Come along, Mimi, there's a good doggie.' Dragging the spaniel behind her, she went on her way.

To her cosy home, Maddie assumed. The dog to its warm basket.

At the vision she had created, she groped for her handbag. The small amount of money it contained was all that stood between her and the workhouse. She suddenly realised she had left behind the bag and all her worldly possessions. She couldn't go back for it. Knowing now what she did, she couldn't face her father again.

With that thought, the misery she was struggling to contain suddenly became too much for her. Tears danced precariously on her bottom lids and fell. She succumbed then as her whole sorry situation crowded in on her. Burying her face in her hands, rocking backwards and forwards, Maddie wept.

It was Sarah who eventually found her.

It was almost dark, too dark to be out aimlessly searching, but none of them would give up, the thought of Maddie in a distressed state and unfamiliar territory urging them on. George was beside himself and Sarah knew he would not rest until he had found his daughter and she was safe.

Reluctantly she was making her way home, having covered every conceivable nook and cranny she could think of. She'd almost dismissed the park as she had passed by the gates; it was delightful in the daytime but dark and eerie at this time of night and the thought of venturing inside on her own unnerved her. She presumed Maddie would feel likewise. It would be locked up anyway at this time of night unless the attendant had forgotten, which he had been known to.

Regardless, she stopped and looked through the railings. From what she could see it did look deserted but automatically she tried the gate. It swung open. Sarah shook her head. It was a wonder the attendant wasn't dismissed for his neglect.

She stepped tentatively inside, wishing George or one of her children was with her, and nearly turned back before a vision of Maddie lost and alone forced her on.

She had walked a short distance down a path skirting dense shrubbery when muffled sobs reached her ears. Sarah stopped and listened. Peering through the gloom, she could just make out a huddled figure on the bench beneath the oak and hurried over, praying that it was Maddie. It was. Sarah was so relieved to have found her she ran the final few steps and threw herself down beside her, placing a hand on her arm.

'There you are! You've had us all so worried.'

Lost in her own misery, Maddie had not heard Sarah's approach. She jumped up and shrieked in fright.

'It's all right, my dear,' Sarah reassured her. 'I didn't mean to frighten you. I'm just so glad to find you. Well, not knowing the area, you could have landed up anywhere, couldn't you now?'

Maddie stared at her. She hadn't expected anyone to bother to come looking for her and the relieved expression on the kindly woman's face surprised her. But Sarah's finding her in such a state horrified her and Maddie hurriedly turned her head, pretending she was removing something from her eye. When she turned back her tears had been wiped away and there was a forced smile on her face.

None of Maddie's attempts at a cover up escaped Sarah's notice. That smile did not hide the devastation in her eyes. Sarah's heart went out to her. She wanted to throw her arms around Maddie for comfort, try to allay her fears. But she might not take kindly to such an action, Sarah reminded herself. After all, George's daughter hadn't known of Sarah's existence until a couple of hours ago. She must be careful how she handled this situation. It was imperative that she got Maddie to return home with her and hear the rest of her father's story. She decided it would be best to pretend nothing was amiss and hope her ruse worked.

'I expect the fresh air did you good,' she said breezily, rising to her feet. 'But we'd best get off. The others will have returned by now. Given up, I expect.'

Bewildered Maddie looked at her. 'Given up?'

'Looking for you. We've all been out. We were all worried about you, especially your father. Still you're found now and that's the main thing.'

'Oh!' Maddie exclaimed, mortified. 'I'm sorry to have caused you so much bother.'

'It was no bother,' Sarah replied. In a friendly fashion she took Maddie's arm. 'Let's get out of here. I like this park in the daytime but at night it gives me the creeps. Strange how places look so very different in the dark.' She attempted to steer Maddie back down the path. 'I expect you could do with a cuppa. I know I could. And a hot meal. I hope you like faggots?'

Maddie pulled her arm free. 'Mrs . . . er . . . Look, I'm grateful to you all for bothering to come looking for me, really I am. But . . . I can't come back with you.'

Sarah had half expected this reaction but still managed to appear taken aback. 'You can't? Whyever not?'

'Because . . .' Maddie's bottom lip trembled. 'Because I've caused enough trouble. Now I really must be going.' Where to she had no idea but she had to let Sarah think that she had.

She made to walk away but Sarah caught her arm. 'Just a minute, Maddie. I don't understand what you mean by causing trouble?'

Maddie swallowed hard. 'Well, I have. I . . . I interrupted your meal. Inconsiderate of me to do that. I'll . . . er . . . call again at a more convenient time.' She thrust out her hand, then jerked it back. 'It was very nice to have met you. Goodbye,' she said brightly, raising her head as if she hadn't a care in the world and marching off.

Sarah rushed after her. 'We've finished our meal now, Maddie,' she said, walking beside her, 'so you're causing no trouble. And your father will be so upset if I don't take you back with me. Now come on,' she coaxed, again taking Maddie's arm. 'I'll not take no for an answer. While I get you something hot, you can finish your talk with George.' Sarah looked her straight in the eye. 'He has so much more he needs to explain to you.'

'No,' she erupted, stopping and pulling her arm free. Suddenly the reserves of energy she had summoned to try and convince Sarah all was well were all gone. Her whole body slumped. With head bowed, she started to shake. 'Please leave me alone, Mrs . . . Mrs . . . I . . . can't take anymore. I've ruined so many lives – yours too. Please, please, just go away.'

Horror filled Sarah's being. 'Maddie! Oh, Maddie dear, what makes you think you're responsible for anything?'

'Well, aren't I?' she uttered. To her horror, before she could stop herself she started to cry. 'I was a mistake,' she choked out. 'I should never have been born. How can I face my father again knowing that it's my fault he's . . . that he's . . . a bigamist?'

'A bigamist?' Mortified, Sarah could not control her own emotions any longer. She threw her arms around the distraught young woman, pulling her close. Maddie, having nothing left within her, rested her head on Sarah's shoulder, gently sobbing. 'Oh, my dear, dear girl,' she whispered. 'You have it all wrong. Your father is no bigamist. Neither were you a mistake. Nothing of the sort. You were very much planned,' she said, an icy tone in her voice. 'Whatever went on, you were in no way to blame. Not in the least.'

Totally bewildered, Maddie drew back her head, looking her straight in the eye. 'I don't understand?'

Sarah sighed. 'No, I don't expect you do, my dear. This must all seem very confusing. You should return with me and let your father finish his story. You owe it to yourself to hear the truth.'

Maddie stared at her.

'You must,' Sarah reiterated.

Maddie nodded. 'All right.'

Relieved, Sarah guided her back.

Maddie and George were both seated once more in the parlour.

'All I can say, Maddie, is that I'm very, very sorry. I was trying to shield you. Spare your feelings. It didn't work, did it?' He rubbed one hand across the back of his neck. 'I'm finding this very difficult. To me you're still my little girl. I forget you're a grown woman of twenty-six now.'

'Yes, I am, Father. I do understand how hard this must be for you. It's hard for me too. But I'd appreciate your telling me everything exactly as it was.'

'You're right, then there'll be no more misunderstandings.' George took her hands and looked at her earnestly. 'I would just like to put your mind at rest about one thing and that is that your mother planned to have you. You were no accident, Maddie. I don't like showing her in such a bad light, but . . .'

'It's all right,' she interrupted. 'Things . . . certain things have happened of late that . . . well, let me just say I think I understand my mother now far better than I used to.'

He shot her a questioning glance. 'In what way, Maddie?'

'I really don't wish to say at the moment if you don't mind, Father.'

He nodded. 'As you wish. But if ever you do want to talk . . . Maddie, I've never been allowed to be a parent to you, but I am your father in every sense of the word. I want to do the best I can for you.'

She smiled wanly. 'Thank you.'

He settled back in his seat. 'Right, so where did I get to?'

'Mother summoned you to tell you she was expecting.'

'Yes.' His eyes glazed over. 'It was certainly a shock. The very last thing I was expecting to hear. Then came her ultimatum. I was too dumbfounded to answer her at first.'

'What was it?' Maddie asked in a whisper.

'That if I refused to do the honourable thing, she would go to my bosses and tell them how their employee had taken advantage of her. She would make sure I was sacked and left with no reputation. Finding other employment would be very difficult – impossible in the trade I was in.'

Maddie couldn't believe what she was hearing. It was like history repeating itself. Harriet had warned her father, but she had done the actual deed to poor, unsuspecting Gilbert Frisby just because he'd dared to ask her daughter out.

'I felt the fear of God on me then. I didn't love your mother, Maddie. I had no feelings in that way for her whatsoever. Well, I hadn't really got to know her well enough for feelings like that to come about. I wanted to run away, emigrate, anything to get out of marrying her. The thought of losing the job I enjoyed so much didn't matter much then. I'd dig ditches, wash dishes if I had to. But once I had time to think about it, I knew I had to do as she said or I'd suffer the guilt for the rest of my life. My uncle and aunt had always taught me to face up to my responsibilities. I had a responsibility to my unborn child. To you, Maddie. My conscience wouldn't let me walk away. Accident or no, you were part of me. So for that reason only, I married Harriet.'

This confession shocked Maddie greatly. 'You did it for me?' she gasped.

'Yes.' He patted her hand. 'And in that respect I have no regrets. At first it was a very difficult time for me. Having come from people who showed they cared for me deeply, living with a woman with a nature like Harriet's was hard. Despite the money I gave her, and not forgetting what she was making in the shop which was something she never discussed with me, she made it very clear the business was hers alone. The house was always cold, even in summer, and the food she gave me hardly enough to feed a boy. Trying

125

to talk to her about it was a waste of time. Whatever I said fell on deaf ears, and for a while after I dared voice my opinion she would create an atmosphere.'

She did not say a word but Maddie knew exactly what he meant.

George cleared his throat in embarrassment, wondering how best to word to his daughter the fact that Harriet had shunned any kind of physical advances. 'It . . . er . . . didn't take me long to realise that Harriet didn't want a husband in the . . . er . . . physical sense. After a while of trying all I could to make the marriage work, I decided it was best just to go along with her way of things. Call me weak but it made for a much easier life. I suppose I resigned myself.

'When we were first married I made a great effort to get home as often as I could, sometimes not getting there until very late in the evening and starting out the next day before the crack of dawn. But very quickly I found I was planning my appointments so that it was impossible for me to journey back daily. Your mother didn't seem put out by this at all. In fact, she seemed quite pleased, encouraged me even.

'When an area became vacant on the north side of Leicester I jumped at it, Maddie. It wasn't a good area. Mostly rural. Collecting penny policies from some of the company's poorest customers, that kind of thing. A come down from what I had been doing. I was delighted when I got it, although my boss couldn't understand why I wanted it so badly. Me, a newly married man with a baby on the way. How could I explain truthfully and expect him to understand that covering this area meant I would only have to put up with my wife at the weekends? He was happily married himself. But at least life was more tolerable for me then.'

George paused and smiled as a memory surfaced. 'It all seemed worth it when you were born. I can remember that day so clearly. I can honestly say, Maddie, that was the only thing that happened in my marriage to bring me any happiness. I asked Harriet if we could call you Laura after my aunt, but she wouldn't hear of it. She insisted you be named Maude. Where she got the name from I've no idea. To me it seemed such a harsh name for a pretty little thing like you.' He smiled tenderly at her. 'Your mother addressed you as Maude but I called you Maddie.'

Her mouth dropped open in surprise. She had always thought that to be her own idea.

George's voice lowered sadly. 'I soon realised I was expected to have little to do with your upbringing. Try as I might, your mother blocked me at every turn, to the extent that I was hardly allowed to touch you. It broke my heart. You were such a lovely child. Such a delight. You would lie in your cot gurgling quite contentedly. Harriet showed little interest in you. She did what she had to and nothing more. She never talked to you or played with you. She would let you cry for hours without picking you up. If I attempted to . . .'

He shook his head savagely, Harriet's harsh tones ringing in his ears. 'How's she supposed to learn discipline if you keep mollycoddling her?' 'But she's a baby, Harriet. Babies need affection. Teaching them right and wrong comes later, surely?' 'She gets affection,' his wife had hissed. 'Remember, you're not here most of the time. Babies fit in with adults, not the other way around.'

Sighing deeply he looked his daughter straight in the eye. 'And that's how life went on, you and I both doing exactly what Harriet wanted. You seemed happy enough, I can only hope that you were.' He leaned closer to her. 'I was miserable. For me life was just an empty existence.' His voice trailed off and Maddie noticed a spark of tenderness in his eyes as he whispered, 'Until I met Sarah.' He paused and looking at her intently. 'Is this all too painful for you?' he asked, deeply concerned. 'If you want me to stop, please say so?'

It was, very much so, but something she had to endure.

Having heard this much she wanted, needed to know the rest.

'Please go on,' Maddie urged.

'All right, if you're sure. Sarah transformed my life. We met by accident. We were both crossing a busy road, neither of us looking where we were going, and we collided. She dropped her bag of shopping and I helped to pick it up. I offered to escort her home. Maybe with hindsight I shouldn't have done, but I did, and I'm glad of it. Her widowed mother had passed away and she lived on her own in a small flat. "Flat" is exaggerating. Two shabby rooms it was with a shared toilet. It was all she could afford, her job as a shop assistant didn't pay much, but she had made it so homely. She invited me in for a cup of tea.' His voice lowered. 'I fell in love with her over that cup of tea as I was to find out very much later she did with me.

'Please be assured, right from the start I made no secret of the fact I was a married man with a child. I took my vows seriously and had no intention of breaking them. Sarah and I could never be more than friends, I felt. And for well over a year that's all we were. If I was in the area I would call in for a cup of tea and a chat. That's all it was, nothing more. And that's the way it would have continued if it had not been for me buying you that doll.'

'A doll?' Maddie frowned. 'I don't remember ever having a new doll. I had a rag doll I think someone made me.'

'You called it Rolly.' He smiled. 'You couldn't quite say dolly. It was made by your Aunt Laura not long before she passed away.'

'Was it? I didn't know that.' Fancy her father remembering the doll's name.

'Unfortunately she never got to see you. She was too ill by then to travel and your mother wouldn't accompany me or let me take you myself. She insisted you were too young to travel. But the doll I bought really did bring matters to a head. I'd seen it in Arbuthnot's shop window in the High

Street. It was a marvellous doll. It had eyes that closed when you laid it down, a frilly pink dress and hair styled in ringlets. I wanted you to have it. Two shillings and sixpence it was. Too expensive for me in one go. So I saved for it. Weeks it took me. I was always worried they'd sell it and so relieved when at last I had the money. That weekend I took it home. Couldn't wait to see your face.

'Your mother always made sure you were in bed before I arrived back. When she was busy elsewhere I'd sneak in and kiss you goodnight. I woke you then and gave you the doll. Oh, Maddie, I can still see your little face. You were so excited.' His own clouded over. 'Then your mother came in and threw a fit. Accused me of wasting good money on useless toys. She snatched it from you. You were not to be spoiled, were her words. The doll went on the back of the fire.' Maddie gasped, horrified. 'I . . . cannot tell you how outraged I was. That she could do such a thing. You didn't understand what was going on and were heartbroken to lose your new toy. Your mother scolded you for acting such a baby.' He shook his head ruefully. 'You were just coming up to three years old, Maddie.

'I had to get out of the house then, couldn't look at Harriet for fear I'd do something I gravely regretted. The next thing I knew I found myself back in Leicester, wandering the streets. All I could see was your heartbroken little face. I had to see Sarah. Go somewhere where I felt I was wanted. She knew something was seriously amiss as soon as she opened the door and I couldn't help but tell her what had happened. She just listened. Then, before I could stop myself it all came out, the whole story of how I'd landed up in this awful situation. I was so miserable, I cried. A grown man of twenty-five, crying like a baby. I felt utterly humiliated.'

He paused momentarily. 'It was then that Sarah kissed me. She leaned over, took my face in her hands and kissed me. Then she put her arms around me and held me tight. Can you imagine how I felt Maddie? The woman I was married to didn't show one iota of affection towards me and I had forgotten what it was like to be held by someone. I found it hard to believe a woman could want me. There was I, George Ashman, being told by this lovely woman that she loved me. I was deliriously happy.

'We talked all night and come morning it was decided I would approach Harriet and ask her to release me from our marriage.' He stopped and ran a despairing hand over his balding pate. 'It took a lot of courage for me to face her. She's not the easiest person to approach. And she laughed. Your mother actually laughed at me. She said I was a fool. Who in their right mind would want to take on me, a useless cripple? She said I should take a cold bath and come to my senses. And then she refused to discuss it any further.

'I don't know what came over me – if it was just that she had ridiculed the fact that someone could care for me, or her refusal to discuss something so important. But I was incensed. I'm sorry to say this to you, Maddie, but I think it was then that I realised I hated her. She had trapped me into marriage, used me for her own ends, and for that one terrible mistake I was going to have to pay dearly by being saddled with her for the rest of my life. If I hadn't met Sarah then that's more than likely what would have happened. But I had met her and things had changed and I couldn't carry on. I told Harriet that I was leaving anyway, divorce or not, and I was going to take you with me. And I meant it. I didn't want to leave you with her, knowing my daughter would be raised by such a cold-hearted woman.

'Stupid of me but I had thought, taking everything into consideration, that she would welcome the idea. At that time I was of the distinct impression she didn't want either of us. I was badly mistaken. She wasn't prepared to let either of us go.' His voice trailed off and he sighed, 'And that's when she told me, Maddie.' His eyes filled with pain. '"If you think," she said, "that I planned and carried out this whole charade for you to humiliate me with a divorce, then you're more stupid than I thought. I married you for life. I am Mrs George Ashman. My husband is a businessman. I have respectability in this town and that's the way it's going to stay."

'I couldn't believe what I was hearing. "You cold-bloodedly planned that night you fell pregnant with Maddie?" I asked her. She smiled. I can only describe her expression as evil. "Would you have married me otherwise?" she said. "You men are all the same. A pretty face, that's all you want. I was ostracised as a child because I was plain and it didn't change as I grew older. Marriage brings status, and I wanted a man to provide for me. I wasn't going to end up like my mother, scratting for every humiliating penny. People laughing behind her back because she made her living selling the rubbish they were glad enough to buy. Do you know how hard I worked to live that down after she died? Nobody knows what it was like for me. Nobody gave me a thought. I wasn't going to leave anything to chance. I wasn't going to go through life a spinster, and if you think I'm going to have the town sniggering behind my back again, people saying I couldn't keep my husband, then you can think again, George Ashman."

'Despite what she'd admitted to doing, Maddie, it wouldn't have been so bad if she'd made an effort to become some sort of wife to me. But she hadn't, and neither was she a proper caring mother towards you. It's no excuse and I don't feel proud but that's when I lost my temper and to this day I don't know how I held back from striking her. Thank goodness I didn't. I would never have lived with myself if I'd allowed myself to be reduced to that. But I told her in no uncertain terms that I was leaving and taking you with me and I would get a divorce and there was nothing she could do about it. Or so I thought. I should have guessed she had already planned what to do should such a situation come about.

'"Try to divorce me and I'll drag you and that floozy of

yours through the courts, and by the time I've finished neither of you will be able to hold your head up again. I shall tell them how you tricked your way into my home on the pretence of selling me insurance, forcing yourself on me to get me pregnant so I'd have to marry you and you could get your hands on my business. I shall say you've been carrying on with that woman all the time. As for Maude – take her and I'll have the police on you for kidnap. If you want your freedom it'll be on my terms or you won't get it."

"'And what are those?" I asked her. "Go and live with your whore," she said. "I don't want you here. The sight of you sickens me and I'll be glad to see the back of you. Making a good excuse for your absence will not be hard. You can write to Maude and send her a gift at Christmas, I'll see that she gets them. She can make her own mind up when she's older whether she chooses to see you or not. You'll continue to pay me my money every week, the amount to be reviewed annually, and the payments will not cease until Maude leaves home. We can make the necessary arrangements so we don't have to come into contact. I don't want you near Market Harborough ever again or to hear word that you have been. Break any of those rules and I will take the necessary action. I'll leave you to work out what revenge I will choose. Do you agree to those terms?"

'I had no choice but to agree and Harriet knew it. I had no idea she was going to play the part of a grieving widow, nor did I have any idea you never received my letters or presents. So many letters I wrote, Maddie, full of my love for you, begging you to reply to me and arrange for us to meet. I never gave up. I sent the last one only weeks ago.'

He sighed despairingly. 'Sarah couldn't believe what I told her. She couldn't believe anyone could be so callous and thought at first I was making it all up. I couldn't blame her. What sane woman would credit such a story? But I'm glad to say I finally managed to convince her. Both of us were devastated. We so wanted to be together as a married couple and that included having you with us.

'But the threat of Harriet's dragging us through court wasn't the reason we decided to go along with her wishes. You were, Maddie.'

'Me?' she uttered.

'Oh, yes. Your mother's no fool, Maddie. She knew how much I cared for you, knew I'd go to any lengths not to have you tainted in any way. I also knew Harriet meant every word she said. Everything was such a mess. It was all so awful. Sarah said she would stand by me whatever I decided. We both knew in the end that I had no choice but to agree to Harriet's terms. So that's what we did, living in the hope that as you grew older you'd decide for yourself to come and live with us and also that Harriet would tire of the situation and give me a divorce. Which never happened.'

Maddie's head bowed and she clasped her hands so tight her knuckles shone white. 'Oh, Father, you put up with this terrible situation all these years, just to protect me?'

George nodded. 'I love you, Maddie, it's as simple as that. I handed over the money to make sure you had a roof over your head and food on the table, and did not divorce Harriet so that you would not carry the stigma.'

Her eyes filled with tears, a lump formed in her throat. 'Oh, Father.'

'Sarah and I discussed what we would do. It was such a painful time, such far-reaching decisions to be made, and I can't say it's been easy for us, especially where Ruth and Roy are concerned. Due to Harriet's selfishness we have been denied the right to marry and forced to live a lie. Our children cannot bear my name. To all who know us in Leicester we are a married couple, and when the children were old enough to understand we explained to them.'

'They know?' said Maddie, aghast.

'Oh, yes. We've always been very honest, never kept anything back.'

'About me too?'

He nodded. 'Since the moment we told them, they have been desperate to meet their sister. Of course it wasn't possible. Sarah and I were very fortunate that they took it all so well. The fact that their parents are not married has never caused them problems. We knew there would come a time when it might. When they decided to marry and so forth, but we hoped that matters would have been settled by then.'

'I expect,' whispered Maddie, 'you were beginning to give up hope that I would ever leave home?'

'I suspect, Maddie,' he said, face clouding angrily, 'that your mother has made things very difficult for you there.'

He had touched a nerve and the tears already in her eyes flowed in answer.

George watched in increasing distress as his daughter wept. He did something he'd always wanted to do but which had been denied him. He threw his arms around her, pulling her close. 'Oh, Maddie, Maddie, I'm so sorry about all this. I hope you can forgive me?'

'It's not you who should be asking forgiveness,' she sobbed. Head bowed, she drew back from him. 'Father, please would you leave me for a while? I . . . would like to be on my own.'

He looked at her for several moments, unsure what to do. 'Yes, of course,' he said eventually, rising to his feet. 'I'll . . . er . . I'll just go and see about some more tea.'

Maddie heard the click of the door as it shut and her whole body sagged as all she had been told flashed through her mind. Now she saw it, and it was almost too awful to believe. But she had to believe it, she had no doubts whatsoever that her father had told her the truth.

She clenched her hands so tight her knuckles shone. So many lives Harriet had ruined! How could she have done it? How could she live with herself?

Maddie sat for an age, numb with shock, then unexpectedly a sudden feeling of intense relief flooded through her, an enormous weight lifting from her slim shoulders. Despite her uncertain future she was so glad she was away from her mother's clutches, that no longer could Harriet govern her life. She was free to make her own decisions and mistakes. But what was more important to Maddie was that her father could now seek his own freedom and marry the woman he loved. And their children, her half-brother and sister, would get their just entitlement.

And what of her own mother? Maddie pondered deeply and realised with shock that all she felt towards the woman who had given birth to her was a great sense of pity. Harriet would now have to live with the aftermath of her own callous actions. Maddie did not wish her ill, but felt if any punishment was due that would be enough. It was the one thing Harriet feared.

She heard the door open and raised her head to see Sarah poke hers around it, her face deeply concerned. She came in carrying a cup of tea. 'Your father is so upset, Maddie. He . . . we're both worried about how you are taking all this. Please forgive me for the intrusion but I just had to come and find out how you are.' Shutting the door she walked over, put the cup on the table and sat down beside Maddie.

She knew it wasn't just words, Sarah's whole persona radiated sincerity. Maddie warmed to her and managed a wan smile. 'With great difficulty. But I'll be fine once I've let it all sink in.'

Sarah hesitated at first then placed one hand gently on Maddie's. 'Your hearing it all was unavoidable, my dear. You could not have been expected to understand the situation between your father and me had you not been told the truth. Please don't think badly of him. He's a good man and loves you very much. You do know that, don't you?'

Head drooping, Maddie gulped hard to rid herself of the lump in her throat. 'I feel so cheated! I'm so angry that I've spent all these years thinking my father was dead just so my mother could hold on to what she saw as her respectability.'

Her shoulders sagged. 'All those lost years.'

'It's not too late, Maddie.'

She raised her head and looked at Sarah. 'Isn't it?'

'Of course it isn't.' She eyed Maddie hesitantly. 'I hope we can be friends too, although in fact I feel I know you already. Your father has always talked of you as though you were part of our family but didn't live with us, if you understand what I mean?'

Maddie stared in surprise. 'Did he? Really?'

'Oh, yes. So, you see, you're no stranger to us. I'm just happy finally to have met you in person. And he was right, you're very pretty. Ruth has a look of you.' Sarah paused and took a deep breath. 'This hasn't been nice for you or your father but I'm glad it's all finally come out. It's a relief.'

'Yes, it must be. And you must love him very much to have gone along with all this?'

'I do, Maddie. To watch him suffering in silence, year after year, with no end in sight hasn't been easy for me. There've been so many times I've wanted to confront your mother, make her tell you the truth about what was going on, let us get matters sorted once and for all. But I couldn't, it wouldn't have been fair to you. You were the innocent one in all this. Still, maybe we can now. But that's for George and you to decide.'

She paused for a moment. 'My dear, please forgive me for asking but George and I are both concerned over what brought you here. We are glad that you came,' she insisted, 'but we both can't help thinking that something . . . well, has something happened? To you? Or your mother?'

Maddie stared at her. She suddenly felt a great need to unburden herself to this kindly woman who until only hours ago she had not known existed. But she couldn't. She was still reeling, still trying to come to terms with her father's heart-rending story and she hadn't the energy. Besides, to explain fully she would be not only to add to Harriet's already hideous list of crimes but to reveal her own terrible secret. She wasn't ready for that.

Maddie clasped her hands. 'No, nothing's happened. After finding out my father was alive, I wanted to meet him and also felt it was time I left home. I hoped he would help me find somewhere to live and tell me where to start looking for a job, that's all.'

The forced lightness of her tone gave her away. But Sarah felt Maddie obviously had her reasons, and besides she had been through so much tonight that now wasn't the time to unburden herself further. Maddie would, she had no doubt, when she was good and ready. It still did not stop her from being dreadfully concerned about what the girl was hiding. Sarah gave a comforting smile. 'You've no need to look for anywhere to live. You have a home here with us.'

Maddie looked at her, startled. 'Oh, but I couldn't possibly impose.'

'Impose? My dear, you're George's daughter. This is your home too. I won't deny we'll be a bit squashed but we could make this room up for you, if you wouldn't mind sleeping on the sofa until we got you a bed? Between us we'll make it really cosy. We hardly use this room, and you'd be doing me a favour.'

'Would I? How?'

Sarah laughed. 'I've never liked this horsehair sofa. You'll give me an excuse to get rid of it.'

Maddie felt fresh tears stab the back of her eyes. The kindness of this woman!

Sarah sensed what was going through her mind and laid a reassuring hand on hers. 'We're your family, Maddie, and as such this is as much your home as it is Ruth's and Roy's. Now I know you have gone through a lot tonight and we'll all understand if you want to stay quietly in here. I'll bring a tray through and some bedding. But Ruth and Roy are desperate to meet you. Do you feel up to that first?'

Maddie gnawed her bottom lip anxiously. Ruth and Roy. They were her half-sister and brother, her own flesh and blood, the family she had always craved. Suddenly a sense of belonging overwhelmed her and her watery eyes brightened. 'Oh, yes, I'd like that very much.'

Sarah smiled in delight and took her hand. 'Come on then.'

# Part Two

# Chapter Ten

'I wish I knew what this meant.' Staring in confusion at the figures scrawled across the pages of the black leather-bound ledger, Agnes Clatteridge raised her head and looked at her younger sister in the hope she might receive some help. In her heart she knew she was wasting her time. Like Agnes, Alice Clatteridge hadn't a clue.

Closing the heavy ledger Agnes smoothed one hand absently over the fringed maroon chenille cloth covering the dark mahogany table. She sighed again as she glanced around the dimly lit room. Everything about it was dark – dark and dismal. Her sister and she matched the room. They were dressed as ever in dark colours. Always dark grey or black, occasionally brown so long as it was dark brown. Hairstyles severe, no jewellery, and absolutely no makeup whatsoever. In fact nothing frivolous about them at all. As per Father's instructions. And now they were in mourning for him they would have to wear black for at least six months longer as a sign of respect. Even in death he was still ruling their lives.

'Alice, you could show some interest. We have so much to learn. This funeral parlour will not run itself.'

Tutting, Alice let her embroidery drop in her lap.

'I know that. But if you haven't a clue how to interpret the books, then how do you expect me to?' She pursed her lips disdainfully. 'It's all Father's fault for leaving us so ill prepared.'

Agnes sighed sharply. 'I don't think he intended to die

just yet. I believe he had every intention of outliving us all.'
For an instant she felt guilty that neither of them was grieving
for the loss of their father. His sudden death had been a
shock but, if they were forced to be truthful, not entirely
unwelcome. An image of him came vividly to mind. His tall
thin frame looming before her, hawk-like, as if ready to
pounce on his prey; unblinking eyes glaring icily. She
shivered violently. As quickly as the guilt had materialised it
departed and her light grey eyes kindled. 'But I'm not sorry
he did, the old bugger! There was no love lost between us
and he made our lives a misery, one way or another. I'm
glad he's no longer around to do that. There, I've said it,'
she cried triumphantly.

Alice stared at her appalled. 'Oh, Agnes, he was very . . .
very . . .' She couldn't quite bring herself to speak as bluntly
as her sister, having a strong presentiment that, dead or
not, he would still somehow manage to show his disapproval.
A bolt of lightning directed straight at her, perhaps? Alice
shuddered. 'Well, I agree he was what you . . . er . . . said.
But actually to speak it aloud, Agnes, really! *And* you
blasphemed. You know Father couldn't abide bad language.'
Her eyes filled with fear. 'He'll come back and haunt
us.' Her face crumpled. 'You'll have to sleep in my room
tonight. Oh, Agnes!' she wailed.

'Stop it, Alice. Father's haunting us is the least of our
worries. Actually,' said Agnes flippantly, 'it might help if he
did, I've plenty of questions to ask him.' Her face grew grave.
'Our situation isn't what I expected it to be, and I can't
understand it. The business seemed to be doing all right,
and it's not as if Father was overly generous. In fact, you
know as well as I do we had to account for every penny he
grudgingly gave us, so why has he left us so badly off?'

Alice shrugged her shoulders. 'Do you think it could be
hidden somewhere? Father didn't have anything good to
say about banks. It could be under the floorboards or behind
a brick somewhere.'

Agnes sighed again. 'If Father has hidden anything it wouldn't be anywhere obvious. It could take forever to find it.'

'Mmmm, you're right. He was a . . .' Alice wanted to say 'devious old devil' but couldn't quite bring herself to. A sudden thought struck her. 'Perhaps Simpson might have an idea? He's worked for Father since a boy, knew his ways, might have seen him doing something suspicious. It could be worth asking.'

Agnes frowned thoughtfully, then shook her head. 'If Father was up to something like that, he wouldn't allow anyone to see him. He'd have had the curtains drawn tightly, the keyhole stuffed with paper and all the mantles turned low.'

Her sister nodded in agreement. 'But you could still ask.'

'I suppose I could. But how do I tackle a subject like that? Don't bother answering, it doesn't matter. He's an employee, Alice. You don't discuss family business with employees. But I suppose,' she added thoughtfully, 'the subject could be approached indirectly. I'm not quite sure how but that would be all right wouldn't it?' Her eyes suddenly flashed annoyance. 'Just a moment – what about *you* approaching him?'

'Oh, I couldn't,' Alice replied, aghast. 'You're the eldest, Agnes, you're in charge. Things like that are for you to do.'

'Alice, I'm not in charge, we're sisters. Whatever Father left is split between us, and whatever we do, we do as equals.'

'Huh! I expect if Father had realised he was going to die he'd have changed his will, left whatever he had to some good cause. He didn't like us, Agnes. Had no time for us at all. He made no bones about the fact he wanted sons.' Alice's voice lowered emotionally. 'How many times did he tell us we should have been sons for all the looks God had blessed us with?' Placing her embroidery on the arm of the worn leather armchair she rose, stepped across to the mantle over the fireplace and picked up a silver-framed photograph, looking with longing at the faded sepia image inside. 'Why couldn't we have taken after Mother, Agnes?' she asked wistfully. 'It's not fair we both took after him. Mother was so pretty, wasn't she? If she hadn't died having me . . . He never stopped blaming me for that.'

'Alice,' Agnes interrupted, 'let's not go over all this again. Not tonight, please. I have a headache.'

She eyed her sister. There was no missing the fact that they were related. Both were tall for women which only accentuated their slenderness. They had long faces, high foreheads, straight noses and spare lips. All inherited from their father along with wide hands and large feet – the very last features a woman would want to inherit. Had their father encouraged his daughters to dress fashionably or use a hint of colour on their lips, it still wouldn't have done much to disguise the fact that they were tall, thin and plain. There was absolutely no getting away from it.

At thirty-four years of age Agnes had resigned herself to spending her life as a spinster. Not so Alice. Despite reaching thirty-two years of age, with never a glimmer of romance, she permanently lived in hope that a man was out there somewhere who would want a wife for talents such as embroidery and cooking skills and not just as an adornment to his table. Agnes didn't blame her, and despite the fact that the terrible Great War had severely depleted the male population, thus greatly reducing her chances, wished with all her heart her sister's dream might one day come true. She loved Alice very much. But she was right: had their mother lived, their lives would have been so different.

Blanche Clatteridge had been a beautiful woman, small and petite, with a warm and humorous disposition. How she had come to marry dour, forbidding Cuthbert Clatteridge defied anyone's belief. They were so oddly matched. But according to those who knew them it was definitely a love match. Blanche had doted on her husband and he on her. The day before she died, it was said, was the last anyone saw Cuthbert Clatteridge summon a smile.

Agnes suddenly wondered what her father's face would have looked like smiling. His near white skin stretched taut over his bony face, the menacing arch of his great bushy eyebrows, his row of long tombstone-like teeth flashing . . . Despite the fact it was her father she was trying to picture, she shuddered at the horrifying vision she'd created.

Her thoughts were interrupted as she realised Alice was speaking. 'I'm sorry, Alice, what were you saying?'

'I asked just exactly what our financial situation was? You've told me it's not good, but you've not mentioned any figures.'

'Oh, er . . .' To divulge the exact sum was something she had been desperately trying to avoid. When she had very carefully broken the news to her sister of their precarious situation Agnes had been very generous with the truth. She had told Alice that their finances were not as good as she had hoped. The fact was they were extremely poor, bad enough to have rendered her speechless when the lawyer had told her. She hadn't expected to be told that they would only be able to keep both business and household going for four months at the most.

'You're trying to hide something,' Alice accused her. 'Just tell me, Agnes. I've a right to know.'

She scowled in annoyance. 'I did ask you several times to come with me to see the lawyer to hear Father's will. If you had, you wouldn't now be accusing me of doing something I'm not. If I'm guilty of anything it's not wanting to worry you.' Agnes paused for breath. 'If you really want to know the exact amount, Alice, after the estate has been settled we've four hundred and fifty-seven pounds ten shillings and fourpence three-farthing to our name. It's not a lot, I grant you, but . . .'

'Is that all?' Alice exclaimed, deeply shocked. 'I'll say it's not a lot! You were exaggerating when you said Father didn't leave us very well off. We've bills to pay, Agnes. He's left us not much better than paupers. What on earth are we going to do?'

'Hardly paupers, Alice. Paupers don't own property. The house and everything in it is ours plus the outbuildings, machinery and some stock.' She took a deep breath and forced a reassuring smile. 'Business will pick up, I'm sure. We only had our bereavement last week, people have probably kept away as a sign of respect, that's all. Father's by no means the first Clatteridge to die and the business didn't go under before.'

'I'm not so sure it will pick up. I think that now Father has gone, the business has gone too.'

Agnes gnawed her bottom lip worriedly. She wasn't certain whether to tell Alice but the lawyer had voiced a similar concern. Cuthbert Clatteridge had been the last male of the family and as such people might assume that the funeral business would end with him. At which Agnes had reminded the lawyer that he was forgetting there was herself and Alice, who were more than capable of keeping things running. The lawyer had rammed his pince-nez higher on his nose, picked up a sheaf of papers and shuffled them together, saying he hoped Agnes realised what she was taking on. Alice now voicing the same concerns was causing a niggle of doubt as to whether she actually did. Agnes forced the worry away and took a deep breath. 'Well, we'll just have to make sure people are in no doubt it's business as usual, won't we?'

Alice gasped in shock. 'You're not seriously thinking of trying to keep it going?'

'Why, of course. What else can we do? This business is our livelihood. It's been in the family for seventy years. We have an obligation to keep it going. And surely we have to consider our employees? I'm not so worried for Peabody.' She did not say she had never liked him, felt him to be sly and untrustworthy though she had never found anything to substantiate her suspicions. 'But Mr Simpson has worked for father for thirty years, since he was twelve years old. Surely we owe him . . .'

'So? He's not too old to get another job. And, besides, he was paid and received his living accommodation,' Alice cut in sharply. 'I don't see that we owe him anything more.'

'He doesn't get much according to the wages book. And as for his accommodation . . . A room over the stable is hardly a palace.'

'Even so, it's something other people wouldn't turn their noses up at.'

Agnes pressed her lips together, fighting her mounting annoyance at the way her sister was speaking so dismissively of Ivan Simpson. Alice may see him as just an employee but to Agnes he was much more than that. But her feelings were a secret, which she had shared with no one, not even her sister. 'I suppose not,' she conceded graciously.

'Anyway, haven't you forgotten something?'

'Like what?' Agnes looked at Alice frowning inquisitively.

'Like the fact that we're women. I don't know of any other funeral parlour that has women running it.'

The lawyer had mentioned that too and Agnes told him the same thing she was about to tell her sister. 'Personally I don't see what difference it makes. Before the war it was unheard of for women to deliver the post or drive ambulances or do numerous other things come to that. Women doing what are deemed to be men's jobs is becoming commonplace now. So why not run a funeral parlour? Besides, to my way of thinking clients are too preoccupied at the time to be much bothered whether the company they're using is run by males or females.'

'You sound like one of those suffragettes, Agnes,' Alice snapped haughtily. 'I don't agree. But anyway, what do you know about running a business like ours? Not enough . . .'

'That's not true,' she cut in, offended, 'and you know it. I know much than Father would ever give me credit for. I learned over the years by listening and watching. I

147

know just about everything there is to know. If you're truthful so do you. You just don't want to admit it. It's only the financial side I'm truly ignorant of because he never allowed anyone to see the books. But that I can learn too. It's just a case of working it all out. It'll take me time, that's all.' Agnes eyed her sister reproachfully. 'You keep talking about me. Can I remind you once again that there are two of us. It's we, isn't it, Alice?'

Her sister blatantly ignored this and just said, 'But if it all goes wrong we could end up worse off than we are now.' She took a deep breath. 'I think we should consider selling.'

Agnes gasped. 'What? No, Alice. Surely not without giving it a try first?'

'Then we might have nothing left to sell.' Alice paused and eyed her sister worriedly for a moment. She had news to break to Agnes that she probably wasn't going to like and wasn't sure how to go about it.

Agnes noticed her discomfiture and misconstrued it. 'We can do this,' she said, far more confidently than she actually felt. 'We have to, Alice, we need to make our living. I know it's not going to be easy but it's not as if we're starting from nothing. We'll show them all we can do it, you see if we don't.'

Before she could stop herself, Alice blurted out, 'But that's just it – I don't want to.' Her mouth snapped shut and she was acutely conscious that her sister was staring at her, astounded. A dreadful feeling of remorse filled her as she wished wholeheartedly she had picked a better time to tell Agnes of her decision, but then realised there would never be a good time to divulge what she was about to. She had opened her mouth now so had no choice but to get it over with and hope that Agnes would understand.

Sitting back down in her armchair, she clasped her hands tightly and looked her sister straight in the eye. 'I've made up my mind, Agnes. I'm going to take up Aunt Celia's offer. I don't want to live here anymore. I hate it. Hate everything about it. While Father was alive I thought I'd be stuck here forever. Well, now I don't have to be, I can make my own decisions. Going to live with Aunt Celia will begin a new life for me. Scarborough sounds a wonderful place.'

Her eyes filled with excitement. 'Aunt Celia can introduce me to so many people. I'll get to do things I've never been allowed to do before. Go to the music hall and to tea dances. Dress in nice clothes. All sorts of things that Father decided were unseemly.' Her voice lowered. 'I just want to be happy, Agnes. I'm not happy here and never will be if I stay. I know what people call us. You don't think I know but I do. The Sisters Grim.' Agnes's sharp intake of breath was audible. 'Yes, it hurts, doesn't it, Agnes? But we're not grim, are we? It was the way Father made us be. People don't understand that and make fun of us behind our backs. That won't change just because he's gone. Here we'll always be the Sisters Grim. I want to get away from that and the only way is to go and live with Aunt Celia. I might never get another chance like this. She's getting old. She's the only relative we've got. If I turn down her offer even just for a while she might never give it again.' She looked at Agnes pleadingly. 'It was extended to both of us. Why don't you come too? Please, Agnes, say you will?'

As she silently stared at her sister, Agnes's mind whirled frantically. Aunt Celia's letter of condolence had arrived two days ago, just after the funeral, and Agnes, with so much else on her mind, hadn't had time to give the contents much thought after hurriedly reading them. Obviously her sister had. Their aunt had been most insistent about their going to live with her, reiterating the invitation several times in her spidery scrawl. She would love their company, the change of scene and air would do them good, she had plenty of room and there was nothing now to put an obstacle in their way. The obstacle referred to, Agnes had deduced, being their domineering father.

She narrowed her eyes, feeling that in view of Alice's

decision she had better give the matter serious thought. To accept would be the simplest answer. All burdens of responsibility would instantly be lifted from her. All they would have to worry about was getting as much as they could for this property and the goodwill of the business to afford them some capital. Agnes's eyes glazed over. Oh, to start afresh somewhere where no one knew of them or their background! Yes, it did sound tempting.

Over the years they had not seen much of their mother's elder sister, two or three visits at the most. Cuthbert Clatteridge had not encouraged his sister-in-law to call and had not made her welcome when she had ignored his excuses and arrived on their doorstep, complete with enough luggage to last for several months. Inside a week she had departed, having had enough of Cuthbert's unsociable, blatantly rude attitude. Visits to Scarborough had never been suggested, everyone knowing in advance what the answer would be. Agnes felt angry to remember it now. Her selfish father had denied both sisters the right to get to know their only remaining relative. But though they barely knew Celia, Agnes had no doubt they would be made very welcome and life with her would be fun if nothing else. Small as their mother had been, despite her advancing years she still retained her youthful figure and her former beauty was very much in evidence. Celia was a loveable character and, Agnes imagined, very well thought of amongst her circle of friends and acquaintances.

As she pondered more deeply, Agnes absent-mindedly place her elbow on the table and rested her chin in her palm, unaware that her sister was watching her with bated breath.

Should the offer be accepted, she and Alice would have to get some kind of work. Aunt Celia wasn't rich by any means and they couldn't expect her to keep them after whatever capital they received had run out. But that shouldn't be hard. They were both adept with a needle and there were other lines of suitable work they could consider.

Another thought suddenly struck her. Depending on the amount of capital they received, she and Alice could maybe start their own small business. A gift shop on the sea front? She started to conjure up a picture of a shop and to visualise it filled to brimming with tasteful merchandise and a constant stream of well-to-do holidaymakers, she and Alice helping meet their requirements, falling easily into pleasant conversation. They could even offer tea and cakes. Or why not have a tea shop? Suddenly it all appeared most appealing.

If she was truthful with herself, keeping the family business afloat was going to take every conceivable effort, against cut-throat competition and with the odds stacked very heavily against her. Already business that would have been theirs had gone elsewhere. Could she stand up to all that continually, be one step ahead all the time, on permanent watch for not-so-scrupulous operators trying to steal their business in any devious way they could concoct?

She sighed. She had been fooling herself. She wasn't up to it. Her father, damn him, had seen to that. The competition would eat her alive, make her a laughing stock, and by the time they had finished the business would be worth next to nothing as her sister had predicted.

Alice was right. Now Father was dead, it was their one and only chance to start a new life, in a new town, well away from anyone who knew of them. Agnes would be stupid to refuse Aunt Celia's offer. And, just maybe, they might meet men who wanted their kind of women. She could hope, like Alice. Why not? Her mind was made up too.

Agnes raised her head and looked across at her nervously waiting sister. 'I wonder how long it will take to sell up? Not too long, I hope.'

The look she received back was a blank one until her words hit home and Alice's face split into a wide beam of delight. Jumping up, she rushed over and threw her arms joyously around Agnes's neck. 'Oh, Agnes, I knew you'd see sense!' she cried. 'Oh, I can't tell you how happy I am. I wouldn't have felt right, leaving you behind.'

Agnes stared up at her. 'If I'd decided to try and make a go of things here, you'd still have gone and left me to it?'

Alice's arms loosened and she straightened up. 'Yes,' she said without a moment's hesitation. 'If you'd stayed that would be your decision. Mine is to go.' She paused, eyeing her sister guiltily. 'Please don't be angry with me, Agnes, but I went to the Post Office in town today while you were at the lawyer's and telephoned Aunt Celia to tell her I was accepting but I wasn't sure about you. I just felt that if I waited, I'd never get out of here. I love you, Agnes, and I didn't want to leave you behind but . . .'

'It's all right, Alice,' she interrupted. 'I understand. As you said, now Father's gone we can make our own choices.' She smiled tenderly. 'I would have felt so guilty if you had stayed and I'd found out afterwards you did it for me. That wouldn't have been fair.' She took a deep breath. 'Anyway, it doesn't matter because we're both going. All we need to do is wait for a buyer then we can be off.' She ran her eyes disparagingly over the room. 'I can't say that I'm looking forward to packing up this house. I suppose we'll have to get rid of most of the furniture. We can't expect Aunt Celia to have room for any. But now our minds are made up we could make a start in the morning. The sooner the better. I'll make an appointment with the lawyer and he can give us advice as to how to go about matters.' She suddenly noticed the worried expression on her sister's face. 'What is it, Alice?'

She gulped and wrung her hands anxiously.

'Alice?'

'I won't be here. I'm . . . going tomorrow. On the early train. I have to change several times, shan't arrive until late-afternoon. Aunt Celia's expecting me.'

'Oh!'

'I'm sorry, Agnes,' she said ashamed. 'I could put it off, I suppose,' she said, implying otherwise. 'Go next week instead. I'm sure Aunt Celia would understand, in the circumstances.'

'No, no,' said Agnes hurriedly. The last thing she wanted to do was to spoil Alice's enthusiasm at the thought of her new life. 'You mustn't do that. I'll . . . er . . . manage.' Though how without her sister she had no idea. It suddenly struck her that this would be the first time since Alice's birth that they would be parted. She didn't like the prospect, not because of what lay in store for her to deal with but simply because she would miss her sister greatly. She forced a smile. 'Aunt Celia will have your room aired and I expect will have rallied round her friends to come and meet you or arranged to take you to call on them.'

'Yes,' Alice replied excitedly. 'I expect she will. Anyway I'm not quite leaving you to do it on your own. You have Simpson and Peabody to help,' she said brightly. 'I'd only get in the way. Father was always saying I was a hindrance, wasn't he? Anyway if I go on ahead it'll make things easier for you when you follow, won't it? I can . . . well, I can get the lay of the land, can't I? Please say that's all right, Agnes? Please say you don't mind?'

Agnes wanted to tell her she did mind, that she couldn't cope with all that needed to be done by herself, the thought terrified her, but as she looked at her sister it suddenly struck her that Alice's keenness to leave stemmed from fear – fear that something would happen to prevent her.

She knew she had only to ask her sister not to go and out of loyalty Alice wouldn't. But Agnes wouldn't do that. She couldn't bring herself to blight her sister's newfound sense of freedom or the excitement she was experiencing at what she visualised ahead. For the first time in her life Alice was seeing a future for herself. She had had little to look forward to during thirty-two years here and Agnes felt she had no right to spoil things for her now. She would manage by herself.

She slapped Alice playfully on the arm. 'I don't mind,

really. As you said, if you stay you'll only get in the way. I'll get things done much quicker without you here to hinder me.' Tears pricked her eyes and she blinked to try and rid herself of them, not wanting Alice to see that she was getting upset. 'I'll miss you, though.'

'And me you, but it won't be for long, will it? Oh, thank you, Agnes.' Planting a kiss on her cheek, Alice spun round and headed for the door. 'I'd better start packing. I've not much but the sooner I start, the sooner it's done.' She suddenly stopped, spinning back round. 'Trunk! I haven't a trunk,' she blurted, panic-stricken.

'Oh, we've never had any need for them, have we?' Agnes rubbed her chin thoughtfully. 'Ah, yes, Mother's. If I remember rightly, they're in the attic. I'm sure Mr Simpson will get one down for you, if you ask him.'

'Oh, can you ask him, Agnes? I haven't the time,' said Alice, spinning round again and disappearing out of the door.

Agnes stood for several long moments staring after her sister. How would she feel when she waved her off in the morning? She gave a despairing sigh, wishing she could feel excited like Alice, but there was no room for such feelings with the worry of so much to organise. Her thoughts swam haphazardly. Just where did she start? She would make a list, that was the best thing, and work her way through it. But before she could do anything she had to see Mr Simpson about that trunk.

She suddenly realised that in fairness she ought to break the news of her decision to him, give him decent warning of her intentions. As she pondered on that task it struck her that, of all she had to do, telling Mr Simpson was the task she least relished.

# Chapter Eleven

Agnes shuddered, wrapping her cardigan tighter round her as she made her way across the cobbled courtyard towards the stables. It had been an extremely warm day for the end of September but now the nights were drawing in and this one was beginning to turn chilly. Soon winter would be upon them. Agnes did not like the winter months one little bit. Winter to her had always meant a constant battle to keep warm.

Her father had had an aversion to any kind of heating and demanded fires be kept low regardless of how bitter the weather was or how cold his daughters. For at least three months of every year Alice and she had had to suffer the terrible agonies this lack of consideration brought. Chilblains; poor circulation; coughs and sore throats; solid blocks of butter; ice on water left standing overnight; the nightmare of Friday night stripping for baths of tepid water in a freezing cold room, to remember but a few. But, she thought, no longer. If she happened still to be here during this coming winter, whenever she wanted she could have a huge fire in every room without fear of retribution. With the warmth they brought all her other sufferings would be greatly alleviated.

Now that she had made her decision she hoped everything would be signed and sealed well before then but, regardless, the thought of not having to suffer the cold any longer cheered her greatly.

As she approached the stables, before making her way

up the rusting iron stairs to the side which led up to Mr Simpson's abode, she stopped for a moment before the half-open gabled door. 'Ned,' she called softly. 'Come, boy, see what I've brought you.' As she heard his snort of recognition and the sound of hooves she held out her hand, palm wide, and smiled as a brown head appeared. 'Hello, Ned,' she said tenderly as the old horse gobbled up the sugar cubes. Agnes patted his nose.

'Good boy. You like your sugar, don't you?' Suddenly her smile faded as she realised that the horse would have to go. But where? She would have to find a decent place for him, not just anywhere. She had a great deal of affection for Ned who had been with them for over ten years of loyal, unbroken service. She would not rest if she had any doubts he would be well looked after for his remaining days.

It had fallen to Mr Simpson to take care of Ned's well-being and he had done so more than adequately, in fact going so far as to treat him like a member of the family.

The sound of a footfall behind her made Agnes jump.

'Miss Clatteridge, I do beg yer pardon, I didn't mean ter alarm yer,' Ivan Simpson said worriedly. 'I was just on me way to swill me hands under the pump.' He respectfully whipped off his threadbare cap and grasped it between large work-worn hands. 'I'm sorry, really I am.'

'It's all right,' she reassured him. 'I didn't expect you still to be around at this time of night. I thought you'd be upstairs.'

'Oh, no, Miss Clatteridge, I was finishing off a batch of nails for the ironmonger down the road. I've one or two regular orders, as you know, to keep up with. And I've a small carpentry job to do tomorrow for Mr Cullins at number 'undred and two. So I want to get me bits together ready to go straight round in the morning. It's only fixing a window. It really wants a new 'un, it's near rotten, but, well . . . shouldn't tek me more than an hour. I like to keep on top of things for when our main work comes in. And especially if we get two or three in together. As yer know, miss, that can be a nightmare.'

She gave a half-hearted smile. There wouldn't be any more jobs. Although Simpson didn't know it, his nail-making had been a total waste of time. Well, maybe not a total waste. They could sell them with the rest of the stock. What she had to tell him burdened Agnes greatly.

'Is there 'ote wrong, Miss Clatteridge?' he asked her in concern. 'Only yer look . . . well . . . troubled, if yer don't mind me saying?'

'Do I! Oh.' She really ought not to delay. This man had been loyal to her father for many many years, though she would never understand why in God's name he had stuck it, having herself witnessed more times than she cared to remember how callously her father had treated him. So why had he stayed when other firms would gladly have taken him on? At least, she thought, one Clatteridge will treat him fairly. She took a deep breath. 'Mr Simpson, I would like to talk to you. If it's convenient, of course?'

A look of astonishment appeared momentarily on his face. Her father would never have addressed him so civilly, but then Miss Agnes was nothing like him in manner so he should not be so surprised. Whenever their paths had crossed she had always been politeness itself. That was one of the many things he had always liked about her. It was heartening to find she was not going to change now her father was gone and she was in charge. ''Course, Miss Clatteridge. About a funeral, is it?' he asked eagerly. 'Instructions like?'

She froze. 'No, it isn't.' She gazed around her uncomfortably. The yard was not the place to tell Mr Simpson he was about to lose his job and home. She felt he deserved better than this. But where? It wouldn't be deemed right to take him in to the house, she and Alice being two unchaperoned females, but there was nowhere else fitting.

Despite wondering what she could be wanting him for if

it wasn't about a job, he sensed her dilemma and, hoping she wouldn't think he was forgetting his place, spoke up. 'It's warm in the workshed, Miss Clatteridge, the furnace is still lit and I've the kettle on if you'd fancy a mash? We can talk there quite comfortably. And . . . er . . .' he added, choosing his words carefully '. . . we'll leave the door wide just in case yer sister should wonder where yer are. You'll hear her calling then.'

Warmth filled her. He had realised her problem and solved it very thoughtfully. It didn't make Agnes's task any easier.

'A cup of tea would be very welcome.'

He guided her through to the back of the shed by the cluttered workbench where two rickety stools stood. Grabbing up the cleanest rag he could find, he gave one a quick wipe before inviting her to sit down. The pitch black battered kettle was already singing on a little oil stove on the floor and deftly he set about mashing a pot of tea in a chipped brown teapot.

As he was busying himself, Agnes glanced around her. The workshed was very cramped. A small brick furnace was set at an angle against the far wall, its chimney disappearing through the roof. At the moment its iron door was ajar to let out some heat. In the middle of the stone floor stood a long sturdy wooden trestle where the coffins were made. At the moment it was empty except for a metal jig. Stacked down one wall were assorted planks of wood, from pine to mahogany, and down the other, three long lengths of higgledy-piggledy shelves housed containers of nails and screws and all manner of other things needed to complete their work.

For fifty years Clatteridges and their employees had worked inside these walls. She wondered whose turn it would be next.

'Seen some sights has this shed, Miss Clatteridge.'

'Pardon? Oh, yes, I expect it has.'

Ivan grinned. 'Could tell many a tale, I bet, if it could

talk.' He laughed. 'I could tell you a few meself but I expect now ain't the time.' He handed her an enamel mug. 'Excuse the crockery. I've given you the best one. I've more milk and sugar should you need it.'

Agnes accepted graciously and took a sip. 'Thank you, this is very good. You make a fine cup of tea, Mr Simpson.'

A warm glow settled in the pit of his stomach as he sat down facing her. She didn't need to say that. It wasn't good tea and he knew it. It had been made from the cheapest leaves, although he had been more liberal with the quantity in honour of her visit. But wasn't that just like Miss Clatteridge? Normally he would have felt uncomfortable to be facing a superior but he never felt that way with her. It was a pity her father hadn't been more like her, life would have been more tolerable if he had.

'You wanted ter speak to me?' he prompted.

'Oh, yes, I did.' Agnes nervously cradled her mug, studying the leaves floating on top before she took a deep breath and raised her eyes to his. 'Mr Simpson, I want to give you fair warning that my sister and I have decided we're going to sell the business. Once everything is settled up we're going to live with our aunt in Scarborough. I felt it only right you should know as soon as possible.' She took a hurried breath then added, 'I hope this hasn't come as too much of a shock?'

It had. It was devastating news. And not just because he would be losing his job and living accommodation. 'It's . . . er . . . appreciated, your tellin' me, Miss Clatteridge,' he mumbled.

His state of mind was not lost on her. 'I'm so sorry, Mr Simpson. If I thought I could possibly make a success of carrying everything on, believe me I would. But I'm not equipped to step into my father's shoes, I only wish I was. I know you're quite capable of finding yourself another place but should you need any help you have only to ask and I'll do everything I can to assist you.'

'That's very good of you, Miss Clatteridge,' he said gratefully.

'It's the least I can do after your service to Father. I maybe should not say this, but he wasn't the easiest of men to get along with and your loyalty was commendable. It will not be forgotten.' A thought suddenly struck her and she felt that in the circumstances it was the very least she could do. 'I'd like to be able to recompense you, to help with your future. I can't tell you by how much as yet until I have some idea of what we can expect to make from a sale, but I hope that whatever it is will be acceptable to you.'

Her thoughtfulness touched him deeply. She must know his wage had not left much to put by in savings. What bit he did have wouldn't go far now he had to find somewhere to live. His thoughts lingered on the woman seated before him. Plain, thin and tall, there was no other way to describe Miss Agnes Clatteridge, and he knew that was how others saw her. But not him. He saw beneath that plainness. Through the dark drab clothing. Past the thin, shapeless frame underneath. Agnes Clatteridge, to him, was the warmest, kindest woman he had ever had the privilege to meet. And he loved her. Had done since he had been twelve years old and frozen with cold, waiting nervously in the yard to begin his first day at work.

She had found him there as she had come out to pump water, and taken him into the austere kitchen to give him a cup of tea. Her father had descended then, dressed in his long black cloak and seeming like a demon from hell. When he'd spotted Ivan his long thin face had filled with rage and he had thrown him outside then slapped Agnes hard for being familiar with an employee. She had been barely five years old. Ivan had never forgotten that first show of kindness. Neither would he forget the numerous occasions since, when leftovers or anything she felt he could use had been thrust silently at him when no one else was around, without her seeming to care about the inevitable backlash should her actions be found out. There had been no need for words between them. She knew that what she gave him was desperately needed. He knew she did it for no other reason than natural generosity.

His deep love for her was his secret, she had no idea whatsoever and never would. He, a lowly carpenter cum jack-of-all-trades, could never expect the daughter of a businessman, especially Cuthbert Clatteridge, to be honoured by, accept or return his feelings. Even to give her an inkling would, he felt, be to offend her deeply. He would never risk that. He respected her far too much. His feelings for her would go with him to his grave.

Loyalty to Cuthbert Clatteridge? That was a joke. Ivan Simpson detested the very essence of the man. The only reason he had stayed for so many years, suffering his employer's harsh ways and downright rude manner, was Agnes. Leaving would have meant not seeing her again and he couldn't have borne that. But now he would have to as she was selling up and leaving for another town many miles away. The thought crucified him. The remaining years seemed suddenly to stretch ahead down a deep dark void. Without this lovely woman around to brighten his day, life for him would not hold a meaning.

Agnes herself was feeling terrible. She had tried to be businesslike in her approach, as she thought would be expected of an employer, but her outward poise had not in the least mirrored her inner turmoil. What she had just done was the worst thing she had ever had to attempt or would again. For Agnes loved Ivan Simpson; she had done since she was five years old and had first taken pity on him, a shabby, undersized twelve year old, clutching a battered blue billycan to hold his tea, frozen to the marrow in the yard on his first day of work.

Over the years her childish feelings for him had deepened to unrequited love. There was something about Ivan that drew feelings from her that would not die.

He was such a nice man, tender and kind, and so well-mannered considering his poor background. He had never been anything other than courteous to her. He wasn't tall, fat or thin, unduly handsome . . . just ordinary, in fact. But it was still surprising to Agnes that he had never taken a wife, or so far as she was aware courted at all. There must be many women around who would grab at the chance to become his wife. She had often worried about that happening, selfish though she knew it was of her, and been glad that nothing had ever transpired, knowing she would not have coped very well with the knowledge of Ivan's sharing his life with another.

Agnes raised her head to look at him and completely misconstrued his devastated expression. 'I do apologise if I've offended you,' she said hurriedly.

Ivan eyed her blankly. 'Offended me?'

'By my offer of recompense. I would prefer you to look upon it as a thank you.'

'I'm not offended, miss, not at all,' he insisted. No matter what she did, she could never offend him. 'I was just thinking what a kind gesture it was, that was all. And, to be honest, your selling up has come as a shock. I have ter say, it was the last thing I was expecting to hear.'

Face grave, she nodded her understanding. 'I've really no choice, Mr Simpson.' Sighing heavily, she placed the empty enamel mug on the workbench then clasped her hands tightly. 'My father didn't exactly equip my sister and me to carry on in the event of his death. If we don't sell now, we might not have anything left to sell soon. I suppose in the circumstances, your having worked for us for so long, I can tell you that he didn't leave us very well provided for so the business couldn't have been doing as well as I thought. Being inexperienced on the financial side, well, I can't risk devaluing it any further. If I had just myself to consider I would not hesitate to take the risk, but I have my sister to think of.'

'The business was doing well enough, Miss Clatteridge,' Ivan said. And added before he could stop himself, 'I expect yer'd 'ave bin plenty well off if yer father hadn't have bin . . .' He stopped abruptly, realising he was about to speak out of turn. The way his employer had carried on was really none of his business and as such he had no right to speak of it. 'Well, yer know,' he said uncomfortably.

Agnes frowned, confused. 'Know? Know what?'

He gulped, staring at her, a red tide of embarrassment creeping up his neck. He ran a hand through his thatch of iron grey hair, exhaling sharply.

'Mr Simpson?' she urged.

He eyed her, confused. 'Don't yer know, miss?'

'No, I don't, Mr Simpson, and I'd be obliged if you would tell me what my father was doing?' she said sharply.

He suddenly realised that she wouldn't know what her father's pastime had been. How could she? He groaned inwardly. Considering how he felt about her, why did it have to be him who told her? He took a deep breath, fixing his eyes on hers. 'Yer father was a gambler, Miss Clatteridge.'

Her mouth fell open. 'What! No. Never.' She shook her head vehemently. 'My father consigned everyone to hell who did anything of the sort. Gambling? No, I can't believe that.'

'He could damn as much as he liked, miss, but yer father must 'ave gone through a small fortune over the years. And it grieved me, so it did, to see the way he carried on but it wasn't my place to say anything about it. According to Seth Harrop, the chippy I took over from, it started after yer mother passed on. He reckoned it was yer father's way of coping with his grief. I could never understand it meself, but then folks do strange things at times like that. It was like a fever inside Mr Clatteridge. Woe betide anythin' should 'appen and his bets not placed. My God, we'd all suffer then. One of my daily jobs when I was the lad was to go between him and the bookie's runner. Bet on anything that moved he did. Only he wasn't often lucky. Oswald placed a bet for him the very day he died.'

Agnes was staring at him, astounded. 'Oswald Peabody, placing bets for my father? And you before him!'

'And those in between.'

'All of them?' she gasped, mortified. 'Every one of the young lads who have worked for us over the years?'

Ivan nodded, face filling with remorse. 'I thought you must at least have had an idea, Miss Clatteridge. Really I did. I feel so bad, being the one to tell yer.'

She stared at him, horrified. 'I had no idea. Neither has my sister.' She sat frozen in shock. Dear God, she thought, this revelation was dreadful. Had Ivan Simpson any idea of the hours she and Alice had been forced to read the Bible, learning parables and verses off by heart, and woe betide them should they recite anything wrongly. How could her father have been such a hypocrite? she thought savagely.

A sudden anger filled her like none she'd known before. Her father had ruled over her and Alice rigidly, never allowing them to do anything he deemed unacceptable, which had covered just about everything social. Oh, not quite. He had allowed them to go to church. His rules had even extended to their not mixing with the employees anymore than was necessary. To be caught in idle chatter had been a punishable offence. When all the time . . . She clenched her fists in fury. 'And what else was my father doing that you know of, Mr Simpson?' A thought suddenly struck her. 'Women! Are you going to tell me he visited women of ill repute too?'

'Oh, no, Miss Clatteridge.' Ivan vigorously shook his head. 'Not to my knowledge. It was just the gamblin'.'

'Considering the state of our finances, I'm glad to hear it,' she exclaimed. Then her face filled with shame. 'I'm so sorry, I'm not angry with you.' She felt a rush of tears prick her eyes and abruptly rose. She must not break down in front of Mr Simpson. She felt stupid enough for being oblivious to all that had been going on under her nose. 'Please excuse me, I have things to do. Thank you for the tea,' she said, rushing out.

Ivan stared after her. For years he had stood by helplessly, watching in suffering silence Cuthbert Clatteridge's mistreatment of his daughters, especially of his beloved Agnes. And there was nothing he could do about it. To say one word to his employer would have resulted in his own dismissal, without references. The man himself, thought Ivan, had much to answer for. To Ivan's way of thinking, to rot in hell was no more than Clatteridge deserved. Ivan hoped he was, for all the pain he had caused and was still causing now.

Alice found her sister huddled in a chair by the fire, head buried in the crook of her arm, gently sobbing. She was so wrapped up in her own private thoughts that Agnes's misery did not register at first.

'Don't bother about the trunk,' she blurted out as she bounded through the door. 'I've got everything in those two old carpet bags of Father's. Agnes? Oh, Agnes,' she cried, rushing over and kneeling down before her. 'You're crying. Whatever's the matter? Look, I won't go,' she said, placing one hand tenderly on her sister's arm. 'I can call Aunt Celia tomorrow. She'll understand when I explain. We'll both go together when everything's been sorted out. Agnes, please don't cry.'

'I wasn't crying,' she lied, hurriedly wiping away tears with the back of her hand. 'Well, yes, I was but it's just because I'm going to miss you, that's all. I'm being silly. Please allow me to be silly, Alice. You're my sister and I love you.' She couldn't tell her the real reason for her tears. Alice was bitter enough against their father and it seemed had every right to be. There was no need to fuel her hatred further. The man was dead. Alice had a future to get on with. Maybe one day Agnes would divulge what she had learned, but not today. With a great effort she forced a smile to her face. 'You're not going to disappoint Aunt Celia and all the cronies she'll have summoned to meet you? I'm sorry it slipped my mind about the trunk, but anyway you don't need one so that's all right. Now give me a hug, then go and make us both a cup of tea. Then, my girl,' she said, wagging a finger, 'it's bed for you. You've a long day tomorrow and so have I, getting started on things here. Go on now,' she ordered. 'I'm desperate for a drink.'

Alice eyed her warily. 'Are you sure, Agnes, about my going? Really?'

'I said so, didn't I? Now, for goodness' sake, go and make that tea.'

A broad smile transformed Alice's plain face. 'I'm so lucky to have you as my sister,' she said earnestly and left Agnes to her own reflections.

# Chapter Twelve

'Thank you, Mr Simpson,' Agnes said as he helped her down from the small cart they called the box, which had been commandeered to transport Alice and her bags to the station.

The pleasure was mine, he wanted to tell her. 'What would yer like me to do now we're back Miss Clatteridge,' he said instead.

Still straightening her attire, she raised her eyes quizzically to his. 'Do?'

'After I've put the cart away and seen to Ned. There's a lot, I expect. Where would yer like me and Oswald to start?'

'Oh, I don't know.' Agnes stood thoughtfully for a moment. 'I really need to see the lawyer and take advice. That's what I ought to do first, I suppose.'

'If yer don't mind my suggesting it, Miss Clatteridge, now that yer sister's gone, don't yer need to get someone in to give you a hand? Of course, it goes without saying I'll do all I can. Oswald and meself can tek care of things out here, but surely you'll need a woman to help in the house?'

Agnes frowned thoughtfully. She supposed she would. She would be stupid to think she could tackle it all by herself. And it wouldn't be right to ask either Mr Simpson or Peabody into the house to help go through all the family's personal things, deciding what to keep and what to do with the stuff they'd have no room for. But she couldn't deal with that now. All her thoughts this morning had been concentrated on seeing Alice safely on her journey. It had been traumatic for Agnes as she had fought to keep her own spiralling emotions in check so as not to spoil Alice's eagerness.

Standing alone on the wind-whipped platform, watching the train heave and choke on its way without bursting into tears, had taken all her restraint. So distressed was Agnes, she had sat in silence all the way back in the cart. Even the fact that the man she adored was sitting by her side had been of no comfort. But now Alice was gone and she had to get on with the sale of the business and all it entailed. Then it would be her turn to abandon her memories of the sorrow and harshness of these surroundings and begin her own new life.

She gazed around the cobbled yard. Apart from the house which fronted on to the main Uppingham Road – a two-storey, four-bedroomed, early Victorian dwelling which could have been made very comfortable had her father allowed – there were several outbuildings of varying sizes, all allotted their individual functions. An inventory would need to be made of their contents, that much she knew, as well as the contents of the house.

She sighed at this daunting prospect, suddenly feeling very tired. She had spent a fraught sleepless night trying to come to terms with her father's dreadful secret, which had left herself and Alice in such a precarious situation. All her bravado seemed to have drained away now and she felt she couldn't face giving orders or setting about making decisions on all that needed to be done. Tomorrow. She'd begin tomorrow. All she wanted to do right now was curl up in an armchair and just sit and think, hopefully find a part of her mind in which to lock it all away.

'Mr Simpson, take the rest of the day off. And Peabody too. And please rest assured, your pay will not be docked.'

It was the last thing Ivan had expected to hear and he stared in astonishment. 'I beg yer pardon, Miss Clatteridge?'

'You heard me, Mr Simpson. Do whatever you want to

do. We'll make a start tomorrow.'

He stood rooted to the spot, watching Agnes intently as she crossed the yard and disappeared inside the house. The rest of the day off? It was unheard of. Her father, he remembered, had expressed severe anger when the old Queen had died and the country had been given a day's mourning. A smile twitched the corners of his mouth. The old devil would be turning in his grave at his daughter's instructions. The thought amused Ivan.

He scratched his head. A day off? What was he going to do with himself? He'd never had a holiday. He was supposed to have half a day a week, but somehow that had never quite materialised. He himself always found something to do around the yard and Mr Clatteridge had never commented on the fact. Well, he wouldn't. Liked his pound of flesh, did that one. Taking the rest of the day off didn't feel right to Ivan, especially not when he knew Miss Clatteridge wasn't thinking straight with all she was contending with. He'd send Peabody home, though, and the lad wouldn't think twice about it. Be off before the words had left his mouth.

He was a wily one was Peabody. Ivan have never taken to him from the day he sauntered into the yard seeking work after hearing the last lad had left. No doubt his widowed mother had pushed him into it. But then, Ivan's opinion had never been sought. Mr Clatteridge hadn't been a man to ask others for advice, especially not a lowly employee.

The object of his thoughts popped his head out of the shed door. 'Thought I 'eard yer come back. Fancy a mash, Mr Simpson?'

'You can help me unharness the cart first. Then yer can make the tea, then you can go 'ome.'

'Eh?'

'You heard, lad. Miss Clatteridge's instructions. You could use the time to help yer mother. I expect there's plenty of jobs that need to be done around your house.' 'Hovel' would be a more apt description of the place where Oswald, his prematurely aged mother and several young brothers and sisters resided, but at least they had a home with a living parent to call their own. Ivan himself had come straight to Clatteridge's from an orphanage. 'Help me get the cart seen too. Then,' he said, suddenly feeling a desire to be rid of Oswald as soon as possible, 'yer can scarper. I'll mash up meself.'

Oswald didn't need another telling. In minutes the cart was housed. 'I'll be off then, Mr Simpson. See yer termorrow.'

Guiding Ned to the stables, he nodded. 'Don't be late,' he called to Oswald as he shot through the archway that led from the yard into the main street. Ivan sighed. He hadn't even had the thoughtfulness to close the large wooden doors after him, despite knowing they needed shutting. The lazy good-for-nothing.

The next afternoon, on her way back from making an appointment with the lawyer for later that week, Agnes walked into the local Post Office and handed over a card. She had given Ivan's advice much thought as she had sat in contemplation all the rest of the day and decided it should be taken. She would need help and hoped that someone suitable would apply. It would go some way towards getting her used to meeting and conversing with new people. She only hoped she had offered a reasonable rate for the job.

'Would you put that in your window, please?' she addressed the Post Mistress.

'That'll be twopence, Miss Clatteridge.'

Agnes handed over two pennies and left.

Tilly Potter studied the card. 'Domestic help required. Twenty-five shillings a week. Apply: Miss Agnes Clatteridge, 97 Uppingham Road'.

Tilly pursed her lips. 'She's offering twenty-five bob a week. That's well above the going rate.'

'Eh?' queried her husband Cedric as he emerged through

the door from the back, carrying several parcels which he stacked under the counter. 'What yer rattling on about, woman?'

'The elder Sister Grim's just been in. Wants me to put this card in the window. She needs help and she's offering twenty-five bob a week. Might suit our Violet's Flossie. She's desperate for work.'

He glanced over her shoulder at the card. 'She ain't that desperate, surely? Mind you, that's good money.'

'That's because Miss Clatteridge knows she's gonna have trouble getting someone. No, I won't bother mentioning it to Violet. I know she wouldn't set foot in the place with all them dead bodies. I'd take bets no one else around here will either. Miss Clatteridge has just wasted her twopence, if yer ask me.'

'Well, she didn't ask you, Tilly Potter. Now put the card in the window and have done with it. If folks want to pay for the service then it's not for us to question it.'

His wife sniffed. 'But I'm particular about my cards. And Mrs Connor might not take kindly to me putting it next to hers for dressmaking. All these twopences add up, you know. Make a nice little nest egg they do over a year. I can't risk our customers taking offence and going elsewhere, now can I?'

'I suppose not. Well, stick it right at the bottom in the corner, away from all the others,' he suggested.

'That's a good thought, Cedric. That way I'll cause no ill feeling, will I?'

She took several minutes to place the card strategically, not taking the trouble she usually did to check it could be viewed adequately from outside, and went back behind the counter.

'I've never seen her smile. Not once I haven't,' she mused as she gave the counter a wipe.

'Your letter should arrive the day after tomorrow, Mrs Rooney. Well give or take,' Cedric added. He gave his customer her change then turned his full attention to his wife. 'Who haven't yer seen smile?'

''Er. The elder Miss Grim. And those clothes she dresses in! They wouldn't look out of place on my old mother, should she still be alive, God rest her.'

'Well, I don't expect she's ever had much to smile about. Would you have, living her life?' He ignored his wife's comment about Miss Clatteridge's clothes. Women to his mind spent far too much time and effort worrying about what they wore. Tilly was always moaning about her wardrobe, yet she always looked all right to him.

'I 'spose not,' she answered, breathing hard on the counter then giving a stubborn spot a vigorous rub. 'Yes, I suppose if anything I feel sorry for her. I expect it's a huge burden lifted now he's gone. Wouldn't have wished him on anyone as a father. He used to scare the kids something rotten when he launched himself off down the street, that black cloak thing he always wore making him look like the devil himself. There's one thing for sure, I doubt many'll miss him.' She gave a dry laugh. 'His business certainly suited him, didn't it?'

Her husband laughed along with her. 'Most definitely. I wonder who'll take it on?'

'Take what on?' she mused.

'The business.'

'According to gossip they're selling up. And I'll tell yer another thing. The younger Sister Grim has gone. Molly Micklewaite saw 'em this morning in the cart. She had bags with 'er.'

'Can't say as I blame 'er. Who in their right mind 'ud want ter stay in that mausoleum of a place? Oh,' he mused. 'Well, if they're selling, why d'yer reckon Miss Clatteridge needs 'elp?'

'Well, I know I would,' said his wife grimacing. 'I wouldn't fancy having to clear that place out by meself. Anyway,' she said tartly, 'how would I know why she's decided she wants

172

help? We ain't exactly bosom pals, now are we?'

'I thought you'd have known – yer seem to know everything else around 'ere, Tilly Potter. Anyway, selling up meks sense. Can't keep it going, can they, them being women?'

'And what difference does that mek?' Tilly demanded. She folded her arms under her ample bosom. 'Let me tell you, Cedric Potter, women are just as capable as men. I managed fine wi'out you when you were away at war. I ran the Post Office just as good as you, and I raised three children at the same time. Let me see *you* doing that.'

'You've changed your tune just a bit. A minute ago you were saying no one would work for her.'

'And I doubt anyone will, considering. But that don't mean to say she ain't got the brains to handle it all.' Tilly snorted. 'You men think we women 'ud fall to pieces without yer, don't you?'

He shook his head. He was on the losing side of this battle and he knew it. 'I was just trying to make the point that there's some things men do best, that's all, and their kind of business is best done by a man in my opinion.'

'Mmmm,' she mused. 'I expect yer right. And lifting parcels is what you're best at. You forgot to deliver that one this morning.' She pointed to a large brown paper-covered box on the floor behind the door. 'You'll have to take it around for Mr Samuels. It's the parts he ordered for his grinding machine. Needs them urgent. Got a man standing idle waiting for it to arrive.'

Good-naturedly, she leaned over and pecked her husband on his cheek. 'Yer right, Cedric. I couldn't manage without yer. I wouldn't want to. I'll have yer tea ready by the time you get back.' She flashed a glance towards the door as it opened and a customer walked through. 'Get a move on, Cedric, looks ter me like there's a fog coming down. Brrr!' she shivered. 'Winter's coming. Yes, Mrs Stanton. Usual? Paper, envelopes and ink. No ink, just paper and envelopes?

Right you are. What a lot of letters you write! How's that sister of yours in Chapel St Leonards? I noticed you had a postcard from her this morning. Got a cold, hasn't she? Well, I hope she recovers soon.'

Cedric shook his head as he bent to lift the parcel. His wife had no discretion. All the locals knew Tilly knew their business before they did. She read their cards; poked and prodded parcels to work out what was in them; knew who had sent the letters they received. On one occasion Cedric had actually caught her steaming open a letter from Mrs Coggin's wayward daughter, Tilly being desperate to find out what she was up to.

What Tilly herself had got up to while he was away fighting in France didn't bear thinking about.

# Chapter Thirteen

Maddie bent lower, squinting hard to read the words on the card. She'd nearly missed it as she had scanned the others, stuck right down in one corner, part of it obscured by an official notice of postal delivery times. This one must have slipped down, she thought. None of the other cards had offered work, just services, and as such this was the only one of interest to her. She didn't mind taking on a domestic situation and the pay offered was very good. Better than anything else she had been offered today.

It was two weeks since she had fled from her mother. That night seemed a lifetime ago now. So welcome had her father and his family – her family – made her that even after so short a time she felt a part of their life, as if she had always belonged here.

Sarah had been kindness itself, in fact in every way been just the kind of mother Maddie had always longed for. It was such a pity, she had thought, that Harriet did not possess just one or two of Sarah's many good qualities. Had she done life would have been so different for everyone.

Sarah had been as good as her word. Despite Maddie's insisting she should find herself a room, not wanting to put them out, Sarah had won her over. The old horsehair sofa was proving very comfortable and would more than suffice until money could he found to buy her a bed. Her father had bought Maddie a secondhand tallboy from the local pawnshop, as well as a wash stand with one leg loose which Roy had fixed. Ruth had come home with a pretty bowl and jug for her. The three women had sat over five evenings and pegged together a large round clippy rug, using odds and ends of material from Sarah's bit box. It was certainly colourful and brightened the room.

As the three of them worked away on the rug, they had chatted and gradually Maddie learned more about their lives.

Financially the struggle had been hard, at times they had been almost poverty-stricken. Harriet still demanded a rightful spouse's share of her husband's wage. So long as he stuck by their agreement, his own financial situation was nothing to do with her. Consequently Sarah had always had to work, doing anything that would fit around her family – taking in washing, sewing, minding children, even trudging several miles daily to the countryside to pick seasonal fruit – whatever bit of money she earned helping to ease the burden for her beloved George.

Now thankfully the children were earning – Ruth as stockroom clerk for a small leather company specialising in importing handbags and shoes for the wealthy which they delivered mainly to outlets in London, and Roy as an apprentice grinder for a local tool-making factory – Sarah was back full-time behind the counter of the Uppingham Road Co-op, her shop assistant's wage still not much but better than before and regular at least. And she did enjoy her job. Their finances had improved but the pennies still had to be watched.

'When Ruth came along,' Sarah had told Maddie, 'your father approached Harriet and asked her again if she would consider releasing him. She just laughed, told him to go to hell, reminded him of their agreement and of what she would do should he not stick by it. When Roy was born he asked her if she would take less of his money, considering she had an income of her own. She said if George expected her to relinquish any of her rights in order for him to raise his . . . children, then he was a fool. Their agreement was that until you, my dear, left home, nothing would change. And nothing has.' She had stopped her work then and looked at Maddie, smiling kindly. 'But things are different now, aren't they?'

She had merely nodded, still far too shocked by her mother's actions to comment.

Maddie had told them she did not intend going back to Market Harborough. Leicester was her home now, her life was here. She kept to herself that too much had transpired between Harriet and her for her ever to return. Too much trust had been lost, too much pain had been caused. Although not voicing their suspicions, George and Sarah knew she was holding something back but decided it was best to leave Maddie to tell her story when she was ready. They didn't want to push her. It was obvious to both of them that whatever had happened between her mother and herself, it was something momentous.

Satisfied his daughter knew her own mind, George was not going to put the deed off any longer. So far as he was concerned he had honoured his commitment for far longer than he had ever envisaged. Now he wanted a divorce, to be free finally to marry the woman he adored. He planned to confront Harriet this coming weekend. All of them knew he was not looking forward to the ordeal but awaited the outcome eagerly.

Sarah had managed to persuade Maddie to give herself time to settle in, get used to her new family and surroundings before she started looking for a job. The girl had insisted on paying her keep, regardless of the fact Sarah and George said they'd wait until she was earning. But Ruth and Roy contributed, and it was only right she should. She had pressed a pound upon Sarah, hoping it was enough.

Her initial savings of nearly five pounds were now down to one pound, six shillings, a portion of what she had spent going on toiletries and stockings but the larger amount on new clothes. Not brand new, but new to Maddie.

What fun she had had the Saturday afternoon she had bought them. Sarah and Ruth had insisted they come along to help her decide what suited her best. And what good advice they had given her. They had taken her to the best secondhand clothes shop in Leicester. Good quality and all from wealthy owners, so the proprietor had informed them. Whether that was entirely true or not was of no consequence; the clothes were far superior in quality and fashion to anything Maddie had ever been allowed by her mother.

She was thrilled with the results, her transformation startling. Pretentious though she thought it of herself, she couldn't stop trying the new clothes on and parading before the mirror, checking over and over that it was really her reflected back.

One dress was of crêpe-de-chine, pale blue, drop-waisted, sleeveless with a v-neckline and contrasting bow trim. Maddie had felt it was far too extravagant for her but Sarah and Ruth had insisted she should take it. The dress was perfect for an evening out. The other was a pretty leaf green belted day dress which perfectly fitted her slim, shapely curves, previously disguised under her dowdy clothes. Three good wool skirts, three fashionable blouses, a warm cardigan and several pieces of underwear completed Maddie's wardrobe. Her long hair was next. They told her a chin-length bob would suit her. She thought so too and couldn't wait to get it done.

For the first time she could ever remember, Maddie actually looked forward to rising in the morning and not just because she had such nice clothes to wear. She was wanted here, felt at ease, was experiencing family love and unity.

But forgetting all the bad things that had happened was proving a great struggle. The days were filled with so much going on around her she had no time to dwell on the past, but nights were another matter. Lying on the sofa, the night sounds filtering in hazily, her thoughts would wander and excruciating memories return. She knew that forgetting her past was too much to expect. Far too much had happened for her ever to hope for that. What she did hope for was for her pain to ease; that she should be allowed to live the rest of her life in peace. If she was ever to do that she knew she could not have come to a better place. Fate had been kind to her the night she had arrived, a devastated dejected woman with her life in ruins, at her father's door.

Two weeks after her arrival, Maddie felt she should start looking for work. Armed with a list of places to try that Sarah had written out for her, Maddie set off. It was a miserable early-October morning, damp and misty. She had never been job hunting before, wasn't quite sure what to do or say, but dressed in her new clothes was feeling confident and her hopes were high.

She got lost several times, only finding two of the five factories she had set out in search of, and she had had to wait to be seen for an age at both. At each factory interviews had been hurried, taking place in a dim corridor where she had been glanced up and down, and asked what sewing experience she had. The owner of the second factory she had visited had made her feel she should be honoured he was offering her a job sewing garments. The sewing room she would be working in was dark and dingy, the air thick with dust. The hundred or so other workers sat in long cramped rows, heads bent over their machines, the high-pitched drone of which she could still hear ringing in her ears. The pay wasn't bad if you worked hard. Sewing for a living, though, was a reminder of her previous life and for the time being Maddie felt she would prefer to do something different if that were possible. Regardless, it was a job she did not intend to refuse if nothing else came along by her proposed start day the following Monday morning, at six-thirty sharp.

The afternoon was closing in when she decided to start on the trek home. Tomorrow, she decided, she would arm herself with precise directions before setting off. As she walked briskly down the length of the Uppingham Road she realised that a fog was beginning to fall, rapidly thickening. Maddie shuddered and forced her pace. She had trouble enough with her bearings, without being hampered by fog. The thought of getting lost and wandering aimlessly did not appeal. Maddie looked forward to arriving home for the evening meal, listening to events in her new family's daily life and knowing they were eager to hear hers. If she hurried she could give Sarah a hand with the preparations.

Intent on going home, the cards in the Post Office window only caught her eye by chance. Automatically she stopped for a moment to view them. The one right down in the corner . . . Maddie bent closer to read it.

Swirling fog hit Cedric Potter full force as he emerged from the Post Office and he shuddered as the damp air closed in on him. Vision blocked by the bulky parcel he was carrying as well as the fog, he just managed to avoid colliding with the figure bent double to peer through his shop window.

'I'm sorry, me duck,' he apologised profusely. 'Didn't see you there.'

Maddie shot upright and moved aside to let him pass her on the narrow cobbled path. 'Oh, excuse me,' she said. 'Could you tell me in which direction number ninety-seven Uppingham Road is, please?'

He stopped and looked at her keenly. 'The card, is it?'

'I beg your pardon?'

'The job on the card. You interested, are yer?'

'Well, yes, I could be.'

'Mmmm,' he said thoughtfully. She won't take it, he thought, but won't Tilly be interested to know that someone's made enquiries. He wouldn't divulge that he had thought the woman rather pretty. 'It's that way,' he indicated with a nod of his head. 'Not far. Can't miss it even in this fog.'

Maddie expressed her thanks and proceeded on her way.

The fog was swirling more thickly. In places it was only possible to see a few feet ahead. Maddie kept close to the walls, counting off the number on the doors as she passed. She had to cross over several streets, hoping no traffic appeared suddenly out of nowhere. It did cross her mind that maybe she should leave it until tomorrow, it being rather late in the afternoon to be applying for work, but then she thought someone could beat her to it and the job would be gone.

Finally she arrived. From what she could see the house was reasonably large and there were clean nets at the downstairs windows. She glanced to her left and as she did so the fog momentarily lifted and she was afforded a view of the next-door building. It was obviously business premises. A window appeared to show a display. Further over an archway had doors painted with lettering she presumed gave the company's name. The fog closed in before she could view either. What the premises next door were used for was no concern of hers. What lay behind this door was. Without further ado Maddie reached for the knocker.

# Chapter Fourteen

Agnes rubbed her eyes which hurt from straining to decipher her father's scrawl and method of bookkeeping in the large black ledger. She wasn't about to give up, though.

The night was unusually dark due to the fog and she had had to light an oil lamp. As it was old, the light it gave off was not very good. Another legacy of her father's penny-pinching ways. She decided to buy herself a new one. She was tired, having spent another sleepless night and rising early to journey into town to make an appointment with the lawyer, then a visit to the shops to buy provisions she had needed, finally alighting from the tram well before her normal stop to place her card in the Post Office window. She had trudged the rest of the way home on foot laden down with bags. On arriving home she had wanted to do nothing more than curl up in the armchair by a blazing fire, enjoying the feeling of decadently wasting time and money which would set her father spinning in his grave. But she couldn't quite bring herself to do that after a lifetime of being careful. She had stacked the fire higher than normal, though, and the heat it was giving off was very comforting, the dancing flames helping to alleviate the austerity of the room.

When she first opened the ledger an hour or so ago, the columns of figures jumped haphazardly out at her, making no sense. Now, though, she felt a certain amount of satisfaction. The figures were beginning to seem less daunting and their meaning was becoming clear. One of

183

the columns obviously showed the cost of raw materials they had purchased. Another the purchase tax they had to pay the government – only by her calculation that did not appear to be as much as it should be, the figures were inconsistent. Despite her pride at beginning to make some sort of sense of it all, it was still very confusing. The thing she was totally sure of was that the columns were totalled up on a weekly basis. She had only ten more to work through until it all came together. Though she wondered if the effort was worth it since the business was going to be sold, but decided if she and Alice did open a shop or something else, they would need to keep books so her time would not be entirely wasted.

She heard the knocker, the sound seeming to echo down the passage. Closing the ledger, Agnes rose to answer the door, wondering who could be calling.

As she opened it a pretty young woman stared back at her. She seemed a mite nervous.

'Can I help you?' Agnes asked, thinking she had probably knocked on the wrong door.

Momentarily Maddie stared in amazement at the tall, thin, extremely plain woman standing before her. Entirely dressed in unfashionable black and peering at her through the dense fog, she appeared formidable, frightening even. Maddie gulped, her instincts screaming at her to run. But it wouldn't be right to do that. She cleared her throat. 'I've come to make enquiries about the job.'

'The job?' Agnes frowned. 'Oh, the job. I hadn't expected anyone to apply so soon. Please, do come in,' she invited, stepping aside.

An extremely apprehensive Maddie followed her down a long dark passage towards a room near the back. As they entered, she glanced around hurriedly. Despite the fire burning in the grate, the drab, dismal surroundings hit her full force, the forbidding atmosphere cloaking her like thick spider's webs. She shuddered, for an instant transported back to her home in Market Harborough, only this room was worse if that were possible. One thing registered: they were obviously God-fearing people judging by the huge Bible open on a lectern by the far wall.

'Please sit down.' Agnes indicated a fireside chair.

Maddie perched tentatively on the edge.

'Would you like some tea?'

She shook her head.

Agnes sat down opposite and looked at her prospective employee. She was well presented, had an intelligent forehead and direct gaze, her severe hairstyle not disguising a very pretty face. For a moment she was reminded of what God had failed to give her but pushed these thoughts aside. She could not hold against the woman the fact that she had been blessed with pleasing features. Whether she could do the job, whether she indeed wanted it, was the most important thing. It suddenly occurred to Agnes that she hadn't the first notion how to conduct an interview.

There was nothing for it, she felt, but to be honest. She looked at Maddie helplessly, shrugging her shoulders. 'To be honest, I don't know where to begin. I haven't done this before. You don't happen to know, do you?'

Her tone of voice was warm, her helplessness genuine, and Maddie suddenly felt this woman was not frightening at all. The apprehension she was feeling vanished. She liked this woman, there was something vulnerable about her. She didn't know why but Maddie felt an affinity to her somehow, knew instinctively that she was kind. Maddie relaxed back in her chair. 'Actually, if you want the truth, I have no idea. I've never attended a proper interview before.'

Agnes stared at her in surprise then burst out laughing, a high merry chortle. 'What a pair we make, don't we? Are you sure you wouldn't like a cup of tea? I know I would and I'd like you to join me.'

Maddie smiled. 'Then I will, thank you.'

Ten minutes or so later Agnes passed Maddie a china

cup filled with strong sweet tea, just the way she preferred it. 'Now, where will I start?'

Maddie thought for a moment. 'You could ask me my name.'

'Why, how silly of me, of course.' Agnes put down her cup and saucer and held out her hand. 'Agnes Clatteridge. I'm very pleased to meet you. Very pleased indeed. And you are?'

Maddie leaned forward to accept her hand and shook it firmly. 'Maude Ashman. But I prefer to be called Maddie. I'm pleased to meet you too.'

They settled back in their respective chairs.

'Maddie. What a pretty name,' mused Agnes. 'Well, Miss Ashman, I'd better explain the job I had in mind, which to be honest will be difficult. I don't exactly want . . .' She paused. 'Well, I suppose I do.' She sighed in exasperation, annoyed with herself. 'Let me start again. I should explain that my father died recently, last week in fact, and we, that's myself and my sister who's not here by the way – she's gone ahead to an aunt of ours in Scarborough. I'm on my own and I have to go about selling the family business and seeing to this house and, oh, there's all sorts of things that have to be done and seen to and I don't know where to start. I . . .' She stopped abruptly, knowing she was babbling, not at all the conduct of an employer. What must Miss Ashman think of her? 'I'm not making sense, am I?' she said apologetically.

'Not exactly, but I gather you're looking for someone to help you sort everything out?'

Agnes eyed her, impressed. 'Yes, that's exactly what I want. I just want someone I can rely on to work alongside me. And it would be nice if we got on well too.' She clasped her hands and frowned. 'There is one problem, though. I can't say for how long the job will last. It all depends how long it takes me to find a buyer. I suppose I should have put that on the card. How remiss of me.'

'So the job's just temporary?'

Agnes eyes Maddie tentatively. 'Yes, it is.' She leaned forward. 'You seem just the kind of person I'm looking for. Would you . . . is there any chance you might consider taking it?' Agnes knew she wouldn't, of course, she was hoping for too much. Maude Ashman was far too pretty, too intelligent, to want to accept a lowly position like this, even temporarily. She prepared herself for rejection.

Maddie, though, had no hesitation. It was just what she was looking for. It would be the breathing space she needed, and paid too, while she decided the direction in which she wanted to go. 'Yes, I'll take it.'

Agnes tried not to appear too disappointed. 'I understand, my dear.' Then Maddie's response registered. Her eyes widened, her mouth dropped open, her delight readily apparent. 'Oh! You will? Why, that's splendid. Oh, please have some more tea,' she urged her new employee. 'The wage I'm offering – is it enough?' she asked, replenishing Maddie's cup and passing it back.

'It's very generous, I'd say.'

'Is it? Oh, good. So when can you start?'

'When would you like me to?'

'Tomorrow?'

'Six-thirty?'

Agnes's face fell in dismay. 'That early? Do we have to?' Maddie's mouth dropped open. 'I'm sorry?'

Agnes laughed at the look on her face. 'I've had a lifetime of rising at five-thirty. Such an ungodly hour. Especially in the winter. So shall we say eight? And we'll finish . . .' She shrugged her shoulders. 'Whenever. But never after six-thirty. Will that suit you? Those are my only rules.'

Would that suit her? Maddie had been made to rise early too as per her mother's orders, never allowed the luxury of a lie in. To begin her working day at that time suited her very well indeed. And finishing before six-thirty was perfect timing for her to get home in time to help with preparations for the evening meal. A warm glow filled her. Fate had played its part by bringing her here. She could so easily have missed that card. She was going to enjoy working here. It was a pity it was only for a short space of time.

'Eight it is,' she happily replied.

'Now,' said Agnes, 'is there anything else you need to know?'

'I don't think so.'

'Well, if you think of anything, just ask. It's terribly foggy but I'll show you out the back way so you can get a feel for the place, and I'll introduce you to Mr Simpson. He's our carpenter. I'm sure you'll like him. And there's Oswald Peabody. He's our lad.' She failed to comment further on Peabody. Maddie looked astute enough to make up her own mind about him. Agnes glanced at the clock. It was six-forty-five. 'I expect Peabody's gone home by now. You'll meet him tomorrow.' Time enough, she thought. 'Oh, and, of course, I mustn't forget Ned.'

'And what does he do?'

'Ned is our horse.'

Ah, thought Maddie. A horse usually pulled a cart. The family business must have something to do with deliveries of some sort.

'I'll have to find a new home for him,' Agnes was saying, more to herself than to Maddie. 'That's just one of the things I have to do.' Her face filled with sadness. 'I shall miss him when he goes.' Still, she thought, when decisions were made, there were prices to be paid. 'If you've finished your tea, I'll show you around.'

Agnes rose. Putting down her cup, Maddie did likewise and followed her through the kitchen and out into the cobbled yard.

The fog was still swirling thickly. It was very dark now and visibility was bad. Through the fog a dull light shone from somewhere to the right of them. 'Ah,' said Agnes. 'Mr Simpson is still in the workshed. I might have known. Follow me and be careful – there are things lying around. I wouldn't wish you to harm yourself. Mind that barrel of pitch, it's just by the workshed door. Get some of that on you and you'll never get it off.'

'What's the pitch used for?' Maddie asked curiously. Must be something to do with the upkeep of the delivery wagons, she guessed.

'Oh, we use it to line the coffins.'

Maddie stopped abruptly, frozen rigid. 'Coffins?'

Agnes turned to face her. 'Yes. Apart from the odd occasion when we've been desperate, we make all our own,' she said proudly. The horrified expression on Maddie's face registered then and she frowned. 'You did know this was an undertaker's?'

Maddie gulped. 'No,' she uttered. 'Actually, I didn't.'

# Chapter Fifteen

'The Sisters Grim? Maddie, you're not? You're never going to work for them? You must be mad.'

'Ruth, stop it,' Sarah scolded. 'Maddie's quite capable of deciding where she wants to work.' Privately she shared her daughter's views, though should she have voiced them she wouldn't have spoken quite so bluntly. 'Just eat your dinner up before it gets cold.'

'Your mother's right, Ruth,' George piped up, though he too thought Maddie should reconsider her decision.

Ruth forked a piece of sausage. 'But, Mam, I'm only trying to warn her. I mean, who in their right mind would want to work in a funeral parlour of all places? I wish I had working hours like that, though,' she muttered to herself. 'Fancy not having to start work until eight.' Though even considering the late start, nothing would entice her to work in that place. She put the food in her mouth and, still chewing, said, 'People reckon they're witches. Have you seen the way they dress and how ugly . . .'

'That's enough, Ruth. Stop being so unkind,' her mother retorted. 'You can't blame anyone for what God blessed them with in the looks department. As for witches, they don't exist. And stop speaking with your mouth full, it's rude.'

'I think Miss Clatteridge is rather nice,' said Maddie. 'I must admit, though, when I first saw her she appeared rather frightening. But that was before I talked to her. She's very kind, really. I know I shall enjoy working there. And she's assured me she doesn't expect me to get involved in anything other than helping to sort out the house. I won't have to go anywhere near where they deal with . . . well, you know.'

'If you change your mind, you can always look for something else,' suggested Sarah.

'Did you see any dead bodies?' asked Roy keenly.

Shuddering at the thought, Maddie shook her head. 'No. And I hope I never will while I'm there.' The very thought terrified her. Her first reaction on finding out just exactly what the family concern was shook her witless. A great urge to retract her acceptance of the job and run away had overtaken her. But she couldn't. She had made a commitment. Besides, she couldn't bring herself to upset Miss Clatteridge.

Death, her new employer had reminded her, happened to everyone. It was a part of life that was unavoidable. And someone had to take care of burials. It was just a job, if not one to most people's liking. Some people, due to ignorance, feared the dead. But there was nothing to fear. The dead couldn't hurt anyone. It had always been Miss Clatteridge's fixed opinion that those one should fear were the living. Maddie had found a great deal of sense and comfort in her words and with an effort had forced her fears away. Now she was looking forward to starting this job and wanted nothing to mar that.

Sarah thought it time the subject was changed. 'How was your day, dear?' she asked her husband.

'Oh, fine,' he replied absently.

Normally he had much to say, entertaining his family with incidents that had happened on his travels and tales of his customers' antics, especially those who tried anything to avoid their payments, but Sarah knew that as the time drew nearer he was becoming increasingly concerned about his imminent confrontation with Harriet. Not only was he going to tell her that Maddie was now living with them, which was not going to please her one little bit, but he had the daunting task of demanding a release from their marriage. Harriet had no hold over them now but nevertheless facing her wasn't going to be easy. Sarah wished she could accompany him, be a prop, give him her support, but this was something George had to handle by himself.

She noticed her son's glum expression. 'What's the matter, Roy?' she asked in concern.

'Can I still go to the football on Saturday? Leicester's playing Sheffield. Should be a good match. All me mates are going.'

George's head jerked up. 'Why do you think you can't go, Roy?'

'Well . . . I didn't think it'd be right, me going off enjoying meself when you have ter . . . well, yer know.'

George put down his knife and fork, and glanced at each of his family in turn. 'Now listen to me, all of you. What I have to do is for me alone. I want none of you to change your plans. Is that clear?' They all nodded. 'We've never kept secrets from each other and I'll admit I'm not looking forward to it, but it's got to be faced. Now Maddie is away from Market Harborough and I have no fear of her being caught up in any of this, my mind's at rest. Harriet can no longer hold out. I hope to catch the early train back. Enough time to sort matters out, I think. While I'm gone I expect you all to carry on as you normally do. All right? I'll tell you what's happened when I return and we'll face it together like we always do.' He picked up his plate and smiled at Sarah. 'Any more gravy, love?'

Ruth scraped back her chair. 'It's your turn for the pots tonight, Roy. Maddie, are you coming upstairs with me? I'd like your opinion on what to wear.'

'Another date. Who's it with this time?' asked her mother.

'Desmond. He's calling for me, Mam, so don't worry, you can give him the once over. He works in our despatch. I know you'll like him,' she said, heading for the door. 'I've fancied him for ages. Nearly gave up hoping he'd ask me out. He did this morning. Weren't that brave of him?' she said laughing. 'Come on, Maddie.'

This was the first time Ruth had invited her up to her private sanctuary and Maddie felt honoured.

'What d'yer think then?' asked her half-sister, holding a dress up against herself.

'It's very pretty,' Maddie said admiringly, delighted to have been asked. 'Where's he taking you?'

'To the pictures, I expect.'

Though Maddie had never herself had the pleasure of going to the pictures, had no idea what people wore to such a venue, she felt the dress would not look out of place. 'Then I think that dress is ideal.'

Ruth flung it over the back of a wicker chair and looked at Maddie fondly as she sat on the bed. 'I can't tell you how pleased I am we've finally met. All these years I've wondered what you looked like and what kind of person you were. Now I know.'

'I hope you're not disappointed?'

'What? Not at all. I think you're lovely. I couldn't have wished for a better sister. This is the first time we've really been on our own since you came and I want to tell you that since I knew I had a sister, I've been desperate to see you. Dad's always said we have a look of each other. Do you think we do?'

Maddie looked at her searchingly. Ruth, she thought, was so pretty, while her own mother had instilled in her for so long that she was plain she still had trouble thinking otherwise. 'We have the same colour eyes,' she said. 'And the same nose.'

Ruth scrutinised herself in her hand mirror. 'Yes, we do, don't we? And our chins, I think. I wish I was as pretty as you, though.' She clapped her hands. 'It's great having a sister, isn't it?'

Maddie smiled. 'Yes, it is.' And she sincerely thought so too.

'Having a brother's all right, but it ain't the same. You can't talk about women's things with boys, can you? Or go shopping?'

'No, you can't,' Maddie agreed.

Ruth perched beside her on the edge of the bed. 'Was it a shock?'

'A shock?' she queried.

'Finding out about all this? I mean, you knew nothing, did you? About us.'

Maddie took a deep breath. 'It was, yes. I had trouble taking it all in at first. But now . . .'

'Now?' Ruth asked, tentatively.

'I'm so happy.'

'And I'm glad. We all want you to be.' A frown crossed her pretty face. 'She sounds awful, your mother. Was she? Was it terrible living with her?'

Maddie bowed her head and clasped her hands. 'I knew no different,' she said softly.

'No, I expect you didn't. But you do now, don't you?' Ruth's face filled with concern. 'You won't ever leave us and go back to her will you, Maddie? I couldn't bear that to happen.'

She raised her head. 'No, I won't. I'm here for good.' She smiled. 'Shouldn't you be getting ready?'

Ruth jumped up. 'Yes, I should.'

Maddie watched with interest as Ruth's dress was hurriedly pulled on and she sat before her dressing-table mirror to brush her bobbed light brown hair and apply a trace of makeup. Although Maddie didn't think she needed any at all to enhance her features.

Ruth suddenly swivelled around in her chair and unexpectedly asked, 'Have you ever been in love?'

Maddie froze for a moment before answering, 'Yes, I have.'

'You have? Really? True love, was it?'

She nodded.

'It was? Oh!' Ruth exclaimed in awe. 'Did he love you?'

Maddie's eyes became distant as a great sadness enveloped her. A vision of Josh rose before her. He was smiling at her, arms outstretched invitingly. She forced it away. 'I thought so,' she murmured. 'But it wasn't meant to be.'

Ruth eyed her sadly. 'Oh, I see. But you'll fall in love again, Maddie. You will, you'll see.'

I doubt it, she thought. What she might feel for another man, should she be fortunate enough to meet one, would be deep fondness, but love like she had felt for Josh? Never. It wasn't possible.

She pushed the sadness away and smiled brightly. 'I've too much to be getting on with to be worried about falling in love.'

'But when you do,' Ruth urged, 'you must promise I'll be your bridesmaid?'

'If ever I get married, that goes without saying. Now you should really get a move on,' said Maddie, rising from the bed. 'I must go and see if Sarah needs a hand with anything.'

Ruth jumped up from her chair. 'Just a minute, Maddie.'

She stopped and turned towards Ruth who threw her arms around her and kissed her affectionately on the cheek.

Maddie was taken aback for a moment by such a show of affection, something she was not used to. 'What was that for?' she asked.

'Does there have to be a reason to show someone you love them?'

Maddie shook her head. 'No, there doesn't, does there?' And she kissed her back.

# Chapter Sixteen

'Maude living with you! With your whore and bastards? I won't stand for that! You'll send her back or I'll come and fetch her. You had no right enticing her to go. How did you do it, George? What did you bribe her with?' Harriet's face darkened thunderously.

'I didn't bribe her, Harriet, how could I? Maddie was under the impression I was dead. How could you do that? It's despicable, that's what it is. What happened to all the letters I sent her? And the presents? I expect they went on the back of the fire the same as that doll I bought her.'

'You're right, they did. I had every right to tell her you were dead, and everyone else for that matter, because the moment you walked out on us you were dead to me.'

'If you'd tried to be a wife to me, Harriet, that might never have come about.'

She sneered. 'Well, now Maddie knows your sordid secret! Now she knows what kind of father you are. How do you feel about that, George? Proud, are you?'

'Stop it, Harriet. Maddie came to us voluntarily.' His eyes narrowed questioningly. 'And I'm of the opinion that something happened to bring her to us. What was it, Harriet? What did you do to her to make her do that?'

She stared at him, her immediate worry that Maddie had talked thankfully lifted. If she hadn't said anything by now, chances were she wouldn't. What Maude had discovered would remain a secret. Satisfied of that, she felt better able to respond. 'How dare you question me like that?

I've been a good mother to her.'

'No, you haven't, Harriet. You ruled her life so strictly she hardly dared breathe without your permission. You never showed her any affection.'

'What would you know? You weren't here. You've only got her word, and let me tell you, your daughter is a liar.'

'That's not true. One thing Maddie is not is a liar. But you are, aren't you, Harriet? Anyway, you were glad I left. It's what you really wanted. You didn't want a husband. You just wanted my name and the money I gave you, and I suspect to keep Maddie by your side to look after you in your old age. What did you do with the money I gave you, Harriet? Nothing went Maddie's way, did it? Or on making this place homely. You haven't a clue how to make a home, have you? Or more likely you didn't want to. You like living like this, don't you? No warmth, no comforts. That's the kind of person you are.'

She was staring at him. He had never dared speak to her in such a way before. Suddenly she knew he was no longer afraid of her and that thought was a worrying one.

George exhaled sharply. 'Whether you like it or not, Maddie is with us of her own free will and she's staying.'

'I don't believe that! You had something to do with it. And she's selfish, thoughtless. I had no warning, nothing. You don't know your own daughter, George. She's devious, let me tell you. She's . . .'

'Stop it, Harriet,' he ordered firmly, his tone icy. 'Maddie is nothing of the kind.'

'Huh! You can think what you like but I've raised her for twenty-six years, I know exactly what she's capable of.'

'Oh, and what's that, Harriet?'

She ignored his question. She could tell him about the baby. That would shock him. Oh, wouldn't it just! Show him his daughter in her true light. And of course her deceitful relationship with that low-life from across the canal. But to do so would mean he'd probe and ask questions Harriet wasn't prepared to answer. 'You'll send her back,' she demanded.

'She's old enough to make up her own mind, Harriet. Are you forgetting she's a grown woman? She's made up her mind to live with us and there's nothing you can do about it. You know that.'

Harriet did. She had lost control of her daughter. Her life's plan, the one she had made twenty-seven years ago, lay in ruins and there was nothing she could do about it. Soon people would know what she'd been striving to avoid all these years. That she had made a sham marriage. They would talk and gossip would spread and her life would become hell. The thought of being the butt of everyone's joke, just as she and her mother had been years ago, crucified her.

George's shocking announcement that Maude was living with him had struck her rigid. Until that moment she had been absolutely confident that her daughter was licking her wounds somewhere and would soon return, begging forgiveness, and life would return to normal. But that wasn't about to happen. Harriet's mind whirled frantically. She hadn't schemed and carried out her plans just for her daughter to do as she pleased. Who did she think she was? Where was her loyalty?

'I'll come and fetch her myself.'

'You can try, Harriet. Maddie won't come with you. And don't forget, she won't be facing you on her own. She has all of us behind her.'

'You bastard!' she hissed, and clenched her fists in fury. She knew what was coming next.

And she was right.

George took a deep breath and steeled himself. 'I have honoured our agreement, Harriet, for more years than I thought to, you can't deny that. Now I want a divorce.'

'Well, you can't have one.'

'You can't stop me!'

'Oh, I can. I won't agree.'

'You won't honour our agreement after I've kept my side of it?'

'Did you expect me to? If so you're a fool. I'll still drag you through the court. My story will still hold good. People will think me a martyr for putting up with your deceit all these years. They won't blame me for making out I'm a widow, they'll understand totally by the time I've finished. And understand this, George. It's not just Maude's good name you should be trying to protect but your two bastards' as well, because I'll make sure they get dragged into it, rest assured.'

He stared at her for several long moments, knowing that to challenge her or argue further was a total waste of time and effort. He sighed in resignation. 'Have it your own way, Harriet. But I'll hand over no more money. If you want to challenge that then go ahead, you have my blessing.'

With that he walked out of the house.

She stood rigid for several long moments before her eyes glinted unpleasantly. All was not quite lost. Her 'widowhood' was still intact. And the story she had concocted to cover Maude's absence could be elaborated on to include the fact that she had left home for good. She harboured little feeling for her daughter, in that respect wouldn't miss her. The work she had done could be tackled by someone else should Harriet choose to employ them. And what of George's money? What of it? She smirked wickedly. He had no idea that she had never used what he had given her. Every penny was hidden inside a cash box, along with the unexpected windfall she had received last year. It had built into a nice little nest egg, just as she had intended. But he'd never get his divorce. She'd have to be dead before he was free of her.

Face stony now, she walked through to the kitchen where she set about cooking a solitary piece of offal for her solitary dinner.

\* \* \*

Sarah shot out of her chair and into the passage as soon as she heard the sound of the front door. She threw her arms around George, crushing him against her. 'How did it go?' she asked eagerly.

'She won't divorce me,' he whispered.

Secretly Sarah had been expecting as much. 'Well, we've lived like this for twenty-five years, my dear, we can live through this setback too.'

He pulled away from her and scanned her face. 'Are you sure, Sarah? Really?'

'A piece of paper makes no difference to the way I feel about you, George. I've got everything of you, my darling, but your name. If keeping your name is what keeps her happy, then let her have it, that's what I say.'

'And the children?'

'What do you think.'

He nodded. His children, all three of them, would say the same as Sarah. 'But what about when Ruth or Roy want to wed? It'll have to come out then. The fact that we're not married.'

'If their chosen spouses don't understand then they've made the wrong choice, ain't they?'

He hugged her fiercely. 'Oh, Sarah, I do love you. What a lucky man I am.'

'And I agree,' she said, chuckling.

'There's one good thing come out of my visit.'

'Oh, yes, and what's that?' she asked keenly.

'My money to Harriet stops, so we haven't the burden of that anymore.'

She sighed in relief. 'Then that's more than I bargained for.' She eyed him worriedly. 'About Maddie, George. What was her reaction to that?'

'She . . . let's just say Harriet wasn't pleased. But I think she's accepted Maddie is with us now.'

Sarah knew much more had passed between George and his wife, the poor man had probably been to hell and back, but decided to let it drop. He'd tell her the fine detail when he was good and ready. Right now he needed food and rest surrounded by the love of his family.

'Come on,' she said. 'I've had the kettle boiling ready for you and I've your dinner keeping hot.'

Hands clasped, they walked down the passage to where the rest of the family were waiting.

# Chapter Seventeen

'There's a Mr Snood to see you, Miss Clatteridge.'

Agnes raised her head and looked across at Maddie, standing in the bedroom doorway. Frowning, she placed the linen she was sorting down on the bed. 'I've never known Mr Snood call here before. I wonder what he could be wanting? Most odd. It's a bit late for him to be paying his respects. I can't see his doing that anyway. He and my father were more rivals than friends. Oh, there's only one way to find out what he wants and that's to go and see him,' she said, untying her apron. She smoothed her skirt, pulled down the sleeves of her blouse and ran a hand over her head. Tendrils of hair were escaping from the bun at the nape of her neck. 'Do I look tidy enough to receive a visitor?'

'You look very nice,' Maddie assured her.

'Well, I'd better see him then. Would you be kind enough to make some tea?'

'Of course. It would be my pleasure.'

'Thank you,' said Agnes.

Down in the kitchen, busying herself making the tea, all Maddie's thoughts centred on her job. She had been right to take it. Working for Miss Agnes Clatteridge was proving highly enjoyable, apart from the fact that the house was quite eerie, its dark wood and paintwork hiding odd nooks and crannies in endless dim passageways. Several times she had wrenched open doors in walls, expecting to find a cupboard, and been shocked to discover a dust-filled room which had not seen life, except for the collection of creepy crawlies it was home to, for numerous years. But she didn't let that deter her. It was only a house after all and since the curtains had been drawn wide and daylight allowed in, it wasn't quite so bad.

Miss Clatteridge and she had worked hard, side by side, and the closeness between them was building gradually. The more of an insight she gained into her employer, the more she found she liked her. Little by little she was seeing beyond the severe outward appearance to the warm, kind human being who lay underneath. A good man, Maddie thought, would not go far wrong should he take the time and trouble to do the same. Agnes Clatteridge had so much love to give the right person. It was a pity about her severe style of dress which did nothing to endear her to people. A softer, more colourful style and her hair done differently would do wonders for her. If only Maddie could somehow find a way to broach the matter, help her just as Ruth and Sarah had helped Maddie herself.

She had been at Clatteridge's a month now, in Leicester just on six weeks, and it seemed a lifetime. Her previous existence far removed from what she was living now. She did think of her mother, wondering how she was faring now she was alone, but her feelings were pitying not loving.

The tea mashed, Maddie took the carefully set tray through and returned to the kitchen, thinking she would take a cup across to Mr Simpson and Oswald. Mr Simpson was a nice man, very pleasant and most courteous. Oswald she hadn't taken much of a liking to. He was lazy, she knew that much, but she had been too busy to notice much more than that.

Over the last four weeks she and Miss Clatteridge had cleared the attic, an arduous task. Years of dust had had to be disturbed to uncover the secrets that lay beneath.

It had saddened Maddie greatly to stand aside and watch silently while Agnes had dusted off two large trunks, prised them open and carefully removed the contents. They were her mother's clothes, some badly moth-eaten. Maddie knew it had broken her heart to part with them all, except for an elaborately embroidered silk shawl which the moths had missed. She would keep that as a memento of the mother she'd hardly known. The good clothes, albeit dreadfully old-fashioned, had been aired outside, then bagged up to take to the Salvation Army. Hopefully they would find a use for them. The others had been thrown away.

'Your father must have loved her very much to have kept her clothes for all these years,' were the only words of comfort Maddie thought it fitting to express.

Agnes had nodded. 'Yes, I'd like to think that.'

They had found an old rocking horse, its saddle rotting, mane non-existent. 'I remember this,' Agnes proclaimed delightedly. 'I spent many happy hours riding on old Dobbin. That was, of course, until Father decided I was too old for him. Alice never got to use him. We weren't allowed toys then. I know we would have been had Mother not died.'

'Do you remember her?' Maddie had asked.

'Strangely, no, I don't. Funny that I should have memories of Dobbin but none of Mother while she was alive. But I was only two when she died having Alice and we weren't allowed to talk about her afterwards. We do have a photograph, though.'

'I've seen it.' Maddie stopped herself from saying she had thought her mother very pretty, sparing Miss Clatteridge's feelings. 'She looked kind.'

'Yes, she was,' Agnes had replied dismissively, making it obvious to Maddie that she was finding this conversation difficult. 'Now what were we doing? Oh, yes, Dobbin. Seems a shame to throw him out. Oswald has a young sister, I believe. I'll give him the horse for her. Mr Simpson can maybe do something with the saddle.'

The attic finally cleared of all its old clutter – just a few bits that could be worth selling, the rest burned in the furnace by Mr Simpson – and dusted and swept, they were now starting on the bedrooms. Maddie had been helping Agnes sort through the linen cupboard when the knock on the door had come and she had been sent to answer it.

She had taken an instant dislike to the man she found facing her. He was portly, stomach extending well in front of him. The chain of his fob watch, stretched very taut across it, looked to be in danger of snapping. He was well-dressed, but most obviously of all he oozed self-importance.

'Miss Clatteridge at home?' he had demanded in a bellow. 'Tell her Mr Snood wants to see her.'

'I'll go and enquire,' Maddie politely replied.

'If you're going to enquire from her then she's in. Don't fool with me, girl. Tell her I want to see her and that I haven't all day.'

He had pushed past Maddie then and made his own way into the parlour.

Now she was wondering how Agnes was getting on with that oaf of a man. After her remark that he'd never called before, Maddie could not help but wonder what he wanted. In the four weeks she had been here, the callers had all been tradesmen.

'Any tea going, Maddie?'

Her head jerked towards the door to see Ivan Simpson look around it.

She smiled a greeting. 'You smell it, don't you?'

He grinned. 'Well, it's better than what I can afford to mash for meself.'

'I was just about to bring you a mug across.'

'I thought as much so I came to save yer the walk.'

'Come in,' said Maddie. 'You can drink it in here.'

Ivan did not need another invitation. Leaning against the huge pot sink, he supped his tea appreciatively. 'This'd never have 'appened during Cuthbert's day.'

'Cuthbert? Oh, Mr Clatteridge. From what I gather he wasn't a very congenial sort of person.'

'If that word you used means he was awful, then he was.

206

And that's putting it mildly! Best day's work he ever did for his daughters was having that heart attack. I'm not being unkind – far from it, Maddie – but he wasn't a good man at all. Dreadful to work for.'

She eyed him searchingly. 'But you stayed?'

'Yes, I did,' said Ivan cagily and took another sup of his tea. 'Dropped stone dead without any warning, did Cuthbert Clatteridge, out in that yard.'

'Really?'

'Just by the water pump,' he said, turning slightly to point out of the window. 'Only six apart from family turned up for the funeral and I reckon that were out of morbid curiosity to check he'd really gone. Thank God he has, I say. Is . . . er . . . Miss Clatteridge not around?'

'She's entertaining in the parlour. A Mr Snood.'

'Snood?' Ivan frowned, obviously perturbed. 'I wonder what he could be wantin'?'

'Who is he?'

'Snood? He owns Snood's Funeral Parlour on Wharf Street.' Ivan bit his bottom lip thoughtfully. 'He's one to watch out for, is Mr Snood. I don't know him personally but I know his chippy well. Not got much of a liking for his boss, that much I *do* know. I hope Miss Clatteridge realises to be on her guard.'

Their conversation ceased abruptly as they both heard the click of the front door and moments later Agnes appeared. She looked pleased. Ivan looked somewhat uncomfortable to be caught drinking tea in the kitchen.

'It's all right, Mr Simpson, finish your drink,' she said. 'Anyway you might as well hear my news – I've nothing to hide from you. Mr Snood has made me an offer. It's . . . er . . . not what I was led to expect I might get, but at least it's an offer. He wants to expand, and having heard our business was for sale thought it an ideal opportunity for him. He did say he wasn't willing to pay for any goodwill. Well, I can understand that. We haven't been approached for our services at all since Father died, so I can't expect him to consider paying for something that doesn't in truth still exist. Anyway, I shall be giving his offer my utmost consideration.

'Oh!' she suddenly exclaimed. 'I forgot to return Mr Snood's gloves. I picked them up intending to as I showed him the door but it must have slipped my mind. Be a dear, Maddie. If you go through the yard entrance you should just catch him if you hurry.'

She took the gloves and ran.

As she stopped to open one of the tall arched doors she paused as voices reached her ears. She recognised Mr Snood's. Who on earth was he talking to? Politeness made her wait for a moment before she slipped through the gap in the doors and announced her presence.

'I thought you weren't coming, Pargitt?'

'You said two, Mr Snood. It's not quite that yet. I had that coffin ter finish off.'

Mr Snood, thought Maddie, had arranged to meet a man called Pargitt and from the mention of coffins she assumed it must be business they were about to discuss. Though, she thought, outside the entry to Clatteridge's yard was a strange place in which to have arranged their meeting. Nevertheless she felt she had better make her presence known and hand over the gloves before they got any further. She made to open the door wider when what Mr Snood said next made her hesitate.

'And were yer followed?' he asked.

'No, I don't think so.'

'You'd better not have been. Wouldn't do for us to be seen together, now would it?'

Maddie's ears pricked. Worried about being following and not being seen together? This was not a business meeting as she had first thought. Her suspicions mounted as she remembered Ivan's comments about the man and strained harder to hear.

'Did Mrs Snood ask where you were off to?'

208

'She did. I told 'er what yer told me to. I wa' just popping out on an errand you'd asked me to do. She told me to 'urry up.'

'Well, we'd better then, hadn't we? Wouldn't do for Mrs Snood to get wind of what I'm up to. God-fearing woman she is – and fair puts the fear of God up me all right! The less she knows about this the better until it's all done and dusted. Just you and me, that's the way I want it kept. You listening?' he snarled.

'Yes, Mr Snood. Yer know you can trust me.' Pargitt's voice grew louder and more insistent.

'Hush, you idiot,' his employer snapped angrily. 'There's ears everywhere, remember.'

Pargitt sniffed. 'So what's the score then, Mr Snood?'

Maddie heard the other man rub his hands together with a dry rasping sound.

'Well, the rumours we got going worked a treat. I was clever to think of that. She's not had a sniff of a job since the old sod passed over.'

'You owe me five bob fer my part in that,' mumbled Pargitt.

'What?'

'Nothin', Mr Snood.'

'Huh! And me letting it be known to the Undertakers' Association that the place is as good as mine has stopped anyone else from getting ideas. And as we know, don't we, Pargitt, word spreads. I know for a fact no one else has bothered even to make enquiries about the place. Don't fancy fighting against me.' He gave a gleeful chuckle. 'That plain-faced creature fell for my patter. I knew she would. Left her to mull over my offer. She'll accept, she's got no choice. But just in case she dithers, we'll do what we planned. You know what to do now. Just like I told yer. Eh, and no more than a shilling. I'm not made of money.'

'What about my half crown for arranging it?'

'You'll have yer money when I sign the papers. Now get to it.'

The conversation ceased and Maddie knew they had both departed. She stood for a moment going over what she had heard. Mr Snood was up to something crooked, she felt sure he was, but just what she'd do about it she wasn't sure.

She assumed Ivan had returned to the shed when she returned as he wasn't in the kitchen. Agnes was washing up.

'Did you catch up with Mr Snood?'

Maddie realised she was still holding the gloves. 'Oh, no, I didn't.'

'Oh, no matter. Leave them on the hall stand. I'll return them when he comes on Saturday.' She stopped her task and eyed Maddie in concern. 'Is anything the matter? You look rather preoccupied?'

'Pardon? Oh, no. Just . . . er . . .' She wondered whether to tell Miss Clatteridge what she had overheard, but decided to mull it over a bit longer first. Maddie didn't want to cause her needless worry over something she could just have misinterpreted. She forced a smile. 'I'm pleased you have an offer at long last, although I know it means my time here is nearly over. I've enjoyed working for you, Miss Clatteridge.'

Agnes smiled broadly. 'And I've enjoyed having you. I shall miss you, my dear. I hope what I say is not one-sided, but I feel we're becoming friends.'

'Yes, me too.'

'Then we must not lose touch. You must write to me, keep me informed of what's happening to you.' Agnes inhaled deeply. 'I have to say, though, that Mr Snood's offer has cheered me somewhat. I was beginning to think no one wanted this place.'

Maddie pressed her lips together. Something Mr Snood had said came back to mind. Rumours. He had said the rumours had worked. What had that meant?

'To be honest,' Agnes was continuing, 'financially things are getting worrying. If it wasn't for the little we make on the nails and bits of carpentry we'd have nothing coming in. I suppose I really ought to consider letting Peabody go – there's hardly enough to keep him occupied – but I don't really want to do that just in case we get a funeral in. We'd need him for that, you see. I couldn't expect Mr Simpson to manage on his own. Oh, dear, it's all such a dilemma. Still, I'll just about get through if this sale goes ahead. I don't see why it shouldn't, Mr Snood seemed keen enough.'

Maddie eyed her anxiously. 'Miss Clatteridge, what you pay me is generous considering. I would accept less if it would help you?'

'Oh, my dear, what a kind gesture! And it's much appreciated. But I'm quite happy with the way things are. You more than earn what I give you. Until the time comes when I cannot afford to keep you on anymore, I'm happy to pay you fairly. I hope to keep you here until the day I move.'

'You talk as if you've already made up your mind, Miss Clatteridge?'

Agnes looked thoughtful. 'Not quite my dear. I have until Saturday, but to be honest with you, I don't think I have any real choice. No one else has come forward, have they? I shall write a letter to Alice tonight, keep her informed of what is going on. I know she'll be pleased if the sale goes ahead. The letter I received from her this morning was so full of how much she's enjoying herself. It's good to know she's happy and I don't have to worry about her. She's been to several tea parties with acquaintances of my aunt's and to a theatre on the sea front. Oh, it all sounds so very nice.' She sighed distantly, then shook herself. 'Right, come on then, Maddie dear, back to the linen. It won't sort itself.'

As she always did at leaving time Maddie popped her head around the shed door to announce her departure. 'Goodnight, Ivan. See you in the morning,' she called loudly.

'No need to shout, gel, I ain't deaf,' he said, appearing to one side of her.

Maddie jumped. 'I didn't see you there. Thought you'd be at the back of the shed.'

'Well, I ain't,' he said, laughing. Then looked at her, frowning. 'What's up, gel?'

'Pardon? Nothing. Why?'

He shrugged his shoulders. 'Just looks to me like you've summat on yer mind. My mistake. Goodnight.'

'Goodnight,' she said again and made to walk away, then stopped, turning around. 'Ivan, can I talk to you, please?'

''Course.' His eyes narrowed in concern. 'I was right, there is summat wrong.'

'I don't quite know if wrong's the word. I would like your opinion, though, as you're the only other person I can discuss this with, really. I wasn't going to say anything. Well, not just yet until I gave it more thought.' She took a breath. 'But I need to tell someone, just in case there's something not right . . .'

'You ain't mekin' sense, gel. Come through,' he said. 'Oswald's gone 'ome so we won't be disturbed.'

He wiped a stool for Maddie before she sat down, Ivan opposite her, their knees not quite touching. 'Now,' he said, hands clasped, leaning towards her. 'Tell me what's ailing yer?'

'There's nothing ailing me, Ivan I'm just bothered, that's all, about something I happened to overhear. It was when I went to catch up with Mr Snood. I overheard him talking to someone. Pargitt was his name, I think. I'm sure I heard that correctly. Anyway . . .' Maddie related what she had overheard. When she had finished she eyed Ivan worriedly. 'What do you make of it?'

Face grave, he leaned back, folding his arms. 'I don't know. But I can tell yer this – I don't like it. As I said before, that Mr Snood is a slippery customer by all accounts. You sure that's what you 'eard?'

'As sure as I can be. Of course, he might not have been

talking about his business with Miss Clatteridge. But I'd guess he was.'

Ivan sat in silence for a moment, Maddie looking on. 'I think so too. He's up ter summat,' he finally declared. 'I can feel it in me water. But how we'll go about finding out is another matter.' He felt a surge of protective sympathy towards the woman he loved and before he could stop himself, blurted out, 'If he's planning 'ote to cause Miss Clatteridge grief then he'd better watch out.' Maddie jumped, startled at the savagery of his tone, which Ivan noticed. 'Well, what I mean is,' he continued, 'Miss Clatteridge is me boss. I can't stand by and let him do wrong against her, now can I?'

'No, you can't,' agreed Maddie. 'Neither can I.'

'Right,' he said, relieved, hoping he had given reason enough for his outburst. It wouldn't do for Maddie to get suspicions of his true feelings towards Agnes; they must remain his secret. He wouldn't want Maddie knowing what a fool he was. He liked her. Thought Agnes had made a good choice in taking her on. Maddie, in her own way, was doing a lot for Agnes. Since her arrival a new woman was emerging. One who did not carry herself quite so stiffly and was certainly more talkative. He loved Agnes regardless, but the changes taking place were making her more endearing if that were possible. Ivan sighed forlornly. Despite knowing it was selfish of him, he hoped no other man took notice.

'Anything wrong, Ivan?'

'Eh? No,' he answered more abruptly than he'd meant to. 'Listen, I don't think we should say anything to Miss Clatteridge just yet.'

'You don't?'

He shook his head. 'I want time to think on this. Mull it over, like. No point in worrying her unnecessarily. She's enough on her plate. Need to be sure before we say 'ote.' He paused for a moment. 'I might just pop over Wharf Street way tonight, see if I can find Bert Knapp. He's Snood's chief chippy. I'll tek him for a pint. See if I can find out anything.'

'Such as?'

He shrugged his shoulders. 'You never know, do yer. Might be summat and nothin'. Better than doing n'ote.'

A thought struck Maddie. 'I could ask my father if he knows anything about Mr Snood. He comes into contact with all sorts in his line. Actually Mr Snood might even be a customer of his firm.'

'That's worth a try an' all. You get off home then and we'll talk in the morning. Try not to worry, Maddie.'

'I won't, but I like Miss Clatteridge.'

So do I, thought Ivan, and more than like. And woe betide anyone who thinks they can ride roughshod over her and hope to get away with it!

# Chapter Eighteen

They were all sitting around the table talking, the only difference being that Sarah was unusually quiet.

'Mam? Mam!' Roy repeated. 'Can I have that last piece of pie or what?'

'Eh? Oh, sorry, Roy, 'course you can. Custard?' she said, reaching for the jug. 'Do you want any more rhubarb pie, dear?' she asked George.

'No, I'm full, thanks. That was grand, as usual,' he said appreciatively, rubbing his stomach. When he received no reply he eyed her in concern. 'You all right, love?'

'Mmmm? Oh, yes, I'm fine, just tired. We were very busy at work today. I never got time for a proper sit down. We had two assistants off sick. If you don't mind,' she said, scraping back her chair, 'I'll make a start on the pots and then I'm going up.'

'I'll see to the dishes,' offered Maddie. 'It's my turn anyway.'

'And Ruth's ter dry,' piped up Roy.

'I hadn't forgotten,' his sister snapped.

'You get off upstairs, love,' said George. 'I'll bring you a cuppa up, shall I?'

'Yes, I'd like that. Ta.'

She went round the table kissing each in turn on the cheek, including Maddie. 'Goodnight, everyone,' she said as she left the room.

'Is Mam all right, Dad?' asked Ruth. 'That's the second time she's gone ter bed early this week.'

'Yes, it is, isn't it?' he mused thoughtfully. 'But I'm sure she's just tired like she says, so stop worrying.' His instructions to his children didn't stop him feeling concerned, however. He'd make Sarah a cup of tea and go and talk to her, to be sure she wasn't hiding anything. Come to think of it, she did look a little peaky.

Ruth and Roy had finished their share of the chores and had departed, and Maddie had begun to stack the dirty plates when she remembered she had wanted to ask her father about Mr Snood. 'Father, can I talk to you for a moment?'

'Of course. If it's private we could shut the door in case Ruth or Roy come in.'

'No, it's not private. Not really.' Besides, nothing was private in this house. The family kept no secrets and so she felt quite at liberty to ask her father what she wanted to know. After years of not being able to talk freely on any matter, being able to now, and being listened to and offered advice, was quite a revelation and something she welcomed.

'Do you happen to know a Mr Snood at all?' she asked, sitting down. 'I don't know whether he's one of your customers or not?'

George shook his head. 'No, not a Mr Snood. Wait a minute – the Snood you're referring to – is he the one who has the funeral parlour?'

'Yes, that's him. Do you know him?'

'Not personally. Just of him. I'm not sure if he uses our company for his insurance needs. He might not even have any. Lots don't bother or can't afford it. Why are you asking about him, Maddie?'

She told him what had happened.

'Oh, I see.' Thoughtfully George took off his spectacles, wiped them, them put them back on. 'I could make discreet enquiries?'

'Would you, Father. I'd be most grateful. I'm worried for Miss Clatteridge, you see.'

He smiled. 'You like her, don't you?'

'I do. Very much.'

'I'll see what I can do. Now I'm off to make your mother – sorry, Sarah – that cup of tea.'

Thoughts of Harriet flashed immediately to mind and Maddie became worried. 'Father, do you think my mother will be all right now that she's on her own? I mean, if she took ill there'd be no one to care for her, would there?'

He rose from his chair and came around the table to join her. He put his arms around her and pulled her close. 'Listen, my dear, I'm not a God-fearing man but I do know that the good book says "What ye sow, so ye shall reap". Your mother made it impossible for people to live with her.' He looked down at her meaningfully. 'I am right, aren't I, Maddie? She didn't make your life very easy, did she? You found it impossible to live with her any longer so you came to us, right?' She nodded. It was the truth. 'Well, then, I'm afraid your mother is suffering the consequences of her own actions. She'll not change her ways. I gave up any hope of that years ago. You're happy here, aren't you?'

'Oh, Father, more than I can tell you.'

'Well then, let Harriet get on with her life, and you, my dear, get on with yours. If your mother was ever ill enough to warrant being taken care of, word would get to us. So stop worrying.'

Maddie smiled. 'Yes, I will.'

He eyed her searchingly. 'My dear, if you've had a change of heart and want to go back, I . . .'

'No, Father! No, I've not. This is my home now.'

He sighed in relief. 'I'm glad to hear that. Now, Maddie, I'd like to take Sarah that drink, see how she is.'

'Yes, of course. And, Dad, thanks.'

Fierce love for his daughter filled him. She had called him Dad for the very first time.

Minutes later he entered the bedroom he shared with Sarah. She appeared to be asleep. He tiptoed across the room and placed the cup on the table by the side of the bed in case she woke up.

'Thanks, love.'

'Oh, you're awake.'

'Just dozing. I heard you come in.' She eased herself up to a sitting position, pulling the pillows up behind her back, and picked up her cup.

He sat on the bed beside her and looked at her tenderly. 'Is it just tiredness, love?'

She cast down her eyes. She didn't want to worry him but had never lied to him and couldn't start now. 'I don't know, George dear. I'm very tired, yes, but I don't feel quite right either.'

'Oh! In . . . er . . . what way, Sarah?'

'Just a bit under the weather. A bit peculiar, that's all. Could be me age. I am forty-three, remember.'

'Just a spring chicken! You don't look a day older than the one I met you. You're still a beautiful woman, Sarah.'

She patted his hand. 'I'm glad you still see me that way.'

'And I always will. Will you go to the doctor? Let him take a look at you? Please, Sarah?'

'But that'll cost a shilling, George, just to visit.'

'Sarah, remember I don't have to hand Harriet any more money. Besides, you're worth more than a shilling, especially where your health is concerned. Now you'll go tomorrow, promise me?'

'All right, all right, but you're fussing for nothing. I'm just under the weather, that's all. Now skedaddle. Let me drink this tea and have a sleep.'

He rose, leaned over and kissed her lovingly on the mouth before he left.

Maddie did not manage to see Ivan until mid-morning, volunteering to take him and Oswald both a mug of tea.

'They make their own,' Agnes had replied when Maddie had made her offer.

'Yes, but Mr Simpson prefers what we have. Better quality

218

leaves. There's plenty in the pot. It's a shame to let it go to waste.'

'Yes, it is.' Agnes had no objection to anything of this nature where Ivan was concerned. 'Take him a piece of the fruit cake that I baked,' she said. Then a thought struck her and she hurriedly added, 'Peabody too, of course.'

Tilting her head, eyes narrowed, Maddie looked at her thoughtfully.

'Is there anything the matter?' Agnes asked. 'Only you're looking at me rather strangely?'

'Am I?' Maddie hadn't realised and mentally shook herself. 'I didn't mean to. I was . . .' What she had been thinking of was Agnes and Ivan. There was something about them both she couldn't quite fathom. It had to do with the way they acted towards each other. Just little things: a hurried glance, the way they stood when in each other's company. And like now, Agnes insisting that Ivan be taken a piece of cake, Oswald only as an afterthought. It wasn't the fact of the cake, though not many employers would give their employees cake, let alone tea, it was the way Agnes had spoken. There had been fondness in her voice, only slight but it had been there, Maddie was certain. And that went for Ivan too whenever he spoke of Miss Clatteridge. Maddie couldn't, though, divulge to Agnes what had been going through her mind. 'I'm thinking about Sarah,' she said. She didn't like telling a white lie, but it wasn't entirely untruthful. She had been thinking of Sarah, knowing she was going to see the doctor today and wondering what his diagnosis would be. 'She's been feeling under the weather just lately.'

Agnes patted her arm. 'She'll be fine, stop worrying.' Her ears suddenly pricked. 'Oh, did I hear the door? Be a dear, Maddie, go and see who it is, please.'

'Who was it?' she asked when Maddie returned, puzzled by the annoyed expression on her face.

'A man enquiring after your services. His mother's just died.'

'Oh, really?' Agnes exclaimed, beaming brightly. 'Thank goodness! We could do with the money even though Mr Snood is keen to buy the place Did you show him through to the room at the back of the Chapel of Rest, like I asked you when a customer called?'

'No, I didn't.'

'You didn't. Why not? Oh, never mind. Where is he? In the parlour? I'd better go and see to him,' Agnes said, untying her apron and heading for the door.

'Miss Clatteridge, stop!' called Maddie. 'I didn't manage to put him anywhere. When I explained I'd fetch you to speak to him, he said he wanted the undertaker. I told him that you *were* the undertaker and he said he wouldn't deal with a woman and would go elsewhere. He just left, Miss Clatteridge.'

Agnes's face fell. 'Oh, I see.' She sighed deeply. 'My sister was right. She said people expected to be dealt with by a man. I don't see what difference it makes, really I don't. Isn't it more important that the job is done properly and considerately, not whether it's by a male or a female?'

'It wouldn't matter to me, Miss Clatteridge. I expect I'd be too upset at the time to be bothered.'

'My sentiments exactly. Obviously, though, we are in a minority in thinking that way. I've made the right decision to sell, then, haven't I?'

Forlornly, Maddie nodded.

Agnes forced a smile to her face. 'Better take this tea over to Mr Simpson and Peabody before it gets any colder.'

Maddie picked up the tray and took it to the shed. Ivan motioned her outside, out of earshot of Oswald.

'Did you ask your father?'

'I did. He doesn't know Mr Snood personally but he's going to make enquiries. But I've something else to tell you.' She explained about the caller they had just received.

'What?' snapped Ivan. 'Bloody fool! Miss Clatteridge woulda done a good job for him.' He frowned thoughtfully.

Something Maddie had told him about Mr Snood's conversation flashed to mind. What was it again? But for the moment it had escaped him. 'Let's hope your father can find out summat.'

'What about you?' she asked.

'I managed to find Bert Knapp in the White Swan, his head in a pint. He was quite willing to talk about Snood. As yer already know, Knapp ain't got much of a liking for his boss. He couldn't tell me much, though. Just that it's known among the workers that Pargitt is the one stuck up his backside.'

Maddie thought she had misheard him. 'I beg your pardon?'

'Sorry, Maddie,' Ivan said in embarrassment. 'Er . . . close to him. They've bin seen huddled together on one or two occasions, whispering. Definitely suspicious, don't yer think?'

'If they were whispering it would be.' She eyed him keenly. 'So what are we going to do then? Do we tell Miss Clatteridge?'

'No, not yet. I had a good think last night when I got back. These rumours . . . If anyone likes to listen to rumours and spread 'em round 'ere, it's Tilly Potter.'

'Who's she?'

'She's the Post Master's wife. Let me see if I can find out from her just what's what. Then we'll decide whether to tell Miss Clatteridge. She can mek up her own mind. I'll go and see Tilly Potter tomorrow. Shouldn't tek me long. I'll think of some excuse should Miss Clatteridge notice me missing.'

Sighing loudly, he ran a hand over the top of his head, glancing round him. 'There ain't hardly 'ote left to do around 'ere. I have a job keeping Oswald at it. I've enough nails made to keep our regulars happy for weeks to come. The workshed's like a new pin. So are the rest of the buildings, ready for inspection by any possible buyer for the place. Yer could sleep on the stable floor.' He laughed. 'I got Oswald to give Ned's home a good going over. Weren't happy about it, wasn't Oswald. He grumbled like hell all the time he was doing it. I've done all the lists of stock too. So, yer see, me slipping out won't cause a problem. It's not like we're up to our eyes in work, more's the pity. Some business coming in while the sale went through woulda stopped Miss Clatteridge being so worried about money . . .'

He stopped abruptly and said quickly, 'I'm rattling on. Sorry, Maddie.' Red spots of embarrassment appeared on his cheeks. 'She's been decent enough to me, 'as Miss Clatteridge,' he said gruffly. 'I'm just bothered for 'er, that's all.'

I'm beginning to think it's a lot more than bothered you feel, thought Maddie, but said, 'I can understand how you feel, Ivan. I think she's nice too. So what do I do in the meantime?'

'Not much you can do. Just keep yer ears open. Maybe yer dad will come back with summat.'

'Yes, let's hope.'

Maddie arrived home as normal at a quarter to seven that evening and walked into an usually quiet house. In fact there were no sounds at all. None of the usual chatter or noises coming from the kitchen. Someone was home, though, there was flickering light from the gas mantles shining through the crack of the back room door.

She hurried down the passageway, stripping off her coat en route, and on into the back room to find Ruth and Roy sitting silently at the table, arms folded, heads bowed. By the look on their faces she knew something was wrong. She laid her coat over the back of a dining chair.

'What is it?' she asked, fear building inside her.

They both raised their heads to look at her.

'It's Mother,' said Ruth.

'Sarah? Has something happened to her?'

'We don't know,' uttered Roy.

'Where is she?'

'Upstairs with Dad.'

'She went straight to see the doctor from work, didn't she? Is . . . is she ill?'

'We don't know,' said Ruth. 'She came in and ran up the stairs without saying anything to us. But I know she was crying.'

'Crying?' Maddie's fear mounted. 'Oh!'

'I tried to talk to her but she'd locked the bedroom door,' said Ruth.

'Locked it?' Maddie frowned. This wasn't like Sarah at all. Dear God, she thought, the doctor must have given her some dreadful news for her to act like that. She felt tears prick her own eyes. Sarah had come to mean so much to her, and if she felt this way, how must Ruth and Roy be feeling? 'And, Dad's with her, you say?'

They both nodded.

'When he arrived home,' said Ruth, 'we told him what had happened and he said to stay here while he went up to see her. They've been up there ages.'

It was serious, Maddie thought. She took a deep breath, not quite knowing how to handle the situation, and not wanting to say or do anything to cause further anxiety. Her brother and sister were worried enough as it was. 'This might have nothing to do with her visit to the doctor. Could be something that happened at work.' She hoped she sounded more convinced than she felt. 'Let's make a start on the dinner. Come on, Ruth,' she said, heading for the kitchen. 'Roy, will you set the table, please?'

Upstairs, George and Sarah were sitting on the bed, wrapped in each other's arms. Sarah was quietly sobbing.

'This can't be happening, George. Why me? Why now? I'm forty-three.' She raised her head and looked at him through swollen tear-filled eyes. 'The children!' she exclaimed. 'What are they going to say? How will they cope with this?'

He held her tighter to him and tenderly said, 'Sarah, my

love, it's a baby you're having. It's such wonderful news, the children will be delighted, you'll see.'

Giving her eyes a wipe with her sodden handkerchief, she bit her bottom lip worriedly. 'Do you think so?'

'You know them as well as I do, Sarah. You know they will.'

'Are you sure they'll not be ashamed.'

'Ashamed?'

'Oh, George, I'm forty-three. Fancy me being nearly five months gone and not noticing. I thought I was getting thicker round the waist but presumed it was just middle-aged spread. I was worried me monthlies had stopped because I was changing. I never dreamed it was this.'

'You're not the first woman to have a baby at your age, Sarah.'

'I know that. But I was looking forward to our grandchildren, I never thought to have another child of my own. I've been so blessed already, I never gave this a thought. And we'd such plans now you don't have to hand over all that money to Harriet. All the things we were going to do to the house . . .' She looked tenderly into his eyes and ran one hand down the side of his face. 'But that's not important, George. What is, is you being able to take things easier. I wanted that so much. It isn't fair on you. I'm so sorry.'

'Sorry? Oh, Sarah, you didn't exactly do this all by yourself, did you? Has it really come as a surprise, considering the loving way we still are with each other?'

She coyly averted her gaze. 'I suppose not,' she said, embarrassed. George was right, she thought. The way they made love was just as fierce, passionate and frequent as in the early days when they had first got together. Considering that, her falling for this baby should not have come as so much of a shock.

'As for the money, Sarah, we'll still be better off than we were, even without your wage. I gave Harriet a good sum each week, don't forget. Anyway, I'm glad you're going to be giving up work. It's about time you took it easier.'

'George Ashman, how can you say that?' she retorted with a twinkle in her eyes. 'Looking after a family is damned hard work. And, don't forget, I've not the energy I had when Ruth and Roy were little.'

'I know kids are hard work, love. I did my fair share in raising our two. But the difference this time is that you won't be having to work right up to the last minute, and when the baby comes you'll be at home just looking after it and us. You'll be able to enjoy this one.'

She sighed, eyes misting over. 'Yes, I will, won't I?'

He smiled. 'Mind you, it's my guess you won't get much of a look in when it does come. Maddie and Ruth will be fighting each other to care for it.'

Sarah laughed as well. 'I can picture them now.'

'That's better.' He eyed her for a moment. 'You are happy about this baby, aren't you, my love?'

'At first I wasn't. I was too worried about how you and the children would react.' She looked deep into his eyes. 'But, yes, I do want it. I want it very much. It's obvious you do too. I don't care whether it's a girl or a boy so long as it's healthy.'

'Nether do I.' He looked at her in concern. 'You told me the doctor said you'd be all right, Sarah. You are being truthful with me aren't you?'

She nodded. 'I've never lied to you, not once in all the years we've been together, George, and I'm not about to start now. There's nothing wrong with my constitution. After he'd examined me, he pronounced me as strong as a horse. He only thinks it best I give up work because I stand on me feet all day and I could end up with really bad varicose veins.'

'Then that's what you'll do. Tomorrow you'll give in your notice. You will, Sarah, won't you?'

She patted her stomach. 'I wouldn't do anything to risk our child George.'

'And I wouldn't do anything to risk you. So from this

moment forward it's feet up. Are you listening?'

'I'm listening. George?'

He drew slightly away and gazed at her. 'Yes?'

'I do love you.'

'I love you, too.'

He leaned over and kissed her tenderly. 'You've made me a very happy man, Sarah,' he said, voice thick with emotion. 'Now don't you think we ought to go and tell the children? Because at the moment they think you're terminally ill or something.'

'Oh, goodness!' she said, jumping up. 'I can't have that. Oh, the poor dears. Whatever was I thinking of? Come on,' she said, grabbing his hand.

'A baby?' Ruth cried. 'Oh, Mother, that's . . . oh, it's such wonderful news!' She jumped up from her seat and rushed over, throwing her arms around Sarah and hugged her tightly.

'Aren't you too old?' blurted Roy.

'That's enough from you, young man,' scolded his father.

'I . . . I didn't mean it nasty, Dad. I . . . well . . .'

'You're not ashamed of me, are you, son?' Sarah asked worriedly.

'Ashamed? Don't be daft, Mam. I'm pleased, honest. I thought you were going to tell us you were dying or summat. But that's just it. Arthur's mam did when she had hers and she were your age. I'm just . . .'

Sarah took him in her arms, smoothing one hand over his head. 'She wasn't a well woman, Roy, She'd had thirteen children already. She was worn out. It was just one of those things.' She pulled away, fixing her eyes on his. 'Nothing's going to happen to me, you hear? The doctor's told me I'm as strong as an ox. All right?'

He nodded. 'It's just that I love yer.'

'I know, I know.' She kissed him on his cheek, then turned to look at Maddie. 'How about you?'

A great surge of emotion had exploded within her when Sarah and George had broken their news. It had brought painful memories flooding back of her own baby and of how much she was still missing her. Will this pain ever leave me? she thought. Will there ever be a day when I don't think of her, wonder about the people who have her now, if they love and protect her? The worst thing of all was that she could not tell anyone, nor share this incredible pain. It was something she had to shoulder all by herself. She wanted desperately to rush out of the room, throw herself on her sofa and weep bitter tears. But she couldn't, she wouldn't be able to explain herself. And, worse, to act so selfishly would only mar the joy of their announcement for Sarah and her father.

'Why, Maddie!' exclaimed Sarah. 'You're crying.'

'With happiness,' she said hurriedly, quickly wiping away the tears she hadn't realised were there. 'I am so happy for you both.' And she was. It was only her memories that were causing her distress.

The rest of the evening was spent sitting around the table discussing the forthcoming event. It wasn't until Maddie was about to excuse herself to retire to bed that she suddenly remembered Miss Clatteridge's plight and her father's promise to make some enquiries.

'Dad, did you manage to find out anything about Mr Snood?'

'Mr Snood? What about him? Who is he anyway?' asked Roy.

'Yes, spill the beans, Maddie,' urged Ruth.

'Be a change to talk about something else besides this baby,' piped up Sarah.

Maddie explained to them.

'Oh,' said Roy. 'It's like one of them penny mystery stories.'

'Which you read too many of,' declared his mother. 'But I must admit, it is all very intriguing. So did you find out

227

anything, dear?' she asked her husband keenly.

George laughed. 'I feel I'm being interrogated! I'm afraid to say I didn't. He's no policies with our firm, so I drew a blank there. I discreetly asked a couple of my business customers whether they knew of him.'

'And did they?' Maddie asked hopefully.

'No.'

'Oh!'

'Yer not going to give up though, are yer, Dad?' asked Roy, folding his arms and leaning on the table.

'No, I'm not. I'll try again tomorrow.' George paused for a moment. 'I tell you what I will do. Snood's parlour's a bit off my patch but I'll go there tomorrow and see if I can talk to him. Don't worry, I won't mention a word about this. He'll think it's a business call. But I should be able to get a feel for him.'

'Oh, Dad, that's a marvellous idea! Thank you so much,' enthused Maddie. 'And Mr Simpson is going to call upon the Post Mistress and try to get to the bottom of the rumours.'

'That's a good idea too,' said her father. 'Whatever these rumours are that have been spread, then Tilly's the one who'll throw some light on them. Why don't you ask Mr Simpson to come around tomorrow night and we can all discuss our findings?'

'He won't mind us sticking our noses in, will he?' asked Sarah.

Maddie eyed her for a moment. 'I don't think so. He wants to get to the bottom of this as much as we do. No, I'm sure he won't mind, just be glad of any help.'

'Ask him to come to dinner,' Sarah offered. 'To my mind such things are best sorted on a full stomach.'

'Can I? Oh, I'm sure he'd be delighted.'

Ivan was honoured to be asked and greatly relieved to have Maddie's family's help in this matter, not offended by their intrusion in the least. After all, if they were correct in their assumptions, Miss Clatteridge's future was at great risk.

The next evening at seven they were all sitting around Sarah's table, ready to begin their discussion, appetites more than adequately appeased by large helpings of mutton stew.

Maddie was beside herself, wanting to know what news the day had brought, not having had a chance to ask Ivan as he hadn't found it possible to slip away to the Post Office until late-afternoon due to Agnes's decision to spend the day in the washhouse, laundering the linen and towels she was taking with her to Scarborough when the time came for her departure. It was an usually good drying day for the middle of November and she didn't want to waste a moment with such a large amount to do.

They had laboured hard. Fires had been lit under the huge brick boiler and they had both dollied, then mangled, pegged, unpegged, folded and packed away. Both women were exhausted by the time Agnes declared a halt and they retired to the sitting room over a tray of tea and the rest of the fruit cake.

Hence it wasn't until after four that Ivan had felt it safe to make his escape without Agnes around to ask where he was going. Maddie did not get an opportunity to catch him before she left for the night as Agnes insisted on her departing by the front door and had waved her off down the street, not giving Maddie an opportunity to slip back in unnoticed.

On Ivan's arrival at the house at six-thirty, as arranged, they were all immediately ushered to the table by Sarah to sit down to eat. The conversation had dwelt on everything bar the one topic Maddie was so desperate to discuss and she was bursting with impatience by the time her father pushed his empty plate from him.

Thank goodness, she thought, the time had finally come. She opened her mouth to ask Ivan how he had got on when to her dismay Sarah beat her to it.

'More tea, Mr Simpson?'

'Please,' he responded, picking up his cup and holding it towards her. 'That wa' a delicious meal, Mrs Ashman.' No one batted an eyelid at his obvious assumption. 'Not the circumstances I would have wished to be invited in, but all the same I'm much obliged.' He didn't tell them that this was the very first home-cooked meal he had eaten, sitting around a family table, apart from the Christmas dinners he had shared with the Clatteridges. But they could hardly have been classed as family occasions, far from it, not with Cuthbert presiding over proceedings, his beady eyes ever watchful, everyone else present frightened to make one wrong move. Usually Ivan's own attempts at cooking or whatever Agnes slipped him were taken in solitude in his room over the stable. He did hope they'd ask him again.

'You're more than welcome, Mr Simpson, and you must come again.'

'Thank you, Mrs Ashman, I'd be delighted.'

'Right,' said George, 'we all know what we're here for.' And with a twinkle in his eye added, 'I know Maddie's been desperate throughout dinner to start the proceedings. So let's get the dishes stacked and we can begin.'

In under three minutes the table was cleared, dishes piled in the kitchen, and they were all seated around the table again.

'So,' said George, taking charge. 'Let's make a start. I'll go first, shall I?'

They all nodded in agreement.

'Not much to tell you, I'm afraid. I did manage to get to see Mr Snood. He wasn't interested in insurance. Wasn't a believer in it but might change his mind in the future, he said. At the moment all his money was tied up in other things. I couldn't get anything else out of him. He came across as a man who thinks well of himself, that's all I can say. I wasn't with him above five minutes. What about you, Mr Simpson? I hope you fared better than me? Maddie said you were hoping to see the Post Mistress to check out these rumours.'

Ivan folded his arms and leaned on the table. 'I didn't think I wa' going to get to, I thought Miss Clatteridge and Maddie'd never finish the washing. I managed to slip away just after four. I didn't need to ask Tilly Potter anything. She asked me.'

She would, thought Sarah, knowing the woman well. But wouldn't voice her thoughts and interrupt with a flippant comment.

'I've only ever had the need to visit the Post Office twice in me life but Mrs Potter knew who I wa' and where I worked. She asked what was I going ter be doing with myself once Clatteridge's had been sold. I asked her how she knew Clatteridge's was for sale. She said she couldn't remember who'd told her. Then she said she thought Molly Micklewaite had, but couldn't be sure.'

'Tilly's a nice enough woman,' piped up Sarah, 'but to my mind the trouble with her is that she listens to that much gossip, and adds so much to it herself when she's telling others, she doesn't know if she's coming or going.'

'I 'appen to agree with yer, Mrs Ashman. Anyway, I was waiting for me change after paying for me stamp and racking me brains on how to ask her if she'd heard any talk about Clatteridge's and what it was about, when she said, "Shame, in't it, what happened about Minnie Tallon? You'd a' thought Miss Clatteridge would have made an exception, being's she lived so close." "I'm sorry, I don't follow you," I says. She looked at me as though I was stupid. "Well, did you not know that two days after her father passed on, Miss Clatteridge sent word to Jessie Victor and Cissie Gower . . ."' He paused and flashed a glance around the table. 'They're local women who do most of the laying out around these parts.' Then he continued, 'Apparently they were told that any dyings that they'd have normally sent to Clatteridge's were to be reported straight to Snood's in future. Now the old man was dead, business was ceasing. A man gave 'em both two shilling for their trouble, apparently. "What man?" I asked. "The man Miss Clatteridge sent to tell 'em – what man d'yer think I was talking about,"Tilly told me. "Anyway, I told Cissie I'd help out by telling everyone who came into the Post Office. I didn't ask no payment from her for me trouble neither, so don't you go thinking I did. Just doing my bit to help."'

Ivan drew breath deeply. 'I left then, learned all I needed to. But not before I told her that the rumours were untrue. Clatteridge's was still operating as normal and whoever had started them rumours must be a thoroughly bad lot. "I trust you'll do your bit in putting people straight," I said to her. And she will. I left her feeling thoroughly ashamed of 'erself, I can tell yer.'

'Good for you,' piped up George. He ran a hand over his chin thoughtfully. 'Well, you certainly found out more than you bargained for, Mr Simpson. At least we know now just what the rumours were.' He looked across at Maddie. 'That caller you told me of, the one who refused to have his mother buried by a woman undertaker . . .'

'What about him?' she asked.

'Seems a bit odd to me.'

'Me too,' said Sarah. 'If anything should happen to any of you, God forbid, I'd be far too upset myself to be bothered whether the undertaker was a man or not.'

Ivan gasped, it suddenly occurred to him just what he had been trying to remember a few days ago. 'Why the . . . so and so,' he proclaimed, just managing to curb a profanity. 'That's what Snood was arranging with Pargitt! That man who called was paid to do it. It's my bet his mother is still very much alive.'

'I'd come to that conclusion myself, Mr Simpson,' said George. 'The fact is, Maddie, you misinterpreted nothing of what you overheard.'

'He's not a nice man this Mr Snood,' said Sarah.

Maddie agreed tight-lipped. 'If he's done all this, then no, he's not.'

'Snood must have plotted his nasty little plan as soon as he heard Mr Clatteridge had died.'

George nodded. 'Seems very much that way to me.'

The room lapsed into silence. Sarah rose. 'I'll make some tea,' she said. 'Ruth, please come and give me a hand.'

Without a word she followed her mother into the kitchen.

'Oh, Dad, this is awful,' Maddie groaned. 'How could Mr Snood be so sly.'

'People do all sorts when they want something bad enough, Maddie love. He saw his chance to buy Clatteridge's cheap and obviously wasn't bothered how he got it. In my line of business this is mild, believe me.'

'I can't imagine,' said Maddie. 'This is terrible enough.'

'I could tell you a few stories,' said Ivan. 'You wouldn't believe some of the things people get up to when a relative passes on.'

'He's right,' agreed her father. 'Like Mr Simpson, I meet all sorts. I knew a man once who murdered his own mother to get her burial money.'

'You did?' gasped Roy, enthralled. 'How come you've never told us before?'

'Not the sort of thing you tell to children. You were nothing but a baby at the time. Hardly the ideal bedtime story.'

'Well, we ain't kids anymore so you can now, can't yer?' Roy pleaded.

Maddie was enthralled too. 'Yes, please do, Dad?'

'All right.' George slid his spectacles higher on his nose and relaxed back in his chair. 'Mrs Collins was a kindly old duck. Wouldn't harm a hair on anyone's head. She'd saved all her life, many times going without to make sure she kept up her payments on her policy so she could have a real posh send off when her time came. It was all she lived for. "Damned sure," she used to say to me, "I'm gonna go out of this world a better way than I came in." She died real sudden. I'd seen her on the Friday night and she was as right as rain, no ailment to my knowledge. By Sunday morning she'd gone. The son got his hands on the insurance payout and arranged the cheapest funeral he could. He pocketed the rest.'

'He didn't?' gasped Maddie.

'Yes, he did. It was only because I attended out of respect for his mother that he was found out. Each week I'd had to listen to what she had planned and agreed with her son should be carried out. Brougham and single for the vicar; carriages and fours, all decked out in their finery, for the mourners; hearse and black-plumed pair for herself. A shroud made special from best linen and a walnut coffin with solid brass handles and name-plate. And a big spread: ham on the bone, trifle, best sherry for the women, whisky and ale for the men. None of that comes cheap, the plywood box her son ordered certainly did. The mourners walked, and got paste sandwiches and a cup of tea for their efforts. The old lady would have been so upset if she'd known that saving for all those years was a total waste of time.'

'But how did you know he'd killed her, Dad?' Roy asked, agog.

'He told me himself.'

'He did?' gasped Maddie.

'Didn't realise he had, of course. But when I went to hand over his dues he remarked it was a good job his mother had had that policy to bury herself with as he'd used his last threepenny bit for the gas the night she'd died.'

Roy frowned. 'I don't see . . .'

'That threepenny bit, son, wasn't used to light the gas mantles, it was used to gas her while she was asleep. Of course, I'd no proof. There's many that never carry out the deceased's instructions. Can't brand everyone a murderer just going by that. But I didn't like the way he grinned when he grabbed that money off me. I was suspicious enough to alert the police just in case. They got the truth from him, eventually.'

234

'Did they hang him, Dad?'

'Roy!' his father rebuffed him sharply. 'Yes, as a matter of fact, they did.'

'Oh,' he mouthed. 'Fancy you knowing a killer!'

'It was a long time ago.'

Sarah returned along with Ruth, carrying the tea things. 'You telling that story about poor Mrs Collins, are you, dear?'

'I was.'

'Oh, did I miss something?' asked Ruth.

'I'll tell you later,' offered her brother.

'Poor Mrs Collins,' said Sarah, putting a jug of milk down on the table. 'What we think Mr Snood is up to is nothing to what her son did to her.'

'It's bad enough,' erupted Ivan hotly. 'Snood's trying to fleece Miss Clatteridge of a fair price for her business. That's wrong whichever way you look at it, and in my opinion he should be strung up too!'

Mouths open at his furious outburst they all stared at him.

I wonder, thought Sarah, as she studied Ivan, if Agnes Clatteridge has any idea how much her employee cares for her? No, more than cares, loves her.

Shocked at his lack of restraint in front of this gathering, Ivan reddened. 'Well, er . . . 'tain't right, is it? It's not even as if Miss Clatteridge was left well off. She weren't, yer know. That father of hers left her in a right bad state, through . . . not taking care of his money when he was alive.'

George cleared his throat. 'You're quite right to be annoyed, Mr Simpson. After all, Miss Clatteridge is your employer and she's also been good to Maddie. I've not had the privilege of meeting her personally but from what Maddie tells us, she sounds a damn fine woman and doesn't deserve to be treated like this by anyone.'

'You're right, Dad,' Maddie agreed. 'No one deserves to be, 'specially not Miss Clatteridge. So what can we do about it?'

'I know what *I* can do,' said Ivan, scraping back his chair.

235

'Where are you going?' Maddie asked him, astonished.

He stood up. 'To see Snood, that's where.'

'Sit down, Mr Simpson,' ordered George. 'You're angry. It's best not to tackle something like this when your dander's up. See sense, man, and sit down. Let's discuss this, decide what best to do.'

'With all due respect, Mr Ashman, what is there ter discuss? All we have is rumours and hearsay. All of which I 'appen to believe are true.'

'And I agree with you, Mr Simpson,' said George, rising also. 'All my instincts tell me so. But we can't accuse him without . . .'

'We've no choice, Mr Ashman,' Ivan cut in. 'There ain't time, you see. Mr Snood is calling upon Miss Clatteridge for her answer on Saturday and it's Thursday today. That gives us a day. What can we do in a day that'll stop him? Not much that I can see. So I'm going to call on him, tell him what we know and that I'm going to tell Miss Clatteridge.'

'He'll laugh at you, Mr Simpson.'

Ivan's eyes narrowed. 'We'll see who's laughing when I've finished with him.'

'I'll come with you,' said George. 'I'll just get my coat.'

'Me too,' said Maddie, hurriedly rising.

'Can I come an' all?' urged Roy.

Sarah's face filled with horror. 'Roy, sit down,' she ordered. 'This is nothing to do with you. George, should you really be getting this involved? And you, Maddie . . .' She wrung her hands anxiously. 'Look, shouldn't we at least ask the authorities for their help?'

'There's nothing they can do,' said George. 'Mr Simpson and I will go and have a talk with Snood, see if we can make him see reason. Maybe once we've had a word he'll . . .'

Ivan raised his hand in dismissal. 'I'm grateful for your offers, all of you, but I feel it best I deal with this alone. You've your job to consider, Mr Ashman. Snood could take umbrage and cause trouble for you. Maddie, this is no business for a woman. I've nothing to lose but Miss Clatteridge has and that's all that concerns me. Thank you for the meal, Mrs Ashman. I'll see meself out.'

They all stared after him as he marched from the room and out of the house.

'What's the meaning of interrupting me at dinner?' snarled Snood. He glanced Ivan up and down scathingly, then fixed angry eyes on him. 'Well, man, what's so important that it couldn't wait 'til tomorrow? Miss Clatteridge that desperate, is she, to clinch our deal that she's sent you round? Well, you can tell her from me I don't do business with lackeys. So yer can scarper. I'll see her as arranged, Saturday afternoon at two.'

Ivan fought desperately to suppress his anger. 'Miss Clatteridge doesn't even know I'm here,' he said evenly.

Snood frowned quizzically. 'Well, why are you then?'

Ivan took a deep breath to steel himself. 'I want yer to drop yer offer.'

'What?'

'You 'eard me correct, Mr Snood, or I'll tell Miss Clatteridge what yer up to. I know, you see. I know all you've done just to get the place cheap from her. About the rumours. About paying that bloke to come calling and say what he did. And yer let it be known around the Undertakers' Association that Clatteridge's was all but yours before you'd even been to see Miss Clatteridge with yer offer. You were 'eard discussing it all outside our yard, just after yer left yer interview with her.' Ivan saw a flash of fear cross Mr Snood's face and, taking a deep breath, puffed out his chest. 'If you won't do as I ask then I'll tell Miss Clatteridge, so I will.'

Mr Snood grabbed his arm and dragged him outside, pulling the door to behind them. 'Now you listen here,' he snarled, wagging his finger, eyes glinting menacingly, 'you ain't got nothing on me. You can't prove nothing neither. Tell Miss Clatteridge, go on. I'm a businessman, you're just a twopenny ha'penny chippy.' A smirk crossed his lips. 'Let's see who she believes, eh? Let me tell you, it won't be you. You'd better start looking for somewhere else to work, 'cos you won't be working for me when I take over that place.'

'That don't bother me one bit, Mr Snood. What does is what you're trying to do to Miss Clatteridge. If yer don't drop yer offer, I'll take a leaf out of your book. I can spread rumours too. I'll let people know how you use cheap wood and charge over the odds for best. Dyed the right colour and polished up, most of the bereaved don't notice the difference, do they? And what about brass handles? I'll put it round how yer pass off brass-plated for solid. And shrouds – using old ones you've took off bodies before the lid is closed and charging for 'em as though they were new. I could go on, Mr Snood. I've bin in this business all me life, I know what other operators get up to.

'One thing I'll say for Mr Clatteridge: he might have been a hard man to work for, but he never did 'ote so diabolical. And whether you have or not won't mek no difference betime I've finished. People listen to rumours as you should know, Mr Snood.'

'Why you . . . How dare you threaten me?'

'I dare, Mr Snood. But yer wrong, I ain't threatening yer. *I will do it.* I'll ruin your business if you go ahead with this offer.'

Mr Snood's face turned purple with rage. He raised one fist ready to strike.

'Do that, Mr Snood, and I'll make such a noise it'll bring Mrs Snood running. I'll tell her it all then, let's see what she has to say.'

'You bastard!' Snood erupted, dropping his arm and unclenching his fist. 'Get out of me sight,' he hissed.

'Not 'til I have yer promise. Though whether that's worth much I'm not sure, considering.'

'I . . . I promise,' he muttered.

'What was that, Mr Snood? I didn't quite 'ear yer.'

'I promise,' he snarled, slightly louder.

'Thank you, Mr Snood. I'll expect yer to inform Miss Clatteridge of yer change of heart first thing in the morning. If not . . . well, yer know what'll happen. Nice doing business with yer. Goodnight.'

And Ivan marched off, leaving an infuriated Snood glaring after him.

Maddie arrived first thing in the morning to find Agnes very upset.

'Are you all right, Miss Clatteridge?' she asked, shutting the door behind her as she took off her coat. A thought suddenly struck her. 'Mr Simpson . . . nothing's happened to him, has it?' After his departure last night, she had lain awake worrying over what had transpired, mind conjuring up all sorts of fears. She hadn't caught sight of him as she had crossed the yard, only Oswald. He had been sweeping up. As soon as she had stepped through the archway, he had stopped what he was doing, leaned on his brush and leered at her. Maddie had lowered her head and hurried away, painfully aware his eyes had not left her until she disappeared inside the kitchen.

Agnes raised her head, frowning. 'Mr Simpson appeared well this morning when I saw him. Why do you ask?'

'Oh . . . er . . . no reason. Just the first thing that struck me. You're upset about something, aren't you, Miss Clatteridge?'

She sighed. 'Yes, I am. When I came down this morning I found this had been pushed through the letter box,' she said, flapping a piece of paper in her hand. 'Must have been delivered while I was still sleeping. I can't understand it, Maddie. It's from Mr Snood. He's withdrawn his offer.' She sank down on a kitchen chair, rubbing her hand worriedly over her chin. 'He doesn't give any explanation.'

How Maddie managed to prevent herself from shrieking in jubilation was a mystery to her. It did hurt her to see Miss Clatteridge so upset and bewildered but she would have been more so had she known exactly what Mr Snood had been trying to do. God bless you, Ivan, she thought. I don't know what you said or did but it obviously worked. She wanted to run over to him now, find out whether he knew about the letter, congratulate him on whatever it was he had done. Then she wanted to go and tell her family to put their minds at rest. But doing anything would alert Miss Clatteridge and then explanations would have to be given.

All Maddie could do was say, 'Oh, Miss Clatteridge, I'm so sorry.'

'I wonder if I should go and see Mr Snood?' mused Agnes. 'Maybe this is a ploy to get me to consider dropping the price even further. I'll have to explain I can't. If I go any lower . . .'

'Oh, no!' Maddie cried, then realised her mistake. 'I mean, you might embarrass him, Miss Clatteridge. Maybe even at the low price he was offering, when he worked it all out he couldn't afford to go ahead.'

Agnes looked at her thoughtfully for a moment. 'You could be right. I assumed he knew exactly what he could afford when he came to see me. Oh, dear, what am I going to do now?'

'Something will turn up, Miss Clatteridge,' she said, more confidently than she felt. Something had to, she prayed. It wasn't fair that this lovely lady had so much to worry about. 'Someone else will come forward. There's someone somewhere who wants to buy a place like this. It's just finding them, that's all. Maybe the right people haven't heard it's for sale. Why don't you ask the agent for his advice?'

'I could. Yes, I could indeed. I know he's been trying his best for a sale but I could talk to him about what else we could do to arouse interest. Yes, I will, Maddie. I won't let Mr Snood's withdrawal get me down. Something will turn up just like you said.'

Maddie hoped so for Miss Clatteridge's sake.

# Chapter Nineteen

Maddie arrived for work the next morning to be greeted by Oswald. Usually he was somewhere around when she entered the gates and would stop what he was doing and watch her closely. As she slipped through the gap today he was immediately beside her.

'Mornin', Maddie,' he said, falling into step beside her. 'I'm off to the music hall ternight. Got tickets, I have.'

She slipped on an icy patch and he grabbed her arm to steady her which she hurriedly pulled free, feeling distaste at his touch.

'That's nice for you,' she replied evenly, quickening her pace. 'I hope you enjoy yourself.'

'I will. Fancy comin'?'

She stopped abruptly. 'With you?'

He frowned, puzzled. 'Yeah, why not?'

'Oswald, you're much younger than I am.'

'Not by that much. Anyway, don't bother me none.'

'Well, it does me.'

The thought of going to a music hall was appealing, but the idea of going anywhere with Oswald repelled her. Besides, to accept an invitation from any man was beyond her. She still held too many feelings for the man she had lost. Maddie knew it was stupid of her, Josh was gone from her life forever, but she felt that to look at any other man in a romantic way would make her somehow disloyal.

'Thank you for the offer but I'm busy tonight,' she told Oswald now. 'I'm sure someone else would be glad to accept.'

'Wadda about termorra then? We could go for a drink.'

'I'm busy then too, Oswald.'

He grabbed her arm and pulled her to a halt. 'What's up, Maddie? Ain't I good enough fer the likes of you or summat?'

'It's not that at all,' she said sharply, indignantly wrenching free her arm.

'Well, why won't yer come then?'

'I've already told you, you're too young and I'm busy.'

'I don't believe yer.'

He was right not to.

'Oswald, if you don't stop pestering me, I will mention it to Mr Simpson.'

Thankfully she arrived at the kitchen door and managed to disappear inside before he could proposition her further. She would have to avoid him as much as possible in future before she ran out of excuses and had no option but to tell him the truth. Despite her dislike of Oswald, she didn't relish the thought of hurting his feelings.

Later that morning Agnes and she both happened to be in the kitchen when there was a knock on the door and Ivan came in. He looked pleased.

'Miss Clatteridge, I've just had a visit from Wilson's chippy.'

'Wilson's?' queried Agnes. 'Oh, yes, Wilson's are the undertakers in Evington. What did he want?'

'Our 'elp. Mr Wilson personally sent him. Seems they've got four come at once.'

'Four? Really! How fortunate for them.' Agnes's tone held no sarcasm, just genuine pleasure for a fellow undertaker. 'What do they want with us?'

'One of the four is from a monied family. They want a top quality mahogany with solid brass trimmings. Engraved too. Want to know if we can muckle one up quick smart, 'cos with the others they ain't got the time but didn't want to turn the work away. They heard we weren't busy so come here first.'

From the corner of her eye Agnes suddenly spotted the bewildered expression on Maddie's face and laughed. 'They want us to make them a coffin, my dear. Their carpenter won't be able to manage four together. It's a pity it's just the coffin they want. The full burial would have brought in much-needed money. Never mind.' She turned her attention back to Ivan. 'I hope you told him we would, Mr Simpson?'

'I did. I checked out our materials and we've more than enough to do the job. If I start on it now and work through, I can have it done by the morning. They want it vanning to their premises before nine so they can tek it up to the house ter put the body in for viewing.'

'They want us to deliver it too?'

He nodded.

'Good. We'll charge for that as well. Thank you, Mr Simpson.'

When he had left Agnes turned to Maddie, rubbing her hands. 'Better than a kick in the teeth. Isn't that what people say when something small but good happens?'

She laughed. 'It certainly is.'

Maddie was in good spirits the next morning. Talk at home still centred mainly around the new arrival in three months' time. Last night names had been discussed. There were several possibilities but nothing definite had been decided. There was plenty of time for that, Sarah had laughingly told them all as she had begun her task of balling up a cone of white wool which she had purchased to begin knitting the baby's first matinee coat.

Ruth had again requested Maddie's presence while she got ready to go out for a night with her girlfriends to a tea dance held regularly in rooms in Churchgate. 'It's such fun,' Ruth had told her, 'and you don't have to dance if you don't want to as there's plenty of tables just to sit at and chat.' But Maddie wouldn't be left sitting long, she had been assured. The nice men who went there would be swarming around her, especially if she wore that posh frock that hadn't seen daylight since she had taken it home. And when she did get around to having her hair cut she'd be pestered mercilessly. Maddie thought her sister was exaggerating her chances but kept her thoughts to herself. Ruth was only trying to be sisterly. Maybe one night Maddie would join her, but not yet, she wasn't ready.

On arriving at the yard that morning she had popped her head inside first to check for Oswald's presence. Thankfully there was no sign of him and she rushed across cobbles before there was.

Agnes arrived moments after, dressed in her outdoor coat, announcing she was taking Maddie's advice and travelling into Leicester to visit the agent, wanting to arrive early to ensure an interview. She left straight away, telling Maddie to take the morning quietly, which Maddie thought rather nice of her.

She was just mashing herself a pot of tea, having decided that she would busy herself giving the kitchen a thorough clean while Agnes was out on business, when she heard the sound of galloping hooves on the cobbles in the yard and the screech of the box cart as it came to an abrupt halt.

Before she even had time to put down the kettle she was holding and investigate what was happening, she heard Ivan shouting urgently.

'Miss Clatteridge, Maddie, come quick! Oswald! Where are yer, Oswald?'

Almost dropping the kettle Maddie wrenched open the door, shot through it and out into the yard. The box cart was parked askew, Ned snorting breathlessly, streams of warm breath billowing from his flaring nostrils in the icy air.

'What on earth has happened?' she cried, arriving at the side of Ivan who was desperately trying to prise open the lid covering the back end of the box cart.

'Blast this, it's stuck. Oh, there yer are, Maddie,' he cried, relieved. 'There's been a terrible accident. Oh, just terrible.

Where's that lazy so and so . . . Oswald!' he shouted. 'Get out 'ere quick and bring a crowbar with yer.'

Oswald appeared, wiping sleep from his eyes. It was obvious what he had been doing while he thought his boss was away for a couple of hours. 'What's up?' he asked, stifling a yawn.

'Where's the crowbar?'

'What crowbar?'

'The one I asked yer . . . Oh, never mind, I'll be quicker gettin' it meself.' As Maddie and Oswald looked on bemused, Ivan darted into the workshed and moments later reappeared, a crowbar in his hand. Like a man possessed he rammed the end of the jemmy into the crack at the side of the lid and fought frantically to free it.

'Ivan, what is going on?' Maddie demanded.

'I told yer, a terrible accident. We might need the doctor.'

'Doctor?'

Just then the lid shot up. 'Thank God!' he proclaimed. 'Oswald, 'elp me slide this coffin out and tek it into the Chapel of Rest. Sharp, lad.'

Maddie's eyes flew to the coffin. Just the end of it was visible, but she still recognised it as the one Ivan had made especially for Wilson's. She had been reluctant to view it due to its morbid association but Ivan had been so proud of his swift handiwork she felt unable to hurt him by refusing. She felt he had been right to be pleased with his efforts. Considering the time in which he had produced it, the coffin was a beautiful piece of carpentry. He was indeed talented at his craft.

'I thought you were delivering that this morning?' she said. 'Why have you brought it back?'

Ivan had managed to slide the coffin partway out of the back of the box cart and was struggling under its weight. 'Not now, Maddie,' he said breathlessly. 'Oswald, get the end, quick! Now, lift. Watch out, you're dropping your end . . .'

His sallow, acne-marked face contorted, Oswald replied, annoyed, 'I know! It's bloody heavy, that's why.'

'Well, it's bound to be. There's a man inside. Now lift higher before he suffers any more damage when we drop him on the ground.' Ivan flashed him a warning. 'Oi! And curb yer language. There's a lady present.'

Maddie was staring, astounded. There was a man inside the coffin? 'He's not dead, is he?' she uttered.

'I 'ope not, Maddie. If he is then I'm the cause.'

Her mind raced frantically but they had reached the door to the Chapel of Rest and Maddie could ask no more questions.

The room was near pitch dark, the black curtains at the small windows tightly closed, and Maddie, never having been in this room before, shuddered as she felt its eeriness envelop her, acutely conscious of its use. She stood stiffly in the doorway as Ivan and Oswald, hampered by the dim light and the weight they were carrying, struggled over to the long black-covered trestle in the centre of the small room and heaved the coffin on top.

'Light the candles, Maddie,' Ivan ordered as he slid off the lid and laid it on the floor. 'Can't see a thing in here. There's matches in that little cupboard just by the side of yer. Oswald, pull back the curtains, we need more light. Maddie, will yer hurry?' he snapped.

'Oh!' she exclaimed. To light the candles would mean having to enter the room. Frozen to the spot, she shuddered violently.

'For goodness' sake, Maddie, what's the matter with yer?' Ivan scolded as he shot over to the cupboard and took out the matches. 'There's nothin' 'ere ter frighten yer.' He grabbed her arm, pulling her inside. 'It's just a room, Maddie, and even if there wa' a dead body in 'ere, the dead can't 'urt yer.' His voice dropped worriedly. ''Sides, I'm hopin' this one ain't dead.'

He let go of her arm. As Oswald drew the curtains, dim

light filtered through the small glass panes and from where Maddie stood she could see to the back of the room where there was a long cabinet draped in black cloth on top of which stood a large silver cross, to either side two huge brass candlesticks. Ivan struck a match and lit the thick white candles. Flames flickered and sprang into life, shadows dancing on the walls. Again Maddie shuddered. The light, although welcome, was still not enough to lift her feeling of absolute revulsion. She didn't want to be in here.

'Shall I . . . shall I go and make some tea?' she offered as a means of escape.

'No, Maddie,' Ivan erupted. 'For God's sake, will yer get over 'ere and tek a look at this man?'

Seeing she wasn't about to obey him, Ivan sprang over, grabbed her arm and dragged her across to the top end of the coffin. 'What d'yer think, Maddie?' he asked. 'Do we need a doctor or what?'

With a great effort she forced herself to look down. As her eyes fell on the face of the man in the coffin she gave a gasp then a piercing scream. Simultaneously the man's eyes flickered open to fix on the face peering down at him, flames from the candles lighting it grotesquely. Eyes wide, his head lifted slightly and his hands came into contact with the padded sides of the coffin. His mouth fell open, face contorting in terror as the knowledge of where he was lying struck him full force. 'I'm dead. Oh, God, I'm dead,' he moaned, and slumped back, eyes shut.

Maddie screamed again. 'Oh, no! NO! NO!' she cried, bursting into a torrent of hysterical sobs. Wrapping her arms around herself, she rocked backwards and forwards, Ivan and Oswald staring at her in shock.

'What is going on in here?' a voice demanded.

Ivan and Oswald both spun around to see Agnes framed in the doorway. 'What's wrong with Maddie?' she asked, face wreathed in worry as she advanced into the room.

'Dunno,' muttered Ivan, totally at a loss. He had known

Maddie had been extremely reluctant to take a look at the man but this reaction from her was utterly unexpected.

Agnes hurried across to the distraught young woman, putting an arm around her shoulders. 'It's all right, Maddie dear, I'll get you out of here,' she said. As Agnes prepared to guide the sobbing Maddie away she flashed a frosty glance at Ivan. 'My instructions were disobeyed,' she said crossly. 'I specifically requested that Maddie was to have nothing to do with this side of the business. So what is she doing in here? And, for that matter, what is that coffin here for?' She raised her free hand in warning. 'Let me see to Maddie first, then I'll be back. And I'll be expecting answers.'

Minutes later a shocked and trembling Maddie sat perched in the armchair by the parlour fire, staring down into the cup of tea she was cradling in her hands. Agnes was sitting opposite, eyeing her in concern. 'Are you feeling better, dear?' she asked kindly. 'It's a good job I returned. It was threatening rain and I came back for my umbrella to be on the safe side. I can't apologise enough to you, Maddie. I gave strict instructions you were never to be asked to do anything connected with the burial side of the business. I don't know what Mr Simpson was thinking of, really I don't.' She stepped over to Maddie and placed a hand on her shoulder. 'Will you be all right for a moment while I go and find out what is going on? I'm concerned about that coffin not being delivered. We made a firm commitment. I must go and see to things. I won't be long, I promise.'

Without lifting her head, Maddie nodded.

It was a good twenty minutes before Agnes returned. 'How are you feeling now? Better, I hope?' she said, sitting back down, her hands in her lap.

Sniffing, Maddie lifted her head. 'Yes, I am, thank you. I'm so sorry for causing a scene, Miss Clatteridge. I don't know what came over me.' She paused momentarily. 'Is he . . . is he dead?' she whispered.

'Dead? Who? Oh, the man in the coffin. No, far from it.

He's in the kitchen, having a cup of tea with Mr Simpson. He suffered no more than a bump on the head. He fainted, that was all, when he realised what he was lying in. And I suspect seeing you peering at him didn't help. Must have thought you were an angel or something. He was sure he had died.' She fought to control the mirth that was building. 'Oh dear, if the situation weren't so terrible it would be very amusing.'

'It seems Mr Simpson, in his rush to get the coffin delivered on time, was pushing Ned too hard. The wheels of the cart slipped on an icy puddle and it skidded sideways. The back end caught a ladder which unfortunately this man was climbing. He fell off, hit his head on the cobbles and passed out. Poor Mr Simpson thought he had killed him. That part of town is usually quite busy in the morning but for some reason today there was no one around. Mr Simpson did the only thing he could think of which was to put the man inside the coffin and bring him back here. Let me assure you, apart from a bump on his head, Mr Jenks is no worse for his experience, thank goodness . . .' Her voice trailed off at the look on Maddie's face. 'What is it, my dear?'

'You . . . you did say his name was Mr Jenks?' she uttered.

Agnes nodded. 'Joshua Jenks he introduced himself as. Why?' She frowned. 'Do you know him?'

Maddie froze. She hadn't been wrong then. It *was* Josh. Her Josh. The last person she had ever expected to see again. She nodded slowly. 'Yes, I do.'

Agnes stood up. 'Then you must come and greet him properly.'

'Oh, no,' cried Maddie, alarmed.

'Whyever not?'

'I . . . I just can't.'

'Can't? Are you on bad terms or something?'

'No . . . not exactly. Well, I don't know. But Jo— Mr Jenks might not be pleased to see me, that's all.'

Agnes sank down on her chair again, eyeing Maddie

closely. 'It's not for me to pry, Maddie, but from what I know of you I can't imagine anyone not being pleased to see you. Did something unpleasant happen between you, is that it?'

'Yes,' came the low response. Maddie locked eyes with Agnes. 'We were engaged to be married. Something happened which forced us to part.'

'Oh, I see.' Agnes observed her thoughtfully for a moment. 'And you still think a lot of Mr Jenks, don't you?'

She nodded.

'The fact is, you still love him?'

She nodded again.

Agnes sighed in distress, deeply aware of Maddie's pain, which was so apparent she could almost reach out and grab it. She realised how little, if anything, she knew of Maddie's past. As weeks had passed, with them working closely alongside, her fondness for Maddie had grown and she had come to regard her employee very highly. Agnes corrected herself. No, Maddie was now more than an employee to her, she had become a friend. Seeing her so obviously grieved was troubling.

The man Maddie thought so much of was in the kitchen recovering from his accident; very shortly he would leave and probably their paths might never cross again. What did Agnes do? Did she let them walk away from each other or did she bring them together? The burden of responsibility was heavy. What she did now could have a dramatic effect on Maddie's life. Was it her place to intervene or should she do nothing and leave Maddie's future for fate to sort out. Was it not fate, though, that had brought Mr Jenks to this house?

Agnes made a decision. Whether right or wrong, she just knew she could not sit back and do nothing.

She rose and headed for the door.

'Where are you going?' Maddie asked.

'I have something I must do,' was Agnes's matter-of-fact response.

Maddie heard the door click shut and her heart thudded painfully. Only feet away from her, on the other side of the wall, was the man she loved more than life itself. In moments he would be gone. She felt a great urge to run to him and beg his forgiveness for what her mother had done to them. It was taking all the courage she could muster to control it, but somehow she must. There was no point in her announcing her presence to Josh. What good would it do? He was a married man with a child, maybe two now for all she knew. Presenting herself to him was bound to rake up the past, bring back memories he had put behind him. It would be unforgivable of her to cause Josh further unnecessary suffering when enough had been dealt him already. His mother had said he was happy now and that was how she must leave him. He was getting on with his life, so must she.

She heard the door click as it opened, felt someone entering the room. 'Has he gone?' she faltered, fearing the answer.

When no reply came she lifted her head and turned towards the door. She gasped in shock, jumping up. 'Oh!' she exclaimed.

Slowly Josh strode towards her to stand just inches away. 'Maddie?' he said. 'Oh, Maddie. It really is you.' His deep blue eyes bored into hers, drinking her in. 'I couldn't believe it when Miss Clatteridge told me you were here. I thought I'd dreamed I'd seen yer. But it *was* you . . . I never imagined it could be. It was you looking down on me. Oh, Maddie, Maddie, me darlin', I never thought I'd see you again.' He took one more tentative step towards her. 'You don't know how long I've prayed this would happen, that somehow we'd meet up again. You . . . you are pleased to see me? Please tell me you are, Maddie?'

She was far too stunned to speak so she nodded.

He covered the final distance between them and threw his arms around her, crushing her to him. 'I've missed yer so much. Not a minute 'as gone by when I haven't been thinking of yer.'

Maddie's mind was whirling, not believing what she was hearing. She was having terrible difficulty convincing herself that these were really Josh's arms enveloping her. She eased herself slightly away from him and looked up into his face. 'You wanted to see me? But, Josh, how could you after what happened? My mother . . .' Her head drooped. 'How can you ever forgive me?'

'Forgive you! There's nothin' to forgive yer for. Look at me, Maddie. Look at me, I said.'

She lifted her head and gazed into his eyes.

'When my mother told me what yours had said to her, I was devastated, Maddie. My whole world caved in like my very soul had died. I knew you wouldn't just up and leave me, Maddie. I knew your mother had everything to do with it. She was lying when she told me mother you'd accused me of forcing meself on yer, that I got yer pregnant on purpose to get my hands on her business.

'I went round to see her, begged her to tell me where yer were. She laughed, Maddie. Told me that if I thought I'd allow her daughter to marry a low-life like me, then I was mad as well as stupid. I begged her then, Maddie, pleaded with her like a madman not to get the baby adopted. I was its father, I said, bring it to me. My family would help me raise it.' He stopped and Maddie felt him shudder. 'She said that what she decided to do with the baby was nothing to do with me. She would see me in hell before she lived in the same town as my bastard. She wasn't risking people ever finding out and pointing the finger at her.'

'Oh, God!' Maddie groaned.

'She slammed the door in me face then, Maddie, telling me that if I ever dared show up again she'd call the police.' He felt her body sag against his and tightened his grip on her. 'I was like a man possessed. I looked everywhere for yer. Everywhere I could think of. But there was no sign, nothing. I locked meself away for days afterwards. Wouldn't leave the house. My mother was beside herself and so were the rest of me family. They didn't know what to do for me. I couldn't eat or sleep. All I did was cry. I couldn't carry on like that. I knew I had to get away, start afresh. So I came here.

'But I never gave up hope, Maddie. Every night I've prayed to God he'd somehow send you to me.' He looked down at her, the immense feeling he still held for her plain to see. 'And He's answered me, ain't He?' He eyed her beseechingly. 'Maddie, tell me you still love me? Tell me you still want me as bad as I do you? Please, Maddie, please?'

'Oh, I do, Josh, I do. There's never been anyone else for me but you. I just can't believe you're here. I'm worried I'll wake up and it'll all have been a dream. Oh, Josh,' she said, trembling, fat tears rolling down her face. She buried her head in his shoulder and sobbed.

'Don't cry, Maddie. Please don't cry,' he whispered, distraught.

'I can't help it.'

After several long moments she pulled slightly back and looked up at him. 'I went to see your mother, Josh, just before I came to Leicester a couple of months ago. She told me what mine had done. That's why I left Market Harborough. I'm living with my father and his family now. That's another story.' She stopped abruptly, eyeing him, afraid to ask him a question, terrified of the answer. 'Your mother . . . she told me you were . . . that you were married with a baby on the way. Are . . . are you married, Josh?'

He shook his head vigorously. 'No, Maddie, I'm not. The only woman I would ever marry is the one I'm holding now. Me mother was angry, Maddie. She was hurt and wanted to hurt you for the pain you'd caused me. Don't think badly of her, she was only trying to protect me.'

'I don't think badly of her, Josh. I know she loves you. But when she told me what she did it was like someone had ripped my heart out. I tried so hard to forget you, get on with my life.'

His eyes narrowed in alarm. 'And did you?'

She shook her head. 'No, I couldn't. My feelings for you are just as strong as they've ever been.'

He leaned forward then and kissed her, long, deep and passionately. She responded willingly, savouring the feel and the smell of him, the sense of belonging inside his arms. Finally he gathered her to him again, crushing her so tightly she could hardly breathe

'You'll marry me, Maddie. Now, right now. I'll not wait, not risk losing you again. You will, won't yer?'

Great joy exploded within her. 'Yes!' she cried. 'Yes, Josh. Yes.'

They stood for a moment, locked in each other's arms.

'Maddie,' he said softly, voice thick with emotion, 'there's something I need to ask yer.'

Her heart thumped painfully. She knew what this was about.

'Our baby, Maddie? What was it?'

'A girl,' she whispered. 'She was beautiful, Josh. She was perfect in every way.'

'Oh, Maddie,' he sighed painfully. 'Your mother had no right to do what she did. No right at all.' His tone lowered savagely. 'How could she give her to strangers? Could we get her back, Maddie? Will your mother tell us where she is?'

'Oh, Josh, if only she would! If only it was possible to get her back.'

He stepped slightly away, hands gripping her arms, face filled with urgency. 'There must be a way. If your mother won't tell us, someone else must know what happened to her. Someone must, Maddie. After we're married, the two of us will go and see your mother. She'll have to tell us then. She's our child, *ours*, and your mother's no right to keep her away from us. Not when she must know where she is.'

Brightness filled Maddie's eyes as hope which she'd thought never to feel again flowered within her. She had Josh back. With their daughter too, her life would be complete.

Only one thing marred her joy. The thought of confronting her mother again, even with Josh beside her, was daunting. But if it meant there was a slim chance of getting her baby back she was prepared to face anything.

George shifted uncomfortably in his chair. He'd always known an occasion like this would come, but not out of the blue. He wasn't prepared. For any man to give permission for a beloved daughter to wed was hard. It was proving extremely difficult for George. He felt that he was just getting to know his eldest child, making up for so many lost years, and now it seemed he was about to lose her again.

He hadn't known of this man's existence until fifteen minutes or so ago when Maddie had bounded into the room, radiant as he'd never seen her before. She had been unable to control her excitement and had blurted out the fact that she had someone with her she wanted them to meet.

He had to admit, though, his first impression of Joshua Jenks was very favourable. Instinct told him the young man was honest and genuine and there was no doubting the depth of his feeling for Maddie. Neither was George in any doubt of Maddie's feeling for Joshua. They both loved each other deeply. In the light of that he knew he had no right to refuse or ask for a delay, and anyway Maddie was above the age of consent. Josh did not have to be here at all to ask for her father's permission. It told George much about the man.

When Josh had asked to talk to him privately, Sarah had immediately despatched a reluctant Roy off to a friend's house then ushered the girls into the kitchen to make some tea. They were in there now and it wouldn't surprise George if they had their ears to the door.

He took a deep breath. 'So, Mr Jenks, you want to marry my daughter, you say?'

'Yes, I do, sir.' A nervous Josh raked his fingers through his thatch of hair and inched to the edge of his chair. 'I know this might seem very sudden to you, Mr Ashman, but I've known Maddie for four years or more. We had an understanding. But . . . well, sir, her mother didn't take kindly to me and we were forced to part. Neither of us wanted that, but we had no choice. When I met up with Maddie again today it was like a miracle, for both of us, sir. Our feelings for each other hadn't changed a bit. Neither of us wants to wait. We can't see the point. That's, 'a course, if we have your permission?'

So, thought George, that was why Maddie had come to Leicester. Harriet had been up to her usual tricks. How come he wasn't surprised? He was hurt, though. Hurt for Maddie and what she must have suffered due to her own mother's boundless selfishness.

'Can you provide for Maddie well enough?' he asked.

'I can, sir. Until now I was quite happy to earn enough to keep me going and put a bit past. I'll work harder now I've Maddie. Well, I've good reason to.'

'And what is it you do?'

'Window cleaning, Mr Ashman. I'm a machine mechanic by trade, but when things happened between meself and Maddie I decided a change was what I needed. When I first came to Leicester I took anything I could, then I was lucky enough to be asked if I fancied cleaning a few windows to help a man out with his round and I liked it so I stayed. I've got me own round now. Cost me a fiver and it's bin worth every penny. You're yer own boss, see, Mr Ashman, you can set yer own pace. I intend to build it up. I can afford ter rent us a little house. Nothing grand, but that won't be for long, I can assure yer.'

George nodded, impressed.

In his nervousness, Josh inched further to the edge of the

chair and nearly fell off. He shuffled back, embarrassed, hoping his future father-in-law hadn't noticed. 'Mr Ashman,' he blurted, 'I love your daughter. I'm honest, reliable, and I'll be the best husband to her, I promise, 'til the day I die.'

'Seems fair enough to me. But let me assure you, Mr Jenks, should you not, you'll have me to contend with. Like you, I love my daughter.'

Josh stared. 'You're giving your permission, Mr Ashman?'

George rose, extending his hand. 'I'm giving my blessing. Welcome to the family. You can call me Dad.'

In the kitchen Maddie was pacing worriedly.

'Maddie, for goodness' sake, will you stop that? You're wearing a trench in the slabs. And, Ruth, get your ear off that door.'

'I can't hear anything anyway,' she grumbled, and looked at her sister in awe. 'He's so good-looking, Maddie. No wonder you weren't keen to come to the dance with him in the closet.'

'Ruth, stop being coarse,' her mother scolded. 'But I have to agree, Maddie, he certainly is a handsome man and very well-mannered. You had an understanding, you say, and drifted apart and met up again for the first time today in well over a year?'

Maddie stopped her pacing and nodded.

'Like one of them penny romances,' said Ruth, sighing longingly.

'Hardly romantic,' said Sarah. 'Maddie's just told us he landed up in a coffin, remember. That must have been terrible for him,' she said, fighting to control her mirth. 'And poor Mr Simpson, thinking he had killed him. Oh, dear.' She couldn't stop herself then. The laughter was so infectious they all joined in.

'What's so funny?' said George as he entered the kitchen. 'This is supposed to be a solemn occasion when a man asks a father for his daughter's hand in marriage. That tea mashed yet, Sarah?'

'Did you agree, Dad? Did you?' pleaded Maddie.

He purposely eyed her blankly, but there was a twinkle in his eyes. 'Pardon? Oh, I forgot about that. Well, you'd better come through and ask your young man yourself, hadn't you?' he said matter-of-factly as he turned and headed back out.

'George!' Sarah called. 'Oh, your father,' she erupted, annoyed. 'He's enjoying keeping us on tenterhooks. Quick,' she said to Ruth. 'Bring the tea tray through. Come on, Maddie,' she ordered, grabbing her arm and propelling her after her father.

# Chapter Twenty

'What about this material, Maddie? It's such a rich cream and the fabric would look lovely made up just as you described.'

Maddie came over to join Agnes and fingered the material. 'Yes, I do like that. You've made my choice, Miss Clatteridge, thank you. I want six yards, please,' she said to the assistant behind the counter of Marshall and Snelgrove's drapery counter. 'It's not curtain material, is it?' Maddie whispered to Agnes.

She giggled. 'I don't think so. If it is, does it matter? It's just what you wanted.'

'Yes, it is. It's perfect.'

The material was measured out and parcelled up and another fifteen minutes was spent choosing cottons, hooks and eyes and braiding to adorn the dress Maddie was going to make. Her wedding dress.

'Sarah is helping me to cut it out tonight.' A thought suddenly struck her. 'Would you like to come around, Miss Clatteridge, and lend a hand? Your help would be much appreciated.'

Agnes stared at her astounded. 'Are you sure you want me to come? What about your family? Shouldn't you ask them first?'

'Why? They'll be delighted to meet you at last. They feel they know you already as I speak of you so often.' Maddie's eyes twinkled. 'All nice things let me assure you, Miss Clatteridge.'

'I'm glad to hear that,' she replied, smiling.

'So will you come? This is the ideal opportunity. It'll be nice for you to meet my family before the wedding day.' Her face suddenly grew worried. 'That's if you don't mind lending a hand, of course?'

'Maddie, I'd be honoured too. Thank you for asking me. I'm quite adept with a needle, you know.'

'Yes, I did know. I've seen samples of your handiwork, Miss Clatteridge, and if I say it myself, I thought I was a neat sewer but you're much better than me.'

'Oh, go on, there's no need for such flattery, Maddie dear. I'll still help sew your dress without such praise.'

She laughed. 'I was speaking the truth. Oh, look,' she said, stopping before a sign pointing to the shop's refreshment area. 'There are plenty of free tables. Have we time for a cup of tea? My treat. My father gave me some money towards my trousseau, I'm sure he won't mind my squandering a few pennies of it. I've spent all my savings on accessories. I do feel extravagant. Maybe I should have made do with second-hand.'

'Second-hand? Not on your wedding day surely, Maddie? If you hadn't had the money saved that would be different.'

She smiled brightly. 'Yes it would, wouldn't it? I do want to look nice for Josh.'

Nice? thought Agnes. Maddie would look stunning. She was such a pretty girl with a figure for which she herself would give anything. Why did Maddie always undervalue herself?

'Well, what about this tea?' she said, cutting into Agnes's thoughts.

'Pardon? Oh, er . . .'

Maddie eyed her anxiously. 'Have I suggested something I shouldn't have, Miss Clatteridge? I do appreciate your letting me shop during working hours. Have I overstepped my position? If I have, I'm very sorry.'

'Nothing of the sort,' Agnes said sharply. 'Anyway it was

at my insistence we came out. I was being selfish. I wanted to help you choose your wedding dress material and the other things you needed to buy.' She wondered if Maddie realised how exciting their excursion into town had been for her. 'It's just that . . . well, I've never actually taken tea out before.' She had never been shopping like this before either, but did not want to confess that, she felt embarrassed enough voicing her last declaration.

Maddie stared at her. 'What, never, Miss Clatteridge?'

She cleared her throat. 'No. Father didn't approve.'

'Well, if it's any consolation, I only have once or twice. My mother didn't approve either.' She saw the strange look Agnes was giving her. Of course, she had mentioned her mother for the first time. She knew Agnes assumed Sarah wasn't her real mother because she had always addressed her by her Christian name. Agnes must presume that Maddie's own mother was dead and that her father had remarried. Oh, how complicated life had become. She didn't feel it was her place to inform Agnes of her father's and Sarah's situation, nor did she feel she could cover up her slip by elaborate lies. All she decided to say was, 'Sarah is my father's second wife. My own mother lives in Market Harborough. Let's be daring and have tea.'

'This really is delicious, Maddie dear. I'm so glad you persuaded me to come in.'

'Have another scone?' offered Maddie, pushing the half-empty plate of cakes towards her.

'Oh, no, I couldn't really. I've had two already.' Agnes gazed around her. After they had given their order the seats around them had started to fill. Next to her sat a couple, obviously very much in love by the way they were acting with each other. 'I wonder,' she said wistfully, not realising she was voicing her thoughts out loud, 'if anyone will ever care for me enough to want to hold my hand over a table in public?'

Maddie looked at her. There is already someone who cares for you very deeply and would be only too willing to do that, she thought. But she couldn't say as much.

'Never give up hope, Miss Clatteridge,' she said. 'I never thought anyone would love me as much as Josh does.'

'Really? You surprise me, Maddie. I'd have thought you had many beaux chasing after you. I think I *will* have another scone. They really are very light.'

'What are you going to wear for my wedding, Miss Clatteridge?'

'Oh, my wool dress, I expect.' She picked up a scone, put it on her plate and began to butter it. 'I hadn't given it any thought, too engrossed in your plans.' Her thin face beamed. 'I can't tell you how happy I am for you, my dear.' She stopped her buttering, eyes glazing distantly. 'It's like a fairy story, isn't it? Your meeting up again so unexpectedly.' She resumed her buttering. 'Josh's bump on the head has gone down now, I trust, Maddie, and he's no worse for his ordeal?'

She laughed. 'None. He actually thinks the whole thing quite funny. He tells me he would have suffered any amount of damage to have found me again – although he did say he'd sooner Mr Simpson had slung him across his shoulder to get him back to the parlour instead of what he did do.'

Amusement sparked in Agnes's eyes. 'Yes, well, I don't blame him.'

'Thank you, Miss Clatteridge.'

'What for?'

'For what you did. I wouldn't be getting married if you hadn't intervened.'

'You've already thanked me, Maddie dear. Several times, in fact. Now please let that be the end of it. I did take a risk in telling Mr Jenks you were in the other room and I was concerned matters could have turned out very differently. I'm glad to say they didn't.'

'So am I.'

Agnes made to take a bite of her scone but changed her mind and asked, 'Will you be wanting to leave me after the wedding, Maddie?'

She frowned. 'Leave you? Oh, no, Miss Clatteridge. The day I leave you is the day you leave for Scarborough. That's providing of course, you are still happy to employ me? Josh and I have talked about this and he is quite all right about my working. He's happy to go along with whatever I want to do.'

Agnes sighed in relief. 'I was dreading the thought of losing you, my dear, although pleased by the circumstances.' She leaned over and patted Maddie's hand. 'From what I've seen of him, I approve very much.'

A warm glow filled Maddie. The opinions of those close to her mattered very much and that included Miss Clatteridge. Her glance caught the bag on the vacant seat to the side of her containing her wedding dress material. 'I can't wait to make a start on my dress,' she said excitedly. A thought suddenly struck and she looked at Agnes tentatively. 'Er . . . the dress you're wearing for my wedding,' she asked casually. 'Your best black are you referring to?'

'Pardon? Oh, yes. I have a brown but I'm still in mourning, my dear.'

Maddie reached for the teapot, busying herself refilling their cups. How could she tell Miss Clatteridge that her style of clothes made her look hideous? But an opportunity had arisen in the guise of her wedding to broach the subject of Miss Clatteridge's unbecoming style of dress, and Maddie felt obliged to seize it. She might not have the opportunity again. But she had to be very careful to act without upsetting her friend, the very last thing she wanted to do. 'Miss Clatteridge, could you not wear something a little brighter? I'm sure it wouldn't be seen as disrespectful, not considering the occasion.'

Agnes stared at her thoughtfully. 'Do you not think so? But I haven't anything in my wardrobe that's brighter.'

'You could make something?'

'I could, but there isn't time. Your wedding is in two weeks, and I haven't a sewing machine. Father wouldn't allow us to have one. He said were not our hands adequate enough? I don't mind hand sewing but it's so laborious.'

'We have a sewing machine. I'm sure Sarah wouldn't mind us using it to help you get started.'

'It's a very kind offer, Maddie, but I couldn't take such a liberty. Besides, you have enough to do as it is.'

'It wouldn't be a liberty and I have plenty of time to make my dress. Don't forget, Sarah and Ruth are helping too. But, all right, why don't you buy something to wear?'

'Buy something? Oh! I've never bought a dress. I've always made everything I've worn, Father insisted. No, I couldn't. I really cannot justify spending good money on such a frivolous item. I'll wear my black dress.'

But suddenly the idea of having something new to wear to Maddie's wedding held such appeal. If ever Agnes had felt there was a time she wanted to look nice it was for Maddie's special day. She always felt so self-conscious in everything she wore, it would be such an exciting prospect to have something of her own choosing. But she couldn't justify the expenditure, not when the serviceable clothes she possessed still had many years of life left in them.

Then she remembered how her father had squandered his money. Remembered his harsh ways; the rigid rules her sister and she had been governed by. Memories of them sitting silently round the table eating cold porridge washed down with icy water while their father had tucked into liver and onions, just because they had dared to run barefoot through the dewy grass, their skirts around their knees. 'Hussies and harlots!' he had screeched at them before giving them a whipping. She had been seven at the time, Alice barely five. And all the time he was gambling away good money, had wasted a fortune according to Mr Simpson.

Agnes's lips tightened. Father had been such a hypocrite.

Why shouldn't she have a new dress? Why shouldn't she indeed? She had no one now to justify herself to, be frightened of. She was in charge. In truth she was wearing her black clothes now not out of respect for her father but because it was expected by society. Wasn't that hypocritical of her? Her eyes sparked. 'You're right, Maddie dear. I do need a new outfit for your wedding and I shall have one. Nothing too frivolous and not too expensive and definitely not black.'

Maddie beamed. She was going to have such fun helping Miss Clatteridge choose an outfit to wear for her special day and it wasn't before time. A thought struck her. Dare she? Dare she push her luck any further? It was worth a try. She had just succeeded where she had feared she'd fail.

'I'm going to have my hair cut on Saturday afternoon. Sarah and Ruth suggested a style which I think will suit me. I had to think about it, though. I've had this style for years and sometimes change can be frightening. Anyway I've made up my mind. Why don't you come with me?'

'To watch?'

Maddie shook her head. 'No, to have yours done too. A Marcel wave would look a treat on you.' It would go a long way to soften Agnes's sharp features, Maddie knew.

'Oh, I couldn't,' she said aghast, patting the tightly wound bun at the back of her head. 'A new dress is one thing . . .' She paused, looking at Maddie keenly. 'Do you think I should?'

With a sparkle in her eye, Maddie nodded.

'Then I will. It's about time I struck out, Maddie, did things I want to do, dressed the way I want.' She scraped back her chair. 'Come along, my dear,' she ordered. 'Let's go shopping before I change my mind.'

Several hours later the two women made their way home, laden down with bags. In the end Agnes had purchased more than Maddie. She was still having trouble believing

265

her employer's behaviour. This was a Miss Clatteridge the likes of whom she had never envisaged.

The styles and colours they had chosen together were soft, not exactly the height of fashion but definitely much more becoming on Agnes's long straight frame than any she had previously worn. There really was no comparison. They made her appear slender instead of thin. The hemline of her four new skirts and three dresses had ridden up dramatically from ankle-length to just above her calves and Maddie had been surprised and delighted to discover Miss Clatteridge owned a pair of very shapely legs.

Maddie herself liked best the blue-grey, drop-waisted dress she had chosen for the wedding. The sleeves were elbow-length, the neckline scooped gently across the shoulders. Agnes looked lovely in it, a woman transformed. As she had sought the mirror to view herself, when on Maddie's insistence she had tried it on, she had actually passed by it, not realising the reflection that had caught her eye was actually herself, thinking it was another customer.

'Oh, Maddie!' Agnes had declared in disbelief when she had studied herself. 'Is that really me? It can't be.'

Maddie had joined her, smiling. 'You look beautiful, Miss Clatteridge.'

'That is an extreme exaggeration but I'll agree that I do look nice. What you wear really does make a difference, doesn't it?'

Maddie knew that only too well herself and had nodded.

On finally arriving home a thankful Agnes plonked her bags down on the table, sighing heavily. She stood back and looked at them. Suddenly her face crumpled worriedly as what she had just done struck home and all her new resolve began to disintegrate. 'Oh, I must have had a brainstorm. Maddie, what have I done? All that money I've just wasted. I didn't go out with the intention of spending any on myself and I must have spent at least thirty pounds. Oh, dear,' she groaned clasping her hand to her mouth.

'With due respect, Miss Clatteridge,' Maddie said, putting down her own bags, 'I think you did very well with all you have for that money.'

'Really?'

'Absolutely. Those skirts had been reduced in the sale and so was your new coat, which I must say looks a treat. The dresses . . . Well, they weren't that expensive, considering their quality. The special one you chose for my wedding was maybe a bit extravagant, we could have made it for a fraction of the price. But . . . to hell with it, Miss Clatteridge! You fell in love with that dress. Why shouldn't you have had it, or the rest for that matter?'

Agnes stared in surprise at this blasphemous outburst, then a smile lit her face. 'You're right. Why shouldn't I indeed? I shall look forward to wearing it so much.' She patted her hair. 'Complete with my new wave.'

'You're still coming with me to get it done?'

'I've gone this far, my dear, I can't stop now.' Agnes's smile grew wider. 'Won't Alice get a shock when she sees me?' Her smile faded. 'I forgot to mention, I had another letter from her this morning asking again how the sale was proceeding. Oh, I do hope those people the agent sent around yesterday decide to go ahead. Only I'm very much afraid they won't. As I told you, the first man wasn't very keen on the area. He wanted somewhere in a more affluent situation. Told me there wasn't that much profit in plain pine which was all he suspected the people around here could afford. Anyway I saw his face after he had looked over the books. He wasn't impressed, I could tell, and muttered something about the business not being as good as he had been led to believe by the agent. I was a bit embarrassed. It's weeks now since we had a funeral to deal with and the agent had told him we were flourishing.

'As for the other undertaker who came, he wasn't too concerned with the way matters had dropped off, said he'd soon get it going again once he was installed. His wife wasn't keen on the house, though. I heard her say something to her husband about there not being a water pump in the kitchen and having to go outside in all weathers. She wasn't pleased about that.' Agnes glanced around the drab room. 'It's not just the water pump, I know. This whole house is so dreary. Enough to put any woman off. I haven't the money to brighten it up to encourage people. It would cost me far too much. More than I spent today.'

'Stop feeling guilty, Miss Clatteridge. The house has great potential. Anyone wanting to buy the business and live here will see that, and the cost of paint and wallpaper won't be an issue. Someone will come along. The agent told you he was going to do his best to push it, didn't he, and he's proved his worth by sending those people who came yesterday. So he prettied up his descriptions a bit. That's what they do to get people to view, isn't it? At least something is happening now.'

Agnes smiled wanly. 'Yes, you're right as usual, my dear. I'm still cross though that he took it upon himself not to tell people about it after he heard of Mr Snood's interest. Still, that's all over. Let's hope the next people who arrive do go ahead. But after my hairdo, my spending will have to stop. If you don't mind, would you put the kettle on? I'll take my clothes upstairs then I must get the ledger out and try and work out what my situation is after this afternoon's expensive excursion.'

It's not going to be good, she thought. And neither would it take her long to work out. Her many hours of poring over the ledger, night after night, after Maddie had gone home and she had cleared away her solitary meal, had started to make sense of the columns. She filled in the ledger weekly now, although considering how little they were doing, it wasn't a large task. The bit coming in from the nail-making and odd carpentry jobs did help a little to ease their outgoings, as had the revenue from the coffin they had supplied for Wilson's, but she had still had to supplement her income from the money her father had left. Except for her madness of today, she had been extremely careful but regardless the balance was dropping.

She heard a knock on the kitchen door and her name being called.

'In here, Mr Simpson. Come through.'

The door opened and Ivan came in. Both women looked at him.

'What is it, Mr Simpson?'

'Oh, yer back,' he cried. 'In the family room.'

'What is?' she asked, frowning.

'The couple. Mam's passed on. They've been waiting an hour. I told 'em you were out on business. I did right, I 'ope?'

Agnes's mouth dropped in disbelief. Maddie's too.

'A funeral?' Agnes cried. 'They've come to me to arrange a funeral?'

'Really, Mr Simpson?' Maddie interrupted.

He nodded. 'Said Tilly Potter sent 'em. Want the best they can afford apparently. I told 'em they'd come to the right place. Miss Clatteridge'd do 'em proud.'

Agnes clapped her hands in utter joy. 'Oh, Mr Simpson, Maddie. Oh! I look a mess. I . . .'

Maddie grabbed her arm. 'Take a deep breath, Miss Agnes. Calm down. You look fine. That's better. Now go and deal with them. I'll bring some tea through, shall I?'

'How kind of you, Maddie. Yes, that's the least we can do for keeping the poor people waiting,' she said, heading for the door. She paused then and addressed Maddie. 'You called me Miss Agnes. I like that, dear. In future you will address me as such.'

With that she was gone, leaving Ivan and Maddie staring at each other. There was no need for words.

# Chapter Twenty-One

'There you go, Sarah,' said Maddie, handing her a mug of steaming tea.

'Ah, thank you, my dear,' she replied gratefully accepting it. 'Ruth said for me to say her goodnights. She's gone up. So will I after I've finished this. I told your father I wouldn't be long over an hour ago. Still, I expect he'll be fast asleep and not notice what time I came to bed.' She relaxed back in her chair, eyeing Maddie who was sitting opposite her, feet resting on the fender. 'Isn't this cosy, just the two of us for a change?' She sighed contentedly. 'It was so nice meeting Miss Clatteridge properly at long last. Of course, I've seen her around but I didn't realise what a lovely woman she is. I know what you've told me of her, Maddie, but then I think you speak well of everyone. It was good to find out for meself. I know it's awful of me but I was itching to try and bring up the subject of her clothes. They do nothing for her, do they? It's such a shame.'

'I did though,' Maddie said with a twinkle in her eye.

'Did what?'

'Something about her clothes. When we went shopping today I managed to persuade her to buy a dress for my wedding.'

'Not black, I hope, dear?'

'No. It's a lovely soft bluey grey. She looks a different person in it. And that's not all. She bought skirts, day dresses, and a coat too. And . . .'

'There's more?'

Laughing, Maddie nodded. 'She's coming with me to the hairdresser's on Saturday to get her hair cut and waved. She looks a new person in her clothes, and with a new hairstyle as well, I know it's going to make such a difference to her.'

'So do I,' Sarah said sincerely. 'People round here are frightened of her because of the way that father of hers made her dress, and her sister too. He never let them mix. Shame on him, I say. But you can't blame them, Maddie. She did look . . .' Sarah shrugged her shoulders. 'Well, frightening. 'Course her occupation doesn't help her none, does it? But she's not frightening at all. You should congratulate yourself, Maddie, achieving what you did. When you've spent a lifetime doing things certain ways change doesn't come easy, so she's to be congratulated too. You, Maddie, are so thoughtful, taking the trouble. Not many women with as much on their minds as you have at the moment would bother.'

She sighed. 'It's all happening so quickly, isn't it?'

'Yes, but you can't wait to marry Josh, can you? And why should you? It was quite funny how you wouldn't let the poor lad across the doorstep tonight.'

'Well, I couldn't, could I? He'd have seen what we were doing. He understood anyway.' Maddie's face filled with excitement. 'I can't wait to see the little house he's found for us to rent. He's warned me it's not up to much but it'll do us 'til we can move to something better. I don't care what it's like, to be honest. So long as we have somewhere. I like the fact it's very close, handy for here and for work.'

'I'll say one thing,' Sarah said, impressed. 'He ain't letting the grass grow under his feet, is he? He does what he says he's going ter do. You want to keep well hold of him, Maddie, me duck. Not many men like that around.' She grinned. ''Cept for yer dad, 'course.' She took a sip of her drink while casting her eyes around the room then settled her gaze on the part-made dress hanging on a coathanger on the back of the door. 'It's going to look beautiful when it's finished.'

Maddie looked across at it too. 'Yes, it is. Thank you so much for all you're doing.'

Sarah smiled tiredly. 'It's my pleasure.' She laughed merrily. 'Your poor father couldn't believe his eyes when he arrived home after a late visit with a client and found this room in such a state. He was expecting to put his feet up after his dinner for a quiet read of his paper. I had warned him what to expect when he left this morning but he obviously forgot by the look on his face when he opened the door tonight.'

'It is a mess, isn't it? Maybe I should try and clear up a little,' offered Maddie, attempting to rise.

'Sit where you are. Tidying up will be a waste of time. I shall only get everything out as soon as you've all gone to work in the morning and it'll be back in the same state. So what's the point?'

'You're supposed to be resting, Sarah. You are expecting, remember.'

'I am resting. Helping you with your dress isn't work to me, Maddie, it's too pleasurable.'

'You are kind, Sarah. I do appreciate it.'

She stared, taken aback. 'Why should I treat you any differently from your sister?'

'Well . . . Ruth *is* your daughter.'

'And you're not, is that what you mean? No, I'm not your mother unfortunately. I only wish I was.' She looked fondly at the younger woman for a moment. 'We never have the chance to talk, just the two of us. There's always someone around. Please let me take this chance to tell you I'm not trying to ease my way into your affections and take your own mother's place, believe me. I just wanted . . . Oh, Maddie, you're such a lovely girl. Your arrival here has brought us such happiness. Your father's so proud of you, I can't tell you how much.'

Maddie's bottom lip began to tremble and tears pricked

her eyes as all of a sudden everything crowded in on her. It was all too much. The unexpected arrival of Josh, the rush to get things done for the wedding, but most of all Sarah's generous acceptance of her. 'I don't deserve your kindness,' she murmured.

'Don't be silly, of course you do.'

'But I don't. And you wouldn't think so much of me and neither would Father is he knew . . .' Maddie's head drooped. She suddenly felt a great need to unburden herself of her dreadful secret. She had to, she couldn't carry it around anymore and let her family believe so well of her, when the truth was she wasn't such a good person. 'I don't deserve it, Sarah. I've been dishonest with you. It's unforgivable of me, considering the way you've all been so open with me about everything that's happened.'

'Dishonest? What are you going on about, Maddie?' Sarah asked, confused.

A sob caught in the back of Maddie's throat as she uttered, 'I have a dreadful secret. I couldn't bring myself to tell you.'

'Maddie, you don't . . .'

'Please, let me finish, Sarah.' She raised her head and stared her straight in the eye. 'I know you've always suspected that something awful brought me to Leicester, not just deciding I wanted to start a new life. You were right to think that.' She wrung her hands. 'I had a baby,' she blurted out. 'A daughter. Mine and Josh's. She's nearly two years old now.'

'Oh, Maddie!' Sarah's shoulders sagged in distress. 'What happened?'

Maddie sniffed. 'My mother realised I was expecting before I had the courage to tell her. She took me to the house of a woman far away from us and left me there until after I'd given birth, with no means of leaving. She told Josh awful lies to cover up what she'd done. She wouldn't tell him where I was, nothing. When my baby was born she came to take us both home, or so I thought. While I was getting ready she handed my baby over for adoption.' Her face crumpled in pain. 'What do you think of me now? My father will despise me, won't he? He, you and everyone else thinks I'm such a lovely person. Well, now you know I'm not.'

'Oh, Maddie,' Sarah whispered softly, the other woman's desperate pain filling her being. How could Harriet have done that to her, acted so callously? To her own grandchild too. Now Sarah knew the reason for the sadness of the dispirited woman who had first arrived on their doorstep so unexpectedly. And why Maddie had almost cried when she had announced the arrival of her own baby. Sarah suddenly felt dreadful. She patted the side of her chair. 'Come and sit here beside me. Come on.'

Obediently Maddie got to her feet and went over, dropping down to sit on the floor next to her. Sarah ran her hand gently over Maddie's hair.

'You poor child. Yes, you're right, I did think there was more to what you were telling us, as did your father. But we knew you'd tell us when you were good and ready. You think I'm shocked? That your father will disown you?' Sarah shook her head. 'You're with a woman who has lived in sin with a man for twenty-five years. We've two children, born out of wedlock, and another on the way.

'But, Maddie dear, even if none of that had happened, if your father had got his divorce and we were respectably married with the children bearing his name, we would never, ever think badly of you. I'll always be grateful for the way you've been with me. You could have hated me, Maddie, thinking I took your father away. And I wouldn't have blamed you if you had. Anyway, you're not the first it's happened to and you won't be the last. It's times like this when families are supposed to be understanding, my dear. And we are. Do you want me to tell your father or shall I leave it for you to do? Or it will go no further than me if that's what you want?'

Maddie eyed her beseechingly. 'Would you tell my father for me? He really ought to know. I can't tell him, I feel so ashamed still.'

'And I've told you, you shouldn't, so stop it. What's happened has happened, you can't carry the blame for the rest of your life. I know your father, Maddie. His anger will be all for Harriet. She took your baby away. She stopped you and Josh from being together. You could have been a family. That was unforgivable of her. If she hadn't made it impossible for you, forcing you to sneak around behind her back, none of this would have happened, would it? If anyone's to blame your mother is, Maddie.'

She pulled a handkerchief from her cardigan pocket and dabbed her wet eyes and blew her nose. 'Josh wants us to go and see my mother after we're married, ask her if she'll tell us now what she did with our child so we can try and get her back. I want her back, I desperately want my baby back,' sobbed Maddie. 'Josh feels the same too.'

Sarah sighed. 'It's worth a try, I suppose.'

'You don't think she will?'

'Do you, my dear?'

Maddie shook her head. 'I know it'll be a waste of time. I don't want to put Josh through it. He's suffered so much through my mother already. I know what our reception will be.' She wiped away fresh tears. 'It's stupid of me, I know, after all she's done, but I still can't help worrying about her now she's all alone.'

'She's your mother, Maddie, and being the sort of person I know you are, it doesn't surprise me to hear you feel like that. I wish I could go with you for support, but that's out of the question.' Sarah suddenly had a thought. 'Where you had your baby, would they know who adopted her?'

Maddie sighed. 'Mrs Baldicott. She was a lovely old lady, and treated me so well. I grew really fond of her. At the time I begged her to tell me but she said even if she knew she couldn't, it was more than her job was worth. I couldn't expect her to risk everything for me. She's a widow, it's her only income.'

'No, I suppose not.'

They lapsed into silence, each with her own private thoughts.

Maddie suddenly sat bolt upright. 'I could go and see my mother by myself. Try and reason with her. She . . . she might be different now, mightn't she, Sarah? Now that she's been on her own and has had time to think, she could be sorry for what she's done. She could be a changed person, couldn't she? I'm stronger now too. She can't bully me like she used to. And I have to consider Josh. I really feel I couldn't put him through the ordeal of facing her again.' She took a deep breath. 'Yes, that's what I'm going to do. If I achieve nothing else, I can see she's all right, can't I? I'll go tomorrow. I'll explain to Miss Clatteridge I've important business to attend to, I know she'll understand.'

Sarah eyed her sharply. 'Are you sure about this, Maddie?'

No, she wasn't, not really, but what else could she do? I have to do this,' she said, and gave a wan smile. 'I do feel so much better now that I've told you about the baby.' She raised herself, leaned over and kissed Sarah affectionately on the cheek. 'Thank you so much for being so understanding. I love you, Sarah.'

She smiled tenderly. 'Oh, Maddie my dear, I love you too.' She reached over and put her arms around Maddie, giving her a hug. 'Go to bed,' she ordered. 'I'll be just behind you.'

As Maddie left the room Sarah's face creased in concern. Maddie was heading for trouble, and Sarah wanted desperately to try and stop her. People like Harriet did not change. They saw no wrong in what they had done. In Sarah's opinion, Harriet did not deserve her daughter's concern. But she knew Maddie had to do this to set her own mind at rest. Sarah suspected Maddie was wasting her time but sincerely hoped she herself was wrong.

# Chapter Twenty-Two

Maddie paused as she turned the corner of the street and stared nervously down it. These familiar surroundings, an area she had grown up in and knew like the back of her hand, suddenly seemed so alien, offering no feeling of belonging whatsoever. Only yards away was the person responsible for her fleeing the town of her birth a few months before. Then she had been a woman whose very soul had been destroyed. So much had happened during the short intervening period. Maddie had discovered truths so shocking she had had to search to the very depths of her being to understand and accept that people could act so deviously to get their own way. With the help of her new family, with their love and support, she had managed to acknowledge it, then put it all aside. To forget was impossible, she knew, but no longer did the cruelty her mother had inflicted on her affect her daily life.

Yet here she was again, by her own choice, preparing to stare her tormentor in the face. Sarah had taken her aside that morning as she was getting ready to leave and asked her if, now she had slept on it, she was still determined to go today? Sarah was deeply concerned for her, that much had been apparent.

In fact, Maddie hadn't slept a wink. She had tossed and turned all night, going over and over what she was about to undertake. But she had no choice. She had to do it. Now that time had passed and she was herself about to embark on a new phase of her life, she had to try and put matters on an even footing with her mother, at least be on speaking terms if nothing else and set her mind at rest that Harriet was faring all right on her own. And there were questions she had to ask that only her mother could answer. But now she had actually arrived, the determination that had steeled her throughout her journey on the slow train suddenly vanished. All she wanted to do was turn and run, back to the security of Josh and her family.

An image of Josh's face swam before her, his handsome features soft with love, and courage and strength flowed through her. She was doing this not only for herself but for him. For Maddie that was reason enough. Taking a very deep breath, she pushed all her fears aside. As she was about to enter the shop a booming voice just behind her made her jump and she spun around.

'Maddie Ashman. Well, well, well. How good it is to see you.'

'Mrs Green! Goodness, you startled me,' she said, exhaling sharply. 'It's nice to see you too.'

'I'm so glad you're back,' said the woman with obvious sincerity. 'Old lady recovered now, has she? Your mother's a saint to let you go off again. I have missed you, my dear. I've been getting what I needed done at Pringle's across town but the girl they have there doesn't hold a candle to you. I'll be in first thing in the morning. How's your mother by the way? To be honest, I haven't been into the shop since you went off so suddenly.'

Maddie gnawed her bottom lip uncomfortably. 'I'm just about to find out, Mrs Green. I'm just paying a visit myself.'

'A visit? Oh, you're not back for good then?'

Maddie shook her head.

The rotund face looked dismayed, monstrous jowls wobbling dangerously. 'Oh, that's a shame. That means I'll still have to patronise Pringle's. When will you be back?' she asked hopefully.

'I won't, Mrs Green.'

'Oh! Never?'

Maddie swallowed hard. 'I have a life in Leicester now.'

'Really? I'm sure your mother said the old lady lived in a village near . . . where was it . . . Coalville, I think.' She eyed Maddie quizzically. 'Is your mother going to be joining you?'

'I can't answer that, Mrs Green.'

'Oh, well, I expect she'll have no choice soon if her business continues to drop off as I know it is. She lost much of her custom when you went, my dear. It was a good little shop once but times change, don't they, and your mother doesn't stock the sort of thing I use now. Except for the basic white and black cotton. And, of course, spare suspenders.' Realising she was speaking of delicate articles of women's clothing, her loud voice was lowered dramatically. 'But I wear blue now as well as my pink and I can't get blue at Ashman's. Yes, you have to move with the times, don't you, dear?' Her voice rose again. 'Pringle's have and that's why most people who shopped at your mother's go there now. And they sell very nice lingerie, you know. And of course Woolworth's have such a good selection of cottons and the like at very reasonable prices. I have to watch my pennies. Well, must be off. I do wish you well. Good day.'

'Good day, Mrs Green.'

Maddie felt even more worried. According to Mrs Green her mother wasn't doing very well at all. Despite herself, Maddie couldn't help but feel sorry.

The bell on the door jangled dully as it was opened and Harriet glanced up. A look of utter astonishment fleetingly crossed her face when she recognised the person who was entering, to disappear just as quickly. Stony eyes glared at Maddie, thin lips twitched into a sarcastic grin.

She was horrified by the sight of her mother who didn't look well. Harriet had always been thin but she appeared gaunt now, lines criss-crossing her drawn face. Her fine hair was sparser, patches of scalp visible. Her clothes too looked in need of a clean and press. Her movements were slow, laboured.

'You took your time.' Her voice was cold and hard. 'Got fed up living with that whore and her bastards, did you? I bet that was a shock. Well, now you know what that father of yours is really all about and what I had to put up with all those years. I must say, I didn't think you'd last this long with them. Where are your bags?'

Maddie was staring at her, shocked by her savage tone and foul language. 'Bags? Oh, I haven't brought them,' she replied absently, still shocked by her mother's state.

'Ah, left them at the station, have you? Decided to test the water first. I see. Well, go and fetch them,' Harriet commanded. 'Your room's just as you left it.'

A great desire to turn and run overwhelmed Maddie. It took all her strength to control it. She stepped back, flattening herself against the glass in the door. 'I . . . I haven't come to stay, Mother. My home is in Leicester now.'

Harriet's lips pressed tightly together, eyes narrowing darkly and nostrils flaring. 'Well, why have you come then?'

'To see you. I was concerned about you.'

'Concerned!' she hissed. 'I don't want your concern. I want nothing from you. You walked out on me, remember, after all I did for you.'

'Mother, please.' Maddie took a tentative step forward. 'Don't be like this. How are you managing?'

'Perfectly well. I don't need you to survive. Is that it?'

'Pardon?'

'Have you got what you came for? If so, go.'

'Mother, please. You don't look well. Let me help you . . .'

'I've told you, I'm fine. Perfectly capable of looking after myself.'

Maddie sighed. 'All right, Mother.'

'So is that it?' she spat again.

'No, it's not. I . . . was hoping we could talk. I was hoping we could . . .'

282

'Could what, Maude?' she demanded icily.

'Be friends?'

'Friends!' spat Harriet. Then she laughed, a nasty spiteful cackle. 'You really amaze me. Friends indeed. Why, you're the most ungrateful, disloyal specimen of a human being a mother could ever be saddled with as a daughter. Mind you, what can I expect with who fathered you?'

A great anger surged through Maddie. Before she could stop herself, she cried, 'Don't speak like that about my father. He's a good man, kind, and I love him. As for his wife – yes, and she *is* his rightful wife, Mother – she's a good woman and neither of them deserves the way you've treated them.'

Harriet's face contorted furiously. 'I'll not have you speak of them in such terms in my house. Now get out. Go on,' she ordered.

Maddie faced her, eyes blazing. 'No, I won't. I came here with the best of intentions but I was wasting my time, wasn't I? I hoped you might have changed. How foolish of me. I'll go, Mother, and I'll not return now you've told me what you really think of me. But before I do I want to tell you that I'm getting married. To Josh. Remember him, Mother? He's the man you told such lies to. He's the man whose baby you gave away. I want you to tell me where our daughter is. I won't move from this spot until you do.'

'Well, you'll stand there forever then, won't you, because I'll tell you nothing.' Harriet moved around the counter and came to stand before Maddie, looking her up and down scathingly. 'Look at you, dressed in your trashy clothes. You've turned into a low-life like them. I'm ashamed of you.' She pushed Maddie aside and opened the door. 'Now get out. Get out, I said, and don't dare darken my door again, do you hear?' Eyes suddenly flashing wickedly, she pushed her face closer to Maddie's, lowering her voice maliciously. 'Oh, and something else to tell your father. That money he gave me – I've never spent a penny. Not one farthing in all these years. Tell him he's left me very well off. Tell him I said thank you. Now get out!'

With that she pushed Maddie out of the door and slammed it shut so hard the glass rattled and the dusty bell above fell off.

Harriet watched for a moment as Maddie, head bowed, walked off down the street, then walked through to the back. The fury that filled her was so intense she shook with its violence. How dare Maude come back, saying she wanted them to be friends? Friends! Harriet had never needed a friend in her life and certainly did not want one in the guise of a daughter. Or rather harlot, she thought. After all Maddie had done, to walk calmly into the shop as though nothing had happened! And the worst of it was the way she'd been sticking up so blatantly for that sorry excuse for a man and the hussy with whom he lived in sin.

Suddenly a vice-like grip tightened round her heart and her hand flew up to clutch her chest. Harriet opened her mouth to scream but all that came out was a gurgle as she breathed her last and her lifeless body crumpled to the floor.

As soon as he heard the key in the lock Josh ran down the passage to meet Maddie. 'Sarah told me where you'd gone. Oh, Maddie!' he cried, gathering her to him. 'You shouldn't have gone on yer own. I wanted to go with you.' He felt her slump against him and lowered his voice. 'It was bad, wasn't it, my darlin'?'

'Yes,' she sobbed. 'It was dreadful. I'd gone with so much hope . . .' Her voice trailed away. She couldn't tell anyone, not even Josh, what had happened. It was just too terrible.

He sensed her deep distress and said nothing, just held her tightly.

'She wouldn't tell me anything about our baby, Josh, I'm so sorry.'

'Don't worry about that, Maddie love. We'll find out some other way. You're home safe and sound and that's the main thing. Come on through, your father and Sarah have been

284

worried sick. She's had the kettle permanently boiling its lid off ready to mash you a cuppa and she's kept your dinner hot in the oven.'

A warm feeling of belonging washed through her. Gripping his hand, Maddie walked with him down the dimly lit passage to where the rest of her family anxiously awaited her.

# Chapter Twenty-Three

'Well, Mrs Jenks, I think it's all going off really well. What do you say?'

Maddie gazed around her happily. There wasn't one person in this room who wasn't delighted for Josh and her. And they had shown it in such a wonderful way. When it had become known that a reception was beyond their means, everyone chipped in. George and Sarah had insisted their house be used and had provided most of the food, the rest being kindly donated by neighbours. Roy and Ruth had rearranged the furniture to allow access to the food and drink, leaving plenty of space in the middle for dancing for those who wished, with seats against the walls for those who preferred to chat. Agnes had provided the drink and had organised a professional photographer to take a selection of photographs of their special day. Ivan had dipped into his savings and bought them a silver frame. The Jenks family had all pitched in together and bought the happy couple sheets and towels. Other friends and neighbours had arrived bearing gifts. Except Oswald Peabody. He just brought himself.

Maddie gazed up at her new husband, eyes shining. 'The day has been perfect, Josh. I couldn't have wished for better.'

He looked down at her fondly. 'Would you sooner have delayed things 'til we'd saved and been able to afford a posher do?'

'What? All that pomp and ceremony! No, thank you. And

besides, that would have meant having to wait and I wasn't going to.'

Josh increased the pressure of his arm around her waist, pulling her closer to him. He had several times caught her unawares looking wistful and had known she was thinking of their child, feeling that the day was not quite complete with her absent. He didn't want to spoil her enjoyment though by raising the subject. 'Happy?' he whispered.

She was ecstatic but for one solitary regret. She knew Josh was feeling it too. She had caught him several times with a faraway look in his eyes. One special person was missing from their special day: their daughter. But Maddie didn't want to spoil his happiness by mentioning it. 'Never been more so,' she whispered back. 'I'm so happy, Josh, I could walk across hot ashes and not feel the pain.'

'You look beautiful, Maddie. I couldn't tek me eyes off yer when you walked into the chapel. I can't believe you're really my wife at last.'

'If you've told me that once, you've said it a dozen times today.' she said, laughing.

'Well, let me say it again. You look beautiful, Maddie.'

'Thank you, kind sir,' she said, giving a mock curtsey.

She turned her attention to their guests. 'My family and yours are getting on so well, but then I never doubted they would.' She looked up at her husband. 'Your mother is happy about us marrying, isn't she, Josh?'

'Maddie, she's over the moon. Stop worrying.' He started to laugh. 'Look at me sister with your Roy. Eh, that's not sherry they're drinking, is it?'

'No, it's dandelion and burdock.'

'That's all right then.'

They both lapsed into silence, each savouring the atmosphere, storing memories to resurrect in the years to come.

Across the room Ivan Simpson was standing with his back against the wall nearest the door, sipping a glass of dark ale, eyes fixed on Agnes who was engrossed in conversation with Sarah.

Agnes looked lovely. He wanted to gather her into his arms and declare his undying love for her. He sighed. Her transformation was breathtaking, so much so that the first time he had seen her crossing the yard late the previous Saturday afternoon, sporting her new Marcel wave and dressed in a smart new coat, his mouth had opened wide enough to drive a tram through, eyes popping near out of his head. He had been unable to move, despite the fact that she was aware he was watching her.

She was so much softer-looking. Not that it mattered to Ivan. He had loved her the way she was before. But now he was a worried man. It wasn't the thought of her eventual departure for Scarborough that was causing his present unhappiness. It was the knowledge that someone of her own sort was definitely going to notice her now and snap her up and Ivan couldn't bear the thought.

Lounging beside him, Oswald Peabody was slyly ogling Maddie over the top of his glass. He was inwardly furious. He had set his cap at her. Then Jenks turned up out of the blue and in an instant, seemingly, had married her and all Oswald's hopes lay shattered. He wouldn't have minded so much if he hadn't lied to his friends about his conquest, telling them how this older woman at work was all over him. Now they knew the truth, he was suffering constant taunts and snide comments.

He suddenly realised that Ivan had spoken to him. 'What?' he responded, easing himself away from the wall.

'I said, I'm off.' Ivan could no longer bear to watch Agnes, his mood of depression worsening by the second. He wanted to return to his room, shut out the world and wallow in self-pity.

'Yeah, me too,' Oswald mumbled. 'N'ote round 'ere for us, is there?'

'You're not leaving so soon?' Maddie said as Ivan, Oswald

behind him, came to say goodbye.

'Yes, stay a little longer. Me father's going to play some tunes on his fiddle soon. We're going to have some dancin',' said Josh.

Ivan looked across at Albert Jenks, eyebrows raised. 'Plays the fiddle, eh?'

'Amongst many other talents. He's better at cobbling shoes, though, me mother reckons. She says his fiddle playing sounds like cats screeching.' Josh laughed. 'He's not that bad. Why don't you stay and judge fer yerself, Mr Simpson?'

'No, if yer don't mind, I'll pass. I, er, have a few things I want ter do back at the yard.' He leaned over and pecked Maddie on the cheek. 'Thanks fer asking me, Maddie love.' His eyes twinkled fondly. 'Yer do look beautiful. See yer Monday, eh? Tarra.'

'Thank you for coming, Ivan. Goodbye. Goodbye, Oswald.'

He grunted something inaudible as he followed Ivan out.

'I like Ivan Simpson. He seems a thoroughly decent sort. Can't say the same fer that young fellow, though,' Josh remarked.

'Off home then, lad?' Ivan asked Oswald as they stepped out into the street.

'Nah,' came the sullen response. 'Thought I'd go fer a pint down the local.'

Ivan looked unimpressed. 'Thought yer'd have had better things to do with yer money?'

'Money! Huh,' he growled. 'What bit I get paid you're referring ter, eh, Mr Simpson?'

'Oi, Oswald me lad, you should count yersel' lucky. You gets paid more than most in our business fer what you do. Miss Clatteridge put yer wage up the other week, I know she did.'

'Not by much, she din't.'

'Better than a slap in the gob, ain't it?'

'S'pose.'

Ivan thrust his hands deep into his trouser pockets and looked up and down the street. He sighed audibly. 'I'm off then. And if you've n'ote better to do than piss yer money up the wall, yer'd better get off too. See yer Monday first thing sharp.'

'Yeah, tarra, Mr Simpson.'

They each went their separate ways.

Oswald had slouched along for several yards before he realised someone was walking alongside him. He stopped abruptly and turned to face the man.

'A' you following me or summat?' he snarled at the youth alongside him.

'Hardly followin', am 'a, Oswald Peabody?'

Oswald's eyes narrowed questioningly. 'How d'yer know me name?' he demanded.

'I made it me business ter find out. I've bin watching yer, see.'

'Watchin' me! Wa' for?'

'Checkin' yer out. I reckon you look like a man who wouldn't turn up 'is nose at the chance of earning an extra bob or two.'

The boy's eyes sparkled keenly. 'How?'

'Are yer interested?'

'Might be.'

'Off ter the pub, weren't yer?'

'Mighta bin.'

'I'll join yer. We can find a quiet corner and discuss it, if yer like?'

Oswald looked at him, then nodded. 'Okay. N'ote ter lose, 'ave I?'

'Excuse me a minute, son,' said Sadie Jenks, squeezing her large round body between Josh and Maddie. 'I want a quiet word with this wife of yours. Women's talk. Go on, skedaddle.'

Maddie smiled. 'I wouldn't mind a glass of lemonade, please, Josh.'

'An' I'll 'ave a stout,' said his mother.

Sadie hooked her arm through Maddie's and pulled her aside. 'I just want ter get things straight between us, me dear, and don't look so worried. I've not 'ad a chance since we arrived. I must say, yer dad and Sarah 'ave made us most welcome. Very good of 'em to squash us all in like this and fer you to give up yer bed last night and share wi' yer sister. Good of yer all. Well, we couldn't afford lodgin's.'

'It's the least we could do, Mrs Jenks. And we were only too glad to. It meant everything to Josh and me that you all came here today.'

'There's no way I'd 'a missed our Josh's wedding. Not on your nelly. An' it's all bin quite exciting really. I ain't never bin ter Leicester before. 'Tain't such a bad place from what I've seen of it.' Her jolly face grew serious. 'Look, Maddie love, we didn't get off to a very good start, did we?'

'Mrs Jenks . . .'

'Let me finish, me duck. It's all my fault. I took yer ter be the same as yer mother. I was wrong ter do that. It was 'cos I wa' upset for our Josh. Anyway, I just want ter ask if we can start afresh like, 'cos I'd like us ter be friends?'

'Oh, Mrs Jenks, so would I. If ever you want to come and see us, you'll be more than welcome. And Josh and I will come and see you as often as we can.'

Sadie's face filled with joy and relief. 'Oh, yer a lovely gel all right. Our Josh 'as done 'imself proud.' She threw her powerful arms around Maddie and crushed her in a hug. 'Welcome ter the family, me duck.' She released her hold on Maddie and turned her attention to the spread on the table. 'Better get a sandwich afore it all disappears.'

'Where's me mother gone?' asked Josh, handing Maddie a glass filled with home-made lemonade.

'She's there, look, at the table.'

'Oh, ah.' He eyed Maddie searchingly. 'Everything all right between you and her?'

She smiled broadly. 'Everything's fine. She was just welcoming me to the family. She's a lovely woman, Josh. All your family are so friendly.'

He leaned over and kissed her. 'Thanks. I'd better take this to her before she starts complaining. Did I tell you that new hairstyle looks great?'

'Only a dozen times! For goodness' sake, give your mother that drink before you spill it,' she said, laughing.

'Enjoying yourself, Maddie?'

'Hello, Miss Agnes, Yes, thank you. Are you?'

'Oh, I'm having a wonderful time. This is the first wedding I've been to.' Absently she patted her week-old hairstyle. 'I hope I get asked to another. I shall have so much to write to Alice about.' She paused, casting her eyes hurriedly around the room. 'Er . . . have you seen Mr Simpson at all?' she asked casually.

'He's gone home, Miss Agnes.'

'Home? Oh.'

'Said he had things to attend to.'

The fleeting look of disappointment that crossed her face was unmistakable. 'Oh, I was just wanting to see if he was all right. As his employer I felt it my duty.'

Maddie did not believe a word of what she said, but declined to comment. 'He was his usual self, Miss Agnes. I think he was just ready to go.'

'Yes, well,' she murmured, feigning disinterest. 'Oh, Mr Jenks is getting out his fiddle. Your father has promised me a dance.'

'*Can* he dance?' asked Maddie.

'He doesn't know himself, dear, and I don't know if I can. We're going to see if we can together. Oh, isn't it exciting?' said Agnes, hurrying off.

Josh came back to join Maddie. 'Well, Mrs Jenks, everyone seems to be enjoying themselves. Everyone's occupied. Sarah is talking to my mother. Me dad is providing the entertainment. Me sister and Roy are squashed together on the settee, staring adoringly into each other's eyes. Budding romance in the meking there, if I ain't mistaken. Your dad and Miss Agnes are about to dance once me father gets into tune. And all the rest of the neighbours and friends are eating, drinking and making merry. Who else is there? Where's your Ruth?'

'She's around somewhere. I saw her a while ago chatting to Bill Wiggins from next door.'

'That good-looking lad that came in with his mam and dad an hour or so ago?'

'That's him.'

'Probably kissing and cuddling up the entry by now then.'

Maddie nudged him. 'Josh, really,' she laughed. 'Good luck to her if she is. She can look after herself, can our Ruth.'

He turned and looked at her. 'So?' he said, cocking an eyebrow.

'So?' she repeated, frowning.

He smiled wickedly. 'So is it safe for us to slip off?'

A pink tinge flushed her cheeks. 'Won't anyone miss us?'

He shook his head and grabbed her hand. 'Too bad if they do. Come on, Mrs Jenks. We've a house of our own to go to.'

# Chapter Twenty-Four

'Oswald, are you listening? The strip of black board needs putting up against the window, advising everyone who passes to be respectful as there's been a death in the house. Please secure it as quietly as possible. And don't forget to take the bale of straw with you to spread on the cobbles outside and dull the noise of the horses and carts passing by.' Agnes paused thoughtfully. 'Now have I forgotten anything? Oh, the wreath to hang on the door. It's outside by the doorstep.'

'I do know all this,' he muttered sulkily. 'I 'ave done it before.'

'I'm quite aware of that,' said Agnes, putting on her coat. 'I just want everything to be right. Remember, it's our task to guide the poor bereaved family through these dark days. Our job does not finish until the family are safely back home after the funeral service. Now, so far as the Dunns' funeral is concerned, there's no need to polish the hearse, it's just the dray we'll be using. I must check with Maddie to make sure the black cloth we drape it with has been washed after the last time it was used . . . Oh, yes, and organise the pall-bearers. There's only the father and an uncle so we'll need another four. Jones, Biggins, Fellows and Bogs, I think. They're all about the same height and I know they could all do with the bit of money they get for doing it. Although I must have a quiet word with Mr Bogs. His black suit is really threadbare, not up to the standard I like to see my pall-bearers keep.' She frowned thoughtfully. 'I expect another suit is well beyond the poor man's means.

I'll speak to him, see if I can help.'

Oswald's unattractive features twisted in a scowl. Old man Clatteridge never made all this fuss, he thought, just barked out orders and let his workers get on with it. Now here *she* was treating him like an imbecile and acting as if she was personally responsible for guiding the souls of the dead. Most folk round here, he thought wickedly, were bound straight for hell from what they got up to while they were alive.

Still, his daily work wasn't such a bind now that his mind was occupied with the deal he had struck. Could be very lucrative, he'd been told. And after he'd thought about it, he was in no doubt that it could indeed. It was risky, 'course it was. Making money on the side didn't come without its dangers. But the money in his pocket and what he could do with it far outweighed thoughts of what would happen if he was discovered.

'Oh, the flowers . . .'

'Flowers!' he exclaimed. 'What, them ones, Miss Clatteridge?' he queried, staring at the bunch on the table. 'You ain't expecting me to walk through the streets wi' a bunch of flowers, are yer?' Oswald looked at her aghast. 'I mean, I'll 'ave me hands full wi' everything else I've ter carry.'

'Yes, of course. I'll take them myself,' Agnes said, pulling on her gloves. 'Well, off you go then. I'll be directly behind you. And please remember, Oswald, act courteously at all times. You're a representative of Clatteridge's.'

'Yes, Miss Clatteridge,' he muttered, turning away from her and heading out of the door. It was not until he was out of sight that he pulled a disgruntled face and stuck two fingers up.

'Oh, what lovely flowers for this time of year, Miss Agnes,' Maddie declared, arriving in the kitchen laden down with a full basket of dirty washing.

Agnes eyed her blankly. 'Pardon, dear? I was miles away. Going over in my mind everything for the Dunn family.'

'I was admiring the flowers. For you, are they?'

Agnes smiled. 'No, dear. Who do I know would buy me flowers? No, I bought them to place in the room where the body is to lie.' She lowered her voice. 'You see, Maddie dear, after a few days . . . I thought the flowers would be a nice touch and help scent the place. The family aren't very well off. In fact, I've had to cut our price to the bone so they can afford to bury their daughter. Oh, such a terrible state of affairs! Only fourteen and struck down by the influenza. She was well one day, a week later gone. She's to be all in white, of course, because she was virginal.' Agnes pulled a face and added, 'Well, I hope so at her age. I did suggest we brought her body here to lie in the Chapel of Rest but the poor mother can't bear to part from her daughter until she really has to.'

Maddie tried not to shudder. 'Oh, I see. I thought I'd set to with the washing while you were out,' she said to change the subject.

'Thank you, dear. I hope to be back before twelve-thirty so you can get off to see to your husband's dinner. Although I might have a problem because the bereaved do like to talk about their loved ones and I don't like to rush away. I feel it's very much part of our job to listen to them. It all helps ease their grief, doesn't it?'

'You're so kind, Miss Agnes. I don't suppose many undertakers would do the extra things you do.'

'I like to think that Clatteridge's is a bit special. Oh, that reminds me. I had a letter of introduction from the agent today for a Mr and Mrs Moss. They're in a village situation at the moment but want to move to town and are looking for a suitable place. Let's hope they like this one enough to make an offer.'

Six potential buyers had been shown around now and not one had taken matters further, which was most discouraging. Agnes did not say as much but Maddie knew the situation was deeply worrying for her. At least once a week a letter arrived from her sister wanting to know what was going on. Agnes was running out of excuses. Still, with business coming in steadily now, her main worry over money had been greatly relieved and she was being kept fully occupied and seemed to be thriving on it all.

Maddie smiled as she watched her bustling about readying herself to see her clients. Despite being dressed in black, which for work purposes was only fitting, she looked very efficient and smart in her flattering blouse and skirt and a good wool wrapover coat, its single large button fastening at the hip. A cloche-style hat was pulled down over her Marcel wave.

'Right, I'd better be off then,' Agnes announced, picking up her handbag.

'I hope it all goes well,' said Maddie. 'Don't worry if you're late back. If Josh arrives home and I'm not there, he'll help himself out of the larder. He never makes a fuss.'

'He's so good your husband, dear. A real treasure. But in this weather, with what he does for a living, he needs a hot meal inside him in the daytime. And of course you're still newly-weds . . .'

'Miss Agnes!' Maddie cut in, laughing. 'We've been married nearly two months. We had our first disagreement last night.'

'Oh, you didn't, dear?' Agnes gasped in concern.

'Don't look so worried, Miss Agnes, it was only over where we'd put the table and chairs we bought last week from that couple who were selling them. I thought they would look best by the window, Josh said by the wall under the mantles so he could see what I was trying to poison him with.'

'Who won, dear?'

'Neither of us. We both decided on the middle. The room looks really nice.' Well, as nice as they could make it, she thought, with what little they had by way of furniture. The house, if she was honest, was not in a good state of repair, the rooms small and narrow, the amenities outside shared between several other families. But at least it was not damp or riddled with bugs, as were many of the surrounding near-slum properties. Josh had been lucky to find it, the landlord being a very pleasant old gentleman who wasn't charging an extortionate rate for what he was offering, and until the day came that they could afford to move to something better, Maddie was perfectly content to live there with her husband. If truth be told, she'd live in a shack to be with Josh. 'You'll have to come round for tea,' she invited.

'I'll look forward to it.'

'And we've had our first Christmas together . . .'

'Oh yes, Maddie dear, wasn't that wonderful? I thought you were so brave, considering you'd only just got married, inviting all your family round for the day and including me and Mr Simpson.' Her voice lowered. 'Pity he didn't manage to come,' she said, more to herself than Maddie. 'I think he would have enjoyed himself. I didn't like the thought of him being in his room all by himself. On previous Christmases, give Father his due, Mr Simpson was always invited to our table for dinner.' She took a deep breath. 'Still, it was such a lovely afternoon. All that food you managed to cook, and helping gave me such pleasure. Then we had carols and opening our presents. I have to say again, Maddie, I really am delighted with that brooch you bought me. It's so pretty.'

'It wasn't expensive, Miss Agnes. We just hoped you'd like it.'

'What it cost is not important, dear. It's the thought that counts. You had enough to buy for as it was. Anyway, apart from deeply missing my sister, it was the best Christmas I've ever spent.'

Agnes had told her this several times already.

'Josh and I wanted to do it by way of thanking everyone for helping make our wedding so special. And, of course, I didn't want Sarah to have the burden, what with the baby on the way. She would have insisted we all went around and

I know we'd all have helped but I didn't want her to have the fuss and worry of it all, so I got in first. Anyway, I really enjoyed it too. It seems like only yesterday, doesn't it?'

'It does, dear, and what is it now – the middle of February? I can't wait to see the back of this dreadfully bitter weather myself. Burying people isn't the happiest of jobs at the best of times, but believe me it can be utter misery, standing blue with cold, trying hard not to shiver by a graveside. Still, I shouldn't be complaining, I'm far too gratified that people are coming to us now instead of going elsewhere. At least we have the goodwill back as an incentive to buyers. Now I've got my bag . . . my hat's on my head . . . What else? Oh, the flowers,' she said, picking them up. 'Mr Simpson is on hand should you run into difficulties, Maddie, though I don't envisage you will. And I'll do my best to be back.'

'Stop worrying, Miss Agnes. You might think of me and Josh as newly-weds but I feel like we're old hands at it. Now go on.' And Maddie laughingly shooed her off.

Humming a merry tune to herself, weighed down by the laundry basket, she made her way across the yard, hoping the fire underneath the boiler had heated the water sufficiently to boil the sheets. She raised her eyes. Dark clouds were gathering and rain, or more likely snow, was threatening. Miss Agnes was lucky she didn't have to have wet washing dripping in her kitchen, or suffer the terrible condensation it caused, like most people around these streets did. There was a small room just off the main laundry building that had cradles hung from its rafters and in bad weather washing hung in there, dried rapidly by the warmth of the fire under the boiler.

Maddie was feeling so happy in herself. Settling into marriage with Josh had been practically effortless, their both falling into living together easily, and she saw the years stretching ahead filled with joy. Her family, particularly Ruth and Roy, ever eager to escape their parents' watchful eyes, were frequent visitors as they themselves were to George and Sarah's. A trip to the Jenks family had not yet been attempted, Josh not pushing as he felt it was too soon for Maddie to return to the town after her last painful experience with her mother.

Now that their wedding was out of the way Maddie and Josh talked often about what, if anything, they could do to find their child. They had explored all sorts of possibilities, even to scouring surrounding areas on the lookout for a child who appeared familiar. That, they both knew, was a silly idea. Their child could take after either or neither of them, with features inherited from forbears, and the adoptive parents could live anywhere.

A visit to Mrs Baldicott had been suggested and was, they knew, the only option left open to them. They were going to journey to see her as soon as the weather improved a little and work on both sides allowed them a free Saturday, Maddie knowing it would not be right to call on Mrs Baldicott on the Sabbath as the old lady liked to attend two church services and spent the rest of the day resting her aged legs, sitting by the fire with her current charge, either knitting or sewing garments for the new arrival. Well, that was what she had done with Maddie at any rate. From what she knew of older people, they did not like change.

Maddie prayed Mrs Baldicott would somehow be able to find it in herself to furnish them with the information they sought. She knew that the old lady was under her own moral code not to divulge information but maybe the change in their circumstances would sway matters in their favour.

Maddie smiled to herself as she thought of her work. All the rooms in the house had been sifted through and what Agnes was taking with her crated up ready for the eventual move. Now Agnes was fully occupied elsewhere, Maddie's job had become that of housekeeper. She cleaned and washed and shopped for Agnes, always making a point, no matter how busy she was, of making sure a hot meal was cooking in the oven for Agnes by the time she left. She purposely prepared too much, knowing that what Agnes did not eat went straight across to Ivan. She had never mentioned this so neither did Maddie. She was also more than willing to lend a hand where required so long as it did not bring her into direct contact with the bodies, her revulsion at the very idea still as strong as ever. Despite Maddie's receiving a more than adequate wage for her work, Agnes was always very grateful for all she did and was forever thanking her, much to Maddie's amusement.

As she made to enter the laundry Ivan came out of the workshed. 'Hello, Maddie me duck. Busy, I see? Oh, and the stew last night was very tasty, but I like me gravy a bit thicker.'

'Cheeky devil!' she giggled.

'Miss Clatteridge out, is she?'

She nodded. 'Just left to see the Dunns.'

'Ah, right. I was just hoping to catch her to tek a look at the coffin for the gel. She likes to give her approval, does Miss Clatteridge. I ain't disappointed her yet, though, so I'm sure she'll be 'appy wi' what I've done. Mind you, you can't fancy up plain box wood however much yer try.'

'Where's the undertaker?' a deep voice demanded. 'I've been hammering on the front door but I got no reply.'

They both looked over to a man standing just inside the yard, having slipped through the arch unnoticed. He was tall, very good-looking and extremely harassed, judging by the look on his face. Maddie knew straight away he was a doctor by the black Gladstone bag he was carrying.

'Miss Clatteridge is out, Doctor,' she replied, putting down her full basket and making her way across to him. 'Can I give her a message?'

'*Miss* Clatteridge? Oh, of course, I had heard the daughter had taken over when the old man passed on. I've had good reports too. My patients tell me they're very impressed by the service they get from her.' The man scratched his head, thoughtfully. 'Message? No, I need her now. Terrible case.

I've just returned home after my rounds and my wife met me at the door. Have to go now, I'm afraid, this can't wait. The police are anxious for me to get there.'

Maddie looked perplexed, not quite sure what to do.

Ivan saw her dilemma and stepped over to take charge. 'What sort of case is it, Doctor? Nasty disease? 'Cos if it is the Infirmary mortuary is the best place. . .'

'I know that, man,' he snapped agitatedly. 'I'm a doctor, remember, and the police would hardly be present if that were the case. According to the message my wife received it appears the cause of death was a car accident. I've no other details until I get there. I don't know what I'm going to find either.'

Car, thought Ivan. Must have money. In his mind's eye a huge funeral procession loomed. The black glass-sided hearse would be gleaming; a well-groomed Ned decked out in plumed headdress. He saw a mahogany, no, walnut casket with solid brass trimmings. Oh, how he enjoyed working with such lovely wood. He couldn't wait to get started. But more important to Ivan was the revenue it would bring in for Miss Clatteridge. Damn and blast! he inwardly fumed. Of all the times for her to be out on business.

'Er . . . look, if Miss Clatteridge isn't available I'll nip over to Snood's,' said the doctor. 'They're the nearest undertakers to here, I think.'

At the mention of Snood's Ivan bristled. 'I'm sure we can handle this, Doctor. I can collect the . . . er . . . unfortunate deceased and Miss Clatteridge can visit the relatives as soon as she gets back, to find out their wishes and arrange matters.'

'Two.'

'Eh?'

'Bodies. There's two.'

'Really? Oh, dear,' Ivan said gravely. 'I'll get the box cart and follow yer in yer trap, Doctor.'

'Yes, all right. I wonder if I should send for an ambulance?'

303

he mused, then said, 'No, there's no point in wasting resources when those still alive are in need. My wife is very precise with her messages and these people are past hospital treatment. Bring the box cart then, and be quick about it, man.'

'Be with yer in two ticks, Doctor. Where is it we're going?'

He consulted his notebook. 'Number two Grange Lane, Thurnby Hill.'

'Them's decent houses,' Ivan whispered to Maddie, taking her aside. 'Explain to Miss Clatteridge as soon as she returns, won't yer?'

'Yes, of course,' she replied as he disappeared into the stable.

The doctor acknowledged Maddie with a hurried glance and a nod of his head before making to rush away, then stopped and turned back. 'You, miss,' he called, 'you'd better come too.'

'Me?'

'I'll need someone to help deal with whoever's in the house until Miss Clatteridge can take over. Get your coat,' he ordered. 'You can travel with me in the trap.'

His decisive manner told Maddie there was no point in refusing.

In other circumstances she would have found the journey exhilarating and exciting, never having ventured this far along the road she worked and lived off or realised it extended so far. There were many questions she would have liked to ask the doctor but she kept silent, not wanting him to realise the extent of her ignorance.

A half mile or so along, terraced houses, new semis and shops had been left behind, giving way to open countryside, the cobbled road to rutted mud. Intermittently the red gabled roofs of several imposing houses were visible over high laurel hedges. Presently they came to a scattering of smaller gabled properties on the edge of Thurnby village and the doctor expertly began to guide his trap through a brick-pillared gateway. One of the pillars was practically demolished, the remains of the cause of the damage embedded at the base of it.

At the sight of the crushed vehicle Maddie froze and turned her head away. The doctor immediately pulled the trap to a halt. A policeman appeared.

'Dr Giddons,' he said, introducing himself as he alighted.

'Ah, bin waiting for yer, sir.' The policeman eyed Maddie questioningly.

'Oh, this is Miss . . .' the doctor began.

'Mrs Jenks,' Maddie answered for him.

'She's from the undertakers,' said Dr Giddons.

Ivan pulled up behind them and jumped out. 'D'yer want me to make a start, Doctor?'

'No. I don't want anything touching until I say so. I have to determine the cause of death first.'

'I think that's obvious, don't you?' the policeman remarked.

'Oh, so you trained as a doctor before you joined the police, did you?'

The constable shuffled his feet uncomfortably. 'D'yer want me to stay or go up to the house to find the Inspector, tell him you're here?'

'No, Mrs Jenks can do that. I'll need your help.' The doctor held up his hand to help Maddie down. 'Tell the Inspector I'm here, Mrs Jenks, then see what needs doing.'

She gulped. She hadn't a clue what he meant but all she said was, 'Yes, Doctor.'

She walked up the short drive which led to a pretty red brick house, the bare stems of a climbing rose scrambling up the front wall and over the top of the door. The gardens she passed were bare of flowers but green with shrubbery and very well-kept. Before she reached the door it opened and a large man in a macintosh strode out. 'That dratted doctor turned up yet?' he wondered aloud. He spotted Maddie. 'Who are you?'

'Mrs Jenks. I'm from the undertakers, Inspector.' She assumed this was he. 'The doctor's dealing with matters at the end of the drive.'

'About bloody time!'

'What do you want me to do, Inspector?'

He looked at her blankly. 'I dunno. What you normally do, I expect.'

With that he slapped his trilby on his head and strode purposefully off, macintosh billowing, leaving her staring after him.

Maddie took a breath and looked at the house. What would Miss Agnes do now? she thought. Go and speak to the relatives, was her answer. But what did she say? Maddie shrugged her shoulders. She would have to use her instincts.

Tentatively she walked through the door into a very tastefully decorated hallway. To the left of her, halfway down the wide hallway leading towards the back, was an occasional table on top of which stood an ornate vase filled with wax flowers. The stairs leading to the first floor were in front of her. Several landscape prints hung on the walls.

'Hello,' she called.

There was no response.

As she stood and listened she could hear the soft sounds of someone crying. They appeared to be coming from somewhere down the hallway. Listening intently, Maddie followed the sounds.

She eventually found the woman sitting at the kitchen table, her head bent, face buried in a large piece of towelling. She was obviously a maid judging by the black dress, white cap and apron she wore.

'Excuse me,' Maddie said softly, 'could you tell me where I can find the relatives, please?'

The maid's head shot up, face blotchy, swollen eyes red-ringed. She sniffed. 'Ain't none. I've already told that Inspector. Anyway, who are yer?'

'I'm Mrs Jenks, from the undertakers.'

'Oh, God,' the maid wailed, again burying her head in the towelling. 'I can't believe it. I can't. Lovely people, 'specially the Missus. Best job I've ever had.'

Maddie sat down on the chair nearest her, leaned over and placed a hand gently on the maid's arm. She was only young, eighteen or nineteen at the most Maddie guessed. 'Would you like me to make you a cup of tea?' she asked.

The girl shook her head. 'If I see anymore tea I'll scream. That's all I did for that blasted Inspector, mek tea and get asked questions I don't know the bloody answers to. I'm only the maid. I ain't bin 'ere all that long. They'd just bought the car. Mr Bingham were tekin' the Missus fer a quick spin. Said they wouldn't be long. Missus were ever so excited. Foreign she wa'. When she got excited 'er arms went everywhere, talking 'er own lingo which yer can't understand a word of.' She shuddered, sniffing back the tears. 'I saw it 'appen. I wa' standing at the door waving 'em off.'

'You did?' Maddie asked, shocked.

The maid nodded. 'A dog shot out the 'edge and Mr Bingham swerved to avoid it and 'it the stone pillar. It collapsed on top of them. Ohhh!' she wailed. 'I can still hear the Missus screamin'.'

'There, there,' Maddie soothed. 'Look . . . er . . . I don't mean to upset you by asking more questions but I'm really here to talk to the relatives. I need to know where they are?'

The maid's face became even blotchier if that were possible. 'And I've already told yer, there ain't none.'

'Oh, dear,' said Maddie. 'There must be someone, surely?'

'There's no one I know of.'

This is dreadful, thought Maddie.

'Inspector sez lawyer'll have ter deal wi' it all. Got the papers he did out the bureau.' She wiped her face, blew her nose noisily, scraped back her chair and stood up. 'He sez I can go 'ome.'

'Are you sure you're feeling all right to?'

307

'Yeah, he sez it's best place fer me. Me mam'll look after me. What about 'er?'

'Sorry?' Maddie said, eyeing her blankly.

''Er,' she repeated, inclining her head over Maddie's shoulder.

Frowning in bewilderment Maddie turned her head to look behind her and then gasped. 'Oh, my goodness!'

Huddled right inside a narrow gap between the back wall and the side of the pantry Maddie could see a little girl of about two. She had her thumb planted firmly in her mouth, large blue eyes staring unblinkingly.

'Oh, but she's beautiful. The poor little mite!' said Maddie emotionally. 'What's her name?'

'Penelope. They called her Penny. Loved 'er they did. Treated that kid like bloody royalty. Me mam reckoned it weren't 'ealthy the way they pampered 'er.'

'Oh, but I can see why they did,' Maddie declared wistfully, gazing at the child and momentarily forgetting the gravity of the situation.

'Yeah, I s'pose she ain't a bad kid,' the maid sniffed begrudgingly. 'Can't stand 'em meself though.'

'What did the Inspector tell you to do with her?' Maddie asked the maid who was by now pulling on her coat.

She shrugged her shoulders.

Maddie swivelled around in her seat, giving the maid her full attention. 'Well, he must have said something?'

'He didn't ask about 'er.'

'Didn't ask? You mean, he doesn't know?'

The maid shook her head. 'I wa' so upset meself, I forgot to mention 'er.'

'What?' Maddie cried, fighting anger. 'Were you just going to go off and leave her here?'

'Well, no, but you're 'ere now, ain't yer?'

'Yes, but I'm from the undertakers. I've come to assist with the funeral arrangements.'

'Well, ain't she part of 'em? I can't tek 'er wi' me. Me

mother'd go mad. I'm worrying I won't get me wage this week now. Look, I godda go. I'm too upset, really.'

Bursting into a fresh torrent of tears, she ran from the room.

Maddie's shoulders sagged. She looked at the little girl helplessly, her heart going out to her. At this moment it appeared that the child had no one. Maddie wondered if she sensed the tragedy going on around her. Easing herself off her chair, mindful any abrupt movement could upset the child, she slid on to her knees on the cold red tiles. 'Hello, sweetheart,' she said, holding out her hand and smiling warmly. 'Would you like a drink? Milk? Do you like milk? Take my hand and show me where the milk is. All right, Penny dear?'

The child stared at her for several long moments, Maddie waiting patiently, then taking her thumb out of her mouth she struggled to her feet. Maddie gently put her arms around her and picked her up. 'My, you're a lump,' she said, smiling. 'Now can you point to where the milk is kept?'

The child looked at her then pointed her tiny finger towards the larder to one side of Maddie. 'Good girl,' she said. 'My, you are clever, aren't you?'

Maddie found the milk and a clean cup amongst the several the Inspector and the maid had used between them. She filled it with milk and gave it to the child, who grabbed it and drank greedily.

'My, you were thirsty,' Maddie said. 'Would you like some more?'

The child nodded.

The process was repeated.

'Now,' said Maddie, 'why don't we go and find that nice policeman and find out what we're to do with you, eh? All right, so that's what we'll do then.'

After finding the child's coat, she put it on. She took hold of her hand, Penny toddling alongside her, and went in search of the Inspector.

The activity that greeted her at the end of the drive shook Maddie rigid. Realising it was no place for a child, she hurriedly turned and retraced her steps. 'I tell you what, Penny, why don't we go and see what toys you have and we'll play a game while we wait for that nice policeman to come back,' she said as they re-entered the house.

Upstairs Maddie found a room that was filled with all sorts of toys, and taking out a box of wooden bricks she settled herself on the rug in the middle of the spacious room, the little girl to the side of her, and began to pile bricks on top of one another. They collapsed and the child giggled. Then she joined in with her own clumsy attempts. Maddie watched her, fascinated. Time passed as they played. At length Maddie raised her head and realised it was growing dark.

'My goodness,' she exclaimed, scrambling up. 'I think it's time we put all the toys away and went back downstairs. What do you think, Penny?'

Thumb in her mouth, the child just looked up at her with big blue eyes. 'My, you'll break a few hearts when you're older,' Maddie said tenderly. Though you're breaking mine now, she thought.

Hurriedly she packed the toys away, gathered the child up and went downstairs. The house was empty. They were taking a long time to deal with matters at the end of the drive. She ought to go and see what the situation was. She needed to tell them about the child. The poor little mite must be hungry and Maddie could tell she was getting tired. She also wondered why Miss Clatteridge hadn't arrived, then it struck her. In the doctor's urgency for them to depart, she hadn't left Miss Clatteridge a note informing her of the situation.

Placing the child on the floor, Maddie rummaged around in the larder, finding a biscuit in a tin. Squatting down before her, she gave it Penny. 'Now you stay here just for a moment while I go and find someone. I won't be long, sweetheart.'

She didn't like the thought of leaving the child unattended and as swiftly as she could ran from the house and down the drive. As the gates came into view she stopped abruptly.

There was no sign of anyone. The area was deserted, the only evidence of the terrible accident hidden under a large tarpaulin.

Maddie stared around her in dismay. Were they coming back or had they all forgotten about her?

Frowning worriedly, she retraced her steps and entered the kitchen, thankful to find Penny just where she had left her. She knelt before her, mind racing frantically. What on earth was she to do? It was getting late. There was only one thing for it. The child would have to spend the night with her and Josh and matters would be dealt with in the morning.

After gathering together items of the little girl's clothing and having the foresight also to include a couple of soft toys and the box of bricks, she dressed the child warmly, pulled the front door securely behind her and set off.

The journey was slow. Maddie weighed down by the child in her arms and the bag containing her belongings. The long road that had fascinated her several hours ago now seemed endless. And to make matters worse the evening had turned bitterly cold and it was beginning to snow. She was tired herself, frozen to the marrow, but all her concern lay with the child in her arms and she hurried along the slippery road as fast as she could.

Exhausted and bedraggled, she arrived home much later, Penny's sleeping head on her shoulder. It was just approaching seven o'clock and the snow was falling thickly. As soon as Maddie managed the struggle to insert her key in the lock it was opened by an extremely worried Josh. He looked at her, the child, then back at Maddie questioningly.

'I'll explain in a minute,' she said, stamping her numb feet on the straw mat just inside the door.

He took the bag from her and followed her down the dark hallway to the room at the back. The fire was blazing, the table set for dinner, and an appetising aroma greeted Maddie. She laid the child down gently in the old armchair they had picked up from the pawnbroker's for next to nothing, and quickly grabbed Josh's jacket from the back of the door to cover her with. He meantime watched silently.

Satisfied the child was comfortable, Maddie turned and looked at her husband.

'It can wait a minute longer,' he ordered, putting the bag down. 'You're soaking wet. Get yourself dry and then sit by the fire while I mek you a cuppa. Then you can tell me. I'm just glad to see you home, I've bin worried sick.'

Too tired to argue she did as he said and ten minutes later, Josh sitting in his armchair, Maddie by his feet, cradling a mug of tea, she told him what had happened.

When she had finished he sighed. 'Sad state of affairs. Well, yer did the right thing, me darlin', bringing the kiddy back here. There was n'ote else yer could do.'

'You don't mind?'

'Why should I? You know me better than to ask that, surely?'

'Yes,' she said, smiling tenderly. 'I do.' She glanced sadly at the sleeping child. 'I really ought to go round and tell Miss Agnes about the little girl.'

He put his hand on her shoulder. 'You'll stay put. The mornin'll be soon enough. N'ote else can be done tonight, it's too late. That kiddy needs a good night's sleep after what she's bin through, and so, me darlin', do you. When we've had dinner I'll sort something out for her to sleep on. Now you sit there while I go and dish up. It's just sausage and potatoes. You know I can't mek gravy for love nor money.'

'I don't care what it is, Josh, I could eat a horse.'

'Well, let's hope it don't taste like one!' he laughed as he rose and made his way into the kitchen.

Maddie raised herself to look more closely at the child and check she was all right before settling herself again, feet resting on the fender, to thaw out before the fire. Not many women, she thought, would have returned home to a husband who'd welcome in a little stranger as Josh had. Nor would a blazing fire and a meal be waiting them. She was certainly a lucky woman.

She heard an urgent knock on the front door.

'Stay there, I'll get it,' ordered Josh.

She heard voices and moments later he returned, followed by Agnes.

'Oh, Maddie dear, I was so worried about you!'

'You won't mind me, will yer, Miss Agnes? I'm just seeing to the dinner.'

'No, of course not, Josh, please carry on.'

'Won't you sit down?' Maddie offered, moving aside to allow Agnes to sit in Josh's armchair.

'Thank you, dear. I'm sorry to intrude at this time of night, but I had to see you were home safely. When I returned from seeing the Dunns, it was after one o'clock. I didn't know what to think when I found the place deserted. I thought you'd gone home to see to Josh's dinner. Then, when you didn't return and there was no sign of Mr Simpson, I became worried. Of course, Peabody hadn't any idea as he'd been at the Dunns' most of the morning.' Tightening her lips, she shook her head. 'That young man takes such a long time to do things, doesn't he? But that's another matter.

'Then those people turned up – you know, the Mosses to have a look round. I heard Mr Simpson return about three but couldn't just abandon the visitors. It was well after five before they left. They seemed very keen, I have to say. Anyway, as soon as I had said my goodbyes to them, I went straight to see Mr Simpson. He explained what had happened. Such a terrible thing, wasn't it, dear? He told me he'd left you up at the house with the doctor and we both thought, as time wore on, that the good doctor had driven you straight home. Well, that was until I had a courtesy visit from him just now.

313

'When he was leaving I thanked him for taking you home and he said he hadn't. When he went to look for you at the house after Mr Simpson had left, he found it empty.'

'I was upstairs,' explained Maddie.

'Oh, I see. Well, he presumed you'd made your own way home. The police had left by then too with all they needed. I suppose with all that was going on there was bound to be a little confusion. I know you're very capable, Maddie, but I had to come and see you were safe. You are all right?' Agnes frowned then as a thought struck her. 'Why were you upstairs when the doctor came to look for you?'

Maddie's eyes filled with sadness. 'I was looking after a precious penny.'

'I beg your pardon?' she said, bewildered.

Maddie nodded and turned, looking back at the armchair behind her. Agnes followed her gaze, mouth dropping open at the sight of the little bundle nestled in its depths. She rose to her feet and peered down. 'I thought I was mistaken but it's a child!' she exclaimed. 'Whose . . . Oh, my goodness, is this the child of the deceased couple?' she said, shocked, hand before her mouth.

'The maid forgot to inform anyone.'

'She *what*? How on earth could a thing like that have slipped her mind?'

'Well, she was very upset, she witnessed the accident, but I still feel it was inexcusable of her.'

'It certainly was.' Agnes stared down at the child, eyes filling with tenderness. 'Isn't she a lovely little thing?' She smiled at Maddie warmly. 'It was good of you to bring her home with you, my dear.'

'I couldn't do anything else, Miss Agnes, could I? From what the maid said the couple doted on her. You should have seen her bedroom. It was filled with toys and clothes enough to stock a shop.' Maddie gave a deep sigh. 'I wonder what will happen to her now?'

'Relatives will take her, I expect. That's what usually happens in cases like this.'

'The maid said she didn't know of any.'

'What? None at all? Oh, she must have that wrong. They can't both have been without relatives. We'll know more when the solicitor makes contact. The doctor told me the police were going to inform him of the tragedy as soon as possible. I can't do anything with the remains until I receive instructions. The solicitor will pay a call on me in the morning, I expect. In my experience solicitors are full of their own importance so I do hope it's at a convenient time as I've a hundred and one things to do. We've two funerals, one in the morning, the other later in the afternoon. Timing's very tight as it is.'

'I'm sure you'll manage,' Maddie said, smiling.

'I'll have to, dear. But I couldn't without you and Mr Simpson, that's for certain.'

They both looked down again at the child.

'Josh is going to make her up a little bed on the floor in our room,' said Maddie. 'We'll make sure she's comfortable.'

'That's good of you, my dear. What about bedding?' asked Agnes, mindful that Maddie had precious little, her married life just starting. 'I've some things you can have to help. A couple of blankets I didn't part with just in case. I'm glad I didn't now. I'll send Mr Simpson around with them shortly. I know he'll still be working in the shed and he won't mind. Now I'd better go and leave you to eat your meal and sort the little one out. I suggest you bring her with you in the morning, ready to hand over to whoever's going to take her.' She patted Maddie's arm affectionately. 'Goodnight, my dear. Goodnight, Josh,' she called.

He popped his head around the kitchen door. 'You off, then, Miss Agnes? Thanks fer calling.

'You ready to eat your leg of the horse?' he asked after Maddie had shown Agnes out.

She nodded. 'Yes I'm ready to risk it. Penny must be

hungry but I don't think we should wake her.'

Arms around each other, they both looked down at the sleeping child.

# Chapter Twenty-Five

'What do you say, Josh? Can she stop with us?'

Sighing, he shook his head. 'I'm not sure if it's best, Maddie. It's you I'm worried for. Worried you'll get too attached to her.'

'And you won't? I saw your face this morning when you thought the authorities were about to fetch her. You had tears in your eyes, I know you did.'

'Well, maybe I had, she's a lovely little kiddy. I know she's only bin with us a week but . . .'

'I know, Josh,' Maddie said softly. 'We've both fallen in love with her, haven't we?'

He nodded. 'Hard not to. You told me that maid said her folks spoiled her, but she don't act spoiled, do she? Where is she anyway?'

'Miss Agnes is playing with her. Offered to watch her so I could speak to you without interruptions. She adores her too. It's so good of her to let me take Penny to work with me while we wait for news. It's a wonder we get any work done. You should see the way Miss Agnes runs around the house playing hide and seek with her, it's so funny. She has Penny in fits of giggles. And as for Ivan – he has her sitting on the stool for hours, watching him work away. It's amazing to see a child just sit like that. It's funny, though, the only person Penny won't go near for some reason is Oswald.'

'Children sense things,' said Josh matter-of-factly.

'Anyway, if you agree we can keep her, Sarah is going to watch her while I go to work.'

'And she's all right about that?'

'Josh, she's delighted. Says it'll get her in practice for when the baby arrives. She offered, honestly. Said a funeral parlour is no place for a kiddy, even though Miss Agnes was quite happy about me taking her there. She said if you agree we can keep her until the family come forward, she'll start this afternoon.'

He sighed again. 'Apart from Peabody it seems Little Miss Twopenny has us all wrapped around her little finger. So tell me again what the solicitor said?'

'Tell me if she can stay with us first?'

'Maddie . . .'

'All right. As you already know the lawyer has no information about any relatives and has decided to put advertisements in newspapers to see what happens. In the meantime there's not much else he can do. Mrs Bingham was German but from whereabouts in Germany he hasn't a clue. So it's a case of finding Mr Bingham's family.'

'Strange state of affairs, if you ask me.'

'What do you mean?'

'The solicitor not having any details of his family.'

'Maybe they're all dead.'

'What, all of them?' Josh shook his head. 'Summat don't feel right somehow. Anyway, what happens to any money they left? Who get's it?'

'Mr Grantham didn't divulge that information, Josh.'

'No, I don't suppose he did.'

'He's placing advertisements in local papers to start with and if that turns up nothing he'll widen the search. It could take a while. In the meantime we just have to wait.' Maddie eyed him expectantly. 'So can we keep her until then?'

'Mr Grantham did say it was all right?'

She nodded. 'He was surprised how well she's adapted to being with us, considering. I think he was only too glad we offered. Saves him the trouble of finding people to look after her in the meantime. And the authorities are only too glad not to have the bother either. The children's homes are bulging as it is.' She shuddered at the thought of Penny's being incarcerated in one of those dreadful places. 'So can we, Josh?'

She saw him hesitate and wrung her hands. 'Josh, I know you and Sarah think I'm using this child to fill the space left by my own baby. Neither of you has said as much but I know you're thinking it. I'm right, aren't I?'

He eyed her gravely and nodded.

Maddie's face fell in dismay. 'Oh, Josh, I'm not, please believe me. How could you think the child I gave birth to could ever be replaced?' She sighed, long and deep. 'I admit, I watch Penny, I hold her, and especially when she's sleeping there's something in me that . . . I can't explain it, it's like this child *belongs* to me. But I know she doesn't. It's just that she's lost her own parents and she's so little and vulnerable and I want to do anything I can to protect her until her own people turn up. That's not wrong of me, is it? I can't replace her own mother but I can try while she's with us can't I? Then it's for her own family to take over.'

He sighed. 'So long as you understand that she'll have to go sooner or later, Maddie. I just can't bear the thought of you getting hurt again when you've already suffered so much.'

'I know you're trying to protect me, my love, but there're some things you can't shield me from. Let's just enjoy little Penny while we can. I can't promise not to be hurt when the time comes for her to leave, and I know you'll be as upset as me, but that's something we'll face together.'

He eyed her searchingly. 'All right, Maddie.'

Her eyes lit up. 'So she can stay?'

'I don't know why you're asking me. You know I can't refuse yer nothin'.'

'Yes, but I'd still go with whatever you decided, you know that, Josh.'

'Yes, I do.' But there was no real decision for him to make. Maddie was right. He could no more bear the thought of

Penny going to strangers than Maddie could, and he too would miss the child deeply when it was time for her to leave. 'We'd better clear out the little room then, make it a proper bedroom for her, if she's stopping longer than we thought.'

'Oh, thanks, Josh,' Maddie cried, joyfully throwing her arms around him.

'Hang on a minute, I ain't finished.'

'Oh?' she said, stepping back and eyeing him worriedly.

'I want you to write to Mrs Baldicott and ask her the first Saturday it'd be convenient for us to call on her. We need to make a start finding our own child, Maddie. If Mrs Baldicott can't for whatever reason tell us anything then we'll rack our brains as to what else we can do to find her. Now Sarah and George know our secret, we could even rope them into helping us.'

'I'll write to Mrs Baldicott tonight.'

'Good. Now I'm off back to work,' he said, kissing her on her cheek. 'And you'd better get back too. I'll finish sharp so I can read madam a story before her bedtime. Oh, and there's summat I want ter discuss with yer. It's just about work, it'll keep.'

Later that afternoon Agnes walked into the kitchen. 'Maddie, you can finish now if you want to.'

She put down the potato she was peeling and turned around to her employer. 'I've not finished preparing the meal yet.'

'I can do that. With no funerals today I've caught up with all I need to do. Tomorrow's burial is well in hand. Don't you want an early finish?'

'Yes, that would be nice. I could have a cup of tea with Sarah when I pick up Penny. It's not often we have time on our own.' She eyed Agnes thoughtfully. 'Please excuse me, Miss Agnes, but you've something on your mind, that's obvious. Do you want to talk about it or do you want me to mind my own business?'

'You're very observant, Maddie dear. I didn't think it showed.' Agnes took a deep breath. 'It's just a little bit confusing for me. I don't really know what to make of it.'

Maddie flattened her back against the pot sink, folded her arms and looked at her. 'Make of what, Miss Agnes?'

'Well, you remember me telling you about the Mosses coming to view? Seemed really keen and the price was just about right for them. Mrs Moss wasn't at all bothered about there not being a water pump in the kitchen. She said she was used to going outside. They went away saying they'd be straight around to the agent's to sort out the details. Well, I never heard anything until this morning when I received a letter from Mr Moss. He wrote asking if I thought it fair to quote one price then, when someone is interested, put that price up. His tone was very angry. I went out this morning, didn't I? Said I was going into town. That was true, Maddie, but my sole intention was to see the agent. He was quite furious that Mr Moss had written to me. Said all dealings should go through him. He said he didn't know what Mr Moss was going on about. The price was the price, and besides he hadn't heard from them again after they left his office to come and view this place.'

'Very strange,' mused Maddie. 'Did the Mosses seem all right to you?'

'Perfectly, dear. They were a charming couple. Most odd, isn't it? Still, nothing I can do. I really was hopeful about them too. Anyway enough of this.' Agnes forced a smile. 'Now off you go. Give Mrs Ashman my best and I'll see you in the morning.'

'You look tired,' Maddie said as Sarah opened the door. 'Penny hasn't been too much for you, has she?' she asked in concern.

'Too much? Maddie, the child's keeping me occupied. I'm not used to having so much time on me hands. She's been a little darlin', as usual. It's a shame she doesn't talk much. Our Ruth was chattering away at her age, even though I couldn't work out what she was saying. I suppose little Penny's gone through so much, it's understandable. She must be so confused and I reckon she's a bit on the shy side. She'll talk when she's good and ready. Anyway, we went for a walk in the park and she had a nap this afternoon. I'm not tired, Maddie love.' She wasn't, it was worry that Maddie could see on Sarah's face. 'I just wish everyone would stop fussing.'

'We're not fussing, Sarah,' Maddie said as she followed her down the passage. 'We just care about you. You are keeping well, aren't you?'

She sighed. 'You asked me that yesterday and I'll tell you the same today. I ain't ill, I'm having a baby. Sit yerself down, I'll mash a cuppa.' She addressed the child playing on the rug with a toy train Ivan had bought for her from a man he knew who whittled toys from old bits of wood to supplement his living. 'Penny want a crust to gnaw on? Oh, good girl. She nodded, Maddie,' Sarah exclaimed in delight. 'Did you see her? She understands everything you say.' She held out her hand. 'Come with Auntie Sarah then into the kitchen and let's see what we can find, eh?'

'I'll make the tea,' offered Maddie, swinging the kettle over the fire.

They all trooped through to the kitchen.

Maddie began to gather cups together and fill the jug with milk. 'Ruth and Roy all right?'

'Fine,' Sarah said, her back to Maddie, spreading a crust of bread with butter for Penny. 'Ruth's off out tonight. Eh, and I think our Roy's got himself a girlfriend.'

'Really?' Maddie smiled, scooping a spoon of tea out of the caddy to put in the pot. 'What's she like?'

'Dunno. I haven't seen her. I don't know what her name is either. In truth I'm only guessing. But our Roy's washed his neck three times this week without me telling him, that's how I know.'

Maddie laughed. 'Oh, Sarah, you are funny.' She watched Penny take the crust. 'How's Dad?'

Sarah sat bolt upright and flashed her a strange glance. 'Fine. He's fine. Why d'yer ask?'

Maddie frowned. 'I always ask how Dad is, don't I?'

'Yes, 'course yer do. Sorry, Maddie, I'm still fuddled from me sleep.'

'Is there anything the matter, Sarah?'

'Matter? No, why should there be? Did you warm the pot before you put in the leaves?'

'Yes, I did. I might stay a bit longer tonight and wait for Dad to come in. Is that all right?'

'Why?'

Maddie shrugged her shoulders, bemused. 'Because he's my dad and I haven't seen him all week. Isn't that reason enough?'

'Oh, Maddie love, forgive me. Yer dad's had to go away for a few days . . . on business. I'm just missing him that's all.'

'Why didn't you say so, Sarah? I was beginning to think something was wrong. When will he be back?'

'I dunno,' she said, a bit too hurriedly for Maddie's liking. 'He didn't say. He should be back before the weekend, I think.' There was something wrong, Maddie knew Sarah well enough by now to see that. But whatever it was, Sarah was obviously not going to tell her.

'Shall we go through?' she suggested.

'Er . . . yes,' Maddie agreed reluctantly.

'Come on then, Penny,' Sarah said, taking the child's tiny hand.

Later that evening, Penny had been settled down for the night and Maddie was curled up in the armchair, an open book in her lap, staring thoughtfully into the dancing flames of the fire.

Josh lowered his newspaper and looked across at her. 'Good book, is it?'

'Pardon?'

'Your book. It's that good you haven't read a word of it for the last hour. What's bothering yer, Maddie?'

She smiled wanly. 'Nothing. Well, that's not entirely true. Just a couple of things. Maybe something and nothing.'

'Oh? It obviously has you bothered. Come on then,' he said, folding up his paper. 'Tell me.'

She smiled at him tiredly and closed her book. 'Sarah acted really strangely with me today when I asked how my father was.'

'Strange? In what way?'

Maddie shrugged her shoulders. 'That's it, Josh, I don't know. It was just the way she acted . . . But then, I was tired myself and worried that Penny was too much for her. Sarah's nearly seven months pregnant after all. But she insisted that having little Penny around was doing her a world of good. Anyway it was nothing to do with the child. It was how Sarah reacted when I asked about my father.'

'They've maybe had a row or something.'

'I've never known them to, Josh. Oh, maybe it was just me. I'll be seeing her again tomorrow so I'll see how she is then. She said Father was away on business.'

'Ah, that's it. She's missing him, that's all.'

'That's what Sarah said. You're right, I'm being silly.'

'I wouldn't call it silly, Maddie. You care for her very much, don't you?'

'Yes, I do.'

'So what was the other thing that was bothering you?'

'Oh, again, something and nothing.' She related to Josh what Agnes had told her. 'I wouldn't have thought anything of it but after what Mr Snood tried to do . . . Of course, we kept that from her. Miss Agnes knows nothing about that.'

'Yeah, best thing too.'

'But you can see why I took notice?'

'Mmmm, I can.'

'Do you think there's something to it, Josh?'

'Can't see what.' He paused thoughtfully. 'I'll mention it to yer dad when I next see him, though. See what he thinks just to be on the safe side.'

'So you think there . . .'

'I don't think anything, Maddie,' he cut in. 'But I like Miss Agnes and I wouldn't want to see anything bad happen to her. I'll just mention it to your dad when he returns from his business trip ter put our minds at rest. Now you just forget about it. You've got enough on yer plate with that little mite upstairs.'

Maddie smiled. 'All right.'

'So, d'yer feel better now?'

She nodded. 'Yes, thank you.'

'And I can get back to reading me paper in peace now, can I?'

'Oh, but didn't you say this morning you had something to discuss with me?'

'What? Oh, yeah, how could I have forgotten about that?' Josh clasped his hands and leaned forward, eyeing her intently. 'I've bin offered a round. Not a bad one either. Wally Cribbins passed on last week and his widow's put it up for sale. She's given me first offer. It's in town, mostly businesses, some houses. It's worth considering, Maddie.'

'What about your own round? Can you do them both?' she asked. 'You work very hard as it is, Josh. And how much is she asking?'

'Ten pounds. And, no, I can't do them both. Before you say anything, let me tell yer what I thought then yer can give me your opinion. I've five pounds saved, Maddie.'

She gasped. 'Five pounds? How on earth have you managed to do that?'

'By being careful. Walked when I could have taken a tram, them sorta things. And I don't booze money away at the pub, do I? And with your wage coming in, Maddie, well, that helps us too. It soon mounts up. But that money was intended for another house for us. I was wanting to surprise you. But, well, what I was thinking was to offer Mrs Cribbins the five and pay the rest off. I think she might agree 'cos she knows I'm genuine and she needs the money. Me and her Wally got on well enough. Then, for my own round, I was thinking of getting another bloke in, and paying him.'

Maddie frowned. 'I don't understand.'

'I'd employ him, Maddie. Pay him a decent wage for the job and keep the rest. I know a number of blokes I can trust who'd be willing.'

'Oh, I see. Well, then, you must do it, Josh.'

His eyes shone. 'Really? Yer don't object?'

'Absolutely not.'

He flung his arms around her, hugging her tightly. 'Thanks, Maddie.'

'What are you thanking me for?' she said, laughing.

''Cos there's no way I'd have gone ahead if you hadn't been happy about it. You know that.'

'Yes, I do, but I am happy, so get on with it.'

'You don't mind staying here a while longer? Or having ter keep working 'til I get things off the ground?'

'I love my job, you know that, Josh. And as for this house, there's many in a lot worse than this, so stop worrying. I'm quite happy to stay here forever if necessary.'

'You won't have to if my plans work out. I want a few rounds, Maddie. That's me intention. Oh, I do love you,' he said tenderly. 'Do yer fancy an early night?' he asked meaningfully.

'Mmmm,' she agreed thoughtfully, eyes humorous. 'That's a good idea. I am tired.'

'Not that tired, are yer, Maddie?' he asked huskily, kissing her lips.

She giggled. 'You lock up and I'll see you upstairs,' she said, pushing him playfully away. 'And be quiet when you come up so you don't wake Penny or you'll be disappointed.'

# Chapter Twenty-Six

Ivan sat upright and peered around him in the darkness – something had woken him. He sighed miserably, lying back down, wriggling to get comfortable on the lumpy straw mattress. He hadn't been fully asleep anyway, restlessly tossing and turning, the same as he did every night now. Agnes Clatteridge was the cause, damn the woman. Why did she have to go and make herself so attractive? Agnes had always been beautiful to him. Now he felt all male eyes were on her and it could only be a matter of time before one of them took matters further.

Ivan wasn't selfish, he wanted Agnes to be happy, but he wanted her to be happy with him.

He sighed again, pulled the worn blankets aside, swung his legs over the side of the narrow iron bedstead and got up, plodding across to the window overlooking the yard. Moving the bit of old curtaining aside, he peered out, looking skyward. The weather was definitely improving. Low cloud meant a frost was unlikely and the warmer weather had removed the threat of more snow. He was glad spring was beginning to put in an appearance, knowing Agnes didn't like the cold.

He was just about to step away and return to bed when something across the yard caught his eye. He strained harder, pressing his face right up to the glass. That was strange, he thought. It looked to him like the Chapel of Rest door was slightly open and he was positive he could see a flicker of light through the crack.

Ivan groaned. Oswald obviously hadn't done his duty for the night by blowing out the candles and securing the door properly. The casket containing the deceased whose funeral was arranged for the morning had been placed there earlier in the day and Agnes had insisted that candles be lit in case any last-minute visitors called to pay their respects.

He would have to go and do the chore himself, despite the fact there was no threat from any outside intruder, the gates to the yard having been secured by him personally before he retired for the night. But candles left burning in a breeze could cause a fire. He'd speak to Oswald severely in the morning. The trouble with that lad, fumed Ivan, as he pulled on his old coat over his long johns, was that he was too lazy by far, over eager to race away come leaving time.

He lit his oil lamp and made his way out.

He had reached the bottom of the iron staircase by the time he'd realised he'd forgotten to put on his hob-nailed boots and the soles of his feet were sopping wet. Oh, he'd suffer that, he thought, he wasn't going back now. He had arrived at the Chapel of Rest's door and was about to pull it open and enter when he stopped abruptly, hearing a low voice. His heart raced. Someone was inside! But who on earth could be in there at this time of night? Certainly not Miss Clatteridge. So far as he knew she hadn't taken to talking to herself, or the dead for that matter.

Heart hammering, he put down the lamp and inched the door open wide enough to peep through. The sight that met his eyes froze him rigid.

Two men stood bent over the open casket. One, a man he did not recognize, held a scalpel in his hand, raised ready to do his business. There was a large black Gladstone bag by his feet, containing what looked like glass jars holding some sort of liquid which gleamed eerily in the flickering candlelight. Ivan's eyes went to the other figure. It was Oswald.

Ivan knew immediately what they were up to.

A great fury filled him and without a second thought he snatched up the lamp, raised it high and pushed open the door.

'And who d'yer think you two are?' he hissed. 'Burke and Hare?'

Shocked, the two of them spun around, faces paling.

'Who's he?' the stranger asked Oswald. 'You said we'd not be disturbed.'

'Then you're a fool to 'ave listened to 'im,' snarled Ivan, stepping forward.

'Now look here, my good man,' the stranger addressed him. 'It's not what you think . . .'

'Oh? Tek me for an idiot, d'yer?' he erupted. 'Get yer stuff and get out.'

'Now look . . .'

'I'd leave while yer still can,' Ivan warned him.

The stranger flashed an angry glance at Oswald before grabbing his belongings and leaving hurriedly.

'Not you, Oswald. You stay where yer are.'

'Look, Mr Simpson,' he blurted, stepping nervously away from the black-draped trestle holding the casket to flatten his back against the side wall. 'I can explain . . .'

'There's n'ote to explain, lad,' Ivan said gravely, shaking his head. 'I had you down as some things, but stooping so low as to desecrate bodies . . . Doctor, was he?'

Oswald hung his head. 'Learning ter be.' He looked up, eyes pleading. 'It's medical science, Mr Simpson. They can't get enough innards to practise on. This is the only way they can do it.'

'Who told yer that?'

'The bloke what first approached me.' Oswald's eyes narrowed. 'Look, Mr Simpson, there's money ter be made. The doctor gave me half a crown for letting 'im in.'

'And how'd you do it? I secured the gates meself tonight.'

'I din't go 'ome. I 'id in the stable 'til I 'eard the doc knock, then I let 'im in.'

'How did he know to call tonight?'

Oswald sniffed. 'I tells the bloke when we have summat in the Chapel of Rest. He let's me know then if they're interested . . .'

'Oh, they pick and choose, d'they?'

Oswald nodded. 'Depends what they need at the time and which bits they want.'

'Bits?' spat Ivan. 'Them's people's bits yer referring to,' he exclaimed, horrified.

'But they're dead so what's the difference? They don't know.'

'But *you* do. And so do I now. D'yer fancy someone cutting you up without yer permission when yer time comes, eh?'

Oswald shuffled uncomfortably. 'I dunno what yer problem is, Mr Simpson. They're dead, where's the harm taking a few bits for the doctors to practise on? It ain't like they're gonna need 'em anymore, is it?' His eyes glared defiantly. ''Sides we ain't the only place that lets the hospital folk 'elp 'emselves.'

Oswald shrank back at the look of utter disgust on Ivan's face.

'I don't give a toss what other parlours get up to. This is a decent place. Decent and honourable. Did you give a thought ter what would happen if you'd 'ave bin caught? No, I bet yer didn't. All you could think of was the money yer were getting. Did yer think of Miss Clatteridge? What this woulda done to her? This carry-on could 'a bin the ruin of her. She could 'a landed in jail as well as yerself.' Oswald opened his mouth to speak but slapped it shut as Ivan's hand came up in warning. 'Don't dare. Don't dare suggest I go along wi' any of this. You make me sick,' he spat. 'How many times have yer done this, eh? How many?'

'Once or twice.'

'What?' Ivan eyed him, horrified. 'You're lucky I don't take me fist ter yer. But yer ain't worth it, Peabody. Yer ain't worth the effort.'

330

Oswald eyed him fearfully 'What yer gonna do, Mr Simpson?'

'I ain't gonna do nothin' and yer can wipe that smirk off yer face. The only reason I ain't gonna get the authorities involved is 'cos I don't want Miss Clatteridge dragging into none of this. Now you get out of 'ere before I change me mind.' As Oswald shot past him Ivan grabbed his shoulder and jerked him to a halt, looking him straight in the eye. 'Just be warned, Peabody. If I ever so much as catch a glimpse of your ugly mug anywhere near this place again, I'll 'ave yer. A' yer listening?'

Terrified, the boy nodded.

Ivan pushed him forcibly away. 'I'm glad we understand each other. Now get out.'

After he had gone Ivan stood rooted to the spot, calming himself. He was sill having trouble believing what he had just, by sheer accident, discovered. Thank God, he thought, he'd decided to look out of the window or there was no telling what might have happened had Oswald's betrayal gone on. Miss Clatteridge must never find out about this. It would mortify her. Taking a deep breath, he blew out the candles, locked the chapel securely the back gates too, and returned to his room. He did not sleep.

The next morning he approached Agnes. 'Peabody ain't turned up, Miss Clatteridge.'

'Oh, do you think he's ill or something?'

Ivan thrust his hands deep into his pockets. 'He . . . er . . . was all right yesterday. To be honest, Miss Clatteridge, the lad's a waste of your good money. Neither use nor ornament. There's plenty of good lads around that'd jump at the job 'e has and do far better.'

'Are you suggesting we get rid of him, Mr Simpson?'

'I am, yes.'

She looked at him for a moment. 'Then I trust your judgement. Can I leave you to do it?'

'You can, Miss Clatteridge.'

'I'll make up his dues. Can I leave you to take on a replacement too?'

Ivan was surprised. 'Me? You want me to hire a lad?'

'Of course, Mr Simpson. You're better qualified than I am. You'll be in charge of him, know what you'll be expecting him to do, and you'll need to be sure you'll get on with him. So can I leave you to see to it then?'

Ivan puffed out his chest. 'Yer certainly can, Miss Clatteridge. Yes indeed yer can.'

# Chapter Twenty-Seven

'A letter? For me?'

'Got your name on it, Mrs Baldicott. Mrs Baldicott it sez. Look, there,' the postman said, pointing. 'It's all the way from Leicester.'

Nancy Baldicott's eyes narrowed quizzically. 'But I can't recall knowing anyone in Leicester. No one that'd be wanting to write ter me, at any rate.'

'Well, yer must know someone else I wouldn't be delivering this to yer, now would I, eh?'

She frowned. 'No, I expect not.' Then, tongue in cheek, said, 'Who's it from?'

The postman's eyes narrowed indignantly. 'How should I know, less you're accusing me of tampering with His Majesty's mail?'

She laughed. 'I wouldn't put n'ote past you, Sidney Box. I remember when you used ter run round with no arse in yer britches, yer mam 'ollering 'er 'ead off callin' yer name 'cos yer'd scarpered wi'out doin' yer chores. Nine times outta ten yer were up ter no good. I lost count of 'ow many times I caught you in my garden scrumping me Granny Smiths.'

He reddened. 'All right, all right, no need to rake up me mis-spent youth.' Sid thrust the letter at her. 'D'yer want it or not?'

''Course I do. It's addressed ter me, ain't it?' Taking the letter from him, she eyed him for a moment. 'Can yer do summat for me?'

'Want me ter read it for yer, is that it, Mrs Baldicott?'

Her eyes narrowed haughtily. 'I'll have you know, Sidney Box, I can read it meself, thank you.'

He looked surprised. 'Yer can?'

''Course,' she said briskly. 'That's shocked yer, ain't it? A few years ago we had a particularly bad winter. I had a young gel stopping with me. She used ter read ter me ter pass the time in the evening. She asked me if I wanted her to teach me to read. I thought she'd be wasting 'er time meself, but she insisted. I took to it like a duck to water. Soon learned enough to get me by.' Nancy flapped the letter and cackled. 'Any more than six letters gets me a bit flummoxed, though. So just in case, yer can hang on a minute, see if I need yer.'

'I will, on one condition.'

She folded her arms under her ample bosom, eyeing the young postman warily. 'Oh?'

'I get a cuppa and a slice of your famous slab cake.'

Nancy sniffed. 'Deal. Come on in, yer young scallywag.'

Ten minutes later she clapped her hands in delight. 'Well, well, well. Once my gels 'ave left me I rarely 'ear from 'em again, so I never expected to 'ear from young Maddie. Or Mrs Jenks as she is now. You did say that word was Jenks?'

'That's right.'

'Well, I never, Mrs Jenks.' Her eyes narrowed thoughtfully. 'I could swear that young man that left 'er in the lurch was named Jenks,' she muttered. 'I could be wrong, though. Age gets yer like that.'

'What was that, Mrs Baldicott?'

'Eh? Oh, just talkin' ter meself. Mmmm,' she mouthed thoughtfully. 'I 'ave a terrible suspicion I knows exactly what she wants to come and see me about too.' She sighed forlornly. 'Oh, Maddie me duck, you know I can't tell yer 'ote even if I wanted to. Coming all this way will be a waste of your time and good money.' It was a shame, she thought. Of all the girls she had seen through their troubles over the years, Maddie was the only one she could truly say she would have enjoyed seeing again. Nancy took a deep breath. 'Will yer do me another good deed?'

Sid leaned towards her, grinning mischievously. 'Depends what it is, Mrs Baldicott.'

She slapped his hand. 'I ain't in the mood fer games, young Sidney. Will yer do me a favour or not?' she snapped.

'Yeah, 'course,' he replied sulkily. 'I was only gonna ask fer another cuppa and slice of cake.'

She tutted disdainfully. 'Help yerself while I go and hunt for the implements. I want you to post me a letter. And don't worry,' she added, 'I'll give yer the pennies for the stamp.'

# Chapter Twenty-Eight

'There's still no word from Mrs Baldicott,' Maddie remarked as she dished up the dinner. 'Is that enough potatoes? I've done plenty if you want more. Put Penny's on the window to cool, would you, Josh, please?'

He did as she bade, then eyed his plate. 'I'll have another couple, love, I'm famished. Oh, pie,' he said appreciatively as she opened the oven door. 'What's in it?'

She laughed, eyeing him teasingly. 'It's called Surprise Pie because you get a surprise when you eat it. Sarah made it for us. I'll be getting a surprise too because she wouldn't tell me either. It was nice of her to make extra for us, wasn't it?'

'She's a good woman is Sarah. Anyway, to answer yer, yer only sent it on Tuesday.'

'Sent what?'

'The letter to Mrs Baldicott. By the time it's delivered and her reply gets back yer looking at next week, I reckon.'

She sighed. 'I expect you're right.' She looked at him in concern. 'I hope she'll agree to see us, Josh.'

'Maddie, just sit down and eat yer dinner and try to put it out of yer mind for a bit. Come on, Twopenny-ha'penny,' he said, picking Penny up and making her comfortable on a chair at the table. The child protested loudly. 'Now, now,' said Josh patiently. 'Yer can play with yer toys after you've eaten else yer won't grow big and strong. Maddie, where's that strap we use to secure Twopenny to the chair so she don't fall off?'

'Er . . . it's there, look, on the back of the door.'

Fifteen minutes later Josh put down his knife and fork and sighed loudly in satisfaction. 'That Surprise Pie was grand. Corned beef and potato and there was summat else in it. What was it, Maddie?'

'Turnip, I think. Whatever it was it was very tasty. There's some left.'

'I'm full, thanks, love. If there's enough for two we'll have it tomorrow, save you cooking.' He eyed her expectantly. 'Any pudding?'

'I thought you said you were full?' she replied, pretending to be annoyed.

'Oh, Maddie love, I can always manage a pudding. I meant, I was full up with dinner.'

'Good job I did plums and custard then, isn't it?'

He jumped up from his chair. 'I'll get it.' As he passed by he kissed her on her cheek. 'I only married yer fer yer cooking.'

As he was tucking into his pudding, she eyed him questioningly. 'Aren't you ever going to tell me then?'

He lifted his head, frowning. 'Tell yer what?'

'Stop playing games, Josh,' she said, feigning annoyance. 'Did Mrs Cribbins accept your offer or not?'

He grinned sheepishly. 'I was saving that 'til later,' he said, teasingly.

'I can't wait until later, I think I've been patient enough. So?'

He beamed jubilantly. 'As a matter of fact, she did.'

Maddie's own face lit up with delight and she clapped her hands. 'Josh, that's wonderful news. All you need do now is set on a man to help you.'

'Already have. Danny Long. Good lad he is and trustworthy. He's happy with the pay I'm offering and I've told him if he gets any new customers I'll give him a bonus.'

Maddie folded her arms and leaned on the table, eyeing him proudly. 'I'm really happy for you, Josh, I know how much you wanted this round. Oh, who's that at the door?'

'Sit there,' he said, rising. 'I'll get it. I hope it ain't visitors. I was looking forward to a quiet night with just the three of us.'

As he left to answer the door, Maddie turned her full attention to the little girl and her face lit up merrily. 'You've more on your face than in your belly.'

Penny, heaped spoon raised precariously, looked at her innocently through large blue eyes. She giggled, showing several milk teeth and bare gums. The spoon tilted further, spilling its contents.

Maddie laughed and got to her feet. 'Oh, I see, feeding the table now, are we? Come on,' she said, easing the spoon from Penny's tiny hand. 'Let's get you cleaned up then you can play for a bit longer before bedtime.' She wiped the remains of the meal from face and hands, unstrapped Penny and picked her up, kissing the child affectionately on the cheek. 'Uncle Josh is going to read you a story. What would you like tonight? Three Little Pigs?'

Voices approaching down the passage reached her ears and she looked up.

'It's yer dad, love,' Josh announced as he entered, followed by George.

She was so delighted to see her father that the flatness of Josh's voice and the grim look on both faces went unnoticed.

'Dad!' she exclaimed, putting Penny carefully down on the floor. She was about to rush over to him when his expression registered and she froze. 'What's wrong, Dad?' she demanded.

Josh scooped up Penny. 'Come on, Twopenny. Let's get you ready fer bed.'

Instinctively Maddie knew that it was something very serious. 'Just a moment, Josh,' she cried, eyes darting from him to her father. 'What's going on?'

Josh flashed a glance at George before answering. 'Yer dad needs ter talk to yer, Maddie.'

'Be as quick as you can, Josh. Maddie's going to need you,' George whispered to him.

Face sombre, he nodded and hurried away.

George sat down on the lumpy settee, patting the space to the side of him, simultaneously putting on the floor a tin box which he was carrying. 'Sit down, Maddie.'

Heart thumping erratically, face grave, she sat down next to him, eyes fixed on his. 'It's not Sarah, is it, Dad?' she blurted. 'The baby? Nothing's happened, has it?'

He shook his head. 'Sarah's fine, love. Look . . . er . . . it's your mother, Maddie.'

Her heart pounded harder. 'My mother. What's happened to her? Is she ill?'

He took a deep breath. 'There's no easy way to tell you this, love. Your mother, well . . . she's dead. I'm so sorry.'

'Dead!' gasped Maddie, stunned. 'I can't believe it.' She wrung her hands. 'How? How did she die, Dad? Was it an accident? What?'

George averted his gaze uncomfortably. He could never tell Maddie the truth about Harriet's death, it was just too terrible, something he himself was still finding it hard to deal with. He had been told her body had been discovered by a neighbour who was curious about the strange smell she had caught a whiff of when she had walked past the shop. She had entered out of curiosity and was still recovering from shock at what she had found in the back room: Harriet's decomposing body.

An autopsy revealed she had been dead for at least a month, so far as they could tell from a massive heart attack, not helped by the fact that she was dreadfully undernourished. From what the doctors had told him George knew that Harriet's death must have happened soon after Maddie's visit to her, but had decided not to mention a word of this.

The death had been ascribed to natural causes. Informing the authorities of Maddie's visit could have resulted in their deciding to question her, that no doubt leading to Maddie's discovering the terrible circumstances of her mother's death. He could not risk that. Maddie had already shouldered more than enough hurt and pain at her hands. He knew she would feel needlessly guilty and torture herself for the rest of her life, wondering if there was anything she could have done to avoid this situation.

He took Maddie's hand gently in his. 'It was heart failure, my dear.' He gave her hand a tender squeeze. 'I was assured she didn't suffer.'

A grim-faced Josh returned and perched on the arm of the settee, sliding his arm protectively around Maddie's shoulders. She turned her head and looked at him. 'Dad told you at the door, didn't he?' she whispered.

He nodded. 'I'm so sorry, Maddie.'

She lowered her gaze to her hands. 'It's terrible of me, I know,' she said softly, 'but I can't feel much at all. I should be dreadfully upset, devastated even, should be crying my heart out. But all I feel is sorry that she died without any of her family around her. But she didn't want her family, did she? It's just sadness I feel for the closeness we could have had but didn't.' She wrung her hands, voice barely a whisper. 'Is it wrong of me to feel like this?'

'No, it isn't, Maddie,' her father said earnestly. 'My dear, how can you expect to feel love for a person who never showed you any? In fact, spent her life causing you nothing but pain.'

'But she was my mother, I should feel more than merely sorry that she's dead.'

Josh's arm tightened around her shoulder. 'She mighta given birth ter yer, Maddie love, but mother ter yer she wasn't.'

She took a deep breath. They were both right, she knew, but it didn't make her feel any better. She looked at her father. 'When's the funeral?' She looked at Josh, putting a hand on his arm. 'I wouldn't expect you to come.' She turned back to her father. 'It will be just me and you, won't it?' Her face filled with sadness. 'There's no one else, is there? No friends. Maybe Mrs Green and one or two of her old customers will attend. I'll contact them anyway, leave it to them.'

George raked one hand over the top of his head, body sagging tiredly. 'Maddie your mother was buried this morning. I was the only one there.'

'Buried today?' Her face creased in bewilderment. 'I don't understand? I should have been told. I should have been there to pay my last respects. She was my mother.'

'Maddie, listen to me,' George said firmly. 'By the time the authorities summoned me with the news and I'd travelled to Harborough, your mother had been dead for two days already,' he lied. 'You know the formalities better than me, considering where you work. She had to be buried the next day. Even if I'd got word to you, you'd never have arrived in time. You've got to remember I was very upset myself. Your mother and I might not have got on but I never wished her ill.'

A lump formed in Maddie's throat. She was being selfish, hadn't considered her father's feelings, only her own. She took his hand. 'I'm sorry, Dad, I wasn't thinking straight. You did what you had to, I understand that.' She sighed forlornly. 'I didn't mean to get angry with you, I'm just . . . just . . .'

'I know, my dear, this has all come as a terrible shock.'

She nodded and sat in silence for a moment. 'Will you take me to her grave?' she asked finally. 'I can pay my last respects there.'

He patted her hand. 'Of course I will, my dear.'

'What about the house?' she asked. 'You'll need a hand clearing it out.'

'I'll help too, if you want me,' offered Josh.

George flashed a grateful smile at him, then brought his gaze back to his daughter. 'It's done, Maddie,' he said softly.

She stared at him. 'That too?'

The house and its contents had been cleared on the orders of the sanitary department. They ordered its fumigation and fresh whitewashing to eliminate any risk of disease. The furniture and Harriet's personal belongings were burned for the same reason. But he could not divulge this to Maddie either.

'I just thought it best,' he told her. 'The landlord insisted,' he added to placate her.

'Oh, I see,' Maddie said tonelessly. 'Next tenant lined up already, I expect, as soon as he heard about my mother.'

'Your mother wasn't much for bits and pieces, you know that, Maddie, so there wasn't a lot for me to clear. I decided to give it all to the Salvation Army to divide amongst the needy. As you know, she had no jewellery. Except, of course, for this,' he said, fishing in his pocket and pulling out Harriet's wedding ring which he held out towards her.

Maddie took it, placed it in the palm of her hand and studied it intently. She raised her eyes to his. 'This had no meaning, did it, Dad? She didn't wear it for the reason it should have been worn. In the light of that, I can't wear it either.' She handed it back to him. 'You do what you want with it.'

He laid a hand on her arm. 'You don't want it as a keepsake, Maddie?'

'No,' she said firmly. 'I know she wouldn't want me to have it so I wouldn't feel comfortable about keeping it.'

'As you wish,' he said, putting it back in his pocket. 'Oh, there was this,' he said, picking up the tin box the authorities had given him. 'This was found . . . I found it in the back of her wardrobe.' He put his hand in his inside pocket and pulled out a key. 'This was on a chain around her neck.'

Maddie looked at the tin then at him. 'Why are you giving it to me?'

He eyed her closely. 'There's money inside, Maddie. A lot, judging by the weight, and I feel in the circumstances whatever your mother left should go to you.'

She frowned. 'But I don't understand how Mother could have left any money. Mrs Green told me the business had been doing very badly and the shop certainly didn't look well stocked to me. Oh!' she suddenly exclaimed as memory returned. 'I know what's in here. I have no right to this money, Dad. It really belongs to you and Sarah.'

'Us?' he asked, puzzled.

'Open the tin and I'll explain,' said Maddie, handing the key back to him.

George put the key in the lock and turned it, then lifted the lid. On seeing the contents his jaw dropped in amazement. He stepped across to the table and tipped out the contents in a jangling heap. He stared agog at the mound of coins. 'There . . . why, there must be a small fortune here. I don't understand . . .'

Maddie rose to join him. 'It's all the money you paid her, Dad. She told me the day I visited her that she never spent a penny of it.'

George's face darkened angrily. 'How could she? Harriet insisted on having half my wage off me every week. She knew how I struggled. That Sarah and the children suffered because of it.' He shook his head disbelievingly. 'I don't understand how her mind worked, really I don't.'

'I'm sorry if this hurts yer, Maddie, George, but I have ter say that to my mind it probably gave her pleasure to know how much hardship she caused,' said Josh.

Maddie sighed. 'Knowing what I do of my mother, I have to agree with Josh, Dad.' She laid a hand on his arm. 'It's yours and Sarah's, though, all of it, there's no doubt of that.'

George exhaled sharply. 'I can't deny we could find good use for this but it gives me no pleasure having it this way,' he said gravely. 'It won't Sarah, either.'

Josh joined them at the table. Thoughtfully he picked up the tin box. 'Yer wouldn't think such a small box could hold so much.' Something wedged inside the lid caught his attention and he prised it out. 'It's an envelope,' he said, handing it to George. 'Got something inside it.'

It was folded in half and George flattened it out. 'It's not addressed to anyone,' he said, frowning.

'Open it, Dad,' Maddie urged.

He ripped open the sealed flap and pulled out the contents. As he did so their jaws dropped.

George counted off the crisp white five-pound notes. 'There's a hundred pounds here,' he gasped. 'I wonder where it came from?'

'Profits from the shop?' offered Josh.

'Could be, I suppose. Wait a minute, what's this?' he said, peeling off a piece of paper stuck to the back of the last note in his hand. 'Why, it's a carbon copy of a receipt!' he exclaimed. As he scanned it, his face paled alarmingly.

'What is it, Dad?' Maddie asked him, frowning.

'Er . . . nothing,' he stuttered, stuffing it in his pocket.

His whole manner alerted her suspicions. 'It has to be for something. You did say it was a receipt?'

'I was mistaken. It's just a blank piece of paper, that's all,' he answered too hurriedly for Maddie's liking.

Her face creased knowingly. 'It wasn't blank, was it, Dad?' she accused. 'Whatever that receipt was for has something to do with me and I want to see it,' she challenged, holding out her hand.

'Maddie, what's got into you?' Josh asked, grabbing her arm.

'Dad?' she demanded, ignoring her husband.

George's whole body froze. He stared at her for several long moments then, resigned, delved into his pocket, pulled out the piece of paper and handed it to her.

Maddie smoothed it out and stared down at it.

'What does it say?' Josh asked.

'It's for . . .' She froze, face stricken, the receipt falling out of her hand to flutter to the floor. With an agonised wail she doubled over, clutching her stomach and sobbing wildly.

Completely shocked and bewildered by his wife's unexpected reaction Josh stared at her then grabbed her, holding her protectively. 'Maddie, what's wrong? Please tell me?' His attention returned to George. 'What was that receipt for?'

'Tell him, Dad,' wailed Maddie.

George's whole body sagged. 'It's a receipt for a baby girl. Josh, I'm so sorry.'

He stared, stupefied. 'What? But I don't understand . . .'

Maddie pulled away from him, her tear-blinded eyes staring straight into his. 'It's dated the tenth of April 1926. The date my mother handed our baby over, Josh. She *sold* our baby. Took money for her.' Her voice rose hysterically. 'It wasn't enough just to give her to some deserving couple, not for *her* it wasn't.'

As Maddie's words slowly sunk home Josh let out a deep groan and tears spilled down his face.

Maddie ran one hand tenderly down the side of his face. 'Oh, Josh,' she whispered. 'I thought she could do no more to hurt me . . . us. I was wrong, wasn't I? Oh, so very, very wrong.'

Her eyes suddenly blazed with anger. She jumped up, went to her father and grabbed the notes out of his hand. 'I know where these are going,' she cried, crushing them tightly. She swung back her arm and flung the bundle into the fire. They all watched as the paper caught light to burn brightly, flames licking upwards then giving way to blackened ashes which withered and died.

Tears streaming down her face, Maddie fled from the room and up the stairs.

Stricken, Josh stared after her. Then he rose awkwardly, looking at George. 'She'd no heart, had she? She was evil. There's no other word for her. I'm glad she's dead,' he spat savagely. Bending down, he picked up the receipt Maddie had let drop and stared at it, sighing painfully. 'There's a signature on this but I can't read it.' He shuddered, a wave of great sadness washing through him. 'This is all we've got to show for our child. That we ever had her.' His face contorted bitterly. 'I wonder if *she* took this out and looked at it often. I wonder if this was why she had kept a copy, so she could . . .'

'Stop it, Josh,' George ordered. 'Stop torturing yourself. Throw it away.'

Josh shuddered. 'I can't . . . I can't do that. I feel if I did I'd be wiping out all memory of our baby.'

George laid a hand on his arm. 'Then don't just yet, until you feel able. But hide it, Josh, so Maddie doesn't find it.'

Sniffing, he nodded and folded the receipt neatly. He put it in his pocket, to hide it later in a place where Maddie would never look.

George could find nothing to say to bring even a morsel of comfort to the man who had married his daughter, a man George had come to respect very much. He eyed him sadly. 'You'd better go and see to Maddie. You'll be needing each other at this moment more than ever. Me and Sarah will be round in the morning. I'll see myself out, son.'

After Josh had left George stood for a moment staring blindly into space, then he lifted his eyes. 'I hope wherever you are now, Harriet, you're truly satisfied that you've finally punished your daughter.'

Grim-faced, he walked across to the table, scooped up the coins and put them back in the box. He closed the lid, and quietly let himself out, the sounds of two people's grief ringing in his ears.

Much later that night, in a deserted, dimly lit church, George turned to Sarah. 'You're sure about this, my love?'

She nodded. 'We agreed, didn't we? Neither of us wants any part of it. Let's just hope it brings happiness to people who'll benefit.'

Standing side by side, together they painstakingly slotted every coin into the poor box.

When their task was complete George put the tin box aside to discard later and said emotionally, 'It's finally over, isn't it, love?'

She sighed. 'For us it is, George. I'm not so sure if it is for Maddie and Josh. The damage Harriet caused them I doubt will ever heal.' She looked at the man she loved, smiling wanly. 'But they say time heals all. Let's hope so, eh? In the meantime we can only support 'em as best we can.'

He sought her hand and gripped it tight. 'Come on,' he said. 'Let's go home.'

# Chapter Twenty-Nine

'Let's talk about something else,' said Agnes diplomatically, picking up the teapot. 'More tea, Maddie dear?'

She leaned over, holding out her cup. 'Yes, please.' She watched silently as Agnes refilled her cup, then her own, and settled back in her chair, sighing deeply. 'Miss Agnes, I've already stressed I don't want people pussyfooting around me. I appreciate you're trying to spare my feelings but I'm all right, really. Besides, it's not as if we can avoid talking of death, all things considered, can we?' she said lightly. 'I want to hear all about you leading the funeral. I want to hear every detail. I was so disappointed you didn't get back before I finished for the weekend. That's why I'm here, so please go on.'

Agnes eyed her in concern. She had to agree that on the surface Maddie appeared to have coped with her mother's death remarkably well, but Agnes wasn't convinced Maddie was being entirely honest about her mental state. There was something she could see in the younger woman's eyes. Maddie had such lovely eyes that sparkled with life, or had done until a week or so ago. There was a dullness, a haunted look, in them now. It was understandable considering her loss, but Agnes felt it went deeper than that. The sadness wasn't just in Maddie, it was in her husband too. There was something different about the pair of them that she couldn't quite put her finger on. But, she had reasoned with herself, people tackled grief in such different ways and she herself was probably just overreacting since she felt such affection for Maddie and her husband.

Agnes was, though, delighted to go along with Maddie's wishes. She really did want to talk of her morning. 'I was so honoured, my dear. I didn't suggest it, you know. People have taken to dealing with me, a woman, better than I ever expected but I still feel they assume a man will lead the funeral party. To be asked to by Mrs Dunn was such a privilege.'

Maddie smiled warmly. 'I was thinking about you when you left this morning. I knew you were nervous, and I know I'm repeating myself now, but I thought you looked just lovely in your outfit. So smart. The milliner certainly did a first-class job of altering your father's top hat to fit you and making it more feminine by adding the black feathers. So much better, I think, than the severe black ribbons undertakers usually have around their hats. Anyway, it all went well then, did it?'

'Yes, very. Well . . . almost.' Agnes paused for a moment to check on Penny who was playing happily on the rug, her childish chatter a delight to hear.

'Not that I know much about children, but I can't get over how contented she seems. You and Josh are doing a splendid job with her.'

'Thank you.' Maddie smiled, directing her gaze towards the child. 'She's very good but occasionally has her moments. She can lift our roof with one of her tantrums. Usually that's because she's tired but fights sleep. And meals! She gets more down herself and on the floor than in her mouth, but she refuses to let either me or Josh feed her. Sarah told me Ruth and Roy were just the same. And she's started to say a few words, so she's overcoming her shyness.'

'Mmmm,' Agnes said distractedly as all her own maternal instincts came to the fore. She had always managed to quash these feelings whenever they had surfaced previously, in fact had managed to persuade herself that mother she would never be, but watching the little girl now she found it impossible to believe that. 'She's so beautiful, isn't she?' Agnes said wistfully. 'She has a look of you, you know. If I didn't know better, I wouldn't know she wasn't yours.'

'That's because we're both dark and have blue eyes. At Penny's age it's difficult to tell what she'll look like when she's older. And people do say, don't they, that children grow to feature the people who care for them?' Maddie laughed. 'Sarah said Ruth and Roy resembled the coalman more than either herself or Dad.'

Agnes laughed too then said, 'But there's no doubt our little Twopence is going to break a few hearts when she's older.' She's breaking mine now, Agnes thought. With a great effort she forced her attention away from the child. 'How's Sarah?'

Maddie laughed again. 'The same as when you asked me yesterday, Miss Agnes. Getting fatter! She hasn't long to go now. Just a month of so. And still no name decided.'

Agnes took a sip of tea. 'Well, to me the name of the child is the least pressing concern. Its safe arrival means much more. And, of course, the welfare of the mother. More tea, dear? Or cake?'

'No tea, thank you. I'm awash with it. But I will have a little more cake. It really is delicious. You're a good cook, Miss Agnes.'

She blushed. 'No more than you are.'

Maddie grinned. 'All right, we'll agree that we can both make a decent cake.' She eyed Agnes keenly. 'So, are you going to finish your story? You said the funeral this morning went well – or almost. So what "almost" went wrong?'

Agnes's eyes sparkled. 'I nearly had a fit of the giggles, that's what nearly happened, and believe me if I had it would have been a dreadful thing for me to do, considering.'

'Oh, yes, it would have,' Maddie said, aghast. 'So what caused it?'

'Old Mrs Stoppard.'

Maddie frowned. 'Who's she?'

'Oh, of course, you wouldn't know of Mrs Stoppard, not having grown up around here, and I've never mentioned her to you before because she's just such a fixture. Mrs Stoppard attends all the local funerals. It makes her day. She loves a good cry, sings hymns the loudest, and eats most of the food at the wake afterwards.'

Maddie was looking at her mystified. 'She gets invited to them all?'

'Oh, no, dear, what she does is invite herself. So naturally I expected her to be at this one. What I didn't expect was for her to be trotting along beside me while I was leading. "'Ello, Miss Clatteridge," Agnes said in perfect mimicry, a gift Maddie hadn't known existed before. "'My, gel, yer do look posh. Like yer 'at. It suits yer it does. Was that yer dad's 'cos it looks fermiliar ter me? Talkin' of yer dad, you've fair come out yerself since 'e passed on. I think 'e done you a favour, gel. Anyway, I'm lookin' forward to this one I am. I've 'eard there's 'am and tongue, better than yer usually get – paste. Huh, ain't got a liking fer paste. 'Ad a right dose of the trots the last time I 'ad it. I gotta rush, Miss Clatteridge, else you'll be there afore me and that won't do, will it?" And off she went.

'How I kept a straight face I don't know. She was in church, bless her, singing and praying her heart out. She certainly had her share of food afterwards too and helped herself liberally to the sherry. The last glimpse I had of her was as she tottered off home, her hat on back to front.'

Maddie was laughing so much at the vision Agnes had summoned up that tears were spilling. 'Oh, Miss Agnes,' she said, dabbing them away with her handkerchief. 'Does no one say anything to her?'

A warm glow filled Agnes. It was good to see Maddie laughing so heartily, that haunted look in her eyes gone. 'No one has the heart to say a word to her. She's a harmless old body. No family. It's her only pleasure in life. People just expect she'll be there. In fact, I've even known the Reverend Pickles hold a service up because Mrs Stoppard hasn't arrived.'

The clattering of the letter box reached them then.

'Too late for the postman,' Agnes said, rising.

She disappeared and returned moments later, a letter in her hand. 'No stamp, so someone has just pushed it through the letter box.' She slit it open and pulled out the sheet of paper inside. 'Oh!' she exclaimed, sitting back down.

'It's not bad news, I hope, Miss Agnes?'

She raised her head and looked across at Maddie. 'Well, no. At least, I think not. It's from Mr Snood.'

'Mr Snood?' said Maddie, frowning. Suddenly she remembered that just before recent events she had expressed her concern to Josh about Agnes's business worries. He was going to speak to her father about it. With all that had happened it had been completely forgotten. What could Mr Snood be writing to Agnes about? Especially since Ivan had told them he had dealt with that matter, leaving no one in any doubt whatsoever that he had warned Mr Snood off. Desperate though she was to know what was in the letter, Maddie could not be so rude as to ask Agnes blatantly.

She need not have feared as Agnes volunteered the information herself.

'He's asking me to reconsider his offer to buy the business. Says his financial circumstances have changed and since he understands no one else has come forward it seems only right that I should be prepared to accept less. Five hundred pounds less to be exact. Oh, dear, that's an awful lot of money. He's right, though, no one else has made a definite offer, only him. I shall have to consider this seriously. He wants my reply by Tuesday latest.' She frowned, bewildered. 'Maddie, where are you going?'

'I've . . . er . . . just remembered I've an errand to do.'

'Oh, I see, dear. 'Til Monday morning then. Have a pleasant Sunday. Bye bye, Penny,' she said, waving to the child. 'Please give my regards to Josh, and of course Mr and Mrs Ashman.'

'I will, I will,' Maddie blustered, making hurriedly for the door. 'Thanks for the tea, Miss Agnes.'

As she hurried across the courtyard, Ivan came towards her. 'Eh up, Maddie,' he whispered urgently. 'I was watching out for yer. Has Miss Clatteridge had a letter from Snood?'

Hitching Penny more comfortably in her arms, she asked, 'How did you know, Ivan?'

'I've just 'ad his chippy pay me a visit. It seems he overheard Snood and Pargitt talking. Heard Snood tell Pargitt to deliver a letter here and be quick about it. Bert Knapp thought, considering what we discussed before, I might be interested in knowing.'

'Well, you're right to be interested, Ivan. Mr Snood has reinstated his offer, only this time this it's five hundred pounds less.'

'What? The bastard!' spat Ivan, then blushed. 'Oh, Maddie me duck, fergive me for blaspheming.'

'It's quite all right, Ivan, your words describe my feelings exactly.'

His face flushed angrily. 'I told that Snood not to come near Miss Clatteridge again and that 'e'd better not play any more tricks else 'e knew what I'd do. I'm goin' to see him right now and . . .'

'No, Ivan. Not yet you mustn't,' Maddie warned. 'There's something I haven't told you. It's . . . well, it's something and nothing. I told Josh and he was going to speak to my father, see what he had to say, but with my mother dying and . . . well, it slipped our minds.'

'That's understandable, Maddie. So what is this summat and n'ote yer told Josh about?'

Maddie told him about the letter Agnes had received from the Mosses accusing her of raising the price once she knew they were keen to buy the place, which of course wasn't true, and of Agnes's visit to see the agent who, according to her, was not pleased about the Mosses writing directly to her. In fact, quite angry.

Ivan stared at her blankly, mind whirling. Finally he said, 'I smell summat fishy goin' on but I ain't got a clue what. I'm definitely gonna see Snood, ask 'im what he's playin' at.'

'No,' said Maddie. 'Ivan, you can't. The Mosses might just have been mistaken and Mr Snood might be perfectly innocent. There've been no more rumours. There can't have been or business wouldn't be so brisk, would it? And he's right, no one has bought the place, so his offer might be perfectly genuine this time.'

'I doubt it!'

'Doubts aren't enough to convict someone, Ivan. You have to have facts. I'm going home to see Josh. Why don't you come around later this evening? I'll ask my father too. We can all discuss it. You mustn't do anything until then. We could be ruining Miss Clatteridge's chances of selling up and we can't risk that.'

He exhaled loudly. 'Yer right, gel. I wasn't thinking straight. It's just . . . just . . .'

She smiled knowingly at him, placing a hand on his arm. 'I know, Ivan. You just have Miss Clatteridge's best interests at heart.'

He shuffled his feet uncomfortably. 'She's me boss, that's why,' he said gruffly. 'I'll come round ternight then. About seven?'

'Seven will be fine.'


Maddie refilled three glasses with foaming beer from a jug fetched from the pub down the road and her own cup with tea and sat back down in her chair at the table.

George rubbed one hand thoughtfully over his chin. 'Well, taking it all into account, I can understand your concern but there's nothing definite to go on.'

'So we can't do anything?' asked Maddie.

'It's not a case of whether we can do anything, my dear, it's what. Snood, as we know, was up to no good and Mr Simpson dealt with him. There's no evidence that Mr Snood's offer this time isn't genuine, and let's face it, any businessman will want to get what he's after at the cheapest price. There've been no offers made so why shouldn't he put in a lower bid? So far as I can see he's not broken any rules and, Mr Simpson, you did tell us you'd threatened him that should anymore rumours be spread around you'd deal with them in your own way. Have you heard any? Has any of you? Has anything for that matter happened recently that has affected Miss Clatteridge's business?'

They all solemnly shook their heads.

'Well then, you've nothing to go on.'

'But what about the Mosses' complaint to the agent? Don't yer think there's summat in that?' asked Josh.

'I honestly don't know,' George said, perturbed. 'People make mistakes all the time. They could have misheard something, just got it wrong.'

'That's what I thought,' mused Maddie.

Ivan exhaled sharply. 'So we just sit back and let Miss Clatteridge accept Snood's offer? Is that what yer saying, Mr Ashman? 'Cos I tell yer, I still feel in me bones summat ain't right.'

'I have ter agree,' said Josh.

'I'm sorry, but I don't see what we can do. And let's face it, time's not on our side.' George paused thoughtfully. 'I suppose I could always . . .'

'What, Dad?' cut in Maddie keenly.

'It's just an idea but I could drop by the agent.'

'And do what?' asked Ivan, mystified.

'Show an interest in the funeral parlour, see what happens.'

'Yes, you could, Dad,' Maddie enthused. 'At least it's better than doing nothing.'

'Don't build your hopes up, Maddie, it's just a long shot.'

'But you do think he could be up ter summat, Mr Ashman?' pressed Ivan. 'D'yer think him an' Snood are in this together?'

'Mr Simpson, you're determined to pin something on Snood, aren't you?' George said tersely.

Folding his arms, Ivan leaned on the table. 'I'll tell yer this for n'ote, Mr Ashman. If Snood ain't lurking somewhere behind whatever dirty work's going on then I'll personally be the first to congratulate the bloke when he takes over. I'm that positive.'

George eyed him, convinced. 'In my game we have to rely on our instincts, so I can appreciate what you're saying, Mr Simpson. I've a couple of calls to make in Leicester on Monday morning, I'll call on the agent as soon as I can.'

'It's cutting it fine, ain't it? Snood's expecting Miss Clatteridge's reply on Tuesday,' said Ivan worriedly.

'I'm well aware of that, Mr Simpson. Please put your mind at rest I'll be acting with all haste. We'll meet again here on Monday evening, shall we, at the same time? Is that all right with you, Maddie?'

'Yes, of course, Dad.'

George scraped back his chair. 'Now, if you'll all excuse me, I want to get back to Sarah.'

'She's all right?' asked Maddie.

'She's fine. Said she's had a couple of pains today but it's just the baby settling, getting ready to be born. I don't like leaving her unnecessarily, Maddie, you know that.'

She rose and walked around the table, putting her arms round her father to give him a hug. 'Give Sarah my love and tell her I'll see her tomorrow,' she said, then kissed him on the cheek.

'Goodnight, all,' he said as he left.

Maddie sat back down. 'If there's anything to find out, my dad will find it. Trust him, Ivan, and stop worrying.'

He wished he could.

★ ★ ★

Later that night Josh climbed into bed and cuddled up to Maddie, pulling her close against him. He loved the feel of her, smell of her, could think of nothing more enjoyable in his life than their private times alone in their bedroom. What really thrilled him, though, was that he knew without a doubt his wife felt exactly the same about him.

He kissed her neck and she snuggled her back against him, sighing contentedly, then turned towards him, pulling him to her, kissing him passionately. He responded willingly. Their lovemaking, as always, was tender, eager, building to a fierce crescendo and, when each was satisfactorily spent, to lie in each other's arms, fulfilled and secure, before they slept.

Josh kissed Maddie's ear and stroked his fingers gently down her neck. 'I love you,' he whispered, snuggling warmly against her and closing his eyes.

'Mmmm,' she murmured dreamily. 'I love you too.'

'Are you all right, Maddie?' he asked softly.

'I'm as all right as you are,' she responded in a whisper. They both knew exactly what each referred to.

'Goodnight, Josh,' she said tenderly.

'Goodnight, my sweet.'

Silence fell, only the sounds of the night infiltrating the bedroom. Maddie was just about to doze off when Josh unexpectedly said, 'He's a dark horse, ain't he?'

'Who is?' she said, yawning.

'Ivan.'

She turned towards him, wide awake now. 'What do you mean, Josh?'

He kissed her lips and put his arms around her, pulling her close. 'I mean just what I said – he's a dark horse. If Ivan Simpson's not in love with Agnes Clatteridge then I, my darlin', ain't your husband.'

'You'd better be,' said Maddie, giving him a peck on the lips, 'or I'm a right harlot after what we've just done! So,' she said, frowning thoughtfully, 'I wasn't imagining it then.

Miss Agnes feels for him too, I know she does.' She sighed despairingly. 'I wish there was a way we could bring them together.'

'Maddie, it ain't fer either of us ter say anything. It's only what we've noticed and we could be wrong.'

'But we're not, though, are we?'

'I wish I'd never mentioned it now,' said Josh, yawning loudly. 'I didn't want a long discussion, I was just passing comment. Come on, Mrs Jenks, turn over and get to sleep.'

Considering what thoughts they had running through their minds, they both slept surprisingly soundly.

# Chapter Thirty

George took an instant dislike to Millburn Cresswell as soon as he set eyes on the man. He was young, in his mid-twenties George guessed – a fact which had taken him by surprise since he'd been expecting a much older man to run the business. Cresswell's boyish features were enhanced by big baby blue eyes surrounded by long dark lashes. His thick black hair was parted down the middle and plastered down with brilliantine, or it could be candle wax, George mused, considering how greasily it shone. His suit was dark brown and well-cut, the stiff collar on his white shirt buttoned with at the very least gold-plated studs. Across his waistcoat hung a thick gold chain, on the end of it a gold fob watch.

It wasn't his good looks, or expensive tastes that annoyed George, it was his arrogant manner. Cresswell sat back in a huge red leather chair, well-shod feet crossed on his desk, a cigarette clamped firmly in the corner of his mouth. The air was thick with smoke and the room stiflingly hot, all its window firmly closed.

George's immediate thought was to wonder where exactly Cresswell got the money to dress so expensively, considering he was not long enough out of nappies to have made his fortune. Neither was he the only land and property agent in Leicester, and competition had to be as fierce as in other trades.

The elderly clerk who had shown him in was obviously afraid of his boss, to judge from his subservient manner.

'A Mr Ashman to see you, Mr Cresswell,' the clerk

announced in not much more than a whisper, head bowed, hands clasped prayer-like.

Cresswell flashed George a false smile showing a row of gleaming white teeth and with a flick of his wrist indicated a chair to the front of his desk. 'And what can Cresswell's do for your good self?' he said nonchalantly, flicking off a speck of ash that had fallen on the front of his jacket.

George was not in the best of moods and Cresswell's manner was not improving matters. Miss Clatteridge's problem had caused him a sleepless night. Sarah had not slept either, uncomfortable in the late stages of pregnancy, and they both of them had tossed and turned all night.

George's appointments that morning had taken far longer than he'd intended and he had worried throughout that he was not going to have time to make his visit to Cresswell's before they closed for lunch.

He fixed his eyes firmly on Millburn Cresswell. 'I understand your firm is handling the Clatteridge sale?' he said matter-of-factly.

George watched the other man closely. Not a muscle on Cresswell's face twitched.

'That's correct,' he said nonchalantly, drawing deep on his cigarette. 'You interested, Mr . . . er . . .'

'Ashman.' And George couldn't help adding, 'Your clerk did tell you my name. And, yes, I am interested.'

Cresswell scrutinised him. 'You don't look like an undertaker,' he said bluntly.

'I'm not,' replied George, anger rising at his impertinence.

'Well, if you're not, why are you interested in a funeral parlour?'

George's eyes narrowed. 'I don't see that has to do with you. Your job is to sell the property, isn't it?'

Cresswell sniffed haughtily. 'Quite right. I'll have my clerk get the particulars and an order to view,' he said, leaning sideways to slap his palm down hard on a brass bell on his desk.

Instantly the clerk entered.

'Particulars of Clatteridge's and an order to view,' Cresswell snapped. 'Wednesday morning suit?' he asked George.

'No, I'm afraid that won't do. I want to go this afternoon.'

Cresswell shook his head. 'Not possible.'

'Why not?'

'I have other appointments.'

George was relieved at this fact, worried he wouldn't think of a plausible excuse for the agent not to accompany him. 'That's by the by. I'm quite capable of viewing by myself. Make the order out for two,' he said dismissively, getting to his feet. 'If I like what I see, I'll be back around four. You'll be here then, I trust?'

'Four, you say? Yes, I'll make sure I am.'

Cresswell scribbled hurriedly on the order his clerk handed to him then gave it to George.

He looked at the order, then at Cresswell. 'Will this property go for auction?'

Cresswell shrugged his shoulders. 'I haven't bothered to fix a date because although several people have viewed they've taken matters no further.'

'I see. So in your opinion there's a good chance Miss Clatteridge would accept a reasonable offer?'

'She's very eager to sell and unless we get an influx of interest, prompting the need for an auction, I think she would.'

George folded the order and put it in his pocket. 'Good,' he said. 'I'll return at four.'

Two appointments concluded satisfactorily and a dozen or so dues collected, George limped across the town hall square, skirting the ornate fountain in the centre en route to Horsefair Street where Cresswell's offices were situated above a tobacconists. It was ten minutes to four. He stopped for a moment. He didn't want to appear too eager and his game leg was suddenly beginning to ache so he parked himself on a vacant bench.

It was quite a pleasant afternoon, the early-April sun warm on the back of his neck. Mothers were taking a rest from shopping and, bags by their feet, sat chattering in groups while their children played hide and seek, tag and hopscotch nearby. Several street vendors were plying their wares of hot pies and potatoes, their cries mingling with those from the market nearby.

George noticed none of the hustle and bustle going on around him, far too preoccupied with his impending visit to Cresswell's.

Apart from his instinctive dislike of the man, so far Cresswell had displayed no sign, no hint, of anything untoward. George wished he could plan his next moves but he couldn't. He had to play it all by ear and depend entirely on his instincts and Lady Luck being on his side. He hoped they were both with him this afternoon, for Miss Clatteridge's sake.

The clock struck four and he rose.

The clerk greeted him as he entered. 'Good af'noon, Mr Ashman. Mr Cresswell isn't back yet. Would yer care to sit and wait?'

George sat stiffly on a hard wooden chair and as he waited was conscious of the clock on the wall above the clerk's desk ticking loudly. Time was passing. He himself had to be across Leicester for another appointment at five o'clock.

It was half-past four by the time Cresswell breezed in. He seemed momentarily taken-aback when he spotted George, who instinctively knew he hadn't expected to find him sitting there.

Fixing a smile on his face Cresswell strode across to George, thrusting out a hand. 'Apologies, Mr Ashman.' He grasped George's hand, shaking it hard. 'Come through, come through,' he urged.

George followed him into his office and sat down. Not wanting to waste time on congenial chit-chat he immediately launched his attack and prayed it would achieve the desired result. 'I like what I saw and I want to make an offer. I don't see any point in messing about, so my offer is for the full asking price.'

'Ah,' said Cresswell, twining his fingers and sitting back in his chair. 'I was afraid of that. I've just come from Clatteridge's. My appointment didn't last as long as I thought so I went along hoping to catch you, do my bit as agent. Sorry I missed you, but I had a very interesting conversation with Miss Clatteridge. She told me you seemed very keen and has therefore decided to up her price. I tried to persuade her otherwise, most foolish in my opinion, but she insisted.'

George was delighted to have caught him out. Cresswell was lying, had no more been to the funeral parlour that afternoon than George himself had. It was just as Ivan had said. This man was certainly up to no good. All George had to do was prove it and who his accomplice or accomplices were. Give the man his due, though, George thought, he was very convincing. An actor couldn't have done better. Trouble was, Cresswell had bargained without George's instincts which had become finely tuned throughout years of dealing with unscrupulous types, some of whom would risk anything to get their greedy hands on money that wasn't rightfully theirs.

Face expressionless, he asked, 'By how much?'

'Another thousand.'

'Mmmm,' George mused, playing for time. His astute mind whirled and a plan to trap Cresswell took shape. He hoped the man took the bait.

'You and I both know, Cresswell, that that property isn't worth another thousand. In fact, less for the right people.'

Through narrowed eyes, George watched Cresswell intently but the man's face remained deadpan.

'Less?' he said quizzically. 'I don't understand?'

George gave a knowing smile. 'I think you do, Cresswell.

I really want that property and I understand from a . . . let's say, mutual friend, that we can come to an arrangement. The only problem is that our mutual friend happens to be interested in the property too. Whatever he's paying you to get it cheap for him, I'll match it and up it by . . . shall we say another couple of hundred?'

Cresswell stared at George who could almost see the man's mind ticking over rapidly. Just to make sure it was running along the lines George wished it to, he said, 'I'll give you a name, shall I?'

Eyes narrowing, Cresswell asked, 'And that is?'

George took a deep breath. 'Snood.'

Cresswell leaned back in his chair. 'Just who are you?' he asked warily.

'I've told you, a friend of Mr Snood.'

'If you're that much of a "friend" then you'll know I don't double deal.'

George's heart leaped, his palms moistened. He was nearly there, all he had to do was keep calm. 'I wouldn't dare accuse you of such, Mr Cresswell. But maybe I happen to have seen a side to Snood you haven't. We were introduced by an acquaintance, someone you've done business with. I wanted another opinion from someone who'd had dealings with you too. I haven't made my money by foolishly trusting in people's word. Far from it. Especially considering the circumstances surrounding this situation. Snood was only too glad to tell me of your arrangement. I must admit, I was favourably impressed by his recommendation. He praised you very highly. I have to say he had drunk a little too much whisky at the time or he probably wouldn't have blabbed to me of his intention not to pay your "retainer".'

Cresswell's face filled with sudden rage and before he could stop himself, he spat, 'What?' Then, realising his mistake, he quickly recovered his composure. He opened his mouth to speak. George, knowing he was about to make an excuse for his outburst, decided not to give him the opportunity and stopped him by asking, 'Have you had dealings with Snood before?'

Cresswell shifted uneasily in his chair and George could see a fine film of sweat covering his brow. 'I don't discuss personal details of my business associates,' he said gruffly.

'Very commendable. I hope you'll treat any arrangement we enter into with the same discretion. I won't insult your intelligence then, Cresswell. You'll already know that Snood isn't exactly a trusting type. I expect you've made the necessary arrangements to cover yourself in that event?' Wondering if he was doing the right thing, George rose. 'Neither of us has time to waste. I'll say good day.'

Holding his breath as a terrible presentiment told him he had just overplayed his hand, George walked away and had got as far as the door when mercifully Cresswell called after him.

'Just a minute, Mr Ashman, let's not be hasty. Sit down, please.'

Relief flooded through him. George purposely hesitated for a moment, then slowly walked back and sat down again.

'Can I get you some refreshment, Mr Ashman?' Cresswell gushed, leaning to one side of him to open the door of a well-stocked drinks cabinet. 'I've a good malt whisky or . . .'

'No, thank you,' George cut in. 'I'm in a hurry, Cresswell. Say what you've got to say.'

Shutting the cabinet door, he leaned forward, clasping his hands, eyes wary. 'Look . . . you're right. I had a deal with Snood to get the Clatteridge place as cheaply as possible. I've spent a lot of time and effort in getting to the point where Miss Clatteridge will readily accept a low offer. I can't . . .' He paused in embarrassment. 'I can't afford to lose my fee on it. And there's the matter of my associates. If they find out Snood's intentions they could follow suit and I'd be done for.'

'So what are you suggesting, Cresswell?' George asked, pretending ignorance. George knew exactly what Cresswell wanted to do. And couldn't wait to give him his answer.

'You seem an honest man, Mr Ashman, and in view of what you've told me, I'm willing to break my agreement with Snood and transfer my allegiance to you. Miss Clatteridge was considering an offer from Snood for four and a half thousand, including the goodwill and stock. You'll agree it's at the very least a thousand less than it's worth. Snood was paying me three hundred pounds. You said you'd up whatever he was paying me by two hundred. So that's five hundred. Which leaves us both on the winning side. Do we have a deal?'

George looked at him blankly for several long moments. 'No,' he said firmly.

Cresswell stared at him. 'I don't understand. I thought you wanted the Clatteridge place? I doubt I can get it any cheaper.'

'Cheaper's not what I want.'

'It isn't?' he asked, deeply perplexed. 'What is it you do want then?'

George's eyes narrowed. 'I'll tell you what I want, Cresswell. I want you to tell Snood your arrangement is off and that he's to withdraw his offer in writing to Miss Clatteridge. If he hasn't done so by first thing tomorrow morning, I'll tip off the police he's up to no good and they'll turn his place over. Then I'll have rumours spread about his underhand dealings with regard to burials. Doesn't matter if it's true or not, people will believe it and won't use him. By the time I've finished, he'll be bankrupt. Tell him all this, make him understand I'm deadly serious. And as for you, Cresswell. Well, the same goes for you.'

His eyes were bulging, face panic-stricken. 'What?'

George eyed him in disdain. 'You heard me, Cresswell. The game's up. I owe you no explanation and I'm not going to give you any. I'll leave you guessing as to how I became involved in all this. But let me assure you: either you do what I say or you'll suffer the consequences. Fancy a stretch in jail, do you? Because I've enough on you to put you there for several years. In case you doubt I've no proof to back up what I say, I know of several people,' he lied, 'who have had dealings with you. The authorities have only to question them for all sorts of interesting facts to come to light, and don't think for a minute I'm bluffing. Though, by the look on your face, I can tell you know I'm not.'

'Just who are you?' Cresswell faltered.

It gave George great pleasure to see that he was a very worried man.

He rose, placed his hands flat on the desk and leaned forward, menacingly. 'Someone the police will take notice of.' He straightened up. 'Good day, Mr Cresswell.'

He strode from the office. He was halfway across the outer room before he dare heave a sigh of relief.

The elderly clerk slipped off his chair and rushed to open the door for him. 'Good af'noon, Mr Ashman,' he said politely.

'Good day,' George responded, then paused, eyeing the man in concern. 'If I were you, my good man, I'd start looking for another position quickly. I happen to know that Cresswell's won't be in business for much longer.' Then George realised this man would not find other employment readily and the thought bothered him. 'The Amicable Refuge on Queens Street is always on the look-out for a good clerk.' Which was true and someone like this elderly man would be very suitable for the Amicable's requirements. George himself would put in a good word for him, he felt it was the least he could do since he was responsible for putting his job in jeopardy. 'Present yourself first thing tomorrow,' he said. 'Tell them Mr Ashman recommended you.'

'I will, sir, thank you,' the clerk answered, somewhat bewildered.

Maddie, Josh and especially Ivan were delighted with George's news when he gave them it later that evening but all of them spent a worried night waiting to see if Millburn Cresswell heeded the threat.

Maddie was to receive her answer as soon as she arrived for work the next morning. She walked into the kitchen to find Agnes sitting at the kitchen table, a letter clutched in her hand.

'What's the matter, Miss Agnes?' she asked tentatively. She hoped it was what she thought it to be, confirmation that Snood was not about to get his greedy hands on this property, but she was far from happy it was causing Agnes such distress.

Agnes raised her head, her face troubled. 'I've received another letter from Mr Snood. He must have pushed it through the letter box early this morning. He's withdrawn his offer. With no explanation whatsoever. I don't understand. Oh, dear, I had pinned my hopes on finally having this place sold. And Alice will be so disappointed.'

Maddie felt mortally guilty for having to pretend she was as bemused by the contents of Mr Snood's letter as Agnes, but unless she wanted to give away their involvement she had no choice. She sat down next to her employer. 'I don't know what to say, it's terrible of Mr Snood to treat you so badly.' And she added before she had time to think and stop herself, 'I hope they both get what they deserve.'

'I beg your pardon?' said Agnes, bewildered. '*Both* get what they deserve?' she repeated. 'What did you mean by that remark, Maddie?'

A knock sounded on the door and Ivan entered. He took one look at Agnes's worried face, flashed a hurried glance at Maddie and said, 'I came to tell yer everything's set for this aft'noon's burial, Miss Clatteridge, but . . . is summat wrong?'

She looked across at him. 'Yes, in a manner of speaking. I've had a letter from Mr Snood, withdrawing his offer. It's most remiss of the man to act in such a way. This is the second time he's done it. I'm not going to tolerate it, though.

I shall pay a visit to Mr Snood and give him a piece of my mind. Then I shall go and see the agent, ask him to sell to the first person who makes me an offer. I don't care how much I have to drop. I want it done with once and for all.'

'No, yer can't!' Ivan blurted out without thinking, then hurriedly clamped his mouth shut, eyes guiltily cast down.

'Can't?' Agnes said. 'And why can't I, Mr Simpson?'

Maddie gasped, horrified.

Agnes looked at them both hard. 'Something is going on that I don't understand.' She rose, folded her arms, fixing her eyes on them. 'You both know something about this state of affairs, don't you?'

'No,' they said simultaneously.

'Then why do you both look so guilty?'

'We don't,' they insisted.

Her frown deepened. 'But you do.' Suddenly a terrible thought struck her and her face filled with shock. 'No, it can't be true,' she murmured in distress. 'You both . . . you're not . . . you can't have anything to do with the fact the business hasn't sold? Somehow put people off?'

'Oh, no, Miss Agnes!' Maddie cried.

'We ain't done nothing of the kind,' insisted Ivan.

'We care for you far too much, Miss Agnes, ever to do anything against you. Well, not in the way you're thinking.'

'And what is that supposed to mean?' she demanded.

Looking at Ivan, Maddie gnawed her bottom lip anxiously. 'We'll have to tell her.'

'Tell me what?' Agnes snapped.

He shuffled his feet uncomfortably. 'It was me,' he said, stepping forward. 'Yer can blame me for everything.'

'That's not true,' said Maddie. 'I'm as much to blame as anyone. I started it all with what I overheard.'

'It was me, I tell yer,' insisted Ivan. 'I was the one . . .'

'Stop it, the pair of you,' ordered Agnes. 'Sit down,' she commanded. 'I think you'd both better start at the beginning.'

371

Like sheep to the slaughter they both obeyed.

It was Maddie who started the tale by telling Agnes what she had overheard and it was Ivan who finished by explaining George's visit to Cresswell's the previous day and its outcome, hence the letter she was still clutching in her hand.

Agnes stared at them both, mortified. 'If I didn't know you both so well, I'd have trouble believing this.'

'But you do believe us?' asked a worried Maddie.

She nodded. 'Yes, of course I do.'

'And you're not angry with us?'

'Angry? Oh, my dear, how on earth can I be angry? You have saved our inheritance.' She took a deep breath, clasping her hands. 'I didn't realise how much you must all care for me, to take such trouble on my behalf.' Gratitude filled her eyes. 'It seems I have a lot to thank you all for. I couldn't understand why this place,' she said, glancing around, 'wasn't attracting much interest, even if the house needs brightening up. It just didn't make sense.'

'And now it does, Miss Clatteridge?' asked Ivan tentatively.

She nodded. 'Yes. But what a fool I've been! I put all my faith in that man. Trusted him. I can't believe he was doing all this and I never noticed anything amiss. Mr Snood too. I should have known, shouldn't I?'

'With due respect, Miss Agnes, how could you have? My dad said it took all his skill to pin Cresswell down. He's very good at business but he said this was touch and go.'

'He did?'

Maddie nodded. 'Mr Cresswell is a very clever man.'

Agnes smiled wanly. 'But, thank goodness, not so clever as your father, Maddie. Anyway he certainly had me fooled.'

'And not just you, Miss Agnes,' Maddie told her. 'Dad reckons he's done this plenty of times before.'

'Well, he won't do it anymore,' she replied with conviction. 'I shall go to the police and tell them all about this, leave them to decide what best to do because I would hate anyone else to find themselves in a similar position.' She smiled gratefully. 'I will visit your father, Maddie, and thank him for his trouble.'

'He was only too glad to help, Miss Agnes.' She took a deep breath with relief. 'What will you do now?'

'Now?' Agnes sighed forlornly, shaking her head. 'I don't know. Find an honest agent, I expect, and start all over again? I have to sell the place. Oh, dear, I don't think I can bear it.'

'Then why sell?' Maddie said. 'It's doing so well now. Isn't there any way you could keep it on?'

Agnes frowned thoughtfully. 'Keep it on? I hadn't given that possibility any thought. You're right, though, things are running very smoothly at the moment, plenty of work coming our way. The bank balance is certainly beginning to look healthy. And I so enjoy it. But I have no option but to sell. Alice wants her share of our inheritance and rightly so. Anyway, I've nothing to keep me here in Leicester. I was all set to start a new life in Scarborough, and Alice and my aunt will be very disappointed if I don't join them.'

Face pinched, Ivan jumped up. ''S'cuse me,' he mumbled. 'I've things ter see ter.'

They both stared at him as he hurriedly left, closing the door firmly behind him. Maddie felt she knew only too well the reason for his speedy departure. Agnes didn't and was puzzled. 'Did I say something I shouldn't have, Maddie? Mr Simpson suddenly acted most oddly. Have you any idea why?'

Maddie looked at her, thoughts whirling. Agnes had actually asked for her views on Ivan. Should she divulge what they were? Should she risk it? She might never get another opportunity. Now that Snood and Cresswell were out of the way a buyer for the business could present themself very quickly and then Agnes would depart for pastures new with never an inkling how Ivan felt for her, no opportunity to decide if she returned his affections or not. It was obvious that neither of them was ever going to find the courage to admit their feelings to each other. If something wasn't done both of them could live the rest of their lives as very lonely people. That was the last thing Maddie wanted for them.

Then she remembered how Agnes had taken it upon herself to act as she had felt fit in a similar situation. If it wasn't for her doing so, Josh and Maddie might not be happy together now.

Her mind was made up.

'Yes, it was something you said that upset him, Miss Agnes,' Maddie said. She rose and rushed to the door, pulling it open and calling across to Ivan who was halfway across the yard, 'Have you a moment, please?'

He turned and looked at her. 'I'm busy,' he grunted.

'Ivan, please come now, it's urgent.'

His face filled with alarm. 'Is it Miss Clatteridge?'

Maddie nodded, 'Very much so,' she said, going back inside.

He ran across the yard as fast as his legs would carry him.

'Maddie, what's going on?' demanded Agnes, perplexed.

Maddie blatantly ignored her, waiting for Ivan to arrive. He did seconds later, a mite out of breath.

'What's 'appened to Miss Clatteridge?' he cried. His eyes immediately sought Agnes and on finding her in perfect health, sitting exactly where he had left her moments ago, he exhaled in relief then frowned bewilderedly at Maddie. 'I thought yer said summat was wrong with Miss Clatteridge?'

'There's nothing wrong with me,' said Agnes sharply. 'Maddie, what on earth has got into you?'

She took a deep breath, the affection she felt for these two dear lonely people beaming from her eyes. 'I'm fond of both of you and it grieves me to see what's going on. You care for each other, I know you do. Josh has seen it too so it's not just me. Now, for goodness' sake, will you talk to each other before it's too late?'

Without giving either of them the chance to respond she made a rush for the door and departed.

Feeling she had done the right thing, but still deeply worried her actions could have unforseen repercussions, she headed across the yard towards Ivan's shed where she intended to await the outcome.

As she arrived she realised a shabby young man was hovering uncertainly just by the door. He seemed vaguely familiar but she didn't know why.

'Can I help you?' she asked.

He whipped off his threadbare cap, fiddling nervously with it. 'I wa' wondering if there wa' any work goin', Missus? I'll tek anything, I ain't fussy. I'm 'ard worker, do 'ote yer ask of me. I don't cause no bother neither.'

Her heart filled with pity for this shabby young man who looked in dire need of a hearty meal and several nights' sleep. He was one of thousands wandering up and down the country in search of work. As it happened, though, this one might be lucky. The lad that Ivan had hired after dismissing Peabody had proved very adept at his work but found he hadn't the stomach for the line of business Clatteridge's operated. He had left two days before.

She smiled at him warmly. 'As it happens we might have. But first, you do know this is a funeral parlour?'

'I do, Missus. Read the sign on the door as I came in. That dun't bother me none. Someone 'as ter do it, dun't they? Me mam reckons it's the living we should be afraid of, not the dead.'

Miss Agnes and this man's mother would get on very well, Maddie thought. She wished she could feel the same. She had worked at Clatteridge's for nearly a year but the terror she had felt on her first day was still as strong as ever. Certain places in the establishment she still would not venture into unless it was absolutely necessary.

'Mr Simpson – that's the man you'll be needing to see – is busy at the moment, so would you mind waiting?'

'I'll wait all week, Missus, if it'd mean the chance of a job.'

She smiled. 'I don't think he'll be that long. Would you like a cup of tea while you wait?'

'Oh, ta very much,' he said gratefully.

Maddie took him into the shed and sat him down on one of the stools, then busied herself mashing a pot of tea, glad to have something to occupy her.

As she handed him an enamel mug of hot sweet tea, she frowned. 'I seem to know you. Have we met before?'

He accepted the mug and before answering supped greedily. Maddie realised it had been some time since he'd last had nourishment and wished she could offer him some food. 'I dun't think so,' he replied eventually.

'I think we have,' she said, sitting down on the stool opposite. Then recognition suddenly dawned. 'I know now. You're the young man on the train.'

'Eh?'

'The day you came to Leicester. Last May it would have been. Don't you remember me?'

He looked hard at her. 'Oh, ah, I do. You're the lady who wa' sittin' opposite me.'

'That's right. So how have things gone for you?' Maddie realised her question was pointless. It was so obvious this young man hadn't fared well at all.

He hung his head. 'Not so good. It weren't fer the lack of trying, Missus. I got work all right, and worked damned 'ard, but that didn't mek no difference. When things got tight I wa' the first ter be paid off. The last job I 'ad wa' for a decorating firm. I did all the running around, 'elped ter mix the paints and do all the dirty jobs so the trades could get on with the proper work. But the gaffer wa' one for cuttin' costs and I wa' a cost he decided to cut. Said the blokes'd 'ave ter do their own labouring. They weren't 'appy, threatened ter walk out, but that made no difference.' He sighed forlornly. 'To be 'onest, Missus, if I don't get summat 'arf decent today, I'm goin' back to Ket'rin. 'Tain't me I'm bothered about, you understand, it's me mother. She needs the money I send her. I won't be able to send her 'ote this week and I dun't know how she's gonna manage.'

Maddie's heart bled for him and his plight. She wished she had the authority to hire him. 'Mr Simpson shouldn't be long,' she said reassuringly. 'Would you like some more tea?'

He nodded vigorously. 'Ta, Missus, ta very much.'

Maddie's nerves were at breaking point by the time Ivan appeared over an hour later. She had exhausted all conversation with Ronald Smith, the young man, and for the last twenty minutes had been pacing the shed, stopping now and again to straighten things that didn't need straightening, glancing out of the door for any signs of Ivan only to be disappointed and begin her pacing again. She was just about to put the kettle on again when she realised he was standing behind her. She spun around and the grave expression on his face sent her heart plummeting.

'Miss Clatteridge wants ter see yer,' he said gruffly.

'Oh, thank you.'

Maddie hurriedly explained the presence of Ronald and rushed off.

Having run across the yard, she paused before the kitchen door to calm herself and then, expecting the worst, entered.

Agnes was sitting at the kitchen table, her face blank. 'Please sit down, Maddie,' she said tonelessly, inclining her head at the chair nearby.

Heart thumping painfully, Maddie sat, thoughts whirling. She should never have said what she had. She should have kept her own counsel. Miss Agnes was going to dismiss her and she had every right to do so. She'd had no right to compromise her employer in such a way, not to mention the embarrassment she must have caused Ivan. Maddie gulped hard and lowered her head. 'I'm so sorry, Miss Agnes. I can only ask your forgiveness though I don't deserve it. I'll collect my things and leave straight away.'

'That's your right, if you wish,' Agnes replied matter-of-factly. 'But I'd like to get something settled first.'

Maddie sighed forlornly and steeled herself for a severe reprimand for her unforgivable behaviour.

'Mr Simpson will speak to Josh himself.'

Raising her head, Maddie frowned quizzically. 'Speak to Josh? I'm sorry, I don't understand. Josh has nothing to do with this, Miss Agnes.'

'Oh, but he has. You wouldn't like me to approach him about your being my matron of honour without asking you first, would you? It's only right that Mr Simpson should be the one to ask Josh to be best man at our wedding, now isn't it?'

Maddie's mouth dropped open in shock. 'Wedding?'

A slow smile spread across Agnes's face, her eyes shining euphorically. 'Ivan has asked me to marry him and it's all your doing, Maddie dear.'

'Oh!' she gasped. 'Oh, Miss Agnes,' she cried jumping up and throwing her arms around her. 'Oh, I'm so delighted.'

'That's very apparent, dear,' Agnes said, laughing. 'Oh, Maddie dear, how can I . . . we . . . ever thank you?'

Maddie drew away. 'You have, Miss Agnes, I'll be the most honoured matron of honour there's ever been. I'm so happy, Miss Agnes, I can't tell you how much. And I was so afraid . . .' she exhaled loudly. 'Oh, so afraid I'd caused you both . . . Oh, Miss Agnes,' she erupted, 'please tell me your plans?'

'I shall be delighted to, my dear. We're going to be married as soon as we can and we're going to keep on the parlour. Mr Simpson . . .' she giggled shyly '. . . Ivan, is going with me to see the bank manager and find out what mortgage we can arrange so I can settle things with Alice. Above all I must see she is well provided for with her rightful share.'

'Will she be happy for you?'

'Oh, yes. My sister and I are very fond of each other.

She'll be shocked but delighted, I can assure you, though disappointed I won't be joining her. But she has a good life in Scarborough, she's very happy there, so I have no worries on that score.' Agnes eyed Maddie tentatively. 'You will still continue to work for us, won't you, Maddie? My marriage will alter nothing of the way you're treated here.'

'Of course, Miss Agnes. Goodness, I was so worried a few minutes ago I was about to lose my job.'

'That was rather naughty of us, Maddie dear. I hope you'll forgive us, but we wanted to keep you guessing because I wanted to break the news to you myself.'

Just then the door opened and Ivan walked in. Without any embarrassment he walked straight up to Maddie, threw his arms around her and hugged her tight. 'Thank you,' he said emotionally.

'It was my pleasure,' she murmured.

He pulled away, stepped over to Agnes and put a loving arm around her shoulder. 'I'd like to introduce yer to our new lad. Ronald!' he called. 'Come through, son. Come and meet the ladies who run this place.'

The women in question laughed heartily.

The house had never known such happiness within its walls for many a long year.

# Chapter Thirty-One

A delighted Nancy Baldicott eyed the two young people before her. 'My, yer a sight fer sore eyes, the both of yer. I 'ave ter say I never expected ter see you, young man, but I'm glad to see things have worked out. Marriage suits yer, Maddie love, indeed it does.'

She smiled warmly. 'Thank you, Mrs Baldicott. I'm glad to see you're well too.'

'Oh, can't complain, gel. Me bones creak a bit more than when you were with me but me health's still good. Mrs Rumkin sends her regards. You remember her, don't yer, me duck?'

'I do indeed. I was rather fond of Mrs Rumkin. Please give her my regards too.' Maddie turned her attention to Josh, sitting by her side at the kitchen table. 'Mrs Baldicott and her neighbour Mrs Rumkin look like two peas in a pod.'

'Only I'm better lookin',' said Nancy, tongue in cheek. 'More tea or cake? What about you, Mr Jenks. You'll 'ave another piece of me slab cake? Famous I am for me currant slab.'

'It's very good,' he said sincerely. 'I don't mind if I do.'

Mrs Baldicott busied herself refilling their cups and cutting the cake, her thoughts running rife. What a dilemma she faced. The worst one she had ever had to face in her life and she didn't know what to do. The young couple sitting before her, she knew without a doubt, had journeyed here today to ask her a special question. It had still to be broached but shortly it would be, she knew, and the answer she had no choice but to give was going to grieve them both deeply. Maddie had told her her mother was dead, at which Nancy had expressed her sympathies though truthfully she felt that dying was the best thing Harriet Ashman had ever done for her daughter. But that knowledge had put her in a very difficult situation. She herself was now the only person who knew of their daughter's whereabouts, their only hope of ever having a chance to reclaim her.

Nancy pushed Josh's cup closer and sighed. Actually seeing them together, witnessing their love, had she the right to refuse them this knowledge, forcing them to spend the rest of their lives mourning the loss of their child?

Secretly she eyed them both. Despite their joint heartache they did look happy, content, as loving as any couple she had ever come across over a long eventful life. It gladdened her heart, having witnessed so much sorrow and misery.

So many different reasons brought girls to her door and most cases were painful but never had she had to face this moral dilemma before. One or two girls or relatives even had returned to her years later and asked for information about the babies but she had always refused. She had to think of the people who took the children and raised them; it would hardly be fair to them for the mothers to turn up years later and demand their children back. What was done was done, in her view, and best for all concerned left that way.

But this situation was different. And it was Maddie who made it so. Despite herself Nancy had become strongly attached to the girl during her stay and despite her own doubts at the time over Maddie's tales of the baby's father, still felt that if ever there was a case of injustice this was one. Even Betty Rumkin had agreed that Harriet Ashman had had no right to do what she had. Any doubts Nancy had had were now dispelled by the sight of the two people facing her across the table. That baby, she knew, had been conceived purely out of love and, if it had been allowed, would have been cared for by parents who adored her.

Nancy took a deep breath. Rightly or wrongly, regardless of the repercussions, she had to tell Maddie and Josh what she knew. Maybe just once a story could have a happy ending.

She rose silently, walked across to a cupboard in the recess by the range and rummaged through a box. Finally unearthing what she was looking for, she went back to the table, sat down, and without hesitation pushed a piece of paper towards Maddie.

'You never got this from me,' she said.

Puzzled, Maddie picked it up and read the words on it. She gasped, eyeing Nancy with a mixture of surprise and profound gratitude.

'Don't say anythin', me duck. Just finish yer tea and be on yer way. It's not far, a short train ride. If yer hurry yer'll arrive about two. I hope yer find what yer lookin' for.'

Hand in hand, Maddie and Josh silently walked from the station down a rutted lane, past the village shop-cum-Post Office, two public houses and a school, until they found the street they were looking for. It was tree-lined, the houses all double bay-fronted Victorian villas, the gardens fronting the properties neat and tidy. Apparently the occupants were far removed from the lowly working classes.

As they approached the house they were seeking their pace slowed and Maddie's grip tightened on Josh's hand. They looked at each other emotionally.

'Oh, Josh,' she murmured. 'I can't believe our child is so close.'

He inhaled sharply and gave a tight smile, squeezing her hand reassuringly.

Hearts thumping painfully, they passed a high hedge and stopped just before a low gate. In the long garden to the front of the house a man squatted, clipping daffodils from a clump and carefully laying each flower in a trug. A child, wrapped warmly, was darting about close by, her dark curls bouncing.

Maddie gasped, drawing back against the hedge. 'That's our child, Josh. It has to be. Oh, she's beautiful!'

He was too choked to speak. He gave her hand another squeeze and, like Maddie, stared transfixed at the scene being played out before them.

The child toddled up to the man. He lifted his head and smiled at her, the deep affection he felt very obvious. He held out a flower. 'For Mummy,' he said.

The child grabbed at it with a podgy hand and giggled.

The front door opened and a woman appeared. She was smiling, wiping her hands on a white lace-edged apron that covered the skirt of her well-cut blue woollen day dress. 'Dinner's ready, you two,' she called, her voice refined but warm.

The child turned and tottered over, the flower outstretched. 'Mama,' she said, handing it over.

The woman squatted down and gathered the child to her, gently easing the gift from her hand. 'That for me?' she said, kissing her cheek. 'Oh, thank you. Are you going to help Mummy arrange the flowers in a vase?'

The child giggled happily.

The man joined them. He handed the basket filled with spring blooms to his wife and scooped up the child, then placed his other arm protectively around the woman's waist.

As they all went inside the house Maddie was filled with a great urge to run into the garden and snatch her child, disappear with her and Josh, but she knew she couldn't do that. Love told her such an action would be wrong.

The child was no longer theirs. She and Josh might be her natural parents but these people were her true family now. It was they who had loved and cherished her, cared for and protected her for all but several days of her short life. By taking the child away, she and Josh would cause suffering and torment for everyone, the likes of which they themselves knew only too well. But, most importantly, the damage done to the child would be irrevocable.

Maddie couldn't do it, wouldn't be able to live with herself, and as she lifted her sad eyes and looked at Josh she knew without doubt his thoughts mirrored her own.

She clutched his hand so tight her nails cut his flesh. 'Let's go home,' she murmured.

Josh stared at the woman he loved more than life itself, saw the unbearable grief she was enduring. 'Are yer sure, Maddie? It's now or never.'

Now or never. What an air of finality those words contained. She took a deep pain-filled breath and nodded resolutely.

Silently, hand in hand, they retraced their steps to the station.

# Chapter Thirty-Two

Agnes Simpson breezed into the kitchen, put her handbag down on the table and took off her coat which she laid on the back of a chair for the time being.

'I won't ask if you've coped all right, Maddie. I know the business is in safe hands with you and Ronald when I have to go out. Ivan made a good choice in taking him on, such a nice lad and very willing. That reminds me, I thought some new curtains would brighten up the room above the stables for him. What do you think, Maddie?'

'I think he'd appreciate that very much. I'll help make them.'

Agnes walked over to her. 'That looks nice,' she said appreciatively, seeing the filling Maddie was preparing to put into a pastry-covered dish. 'Smells nice too. What is it?'

'Sarah's Surprise Pie. I thought you and Mr Simpson would like it for your dinner. I didn't know how long you'd be at the station. You're back quicker than I thought you'd be.'

'The train arrived and left on time.' Agnes sighed. 'It was quite sad seeing Alice off, but it was obvious she couldn't wait to get back to Scarborough. Leicester holds nothing for her any longer. I've promised her Ivan and I will pay a visit as soon as we can spare the time. It's a pity Aunt Celia couldn't manage to come for the wedding. Still, at least Alice did.'

'She told me just after she arrived that she wouldn't have

missed it for anything,' said Maddie, slapping a piece of pastry over the top of the dish and beginning to crimp together the edges. 'Oh, it was such a lovely wedding,' she mused. 'All those people who turned out to wish you and Mr Simpson well. I'll never forget them all cheering when you both arrived back from the Register Office in the box cart all decked out in orange blossom. Me and Josh, Sarah and my father, Ruth and Roy and Ronald, all crammed into the hired brake, cheering along with the crowd. I thought we'd all fall out,' she said, laughing at the memory.

She stopped her task and turned to face Agnes, studying her for a moment. Agnes looked radiant, happiness oozing from her. Ivan too was a changed man since Maddie herself had intervened, giving them an opportunity to declare their feelings for one another. She was so glad she had taken the chance. With both of them it was as if someone had lit an inner light and its beam was glowing out. Maddie knew without a doubt that theirs was a partnership that would be as loving and happy as the one she shared with Josh, one that would last a lifetime. She smiled warmly. 'I can't believe it's all over.'

'All over?' Agnes said, sitting down at the kitchen table and reaching for the teapot. Satisfied the tea was not long made she began to pour herself a cup. 'It's just beginning, surely?'

'Oh, you know what I mean,' Maddie laughed. 'The wedding is over, not your marriage. My goodness, I thought Josh and I got married quickly but it was only just over a fortnight ago that Mr Simpson asked you to become his wife.'

Agnes smiled secretly. 'He's a surprising man, is my husband,' she said, eyes twinkling. 'Bit like your pie. It's so thoughtful of you, Maddie dear, to make it for us. Tell me what's in it?'

'No,' she said. 'You'll have to wait and see.'

As she sipped her tea Agnes studied Maddie closely. There

was something different that she couldn't quite pinpoint. To those who did not know her well, on the surface Maddie would appear to be her normal self. But Agnes knew different. If asked, the only way she would be able to describe this change would be to say that if Maddie's inner being was lit by a hundred candles, then several of them had recently been snuffed out, never to be relit. She wondered what had caused that.

It was nothing to do with her mother's death. Maddie, Agnes knew, was over that. It was to do with something else. She wondered if it could be connected to the day Maddie and Josh had made a journey together to the countryside, telling her they were paying a visit to a dear old lady there. Agnes had noticed Maddie was very quiet, withdrawn even, after she had returned, but she herself had been so happily caught up in her wedding plans that she hadn't taken the time to dwell on this fact as she would normally have done.

'Maddie,' she asked, 'are you all right, dear?'

Maddie eyed her in surprise. 'Yes, of course. Why do you ask?'

'Oh, just wondered. You . . . I don't know, my dear, you seem a little preoccupied at times. Nothing wrong, is there?'

Maddie stared at the woman she had come to regard so highly and suddenly felt guilty. She had thought she had hidden her recent trauma. Obviously she had misjudged how deeply Agnes cared for her. But to share with her the story of her child, no matter how understanding and sympathetic Agnes was, would reopen closing wounds, prolong the healing process.

She took a deep breath. 'I'm fine, really. I am worried about Sarah. She's been getting a lot more of those pains . . . settling pains, she calls them, but with her time getting so close now it's natural to be concerned, isn't it? I've asked her if Penny's too much now, she's certainly a bundle of energy, but Sarah insists she's not.'

'I know Sarah well enough to realise, Maddie dear, that she would tell you straight if Penny was, so stop fretting. Er . . . Maddie?'

'Yes?'

'As a matter of interest, why have you suddenly started calling Ivan "Mr Simpson"?'

'Out of respect Miss Agnes, now he's your husband. I felt it only right.'

Agnes rose and stood before Maddie, hands clasped. 'Maddie, my dear, I told you nothing would change on our marriage and nothing has. Now Ivan is Ivan to you as he has always been. And I think it's about time you addressed me just as Agnes. We have become more than employer and employee, haven't we?'

Maddie smiled. 'Yes, we have.'

'Good. And Ivan and I are still invited for Sunday tea, aren't we, dear?'

'Yes, of course. Josh and I are looking forward to it.'

'So are we. I haven't seen much of your husband recently and only briefly at the wedding. In fact, since this all came about, I haven't had any time to speak properly to you, unless it was wedding talk, so how are things? Is his new window cleaning round as profitable as he hoped?'

'Yes, very much so. Josh's so pleased he took the chance. He's already taken on several new customers and is talking about taking on another man to help.'

'That is good news.' Agnes eyed Maddie tentatively. 'Any word on Penny's relatives yet?'

Maddie breathed deeply. 'No, nothing. I think Mr Grantham's had quite a time of it from what he told me and Josh when he came around to see us the other day. I must say, I do like him. He's a very nice man. He's pleased by the way we're looking after Penny.'

'I would have been very surprised should he have found anything to complain about, Maddie. You couldn't treat that child any better if she was your own. Exactly what did you mean when you said Mr Grantham's had quite a time of it, looking for the relatives?'

'Oh, just that several bogus claims have been made. People saying they're related when they're nothing of the kind. I can't understand anyone doing something like that. Don't they realise their story will be thoroughly checked out? Neither have the Binghams Mr Grantham has traced come to anything. He's placing an advertisement in *The Times* and is hoping that will turn up something.' Maddie sighed. 'If not, I don't know what will happen. He's just about exhausted all lines of enquiry.'

Agnes caught a flicker in Maddie's eyes and knew instinctively she was trying to cover up the hope that nothing would transpire, leaving the way open for she and Josh to keep the child with them. It would be wrong of her, she felt, to add fuel to Maddie's hope, when there was still time yet for a relative to show up. 'Well, best not give up yet. There could be a perfectly simple reason why it's taking such a time.' Let's hope it's soon, she thought, before Maddie and Josh got any more attached to Penny, if that's possible.

'Mmmm,' murmured Maddie.

They both jumped as an urgent banging on the back door began. Agnes rushed to open it, finding an anxious young woman staring back at her.

'Mrs Jenks 'ere?' she cried.

Maddie appeared at the door, 'Mrs Tate, what's the matter?'

'It's Mrs Ashman, she sent me ter fetch yer. Baby's coming. I'm off ter get the midwife,' she said, running off.

Maddie's jaw dropped. 'Oh . . .' she exclaimed, flustered.

Agnes grabbed her arm. 'Calm down, Maddie, you'll be no good to Sarah, getting yourself in such a state.'

'But the baby's not due for another three weeks.'

'I know I haven't had the joy of having one myself but as I understand it babies have a tendency to arrive when they see fit, not when others do. Right,' said Agnes, taking charge.

'Clean towels and sheets. I expect Sarah's prepared but I'll bring some along just in case.'

'You're coming too?'

'Of course. I'm sure I can be of help somewhere. Even if I only keep everyone supplied with tea. And Penny will need watching. Go on, Maddie,' she urged. 'I'll only be minutes behind you.'

A flustered Maddie found Sarah in the back room, gripping the back of a chair.

'Oh, thank goodness,' she sighed as a wave of pain washed over her. 'I didn't know what to do, Maddie love. I've felt peculiar all day but the pains started an hour ago. I thought it was them testing pains, but this is it. Lucky Mrs Tate popped in. I didn't want to upset Twopenny,' she said, eyeing the child sitting on the clippy rug surrounded by her toys, staring back at them. 'Poor little mite must be wondering what's going on. Ohhhhh!' she moaned as a severe pain gripped her, fighting to control her outburst for fear of frightening the child.

Maddie clutched hold of her arm. 'I'd better get you upstairs. Agnes is on her way. She'll take care of Penny. Mrs Tate's gone for the midwife.'

'No time, Maddie love,' Sarah uttered through clenched teeth. 'This baby's coming now.'

Panic-stricken, Maddie gulped. 'Now? But it takes hours . . .' she began as memories of her own labour returned.

Sarah transferred her grip from the chair to Maddie's arm, clutching on to her so tightly the bruising would take days to fade. 'Not always, Maddie. Help me get to the sofa in the front room.'

The urgency of the situation suddenly struck home and Maddie pushed aside all her fears as she realised someone had to take control. She just hoped the baby wouldn't arrive before the midwife turned up.

They began the slow painful journey across the room and down the short passage. The distance was measurable in feet but seemed to them both like miles, stopping several times en route to allow Sarah to cope with contractions.

Agnes, her arms filled with clean sheets and towels, arrived at the door at the same time as Mrs Tate and the midwife. As they all rushed in, they stopped in their tracks as the sound of a baby crying met them. They all looked at each other and ran in the direction of the cries. Framed in the doorway they stared astounded at what they saw.

A tired but serene Sarah was lying on the sofa, legs still drawn up, her modesty covered by her rumpled skirt. Maddie was kneeling to the side of her on the floor. In her arms she held the newly born baby.

'Better late than never,' Sarah said jocularly.

Maddie dragged her eyes away from the child and looked across at them all, face filled with wonder, far too overwhelmed to say anything.

Much later Agnes handed her a steaming cup of tea. Sarah had been attended to by the midwife and made comfortable upstairs in her bed, the baby in a cradle by her side. Both were in perfect health and at the moment having a well-deserved sleep. Mrs Tate had returned home to see to her brood; the midwife, having had her cup of tea, had departed too.

Maddie accepted the cup gratefully. 'The baby's beautiful, isn't he, Agnes?'

She nodded. 'You did so well, Maddie. How does it feel to know you played such a big part in his birth?'

'I can't describe it. And it all happened so quickly I didn't have time to think, just get on with it.' She paused for a moment and positioned Penny more comfortably on her lap. 'If anything, I feel bad for Twopenny here. With all that was going on, I quite forgot about her.'

'That's understandable. Anyway she was quite happy playing with her toys.'

Maddie bent over and kissed the top of the child's head. 'I can't wait to see my dad's face when he comes in any minute now. And Ruth and Roy.'

Agnes smiled. 'They'll be absolutely delighted. While you were helping the midwife deal with Sarah and the baby, I took it upon myself to prepare a meal for them all.'

'Oh, that was good of you, Agnes.'

'It was the least I could do. Oh, there's the door now I expect that'll be your father,' she said. 'I'll let you break the good news, Maddie dear. I'll go out the back.'

It took George a few moments to digest what had happened but when it sank in he bounded up the stairs. 'Oh, my dear, I'm so happy,' he said, gazing tenderly at Sarah. He looked down into the cradle. 'He looks like me,' he said proudly.

'I hope he takes after you,' she replied softly. 'Then we'll have two wonderful sons and two beautiful daughters.'

Eyes brimming with love, George leaned over and kissed her lovingly. 'Aren't we lucky, Sarah?' he whispered.

Eyes shining, she nodded.

He looked at her for several long moments. 'Will you marry me?' he asked.

'Oh, George,' she breathed in delight. 'We'll slip off quietly, just us and our family.'

'Yes, just us and our family.'

A commotion erupted below and seconds later feet pounded up the stairs. They both started to laugh.

Sarah looked down at her new son. 'Get ready, my boy,' she said tenderly, 'to meet your other sister and your big brother.'

# Chapter Thirty-Three

Maddie was making her way home, conscious that Josh would have returned from work by now and be wondering where she was. But she knew he would be delighted when she told him the reason for her absence and be understanding about her failure to get word to him. Heavy in her arms, a tired Penny was becoming tetchy. 'Soon have you tucked up in bed nice and warm,' said Maddie soothingly.

She suddenly spotted Josh heading towards her. 'Oh, here's Uncle Josh come to meet us,' she said, pleased. 'Sarah's had her baby,' she announced as they met. 'It's a boy, Josh, and he's just perfect. I delivered him, what do you think about that? Take Penny for me, please. She's getting such a weight, she's about breaking my arms.' As she handed him the child his seeming lack of interest in the new arrival registered, as did the troubled look on his face. She frowned. 'Josh, what's wrong?'

Hitching the child comfortably in his arms, he eyed his wife gravely. 'We've visitors, Maddie.'

'Visitors?' she queried. 'Who at this hour?'

He placed his free hand on her arm, wanting to break the news as gently as he could but knowing Maddie was not going to like what he had to tell her. 'Mr Grantham and Twopenny's auntie.'

Her face fell, horrified. 'Auntie!'

He eyed her. 'Maddie, I know that as time passed yer hoped this wasn't going to happen, I have ter be honest so did I, but . . .'

'I know, Josh, we shouldn't have, should we? It's just come as a shock. I expected some warning so we'd be prepared, that's all.'

'Maybe it's better this way, eh, love?'

She sighed. 'Yes, I expect so,' she said softly. 'Josh, what's she like, the auntie?' she asked urgently.

'I never got a chance to find out, love. As soon as I put me key in the lock they were behind me. I showed them in and came immediately to find you.'

'Oh, dear,' she said worriedly. 'There's no fire lit, nothing. What must they think of me?' She took several deep breaths and steeled herself. 'We'd better hurry,' she said matter-of-factly. Penny started to grizzle and Maddie stroked a hand tenderly over her face. 'She's tired, poor love. I hope the aunt won't mind waiting while I put her to bed before we discuss arrangements. When do you think we'll be expected to hand her over, Josh? A week? Two?'

He eyed her helplessly. 'Dunno, love.'

She stared at him for several long moments. Maddie had tried to prepare herself for this moment and had thought she had, but now she was faced with it she realised she was not prepared at all. Despite all the warnings and the number of times she had reminded herself that Penny would eventually be reunited with her relatives, nothing had prepared her for the painful emotions that were overwhelming her now. She likened it to losing her own child all over again. Josh, too, despite his brave front was, she knew, feeling exactly the same. With all the force she could muster Maddie stiffened her back and said, 'Well, I'd best go and find out.'

She hurried on ahead.

Mr Grantham rose from his seat as she entered the room. 'Good evening, Mrs Jenks. So sorry to be calling at such an unsociable hour . . .'

'Stop apologising, man,' a voice boomed. 'Just get matters dealt with and we can be on our way. Where's the child?'

Maddie's eyes flew to the middle-aged woman seated in her armchair. She was tiny, her round body draped in an expensive ruby-coloured coat, head covered by a matching feather-adorned cloche hat. Her features would have been classed as handsome had they not been clouded with impatience.

Maddie took an instant dislike to the woman and, fighting to hide her feelings, forced a smile to her face. 'You must be Twopenny's aunt,' she said, walking forward, holding out one hand in greeting.

Olivia Fotheringhay blatantly ignored her hostess's gesture. 'Who on earth is Twopenny?' she snapped.

'Oh!' Maddie exclaimed, withdrawing her hand. 'That's what we call Penny.'

'You mean Penelope, surely? I don't hold with the use of sentimental nicknames. People should be addressed by the name they were christened with. So where is she?'

'She?' snapped Maddie, unable to control her rising anger. 'Meaning your niece, I take it?'

'Niece! That child is no kin of mine and I'll not have her described as such.'

Maddie gasped in shock. 'I'm sorry?'

'Mrs Jenks,' Mr Grantham said, stepping forward with an apologetic expression on his face. 'Mrs Fotheringhay has had a long day and is anxious to get the formalities over with. She's still in shock over her brother's death.'

'Don't apologise for me, man. My brother got what was coming to him. If he hadn't married that woman in the first place, I doubt we'd be in this situation now.'

Just then Josh arrived. 'Sorry I took so long . . .' He stopped abruptly, sensing the atmosphere in the room, and went immediately to his wife's side. 'What's going on?' he whispered.

She flashed him a worried glance. 'Something's not right, Josh,' she whispered back.

'What d'yer mean?'

Before she could answer Penny started crying and held out her hands to Maddie. 'Mammy,' she screamed.

'She addressed you as her mother,' Olivia Fotheringhay said disapprovingly. 'You had no right to allow the child to do that.'

'She didn't,' said Maddie, taking the distressed child from Josh's arms. 'She was trying to say Maddie. It just sounded like Mammy, that's all. Look, would you please excuse me for a moment while I put Penny to bed? She's very tired. Then we can discuss . . .'

'Just get the child's things together,' Olivia Fotheringhay interrupted sharply. 'We're taking her with us now. She can sleep on the journey. Nanny!'

Nanny? Maddie looked around her as seemingly from nowhere a tall, thin, sharp-featured woman appeared at Josh's side. Maddie and he stared at her, shocked.

'You're taking Penny now . . . tonight?' Maddie asked, horrified.

'Of course. Did you think this was a social visit?' Olivia Fotheringhay replied off-handedly.

As the nanny tried to take the child from Maddie, Penny let out a piercing scream and closed her arms tight around Maddie's neck.

'Can't you control that child?' said Olivia Fotheringhay coldly. 'I can see you're going to have your work cut out, Nanny. The child has obviously never been disciplined.'

Unable to control herself, Maddie turned on her. 'Penny's tired, Mrs Fotheringhay, that's why she's crying. And your . . . nanny is upsetting her. Twopenny doesn't know her so how can she be expected to go to her without a fuss?'

'Utter nonsense! The child will have to learn to behave herself.' Olivia rose, pulling on her gloves. 'Mr Grantham, will you kindly hurry up and get the formalities over with? I wish to leave.'

'Formalities?' queried Josh. 'What do you mean?'

'Mrs Fotheringhay means your payment.'

'Payment?' said Maddie, confused. 'I don't understand.'

'Oh, I'm sure you do,' said Olivia knowingly. 'Isn't money the whole reason you took the child in in the first place?'

'I beg your pardon?'

'Oh, please don't insult my intelligence, Mrs Jenks,' she responded coldly. 'The child is to inherit a good sum of money. You must have had an idea of that. Money, I might add to which she has no right. I expect you were hoping no one would turn up to claim her so you'd offer to take control.'

'Now just a minute,' Josh piped up angrily. 'Just what are yer accusing us of?'

'Mrs Fotheringhay, with due respect these people had no idea . . .'

'Oh, save your breath, Mr Grantham. I don't know how they learned about the money, I just know they did. Working-class people don't do anything without an ulterior motive. Now can we please just go?'

The nanny made to take hold of Penny again. Instinctively Maddie's hold on her tightened and she stepped several paces back, her whole being screaming at her that matters were far from right. This situation was far removed from the loving reunion she had anticipated.

She pulled Josh aside. 'She doesn't want her, Josh. Mrs Fotheringhay want Penny, I mean. It's got something to do with money.'

He eyed her gravely. 'I gathered the same.'

'We can't hand her over! We can't,' mouthed Maddie urgently. 'They won't treat her right.'

'But what choice have we got?'

Her mind was racing frantically.

The nanny was advancing again, eyes glinting determinedly.

'You don't want Penny,' Maddie accused Mrs Fotheringhay.

'Maddie!' Josh gasped, horrified.

'It's true,' she cried. 'And what did you mean, Penny's

no kin of yours? If she's no kin of yours, why did Mr Grantham say you were her aunt?'

'That is none of your business,' Olivia hissed, incensed.

'Oh, but it is. It was made our business when Penny was abandoned after your brother's and his wife's death and no one came forward to care for her. We looked after her, loved her, so if you expect us just to hand her over when it's obvious you have no feelings for her then you've another think coming. We won't, will we, Josh?'

The older woman's eyes darkened dangerously. 'Either you hand that child over or I have the police fetched,' she warned.

'Then fetch them,' said Josh.

Olivia turned on Mr Grantham. 'Are you just going to stand here and allow this?'

Mr Grantham tightened his lips, trying to hide how angry he was becoming. A solicitor was not expected to allow personal feelings to interfere with professional matters but in this case he couldn't help himself.

He had taken a great liking to the Jenkses who without question had grown to love his deceased client's child. During all the time Penny had been with them not once had he doubted the child was in safe hands. He'd thought it most kind of the Jenkses to do all they had and never once ask for any remuneration.

On meeting Olivia Fotheringhay for the first time this morning when she had presented herself at his office, without prior notification, he had been shocked to say the least. She was nothing like her brother in looks or attitude and not one bit like her sister-in-law whom he had thought a gentle, kind woman. Hildegard and Christopher Bingham had both doted on their child and would be turning in their graves if they could see what was happening.

His eyes grew troubled as he struggled with his conscience. Surely his duty to look after his client's interests extended to the best interests of their child now they were no longer around to see to it themselves? It was his belief that it wasn't in this child's best interests to be handed over to Mrs Fotheringhay, not when he gravely suspected the true reason why she wanted the child and not when a far more suitable alternative was at hand. If he didn't act now his chance would be gone forever.

He eyed the formidable aunt. 'Would you allow me to have a private word with Mr and Mrs Jenks?'

'What?' she hissed, then sighed in irritation. 'If it will mean getting this matter over and done with. Hurry up.'

In the kitchen, the door closed firmly, Mr Grantham faced them both. He clasped his hands. 'What I'm about to do could be classed as improper.'

'What are you about to do?' asked Maddie worriedly, hitching Penny more comfortably in her arms.

'Here, let me take her,' said Josh, then eyed the kindly solicitor. 'Yes just what are yer about to do?' he reiterated.

Looking concerned Mr Grantham said, 'Tell you a story. I first met Mr and Mrs Bingham two years ago when they came to me over the purchase of their house. I found them to be a devoted young couple with a small baby. It wasn't until two days ago that I discovered that Bingham was not their true name. The cleaner who is looking after their house while matters are being settled found an envelope wedged at the back of a drawer inside which was a marriage certificate and adoption papers for the child. The surname of both official papers was Scatterswaite, not Bingham.'

'Adoption papers?' gasped Maddie.

He nodded. 'Acting on the information I gleaned from the documents,' he continued, 'I contacted the Scatterswaite Estate's solicitor and from him I have learned much.

'It appears that Christopher Scatterswaite married Hildegard Schmitt against the wishes of his family. In fact his father was incensed and threatened to cut him off. He'd expected his only son to marry into a titled English family. All the threats the father issued went unheeded. Christopher adored Hildegard and was determined to marry her. Financially he did not need to be supported by the family, having received a large legacy from his maternal grandmother. He wasn't rich compared to the rest of the family but had more than enough to provide a handsome living for them both. Having nothing with which to threaten his son, the father grudgingly relented and appeared to accept the marriage.

'There was only one thing to mar Christopher and Hildegard's happiness. After ten years of marriage the couple had not produced a much longed for child. Knowing how the family would feel about such a matter, they secretly began to explore the possibility of adoption and only declared the existence of Penelope after all the formalities were dealt with. The family were outraged. Marrying a foreigner was something that had been reluctantly forgiven. Bringing a total stranger into the family and expecting them to accept the outsider as one of their own was unthinkable. There was a terrible disagreement and the family did not see or hear from Christopher, Hildegard or their child again, and did not know of their deaths until I made contact two days ago.

'It is obvious to me that for the sake of their beloved daughter, Christopher and Hildegard decided it was best to sever all ties and move away where no one knew of them to start a new life under an assumed name. And that is why the advertisements we placed under the name of Bingham did not bear fruit.' He paused. 'I can see the name Scatterswaite doesn't mean anything to you?'

They both shook their heads.

'The Scatterswaites are a very old family of landowners in Yorkshire. Lord Scatterswaite's a very powerful man. The family are not interested in the child. What they want is the family money to be returned. The child is not of their blood and in their eyes not entitled to anything. I expect when Christopher and Hildegard made their will, they did not for a moment think that they would die together. In the event of either of them dying, money would go to the survivor. As their adopted only child, that money now passes entirely to Penelope. So, whoever cares for her has control of the money.'

'And that's all Mrs Fotheringhay wants Penny for, so she can get her hands on the money?' said Maddie icily.

'I'm very much afraid that is the case, Mrs Jenks. Mrs Fotheringhay made no secret of the fact that the Scatterswaite family intend the nanny to raise the child in a cottage away from the family home. I strongly suspect that by the time Penelope is of age there will be no money left to inherit.' He paused and eyed the dumbstruck couple. 'I would like to ask you a question.'

Maddie and Josh looked at each other. 'Yes, we will,' they said simultaneously.

The solicitor smiled. 'I haven't asked you the question yet.'

'You don't need to,' they said.

He patted their shoulders. 'Then I have your permission to put a proposition to Mrs Fotheringhay?'

'You do,' they answered.

It was fifteen long minutes before Mr Grantham called them both through.

Josh entered first and hurriedly glanced around. 'They've gone?'

The solicitor nodded. 'Mrs Fotheringhay was more than happy to accept my suggestion that in exchange for the child, half of the money should revert back to the family estate. The other half is to be held in trust for Penelope until she comes of age. All in all, I feel Penelope will benefit most from this arrangement and, as her father's executor, I am satisfied that I have acted in her best interests.' Though, he thought, I know what I have done is not quite to the letter of the law. 'I will have the necessary documents drawn up for you to sign as soon as possible.'

Maddie sat down in the armchair and positioned Penny comfortably on her knee. Josh perched on the arm, holding Maddie's shoulders protectively.

She kissed the top of the child's head. Looking at the solicitor she said, 'I feel sorry for that family. They may have got back the family fortune but we're the richer. Our Twopence is worth more to us than all the money in the world.'

He smiled warmly at the family before him. 'And I'm very happy that my clients will be able to rest in peace, knowing their child is so very well looked after.'

The child in her lap turned her head and looked up at Maddie. In a clear voice she said, 'Mamma.' Then turned to Josh, large blue eyes shining lovingly, and gave him a wide devoted grin.

# In For A Penny

For Rosemarie Bailey, a woman of many virtues.

My mentor, confidante, adviser – someone to laugh and cry with – steadfast and faithful. But more important than all of these, my trusted friend.

This book is for you with my love.

## Acknowledgements

The Lloyd Escoffery, with grateful thanks for the wonderful evening we spent reminiscing about your arrival in the United Kingdom in the early fifties. The experiences you shared were invaluable in bringing my character Herchell to life.

With thanks to my increasing army of fans, who are uppermost in my mind when I force myself to sit down at my PC and write when I'd sooner be watching the telly!

To my beloved grandson Liam, for continuously reminding me that at fifty years of age I am very old and at four-and-a-half he can do everything better than me.

To Lynsey – oh, daughter dear, what words can express how proud I am of you – there are none strong enough.

# Chapter One

'Jennifer Jeffries, wadda yer mean yer've no money! I know bloody well yer have, 'cos I looked in yer purse. Holding out on me, well, I ain't never heard the like! Can yer 'ear 'er, Tony?' May Jeffries spun her shapely body around to face the man she was addressing. Realising he wasn't paying any attention, her temper flared and she slammed down the tarnished compact and stick of cheap red lipstick she was holding on the littered table. 'TONY!' she screamed. 'I said, can yer bleddy 'ear 'er?'

A loud grunt came from the huge, balding man slouched in the grubby, threadbare armchair at the side of the cast-iron fireplace. His massive stomach spilled over a pair of dirty grey flannels, the waist fastenings of which were undone to allow room for the massive helping of chips and mushy peas smothered in salt and vinegar he'd just eaten, also affording onlookers an unpleasant view of the top of yellowing underpants. Greying chest hairs protruded through holes in his grimy vest and sprouted from his ears and wide nostrils.

The dark Italian looks he'd inherited from his father, which had once attracted an abundance of females, were scarcely evident now after years of excessive drink, mounds of greasy food and a daily quota of sixty Capstan full-strength cigarettes. Never an active man, Antonio Brunio's only exercise these days was the occasional tumble in bed when May felt obliging, which in recent weeks had not been the case.

1

Stubbing out his cigarette in an overflowing ashtray and taking a swig of beer from the bottle he was grasping, Tony shot an angry glance at her from his bulbous eyes. 'I can 'ear yer. So can the whole bleddy street, I expect.' He scratched two days' growth of beard irritably. 'Shut it, will yer, May, I'm trying to 'ear the bleddy racin' results.' Balancing the bottle on the edge of the armchair, he stretched out one hand towards the wireless set and turned up the sound.

Fuelled by his manner, May's temper erupted to boiling point and before Tony could stop her she jumped to her feet and heaved up the Bakelite wireless set from the small table to one side of him. As he looked on, shocked, she hurled it furiously across the room. It hit the far wall with a crash, the back flying off, glass from the valves inside smashing into smithereens. The vibration caused the half-empty bottle to tumble off the arm of his chair, spilling its contents on to the holey linoleum covering the floor.

The pretty young woman standing just inside the door watched the scene before her with mounting unease. As the wireless set disintegrated against the wall she gasped, unsure whether to leave her mother and Tony to it, or stay in case he retaliated in a violent manner and she was needed to aid May. Despite the fact that her mother was quite capable of taking care of herself, Jennifer Jeffries decided to stay, just in case.

Tony's face darkened thunderously. 'Yer daft bitch! Look what yer done now,' he exploded, struggling to raise his ungainly body.

'Oh, bitch, am I? I'll give yer bitch,' bellowed May. Clenching her fist, she flung out her hand and brought it back hard against his chin. The unexpected blow caught him off guard and, stunned, he fell back into his chair. 'You're n'ote but a useless fat lump, you are,' she screeched, leaning over him to wag a finger in his face. 'Neither use nor ornament. If you got off yer arse and gorra job like yer promised instead of sitting in that bleddy chair all day, swigging beer and workin' out yer bets, then I wouldn't 'ave ter be cadging money off our Jenny, now would I? 'Ow much yer spent down the bookie's terday, eh? 'Ow much?'

'N'ote,' he spat.

She thrust her angry face to within inches of his. 'Yer fuckin' liar! I 'ad five bob in the rent tin this morning. It's gone and you took it, din't yer?'

He shrugged his massive shoulders, indolently. 'I borrowed it.'

'Oh, yeah? Well, when yer borrows, yer pay it back.' Her hand shot out towards him, flapping furiously. 'So give us it back. Now. I wannit now.'

He inhaled sharply. 'Yer know I ain't gorrit. Listen up, May. I'm on a roll. Only need one more 'oss ter come in and I've got the jackpot – twenty quid. I'll buy yer that dress . . .'

'And 'ow many times 'ave I 'eard that? Yer good-fer-nothin' lazy git!' she spat ferociously. May stretched herself to her full height of five foot one inch and folded her arms under her full bosom, her face hard. 'I can't remember the last time you 'ad a winner. I don't think yer've ever 'ad one since I've known yer. That five bob were mine. I worked fer it. Slaved me guts out over a blasted machine, day in, day out. When were the last time you brought anything into this 'ouse, eh? 'Ote legal anyway.'

'I gave yer three quid last week.'

'It was two.' Jenny could not help but speak out, herself harbouring a grudge against Tony for the way he refused to chip in yet still expected his every need to be provided for.

He turned on her. 'And you can keep yer bleddy nose out, yer . . .'

'Oi!' May exploded. 'Don't yer dare speak to my daughter like that. And she's right. It were *two* quid, and it weren't last week, it were the week afore. And I only got that because I

3

caught you drinking the proceeds from those watches with the faulty winders yer flogged for half a crown a time. When I let yer move in 'ere yer promised me all sorts, Tony Brunio. And I've 'ad all sorts, ain't I? But not the all sorts you promised. Where's the television or the carpet yer said yer'd get me? I'll tell yer, shall I? Over the bookie's counter along wi' all the money yer steal off me. Yer think I'm stupid, don't yer? Think I get that drunk I don't know what I've done wi' me cash.' She curled her half-painted ruby red lips disdainfully. 'You make me sick. I can't imagine what I ever saw in yer. I must 'ave bin off me head allowing yer to move in 'ere. Well, I want yer out. Now.'

'Ah, May . . .'

'Don't "Ah, May," me,' she mimicked sarcastically. 'I mean it. Pack yer stuff and gerrout. Go and park yerself on Ivy Biddle. You think I don't know about you and 'er? She's bin after you since 'er old man left. Well, she's welcome ter yer as far as I'm concerned. Now piss off before I tek the poker to yer.'

She made a grab for the object propped against the fireplace and finally Tony, realising she was intent on causing him bodily harm, hauled himself out of the chair and managed to grab her arm before she could grasp the poker, his bulbous eyes now fearful. 'Yer don't mean that, May?' he said worriedly. 'Yer can't.'

With strength that was unexpected in one of her size, she wrenched free from his grasp and smacked her fist into his flabby chest. 'I do. It's my name on the rent book, I can do warra like. I want yer gone by the time I get back. If yer still 'ere when I do, Lou and 'is boys'll come and sort you out.'

'Now look 'ere, May,' he said pleadingly. 'There ain't no need ter do that. Me and Ivy Biddle . . . well, that's a load of twaddle and you know it. I ain't never looked at another woman since I met you.'

4

May knew his statement to be true. He wouldn't try it on with any other woman because he knew no other woman with common sense would so much as look at him. He was a lazy, no-good rotter, a man who had spent his entire adult life living with one woman after another. Stupid women like herself who, believing his charming lies, had thrown caution to the wind and taken him home. Women like herself who were ecstatic to believe they had found a man who would take care of them, lift them out of their hand-to-mouth existence, give them a better life.

And how very wrong that was. Tony was just like all the other men May had had over the years. She always believed the next one would be her saviour, only to be quickly and cruelly disappointed, and at the end of the tempestuous relationship, very much out of pocket, though unfortunately none the wiser. Then just like the other disappointed women before her, she would rid herself of the likes of Tony, promising herself that next time she'd be more cautious, hoping when the time came that she was being.

She glared a warning at him. 'I've had a belly full of yer lies, so don't bother tellin' me no more.' She retreated to the table. Hitching up her worn, faded pink petticoat, she sat down and crossed her shapely legs, revealing snagged stocking tops held up by frayed suspenders. Moving aside a half-empty bottle of sterilised milk, she retrieved her compact mirror from under the edge of a dirty plate and the lipstick which had landed by the bottle of malt vinegar and made to continue applying her makeup. Momentarily she paused, raised her eyes and looked across at the young woman standing by the door, slender hands clasped, pretty face creased worriedly.

Running her fingers through thick, shoulder-length, honey-blonde hair, Jenny sighed despairingly. This situation had been brewing for days. When any male friend of her mother's was in residence, rows were regular occurrences and only to be

5

expected until the man's usually abrupt departure. What Jenny was fearful of was this one turning violent, not because of any action of the huge man standing rigid with shock before them but at May's prompting. As tiny as she was, when May Jeffries was angry grown men cowered, just as the unsavoury Antonio Brunio was doing now.

'Are yer gonna get me that 'alf crown or not?' May barked at her daughter. 'And 'urry up about it. I said I'd meet Lil at eight outside the Newfoundpool Working Men's Club and it's ten to already. The tombola will 'ave started before I get there. And, eh, Jenny love,' she added, her face softening, 'be a duck and run the iron over me blue skirt. It's on the chair in me bedroom. Oh, and me red blouse while yer at it.'

Jenny fought down annoyance. Her mother could be thoughtless sometimes. Not that Jenny begrudged her anything, it was just that she was going out herself to meet a couple of the girls from work for a drink; had been looking forward to it. If she obliged her mother then she'd not be able to go. Two shillings and sixpence was all she had until Friday when she got paid, which was two days away. But regardless of her own financial predicament, if bloodshed were to be avoided tonight then May's request would have to be granted. 'I can't give you all that, Mam, it's all I've got. I can . . . er . . .' Jenny quickly did some calculations in her head, totting up her bus fares and anything urgent she might need until her brown envelope was handed to her on Friday lunchtime. 'Let you have one and threepence.'

May eyed her for a moment then snorted disdainfully. 'That'll do, I s'pose. I'll give it yer back out me winnin's.' She flashed a glance at Tony. 'What you standing gawking like an idiot for? I meant warra said. Pack yer stuff and gerrout or I'll get Jenny to fetch Lou and the boys.'

Half an hour later, Tony's shoes pounded against the bare-boarded stairs, quickly followed by the front door banging shut so hard the old house shook on its precarious foundations.

Standing before the pitted oval mirror hanging lopsided from a thick nail in the wall above the mantel, May tugged the last plastic roller out of her bleached blonde hair, gave it a brush and tweaked it into place before turning to face Jenny, with a sigh of relief. 'Thank God he's gone. Maybe we can 'ave some peace in this 'ouse for a while. I didn't think he'd go so easily, though.' She grimaced. 'I've missed the start of the tombola and it's all '*is* fault. I bet Lil thinks I ain't coming and ain't saved me a seat.'

Jenny propped the iron on its end, gave the shabby red blouse she had just ironed a shake and held it out towards her mother. 'Shall I check Tony hasn't taken anything of ours?'

May gave her a withering look. 'And what have we got that'd be worth anything ter Tony? Worth anything to anybody, fer that matter.' Taking the blouse from Jenny, she pulled it on, easing the ends into her tight-fitting bright blue skirt. 'Sod!' she exclaimed. 'Me button's shot off and it's me only good blouse. 'Ave we a safety?' she said, scanning her eyes across the littered mantelshelf.

'There's several gold ones in the vase. Give the blouse to me, Mam,' Jenny offered. 'I'll sew the button back on. Won't take me a minute.'

May shook her head. 'No time. Not if I hope ter stand a chance of winnin' summat. Thirty bob the prize money is ternight or a bottle of sherry for the booby. Either 'ud do, the mood I'm in,' she added, retrieving a pin. 'There,' she said a moment later, patting the blouse front. 'No one'll know 'cept you and me.' She rammed her tiny feet into badly scuffed three-inch-heeled shoes, then smoothed her hands over her shapely body, giving a provocative wiggle. 'Will I do?'

Jenny appraised her mother. To others her mother appeared cheap and brassy in her tight-fitting clothes, proudly display-ing her bulging cleavage, but May herself was under the impression she looked sexy and attractive. Other girls might be embarrassed to have a mother who flaunted herself. Not Jenny. Her mother dressed the best way she could with what little she possessed, and if what she achieved kept her happy then who was Jenny to dispel her illusions? May had few enough pleasures in her life as it was. Besides, should she ever voice any well-intended observations, her mother wouldn't take them at all kindly, she knew.

Jenny smiled. 'You'll do, Mam. Best-looking woman there tonight,' she said sincerely.

May donned her imitation leopard-skin coat and picked up her battered black handbag, checking its contents. 'Thanks, me duck. Now I'm off,' she said, clicking the bag shut. 'Be back about eleven. Eh, and if Tony dares come back and gives yer any trouble, bang on the wall fer Gloria. She'll sort 'im out good and proper.'

'Gloria not going with you tonight then?' Jenny asked.

'No, she's no money. Between you and me, as much as I love old Gloria, she's the luck of the devil and you can bet yer life she'd win that thirty bob. Wi' 'er out the way I might stand a chance. If I do I'll treat yer to a bag a chips on me way 'ome. All right?'

Jenny gave her mother an affectionate peck on the cheek. 'Can I have a pickled onion too?'

May slapped her playfully on the arm. 'Depends how generous I'm feeling. See yer later.' A thought suddenly struck her and she eyed Jenny quizzically. 'Oh, weren't you goin' out ternight?'

'I was but I changed me mind. Probably go Friday instead.'

'Oh, well, yer can't afford to go out anyway, can yer?' she said matter-of-factly. 'Tarra, love.'

Smiling at her mother's logic, Jenny shook her head. 'No, I can't really. Enjoy yourself, Mam.'

A while later Jenny shivered. Despite the fire being banked high with potato peelings, old bits of wood and a bucket full of slack, the small room still felt chilly. But then no matter how well the fire was stacked, no heat ever really built up here. How could it when it seeped straight out of the ill-fitting window and doorframes or through the cracks in the walls? This hundred-year-old terrace house was just one of many similar in a rundown area known as Frog Island about half a mile from Leicester city centre.

Laying aside a tattered three-month-old copy of *Woman's Own* that her mother had brought home from the factory, Jenny tucked her legs more comfortably underneath her and pulled her thick knitted cardigan tightly around herself. She lifted her eyes and gazed absently around the room. Two threadbare armchairs, a badly stained and scratched oak table covered by a plastic cloth, and a boxwood sideboard, the top of which was littered with odds and ends, practically filled it.

Jostling for space in the corner by the sideboard were piles of dusty old magazines and newspapers plus half a dozen or so empty bottles saved for when money was tighter than normal and a penny or two could be gained for them from the off licence down the road; plus a couple of tattered cardboard boxes holding bits and pieces discarded over the years, all worthless but May refused to part with them.

Despite its shabbiness – the uneven, cracked and damp walls that hadn't seen fresh wallpaper or paint for as long as Jenny could remember; the creaking and in parts rotten floorboards; the dreadfully old-fashioned kitchen where in 1955 they were still having to light a fire inside the brick boiler for hot water which in turn had to be pumped from the hand pump over the pot sink as was done when the houses were first built – this house was not as bad as most in the slums the Corporation were currently clearing. It was at least home to Jenny and had been for all her twenty years. Her and her feisty mother, and a succession of her mother's male friends.

Jenny smiled warmly at the thought of the indomitable woman who had raised her single-handed since her father had been killed in an accident at work just before she was born. Her eyes travelled to the blurred and faded black and white photograph of him and her mother, displayed in pride of place on the mantel. It had been taken on a day out together at the seaside when they had been courting, her mother had told Jenny. Ingellmells the place was if she remembered correctly, and the year was 1934. A hot sunny day in July. They stood with arms linked, and despite the out-of-focus image Jenny could tell they were smiling happily, looking the perfect couple. According to her mother they had scraped together the money for that trip over months.

Jenny sighed. How she wished she could have known the man who had fathered her. According to her mother, Jim Jeffries had been a wonderful man in every way and would have been a wonderful father too, had disaster not struck.

Jenny's thoughts returned to her mother again and not for the first time she tried to imagine how it must have been for May when he died. She'd been alone in the world, hardly out of her teens, and nine months pregnant. Then to lose the man she'd thought she was going to spend the rest of her life with . . . It must have been dreadful.

Looking back, Jenny couldn't for the life of her imagine how May had managed. It was hard enough now she was earning. How bad must it have been then? They were no different from anyone else hereabouts. All the children she'd mixed with had run barefoot, thought nothing of having their shabby, hand-me-down clothes patched with ill-assorted scraps of material, and considered a thin layer of jam on their bread a rare treat compared to the usual dripping or lard. No one expected to see carpets on floors or the walls papered. Besides, should the money ever be found to do so, going to such lengths was a total waste of time as damp crumbling walls and sodden floorboards soon set the mildew creeping again.

It was only as she grew older and her world expanded beyond the immediately surrounding streets that it began slowly to dawn upon Jenny what a desperate life she and her mother actually lived. To pay the rent each week was a major achievement, let alone having enough left to meet the bills and buy essentials. Which usually meant the bills went unpaid. To hide from the rent, tally, coal and milkman was normal practice. But despite the odds they had survived, and it was all down to her mother, although Jenny suspected that money might not have been quite so tight had it not been for the succession of 'uncles' who had come and gone over the years. It was they who had had the most deleterious effect on May's precarious resources, and in turn Jenny's once she was earning. When May gave to the likes of Tony, or they just took, it was to her daughter she turned to make up the shortfall. Why her mother didn't appear to learn from her mistakes was beyond Jenny. Why she continued to pin her hopes for a better future on men who were obviously no more than scroungers was also beyond her. Each one – how many there'd been Jenny had lost count – only brought the same result. Bitter disappointment. One day, she prayed, a decent man would appear and grant May her wish. It wouldn't matter if he had no money so long as he treated her mother with respect and took care of her. Someone who would give, not just take. Jenny loved her mother deeply and wanted the best for her.

The sound of the back door opening and shutting broke into her thoughts and her eyes went to the tarnished tin clock on the mantel. It was only eight-forty-five, far too early for her mother to be back. A bleached blonde head popped around the door, the very same colour May sported because the peroxide was shared, visits to a hairdresser being out of the question for people in this area.

'Hello, Mrs Budgins,' Jenny greeted her warmly. 'Me mam's out. Gone to the club.'

'Oh, she went then. The cow! Borrow the money off you, did she? Well, if she wins, she'd better share it, that's all I can say. Lover boy gone with 'er, as 'e?'

Jenny hesitated for a moment, unsure whether to tell Gloria Budgins what had happened between May and Tony. Her mother's character being what it was, in situations like this Jenny knew whatever she did could be right or wrong, depending on May's mood when she found out. Oh, what the hell? she thought. Gloria Budgins would know something had gone off by the rumpus earlier. Neighbours kept no secrets through these thin dividing walls.

'Tony's gone, Mrs Budgins. Me mam asked him to leave.'

Gloria's eyes flashed knowingly. 'Oh, she did it then, did she? She told me earlier she'd 'ad enough of 'im and was gonna kick 'im out. I thought she 'ad by the row I 'eard. Said as much to my Cyril. "Mark my words, that's another one shown his cards," I said. And I don't know why 'e had to bang the bloody door so hard when 'e left neither. It's a wonder the whole bleddy street didn't collapse like a pack of cards.

'Anyway I'm glad yer mam's seen sense at last. I told 'er that Tony's measure when she first introduced us. " 'E's a sponger, May, if ever I've seen one, no better than any of the others yer've brought 'ome. Get rid before it's too late." But would she? Yer can't tell yer mam n'ote, Jenny love, you know that as well as me. Law unto 'erself she is. Anyway let's 'ope she's more choosy next time.'

Without waiting for an invitation Gloria lumbered into the room, her ungainly body squeezed into clothes unsuitable for a woman of her ample proportions, and plonked herself into the armchair opposite. She was clutching a bottle. 'Cyril's gone down the boozer so I thought May'd like to share this bottle of port. Mighta known she'd get you to cough up and bugger off wi'out me. Mind you, in the circumstances I can't blame 'er for wantin' to get 'erself out, I'd do the same.' She eyed Jenny hopefully. 'Warra about you?'

'Pardon? Oh, I'm not that fond of port, Mrs Budgins.' At least not the gut rot Jenny suspected was in the bottle Gloria was brandishing. 'Besides, I've got to get up for work in the morning and I won't manage if I help you down that.'

'Oh, go on,' Gloria coaxed. 'A drop won't 'urt yer. It's a real treasure trove this bottle. I unearthed it from the coal 'ole this morning. Under a pile of slack it wa'. Cyril musta 'idden it there at Christmas and forgotten about it.' She gave a broad grin, which caused the heavy panstick plastered over her deep crow's feet to crack. 'Well, it musta bin 'im unless it wa' Santa. Not like my Cyril to forget summat like this, is it? Maybe 'e's goin' doolally in 'is old age. Anyway, better down our necks than 'is. Port meks Cyril randy and I can't be doin' wi' any of that nonsense just now. 'E 'ad his ration at New Year, the dirty old bugger, so 'e's gorra wait for 'is next lot in August when it's me birthday.' Her grey eyes twinkled wickedly. 'Mind you, if it were Clark Gable I wa' married to that'd be a different matter. Wouldn't say no to 'im. Get the glasses, there's a duck.'

Jenny eyed the large woman for a moment. Despite this intrusion into her evening, she had a fondness for their neighbour. If ever her mother had a true friend it was Gloria Budgins. Despite their rivalry and constant bickering, Jenny knew the two women harboured a deep mutual respect and in truth neither would have weathered the last twenty years intact without the support of the other, especially through the war. Jenny smiled to herself. Thick as thieves and arch enemies would aptly describe the pair, though both of them would deny it.

Jenny knew that Gloria's offer could not be refused. Gloria was not going anywhere until she decided to and that would only be when the bottle was empty so Jenny might as well relent.

13

'All right,' she said reluctantly. 'But just a spot for me.'

An hour later, bleary-eyed, Gloria raised her half-empty glass of port and gazed at it admiringly. 'Not a bad drop of stuff is this. I wonder where 'e got it from? Not our local offy that's fer sure. The port that robbing so and so sells 'ud strip paint – not ter mention the sherry. God, a tablespoon of that 'ud be enough ter give 'orse a dose of the trots!' She downed what was left in her glass and held it out towards Jenny. 'Fill 'er up, gel.'

Jenny, who as they had talked had drunk far more than she'd intended, fought to concentrate all her efforts on picking up the bottle, but Gloria, a hardened drinker, anticipated its being knocked flying and snatched it up. 'Oi, be careful. A drop spilled is a drop less down my throat. Pass yer glass.'

'I don't think I will, Mrs Budgins, thanks. I've had more than enough. I'm seeing double.'

'Treble's when yer start worrying. Pass us yer glass. We won't see the likes of this stuff fer a long time and if yer mam wa' 'ere you wouldn't be seeing it now. And one thing's fer sure: I ain't leavin' 'til it's all gone, 'cos my Cyril 'ud only polish it off.'

Without waiting for Jenny's response, Gloria leaned over and poured another measure of the ruby liquid into her glass. Having topped up her own she lolled back in her chair, big legs spread wide, obliviously affording Jenny an unpleasant view of thigh-length cotton knickers. 'Oh, ain't it nice to 'ave a natter? D'yer know, Jenny love, I don't think I'd be wrong if I said this is the first time me and you 'ave sat and 'ad a good old gossip. 'Course I always think of you as just a kid, but yer not, a'yer? You're all growed up. And just look at yer. As pretty as a picture. Nothing like the skinny scrap May arrived 'ere wi' all those years ago. How many now . . .'

She blew out her cheeks thoughtfully. 'Twenty years. Well, it must be, you're twenty now, ain't yer? God, 'ow time flies. Seems like only yes'day. She hadn't got n'ote when she

14

arrived, yer know, yer mam. 'Ardly a stick of furniture and
certainly n'ote fer you. Not even a pram. Lent her mine I did
'til the authorities gave her one. And what a contraption that
wa'. I wouldn't 'ave bin surprised to find out it'd belonged to
Queen Victoria. It had ter be scrubbed with carbolic 'cos it
were that filthy then we had to rub it down with Brasso to get
rid of the rust. Took us ages.' Taking a mouthful of port, she
paused thoughtfully. 'Could never understand that meself,' she
said at length.

'Understand what? Oh, if you mean about my mother not
having much, well, it's understandable, Mrs Budgins. They'd
hardly been married any time when my father died. No chance
to get much together.' Jenny spoke brusquely, the drink making
her words come out far more defensively than she'd actually
meant.

Jenny's clipped tones were not lost on Gloria despite her
inebriated state. 'Eh, no need ter get on yer 'igh 'orse, gel. Fer
the love of Christ, none of us 'ave much now, let alone when
our kids were little. No, I meant I can never understand why
May came ter live over this side of town.'

'And why shouldn't she?' Jenny asked, frowning.

'Well, people don't just up and move ter foreign parts. I
mean, I know yer dad was all she had in the world – or that's
what she said – but it don't mek sense ter me that in those
circumstances she'd want to leave people that knew 'er, that'd
'elp her through it. I've often wondered why she chose to live
amongst strangers. I mean, I've lived 'ere all me life. It wa' me
mam's house before mine, and if 'ote 'appened ter Cyril the
last thing I'd do is move somewhere where I don't know a
soul.' Gloria eyed Jenny meaningfully. 'Did yer mam ever tell
you why she just upped sticks like that?'

Jenny felt her hackles rise. She felt disloyal speaking of her
mother like this. 'No, Mrs Budgins, maybe me mam wanted a
fresh start away from painful memories.'

'Mmm, maybe. I never thought on it like that.' She eyed Jenny keenly. 'Is that what she said?'

Jenny sighed. 'Me mam won't talk of the time before she came 'ere. She says it upsets her too much. She loved me dad and I know she still misses him.'

Gloria pursed her lips. 'Yes . . . well . . . she won't find a replacement in the likes she brings 'ome and that's fer sure. I keep tellin' 'er. "May," I sez, "yer won't find anyone decent propping up the bar in the North Bridge pub." But will she listen? Like 'ell she will. Your mam's the most stubborn woman I've ever met.' She screwed up her face haughtily. 'Besides, for all she sez, I bet yer dad wa' no better than the rest.'

Her glazed eyes grew distant. 'I met my Cyril at school. Yer wouldn't think it now but 'e warra 'andsome lad. I thought 'e was a catch because 'e wore clothes wi'out 'oles in. Didn't find out 'til it were too late that the only reason he 'ad decent clobber wa' 'cos 'is mam worked down the second-hand shop on Sanvey Gate and 'ad first pick of 'ote that came in. I wa' smitten by the time I wised up, and not long after wa' expecting our Kelvin. Me fate were sealed then.' She pulled a wry face. 'I s'pose I ain't 'ad it bad, though. Cyril's bin . . . well, Cyril.' She looked Jenny straight in the eyes. 'He's sweet on you, yer know.'

Jenny gawped. 'Mr Budgins is?' she exclaimed, horrified.

Gloria let out a bellow of mirth. 'No, yer daft sod, our Kelvin.'

Jenny shifted position uncomfortably. For as long as she could remember Kelvin Budgins had made that quite plain, been quite blatant about it in fact, much to her embarrassment. At school he'd been forever seeking her out and generally making a pest of himself. But the likes of him hadn't been for her then and certainly wouldn't be now. Thankfully she didn't see much of him now they were both working.

16

To her mind Kelvin was a thoroughly bad lot. When they were growing up, if anything untoward happened in the neighbourhood the first name on most people's lips was Kelvin Budgins. And they were usually right. He'd received more clips around the ear from his parents, and had more home visits from the local bobby, than any other boy in the district. According to local gossip the childish pranks had been followed by more serious misdemeanours and it wouldn't surprise Jenny in the least to learn in the not too distant future that Kelvin was spending a period of time at Her Majesty's pleasure. But Gloria was his doting mother so she chose her words carefully.

'Oh, Mrs Budgins, Kelvin's like a brother to me. I've grown up with him, haven't I?'

'So? I grew up wi' my Cyril and look 'ow 'appy we've bin.' Then on second thoughts she added, 'We've 'ad our moments, lots of 'em in fact, but we're still married. At least yer knows those you grows up with so yer don't get no surprises.'

I don't want any surprises from Kelvin, Jenny thought. At least not the kind he has in mind. 'I think the world of your Kelvin,' she lied, 'I do really but . . . but I've got meself a boyfriend,' she lied again. At least, it wasn't exactly a lie, there was a lad at work she was taken with and she had a feeling he liked her.

Interested, Gloria leaned forward, her deep cleavage appearing to be in danger of escaping its confines. ''Ave yer? 'Bout time you got yerself a steady fella. May's about despaired of you ever gettin' settled. Let's face it, you are twenty, Jenny. On the shelf really. Who is 'e then? Anybody I know? 'As yer mam met 'im? If she 'as then she ain't said n'ote ter me.'

Jenny eyed her blankly for a moment, mind racing. Whatever she told Gloria would get straight back to her mother and if May had an inkling there was a man in the offing, Jenny would never hear the end of it until the potential husband was brought before her mother and scrutinised for his suitability. 'No, me mam hasn't met him. It's nothing serious. Well, not yet. Just a lad from work. How's . . . er . . . how's Sandra?' she asked to change the subject. 'I haven't seen her for a while.'

Sitting back, Gloria sniffed contemptuously. 'She's all right. Least I think she is. Don't see much of 'er these days meself. She's in and out like a bleedin' yo-yo that one. Mind you, 'er shifts down the Robin Hood pub mean we 'ardly cross paths.' She tutted loudly. 'The wage she earns 'ardly pays her board, let alone 'ote else. She'd earn much more in the factory after trainin'. Cryin' out fer overlockers we are. Still, it's 'er choice and as long as she pays her board I don't care where she works. Anyway, I'm sure our Sandra thinks I'm stupid. She thinks I don't know the only reason she took a job in that dive of a place was 'cos she fancied the cellarman. 'E ain't a bad looker, though, if I say it meself. 'E wouldn't stand a chance if I were twenty years younger. Mind you, 'e's got sideburns like brush-heads and 'is clothes . . . well, our Cyril reckons he looks like a stick insect in those pipes 'e wears.'

'Pipes? Oh, you mean drainpipes. All the lads are wearing them, Mrs Budgins. It's the latest fashion.'

'Yeah, it might be, but who on earth will take you serious when yer call yerself a Teddy Boy? Look like a load of nancys ter me. Now in my day there weren't no such thing as fashion, yer were just lucky if you had summat warm on yer back. These days . . . well, it's got ter be the latest or else. When I was young we never had time for youth, too busy helping our folks keep body and soul tergether. I remember . . .'

A loud hammering on the door made both women jump.

'Someone's desperate,' Gloria remarked, frowning, annoyed someone had dared to interrupt her narrative. 'You expectin' anyone, Jenny love?'

She shook her head, rising. 'Unless it's me mam who's had a few and can't get her key in the lock.'

Gloria let out a loud bellow of mirth. 'Won't be the first time she's come home piddled, only usually I'm piddled wi' 'er too.' She flashed her eyes up and down Jenny. 'Want me ter go and let 'er in? You look ter me like yer legs 'ave forgotten their business. That port's done yer good, gel.'

'I can manage, thank you,' said Jenny, sounding more confident than she felt. She hadn't realised what effect the port had actually had on her until she stood up. Her legs did feel rather wobbly.

There was more loud knocking on the door.

'Best 'urry then before whoever it is knocks it off its 'inges.'

Raising her chin, Jenny took a deep breath and, walking as straight as she could manage, headed for the door.

The dishevelled man shivering on the uneven cobbles before her, several brown paper carrier bags of belongings scattered around him, was swaying drunkenly. Jenny sighed in exasperation. She didn't like confrontations and this was the last thing she felt like after drinking all that port, especially not with her mother's ex-lover. As she looked at Tony it did cross her mind to wonder where he'd got the money from to buy his drink. As far as she was aware he had left the house the same way he had entered it nine months before. Broke.

'Me mam ain't back yet, Tony. You know she went down the club,' Jenny said as pleasantly as possible.

He belched loudly and tried to barge his way past her and inside the house but she blocked his way with her body. 'You don't live here no more, Tony,' she reminded him.

He belched again and swayed dangerously. 'May's changed 'er mind. She said she din't mean it. I came ahead of 'er so I can unpack me stuff before she gets back.'

Jenny folded her arms and took a stance. 'Well, she's not told me that so 'til she does, you don't get in. Come back and see her tomorrow.'

His face crumpled. 'Ah, Jenny, don't be like that. Look, it's cold.' His massive shoulders sagged in defeat. 'Okay, I lied. I ain't seen May. Can't I come in and wait?'

'No,' she said sharply. 'I daren't go against me mam's orders.'

He lumbered several steps forward. 'Come on now, Jenny, stop being a daft bitch. Yer know yer man's always blowing her top. She didn't mean what she said. Just let me past, there's a good gel. I only want to talk to 'er, mek her see reason. Let me come in and wait fer 'er, Jenny? I won't cause no bother, 'onest.'

She eyed him for a moment and despite her intense dislike of him could not help but feel sorry at the pathetic sight. He'd obviously nowhere to go and it was cold. There'd be a frost soon. She wouldn't leave a dog out on a night like this, let alone a human being. Risking a reprimand from her mother, she was just about to comply with his request when a voice from behind stopped her.

'Wass goin' on?'

Jenny turned her head to see Gloria weaving her way down the dingy passage.

She squeezed her large frame between Jenny and the door and glared at Tony. 'Oh, it's you. Mighta known it'd be your ugly mug I'd be findin'. What you doin' 'ere? May gave you yer marching orders. You ain't marched far, 'ave yer?'

His face contorted angrily. 'And what's any of this got ter do with you, yer fat cow?'

Gloria scowled back. ''Ow dare the likes of you speak ter me like that?' she bellowed, wagging a podgy finger at him. 'Fat, am I? It's when I get ter your size I'll start worryin'.' She leaned forward and thumped her fist into his huge shoulder. 'You'd mek two of me. Mind you, what can yer expect when all yer do all day is sit on yer arse, fillin' yer face and guzzlin' beer?' She eyed him in disgust. 'May's well rid of you. You bled her dry. Now go and find some other daft sod to believe

20

yer lies. Go on, clear off. And tek yer rubbish with yer,' she added, pointing at his bags.

His lip curled defiantly. 'I ain't goin' nowhere 'til I've seen May,' he snarled.

The large woman smirked. 'Well, you'll 'ave a bleddy long wait 'cos she's gone out on a date. She said she wouldn't be 'ome. Yer see, she's found someone decent for a change. So you ain't got no chance of ever settin' foot in this 'ouse again. That right, Jenny?'

She turned and eyed their neighbour in confusion. 'Eh?' She received a sharp dig in her ribs from Gloria's fleshy elbow. 'Yes, yes, that's right,' she said hurriedly.

Gloria folded her arms, squashing Jenny even further against the wall. 'Now get yerself and yer belongings off our cobbles. I swept 'em meself this mornin',' she lied, never having swept outside since her mother had died fifteen years before, considering it a thankless task. 'Particular I am who stands on 'em. You'd better do as I say or I'll send Jenny for me brother. D'yer rate yer chances against Lou and his sons? If I were you I wouldn't, I've seen what they can do.' She unfolded her arms and grabbed Jenny's shoulders, pulling her backwards. 'Come on, gel, I ain't standin' 'ere any longer talking ter this scum, it's cold.'

After slamming the door, Gloria waddled precariously down the passage and plonked herself back in the armchair, making herself comfortable. Picking up her glass, she knocked back what was left. 'Well, that's got 'im sorted. If 'e's any sense 'e won't pester May again.'

'Don't you think we were a bit hard on him?' Jenny said as she came back into the room.

'Hard? Don't you start feelin' sorry fer 'im. There's only one way to treat the likes of Antonio Brunio, Jenny love. You threaten. That's the only language his type understand. Where's that bleddy bottle?' asked Gloria, casting her eyes around.

21

'By your foot,' Jenny replied, sitting down. 'Is it not empty yet?' she added hopefully, feeling woozy and the call of her bed beckoning.

'It is now,' Gloria said remorsefully, shaking out the last drop. 'Pity I didn't find two, I'm quite enjoying this.' She gave a loud hiccup and laughed. 'I'm pissed!'

So am I, thought Jenny. I've to get up at six-thirty in the morning, too, and I've a job doing that when I've *not* had a drink.

# Chapter Two

'You 'aving one fer the road, gel?' Lilly Russell asked the woman lolling beside her on the long plastic-padded bench. She gave the woman a sharp nudge in the ribs. 'Eh, yer drunken sot, I asked if yer were 'avin another? Last orders 'ave just bin called.'

'What?' With difficulty May turned her head towards the woman addressing her. 'I will if you're offerin'. I'm skint. I'll 'ave a barley wine.'

Lil scowled. 'You'll 'ave 'alf a bitter and like it.' She unclipped her handbag, rummaged inside and pulled out her purse, the contents of which she tipped into her hand and counted. 'Ain't got enough. How much you got, May?'

She put her hand into her pocket and slapped what coins she had on the table they were sitting at. Through hazy eyes she appraised what was left of the money she had taken from Jenny. She eyed the fourpence, all she had left. Oh well, she thought, in for a penny . . . She was sozzled now. Another wouldn't make any difference to her state. She held the coins out towards Lil. 'That's all I've got.'

Lil scooped them up. 'That'll do,' she said, rising.

May watched as her friend weaved her way towards the crowded bar. It was unusually busy for a Wednesday night, even considering the lure of the prize money from the tombola. It had been won by an outsider, much to the disgust of the locals who had voiced their displeasure loudly enough to force the winner into making a hurried exit before all hell was let loose.

May herself had had high hopes of collecting that money. She had been stupid, she knew, to have harboured such a dream. She'd never won anything in her life, never got anything without paying a high price for it, so why should things be any different tonight?

She sighed, annoyed with herself for feeling like this. Alcohol usually made her feel happy for a while, made her forget her problems, but tonight for some reason it was having the opposite effect. It was making her feel sorry for herself. All that bloody Tony's fault, she thought. She was glad she had got rid of him, she'd no doubt she'd done the right thing there, but once again she was on her own, facing life without a man. She sighed sadly. All she wanted was someone, nice and caring, someone who'd look after her and Jenny – Jenny most of all. Though it was a bit late for a father figure. Jenny was all grown up now. It was only a matter of time before the man with whom she would share her life made his appearance. Then where would May be? She shuddered. All on her own.

This was not how she had envisaged her life turning out when she had been a young woman, nothing like it. But then her choices had been dictated by the actions of another. At that time she had not foreseen the years of continual struggle for existence, but more importantly the terrible secrets she'd had to keep – secrets that should they surface, even after all these years, would cause terrible repercussions.

'What's up wi' you, gel? You've a face like doom. I thought we were s'posed ter be enjoying ourselves?' asked Lil, plonking a brimming glass in front of May and taking a sip from her own as she sat down.

May raised her head and eyed her blearily. 'I was just thinkin',' she mumbled.

'I'm surprised yer still can after all you've drunk ternight,

24

gel. What a'yer thinkin' about?'

May's sigh was long and loud. 'Oh, just this and that. About being on me own.' Her eyes glazed over. 'It were all worth it, though.'

Lil eyed her quizzically. 'Wadda yer mean, May? What yer goin' on about?'

She stared down into the murky depths of her beer. 'What I done, that's what.' She drew breath. 'I wouldn't change things, yer know. I'd do the same again even if I knew I'd end up like this.'

Lil frowned. 'End up like this? What on earth you on about? May Jeffries, I'm talking to you.'

May's head jerked up and she stared blankly at her drinking companion. 'Eh?'

Lil tutted. 'Yer gassing away ter yerself like someone from the loony bin. Yer were saying about changing things. Change what, May?'

She grimaced. 'Was I? Oh!' An abrupt silence followed as May suddenly realised with horror that she must have been voicing her thoughts out loud. She'd never done that before. Well, not to her knowledge. She'd better watch herself or before she knew it her babbling would lead to all sorts of terrible secrets getting out. The damage and pain that would cause would be catastrophic even after all these years. 'Oh, er . . . just ignore me. I was rambling,' she snapped and eyed Lil questioningly. 'Where d'yer find a decent man, Lil?'

She emitted a cynical laugh. 'Yer don't 'cos there ain't none. You can 'ave my old man if yer that desperate, May.'

'I'll pass, thanks.'

'Why, what's wrong wi' my Alfie?'

''E's married to you, that's what. Anyway 'e'd drive me nuts, spending night after night on 'is model planes.'

''E drives *me* nuts. Why d'yer think I come down the pub so much.'

'To see Wally Cummings,' May replied sarcastically.

'Oi, keep yer voice down. Me and Wally are just good friends.'

'Mmm,' May voiced knowingly. 'More than good, I'd say. You wanna watch yer step, Lil. Should Alfie find out just what kind of friends you are then I think you'd see a different side to 'im.'

'That's as maybe. But Wally gives me what Alfie doesn't and that's a bit of fun. My Alfie's a good man, May, but since 'e came back from the war 'e's changed. 'E's got old before 'is time. 'E don't . . . well, yer know, I ain't a woman no more to 'im, May. It's like bein' married to me dad. I can't remember the last time he made advances terwards me. I 'onestly think his . . .' she paused and mouthed *'parts'* then resumed her normal tone . . . 'don't work no more. But I need that. I need a bit of fun and romancin'. For the love of God, I'm only forty-four.'

May's eyes flashed scornfully. 'And Wally gives yer that, does 'e?'

Lil nodded. ''E does.'

'Ah, well, it's your life. But I'd be careful. I 'appen ter know that wife of 'is is a right tartar.'

Lil giggled. 'I do an' all. She took the rollin' pin ter Cissy Gibbons when she thought it were her Wally was seein'. Right bloody mess she made of Cissy's head, she did. Anyway, you can talk, the number of men you've 'ad come and go, May Jeffries.'

'Yeah, but I ain't married. What I mean is, I'm a widow. So it's all right for me.' May picked up her glass and took a long gulp. 'Anyway I've decided I've finished with all that. No more men for me.'

'That'll be the day,' Lil replied, unconvinced. 'I'll give yer a week. Two at the most.'

'I mean it, Lil. I've 'ad a belly full this time. I 'onestly thought Tony was different. 'E certainly 'ad me fooled. But 'e

26

was just like all the rest – a bloody waste of time.'

A man approached their table. 'I'm walking your way if yer want escorting 'ome, Lil. Never know who's about,' Wally Cummings said loudly, looking at her knowingly. He turned and winked an acknowledgement at May. 'All right, are yer, May?'

'I'm fine, thanks, Wally,' she answered flatly. After downing the last of her drink, she rose awkwardly. 'I'm off. See yer Sat'day as usual down the North Bridge, eh, Lil?'

'Yeah, I'll be there.' She eyed May in concern. 'You gonna be all right, gel, gettin' home? You're a bit the worse for wear, yer know.'

May grinned wryly. 'May Jeffries always finds 'er way 'ome, Lil, no matter how much she's 'ad, you know that.'

'Ah, well, so long as yer sure. Come on then, 'andsome,' she said, rising to joining Wally. 'It's good of yer to see me 'ome,' she shouted as Wally had done for the benefit of any nosy earwiggers. 'Just 'ang on a minute while I finish me drink.'

May tumbled out of the club doors along with several other regulars. The cold night air hit her and she stood swaying for a moment as she got her bearings.

'You all right, May?' Jim Stubbs asked as he made to walk past her. 'I can go your way if you want seein' 'ome.'

'Yeah, yer can tag along wi' us if yer want,' the man with him offered.

'I'm fine. Get off 'ome before yer wives come looking for yer,' she said, laughing.

'Mine won't,' said the man. 'If I know my missus, she'll be snoring her head off by now.'

'Mine too,' said Jim a mite forlornly. 'See yer, May,' he called, striding off.

'Yeah, see yer,' she responded, waving a hand. She watched the two men as they walked away. Jim Stubbs was a lovely man, quiet and kept himself to himself. His only fault, if indeed you could call it that, was liking a couple of pints on a

27

Wednesday and Friday night. His wife Hilda, a thin, hard-faced woman, moaned incessantly about her lot to anyone who would listen. To May's way of thinking, in contrast to those around her, Hilda Stubbs had nothing to be dissatisfied with. She had a nice little house at the good end of the street and a faithful husband in regular work who never raised his voice or hand to her. Hilda Stubbs should be thankful she had a good man like Jim. But then women like her would find fault if they landed Royalty.

Plunging her hands into her pockets, May set off. On her three-inch heels she had tottered several yards on her way before she realised someone was walking alongside her. She stopped abruptly to face them. 'What the 'ell . . . Oh, it's you, Ron,' she said, surprised. 'Ain't seen you for ages. Thought you'd moved over Humberstone way with that woman. What's 'er name?'

'Maggie?'

'Yeah, that's 'er. So what a'yer doin' around 'ere at this time of night?'

'Bin fer a drink same as you. I'd 'ave bought yer one only yer were busy gossiping ter Lil.'

She eyed him scathingly. 'Too tight, yer mean.'

'No, just didn't want ter interrupt, that's all. I've moved back now, May. Livin' with me mam fer the time bein' 'til I find me own place. It didn't work out between me and Maggie.'

'I ain't surprised,' she said matter-of-factly, walking again. 'What she do, chuck you out when she found out what you were really like?'

'Don't be like that, May,' he said, falling into step beside her. 'It'd just run its course, that's all. Maggie was all right, but she weren't for me. Not like you, May. You're a real woman, you are. You know how ter treat a man.'

Her eyes flashed warningly. 'Don't start all that. I've known you a long time, Ron Bates, and yer patter don't do anything for me.'

'I ain't so sure, May. I reckon yer've always 'ad a fancy for me.'

'Well, yer thought wrong. I ain't never fancied you.'

'Well, I can live in 'ope, can't I? I 'eard you gave that Eyetie the push.'

She stopped abruptly and turned on him, face contorted in anger. 'Who told yer that? It only 'appened ternight.'

'The whole street knows, May. Yer can't keep secrets round 'ere. So what about it, eh?'

She eyed him sharply. 'What about what?' Then she scowled. 'Oh, I get it, yer lookin' fer someone to shack up wi'. Well, yer needn't look at me. I've 'ad enough of men.'

She made to walk off but he grabbed her arm. 'Yer've got it wrong, May. I just meant go for a drink. We can tek it from there. Sat'day, eh? I'll meet you in the bar at eight.'

She looked at him as directly as her inebriated state would allow. Her and Ron Bates? she thought. Oh, well, he wasn't that bad-looking for a man of nearly fifty. He was a big man, like Tony, but from what little she knew not such a slob. Rough and ready would more aptly describe him, but then there weren't many men in these parts who were exactly suave. Most importantly to May he had a job. Well, so far as she knew he had.

'You still workin'?' she asked.

He nodded. 'Why d'yer ask that when yer know I am, May? Bin wi' Imperial Typewriters for twenty-five years. Only broke me service while I was away at war.'

'Just making sure you can pay yer way.' She hesitated for a moment. She'd promised herself she wasn't going to get involved again, but she wouldn't say no to having someone around to take her out whenever she felt like it. She pursed her lips. 'I ain't doin' anythin' Sat'day night, so okay,' she said, nonchalantly shrugging her shoulders, and linked her arm through his. 'Come on, I'll let yer walk me to me door.'

# Chapter Three

'Oh, me 'ead,' May groaned. 'What day is it?'

'Thursday. Why?'

She groaned again. 'I was 'oping it was Sunday and I could go back to bed.'

Jenny put down the piece of toast she was having trouble eating and eyed her mother unsympathetically. What a sight she looked. Matted hair sticking up all ways and yesterday's makeup still streaked across her face. The shabby crumpled dressing gown she was wearing was in dire need of a wash and Jenny made a mental note to add it to the weekend pile.

In truth she was feeling far from well herself. After managing to persuade Gloria to vacate her chair and go home the previous evening, it had taken ages for Jenny herself to get to sleep. Every time she had closed her eyes the room had spun wildly. Then, when she had finally managed to doze, she had been rudely awakened by the thud of her mother falling up the stairs when she had finally returned – that was after Jenny had listened to the seemingly endless operation of May trying to insert her key in the lock then banging the door forcefully in her inebriated attempt to shut it.

Consequently Jenny's morning mood was not the pleasant, cheerful one it normally was. 'You shouldn't drink so much, Mam, when yer know you've work in the morning.'

As she stubbed out her cigarette in the tin lid she used as an ashtray – her fourth that morning since she'd dragged herself from her bed – May gave a hacking cough, then said defensively, 'Yeah, well, I was in need after givin' Tony the boot. Despite what yer think, it upset me.'

'He came back last night.'

May eyed her blearily. 'Who did?'

'Tony. Mam, are you listening to me?'

'I'm listening,' she snapped. 'So what did 'e want?'

'Isn't it obvious? He wanted to come back. Said you didn't mean to chuck him out.'

May scowled scornfully. 'Well, 'e's wrong. I did. You sent 'im packing, I 'ope?'

'I didn't, Gloria did. She came round . . .' Jenny paused, not wanting to go into details about the bottle of port, deciding to tell her mother tonight when she had more time for an inquisition. If Gloria didn't get in before her, that was. At this moment Jenny was very much regretting her part in the port's disappearance and wondering how she was going to survive the day. 'Gloria called in to see you and she was here when Tony came. She gave him what for. I don't think you'll have any more trouble with him, Mam, not after what Gloria said.'

'Good. I don't ever want to clap eyes on him again. I expect Gloria will be around ternight to tell me all the gory details.' Yawning loudly, May eyed the cold slice of toast on Jenny's plate. 'Don't yer want that?'

She shook her head. 'No, I'm not hungry.' She rose from the table. 'Better get a move on or I'll be late. And you'd better too, Mam, you've only got ten minutes before your bus goes.'

'I've only to swill me face, pull me stockings on and put a brush through me 'air. Two minutes at the most. Oh, what I wouldn't give to go back to bed.'

'That'll teach yer,' Jenny said, then felt remorseful. Wasn't she suffering too for doing exactly the same? 'I'm sorry, Mam. Here,' she said, grabbing at her handbag and delving inside.

'This couple of Aspirin should help.'

'Ta, duck,' May replied gratefully. Suddenly a grin split her face as a memory returned. 'Eh, I've a date Sat'day night,' she announced.

Jenny tightened her lips. Here we go again, she thought. 'You have? Who with, Mam?'

May fought for a moment to remember his name. 'Er . . . I've got a date, I know I have,' she muttered. Then she remembered. 'With Ron. Ron Bates.'

'Mam!' Jenny exclaimed. 'Not him? If you're going to be seeing him next you might as well have stuck with Tony.'

'Wadda yer mean? Ron's all right. He's workin'. That's summat, ain't it?'

'I suppose. But he's been married twice, and from what I remember he's handy with his fists.'

'Yeah,' May grudgingly agreed. 'But that's only when he's had a few and I've never known him hit a woman. Anyway,' she snapped defensively, 'I'm only goin' for a bleddy drink wi' 'im, not askin' 'im to come and shack up 'ere.'

Jenny sighed despondently. Judging from the past it wouldn't be long before she did. 'Well, just be careful, Mam,' was all she said.

'I thought yer'd be pleased for me,' her mother protested.

'Miss Jeffries, you're not busy at the moment so please go to the stockroom and fetch the new stock.'

Jenny laid her duster down. 'Yes, Mr Stone.'

Stifling a yawn, she made her way down the two flights of stairs towards the basement. It was only eleven o'clock. Already she felt as if she had been at work all day. Her headache hadn't been eased by the three extremely pernickety customers she had dealt with so far this morning. They'd all left for further deliberations on their purchase and she had then been scolded by Miss Bane, her immediate superior, who

33

herself had been busy elsewhere at the time and so unable to intervene and make the sale.

Arriving in the gloomy basement Jenny stopped for a moment, resting her back against the grey-painted wall. She had earned her two pounds seventeen and sixpence weekly wage from Stone & Son since leaving school at the age of fourteen. May had tried to encourage her to work alongside herself in the garment factory which was several streets away from where they lived, using the lure of a better wage once her training was finished and most of the weekend off. The bribe had not worked. Jenny hadn't wanted to be one of the hundred herded through the gates of the formidable Victorian three-storey building at seven-thirty each morning, to be incarcerated in its long, dingy, dusty rooms, not seeing daylight for hours upon end, bent over a noisy machine, scratching out her living under the scrutiny of eagle-eyed supervisors.

After giving much thought to what else she could do, she had chosen to work in a shop. Despite every minute of her day being governed by the humourless, aged owner Mr Stone and his underlings, she did not regret her choice.

Stone & Son had been successfully selling fine china and crystal to those wealthy enough to afford them for over sixty years. Their premises, a three-storey, red-brick, bay-fronted building were in a prestigious location on busy Granby Street in the centre of Leicester. It was only in the last ten years, at the suggestion of Mr Stone Junior – a greying man as old as the business he hoped to take over when his eighty-year-old father finally succumbed to retirement – that the floor above had been cleared and refurbished to sell quality hardware items and a selection of paints and wallpapers.

Jenny had started off in hardware, to progress two years later to the street-level china floor when the store's elderly management had had the acumen to acknowledge the girl's potential. She had enjoyed her time on the hardware floor, but handling the delicate pieces of china she had grown to appreciate gave her great pleasure. It was even more satisfying to sell a piece to someone she knew would cherish it. One day she hoped to rise above her junior assistant's position to manage the department. It would be a long slow process but she had the patience to persevere.

'You all right, Jenny?'

She jumped. 'Eh? Oh, hello, Janet. Yeah, I'm fine. No, actually, I'm not. Can't wait to get home and go to bed.'

'Like that, eh?' Janet replied, laughing. She was an attractive girl of Jenny's own age, dressed in an identical uniform of severe dark grey, a below the knee dress with matching white collar and cuffs – an old-fashioned style still adopted by the firm and loathed by its young female assistants who secretly moaned it was about time the old duffers modernised. Janet's dark hair, which in her leisure time was worn bouffant at the front and French-pleated at the back, was scraped severely off her face for work and tied neatly at the nape of her neck by a length of grey ribbon. 'So you went out with Jane and Ginny? I couldn't go 'cos I've no money. Had a good time, did you, eh?'

'They probably did, knowing those two. But I didn't go, for the same reason as you.'

'So, why the hangover? It is a hangover you've got. I should know, I've had plenty.'

'Me mother's neighbour came around with a bottle of port.'

'Oh, I like a drop of port,' said Janet enviously. 'Only see it at Christmas, though. Anyway, I shouldn't let the stuffed shirts know yer suffering. They don't take kindly to that, Jenny. Remember how they got rid of poor Mr Sibbins for just smelling of drink the day after his dad's funeral? As if that weren't reason enough to get sozzled! Mr Stone chucked him out without a by your leave just 'cos that stuck-up customer complained. And him having worked here fifteen years, poor sod.

35

'Yes, that was awful,' she continued without taking breath. 'I saw him the other day. He works down the fruit market as a porter now. Couldn't get work in a shop after word spread he were sacked for drinking. Only got the job as a porter 'cos his brother works there and vouched for him. Shame, in't it?' She leaned towards Jenny and took a sniff. 'Yer can't smell 'ote on yer so you should be all right. I godda go. Mr Dodds sent me to fetch a roll of brown paper and he times me to the minute – miserable old beggar. It's all right for him ter slope off for a crafty fag though, when he thinks the management ain't looking. Well, keep smiling, and I'll see you in the canteen at lunchtime. Save me a seat if yer get there before me.' Before hurrying off she gave Jenny a cheeky wink and with a flick of her head added, 'Watch out, lover boy's in there.'

Jenny felt herself blushing. She'd thought she'd managed to keep her liking for the young storeman a secret. Obviously not. If Janet knew, did any of the other girls?

Jenny smiled. She liked Janet. In fact, she liked all four girls of her age group who worked for Stone's. Funds permitting, they socialised together. Usually it was just for a drink, but most Fridays they managed to scrape up the money to go dancing. Leicester had several dance halls but the girls' favourite haunt was the *Palais-de-danse* on Humberstone Gate. Jenny immensely enjoyed these evenings. She was a natural dancer and found the latest steps easy to copy after watching the experts. She'd met a couple of potential long-term boyfriends there, but none had come to anything, Jenny usually being the one to end the friendships amicably.

She rubbed her aching head then gave herself a mental shake. Janet was right. She had better watch her step. Nothing escaped the beady eyes of the owner, his son or the managerial staff, and to lose the job she loved for the sake of a few glasses of port would be catastrophic for her.

She picked her way through the dimly lit rows of stock

shelves until she reached a doorway and entered a brighter room where the storemen carried out their main duties.

As she entered an elderly man standing by a long cluttered bench, busily tying a large brown paper-wrapped box, turned his head to acknowledge her. 'Hello, Jenny love. What can we do fer yer?'

'Hello, Sid,' she said, smiling warmly. 'Mr Stone sent me to fetch up the new stock.'

'Huh, 'e did, did 'e?' Sid Paine grumbled. 'We could do that. It came in yes'day. We could 'ave 'ad it unpacked and took upstairs and out from under our feet. But will they let us? Will they 'ell as like. Our brown basement coats ain't good enough ter be seen on the "floors". Oh, no, wouldn't actually be the done thing ter let the customers come in contact with rough working men while they're buying their posh ornaments.'

'Eh, you speak for yerself, Sid. I ain't rough,' a voice announced from behind some wooden shelving. The body to which the voice belonged made its appearance, struggling under the weight of a box holding part of a Crown Derby dinner service. 'Hello, Jenny,' the young man said, grinning at her. 'I'll help you get the boxes of stock on the dumb waiter if yer just give me a minute or two.'

After acknowledging his offer, her eyes followed the young man as he went about his business, praying that the heat she felt under her collar did not creep up further to show itself on her face. She took a deep breath. Twenty-two-year-old Graham Parker wasn't a particularly good-looking man: he wasn't tall or especially muscular, but there was something about him that very much attracted Jenny. He had such a pleasant personality and she could imagine he would be very kind and attentive should she ever be fortunate enough to be asked out by him.

He must know I like him, she thought. She hadn't tried to hide the fact. Couldn't help but hang on every word he said, laugh the loudest at his quips, jump at any opportunity to visit the basement in the hope of seeing him, to the point where even he must question the fact that she was down here the most out of all the junior assistants. Maybe today might be the one he asks me out, she thought hopefully, and wondered what she could say to encourage him that wasn't too forward of her but enough to give him a lead.

'A'yer busy upstairs?' Sid asked, breaking into her thoughts.

'Pardon? Oh, busy enough for a Thursday,' Jenny replied. 'And you down here?'

'Huh! Need yer ask? Got more than enough ter do, we 'ave. What wi' the stock handling, packing the deliveries, offloading new stock and checking it off – and now we're expected ter be garage mechanics, looking after the van and the Stones' cars. We ain't stockmen no more. More like Jacks of all trades.' He exhaled loudly. 'Could do wi' another man – but will they let us 'ave one? Will they 'ell as like. Still, can't grumble. As me wife sez, it's a job.'

Jenny laughed. 'You love a good moan, Sid. We all know that.' And wondered if he knew the nickname given to him by the junior staff upstairs was 'Moaning Minnie'.

'Eh, less of yer cheek. When you've bin 'ere as long as I 'ave then you've a right ter moan. Come on, Graham, get a move on,' called Sid. 'And put the kettle on whilst yer over there, it's about time for a mash.'

'Right you are, Sid. I'm just coming.'

Graham arrived back, wiping his dusty hands on the bottom of his brown overall. 'You could mek yerself useful, Jenny, and mash for us while I load the dumb waiter.'

'I could but I'm not going to. Just be my luck if Mr Stone caught me,' she said good-naturedly, although she would dearly have loved to have made a pot of tea for Graham, affording him an insight into her domestic skills. Jenny suddenly realised he was staring at her, grinning. Her heart thumped. Maybe this was it, she thought. Maybe he was summoning the courage to ask her out. 'Are you all right?' she asked.

'Is 'e all right?' piped up Sid. ''E ain't never gonna be the same again. Go on, tell 'er, lad. Yer know yer itchin' ter tell someone.'

Jenny eyed Graham quizzically. 'What is it?'

''E's gone and got 'imself engaged, that's what.'

'Ah, Sid, that's my news, that is,' snapped Graham, his expression crestfallen.

Jenny's heart plummeted. 'Oh. I . . . wish you every happiness, Graham,' she said, hoping her voice did not reveal her disappointment.

''E'll need it,' Sid said gruffly. 'You young 'uns can't wait ter tie the knot. Yer think it's all hearts and flowers and roses round the door. Just you wait! You won't be grinnin' like a Cheshire cat in a couple of years – maybe sooner. You'll be wishin' you'd listened ter me then, you will.' Sid stopped what he was doing, stepped over to Graham and slapped him on his back. 'But yer know I wish yer all the best, lad. In all 'onesty, if yer as 'appy as me and Mrs Paine 'ave bin, then you'll do all right. Just mek sure this fiancée of yours can cook as good as yer mother before you take the final plunge. Now, fer God's sake, get that new stock loaded afore we 'ave the management on our tails.'

It was a more sombre Jenny who made her way back upstairs a short while later. She had daydreamed about having a relationship with Graham for several months now, had had no idea during that time he already had a steady girlfriend. She felt foolish and annoyed with herself for wasting her time on someone who was already spoken for. But despite her disappointment she still liked the man and wished him the best.

The day seemed to drag on. The task of carefully unwrapping the delicate stock, buffing and suitably arranging it on display shelves, something she normally enjoyed, wasn't such a pleasure today. Several times she was disturbed by her superiors to help with a sale – usually in the nature of a menial task to make them appear more important to the customer – plus Mr Stone sought her out to run an errand across town, such jobs usually being allotted to the most junior member of staff who happened to be off sick today. The outing did at least afford her a breath of fresh air which helped to relieve her persistent headache.

It was approaching four o'clock. Jenny sighed. Still two hours to go before she finished for the night. Apart from two browsing customers the china floor was empty. After loading the last of the empty packing material on to the dumb waiter for disposal in the basement, Jenny picked up her duster and glanced around in search of something to do. All staff were expected to keep busy every minute of the day. Those caught idling were severely reprimanded.

'What would you like me to do now, Miss Bane?' she asked the tall, thin spinster who always looked at Jenny like she was a nasty smell wafting up her nostrils. 'I've cleared away the packing stuff and dusted and arranged the ornaments like you asked. I put the Coalport figurines in the cabinet by the Edinburgh Crystal. It's a bigger display case and I thought the figures would catch customers' attention better in there.'

Miss Bane's sparse greying eyebrows rose indignantly and her small hazel eyes bulged. 'You've taken it upon yourself to do what?' She clicked her tongue disapprovingly. 'Miss Jeffries, junior members of staff do as they are told. They do not take it upon themselves to do as they like. I instructed the figurines to be placed where they always are – in the cabinet in the centre and so that's where they'll be put. I expect to be obeyed. Understand?'

Jenny fought to control her annoyance at being treated in this high-handed way. It wouldn't have hurt Miss Bane at least to take a look at what she had done. She should have known better, though. Her superior was right. Junior staff were not expected to show any initiative. Nor in truth were senior staff. Everyone did exactly as Mr Stone and son ordered.

'Yes, Miss Bane,' said Jenny evenly. 'I'll do it now.'

She was just about to turn and proceed with her task when the noise of the street door crashing open stopped her in her tracks. Her view being obstructed by a tall display cabinet she instinctively stepped aside to see who had done such a thing. On recognising the huge figure filling the doorway her mouth fell open in shock. It was Tony and she instantly realised he was extremely drunk.

'JENNY,' he bellowed. 'JENNY JEFFRIES – WHERE A 'YER?'

Miss Bane rounded on her, her expression shocked. 'You know this man?' she accused.

Jenny's mind raced frantically, her mouth opening and closing like a fish's. The rules on staff being visited in the shop were very precise and if disobeyed without a very good reason, such as a sudden death in the family, were rewarded with harsh disciplinary action. The response to visits from the drunken ex-lovers of assistants' mothers didn't bear thinking about.

'Well, do you?' Miss Bane demanded.

'Er . . . yes, sort of. He's a . . . he was . . . he's an acquaintance of me mother's. I'll see what he wants, Miss Bane.'

Tony shouted again at the top of his voice. 'JENNY JEFFRIES, WHERE A 'YER?'

'You won't see what he wants, you'll get rid of him. And quick,' the older woman hissed, incensed.

'Yes, Miss Bane. Right away, Miss Bane.'

Jenny sped towards the door, but not quickly enough to stop Tony from lumbering further inside. As he did so his shoulder caught a wall fixture and he cursed loudly. 'Fuckin' stupid place to purra shelf,' he spat.

A Beswick toby jug in the likeness of Mr Micawber toppled dangerously. Jenny just managed to steady it before it fell off the shelf. 'Tony, what are you doing here?' she demanded, fighting to keep calm and her voice low.

'Oh, there y'are,' he cried. 'I thought yer were 'iding from me, gel.' He belched loudly, swayed precariously, then steadied himself by placing both paw-like hands on her shoulders. 'I need some dosh,' he slurred.

'And I haven't got any. You know I haven't, Tony. And you shouldn't be here, you'll get me the sack. Now please go,' she urged.

'Go? I ain't got nowhere ter go, Jenny. Look, just gimme a couple of shillin'. I borrowed, see, and I gotta pay it back. Only I can't, can I? Look, tell yer what, gimme yer key and I'll go and wait fer May. She'll see me right. She bleddy ought ter, seein's she chucked me out wi'out warnin'.'

'I can't, Tony. Now, please,' pleaded Jenny. 'Please go.'

He swayed dangerously again and she thought he was going to collapse. Thankfully he stayed upright.

'I ain't goin' nowhere, gel, 'til yer either gives me some money or the key.' He suddenly spotted Miss Bane glaring at him from behind the serving counter and reared back his head. 'What's that sour-faced old cat lookin' at?' he roared. 'Oi, you, yer ugly bitch, ain't yer never clapped eyes on a good-lookin' bloke before?'

'Well, really,' she uttered, deeply shocked.

Tony turned his attention back to Jenny and bellowed, 'I bet she's never had a good . . .'

'Tony!' Jenny exclaimed, cringing, trying her best to turn him around and steer him out of the door. 'Please go. Please,' she begged. 'Look, wait for me outside. I'll . . . I'll . . . speak to me mother. Try and borrow some money. Just go, please.'

His face darkened angrily and he shrugged free from her grasp. 'Stop doin' that. I ain't going nowhere, I told yer.' He pushed her away so forcefully she tumbled backwards to fall heavily against a full display case. The crash of the case hitting the wooden floor and the cry from Jenny as she toppled over with it rent the air. The clatter of breaking china and tinkling of shattered glass seemed to stretch into eternity.

A voice from the top of the stairs barked, 'What on earth is going on down there?'

Prostrate amid the debris, Jenny looked up and warily traced the progress of the man who ran downstairs and made straight for her.

Looming over her, Mr Stone spoke icily. 'Miss Jeffries, get up and go to my office. You,' he said, spinning round and pointing an authoritative finger at Tony, 'get off my premises now before I call the police.'

Tony glared at him for a moment before meekly turning and stumbling out of the door.

'I'm very disappointed in you, Miss Jeffries. Very disappointed indeed. This is quite disgraceful. Have you anything to say? Well, have you?' Mr Stone demanded several moments later.

Hands clasped, she bowed her head. Of course she had, plenty in fact, it was just she didn't know how to begin to try and salvage this terrible situation. Her mind whirled frantically while she remained acutely conscious that Mr Stone was impatiently awaiting a response. But she could not find anyway to excuse what had happened. All she could hope was that her employer would be lenient with her, take into consideration her five years' previous exemplary service.

She realised he was tapping his fingers on the desk in irritation. Ready to plead her cause Jenny raised her head and fixed her eyes on his – and what she saw gleaming there made her mouth snap shut. She knew without doubt that Mr Stone wanted her to beg for her job and that when she had belittled herself to his satisfaction he would take great delight in enforcing his rules nevertheless. Mr Stone was renowned for being a stickler for rules, especially one of his own making. She knew he wouldn't give an inch for the sake of one lowly assistant who could easily be replaced. Fierce pride rose within Jenny then and overrode her liking for her job. She would not give this man the satisfaction he craved. To hell with him, she thought.

She raised her head defiantly. 'No, sir,' was all she said.

His eyes flashed, disappointment in her response very apparent. 'No,' he grunted. 'I don't expect there *is* much you can say to justify such a despicable display.' He leaned back in his chair and clasped his hands prayer-like. 'You know the rules, Miss Jeffries. They were made very clear to you when you began your employment here. I have no alternative, I'm afraid. I could, in fact, take this matter further in law, but considering your circumstances that would be a waste of time. Nevertheless I see it as only fitting that you should forgo any money due to you, in compensation for the damage caused. Not that it will go very far towards covering it, I hasten to add. I trust you will not expect a reference either. Call in tomorrow for your cards. You may go.'

Jenny stared at him, horrified. She had expected no less than dismissal without a reference but to lose her wage too . . . Only minutes ago she'd had a future. Now that lay in ruins, and all through the actions of one thoughtless, drunken man. And her own stupid pride. Acute misery flooded through her. Unable to control herself, the tears came then, stinging her eyes.

Jenny turned and fled from the room.

# Chapter Four

Face white with shock, May stared at the woman on her doorstep, the fear that was building within her causing her body to shake. She flashed a terrified glance up and down the street then shot her eyes back to the woman. 'You've the nerve of the devil! I can't believe yer've turned up outta the blue like this after all these years. How did yer find us?' she demanded.

'It weren't easy, May. Yer covered yer tracks well.'

Obviously not well enough, she thought. Folding her arms, her face contorted darkly, her eyes narrowed warningly. 'Well, yer can *unfind* us. You ain't welcome 'ere.' She leaned forward and with the flat of her hand pushed the woman hard on the shoulder. 'Now get off my doorstep.'

May attempted to step back inside and shut the door but the woman stopped her. 'I ain't goin' nowhere,' she declared, slapping her hand on the door to stop it closing. 'Yer know what I've come for. And I've rights, yer know that.'

May's mouth dropped open in astonishment. 'Rights?' she erupted. 'After what you did, how can you stand there as bold as brass and tell me you've rights?' She reared back her head, eyes blazing. 'Listen 'ere, milady, you've no rights ter anything. Have yer any idea the trouble yer caused? Any idea what yer put me through? Given any thought at all to 'ow I've managed all these years?' She savagely shook her head. 'No,' she spat scornfully, 'you wouldn't, would yer? Never gave any of it another thought. Just turned yer back and conveniently forgot it all. So why, after all these years, have yer decided to show yer face now? Don't tell me it's remorse or out of love, 'cos I wouldn't believe yer. Yer've always bin a selfish sod and I doubt the years have changed yer.' Folding her arms, she took a firm stance. 'I've no money, and no room to put you up. In fact I've nothing that could be of any use to you. Now go – crawl back into the 'ole yer came out of. Go on! And I never wanna see yer face again, you 'ear?'

The woman's eyes filled with sudden sadness and she stared at May for several long moments before she spoke, her voice low and full of emotion. 'Yer don't understand, May. I don't want nothing from yer. I've not turned up to cause yer trouble. I want to make peace between us. And . . .' she heaved a deep, long sigh '. . . I want ter see me daughter.'

May's face turned purple as her rage at this woman's audacity intensified. 'Oh, so suddenly after twenty years she's yer daughter, is she? Well, madam, for your information . . .' Suddenly May's mouth snapped shut and she stared at the woman for several long moments. Then her face unexpectedly softened. 'Take my advice and leave well alone. It's best all round, believe me. Have yer given any thought to how much hurt this could cause? Not just to *her*, but yerself as well.'

'She's a right ter know about me, May. What did you call 'er? I hope it was summat nice.'

May's face set stonily. 'If yer were that bothered, yer should have named her yerself before yer decided to scarper.'

The woman's face fell. 'Have yer told her about me, May? Anything at all?'

'No, and I ain't goin' to and neither are you. You gave up any rights you had a long time ago. If yer've any sense, you'll tek my advice and leave well alone.'

'I can't, May. I didn't want to tell yer this but . . .' She stopped abruptly and took a deep breath. 'I'm dying.'

46

May froze, stunned. 'What!' she uttered. 'Dying? What d'yer mean, yer dying?' She hurriedly scanned her visitor up and down, her face screwed up disbelievingly. 'Yer don't look like yer are. Yer look as healthy as yer did the last day I saw yer.' Her eyes glinted. 'This another of yer lies, eh? Another of yer conniving ways ter get what yer want? Dying, indeed. You're no more on the road upstairs than I am.'

The woman eyed her beseechingly. 'It's the truth, May, 'onest it is. A few weeks at the most I've got. There's a tumour in me stomach. It's cancer I've got, May. That's what the quack at the hospital told me.'

May stared at her in disbelief, then spat, 'A'yer sure it wa' a doctor yer saw and not the porter?' She flared her nostrils and shook her head. 'I used ter believe yer lies, but not any more.' May glanced up and down the street again and to her horror in the distance spotted the familiar figure of Gloria Budgins, laden down with shopping bags, appearing round the corner.

Her heart hammered worriedly. It wouldn't do for Gloria to see them. It wouldn't take her prying eyes seconds to work out this was no pleasant exchange May and her visitor were having. The resulting questions Gloria would bombard her with then were not to be borne. She had to get rid of her visitor, and quick. Panic-stricken, May flashed an icy glare back at the stranger and hissed urgently, 'Now I told yer ter get off my bloody doorstep. And just be warned,' she said, wagging a menacing finger. 'You dare mek any moves towards *her* and I'll mek sure you wish you hadn't. So if yer know what's good fer yer yer won't show yer face around 'ere again. As I said before, you ain't welcome.'

With that she stepped back inside the house and slammed the door.

Face draining of colour, the other woman stood staring at it for several long moments before she turned and walked back down the street, shoulders hunched in defeat.

A while later Jenny stopped outside the same door to steel herself. The consequences of Tony's actions were worrying her witless, but far more disconcerting was the prospect of telling her mother. May was going to go stark staring mad and Jenny didn't relish one little bit the drama she was about to face. In order to delay it she had dawdled all the way home. But she could delay no longer. Besides, she thought, in an effort to make herself feel better, May's tongue lashing could not be as bad as what she had already faced. Even Janet, her closest friend at Stone's, had not stepped forward to offer any word of comfort, just stood with the rest silently watching while Jenny had collected her belongings and left the shop, her former colleagues all unwittingly making her feel like a criminal at least.

Taking a very deep breath, she mustered all the courage she could and inserted her key in the lock.

The shock of what she found when she arrived in the back room momentarily erased her own troubles from her mind. May was slumped in an armchair, head cradled in her hands. She appeared to be crying.

Dread filled Jenny. She rushed over to her mother. 'What's the matter, Mam? What's happened?' she asked, dropping to her knees before her. On receiving no response her worry mounted and she tried again. 'Mam, it's me, Jenny. What's wrong? What's happened?' she demanded.

May's head jerked up. 'Eh? Oh,' she gasped as recognition dawned. 'Jenny, it's you, lovey,' she said with forced lightness, hurriedly wiping her eyes with an already sodden handkerchief. 'I didn't 'ear yer come in.' She made to rise. 'I ain't got the dinner started yet. I . . .'

Jenny put a hand on May's shoulder. 'Forget the dinner, Mam. I want to know what's upset you?'

'Upset me?' she said with assumed innocence. 'Why, nothing's upset me. It's . . . it's this blasted headache. You were right, I should 'ave known better than to 'ave a skinful when I've work the next morning. I've had an awful day. Come on, shift out me way and let me get the food on the go.'

She made to move Jenny aside, but the girl wasn't about to be dismissed so easily. 'Mam, don't lie ter me. I know something's wrong. You've been crying.' That fact above all was worrying Jenny the most. She couldn't remember the last time she had seen her mother cry.

May's face puckered in annoyance. 'You, gel, are imagining things. There's n'ote wrong wi' me, I tell yer.' She snapped, 'Now stop goin' on about it, yer gettin' on me nerves.'

Jenny's lips tightened. She knew not to push her mother any further. That it was best, unless she wanted to risk her wrath, to drop the matter for the time being.

'All right, Mam,' she said, reluctantly rising. 'But you sit there while I mash you a cuppa. And I'll fish in me handbag to see if I've any Aspirin left.'

She had reached the kitchen door when May unexpectedly asked, 'Was there . . . er . . . anyone outside when yer came in?'

Jenny stopped and turned to face her. 'Not that I can remember. Why? Were you expecting someone?'

May nonchalantly shrugged her shoulders. 'No, just askin'. I . . . er . . . saw some people door knocking when I came home, Jehovah's Witnesses or summat like that, and I wondered if they'd be calling here. If you'd seen 'em I was gonna send you to tell 'em not to bother calling here, that's all. I can't be doing with that lot just now, not wi' this headache. What . . . er . . . about Gloria? Was she lurking around?'

Jenny shook her head. 'No.' She stared at her mother quizzically for a moment then a thought struck. 'Oh,' she said knowingly. 'Have you and Gloria had words? Is that it?'

May looked at her blankly. 'Eh? Oh, yeah, that's right. One of our fights we've 'ad. I'm avoiding 'er. But . . . er . . . don't say n'ote to 'er when yer see 'er, will yer, me duck? It were summat and n'ote, best forgotten.'

Jenny frowned. 'But I've never known Gloria make you cry before, Mam.'

'And I've told yer, I *weren't* crying. Got summat in me eye,' she snapped dismissively, standing up. 'Now can we discuss summat else? Yer meking me headache worse. It's egg and chi—' Her voice trailed off as she looked at Jenny searchingly. ''Ang on a minute,' she said, grabbing her arm. 'You accused *me* of crying – now I'm gonna accuse *you*. You 'ave been, ain't yer? Bawlin' yer eyes out, I'd say.' A look of acute fear filled May's face and her grip on Jenny's arm tightened. 'Why?' she demanded. Her voice rose hysterically. 'There was someone outside – there was, wasn't there? What did she say?'

Jenny gazed at her, bewildered. 'There was nobody, I told you. Mother, what's got into you?'

May eyed her blankly for a moment, her mind racing. 'There's a loony on the loose,' she blurted. 'Accosting young women, telling 'em cock and bull stories.'

Jenny grimaced. 'A minute ago you were rambling on about Jehovah's Witnesses. Now there's a loony on the loose. What's got into you?'

'Stop confusing me,' May snapped. 'There were Witnesses about and there is a loony on the loose, and she's dangerous apparently. So if any strange woman stops yer and tries ter get yer talking, run off as quick as yer can. A'yer listenin'? Well, a'yer?'

'Yes, Mam.'

May exhaled sharply, shoulders sagging in relief. 'So, what's upset yer then? It's summat bad, ain't it? I can tell. Is it a lad? Eh, you ain't pregnant, are yer?' she accused.

'No, Mam, I ain't.'

Jenny eyed her mother gravely, took a deep breath then related her misfortune. When she had finished Jenny thought it

50

must surely be her imagination that her mother seemed indifferent to the whole dire situation. Her suspicions were confirmed, though, by May's totally uncharacteristic response.

'Oh, never mind, me duck. These things 'appen to the best of us. I'm surprised yer've lasted this long, working fer such high and mighties.'

Her daughter's mouth dropped open in shock. 'Eh? But, Mam, I thought you'd go mad, especially since it was Tony who caused . . .'

'Oh, him,' May cut in, flapping one hand dismissively. 'I can't be bothered wi' him just now. 'Sides, what's the point? Wasting good time trying ter find him and giving him what for wouldn't get yer job back.' She gave a sudden grin. 'Maybe the drunken sod did yer a favour, eh, Jenny love? What kinda job was it anyway, selling fancy glass and posh pots to stuck up cows that've got more brass than common sense?' She patted Jenny's arm reassuringly. 'Stop worrying. If the worst comes to the worst I can always get you set on at my place. And they won't bother about references. Crying out for overlockers they are and it wouldn't tek long to train. Not a clever dick like you, our Jenny.'

'But what about money, Mam? How are we going to manage 'til I get another pay packet?'

'Like we always do. On a wing and a prayer.' May shrugged her shoulders matter-of-factly. 'I just won't pay the rent for a couple of weeks, that's all. Eh, and it won't hurt ter miss the tally man neither.'

'We can't do that, Mam,' Jenny replied, aghast.

'Why not? We've done it afore, more times than you've had hot dinners. You used ter think it warra game, 'iding from the rent man.' She grimaced. 'Now let's fer God's sake stop talking about this, it's mekin' me headache worse,' she protested, vigorously rubbing her brow. 'As I was saying, it's egg and chips tonight, so go and peel the spuds, there's a duck.'

Jenny eyed her suspiciously. This reaction wasn't like her mother at all. At the very least she had expected May to rant and rave, cursing and damning all concerned to hell before she stormed off in search of Tony to give him a piece of her mind. And Jenny's employers would not have got off lightly either. May would certainly have told them in no uncertain terms what she thought of them.

Something was wrong. She was lying. Whatever had happened between herself and Gloria was much more than something and nothing. Her mother was hiding something momentous, something that had greatly upset her, and Jenny wanted to know what it was so she could share the burden and help her.

She took a deep breath. 'Mother . . .' she began.

May glared a warning.

Jenny stopped abruptly and sighed, resigned. 'I'll . . . er . . . make a start on the spuds.'

A while later she pushed her plate away. 'I can't eat any more, I'm not hungry.'

May did likewise. 'Me neither.' She rose. 'I'm goin' ter bed.'

Jenny eyed her in concern. 'It's only eight, Mam.'

'I can tell the time, Jenny. See yer in the morning,' said May, leaving the room.

A troubled Jenny began to clear the table. Just as she had stacked the plates there was a tap on the back door and seconds later Gloria entered. She was smiling broadly.

'Oh, not caught yer in the middle of yer dinner, 'ave I?'

Jenny stared at her, surprised. Considering her mother and Gloria were supposed to be at loggerheads, their neighbour was very friendly. 'No, Mrs Budgins, we've finished.'

Gloria eyed the nearly full plates. 'Neither of yer 'ave eaten much. Waste of good food that.' She hurriedly glanced around. 'Where's yer mam? She ain't gone out, 'as she? Only I fancied a natter. Cyril's snoring 'is 'ead off in the chair, Sandra's down the pub and our Kelvin's . . . well, 'e's off somewhere. 'E never tells me where 'e's goin'.'

Jenny's confusion mounted. 'Me mam's gone to bed with a bad headache. She's . . . well, she's upset, Mrs Budgins.'

'Upset? What about?' Gloria asked, frowning.

'Well . . . er . . . me mam told me not to say anything but she's upset about what happened between you and her earlier on.'

Gloria seemed perplexed. 'Me and her?'

'You had words, didn't you? An argument?'

Gloria's frown deepened. 'Did we? When?'

'Today?'

'I ain't seen yer mam today. If she had words then it weren't wi' me.'

'You haven't seen her at all?'

'No,' Gloria snapped, agitated. 'Accusing me of lying, are yer?'

'No, not at all. It's just that . . .' Jenny gnawed her bottom lip anxiously. Why had her mother lied about having an argument with her? Most worrying of all, what was she covering up? 'Oh, I must have heard me mam wrong, that's all. Sorry, Mrs Budgins.'

'Huh, well, 'pology 'cepted. Only 'cos it's you, mind.' Good-naturedly she asked, 'So do yer fancy a natter then?'

'Me? Oh, no, not tonight, if you don't mind, Mrs Budgins. I'm still suffering from that port.'

Gloria let out a bellow of mirth. 'You young 'uns can't tek yer drink, can yer? See me, I was up with the lark. 'Ad the washing on the line afore I went ter work. I bet you 'ad ter drag yerself out your pit. Right, well, if yer don't fancy a natter, I'll pop in and see how Nelly Bates is. The poor old duck loves a visit. Oh, that reminds me,' she said, rubbing her fat hands gleefully, 'I must tell May – Nelly's son Ron is back. Be one in the eye for her 'cos I found out first. I always said that relationship 'tween him and that hard-faced woman across town 'ud never work. I wa' right. Tarra, me duck.'

A while later Jenny wearily rubbed her face with her hands. She could never have envisaged that morning when she had arisen how disastrously her day was going to turn out. Had she had even an inkling of what lay in store she wouldn't have got up. She raised tired eyes to the clock. It was nine. She sighed forlornly. The best thing she could do would be to go to bed and try and get some sleep but she knew that would be futile. She had far too much whirling around in her head to rest. Not only was her own dire situation causing her worry but also her mother's confusing behaviour. Try as she might Jenny could not fathom what could possibly have happened to cause her mother to be so upset and, far worse, blatantly to lie to cover up the fact.

May often evaded the truth or exaggerated when caught on the hop, but Jenny would not class her as a blatant liar. And to tell one that could so easily be discovered ... well, it just didn't make sense.

She uncurled her legs, stood up and paced the room. Up and down she went, stopping now and then to stare into space until suddenly a great desire for a walk overwhelmed her. A walk might do her good, she thought, hopefully clear her head and tire her out sufficiently to get some sleep. She'd need to be alert and look fresh in the morning to entice possible employers into giving her work. And besides, everything appeared so different in the morning, problems not half so daunting as they seemed in the dark of the night. She hoped this was the case here. Not heeding the lateness of the hour, she grabbed her coat off the back of the door and quietly left the house.

The night was cold, a fierce wind rising and thick black clouds rolling across the sky. Heedless, Jenny pulled the collar of her coat up, dug her hands deep into her pockets and stepped forth.

On and on she walked, so preoccupied she was unaware of how far she had ventured. Suddenly a splash of rain hit her and then another. Suddenly alert, she looked skywards and as she did so heavy clouds overflowed and began dispersing their contents all over her.

'Oh, hell,' she groaned as she glanced hurriedly around, then grimaced as it struck her she could not for the moment place where she was. The unfamiliar street she was on was deserted, with no apparent shelter. The rain was lashing down now and she was getting wetter by the second. To the back of her was a building which Jenny thought was disused as its windows were boarded, weeds growing in abundance in cracks and crevices. At the end of the building she could just make out a wide, muddy, near-overgrown lane. Without another thought she made a dash for the lane, hoping it housed an old lean-to or something where she could wait until the deluge subsided.

Halfway down the lane, having jumped puddles, her shoes now caked in squelching mud, she stopped, dismayed. A short distance away the lane appeared to come to a dead end at a high wall. She was almost sodden through now, the bitterness of the weather penetrating her bones, and her urgent need for shelter mounted. She spun around, her intention being to make her way back to the street when she spotted a door in the side of the building. Instinctively she tried the handle. To her complete surprise it opened. She slipped thankfully inside, and forced the door shut behind her against the wind.

The interior of the building was nearly pitch dark and as she fought to accustom her eyes to it, eerie shapes began to loom and she shuddered. She had expected the dilapidated building to be devoid of any contents. Regardless, at this moment she was just too glad to be out of the driving rain to be worried over her possible trespass. Unbuttoning her sodden coat and shaking herself, she tentatively stepped forward, arms outstretched to feel for something she could sit on to wait while the weather moderated. Suddenly she stopped short as a sound reached her ears. It was nothing she could instantly recognise, but a sound all the same which must have been made by something. She froze, ears pricked, hoping she was imagining things. To her horror it came again. A surge of fear shot through her and her heart began thumping painfully. She was not alone. Clenching her fists, taking a very deep breath, she called: 'Who's . . . who's there?'

The prevailing silence was deafening.

Suddenly the scratch of a match striking rent the air, the noise it made seeming to echo off the old walls. After what seemed an eternity the flame flared up, its brightness like a distant beacon in a vast area of darkness. Mouth wide, eyes bulging, Jenny stared at it as seemingly unaided the flame rose upwards then started to move slowly towards her. A scream of sheer terror stuck in her throat as a premonition of danger filled her.

Jenny had thought her disastrous day could not possibly get any worse. She had been dreadfully wrong. It was turning into a nightmare.

# Chapter Five

As Jenny's disastrous day was dawning, in a shabby room in a dismal lodging house on a grimy street off Belgrave Gate, forty-four-year-old bachelor Owen Ford forced his eyes open and peered blearily at the tarnished tin clock ticking merrily away on the old dressing table at the side of his bed. The hands slowly came into focus, reading five-forty-five. Yawning loudly, he ran his fingers through fine greying hair, rubbed his eyes and pulled back the patched, greying sheets on his rickety iron bed, then sat up and swung his legs over the side.

Ten minutes later he was wolfing down his solitary breakfast of toast scraped sparingly with margarine and a mug of thick black tea – the drop of milk in the bottle had gone off overnight. At six-twenty-five he hurriedly put his chipped plate and handleless mug into the antiquated pot sink to wash when he returned home that night, grabbed his cloth cap and shabby donkey jacket from the back of a very worn straight-backed chair, and left the room. At the bottom of the stairs, Owen called out his customary 'good morning' to his sour-faced, slovenly landlady and pulled shut the peeling front door behind him, the only thing on his mind the worry he'd be late for work if he didn't get a move on. He had never been late for work in his life before and wasn't going to start now.

As he strode off down the street, steel-capped boots clattering rhythmically against the cobbles, he was totally oblivious to the fact that in a few short hours such a simple thing as allowing his thoughts to wander – something completely out of character for a normally conscientious man – would prove of immense significance not only to himself but to several other unsuspecting people.

'Ahhh! It's on me bloody foot. I said lift, not drop.'

'I did lift. Well, I tried.'

'Tried? Put some effort into it, lad. Now, on my three – lift. Three!'

'I can't.'

'Can't?'

'No, gaffer, I can't, it's stuck.'

'Stuck! Fer God's sake, wadda yer mean, it's stuck?' Straining his neck in an effort to assess the situation, Owen loudly grumbled. 'You young uns, yer've no stamina. Good job I 'ad stamina during the war or where would we be now? Up to our bleddy neck in Jerries, that's what.' He paused for breath then blurted, 'I can't see a bleddy thing, it's jammed against the wall.'

'That's what I've bin trying ter tell yer, gaffer. What we gonna do?'

Clawing his fingers through his hair, Owen stepped back to survey his end of an ancient woodworm-riddled oak wardrobe, the ornate feet of which were covered in decades of dust and cobwebs. He sucked in his cheeks. He hadn't a clue bar chop the monstrosity into bits and burn it. To his mind that was all this piece of furniture was worth, but he realised his thoughts were unkind considering the poverty of the poor old duck who owned it.

At the other end of the wardrobe, awaiting instructions, seventeen-year-old Trevor O'Neil, who had only started with Wadham's Removals three days previously, perched his skinny backside on a bare-boarded step and absently stroked his sideburns, mind fully occupied with a petrol blue drape suit he was saving up to buy. Decked out in such an outfit he'd become an accepted local Teddy Boy instead of watching from the sidelines. And, more importantly, the girls would flock after him.

In his mind's eye he could picture it all now. Friday night down the *Palais-de-danse*, jiving to the live band's rendition of Bill Haley's 'See You Later, Alligator', eyes glued on the panty-clad backsides of the women as they were flung under legs and over heads, their colourful skirts swirling over numerous nets worn underneath. Hopefully, he himself would be dancing likewise. A blonde would be nice, or maybe a redhead. If truth were told he wasn't that fussy as long as she was attractive enough not to attract derogatory comments from his mates. It was Thursday today. His eyes glinted with anticipation. Only another day to wait.

'Early tea break, Trevor?'

'Eh?' He jumped up, shocked. 'Er . . . no, boss, no. I . . . er . . . thought yer'd gone off ter price that job?'

'Well, you know what thought did. There was no one in so I'll have to go back later. So what's going on?'

Trevor gulped. 'We've a problem, boss.'

'Problem?' William Wadham's eyes narrowed, broad brow furrowing. 'I've only been gone a few minutes. How could you have a problem?'

'Well . . .' Trevor gulped sheepishly. 'Yer'd better tek a look,' he said hesitantly, hanging his head and standing aside.

Bill poked his head around the entrance to the narrow stairway. The sight that met him made his mouth drop open. 'What on earth . . . Owen?' he shouted sternly. 'What in God's name possessed you to try and get that 'robe down the stairs?'

'Oh, yer back, boss,' came the muffled reply.

'Yes, I'm back. Now, explain yourself. I left you in charge of the simple job of bringing the furniture down the stairs.

What possessed you to bring the 'robe this way? A three-year-old could see the stairs are too narrow.'

'It's stuck, boss,' piped up Trevor.

'I'm not blind,' he replied tersely. 'What got into you, Owen?'

'I dunno, boss. I weren't thinking straight,' he offered.

'You weren't thinking at all. Mind on other things, I shouldn't wonder. That lady friend of yours, was it?'

'Lady friend?' piped up Trevor, his face contorting in disgust. 'Mr Ford's too old fer lady friends, in't 'e?'

'Shut up, Trevor,' Bill snapped sharply. 'We need to shift this wardrobe before Mrs Cudbull sees what's going on. She'll think we're a right tuppenny ha'penny outfit. Owen,' he ordered, 'I'll shove from this end and you try to manoeuvre it your end, okay?'

'Okay, boss.'

As he flattened himself against the stair wall to allow his boss to position his shoulder against the end of the offending article, Trevor mused, 'I don't understand. If it went up, surely it'll come down? I mean, the wardrobe can't 'ave grown, can it?'

'It didn't come up this way, Trevor,' Bill replied, agitated.

Frowning he muttered, 'It didn't? Then 'ow . . .'

'Through the sash window. It was hoisted up by ropes. And that's the way we'll have to get it out. Providing, of course, we can get it unjammed first.' Fighting to keep control of his growing annoyance, he added, 'And if you had taken notice of me when I went over the running of the business the day you started then you'd have remembered this. Right,' he called, 'here goes, Owen.'

'Eh up, me ducks, tea's up.'

'Oh, my God!' Bill exclaimed, horrified. 'Hold on a minute, Owen,' he shouted.

Hurriedly righting himself, he jumped down the remaining stairs, just avoiding knocking Trevor out of the way. Luckily he managed to waylay the person who had hired his services just as she was about to poke her head around the entrance to the stairs and witness the predicament they were in.

The shabby old lady who greeted him was dressed from head to toe in black, the only garment alleviating her drabness being a very worn wrap-round apron. Her sparse salt-and-pepper hair was cropped short, parted down the middle and secured behind her ears with kirby grips. She was carrying an ancient *papier mâché* tray on which sat two steaming chipped blue mugs.

'It's very good of you to make us a mash, Mrs Cudbull,' said Bill, sincerely, taking the tray from her while peering around the almost empty room for somewhere to put it down where it wouldn't be knocked over.

'My pleasure,' she said, her grin exposing a set of pink gums. 'I couldn't quite manage the three so I've left yours in the kitchen.' She eyed him hopefully. 'Actually I thought yer might like ter park yer body for a minute whilst yer drink it, you being the boss. Then I wondered if yer'd mind giving me an 'and gettin' some bits off the top shelf in the larder. I don't like ter ask only . . .'

'Of course I will,' he cut in kindly. 'All part and parcel of our service, Mrs Cudbull. But we haven't the time to stop now,' he said, placing the tray on the bare boards by the far wall. 'Your son told me he expects me to have you settled in your new place before lunchtime. Time's wearing on and we've still a fair bit to do.'

The elderly lady clicked her tongue disdainfully. 'Don't take any notice of what 'e says. I know 'e's my son but 'e's bin the bane of my life since the minute 'e was born. 'E 'ad that knowing look, if yer understand what I mean, and 'e's been a know-all ever since. Anyway it's me that's 'aving ter find the money for this move, not 'im, so if I say you've ter tek a breather, then yer tek one.'

Bill smiled gratefully. 'Right you are, Mrs Cudbull. If I'm honest I could do with a couple of minutes' sit down.' And while they were in the kitchen, hopefully Owen and Trevor could remove the wardrobe from the stairs and Mrs Cudbull would be none the wiser.

But Bill had bargained without her.

She patted his arm. 'Why don't yer call yer lads afore this tea gets cold and I can ask 'em what they'd like in their sandwiches. I 'ope it's paste 'cos that's all I've got.'

'You don't need to go to all that bother, Mrs Cudbull.'

'Oh, I do. Keep the workers 'appy, that's my motto, then yer gets a good job done. So go on, call 'em,' she ordered.

Bill was cornered and he knew it. Reluctantly he complied. Trevor, who had been lurking in the shadows at the bottom of the stairs, leaped over, grabbed hold of the mug and was supping from it before Bill could finish issuing instructions.

'Where's yer other bloke?' Mrs Cudbull asked.

Bill eyed her blankly. 'He's . . . indisposed at the moment, Mrs Cudbull.'

She looked worried. 'Really? Oh, dear, I 'ope it ain't serious. Should we fetch the doctor?'

'Pardon? Oh, he's not ill. He's . . . what I mean is he . . . well, he can't exactly get down the stairs at the moment.'

'He can't? Why?'

Deeply troubled Bill looked at her, seeking the best way in which to explain to Mrs Cudbull the problem they were faced with. He needed this job, as small as it was, to be a success. His business was ticking over, just, but survival was a constant worry. He needed Mrs Cudbull to recommend his services to all her neighbours and they in turn to theirs. This tightly packed area of decaying two up and two down terraces was situated in the west of the city, all its residents being forced to move by the council due to their slum clearance policy. He couldn't expect Mrs Cudbull to recommend him if a mess was made of her removal.

There was also the fact that in order to stand a chance at the job in the first place he had cut his price to the bone in the hope it would lead to others and had not made allowance for any docking of payment against damages.

Bill sighed. His back was against the wall. There were many in this city fighting for a living like him. The ending of the Second World War ten years ago had created many jobs but in the long term had cut far more and consequently small one-man businesses making promises of good performance at cheap rates they couldn't fulfil were springing up daily and disappearing as quickly.

William Wadham's business wasn't one of those. He prided himself on a fair rate for a job well done, customer satisfaction paramount, working day and night to ensure he'd be trading until the day he retired.

It shouldn't have been like this, though. He'd never had any intention of going it alone. Another, someone faceless, had been the cause of that. At this last thought a vice-like pain shot through him and memories he had desperately fought to bury began to resurface. Fighting with all his might to block them, he shuddered violently. William Wadham had witnessed sights and suffered enough hardships and physical pain during the war to bring the most hardened man to his knees, but it wasn't any of those that had broken his heart and left invisible scars that would never heal. That terrible event dated from 1936 when he was a young man of twenty-four and had pained him so greatly it had ripped the very soul from him, making him almost suicidal.

Mentally he shook himself. It had taken every ounce of his courage to pull himself out of the depths of despair that had followed that dreadful time in his life. His years of recovery had been slow, just functioning, with no zest or purpose. But with time the pain was now bearable so long as he didn't allow himself to dwell on that period of his life, brood on what might have been if things had happened differently.

Forcing his thoughts back to the matter facing him, he took a deep breath. Despite his craving for success he couldn't and wouldn't try to fool this old lady who, despite her cheery outward appearance, he knew, was very distressed at her enforced rehousal. He looked her straight in the eye. 'We've a slight problem, Mrs Cudbull.'

Her rheumy eyes widened worriedly. 'Oh?'

'Nothing we can't put right. Well, I hope we can,' he added worriedly. 'It's . . . well, it's your wardrobe. I'm afraid we've got it stuck on the stairs.'

She gave a loud sigh of relief. 'Is that all? My God, I thought it were summat serious you were about to tell me. I've never liked that old thing. Would've got rid of it years ago if I could've afforded another. Me dad used ter lock me and me sister in it, yer know, whenever we misbehaved.' She shuddered at the memory. ''Ate that 'robe, I do. If yer can't shift it then leave it for the bulldozers. I'll be glad ter see the back of the damned thing. Haunted me all me life it 'as.'

Bill was staring at her in surprise. 'Oh . . . er . . . right then. If we do damage it, of course I'll compensate you.' It was the last thing he wanted to do but he felt obliged to offer.

'You'll do no such thing, young man.' She eyed him knowingly. 'I might be old but I ain't daft. I know you've priced this job cheap. I picked yer because yer were the only one I could afford. But more ter the point, I picked yer because yer looked 'onest. A damned sight more 'onest than some of the beggars who priced it for me. Anyway 'ow can I expect yer to compensate me for a wardrobe that ain't worth the effort of shifting it?'

Ida Cudbull paused for a moment and surveyed the man before her. She wished she was thirty years younger. By God, William Wadham was a good looker, she wasn't too old to appreciate a handsome man when she saw one. He reminded her of her beloved Bert, God rest him. He had been tall, his chiselled features arranged very pleasantly and topped off with a thick thatch of fair hair which her Bert used to rake his fingers through whenever he had a problem, just like Mr Wadham was doing now. And Bert had had startling blue eyes that had mesmerised anyone who happened to look into them, but whereas his had always twinkled merrily whatever mood he was in, behind this young man's was a definite haze of sadness. Many would not see it, but Ida did. She'd always been astute and the advancing years hadn't diminished that quality.

Mr Wadham had obviously suffered greatly during his lifetime, she thought. At a woman's hands maybe, or more than likely what he'd endured during the war. But he was far from being alone in that. Millions of men, women and children had suffered more than it was humanly possible to comprehend. This young man, like them, would have to live with his grief, whatever the cause, as best he could. At least he was still alive; many hadn't been so lucky.

'Anyway,' she continued, 'me mind's made up. Get it off the stairs as best yer can then leave it fer the 'dozers and be done with it. Me son can put his hand in his pocket for once and get me another. 'E's always bragging 'e's a decent wage, but not much comes my way. Tight-fisted, 'e 'is. I don't know who 'e teks after. One thing's fer sure, it ain't me nor his father. Now come on, young man, and get yer own tea afore it gets cold.'

Bill smiled to himself as he followed the old lady through to the kitchen. She had addressed him several times as 'young man'. He was hardly young. Forty-five he'd be next birthday, and if truth were told at this moment he felt far older than his age.

Ignoring the commotion coming from the stairway as Owen and Trevor endeavoured to remove the wardrobe, Bill lowered himself tentatively onto the rickety chair offered, fearful it could collapse under his weight, and supped on his mug of strong tea, glad that Mrs Cudbull had enforced this break. In truth he was very tired, in body and in mind. Restful sleep was something that only happened periodically, usually when he'd allowed himself time to relax over a few pints down the local, only to feel guilty the next morning over all the chores he should have done but hadn't.

Last night had been typical. After a snatched meal, he'd worked until near midnight, failing miserably in his attempt to catch up with paperwork, a task he detested. Then, when he had finally forced himself to retire for the night, he'd only tossed and turned trying to dream up new ways in which to entice more business. His fatigued mind had been unable to conjure anything up.

He had risen before dawn and been out in the yard tinkering with the old Ford lorry, praying the second-hand parts it was constructed with now, all salvaged from the local scrap dealers, would hold it together for just a while longer. He smiled to himself. Bessie, as he affectionately called the vehicle, had an engine that rattled, clanked and wheezed worse than an old man's chest in a severe winter, but regardless she had served him well and for Bill it would be a sad day when they were forced to part company. But the purchase of another vehicle, unless business greatly improved, was out of the question for Wadham's Removals.

Taking a deep breath, he forced his worries away and addressed Mrs Cudbull. 'I expect you'll be glad to be settled in your new place,' he said to make conversation.

From the chair opposite, cradling her own mug of tea, she replied flatly, 'Not really.'

'Oh?' He frowned, surprised. 'Don't you like your new house?'

She tightened her lips. 'It sounds nice enough. I can't say much more than that 'cos I ain't seen it yet. I asked me son ter take me, but 'e's always too busy. And it's all 'appened so quick, yer see. All of us around 'ere 'ave lived under threat fer years from the Corporation about razing the area. Nothing 'appened, then the war came and went and in the meantime we all forgot about it 'til a couple of weeks ago when we gets a letter out of the blue. Compulsory eviction. We've no choice in the matter. And no choice either in the 'ouse we were offered. Well, not in my case,' she added gruffly. 'Lilly Thomkins next door did. She got the choice of one up Saffron Lane or in Braunstone. Yer know, them big new estates they're building.' Bill did and nodded. 'Me, I just got offered a prefab up the top of the Hinckley Road.' She grimaced scornfully. 'Them prefabs are only make do and mend, only supposed ter last five years at the most. When the Corporation allocated it, they obviously thought the 'ouse 'ud see me out.'

Bill hid a smile. 'I'm sure they didn't,' he said reassuringly.

'I'm sure they bleddy did,' Ida retorted. 'That's all they offered Sid Jones, too. 'E's as old as me, we used ter be in the same class at school. 'E's had the corner shop for nigh on fifty odd years and reckons 'e ain't going anywhere 'less they gives him compensation for loss of his living. They can starve 'im out, 'e reckons. But 'e knows 'e won't get nowhere. Yer get more sense talking to a brick wall than yer do from the Corpo.

'The lot that work there ain't really interested in what their tenants need. I went down to speak to 'em about a couple of things that were bothering me. Some chit of a gel hardly out of her pram told me ter wait in a queue. No please or thank you neither. After an hour I gave up.' Ida sighed despond-ently. 'At least wi' a private landlord yer knows where yer stands. Harry Marsh has bin me landlord for over fifty years. I never thought I'd 'ear meself say this, but I'll miss the penny-pinching old sod I will. At least I knew who I wa' dealing with.'

The old lady gave a violent shudder, her aged face filling with sadness, and Bill's heart went out to her. Leaning over, he placed one hand gently on her arm. 'You don't want to leave this house, do you?'

Sniffing, she sadly shook her head. 'No, I don't. I've lived 'ere all me life. Not all of it's bin 'appy but it's the only 'ome I've known. I've got all me friends nearby – well, those left livin' that is – and me neighbours ain't a bad bunch. They're there when yer need 'em and that's what counts.' She gave a wistful sigh. 'Things 'ave never been easy. When yer poor they never are. I've always 'ad ter live 'and ter mouth, but durin' the war I don't know what I'd 'ave done wi'out me neighbours. Nor them wi'out me come ter that.' She eyed him meaningfully. 'I knows it were 'ard fer you boys that went off ter fight, but it were tough fer us back 'ome, too. We 'ad a dreadful time of it.'

Wringing arthritic hands, her eyes glazed over. 'I 'specially remember the pans of soup. When things were really 'ard and none of us had enough food ter make a meal, we'd all chip in to mek a pan big enough ter feed the whole street. Nelly Gibbons next door always had spuds – whatever else she never had you could always count on her for a spud or two. With Vi Taylor it was bones for the stock. She 'ad a dog, yer see, and Bilson the butcher always kept a bone aside for her. It was 1944 before he found out the dog had passed on in '42, of old age.' Ida gave a wheezy cackle of mirth at the memory. 'Boy, was there 'ell ter pay! But, bless Mr Bilson, Vi still got her bones.

'The kids around 'ere then were a right motley bunch. Still are fer that matter. Always getting a thick 'ear from their mothers for summat they've done, but do 'ote for n'ote them kids would during the war. Well, they 'ad ter. We 'adn't n'ote ter give 'em. They all played their part running errands, following the coal cart fer dropped lumps and collecting 'orse dung for the allotments. We women relied on them fer apples and blackberries in autumn. Packed 'em off in the morning wi' bread and lard and bottles of water, and come evening they'd troop 'ome, 'ands and faces stained black and clothes ripped ter shreds. 'Course they'd ate more than they brought back wi' em but fruit we'd never 'ave 'ad if it 'adn't 'ave bin fer them.'

Her voice lowered emotionally and she raised her eyes to meet his. 'I'll know nobody up there, will I? Nobody well enough to call on if I need 'elp. No kids ter run errands for me. And what about me memories? I won't have none where I'm goin'.' Two large tears settled on her eyelids which she wiped away using the bottom of her apron. 'Oh, don't mind me, Mr Wadham, I'm just a silly old woman.'

He smiled sympathetically. 'I don't think you're being silly at all.'

'Yer don't?'

'No,' he said kindly. 'You're frightened, Mrs Cudbull.'

'Yer right there, young man. I am. Terrified if I'm 'onest.'

'It's understandable.' He cast his eyes hurriedly around the cramped confines of the scullery. It was dire to say the least. Damp had caused the discoloured whitewash to peel and chunks of cement between the ancient bricks had fallen out. Creeping black mould was very much evident. The wooden window frame was rotten and ill-fitting and a cold blast was wafting continuously through. The same with the door. The weight of the discoloured chipped pot sink had over the years loosened its moorings and it was held precariously in place by several bricks, the single brass tap protruding through from the outside wall stained green and dripping steadily. And this was only the kitchen. The rest of the tiny house was just as bad, in fact worse in parts. But, regardless, these damp, mould-encrusted walls were home to the old lady.

Bill's place of abode – a two up, two down terrace in Leamington Street, an area itself somewhere on the Corporation's list for slum clearance – was hardly a palace but it was in better condition than this. It and the houses adjoining were unfit for human habitation and had been for many years. But regardless Bill was fully aware that to voice his opinion bluntly would only add to this dear old lady's distress and that was the last thing he wanted. Pity Mrs Cudbull's son couldn't have shown a bit more care and consideration towards his mother, tried to allay her fear, taken the trouble to accompany her to see her new house, given her some encouragement and reassurance over her daunting move. Had he done so she might not be feeling such dread now.

He thought of his own dear mother, now many years departed, and how she would be feeling in such circumstances. She too had been born, lived her life and died in the little house in Leamington Street. Faced with such an upheaval, he knew his mother too would have felt the same as Mrs Cudbull.

Bill cleared his throat. 'Mrs Cudbull, with due respect, you might be attached to this house and with good reason, but it's hardly fitting, is it, for a lady like yourself to live in any longer? In truth it should have been pulled down years ago.' He smiled at her warmly. 'Those prefabs might only have been put up temporarily but they're really quite nice. I happen to know they only allocate them to special people.' This was a lie but told with the best of intentions. 'You're one of the lucky ones, you know.'

She grimaced. 'Am I? You think so? That's not what me son sez. 'E reckons we've bin palmed off.'

From what he'd perceived of him, his type would, Bill thought. 'It's not for me to question your son, Mrs Cudbull, but I happen to think he's wrong. Most of those houses on the new estates are for families, they cost a lot to heat in winter. And the prefabs have a bathroom.'

'A bathroom?' Her eyes widened in amazement. 'A proper room with a bath in it? Really? Just like the posh folks have?'

He nodded.

'Oh,' she mouthed. 'A proper bath, eh! With taps? No carting the water?'

'With taps. Hot and cold. There's a boiler to heat the water.

And,' Bill continued, 'think of all the rooms in those bigger houses that you'd have to keep clean. And you'd never get any peace with all the kids playing in the streets. No disrespect, Mrs Cudbull, but haven't you had enough of kids knocking on your door for this and that?'

She pursed her lips. 'I s'pose I 'ave. Not that I mind kids, but they do get on yer nerves sometimes.' She frowned thoughtfully. 'Mmm, like yer said, a prefab'd be a lot easier ter keep.'

'It would.' He paused as a thought struck him. 'Mrs Cudbull, have all your neighbours been allocated houses yet?'

'Some 'ave, not all. Why d'yer ask?'

'I wouldn't want to build up your hopes but they could be offered a prefab too.'

A spark of interest lit her eyes. 'Oh, d'yer think they might?'

He nodded. 'But even if they aren't, it wouldn't take a lovely lady like yourself long to become friendly with your new neighbours. Actually I think it's quite an adventure myself. New area, new house, a whole new set of friends.'

Ida eyed him scornfully. 'An adventure? I'm too old fer adventures, young man.'

He smiled. 'You're never too old, Mrs Cudbull. Anyway, how old are you?' With a twinkle in his eye he appraised her. 'Sixty?' he asked, knowing she was much older.

She gave a cackle of mirth. 'Cheeky thing! I'm seventy-two.'

'Seventy-two?' he said, pretending surprise. 'Is that all? There's plenty of life in you yet for new adventure.'

'D'yer reckon? But I've never 'ad an adventure.'

'Well, now you're about to, Mrs Cudbull. And you should take the trouble to enjoy it – you might not get another chance.' He smiled warmly. 'What's the saying? In for a penny, in for a pound.'

She frowned. 'You mean I shouldn't be so half-hearted

about me move, don't you, Mr Wadham. That I should grasp this chance of a new start despite me age?'

He nodded.

She looked at him for several moments then suddenly her worried face broke into a smile. 'Yer right,' she said, rubbing her hands. 'So let's get started then, before I pop me clogs wi' excitement.'

Just then there was a pounding on the back door. It burst open and a woman as elderly and as shabbily dressed as Ida Cudbull charged in. She was brandishing a letter. 'What number 'ouse did yer say you'd bin allocated, Ida?' she shouted excitedly.

'Six,' Ida responded, puzzled by her neighbour's unexpectedly eager question. 'Why, gonna write to me, are yer, Vi?'

'Won't need ter 'cos we're gonna be neighbours,' she cried joyfully.

Ida's mouth dropped open in surprise. 'We are?'

'Yeah. I've got number eight.'

'Number eight. Why, that's next door!'

'I knows that, yer soppy sod.' Vi grinned cheekily. 'So yer'd better get an extra bag of sugar in, gel, for when I comes around to borrow a cup, hadn't yer, eh?'

'Well, I never,' Ida proclaimed, clapping her gnarled hands in delight. 'I'll get two in, Vi, yer can come and borrow as much as yer like.' She fixed shining eyes, full of hope, on Bill. 'Oh, it's just like you said, young . . .'

She was rudely interrupted by a sudden loud crash and the thud of bodies hitting the floor, followed by a stream of curses. Bill sprang up and raced through to the back room. He stopped abruptly. Sprawled at the bottom of the stairs, surrounded by the debris of the disintegrated wardrobe, were Trevor and Owen. Both were writhing in agony, groaning pitifully.

'I think me leg's broke,' Trevor wailed.

Bill sighed deeply and rubbed his hands over his face which was etched with worry. What a dreadful day this had turned out to be. When he had risen that morning he could never have envisaged it ending with two employees hospitalised. The situation was terrible, not just because Bill faced the prospect of trying to run his business single-handed for the foreseeable future, but also because he felt he carried a burden of responsibility for what had happened to Owen and Trevor, and due to that responsibility the least he could do was continue to pay their wages while they were both recovering. How he would find the money to do that, though, was beyond him.

Despite the guilt he felt over the accident, in fact Bill should have congratulated himself on the way in which he had handled the situation. Not only did he swiftly organise an ambulance to get Owen and Trevor to hospital and accompanied them, staying until the medical staff took over, he returned later, satisfying himself they were comfortable, and then completed Mrs Cudbull's move and saw her happily settled, albeit hours later than originally agreed.

Bill allowed himself a smile. The old lady had been remarkable. Not once had she commented on the accident in any way other than to say she was deeply upset for Owen and Trevor's sufferings, mostly blaming herself as she was the owner of the cursed wardrobe. Once Bill had calmed her sufficiently she had bustled about mashing endless pots of tea and doing her utmost to ensure the men were as comfortable as possible until the ambulance arrived. On Bill's return home from the hospital, when he'd insisted in carrying on with her move, she had even rounded up a couple of male neighbours to help him load her sparse belongings on to the lorry. It had been farcical, the men elderly and hardly capable of carrying themselves, let alone anything weighing more than a few pounds, but nevertheless Bill had gratefully welcomed their efforts.

73

He grimaced ruefully. Pity Ida Cudbull's son, when he had arrived home at lunchtime to inspect Bill's progress, had not shown such compassion or offered any help. To his mother's acute embarrassment he had loudly voiced his own opinion of Bill's lax manner of running a business, saying he expected a large reduction in the bill and the wardrobe to be replaced or he would take matters further.

When he had stormed off back to work, Ida had told Bill to ignore her son and, bless her, on completion of the job, to his immense relief, had paid the bill in full, actually adding an extra half crown and insisting he put it towards getting his men something to ease their discomfort. And much to his surprise she had told him she would definitely be recommending his services to all her old neighbours.

Despite Ida Cudbull's insistence to the contrary, Bill felt duty bound to replace the wardrobe. A replacement wasn't a problem. He had several at his disposal, which he admitted weren't up to much, but were in better condition than Mrs Cudbull's before the accident, stored in a dilapidated warehouse he rented for a pittance off the Braunstone Gate, backing on to the canal. The wardrobes stood alongside other pieces of furniture he'd picked up over the years, his intention being to expand into the selling of second-hand furniture. Time and limited resources hadn't allowed that so far and the furniture lay gathering dust until such time as it did.

Bill pushed his grubby shirt cuff back and peered at his watch. It was twenty minutes to eleven. He sighed despondently. While unaware of what the day had in store for him he had planned to finish early tonight in order to tackle some overdue chores at home. A pile of dirty laundry urgently needed his attention and it was well over a fortnight since he'd found the time to pass a brush over the floors and dust the furniture. William Wadham was a man with high standards and his inability to find the time to do any housework did not sit easy with him.

He sighed heavily again and cast weary eyes around him. His business was conducted from a small yard which housed a crumbling, single-storey building, its roof constructed of rusting corrugated tin, leaking in places, the rent charged for the premises being much more than they were worth but still reasonable compared to similar places and all he could afford.

It was situated behind a busy, noisy lumber yard off the Sanvey Gate in a deprived area consisting of mazes of back-to-back terraces, mixed with assorted factories and other business yards, pubs and corner shops, about a half-mile from the centre of Leicester. It was not an ideal place from which to run a hopefully expanding business, reached as it was by means of a narrow cobbled lane. Negotiating the old lorry down it several times daily was a feat in itself and how damage to any of the dilapidated buildings that lined the lane, or to the lorry had been avoided over the years was a miracle.

At this moment in time, and much to his disgust, the premises were in a dreadful state of chaos. Around the yard lay gradually mounting heaps of unwanted metal items pressed on him by customers, either given for nothing or purchased by Bill for pennies. His hope was eventually to acquire a small profit when he'd offloaded the items down the scrapyard, but in his endeavours to keep the removal side of the business afloat, he'd not found time to do so as yet.

In the cramped confines of the building he used as his office, paperwork on past jobs needing to be filed was stacked haphazardly on top of two rickety filing cabinets, several of its drawers jammed or broken. Jostling for space on the old desk he was sitting at were more piles of assorted paperwork needing to be dealt with – in fact they should have been dealt with months ago, including forms for the tax office which were worryingly overdue, plus invoices to be paid and accounts books to be updated. The small table behind the ill-fitting entry door, which held a gas ring, blackened kettle, half-empty bottle of milk, the contents of which Bill could see were rancid, and several tea-stained tin mugs, was grimy to say the least. If the mashing area wasn't a health hazard then the family of mice he suspected resided behind the filing cabinets were. In fact the whole office needed sorting and cleaning out and the landlord made to carry out repairs. That was to say nothing of the yard. But Bill knew he had as much hope of the landlord doing the repairs as he had of becoming rich.

He yawned loudly. Home chores would have to be shelved again; he was desperately tired, but regardless, before he climbed into bed that night he would still find time to launder a couple of shirts and hang them to dry. No matter how low his standards had sunk of late, a clean shirt each day was something he would not give up. He yawned loudly again, stretching out his arms. Tomorrow he had two removals to conduct and the prospect of carrying them out on his own was daunting. His brow furrowed deeply. Help was what he desperately needed until Owen and Trevor were back on their feet. But where would he get reliable temporary help at such short notice? He sighed worriedly, no immediate answer springing to mind.

Hiring good staff these days, when the maximum wage he could afford to offer was not as good as factory work or that paid by a bigger removal firm, was not easy. He had been lucky with Owen. He was as hard-working, loyal and trustworthy as Bill could wish. Until his mistake of today that is. But then, to Bill's way of thinking, no one was perfect. It was just bad luck that Owen's lapse in concentration had resulted in such a catastrophe.

Bill, of course, had compensated Owen for his loyal service with as much money as he could afford. But younger lads were a different matter. Over the years he had employed a succession of them and they had never stayed long, constantly being enticed away by an easier job with a better wage or else being summoned to do their National Service. Trevor had only been with him a matter of days and Bill had quickly realised from his lack of interest that he wouldn't last long, but regardless he had been the best of the applicants the employment office had sent.

Bill glanced at his watch again. His first job in the morning started at seven-thirty, the next at one. He'd also promised to price three jobs – which he prayed that he'd get – plus revisit the one today where the houseowner had not been at home. A more than full day ahead which did not, even if he still had his full complement of staff, leave him any time to sort out then deliver Mrs Cudbull's replacement wardrobe, or to tackle any of his office work. He sat for several minutes deep in thought before he sighed in resignation. There was nothing for it. Despite the lateness of the hour he would have to visit the warehouse now and hope Mrs Cudbull was up and about very early in the morning to take delivery. The daunting task of trying to load the wardrobe single-handed onto the lorry he decided not to think about, shoving it aside along with all the rest of his problems. He just thanked God the deluge of rain that was battering hell out of the corrugated roof above his head seemed, for the time being at least, to have lessened and prayed that it stayed that way until his task was completed.

His stomach grumbled loudly and he realised that the last time he had eaten had been a snatched slice of toast eighteen hours before. Standing, he picked up the lorry keys. Food would have to wait until he returned. That was, of course, if he wasn't too tired to make the effort to prepare it after he had washed his shirts.

# Chapter Six

Jenny swallowed hard and made herself look directly into the anxious face of the man sitting opposite her on a moth-eaten chaise-longue. She herself perched on the very edge of a worn leather armchair. The rain, although slightly lighter, was still bouncing rhythmically off the roof above and inside the building it was cold and damp. Clutching her sodden coat tight to her, she shuddered. 'Honestly, I'm fine now, really.'

Now she was calmer, Jenny didn't know which of them had been the most terrified when they had come face to face, the flickering from a candle making both their faces appear grotesque.

One thing she was sure of was that the piercing scream she had emitted when she had seen his shadowy figure moving towards her had been more than loud enough to wake the dead. So shrill it had caused the man to drop the candle, once more plunging the building into darkness. The sudden loss of light had sent Jenny's own terror soaring to fever pitch and she had somehow managed to convince herself that the end of her life was only seconds away. It had seemed like an eternity as she stood rigid with shock, her heart hammering so hard she thought it would burst, while she listened to the man she expected to attack her scrabbling around for the candle and making several attempts to relight it.

When the flame was rekindled they had both stood, eyes

wide, mouths gaping, eyes locked on each other for several moments before the man had finally spoken, his voice rich and deep with a thick accent Jenny had never heard before. She had to concentrate extremely hard to decipher just what he was saying. It took her several moments to realise he was trying to calm her fears and apologise for frightening her.

But then, this was her very first face-to-face encounter with a man from the West Indies.

Jenny's knowledge of West Indians was scant, consisting of not much more than half an hour's talk followed by a short ciné film given by her teacher as part of a series of lessons on world cultures. The lesson had been interesting but it had left her, like the rest of her classmates, little the wiser about any of the nations they had studied. Buried deep in her mind and almost forgotten were memories of herself as a very young child on several occasions standing alongside her mother, watching a platoon of black American soldiers parade proudly through the town on their way to their billet on the Braunstone Park. The black soldiers, along with those from many other nations, were long gone now and the streets of the city of Leicester were once again mainly pounded by the feet of its Anglo-Saxon population.

That population was slowly changing, however, being swelled by different cultures as immigration to other countries became easier and was actually encouraged by the government, offering a somewhat exaggerated promise of a better life to many.

At the beginning of the fifties, boatloads of hopefuls from the West Indies started to arrive at Southampton docks, carrying their sparse worldly possessions in suitcases. By 1956 a handful of them had found their way to the city of Leicester. Jenny was aware of a growing West Indian presence in the city of her birth. As she had gone about her daily business, she had herself on several occasions passed a gathering of two or three black men on a street corner – which wasn't of particular note to her as white men did exactly the same – and the odd black woman with a child shopping in the market. Preoccupied with her own thoughts, she had not taken much notice of them, nor they of her.

She had heard the grumblings and fears voiced by some of the locals as these strangers to their shores began to make their presence felt. Jenny herself had enough to do coping with the ups and downs of her own life to bother forming opinions on matters of which she hardly knew anything and which didn't particularly affect her. And besides, to her way of thinking, people were people, regardless of their origins.

She realised he was speaking to her again.

'You sure you're all right now, miss?'

She took a deep breath. 'Yes, really.' She shifted uneasily and looked upwards, feeling an urgent need to get home, away from this situation. 'I wonder how long it'll be before this rain stops?'

She brought her gaze back to him and for the first time since her ordeal took a moment to take a proper look. Despite the poor light of the paraffin lamp he had now lit, she realised in surprise that before her sat one of the handsomest men she had ever come across in her life. He was big. Everything about him was large. But he wasn't lardy like Antonio Brunio. Underneath the thick layer of clothes this man was wearing his body was well-toned, that much she could tell. He was, she guessed, not much older than herself. Early-twenties, certainly no more. But it was his face that arrested her gaze. Dark chocolate-coloured skin smoothly covered his firm square chin, broad straight nose and high forehead. He had well-defined lips; black wiry curls cut short. But what held her attention was his eyes. They were large, and they were honest, looking back at her and radiating gentleness. A gentle giant, that's how she'd describe him. Suddenly any remaining fear within her vanished. She knew he was no more of a threat to her than she was to him.

Regardless, there was a niggle of discomfort in her stomach. There was something about this situation that wasn't quite right. It suddenly struck her as odd that if this man had been sheltering from the rain as she had been, he'd had to hand matches, candles, and then as if by magic a paraffin lamp.

Jenny shifted warily in her seat. 'Let's hope it doesn't last much longer. I expect you'll be wanting to get home, too. Oh . . .' Her voice trailed off as suddenly the truth of the situation struck her full force. 'You're living here, aren't you?' This was a question, not an accusation.

His face grew grave and he stared at her for several seconds before he took a deep breath. 'I am,' he answered slowly.

'And the owner doesn't know?'

He shook his head and looked at her worriedly. 'Are you going to tell the owner?'

'I've no idea who he is. Anyway, why should I? I've no more right to be in here than you have.' She looked confused. 'But why are you living here? I mean, well, it's awful. And it's cold,' she added, shivering. 'It's a wonder you haven't frozen to death.'

His lips tightened grimly. ''Tis better than nowhere. It was this or the streets. I came across this place by accident while I was looking for somewhere to spend the night. Couldn't believe me luck when I tried the door and it was open and then I found all this furniture. It was like God Himself was looking down on me. I couldn't get anyt'ing else, you see.'

'You couldn't? But why not? There are plenty of lodging places in Leicester.'

'For you maybe. Not for me. I tried lots of places but every time they gone when I knocked on the door.' His mouth tightened grimly. 'Don't want us blacks living in their rooms. Weren't so bad in London but up here . . .' He shrugged his massive shoulders. 'People frightened of us. Probably t'ink we're goin' to steal their belongings and take advantage of their daughters.'

Jenny was staring at him agog. 'Oh, surely not . . .'

'Well, you explain to me, lady,' he cut in harshly, 'why else I get the door slammed in me face. I got money to pay rent, same money as white people. Money I earned.' He sighed long and loud. 'I'm sorry, I don't mean to shout at you. I just feel so . . .' He shook his head despairingly, voice filled with emotion. 'I had such hopes, such plans for my future. I never thought it'd be like this. And it's so cold! I wish I'd stayed in Jamaica. I wish I'd never come to this Godforsaken mother country.' His bottom lip trembled. 'And I miss my Blossom,' he added miserably.

Jenny stared at him, shocked, his acute misery filling her being. Were people from foreign parts really being treated so appallingly? If this was indeed happening, she had no excuses to offer. Instead she asked, 'Who's Blossom?'

'My wife.'

Jenny's heart went out to him as she tried to imagine how he felt, alone in a strange country, far away from his wife and family and unable to secure a proper place to live. Never having been in that situation, she couldn't. Suddenly her need to go home was overridden by deep concern for this man's plight and a strong desire to find out more about his background. 'How long have you been in England?' she asked.

'About four months, but I've bin away from me home for longer than that. It took nearly three weeks on the boat to get here. We stopped off at all sorts of places picking up people just like me, emigratin'. It was good on the boat, like we were all havin' an adventure. I was so excited about gettin' here and starting me new life but when the boat docked and I looked over the side across the town, I got such a shock.'

'You did? Why?'

'Well, I thought all of England was filled with factories.'

Her eyebrows arched in confusion. 'I'm sorry, I don't understand. Why would you think that?'

'All the chimneys. The black smoke. We don't have chimneys on our houses in Jamaica. We only need the fire to cook with.'

'Oh, I see. It doesn't get cold at all then, where you come from?'

'Not enough for a fire. And I was shocked to see the children.'

'The children? What about them?' asked Jenny bewildered.

'Some had no shoes and their clothes were ragged and dirty. In my country only black children had no shoes and dress like that. All white folks were rich, had nice houses, we worked for them, they were our bosses. It was strange to see . . . well, white folks like us. With no money.'

'Oh. So you thought life in England for white people was just like in Jamaica?' She smiled wryly. 'The people I know all struggle to make ends meet. My mam and me live from week to week, hoping we can pay the rent at the end. Living well, you really have ter be born to it or just plain lucky to win the pools.' She eyed him with interest. 'What did you do for a living in Jamaica?'

'I worked in a shop, wrapping. For fifteen years I wrapped parcels.'

'Fifteen years?' blurted Jenny without thinking, swiftly doing calculations in her head which didn't add up. 'Why – how old are you?'

'Twenty-five. I started at ten in the shop. Before that I helped my father and brothers on a banana plantation. Sometimes I was too tired to eat. Up at five and didn't finish 'til after eight. It was hard work and we didn't earn much, just enough to feed us all really.'

Jenny was staring at him. Her vague memories of the lesson at school had led her to believe that the West Indies were paradise. Life was slow and easy for the adults, a permanent playtime for the beautiful, doe-eyed children on golden beaches edging clear seas. Magnificent bright flowers grew in abundance as did coconuts, bananas and other exotic fruits, many she'd never heard of, just ripe for the picking whenever you were hungry. This man's description of his life at home wasn't mirroring what she had been taught at all.

'But there's no future in plantation work, not for the black people,' he continued. 'I thought the shop would give me a better one. I was wrong. The boss, Mr Harold, he wouldn't let me do anyt'ing else. Said I was a wrapper and that was it.' He laughed, a deep rich bellow. 'I wanted to get on. To do better t'ings. I wanted to prove I was just as good at serving as any white man and was determined to do so. When Mr Harold was out on business I went into the shop to serve the customers. They liked me, I did a good job. I got caught and Mr Harold, he threatened me with the sack if I did it again.'

'And did you do it again? Go into the shop and serve?' she asked, amused at his nerve.

'Yes. Lots of times.'

'And this Mr Harold sacked you then?'

'No, threatened, but I was a good wrapper. He wouldn't get better than me. He could trust me, see.'

Jenny eyed him in admiration. She could relate to what he was saying, judging from her own experiences in the china shop. Its hierarchical system meant promotion was hard-earned and a long time coming but she would never have had the nerve herself to disregard the rules in order to get on. 'So you continued to serve when you thought he wasn't around and he'd threaten you each time he caught you, I take it?'

'Just like that, miss. It was just like that.'

'So when did you decide to come to England?'

'After Blossom and me got married. I tried to get a better job but Mr Harold, he wouldn't let me go, told other bosses I was lazy. I was stuck in that shop being a wrapper. I knew the only way to better meself was to come to England. Lots of people were coming. It was all some talked about. It's a good life in the mother country, they said. Lots of work. Good money. I could get a house. Then I could send for Blossom. I knew I had to come. I talked it over with my family and they all wanted me to go. Scraped together all the money for my ticket on the boat. My grandmother sold her table to help. Blossom, she cried but I told her it wouldn't be for long before I sent for her. We would work together to save enough to buy some land of our own back home and build a proper wooden house with plenty of rooms for a family to grow and I'd start my own business. I'm not quite sure doing what, but anyt'ing so I wouldn't be workin' for someone else.' His face grew sad and he sighed long and loudly. 'England is nothing like I thought. I've managed to send some money home but not much. Not enough for Blossom to come over. And how can I send for her when I've nowhere to live? And 'specially now I know about the baby.'

'Your wife is having a baby?'

He nodded. 'In about three months. I got a letter from her before I left London. She never wrote it – Blossom can't write. The mistress she works for did it for her. I learned to read and write from the nice missionary lady from the church and I was goin' to teach Blossom, we just never got around to it. She didn't want to tell me about the baby before in case I got worried but she couldn't hold off no longer. She wants to come, you see. Have the baby here. Be a family together.

'I made my way to London first. Got a job as a bus conductor. That was decent enough. Money was a lot more than I got back home. I liked the job, it was better than wrapping. But London is noisy, too big, I didn't like it there, and the money just . . . went. People always hurrying about, no time for anyt'ing. I shared a room in a house with four men from Trinidad. We slept on mattresses on the floor and there was big black t'ings running up the wall. And rats. Man, they were big enough to scare me to death.

'We had not'ing to cook on, so we had to eat out all the time. The food was greasy, taste awful, it upset me stomach. Faggots – ugh!' he said, pulling a wry face. 'I never eat anyt'ing so disgusting.'

'There's nothing wrong with faggots. In this country beggars can't be choosers,' said Jenny defensively, then felt ashamed at her sharp tone, feeling that this visitor to her country had a right to express his opinion. And besides faggots, regardless of the fact they were one of Leicester's favourite dishes because they were cheap and filling, were not to everyone's taste. 'So, what kind of things do you eat in Jamaica then?' she asked politely.

'Lots of t'ings. Salt fish, rice and peas is me favourite.'

It sounded disgusting to Jenny but all she said was, 'Oh.'

His face suddenly puckered. 'Oh, what I'd give for some salt fish now.' His head drooped, chin resting on his chest, and his voice was thick with emotion. 'I miss my home so badly. I just want to go back but I can't 'cos I haven't enough money for the ticket. When one of the men from Trinidad told me he had a cousin up here who'd let us live in his house and help us get a job, I jumped at the chance. I used nearly all I'd got on the train ticket. But we couldn't find this cousin – he gone off, no one knew where or when he'd be back. The house he was livin' in, well, it was worse than the one I stayed in in London. I was offered a mattress in a room with six other men and asked to pay ten shillin' a week for the privilege.' He raised his head and looked at Jenny. 'I was desperate for a place to stay. But, lady, not that desperate.' He cast his eyes around him. 'This place, it might not seem much to you, but it's a palace compared to that. The man I came with went back to London but I couldn't afford a return ticket.'

Jenny's mouth tightened grimly. 'And I gather you haven't had much luck in Leicester?'

He did not answer.

'How long have you been here?'

'Four days.'

'Oh, not long then,' she said lightly, hoping she sounded positive. 'What about work? Have you tried yet to get a job?'

He nodded. 'I start on Monday cleanin' the public toilets in the market place. Pay not so good, but it'll do 'til I gets somet'ing better.'

Jenny tried not to show her distaste. The underground public toilets in the market were dire to say the least and a place she avoided at all costs. The kind of people who frequented them would more than likely steal your belongings if they could. Still, Jenny thought, at least this man had a job, which was more than she had. 'Yes, as you say, it's something to be going on with. It's just a thought but have you tried the Corpo?' she asked.

He eyed her blankly.

'Sorry, the Corporation buses. If you liked your job in London well enough, surely you'd like it just as much here too?'

'I been down several times, but the boss man he always too busy to see me. "Come back," he keep sayin'. I keep going back but he still too busy to see me.'

Jenny shook her head. 'That's nothing unusual,' she said ruefully. 'Some people in Corporation positions seem to think they're gods. I had a boss a bit like that too. He seemed to think he owned me lock, stock and barrel because I worked for him. But you'll not give up, will you?'

He nodded. 'I try again tomorrow.'

They lapsed into silence. Jenny suddenly realised he was staring at her. 'Is anything the matter?' she asked, a mite uncomfortable.

'What? Oh, no, miss, no. It's just . . . well, you the first white person I really speak to proper.'

'Am I?' she said, shocked. Though he'd already told her he'd not exactly been made welcome since his arrival in England so she shouldn't really have been surprised. She took a deep breath. 'I'm sorry you've not exactly found us very hospitable. I expect it's as you say, people are . . . wary of strangers. Well, they are, aren't they? Of anything they don't understand.'

He looked worried. 'Are you frightened of me?'

'I have to be truthful, I was when we first met. But that wasn't because you're black, if that's what yer mean. You could have been white, yellow, green or blue – it was the situation that terrified me.' Jenny leaned forward and held out her hand, a broad smile on her face. '*I'm* glad to meet you. My name's Jennifer Jeffries. Jenny to me friends.'

He smiled, revealing very pink gums and a set of big, strong-looking, white teeth. A large hand grasped Jenny's and shook it vigorously. 'Herchell Lloyd George Williams. I'm very pleased to meet you too.'

She laughed. 'Blimey! That's some name. I've no middle names at all.' And with a twinkle in her eye she told him, 'I asked my mother once why she called me Jenny, seeing as nearly every other girl in my class at school was called Jenny too. She said that when I was born she laid me on the bed, called me all the names under the sun, and when she said Jennifer I smiled. So Jennifer it was. It was probably an attack of wind that made me smile. I suppose I was lucky I had the attack when I did – I could have ended up with something really awful, like Florrie or Gertrude. Herchell,' she said, sitting back. 'I've never heard that name before. It's nice.'

'T'ank you. It's common where I come from.'

'Oh, so we're both common then. But Herchell doesn't sound common to me. It sounds . . . grand, like you should be a prince or something.' A thought suddenly struck her and, tilting her head, she raised an eyebrow and said, 'You asked if I was frightened of you when we first met, but I bet I ain't wrong when I say you were just as frightened of me. You were, weren't you?'

'I was,' he admitted. 'I thought you were the owner of this place and I was about to be thrown in jail. When I heard the door opening I dowsed the lamp and sat as still as I could, hoping whoever it was would go away. Then I heard you callin' out and thought you'd somehow seen me.'

'Lucky for you I wasn't the landlord. I've a feeling you wouldn't like the food in prison.' She flashed a hurried glance around the immediate area illuminated by the paraffin lamp. 'You can't stay here, you know. Shame,' she added, bringing her attention back to him. 'You've arranged the furniture nicely.' She exhaled slowly. 'I know they're not very welcoming places but there are hostels for men. One or two in Leicester, I think. I don't know what the terms are but at least you get a bed and I think some sort of meal in the evening. It's got to be better than this at any rate. And,' she added, 'you don't risk a prison sentence for trespassing.'

He scowled. 'I spent me first night here in a hostel. You're right, they ain't very welcoming. All the men were drunk. They were fighting and carrying on. I was robbed of the last of me money while I managed to get some sleep.'

'Oh, I'm so sorry,' Jenny said remorsefully. 'I can understand then why you prefer to stay here.' Her mind worked frantically, wondering what she could do for this man. 'Look, if it'll help I could try to find out if there are places to rent around where I live?'

He looked at her, astonished. 'You'd do that for me?'

'Yes, why not? You need some help, don't you?'

He sighed. 'I do.'

'Well then. There's all sorts of people live in our streets. Irish, Scottish, Welsh.' She pulled a face. 'I'm not keen on the

Welsh meself. Mr Jones is Welsh, he lives several doors up from us. Doesn't like the English, makes no bones about it, so we don't have much to do with him or his family, though his daughter's nice and if her dad hadn't been so strict with her I think we'd have become friends. There are a couple of lovely Indian families living nearby. Mrs Patel I think her name is, she can't speak a word of English but she always smiles when you pass her by. Anyway, I'm sure if there's 'ote going to rent near us you'd stand as good a chance as any. And me trying to help will show you we English ain't all bad.'

He smiled in gratitude. 'I'd be grateful of anyt'ing. T'ank you.'

'You're welcome. Now, when was the last time you ate a proper meal?'

'I had soup and bread at the hostel. It was . . . okay, but not very hot.'

'That's what I thought. You can come round to us for dinner tomorrow night. Might not be up to much but it'll be hot, I promise yer.' Thoughts of just what food could be put in front of her guest, considering their financial status, and just what exactly her mother's reaction would be to her inviting this stranger, came worryingly to mind. Jenny pushed them aside. Her offer was made, too late for retraction, and besides, his delight at her invitation was written all over his face, and Jenny couldn't bring herself to dispel it. 'You can meet me mam,' she continued. 'You'll like her, she's . . .' Her voice trailed off and her head turned to look behind her, eyes staring nervously into the pitch darkness beyond. 'What was that?' she whispered.

'What was what?' he asked.

'That noise?'

Herchell cocked his head. 'I didn't hear anyt'ing.'

Outside the wind was howling, the rain still battering on the tin roof above. Inside, the near pitch-dark expanse beyond the reach of the sparse light the paraffin lamp was giving off seemed to form an eerie damp cloak around the two people sitting on chairs in the small circle of furniture Herchell had arranged. An icy shiver ran up Jenny's spine. Shuddering, she turned her attention back to him. 'It's this place. It's giving me the jitters. I don't know how you can stay here on your own.'

'Jitters?'

She shuddered again. 'It's spooky. I feel like someone's watching us. It's just my imagination, that's all.'

'You were right, young lady, someone *is* watching you. Just what is going on here?'

At the sound of the deep voice so unexpectedly booming out they leaped to their feet, both staring into the darkness and watching open-mouthed as a figure emerged to stand just before them. The flickering light danced over the man's features, making him appear menacing.

For the second time that night, terror ran through Jenny and she clutched her sodden coat tightly to her.

'Well?' the man demanded, eyeing them each in turn. 'Is one of you going to answer me, or do I fetch the bobbies?'

'We . . . weren't doing n'ote, mister,' Jenny faltered, finding her voice. 'I . . . we . . . we're just sheltering from the rain. Honest, that's all we were doing.'

The man advanced further, taking in the arrangement of the furniture. 'Really?' He looked Jenny straight in the eye, face grave. 'I'd say you're lying to me, young lady. You broke into my warehouse first and now you're both living here, aren't you?' he accused.

'No, sir,' Herchell spoke up urgently. 'This lady, she tellin' the truth. She just shelterin' from the rain. I'm the one who goes to jail. It's me that's bin livin' here, sir. But I never broke in. The door wasn't locked.'

'Unlocked? But you're still trespassing on private property and that's against the law.'

'Oh, but you can't send him to prison, mister,' Jenny blurted, panic-stricken at the thought. 'He's only here 'cos he's nowhere else to go. He's only bin days in Leicester and he's bin treated rotten. He's had his money stole. He's . . .'

'All right, young lady, all right. You've made your point.' Bill Wadham sighed, eyeing the two anxious people before him. He was bone weary after his dreadful day and had enough problems to deal with without handling this on top. All he wanted to do was get Mrs Cudbull's replacement wardrobe loaded and be off home.

When he had arrived at his warehouse the full implications of the door being unlocked hadn't quite registered in his fatigued mind. The voices he had heard on entering had brought him up short, making him think he had burglars.

Fuelled by anger that a break-in had taken place and he was in the process of being robbed of the furniture that was to form the backbone of his new business venture – whenever he found the time to begin it – he had crept inside to investigate, fully expecting to be greeted by a gang of men carrying out their illicit task. It hadn't occurred to him to summon the police and let them deal with what could have been a potentially dangerous situation. Of all the things that could have been going on, the very last thing Bill had expected to find, though, was a man and a woman apparently having a cosy chat in a circle of his furniture that had obviously been chosen carefully from the pieces round and about.

He had to admit, though, these two people were not acting like thieves. The girl's story about sheltering did have the ring of truth to it. Her dishevelled appearance was proof enough. He wasn't quite sure about the man's tale, though. There were plenty of places to live in Leicester without choosing a run-down warehouse. The fact that did strike him as odd was that the girl seemed to be quite at ease in the black man's company, though the man's race was of no consequence to Bill. People were people to him. He was only too well aware that the West Indian people, like many other nations, had more than played their part in the war effort, something that was hardly spoken of when credit for the Allied success was being given. But Bill knew that the fact he was standing here a free man, in a country free from aggressors, could not have been achieved without the participation of the West Indian people who had showed unquestioning loyalty to what they regarded as their mother country.

But, regardless, that had nothing to do with the situation here. He took a deep breath. Were these two people in truth lovers? Were they hiding from her family or something? Bill's mind whirled frantically. Did he fetch the police and let them deal with this, or did he take their word and let them go?

Herchell was staring at him, petrified at the thought of landing in jail in this strange country. What would Blossom and his family say then?

He wasn't the only one frightened of being hauled off to prison. Jenny too dreaded being locked up for something she hadn't done, and was even more afraid of what May's reaction would be when she found out. She looked at Bill pleadingly. 'Please, sir, we're telling the truth, honest. You can see for yerself we've done no damage. If we were robbers, would we be sitting here talking?'

Bill sighed. The girl was right. There was no evidence he could see to incriminate them. Besides, he hadn't the energy at this particular time to take matters further. 'All right, you can go. But be warned, usually I visit the warehouse daily and if I see either of you hanging about, I'll get the police and no messing.'

'Oh, but you can't chuck Herchell out! He's nowhere to go,' Jenny cried in alarm.

Bill's jaw dropped. 'Listen, young lady, this is not a lodging house, it's a warehouse, and it's not fit for anyone to be living

94

in. Now I'd just go while the going's good, if I were you. And heed what I said. If I see either of you hanging around here again . . .'

'Oh, yer won't mister, yer won't,' she insisted.

'No, you won't,' agreed Herchell. 'T'ank you, sir, t'ank you. Would . . . er . . . you like me to put the furniture back as I found it before I go?'

His offer confirmed for Bill that his decision had been correct. No self-respecting criminal would offer to tidy up after himself. He hid a smile. 'No, it's quite all right. Just get off, the pair of you, before I change my mind.'

Bill watched as Herchell hurriedly collected his belongings, stuffing items into a shabby brown suitcase, and then the pair of them picked their way through the clutter of furniture towards the door. As they disappeared from view, Bill's eyes settled on a wardrobe. It was made of walnut, along plain lines and in reasonable condition, one of the better pieces on which he'd hoped to make a reasonable profit. But it was ideal for Mrs Cudbull and he didn't begrudge the old dear the few shillings he would have made on it. He suddenly wondered though how he was going to manage to drag it outside then load it on the lorry single-handed. Exasperated, he scraped his fingers through his hair. He must have been mad to think he could tackle that task by himself. An idea suddenly struck him. He felt it was worth a try.

'Hold on a minute!' he called to Herchell and Jenny.

At the entrance the pair abruptly stopped and turned, worried about what was to come. Had this man changed his mind and decided to call the police?

Bill addressed Herchell as he made his way towards him. 'You said you've been living here for a couple of days?'

Gulping, he nodded.

'Right, then, by way of rent would you help me load a wardrobe onto my lorry?'

Astounded, wondering if he had heard the man right, Herchell stared at him.

'Well, will you?' Bill asked. 'I suppose you must think me mad to be asking your help in the circumstances, but you see . . . well, I'm in a bit of a pickle.'

'Pickle?' Herchell asked, frowning.

'In a bit of a jam. Er . . . speaking plainly, I need help.'

A smile of relief split Herchell's face. 'Yes, sir. No problem, sir. Be my pleasure.'

'I'll help too,' offered Jenny.

Relief flooded through Bill. 'Good. Then let's get to it.'

The loading was swiftly done. Bill was amazed at Herchell's strength and his willingness to take instruction and follow it correctly. And the girl had done her bit in the dim light, guiding them through the maze of old furniture and holding open the door. She had even helped cover the wardrobe with tarpaulin and secure it. Due to the lateness of hour and extreme weather conditions, none of this was easy. By the time they had finished they were all soaked through, Jenny for the second time that night.

In the shelter of the doorway, Bill shook Herchell's hand. 'Thank you. I appreciate your efforts.' He turned to Jenny. 'And you, miss. Right then, I'll be off. Er . . .' He eyed Jenny awkwardly. 'I trust you have a home to go to?'

'Yes, I have,' she replied defensively. 'I told you I was just sheltering from the rain. It's Herchell who hasn't a home.' And she added sharply without thinking, ''Cos he's black no one will let him have a room, that's why he was living in your warehouse. Better than n'ote, ain't it? And he's a nice man. It ain't right.'

Bill frowned quizzically. 'Is this true?'

Herchell nodded, shifting his feet uncomfortably. 'Seems that way to me, sir.'

Grimacing, Bill considered this. If it was the way West

Indian strangers were treated, he felt extremely embarrassed to be English. He couldn't find anything to say to excuse it. 'Oh, well,' he blustered uneasily, 'I'm sure not every landlord acts that way. Maybe you've just been unlucky. I happen to know there are several lodging places on Belgrave Gate you could try. In fact my man Owen Ford lives in one. It's my guess his landlady's only interest is that her lodgers can pay their rent. In the meantime there are a couple of hostels . . .'

'He's stayed in one already,' Jenny cut in. 'That's where he got his money pinched. He must think we're all horrible and it's about time he found out different.' Turning to Herchell, she said without thinking, 'You can come home with me. We ain't got much room but I'm sure you won't mind kipping on the settee 'til we find you summat proper. I hope you don't mind that the sofa's a bit lumpy, though. And I'll warn yer, me mam might create a bit. But once she knows the full story she'll be okay. Come on,' she ordered, hooking her arm through his.

'I can't put you to that trouble, Jenny,' protested Herchell. 'I appreciate your kindness, though.'

'You can and you will,' she responded firmly. 'I wouldn't see a dog out in this weather, and neither would me mother. Now come on, I said,' she ordered, striding forward into the lashing rain, dragging him along with her. 'Goodnight, mister,' she called to Bill.

He watched them for several seconds before his better nature took over and he shouted, 'Just a minute, let me at least give you a lift. It'll be a bit of a squash but I'm sure you won't mind. And . . .' his voice trailed off as he hesitated for a moment, wondering if he was about to make a very grave error. But to Bill it seemed a shame that this big man, whom he had to admit did have an honest look about him, after all the other bad experiences he seemed to have had, was about to spend an uncomfortable night on a lumpy settee when Bill had a comfortable spare bed. Spare room, in fact.

It used to be his mother's before she passed on. But he knew that if she had still been alive, she would without hesitation have taken the stranger into her home and made him most welcome. Bill's mother had harboured no prejudices against man nor beast, and had passed on that open-mindedness to her eldest son. He took a deep breath. It wouldn't do any harm for him to offer the use of his room for one night, and might in turn make some amends for the dismal way in which this man had been treated since arriving in this country.

Bill realised they were both staring at him.

'I've got a spare bed,' he said to Herchell. 'You're welcome to it, lad. Just for the night, mind. Be better than a lumpy settee. I've spent a few nights myself on my sofa when I've been too tired to get myself up the stairs and I've suffered the consequences in the morning. Anyway, it'll save this young lady getting into trouble with her mother.'

Herchell was far too stunned by the offer to answer.

Bill laughed. 'I'll take that look on your face to mean you're delighted to accept then, shall I?'

Herchell nodded vigorously. 'Oh, yes, sir. T'ank you, t'ank you.'

'My pleasure. And will you stop calling me sir? My name's Wadham. Bill Wadham. Now, for goodness' sake, let's get off. Oh, I'd better make sure this door's well and truly locked first.' He added with a twinkle in his eye: 'Don't want half the waifs and strays of Leicester using this place as their abode, do I.'

Jenny and Herchell both saw the funny side of his comment and laughed.

The lorry clanked and groaned as it pulled to a juddering halt outside Jenny's front door. The noise it made had several neighbours yelling, 'Fer God's sake, shut that racket! There's people sleeping.' As Jenny clambered out, the door to her house burst open and May, dressed in a rumpled dressing gown, hair filled with pink and blue rollers and a cigarette hanging from the corner of her mouth, appeared on the threshold. Her face contorted thunderously.

Folding her arms, she bellowed at Jenny: 'Where the 'ell you bin?'

Flinching from what was to come, Jenny ignored her, playing for time. She hadn't bargained on her mother discovering she had left the house and wasn't prepared for an inquisition. And the last thing she wanted was the embarrassment of a scene in front of Herchell and Mr Wadham. Let them get off first then May could vent her wrath all she wanted. The neighbours were used to it.

'Don't forget, tomorrow night, about eight, Herchell,' Jenny reminded him as she shut the door. She waved to the occupants as the lorry pulled away. It backfired and a cloud of thick black smoke billowed from its rusting exhaust pipe.

'What's that bleddy contraption running on? Coal?' May grumbled, eyeing the lorry with disdain as she wafted the disgusting-smelling smoke away from her. She took a drag from her cigarette. 'Anyway, gel, I asked you a question,' she barked as Jenny made her way towards her. 'Where the 'ell 'ave yer bin? It's one o'clock in the morning. And what's this about tomorrow night, eh?'

She eyed her mother hesitantly. 'It's a long story, Mam.'

'And I'm listening. Now get inside,' she said, giving Jenny an unceremonious shove across the threshold. 'I'm gettin' bleddy soaked out here. Eh, and was that a black man I saw? What you doing with a black man?'

'His name's Herchell and he's from the West Indies,' Jenny said, stripping off her wet coat as she arrived in the back room. The cold there hit her and she shuddered. 'Is there any tea made, Mam?' she asked hopefully.

'I'll give yer bleddy tea! Stop stalling, sit down and tell me what's bin going on?'

Twenty or so minutes later, May lit her third cigarette since Jenny had arrived home and blew a thick plume of smoke into the air. She knocked the ash off the end into the tin lid she used as an ashtray and pulled a wry face. 'Huh,' she grunted. 'I'm still mad at you for going out like that, late as it was. Anything could 'ave 'appened ter yer. Fancy going into a strange place like that! You'd 'ave bin safer getting wet. That Histall chap coulda bin a murderer for all you know.'

'His name's Herchell, Mam. And I've told you . . .'

'Don't care what yer told me, just don't do it again,' May cut in angrily.

Jenny flinched at her tone. Her mother was renowned for her sudden temper which could flare up without warning and have the recipient quaking in their shoes but she never usually showed such aggression towards her daughter, and certainly not for such a simple thing as going out without notice. She'd done it before, though admittedly not so late in the evening and in such bad weather.

Jenny could understand May having a go at her out of worry, but what she couldn't understand was why her mother was so furious. There was something going on here Jenny couldn't quite fathom and for a fleeting moment it crossed her mind to wonder if it had anything to do with what had transpired earlier in the evening, something she still hadn't got to the bottom of.

What Jenny could not understand, and what was really fuelling May's anger, was a fear so great that even her strong-minded mother was having difficulty controlling it.

May had risen not long after Jenny had left the house, having been unable to sleep, the shock she had received earlier still preying heavily on her mind. On finding the house empty it had struck her like a lightning bolt, May immediately thinking Jenny's disappearance was connected with their visitor. That she had returned and somehow enticed Jenny away. Panic stricken, not knowing what to do, she had paced the back room like a woman possessed, smoking cigarette after cigarette.

The eventual noise of the lorry pulling up at her door had sent her racing to the front window, the sight of Jenny alighting causing such a surge of relief to flood through her that for a moment May had felt faint. Despite not being religious she had thanked God profusely for Jenny's safe return and for the fact that the girl's departure did not appear to have had anything to do with earlier. Regardless, it wasn't in May's nature to let her daughter get away with worrying her so, despite its being innocently done.

'You do that ter me again, our Jenny, and I'll paste yer senseless,' she warned.

'I've said I'm sorry, Mam, what more do you want me to do? I didn't make it rain. And I'm not a young child – I'm twenty, yer know. I don't know why you're making all this fuss.'

'I'm well aware of 'ow old yer are.' She leaned forward and looked Jenny straight in the eye. 'And if yer give me any more lip, I'll knock you to kingdom come, young madam.'

Jenny knew May was just threatening. Her mother had never smacked her in her life. Well, except for the odd wallop when she had misbehaved as a child and in truth had probably deserved it by pushing her mother's patience to the limit.

May took another drag from her cigarette. The smoke hit her lungs and she gave a loud hacking cough. When the spasm had subsided, she blew her nose noisily into a grubby handkerchief. Shoving it back into her ripped pocket, she glared at Jenny in annoyance. 'Yer left all the lights on when yer went out,' she accused. 'I've had ter put another tanner in the meter. The 'lectric woulda lasted 'til tomorrow if you'd 'ave turned them off. I took the tanner out yer purse.'

'Ah, Mam, that were for me bus fare to town tomorrow to look for a job.'

'Yer'll 'ave ter walk then, won't yer? And serves yer right.' A memory suddenly struck May and she eyed Jenny questioningly. 'What's this about eight o'clock tomorrow night? What's 'appening then?'

'Oh, er . . .' Jenny eyed her mother sheepishly. 'I forgot about that. I've . . . er . . . asked Herchell to come around for something to eat.'

'Yer've what? And how d'yer think yer gonna feed this . . . what did yer say his name was?'

'Herchell. He's from Jamaica.'

May's eyes bulged. 'Now 'ang on a minute. I ain't having *him* in my house. Whatever were you thinking of?'

'Mother,' Jenny proclaimed, 'all I was thinking of was asking a very nice man to have a meal with us. He's a stranger here and it's comments like that have made him feel very unwelcome,' she retorted.

'Well, that's just it, he's a foreigner,' snapped May. 'They're different from us. Got funny ways.'

'And we English haven't? Anyway, Tony was a foreigner, and if anyone had strange habits *he* did.'

'Tony weren't foreign, he was Italian. But I'll agree with you he did have some peculiar ways. Anyway if this black man comes to dinner what are the neighbours gonna say?'

'Oh, Mam,' Jenny said in exasperation. 'When have you ever worried about the neighbours? Look, I've asked him now so it's too late. And the least you can do is make him welcome. He's been treated very badly since he arrived here. Had all his money stolen and can't get lodgings 'cos people like you think that just because his skin's dark it makes him a murderer or summat worse.'

'I never said that.'

'Well, what *are* you saying then?'

May couldn't answer her. She just sniffed haughtily and took a long draw on her cigarette.

'Look, Mam, it ain't like you to be narrow-minded. Just be nice to him, eh? I feel sorry for him, that's all. Just want to show him not all English folk are unfriendly.'

'As long as sorry for him is all you feel.'

'Mam! Herchell is married and has a baby on the way. He's very homesick. If you feel you can't sit in his company, you can always go out.'

'Oh, I can, can I? And you tell me how, with no money, now you've lost yer job?' That comment was uncalled for and May knew it. In a roundabout way it was her fault Jenny was now unemployed. And the girl was right. It wouldn't hurt her to be civil to this man for a couple of hours. If her daughter liked him then that was good enough for her. It was just May's nature to make simple things difficult. She enjoyed it. 'And what d'yer propose to give him? Bread and scrape? 'Cos that's all we've got.'

'Oh, I never thought. I don't think he'll be that bothered, though. As far as I know he hasn't had a decent dinner for days.'

'Neither 'ave I,' May grunted, blowing out her cheeks. 'And none of us, including this chap Hossell, are gonna get n'ote decent tomorrow night either. Have you forgotten you've no wage to collect this week? We'll be lucky to scrape enough to pay our dues, let alone 'ote else.' Tutting loudly, she shrugged her shoulders. 'Oh, I suppose the dues can wait, and you could always get summat on tick from the butcher. Tell 'im some cock and bull about yer old granny dying or summat. That'll land us a pound of beef sausage and three faggots. And, eh, mek sure whatever he gives yer is fresh. Just 'cos I can't pay on the nose don't mean he can palm us off with old stuff.' She

103

suddenly narrowed her eyes. 'You ain't asked the other chap too, have yer?' she asked worriedly.

'No, just Herchell.'

'Thank God fer that.'

Jenny gnawed her bottom lip anxiously. 'Herchell doesn't like faggots.'

May eyed her, astounded. 'Wadda yer mean, he doesn't like faggots? Nothing wrong with faggots. Good solid food is faggots. If he don't like 'em, he can leave 'em.'

'Come on, Mam, it ain't right to give a guest what you know he doesn't like.'

May stabbed out her cigarette. 'I suppose not,' she said grudgingly. 'So what does he like then?'

'Salt fish, apparently.'

She pulled a face. 'Salt fish? What on earth's that?'

Jenny blew out her cheeks. 'Dunno. But he likes it with peas and rice.'

'Oh, I've got rice, half a packet left over from the last rice pudding you made. But are you sure these folks from Jamaica eat rice pudding with their main meal? Sounds disgusting to me.'

'That's what he said.'

'Oh, well . . . Anyway, peas ain't a problem either, just remember to put a basin full in soak in the morning.' May paused thoughtfully then proclaimed, 'Salt fish ain't no mystery. Just cod sprinkled with plenty of it before it's fried. There, problem solved. Though I can't say I fancy any of it meself, but for the sake of hospitality I'll grin and bear it.' She gave a loud yawn and stretched herself. 'I'm off ter bed. And being's you're a lady of leisure, yer can get up in the morning and get me breakfast.'

Jenny always got the breakfast. If it was left up to May they'd both go out to work on empty stomachs. But she decided it was best not to comment. 'I'll bring you a cuppa in bed, shall I, eh, Mam? With plenty of sugar?'

May smiled, Jenny's peace offering restoring her good nature. 'And an arrowroot biscuit so I can 'ave a good dunk.'

'We haven't got any.'

'Oh.' She gave a haughty sniff. 'Then I suppose the tea will 'ave ter do.'

# Chapter Seven

'Ah, there you are. Did you sleep well?'

Standing just inside the doorway, Herchell eyed Bill hesitantly. When he had woken a short while ago he had received a shock. In the comfortable bed he had been dreaming of home, transported back to his land of sun, surrounded by the familiar faces of his family, and in his dream he had made tender love to his Blossom under the stars.

As he had woken he had been cruelly transported back to the cold, austere climate he had chosen to come to just a few months ago. He had opened his eyes fully expecting the damp, musty-smelling interior of the old warehouse to greet him. Instead his eyes had settled on rose-patterned wallpaper. The pattern was faded, the paper itself worn very thin in parts, having lined the uneven walls for many long years, and the once-white paint covering the cracked ceiling and old wood-work was yellowing now, but all the same it was a welcoming room.

He had lain motionless for quite a while, recalling the events of the previous night and trying to make sense of them. He had found it difficult. With the exception of the missionaries, whom he'd found a rather strange group of people with their insistence on reading and writing only stories about Our Saviour, white people had never shown him generosity or courtesy before. In all his life he had never been treated by them in such a courteous manner or on equal terms. This attitude was alien to him and, despite having no reason to doubt his two new-found friends, he couldn't quite bring himself to accept this novel situation without wondering what the catch was.

A vivid picture of Jenny rose before him. Before Mr Wadham's offer she had been prepared to take him home, risking her mother's wrath, and he was still reeling from her invitation to sit at their table. He'd never received such an offer before. Never expected to. In Jamaica, black people did not sit at white people's tables, they waited at them after they had done the cooking. His immediate thoughts on waking had been that the events of last night had been just a dream. But they hadn't. Couldn't have been or he wouldn't be in this house.

He realised Bill was still waiting for his answer and took a tentative step forward.

'I slept very well, Mr Wadham, t'ank you. The bed was very comfortable.'

'Glad to hear it. To me there's nothing worse than having a rotten night's sleep to ruin the day ahead.' Bill paused for a moment, taking in the fact that Herchell was dressed for outdoors and already carrying his battered brown suitcase. 'Not thinking of leaving without some food in your stomach, surely? Come and sit yourself down. I'm not much of a cook, I'm afraid. Actually I usually make do with toast, so you being here was a good excuse to have a decent breakfast myself. Two eggs or one with your sausage?'

Herchell's mouth dropped open. 'Pardon?' he uttered.

'I said . . . never mind, I'll do you two. One's not going to be enough to fill a big man like you. Help yourself to tea. And will you stop looking so worried, man? I'm not going to bite you.'

A while later, sipping a mug of tea, Bill watched thoughtfully as Herchell finished off his meal. He had been mulling over a proposition since he had woken that morning and still wasn't quite sure whether to put it to Herchell or not. After all, what did he know about the man? Not much. Still, how much did he know about anyone to whom he offered a job? Only what they told him, and to his cost many times he had found that to be nothing but lies. At least he had witnessed this man's strength when he had helped load the wardrobe last night. And he was polite, which was more than Bill could say about some of the youths he'd employed.

He pursed his lips. The fact was, he urgently needed help. 'Desperate' actually described his need if he wanted to keep his business going. No time to advertise or interview. He had to have help today. This man could be the answer. Bill just had to hope Herchell Williams would be agreeable to his offer. He decided to wait until his guest had enjoyed his breakfast, though, before he put his proposition to him.

It didn't take long for Herchell to demolish what Bill had placed in front of him and it was obvious by the way he ate that he relished every morsel.

'So,' Bill began as he poured them both a fresh mug of tea, 'I know you haven't anywhere to live, but what about work?'

'Work? Oh, I've work, Mr Wadham. Start on Monday as a lavatory attendant in the public conveniences in the market place.'

Bill's heart sank. Mind you, he thought, cleaning toilets was a permanent job, not the temporary one he would be offering until his men were fit enough to return. Regardless, it was Bill's opinion, despite what little he knew of this man, that he was capable of far more than merely cleaning toilets for a living.

'Well, you've a job, that's good. Means your money problems are solved at any rate. And I expect you'll be wanting to spend today getting somewhere to live?'

'That was me plan, Mr Wadham. You did say you knew of

places that might take me. I'd be grateful if you'd give me the addresses.'

'Yes, of course.' Bill thoughtfully rubbed one hand over his chin as an idea struck. 'Would you be interested in a day's work first? I'd pay the going rate, of course, and if we don't get time to suss out some lodgings you could always stay here again tonight. Look for a place tomorrow. I really am desperate for another pair of hands. Would you be interested?'

Herchell didn't need to think twice about Bill's offer. His dark face lit up. 'Yes, sir, Mr Wadham. I'd be very interested. That bed was very comfortable. I had the best night's sleep since I arrived here and I'd be quite happy to do anyt'ing so I get to sleep in it again. I have to be honest and say until last night I've never slept in a proper bed before. We all sleep on matting at home.'

'Oh, really?' It sounded dreadful to Bill. 'I suppose I take a lot for granted and a bed's one of those things.' He smiled. 'So we have a deal then?'

'We do indeed, Mr Wadham,' said a delighted Herchell.

Bill eyed the woman standing before him in utter disbelief. Despite what Herchell had told him about his reception by white people he was unprepared for this response and completely taken aback by it. 'I beg your pardon, Mrs Taylor?'

Mrs Taylor, a small, skinny, middle-aged woman whose pinched scowl reminded Bill of someone sucking lemons, folded her thin arms across her flat chest and took a stance. 'You heard me correctly, Mr Wadham.' She lowered her voice. 'You never mentioned about *him* when you came to price this job. I ain't having no nigger in my house. Don't know what he'll get up to, do I? I've one or two decent bits. And I've me daughter to consider.'

Bill's eyes flashed to the young woman hovering behind her mother in the doorway. She was aged about seventeen, he guessed, with a very shapely figure for a girl of her age. She was of medium height, with a round pretty face which was plastered in makeup, lips ruby red which Bill felt unseemly for such an early hour. Her hair was the brassy yellow-blonde only achieved by bleaching, ends brittle and dry from a cheap home perm. Her hands were fixed tightly against her waist in an effort to emphasise its trimness; full breasts thrust upwards and outwards. She was running her tongue provocatively over her lips, eyes fixed on Herchell who was standing by the lorry, totally oblivious to the young woman's attention. The girl was a first-class hussy if ever Bill had seen one. In his opinion they should worry for Herchell's chastity not Mrs Taylor's daughter's.

Bill felt exasperated. He'd faced many tricky situations in his line of business and had dealt with them to the best of his ability but he wasn't sure how to handle this one. It was totally beyond his understanding that someone could unthinkingly brand another human being with a catalogue of bad traits just because of their colour. He was incensed by this woman's ignorance and fought to keep his anger from showing. 'Well, I'm sorry you feel like that, Mrs Taylor. I'll say good day, then.'

'Eh? Now just a minute, Mr Wadham, I've n'ote against you, just him.'

He took a deep calming breath. 'With due respect, Mrs Taylor, you hired me to do a job. That doesn't entitle you to choose who works for me. Now I can fully vouch for Mr Williams. If that's not good enough for you, I'll take my leave. It's up to you to hire someone else.'

Her face fell in dismay. 'But it's too late – I've to move today.'

'Then if you want to, I suggest you let me and my man get on with it.'

Mrs Taylor sniffed haughtily, glancing up and down the street, on the lookout for nosey neighbours. Several were standing on their doorsteps and the twitching of net curtains across the street could clearly be seen. Typical of these streets, her audience was growing by the second. 'As long as he don't come in,' she said, inclining her head towards Herchell.

'And how do you propose I shift your furniture single-handed, Mrs Taylor?'

'Well, that's up to you. My husband agreed a price for you to do the move. How many people it takes is your problem, not mine.' She eyed Bill sourly. 'I'm surprised at a man of your standing, Mr Wadham, employing a man like that. They don't wash, you know, and they've never heard of knives and forks. And now they're coming over here, taking our men's jobs, stealing the food from out of our babies' mouths . . . We're not safe in our beds, you know. I don't know what the government is thinking of, encouraging them to come. One of them tried to rent a house down the road. Well, we soon put a stop to that, I can tell you. Particular we are who lives in our streets.'

'Oh, really?' Bill replied matter-of-factly. 'When Mr Williams sat at my table last night he certainly knew what to do with the cutlery I gave him, and as for the new bar of Lifebuoy I had on the wash stand, well it was half-gone after his scrub down before he got into bed last night.'

'He's living in your house?' she said, aghast.

'As you so bluntly pointed out, it isn't easy for the likes of Mr Williams to get decent accommodation so until he gets settled elsewhere, yes, Mrs Taylor, he is and a better lodger I couldn't wish for. Now, with all due respect, you are entitled to your opinion but I happen to think you have been listening to people who haven't a clue about life beyond these streets. The local hooligans are more of a threat to your daughter than Mr Williams is, and I would stake my life he's also got more morals about him than the grocer on the corner who robs his customers blind by putting his prices up when things are in short supply. Now, if you'll excuse me, I've another job to start

112

at one and time's running out. Mrs Pickles, I know for a fact, won't be bothered about the colour of the man who's helping her move. She'll just be grateful we've turned up and for the fact that we'll do her a good job. She'll be pleased to let us start earlier. Good day, Mrs Taylor.'

She was staring after him, agog.

Bill made to walk away but Mrs Taylor launched herself off the step and grabbed his arm, pulling him to a halt. 'Look . . . er . . . I was too hasty. Just . . . er . . . keep an eye on him. I'm still not happy about all this but you've got me cornered.' She tossed her head haughtily. 'I'll mash *you* a cuppa, shall I, while you make a start?'

Bill took a deep breath, forcing down a great urge to tell this narrow-minded woman exactly what she could do with her job. But he couldn't risk his business reputation or losing the small profit this move would bring in. With a great effort he forced a smile on to his face. 'That would be much appreciated, Mrs Taylor. *We both* take two sugars,' he emphasised, knowing Herchell had not been included in her offer. But let her dare exclude him. If she did, then Bill would give Herchell his mug. See what she makes of that, he thought, hiding a smile.

# Chapter Eight

Leaning against the lorry just after six that night, Bill watched distractedly as Herchell washed his dirty hands under the outside tap. The water puddled and swirled against the almost blocked drain and Bill made a mental note to clear the dead leaves and debris that had gathered around it. Just another job, he thought, one of many he never seemed to get around to. But at the moment that problem was a minor one compared to all the rest he had, and certainly not important enough to override the idea he was considering.

As the day had progressed Bill had become increasingly aware that he'd be a complete fool to let such a hard-working and well-mannered assistant as Herchell slip through his fingers. As he had watched the man deftly carrying out his instructions and using his initiative to do things without being told, it had struck Bill what an idiot he had been in the past.

He had been so focused on trying to work out ways to bring in business with what limited resources he had, he had failed to look at matters from the most obvious standpoint: his work-force. As he had worked alongside Herchell it had slowly dawned on him that Owen must have spent a large part of his day labouring to keep the younger member of staff focused on the job in hand, keeping a constant vigil on what they were up to. This practice had cost Bill untold lost time and consequently revenue. He should have had the foresight to realise that he needed two men of the same calibre as Owen Ford on board, conscientious and reliable men who would contribute to the business instead of detract from it. Younger workers should be encouraged to take an interest in the business and motivated to stay with the firm when it expanded.

With a man like Herchell to work alongside Owen when he returned, fully recovered, Bill could safely hand over the procured jobs to them, leaving himself free to pursue further work and tackle the things he should be doing as boss of the business, maybe even find time for his household chores on a regular basis and some sort of social life. He knew this made sound business sense, but was also fully aware of the risks involved. Another wage would mean resources stretched to the limit. It meant he himself possibly living on bread and water and hiding from the rent man until Owen and Trevor returned and they were actually earning their money again. But if he wanted to progress, which in turn would afford him the means to give his men a better wage and job security, plus himself more than a basic standard of living, then he was prepared to make the sacrifice. But to start the process, first he had to persuade Herchell that his future working life lay with Wadham's Removals.

'Have you got a minute?' Bill asked him as the big man finished his ablutions and wiped his large hands on a grubby piece of cloth he'd found hanging on a nail behind the door in the office. 'I know you have to be over at . . .' he hesitated, unable at this moment to recall her name '. . . that young woman's house at eight. You've been invited for dinner, if I remember rightly. This won't take long.'

'Yes, Mr Wadham, sure,' Herchell replied, following him into the ramshackle office.

'Take a seat, man,' Bill said, indicating a rickety straight-backed chair piled high with odds and ends. 'Just put that stuff on the floor.' Bill perched on the end of his cluttered desk.

'And don't look so worried,' he added. 'I only want to settle up what I owe you and . . . well, I've a proposition I'd like you to think over.'

'Oh?' Herchell said, sitting down tentatively.

From his wallet Bill extracted a ten-shilling note. He handed it over to Herchell. 'A little above the going rate. You've more than earned it and I'm sure you'll find a use for it.'

In astonishment Herchell looked down at the money in his hand. It was three shillings over his daily rate as a conductor on the London buses and about three shillings more than his weekly pay as a wrapper in Jamaica. Tears of gratitude filled his eyes as Bill's kindness overwhelmed him. 'Ah, me neck back,' he muttered.

'What was that you said?' Bill asked, bewildered, wondering if it was a foreign language Herchell had lapsed into.

He raised his head. 'Eh? Oh, me neck back,' he repeated. 'It's just something we Jamaicans say when we get a surprise. I . . . I just didn't expect so much. Are you sure you've paid me right?'

Bill smiled. 'I don't make mistakes where money is concerned. I can't afford to. Now put it in your pocket and let me tell you what's on my mind.' He took a deep breath. 'First I have to say I was very impressed by how you handled things today – and you certainly showed that Mrs Taylor what you were made of. She was blatantly rude to you, Herchell, unforgivably so, and I apologise for letting her get away with it.'

'No need to apologise to me, Mr Wadham,' Herchell cut in. 'I understand you could have lost the job if you'd spoken up. Customers are always right, no matter what. Mr Harold used always to be telling me that and it's no different here than anywhere else. Anyway, I'm used to people being rude to me.'

'But that's just it, they have no right to be,' Bill retorted angrily. 'But, regardless, I was impressed with your polite manner towards her. She had no complaints when she paid her dues. Anyway, let's not talk about that woman any more, the thought makes my blood boil. Let's get down to brass tacks. You're just the sort of man I need working for me.'

Herchell's jaw dropped. 'You're offering me a job, Mr Wadham?' he asked warily, worried he had misconstrued Bill's words.

'I am, yes. I hope you might consider it a more attractive prospect than the work you were to start on Monday.'

Herchell stared at him agog. 'You mean that, Mr Wadham? Work for you, really?'

'After your efforts of today, absolutely. I have to be honest and tell you my business is just ticking over. I need to build it up, branch out, and I realised today that to do that I need the right kind of people working for me or I'll never be any more than I am now, a backstreet removals firm. I can't price for any more than small house removals because I've not the resources to undertake anything larger. I intend to put that right, Herchell. Somehow I've got to sort this business out and get it ship-shape. I'll start by employing you. That's if you want the job, of course. And I know you'll need time to think about it because you'll be taking a gamble too that I can continue paying your wages.'

Time to think about it? That was something Herchell did not need. He had not been looking forward to starting at the public conveniences. When the man from the Sanitary Department had showed him his place of work he had been utterly appalled and it had taken all his willpower not to refuse the job.

Today's labours had been a revelation to him. Working alongside William Wadham had been an utter joy. He did not bark orders, he asked. He did not talk condescendingly, he politely instructed. He liked a laugh. And after the payment Herchell had been given for his day's work, it was obvious Bill was a fair man. Working for such a man would be a dream come true, one he'd never dared hope would ever be fulfilled. Mr Wadham might think he was taking a gamble, but Herchell didn't. It was his gut feeling that Mr Wadham was as safe a bet as they came. Did he need time to think about it? Only as long as it took to get the words of acceptance out of his mouth.

'I'd be delighted to accept, Mr Wadham. And you have my solemn promise, I'll help you all I can to make the business prosper. Yes, indeed, sir. I'll start as soon as you like.'

Bill smiled broadly. 'I like a man who can make a quick decision. You'll fit in well, Herchell.'

He beamed at the compliment. 'Do you need me tomorrow?'

Bill nodded. 'I could do with you in the morning.' His eyes scanned the cluttered yard. 'I'd like to make a start getting this place in some sort of order.'

'Consider it done then, Mr Wadham.'

'We need to talk about your wages.'

'I'll take whatever you're offerin', Mr Wadham. Gladly, I will. I've never enjoyed meself so much doing a job. Working for you would be a pleasure. I have to be honest and say I wasn't looking forward to starting on Monday at the public conveniences.'

Bill sighed with relief. Taking Herchell on was going to prove one of his better decisions, that much he did know. A great surge of purpose filled Bill and for the first time in decades he felt life might actually hold some meaning for him.

He stood up and slapped Herchell on the shoulder. 'I'm off to visit my man Owen Ford in hospital tonight. I'll ask him if he can recommend any decent lodgings. We could go and inspect them tomorrow if you want to. Don't worry, if we find nothing suitable then you're quite welcome to stay at my place until you do.'

Herchell was far too overcome with emotion to comment.

'Now,' Bill continued, 'you have a dinner date and I've to be at the hospital for seven. Late arrivals earn the ward sister's disapproval, and that is not recommended. She has a face like a British bulldog and a manner to go with it, so we'd best be off.'

As Herchell walked alongside Bill on their way home, for the first time since his arrival in England he thought that maybe his decision to come here had been a good one.

# Chapter Nine

Herchell stared down at the concoction on his plate. It looked disgusting. The piece of cod that had been encrusted with a thick layer of salt before it had been fried was nothing like the fish back home that was lightly salted and then dried in order to preserve it. When required it was cooked gently in water along with spices, or fried with vegetables, and always tasted delicious. The dollop of white gooey-looking stuff which slightly resembled rice was nothing like anything his mother cooked. And as for the peas . . . this green mush was not what he called peas. Peas in Jamaica were red, something which the English he had found out since being here called kidney beans.

But then, in fairness, when he had described his tastes to Jenny that night in the warehouse, he had never envisaged her trying to cook this food for him. Had he done, then he would definitely have been more explicit.

But despite his concern about how he was going to get through this meal and appear as if he was enjoying it, one thing Herchell would never do was hurt these two very kind women's feelings. They had obviously gone to a lot of trouble to make him feel at home and he in return was very grateful to be sitting at their table. He was glad, though, he'd had the foresight to bring with him three bottles of light ale. Jenny's mother seemed to be appreciating it. She'd already drunk one.

He picked up his knife and fork and bravely tucked in.

From under her lashes Jenny watched Herchell, bemused, then looked down at her own plate and scanned the contents. How anyone could eat this with the relish Herchell was displaying was beyond her. She daren't look at her mother. May had voiced her views freely while they had been cooking it before Herchell had arrived. Very tactfully Jenny had asked her mother to be nice to her guest though she did not hold out much hope for this. The odds on May keeping her own counsel were low, and even lower with a drink inside her. Despite knowing it was futile, Jenny said a silent prayer to God that her mother would be on her best behaviour until Herchell had left. Tentatively, she picked up her knife and fork.

'Sorry, we ain't got any jam, Hostel.'

Jenny cringed, looking up at her mother, worried about what was coming next.

Herchell stopped eating and looked across at May. 'I beg your pardon, Mrs Jeffries. Jam?'

'Yeah, fer yer rice pudding. We always have it on ours but we ain't got any to offer yer. Bit boracic this week, being's our Jenny lost her job. But next time yer come, I'll mek sure we've some in.' She looked down at her plate and grimaced. 'Mind you, I ain't never had rice pudding and fish before. I don't somehow think jam would go very well with it.' She took a long draught of her drink, then gave Herchell a grin. 'Still, each to their own. What other funny stuff d'yer eat back home, then?'

'Mother,' Jenny whispered urgently, flashing May a warning look.

'What?' she said innocently. 'I'm only showing interest.' She leaned over and picked up a half-empty bottle of the beer. 'Top up, Tishell?'

'Mam, his name's Herchell,' Jenny hissed under her breath. She flashed him a broad smile. 'Everything all right?' she asked politely.

Mouth full of very salty fish which wasn't pleasant at all, he nodded vigorously. 'Yes, t'ank you,' he lied with the best of intentions. 'It's very nice.'

'Is it?' said May, grimacing. 'I think it's bloody awful meself.'

The comment Jenny had dreaded had been issued and she steeled herself for what was to follow.

'A'yer sure,' May continued, 'this is what you eat back home, Hassell? Honestly?'

'Mother!' Jenny hissed again. 'Will you stop it! You said you'd behave yourself.' She looked across apologetically at their guest. 'I'm sorry, please excuse me mother, she doesn't mean to be rude. But I'll warn yer, she'll get even worse when she's had another couple of beers inside her.'

'Rude! I'm not being rude,' May snapped, hurt. 'I asked a civil question, that's all. So then, Herchell,' she said, finally getting his name right, 'is this really the kind of thing you eat back home? If it is, then all I can say is, thank the Lord I wa' born over here.'

He gulped down what was left in his mouth, then reached for his glass of beer in order to wash the salt away, also by means of stalling while he searched for an answer to May's question. What a dilemma. How could he tell the truth without hurting their feelings? 'Well ... er ... yes, but ... done a bit different.' He prayed that would suffice.

His prayer went unanswered.

'What d'yer mean, different? Didn't we put enough salt on the fish then?' May asked.

'Oh, plenty,' he urgently agreed. Any more, he thought, and he would definitely have choked. Jenny and her mother were only picking at their food. He guessed they didn't like it any better than he did. 'I just meant different in the way me mother cooked it. She added bits and pieces – spices and vegetables – that's all.'

May sniffed. 'Oh, I see.' She pushed her plate away. 'I can't eat any more, I'm full. You can have my fish, Herchell. Don't like to see good food wasted,' she said, picking up her plate and making to scrape the contents on to his.

Before he could stop himself, mortified at the thought of having to eat another portion, Herchell snatched up his plate and held it protectively to him. 'No, it's all right, really, Mrs Jeffries, I've more than enough, t'ank you. You've been more than generous already.'

'Don't be silly. A big man like you could eat twice as much as you've got, so give over yer plate.'

He jerked it further out of her reach. 'No, really, Mrs Jeffries, I couldn't.'

Forkful of mushy peas poised mid-air – the most palatable portion of food on her plate – Jenny was staring with growing unease from one to the other. 'Mother,' she said evenly, 'Herchell doesn't want any more.'

'Of course he does,' May insisted.

It was then that the look of horror on Herchell's face registered and Jenny realised he could no more eat the food than they could. Mirth erupted from her and before she could stop herself she burst out laughing.

'What's so bleddy funny?' May demanded.

'All of this,' spluttered Jenny. She wiped her tear-filled eyes on the back of her hand. 'We've made a right cock up of this meal, haven't we, Herchell? This isn't a Jamaican meal at all, is it? In fact, it's just like me mother said – bloody awful. I'm so sorry.' She stood up and without further ado snatched his plate from him. 'I'm off down the chippy. Pie and chips do you, Herchell? I promise it'll be more edible than this.'

'Thank God fer that,' said a relieved May. 'I'm starving. Get me a pie, Jenny. On second thoughts, in for a penny, get me two. There's money in me purse, sod the rent man.'

A mightily thankful Herchell stood up, reaching inside his

jacket for the wallet that held his day's wage. He needed all he had received to pay his lodgings should he get some, or if not to offer to pay his way at Bill's, but regardless he did not begrudge one little bit buying these two lovely ladies some pie and chips considering what they had tried to do for him. 'Please, you must let me pay and fetch them,' he offered.

'Not likely,' said May. 'You're our guest, so get your bum back on that seat.' Bottle of ale in her hand, she leaned over and topped up his glass. 'While Jenny's away yer can tell me about yer home and what brought yer to England. And yer can stop this "Mrs Jeffries" nonsense. Call me May, all me friends do. Eh, and call in the offy on the way back, Jenny, and get another couple of bottles, I've quite got a taste for this.'

Just then there was a loud rap on the back door and seconds later Gloria popped her brassy blonde head into the room. 'Sounded through the wall like yer were having a party wi' all that laughin' going on. Got fed up waiting fer me invite so I've invited meself. I've brought a bottle with me,' she said, thrusting forth a bottle of draught sherry – cheap gut rot from the local off licence. Her gaze settled upon Herchell, quickly appraising his handsome features. 'So how long's it gonna tek yer to introduce me to this fine young fella?'

'I wondered how long it'd be before you showed yer face,' said May with a twinkle in her eye. 'Pass the sherry over 'ere. And yer can keep yer eyes off Herchell, I saw him first,' she added mischievously.

It was nearing twelve when Jenny, having satisfied herself that Herchell knew the way back to Bill Wadham's house, saw him to the door, with a firm promise that the evening would be repeated soon. She returned to the back room where Gloria was snoring loudly in the armchair, mouth gaping, empty glass in her hand, fat legs spread wide. Last week's pink drawers were obviously in the wash as tonight she was displaying pale blue ones.

Slumped in the chair opposite, May seemed deep in thought when Jenny came in. 'Are you all right, Mam?' she asked in concern. 'Mam, what's the matter?'

Her mother's head jerked up. 'Eh? Oh, I wa' just thinkin'.' She gave her daughter a wide drunken grin. 'Nishe man that Herchell,' she slurred. 'Very nishe man. Plays a mean game of cards. Wake that drunken sot up,' she said, eyeing Gloria in disdain. 'And show her the door or she'll be 'ere all night and demanding breakfast in the . . .' May stopped abruptly. 'Wass that on 'er head?'

Jenny looked across at her. 'Oh!' she exclaimed, horrified. 'Herchell's trilby.' Stepping across to Gloria, she snatched it up. 'I ought to go after him. Maybe he hasn't got too far.'

'Don't be daft! A bloody hat ain't a matter of life or death. I'm not havin' you traipsing the street at this time of night. It's gone twelve. Never know who's lurking,' she added as a vision of her unwelcome visitor of yesterday flashed to mind. 'Yer could drop it around his work place tomorrow. I know where it is. It's behind the wood yard on Sanvey Gate. Anyway, I ain't surprised he did forget his 'at, he'd had a fair few by the time 'e left. Just hope he manages to find his way home. We certainly gave him a good night, d'int we?'

'We sure did, Mam,' Jenny said sincerely. 'Thanks.'

'What yer thanking me for?'

'I just am. You were great, Mam, really made him welcome.' And she had, Jenny thought, after that bad start. May had been on entertaining form all night. The only time she had become unusually quiet was when Herchell was telling the story of how he came to emigrate to England. May had sat riveted, which had amazed Jenny. In all her life she had never seen her mother so engrossed before. It was as if she was sucking in and savouring Herchell's every word. She had even told Gloria to 'shut her trap' when she had interrupted Herchell with one of her quips. Most unusual, Jenny thought. Yes, definitely. Still, Herchell's

story was very interesting and her mother's attentiveness had meant Jenny herself had been able to hear it all properly.

Yes, the evening had been a great success and had achieved what Jenny had hoped. Showing Herchell that not all English people treated foreigners badly. 'I think Gloria took a shine to him,' she commented.

'She'd tek a shine to 'ote in trousers,' May scoffed. 'Mind you, I quite took a shine to him meself. He's a good-looking man. Pity he's married, and more's the pity I'm old enough to be his mother. Ten years younger and I'd have given him a run for his money.'

'Mother!'

May patted her hair. 'Don't *mother* me, I'm only being truthful. Turned a few heads in my day, let me tell you.'

'You still do, Mam.'

May sighed. 'Mmm,' she mouthed. 'But not the kind I really want to,' she mumbled.

'What was that, Mam?'

'Eh! Oh, n'ote, Jenny love. Just ramblin'.' May rose awkwardly and stumbled in the process, just managing to keep her balance. 'I've had more than I thought,' she giggled. 'I'm off ter bed,' she announced, ignoring the fact that the kitchen sink was piled high with dirty pots and the table still littered with empty bottles, glasses, full ashtray and scattered playing cards from their games of rummy.

Fortunately they had been playing for matchsticks as Herchell had completely thrashed the three of them, winning all but one game which May had taken because she had cheated. Gloria had been too drunk to notice May's sleight of hand; Herchell too polite to comment; Jenny too relieved that no one had challenged her mother and risked spoiling the evening.

'You ought to get ter bed too,' May said, yawning. 'You'll need all yer beauty sleep to look good at yer interview in the morning.'

'My interview is on Monday morning, not tomorrow, Mam. Sometimes I wonder if you listen to me.'

'Oi, don't be so bleddy cheeky! I knew you had an interview, just slipped me mind on what day, that's all. Anyway I don't know why yer bothering wi' another shop after the way you've been treated. I . . .'

'Mam,' Jenny interrupted. 'I'm *not* going to work in a factory. I like shop work.'

May sniffed dismissively. 'Your life, I suppose.'

'Yes, it is.'

'Well . . . goodnight then, eh, and don't forget about Gloria,' May said, inclining her head towards the snoring woman slumped in the chair. 'Don't want her ugly mug greeting me when I come down in the morning.'

Upstairs in her icy cold, sparsely furnished bedroom, May lay staring up at the cracks in the ceiling, unable to sleep. The muted sounds of Jenny clearing up downstairs were not what was keeping her awake, neither was it the amount of drink she had consumed. It was thoughts of Herchell. Without realising it, the man had had a profound effect on May. Not a woman to be easily impressed, the reasons behind his emigration to England had struck deep.

Like herself, Herchell had come from very humble beginnings, from good but poor people who lived from day to day, hoping a meal could be scraped together at the end of it and, if really fortunate, the rent be kept up to date. Her own mother and father had worked hard to raise their children and had died young, old before their time, from labouring to survive. And that's all May had expected of life, hadn't realised any more for the likes of herself was possible until she had sat and listened to Herchell. Like herself, he wasn't ashamed of his origins but wanted something better for himself and his family. And the man hadn't just talked about improving his lot, hadn't just spent his days wishing for it to happen, he had actually got off his backside and done something about it. Gone for the whole pound, not settled for the penny, and May admired his guts.

He had left his loved ones behind, the security of his homeland, and travelled thousands of miles to a strange country, not sure what awaited him there but knowing without doubt that life was not going to be easy. And despite what had befallen him since his arrival in England, his enthusiasm and sense of purpose had not waned in the slightest. Come hell or high water, he was going to make something of himself and didn't care what hardship he had to suffer to achieve it.

He had reacted like a child who had been given an expensive toy at Christmas when Bill Wadham had given him a job – which was in fact nothing more than labouring for a living with a backstreet firm – and he was going to seize this chance he'd been given, use it as his first step upwards.

May sighed deeply. She felt she herself hadn't done too badly considering she'd raised a child on her own. She had managed to keep a roof over their heads, food on the table, and life could have been worse, very much so. You only had to look at some of the poor sods living in the same street as them to realise that. Kids with no shoes on their feet, going for days on empty bellies, their dads having drunk their money away down the pub. Jenny had never suffered that, May had made sure. And to a certain extent she had been happy with her lot. But suddenly she wasn't. And it was all Herchell's fault. His thirst for self-improvement had woken in her something that had lain dormant for a long time and now was suddenly breaking free within her. She wanted more from life. Not riches, she wasn't a greedy woman, just something better.

It struck May forcibly that she had pinned all her hopes for a better life on others. And she suddenly realised with horror that she was about to embark down the same path again with Ron Bates.

Oh, she knew she had promised herself she wouldn't, but promises to herself were broken as easily as they were made. Before she knew it Ron Bates would persuade her to let him move in, promising her all sorts which would never materialise, and a year ahead, maybe less, he'd go the same way as all the others, she being left, older, no wiser, certainly no richer, and once again alone.

Without warning a great determination swelled within her. Well, not this time. No more Antonio Brunios and no more Ron Bateses. It had taken fate to bring a stranger to her table and show her that the only way to change your life is by doing it yourself.

And that's what she would do. And like Herchell, she would tackle it full-on. She wanted the pound like him.

But where did she start? It wasn't just one thing in her life that needed working on, in all honesty it was everything.

A vision of herself suddenly loomed. She forced herself to take a long hard look. For the first time she saw herself as others saw her. The pictures shocked her. She wasn't attractive and sexy as she had always thought, but cheap and trashy, her habits questionable. Since the only man she had loved had left her life so abruptly, she had let her standards slip. She drank like a fish and wasn't particularly nice when she was drunk; smoked like a kipper, and if truth be told was slovenly in her habits. She shifted uneasily in her bed. No wonder she never attracted the kind of man she'd always craved. They would never give her like a second look, would be too embarrassed to be seen with her on their arm.

A terrible thought suddenly struck her. If this clear-eyed vision of herself had May shuddering at the sight, what must Jenny have been feeling all these years? The thought didn't bear considering and she forced it away.

Pulling the bedclothes up underneath her chin, May tightened her lips. That was where she would make her start. On improving herself. Less makeup for a start. She knew that for her age she was still a good-looking woman, she didn't really need to plaster her skin with a thick layer of panstick. So she had a few lines. They were laughter ones, she convinced herself, not wrinkles, which in future she would dust lightly with powder. Her hair? She liked her style, it was modern, but maybe a softer blonde would be more appropriate. She'd save – not going to the pub so often for a start would save her a fortune – and treat herself at the hairdresser's. No, better still, one of her mates at work had a daughter training to be a hairdresser at the polytechnic who was always on the lookout for volunteers to practise on. She was ever so good, May's workmate bragged. Well, May would let her practise on her.

Next, clothes. Like all other women of her ilk she bought cheap from the market. Now she'd start making her own as she used to do until she had allowed herself to get to the stage where she couldn't be bothered to get the sewing machine out. Like her hair, the style of clothes she wore needed looking at. Jenny had an eye for classy fashion and would happily advise her. Money would, May was determined, be found somehow for materials, which needn't be expensive. As a seamstress she knew it was the finishing off that made all the difference to a garment.

One thing she must do and that was break the habit of permanently having a cigarette hanging from the corner of her mouth. She liked her fags, had no intention of giving them up, but she'd learn to smoke properly, like ladies do, cigarette held between two fingers and taking short dainty puffs. And she must learn to curb her temper and use of foul language. If she was going to move in better circles she must learn to put her brain in gear before she let rip with her mouth. She wouldn't drink so much either.

May could feel excitement grow within her as she meticulously planned.

Next came the house. She suddenly felt so ashamed of herself. It was a mess, there was no denying it, and it was mostly her own fault that it was that way. For years now it was Jenny who had tackled all the housework because May herself had grown lazy in that department. Cleaning up alone had been a thankless task, especially when the likes of Tony had been in residence. He had thought nothing of leaving his daily debris at the side of the chair for others to move, and to be honest May herself had followed suit. Well, she would clear all the rubbish out. Anything that wasn't of use she'd get rid of.

New furniture was out of the question but a bit of spit and polish on the old would go a long way to improving its appearance. She might be able to pick up a roll of cheap linoleum to replace the back room covering that was wearing very thin. May smiled to herself. The little house might not be in the best state of repair, or in the most salubrious area of town, but with a bit of effort the inside could be made to look much better. At least presentable enough to bring someone decent back to. Because that's what she was going to do.

Once she was satisfied that she and the house were transformed to the best of her ability she was going to set about finding herself a man, one who would look after her, treat her and Jenny well, a man who would want to support her financially, but most importantly someone she would be proud of.

One thing was for certain, she wouldn't find a man like that in the kind of pubs and clubs she frequented, amongst the kind of people she mixed with. She needed to go to better-class places. The kind where you didn't expect the evening to end fleeing a full-blown punch up between men too drunk to know what they were fighting about. The kind of places where a lady was treated with a bit more respect.

She turned over, dragging the covers protectively with her. She would start tomorrow. Before she turfed them out, the pile of old magazines stuffed at the side of the sideboard would give her some ideas. The articles she'd previously scanned and scoffed at, she'd read and digest and use in whichever way she could. She yawned long and loudly. All this planning combined with her consumption of drink had completely drained her. With a warm glow, a new sense of purpose filling her being, she closed her eyes and fell soundly asleep.

# Chapter Ten

'Now don't take that attitude, man. There's no need. I've taken Herchell on, not to take your place but to work alongside you. He's a good man, Owen. I'm sure you'll get on. Is it because he's black? Is that your problem?'

'No,' he vehemently argued. 'I've n'ote against foreigners. Yer know that, boss.' Owen eyed him shamefully. 'It's . . . well, it's as you assumed, boss. My first thought was that you'd brought the chap in to replace me.'

'Well that's daft, Owen. I've no intentions of ever replacing you.'

'I know that, boss. I'm sorry. It's just being in here, it's doing funny things to me mind. Too much time to think, I expect.'

'Well, just think on getting yourself better. I need you back, Owen, fit and well – don't forget that.'

Owen smiled. 'I won't.' He eased himself further up on his hard hospital pillows. His broken bones, legs encased in their plaster of Paris from toe to thigh, one arm from hand to elbow, hardly having had time to begin to mend, pained him excruciatingly and he winced.

'Let me help you,' Bill said in concern, leaping from his chair to aid Owen settle more comfortably by hooking his arm around his back and under his armpit and easing the man gently upwards.

'Thanks, boss,' Owen said gratefully as he lay carefully back. 'Doctor said I'll be in pain for a few weeks yet, but it'll gradually ease when me bones knit together. The tablets help. Sleeping is the worst. Can yer imagine what it's like trying to get comfortable with half yer body in plaster, and not being able ter bend? It ain't funny, believe me.'

Bill cast his eyes across the metal frame over the bottom half of the bed holding Owen's legs up in traction. 'What happens when you forget and try to turn over?'

'Just don't ask,' came the terse reply.

Bill sat down again on the hard hospital chair at the side of the bed. 'What's the food like?'

'Heaps better than I get in me lodgings. Three cooked meals a day and yer gets a choice. Coffee and biscuits at eleven, tea and a cake at three. Better than a hotel, if yer ask me. Not that I've ever stayed in one, mind. And apart from that misery of a ward sister, the nurses are wonderful. Though I can't say as I enjoy the bedbaths.' He pulled a face. 'Bit embarrassing, boss.'

'Really?' Bill said, hiding a smile of amusement. 'I'd have thought you'd have enjoyed that bit.' He glanced down the ward for a moment then brought his attention back to Owen, his face suddenly sombre. 'So, are you going to tell me what was on your mind before you fell or don't you want to talk about it?'

Owen tightened his lips, eyeing him sheepishly. 'I s'pose I do owe you an explanation. But all I can say was that me mind was wandering and that's a fact. It shouldn't have bin. I should have had all me concentration on me job.'

'Well, none of us is perfect, Owen, and I don't hold it against you. I'm just sorry about whatever it was that caused you to land up in this mess.' Bill eyed him knowingly. 'Can I assume I was right in what I said just before the accident – that it *was* something to do with your lady friend that was bothering you?'

Owen inhaled sharply. 'N'ote escapes you, does it, boss?' He sighed heavily. 'Yeah, yer right. Mrs Daily's given me an ultimatum. She wants us to get married.'

'Oh.' Bill stared thoughtfully at his employee for a moment. He'd known the man for over ten years. Owen Ford had been the first employee he'd taken on when he had started his business and he had never regretted that decision. During that time he had come to know him fairly well as they had gone about their work and a mutual respect had grown between them. General chit-chat had gleaned Bill an outline of Owen's homelife, such as it was, of his past; of his likes and dislikes. Owen was, he supposed, attractive to the opposite sex. He kept himself well with the resources he had. But what had always surprised Bill was that the man, despite seeming to have his fair share of liaisons, seemed most reluctant to settle down. He'd never been married as far as Bill knew. 'And . . .' he ventured. 'Do I get the impression you don't want to get married?'

'No, I don't, boss. Not really. The thought, well . . . it terrifies me if yer want the truth.' Owen sighed despondently. 'Mrs Daily . . . Muriel . . . she's a good woman who'd look after me, I've no doubts on that. I get on with her kids. Bit boisterous, but they ain't a bad lot. But . . .' His voice trailed off and his eyes glazed over.

'But what, Owen?' Bill prompted.

Lips pressed tight, the man stared blankly at him. To Owen one's innermost thoughts were private, not to be discussed with anyone, even his boss whom he respected. Men, he had been raised by his dear, long-dead mother to believe, were supposed to be the stronger sex, and how could you live up to that if you let others see your weaknesses, things about you that could be used against you? Not that Bill, he knew, would ever break a confidence or use any trait in another's character to his own advantage, but all the same Owen could not break the habit of a lifetime. He would keep his own counsel.

Besides, disclosing his reasons for refusing Muriel's proposal would mean revealing to Bill parts of his past and having to admit to making a stupid mistake over twenty years ago. He had suffered dearly ever since for that one silly male act of pride, and the way he was heading he would do until the day he died. And that was all to do with a woman.

But what a woman!

His mind flashed back to the last day he had seen her. Her face, that beautiful face, the one he still saw clearly every time he closed his eyes to sleep, was wreathed in bewilderment, totally unable to understand why he was so against her plans. He had not listened to her reasons, tried to understand why she had felt she had no choice but to do as she was about to. Her decision had appalled him. He had been twenty-three years of age at the time, full of his own importance, convinced he was worldly wise when in truth he was almost as innocent in some matters as the day he had been born.

When she wouldn't back down and comply with his wishes and drop what he felt was a stupid idea, he felt his male pride had been attacked and had childishly stormed off to sulk, fully convinced she'd chase after him and give in. But she hadn't, and by the time he had admitted his own pig-headedness, summoned up enough courage to try and put things right, the great love of his life had disappeared, seemingly off the face of the earth and he had never seen her since.

He sighed long and loud. Despite the passing years, his love for her was still as strong as ever and the pain of her loss was just as unbearable now as it had ever been. In the circumstances, marrying Muriel wouldn't be fair on the woman and he knew he could never truly be happy with any other than the one he still loved, the one he had spent all these years mourning, and whom he knew deep down was lost to him forever.

Owen felt he couldn't be truthful to Muriel when he refused her proposal because it would hurt the woman too much to know he didn't feel about her the way he did about another. Neither could he open his heart to the man he had such respect for because he did not want to appear stupid in Bill's eyes for a mistake he'd made so many years ago and lived with ever since. All he said was, 'I've bin too long on me own, boss. I wouldn't tek to marriage.'

'Are you sure, Owen? She seems a very nice woman, what little I know of her.'

'I'm sure, boss.' And to change the subject he asked, 'Why ain't you never married? That's always had me wondering. Yer a good-looking man and I've seen the way women look at yer, though you never seem ter notice.'

'Oh, I notice, but like you I'm a bachelor at heart.' Painful memories threatened and Bill tried to avert them. 'Anyway,' he said lightly, 'I've never met a woman who'd put up with the hours I have to work.' He eyed Owen gravely. 'Take a bit of advice and put Mrs Daily out of her misery if you've made up your mind not to marry her. She deserves to know that at least.'

'Yeah, I will, boss, I will,' he replied, not relishing the prospect. He did after all like Muriel very much, and hated the thought of upsetting her, which a refusal was bound to do.

'Good man. Now, to put your mind at rest, I've been to see your landlady and paid your lodgings and I'll continue to do so until you're back to work. I'll take care of anything you need in the meantime as well. Before you say it, I know I don't need to but no employee of mine is going through the rigmarole and embarrassment of claiming sick entitlement from the government. How much is it anyway? Not enough to stop you lying here worrying. I'm doing the same for young Trevor. Popped in to see him on my way here. He seems comfortable enough on his mother's sofa, with her fussing around him. I know it's no consolation to you, Owen, but I do thank God his injuries are minor compared to yours. A cracked ankle. Six weeks should see him back to work. Though it's my opinion he was none too happy about that, quite put out he didn't suffer as bad as you.'

'Ain't surprised,' huffed Owen. 'Lazy git, that one. Head stuffed wi' being a Teddy Boy. That's all he ever talked about. And girls. No interest in work at all.'

'Well, that's most young men these days for you. His mother was pleased about me paying his wage whilst he was off. She snatched the money out of my hand.'

Owen eyed him in concern. 'I am grateful fer what yer doing, boss, but I know the business can hardly stand it and it bothers me how yer gonna do it.'

'Leave that to me. Me and Herchell between us will keep things going. As I said before, I want you back as soon as possible, Owen. Fully recovered, mind. I want it in writing from the doctor. Then I'm going to build up Wadham's Removals.' Bill spent the next fifteen minutes outlining his plans for the company's future. 'So, what do you think?' he asked when he had finished.

Owen looked at his boss admiringly for several seconds. How lucky and privileged he felt. How many working men, he thought, had a good job with a decent boss to work for, one who laboured hard to look after his employees and many times to the detriment of himself? Owen suspected that on numerous occasions over the years the weekly profits had left hardly anything for Bill himself by the time he'd paid everyone else. But Owen would never demean him by voicing his suspicions. A man who had started a business with nothing more than a ramshackle lorry paid for out of his demob money, and in the face of overwhelming odds managed to keep it going for over ten years, deserved respect to Owen's way of thinking.

He considered Bill's plans and pondered them. He liked the sound of this man Herchell and was looking forward to working alongside him, but best of all he liked the part concerning the young member of staff – Bill's idea of getting Trevor really involved in the operation, building his interest, and then hopefully loyalty and conscientiousness would follow. Owen himself had despaired many times in the past of the way the young lads had used Bill's good nature to their own advantage, despite Owen's endeavours to the contrary. But you'd have to have eyes in the back of your head to counteract some of their wily ways. Lazy and disinterested most of them had been, only showing any keenness when pay packets were being handed over, though they were quick enough to grumble about how much more they could be earning in another job. 'Go, then,' Owen himself had angrily told them. 'Go and work in yer factories or such like, and then come back and tell me if the bosses are as fair as Mr Wadham is.' And most of them had taken his advice and lived to regret it.

Still all that was in the past now according to Bill. His plan was sound to Owen's mind. He couldn't find anything to question in it and nodded in approval. 'All sounds good to me, boss. And yer know you can count on my full support in whatever yer do.'

'I know that, Owen, but regardless, thank you.'

'I think you've got yer work cut out regarding young Trevor, though.'

'I hazard you're right. Still, I can but try.'

'This man . . . sorry, boss, what did yer say his name wa'?'

'Herchell.'

'Funny name that. Still, he sounds a good man and I'll happily have him alongside me. We could maybe handle two removals in one day, even three.'

'That's what I'm hoping for, Owen.'

'Shame we can't get another lorry,' he mused. 'A covered one. Keep the bad weather off the furniture. We could price for posher removals with a decent lorry.'

141

Bill sighed. 'My thoughts exactly. But I can't afford one at the moment, more's the pity, though it's certainly high on the agenda.'

Footsteps clattering on the hospital tiles made Bill turn his head. 'Oh, hello, Mrs Daily. Enjoy your cup of tea?' he said, rising in gentlemanly fashion.

The plump, mousy-haired, jolly-looking woman who was approaching tutted loudly as she adjusted the tatty strip of fox fur trimming on the collar of her shabby black winter coat. 'Weak as dishwater and only lukewarm to boot. But that's 'ospitals for yer. All right, dear?' she clucked, leaning over to give Owen a peck on the cheek, which made a loud smacking noise. 'Had a nice chat with yer boss, have yer, ducky?' She spoke as though he was a child.

After his conversation with Bill, Owen reddened in embarrassment at Muriel's intimate attentions.

Bill saw this and said, 'Thanks, Mrs Daily, for leaving us alone. Just a few work-related matters I needed to discuss with Owen. He's all yours now, though.' Just then the bell announcing the end of visiting time rang loudly. 'Oh, sorry, I've talked longer than I should have,' he said remorsefully.

She smiled good-naturedly. 'Don't you go fretting yerself, Mr Wadham. I know my Owen is your right hand. I just hope you can manage without him while he's off. I don't know,' she said disdainfully, 'what that woman was thinking of letting her child abandon them roller skates in such a silly place. It's a wonder my Owen didn't break his neck. His injuries are bad enough but I expect we should be thankful it weren't worse.'

'Pardon?' Bill said, frowning. 'Roller skates?'

Muriel looked at him as though he was stupid. 'The ones my Owen fell over at the top of the stairs in the house yer were doing the removal in.'

Bill flashed a look at Owen, whose face was sheepish. 'Oh, yes,' he said, a twinkle in his eye. 'Those skates. How could I

142

forget? The woman was very sorry, I can assure you, but I can't hold her responsible for what her six year old did,' he fibbed. 'Well, I'll leave you two to say your goodbyes.' He leaned over and shook Mrs Daily's hand. 'Nice to have met you.' He addressed Owen. 'I'll pop in early next week and . . . er . . .' He flashed a quick glance at Mrs Daily, then back to Owen. 'Think about what we discussed.'

Owen nodded. 'I will, boss, and I'll sort it out.'

As Bill strode off down the hospital ward he heard Mrs Daily ask Owen what that was all about. He was quickly out of earshot so could not catch the reply. He just felt glad he didn't face Owen's task of breaking to Muriel Daily the news that he wasn't going to marry her.

As Bill pushed open the double doors leading out of the ward and stepped through the gap, his attention was immediately drawn to a woman at the other end of the corridor. Her profile to Bill, she was in conversation with a doctor.

He froze rigid, eyes fixed on her, the rest of the world suddenly non-existent. After all these years, there she was. So far, yet so near. How long he had prayed for just such an occasion and now he was presented with it, his legs wouldn't move, his brain wouldn't function.

Only feet away was the woman who had been the cause of all his misery for the past twenty years. A woman he had loved more than life itself and whom he had known had loved him as much in return once. They had planned to spend the rest of their lives together. Until, that was, others had intervened.

Despite not having clapped eyes on her for two long decades he would have known her anywhere. She would be forty-four now, but to him she hadn't aged one iota, was still as beautiful as the last time he had seen her. 'Val,' he murmured. Even saying her name after all this time brought him untold pain, years of pent-up emotion welling within him. It took all his strength not to rush to her now, grab her hand and drag her off

143

with him, regardless of the consequences. But he couldn't do that. She was another man's wife. And that man was his own brother.

The woman turned slightly and Bill held his breath, afraid she would become aware of him. His mind raced frantically. What did he do? There was only one way out of the hospital and that was through the doors behind Val. To go there would be impossible without her seeing him. He couldn't risk that, not so ill prepared. But then he saw her shake the doctor's hand, and before Bill knew it she had gone.

He stood staring blankly at the doors, swinging backwards and forwards in her wake before finally coming to rest. His encounter had all happened so quickly, lasting brief seconds rather than minutes, and now he was wondering if he had imagined it all.

'Are you all right, sir?'

The question shook Bill out of his trance. It was being asked by the young doctor to whom he had seen Val talking. 'Er . . . yes, I'm fine, thank you.'

The doctor continued on his way and a worrying thought suddenly struck Bill. He stepped quickly after him. 'Excuse me, doctor,' he said, catching him up.

The young man stopped and faced him. 'Yes?'

'The lady you were speaking to just now. Is there anything wrong? I mean, she's not ill is she?' Bill asked urgently.

The doctor eyed him quizzically. 'Are you a relative?'

'Yes,' he replied truthfully. 'I'm her brother-in-law. My name is Bill Wadham. I've been visiting an employee of mine who had an accident. The men's ward, just there,' he said, pointing. 'I just happened to see Mrs Wadham when I came out, but she'd gone before I could stop her and ask what she was doing here.'

'Oh, well, in that case I suppose it's all right for me to tell you.' The doctor paused, taking a breath. 'It's not good news,

I'm afraid. Mrs Wadham's father died this morning. She was just collecting his belongings.'

Shaken rigid by this news, Bill's face turned ashen. 'Mr Collier, dead?' he gasped in disbelief, and eyed the doctor questioningly. 'How . . . what . . .?'

'A massive heart attack,' the doctor cut in. 'There was nothing we could do for him. He died just after he got here.' He placed his hand on Bill's arm. 'I'm sorry, Mr Wadham.'

Bill felt as if all the stuffing had been knocked out of him. 'Thank you, doctor,' he uttered, fighting with all his strength to keep his emotions in check. He couldn't believe it. Ernest Collier dead. Poor Val, what pain she must be suffering. Father and daughter had been very close. Bill fought to quash a great longing to race after her and offer his condolences, maybe give her some sort of comfort. But he couldn't do that. Years ago Valerie Collier had made it very clear she wanted nothing at all to do with him and he had no reason to suspect that situation had changed.

He felt a hand cup his elbow. 'Mr Wadham, this has obviously come as a shock. Would you like to sit down in Sister's office for a while? I could get one of the nurses to bring you a cup of tea?' the doctor offered kindly.

Tea might be what the doctor ordered but at this moment just the thought of anything passing his lips nauseated Bill. He gave a tight smile of gratitude for the younger man's thoughtfulness. 'I'll be fine, thank you. I need to get home.'

# Chapter Eleven

Jenny hadn't given a thought to what she would find at Wadham's yard. In reality she hadn't given the matter any consideration as she had walked there that brisk Saturday morning, tightly clutching Herchell's faded trilby as she navigated her way down several busy, grimy terraced streets, past assorted shops, pubs and factories, only stopping for a minute to watch a bargeman skilfully manoeuvre his boat through a narrow canal under the small hump-backed bridge she was crossing by the North Bridge public house before continuing on her way.

Of all the things she could have been thinking of – her desperate need to get a job and impending interview, worrying lack of money, the fact her friends seemed to have abandoned her since her abrupt dismissal from Stone & Son – she was concentrating on her mother.

May had been acting very strangely recently. There was still the matter of her unusual behaviour on the evening Jenny had lost her job, but this morning she had acted even more oddly and Jenny wasn't quite sure whether to be concerned or not. She'd also said some funny things which Jenny couldn't decipher. They'd make sense maybe if someone else had said them, but not coming from her mother.

Jenny's first shock had come when she had risen that morning to see May off to work, still dozy from her late night entertaining Herchell. She had padded her way into the back room to stop abruptly in astonishment on finding a fire blazing in the grate and the table set for breakfast. Coming from the kitchen she could hear the clatter of plates and smell toast burning under the grill.

'Mam?' she called. 'Is that you?'

'Who the 'ell d'yer think it is, yer daft bugger?' said a cheery-faced May, appearing in the doorway. She was carrying a plate of blackened toast and the teapot.

Jenny stared at her mother. There was none of the usual hangdog look after a drinking session, and she was washed, hair tidied, and dressed. This was all most confusing.

'Well, get yer arse on the chair before this lot gets cold,' May ordered, setting the teapot and a plate of toast on the table. 'And if the wind changes, yer face'll stay like that.'

'Oh,' Jenny responded, shutting her mouth. 'Er . . . you all right, Mam?'

''Course I'm all right. Why shouldn't I be?' she answered sharply.

. 'Well, it's just that you're usually the worse for wear the morning after the night before.' Jenny paused, thinking she ought to choose her words more carefully. 'What I'm trying to say is, you're not your usual self, are you, Mam?'

May reared back her head, placing her hands on her shapely hips. 'That's just it, Jenny love, I *am* meself. For the first time in over twenty years I am. And I'll be more so by the time I've finished.'

Jenny frowned. It was the drink, she thought. It had finally pickled her mother's brain.

'Has the old treadle got any needles?' she asked unexpectedly.

'Needles?'

'Yes, yer know, them things yer sew with, Jenny?'

'No need to be sarky, Mother. There were some the last time I used the machine a few months ago to repair that tear in me skirt. Why?'

148

'Just asking,' May answered cagily. 'What about cottons?'

'There's a bag full in the cupboard under the stairs. The ones you pinched from work.'

'Oh, yes. Good, that's sorted then.'

'Why do you need needles and cottons, Mam?'

'Well, why do you think?'

'You're going to be sewing?' Jenny asked, amazed.

'Is there a law against it or summat?'

'No, 'course not. It's just . . . well, I can't remember the last time you used that sewing machine.'

'Neither can I, that's why I'll need you to help me refresh meself 'cos I'm used ter using the industrial ones at work. I'll let you know when. Now,' she said, sitting down and snatching up a piece of toast, 'first things first. I want you out of 'ere this afternoon.'

'Why?'

''Cos I said so. I'm sure you'll find summat to do for a few hours.'

'But there's a pile of washing needing doing, and what about the cleaning?'

'It can all wait. I'm sure you've better things to do. Don't forget you've to tek Herchell's 'at back to him, then why don't yer tek a walk up town and have a browse around the shops? Take a good look at what styles the dress shops are selling. The good dress shops, mind. That should occupy you well enough for a few hours. Now I'd better hurry or I'll be late fer work. Thank God it's Sat'day and we finish at twelve.' Stuffing the remainder of the slice of toast into her mouth and chewing rapidly, May rose. 'Come back about five, that should give me enough time to mek a start.'

'A start on what, Mam?'

May smiled secretively. 'You'll see,' she said, heading for the door.

And that was what had been occupying Jenny's mind all the

way to Wadham's yard. All thoughts of her mother vanished rapidly, though, as she slipped through the narrow gap in the patched, wooden doors. She stood still, eyes darting. For a moment she wondered if she had entered the right place. The fair-sized cobbled yard was a shambles. Apart from the space the old lorry occupied it was crammed haphazardly with all manner of things, almost like a scrapyard.

The single-storey building she presumed was used as the office, appeared to be almost derelict. Weeds were growing up the walls and the guttering edging the rusting tin roof was hanging loose in parts. If there was one thing working at Stone & Son had taught her it was that to be a success in business meant operating in an orderly fashion. This business appeared to be far from orderly.

A loud grating noise attracted her attention and she glanced sideways to see Herchell, oblivious to her presence, puffing and panting in his efforts to manoeuvre a large heavy object. Jenny realised it was a lawn roller, the type used in parks, a very old one judging from the screeching noise its great iron wheel was emitting. She wondered why a removal company would be in possession of such a thing?

Skirting obstacles, she rushed over. 'Here, let me help,' she offered, slapping Herchell's hat on his head and grabbing at the roller's huge metal push bar.

Her unexpected appearance and quick action made him leap sideways. 'Oh, Lord,' he cried, eyes bulging in alarm, hand clutching his chest.

'I'm so sorry,' she cried. 'I didn't mean to frighten you, Herchell.'

On recognising her his big brown face split into a wide smile. 'I thought you was the devil a-comin' for me. But I'm glad to see it's you, Jenny.' His large hand came up to pat his hat. 'Glad to get this back, too. A man is naked without his hat.'

Jenny grinned at his quip. 'You got back to Mr Wadham's okay last night?'

'I got lost a couple of times but I managed in the end. He's a nice man is Mr Wadham.'

'So you kept saying last night. Many times, in fact.'

He grinned sheepishly, then his face grew serious and he asked, 'Jenny, please tell me why Mrs Gloria kept telling me to give over. What does "give over" mean?'

Jenny pressed her lips tight to suppress a smile. 'Er . . . well, you were going on a bit much about Mr Wadham, and "give over" was Mrs Budgins's nice way of telling you to shut up.'

'Oh! Oh, I see. Then I must learn not to go on in future.'

'Herchell, you go on as much as you like. I can assure you Mrs Budgins certainly does when she gets a bee in her bonnet.'

He looked puzzled.

Jenny laughed at his comical expression. 'Oh, never mind. I'm sure you'll learn our English expressions in time, like we'll learn yours. What are you doing with the roller?' she asked.

'I'm tryin' to make a start tidying up the yard for Mr Wadham. But it's going to take much longer than I thought.'

'Yes, it's in a right bloody mess,' said Jenny, looking around her. 'And that lorry's seen better days. I wonder what the people who are moving think when that rolls up at the door? Anyway, I'd better go in case Mr Wadham catches me.'

'Mr Wadham not here.'

'Oh, he's not helping you, then? You're trying to do this all on yer own? What about his other workers . . . Oh, they're in hospital, ain't they? You be careful, Herchell, or you'll end up the same way, trying to lug all this lot around by yourself.' She eyed him questioningly. 'Are you sure Mr Wadham is as nice as you think he is?'

'Oh, yes, he a very nice man,' he said gravely. 'Mr Wadham was here with me this morning but he suddenly remembered he had something to do. Although . . .' His voice trailed off.

'Although what?'

Herchell slowly exhaled, wondering whether to voice his opinion or not. He decided doing so would not be betraying his new employer in any way. 'I don't know him well yet, Jenny, but I do know when a man's upset. And Mr Wadham is very upset.'

'Is he? What about?'

Herchell took off his hat and ran his hand across his thick curls. 'Dunno. Not my place to be askin'. He just apologised to me for leaving me on me own. Asked me to do what I could and finish up when I'd had enough. He left me the keys to lock up.'

Jenny frowned. 'Oh, well, that's different. But you seem surprised by his attitude. Why?'

'Why! Jenny, no boss man has ever apologised to me before nor trusted me like Mr Wadham is.'

'Well, more fool them,' she said with conviction. 'Do you want me to give you a hand?' she offered.

'What, in tackling this lot?' he asked, shocked.

'Yes, why not?'

'Well, you're a woman.'

'Glad you've noticed,' she said, laughing. 'To be honest I've n'ote better to do. Me mam's chucked me out for the day and won't tell me why.' Her brow furrowed deeply. 'She's up to summat, Herchell, and I'm not sure whether to be worried or not.'

He smiled. 'I like your mother. She's a funny woman.'

'Yes, in more ways than one. So do you want a hand?'

'But what about your good clothes?'

She glanced down at herself. 'Oh, you call these good, do you?' she said, laughter in her voice. 'I made these trews two years ago out of remnants they were selling off at Lewis's. Me mam nicked the blouse from her work about the same time and

152

me cardy was knitted from wool I got from the market they were selling off for a tanner a skein, so I don't think we need worry, do you? I will take me coat off first, though. I paid one pound nineteen and six for this from C & A last winter. Took me ages to save for it an' all.' She smiled broadly. 'I've a couple of nice things but I keep them for best, like when I go dancing.'

Herchell listened to his new friend, enthralled. All the clothes he possessed, which amounted to two pairs of trousers – the better ones he was wearing now underneath the shabbier pair to ward off the cold which he seemed permanently to suffer from since his arrival in England – a brown overcoat, a jacket that matched his good trousers, two shirts, both too tight across his broad chest, and one set of underwear, along with his battered suitcase, had been purchased just before he had emigrated second-hand from the missionaries with the aid of his family, they having acquired them as donations from white folks who lived on his island. The two thick pullovers he was now wearing he had paid five shillings for off Camden market from his first pay packet out of dire necessity.

Listening to Jenny confirmed for him that in some ways her struggle for existence was just as great as his. Their cultures may be far apart in many ways but not in every respect.

'Mind you,' Jenny was saying, more to herself than to Herchell, 'whether I ever get to go dancing again is another matter as me friends seem to have deserted me.' She suddenly realised he was eyeing her, bemused. 'Oh, don't mind me, I was talking to meself. Us English are like that, yer know. Mad as hatters. So, *do* you want me help or not?'

'I do,' he said, smiling gratefully. 'But leave the heavy stuff to me.'

'Eh, I'm no weakling. I don't mind lifting. I did at Stone's. Boxes of glassware can weigh a ton.' Being reminded she was unemployed brought a new worry flooding through her. She just had to get that job on Monday, whether she liked the sound of it or not. She hoped they wanted her. 'Come on then,' she said, pushing the thought aside. 'Let's get to it and see what damage we can do between us.' She laughed at the look on Herchell's face. 'As I said before, you'll learn our expressions in time.'

A couple of hours later Jenny straightened herself and stretched her aching back. She looked at the pile of scrap items stacked on the back of the lorry.

It was a shame, she thought, that things hadn't been dealt with much sooner instead of being allowed to lie rotting. Some of it admittedly couldn't have been worth anything when it was first stored in the yard, but other things, like the lawn roller and the two mangles they had unearthed under several rolls of mould-encrusted linoleum, must have been in quite good condition when Mr Wadham had taken possession of them. Before the elements had done their worst.

'He could have put them in his warehouse,' she mused.

In the back of the lorry Herchell stopped what he was doing for a moment and looked down at her, puzzled. 'Pardon?'

'All this stuff. Mr Wadham could have stored it in his warehouse instead of letting it go to rack and ruin.'

'But you've seen it yourself, it's full of furniture.'

'Yeah, but Mr Wadham could have shoved the furniture up or something to make more room. Anything sooner than let all this happen.'

'I t'ink he meant to,' Herchell said protectively of his new boss as he jumped down from the back of the lorry. 'I t'ink he just a very busy man.'

'Yes, I suppose. I wonder what he's going to do with all that furniture? Do you know, Herchell?'

He shook his head as he continued with the loading.

Jenny shrugged her shoulders. 'Well, you'd think he'd sell it or summat, wouldn't yer, instead of leaving it sitting there gathering dust? Still, it's none of my business.' Her eyes settled on one of the rolls of rotten linoleum. 'Shame they're past it, would have done us a treat. There's more worn bits of lino on our back-room floor than good bits.' She eyed Herchell hopefully. 'Any chance of a cuppa, do you reckon? I'm parched.'

Herchell stopped what he was doing for a moment, his face thoughtful. 'I t'ink there's a kettle in the office if I remember right. I don t'ink Mr Wadham will mind if we make tea.'

'I'm positive he won't,' Jenny replied. 'I know I didn't meet him in the best of circumstances but he seemed a decent man to me.'

'He is . . .' began Herchell.

'Eh, don't start all that again,' Jenny cut in good-naturedly. 'I know exactly how much you think of Mr Wadham, and if you keep on telling me I'll scream. I'll give you a shout when I've mashed,' she said, heading over to the office.

The door was badly fitting and Jenny had to push her shoulder against it to get it open. She stood on the threshold and shook her head in disbelief. Just like the yard, the office was a shambles. Piles of paperwork and discarded bits and pieces lay everywhere. The dilapidated structure of the building did nothing to alleviate matters. The bare-bricked walls were crumbling in parts and the place smelt strongly of must and damp. She turned and looked behind the door, staring in horror at the old wooden table on top of which sat the gas ring and implements for mashing tea. It was filthy. Her need of a drink suddenly left her, overridden by her housewifely instincts.

Without further ado she had a rummage around and under the table shoved right up against the outside wall she unearthed a disintegrating packet of Tide washing powder, a chipped enamel bowl, a piece of grubby cloth and the remains of a scrubbing brush. She checked the blackened, battered kettle for water and lit the gas with the matches she found, jumping at the explosion it made as it burst into life.

A good while later she stood back and smiled, pleased at her efforts. The table was now scrubbed, the chipped brown teapot and assortment of huge pot mugs cleaned of stains, several empty milk bottles washed of their rancid remains and ready to take back to the corner shop. The kettle had been refilled from the tap outside and was slowly heating again on the gas ring to make the tea she'd originally set out in search of.

As she waited for it to boil she absently sauntered over to Bill's cluttered desk and idly scanned her eyes across it, settling on a large black ledger, its pages stuffed with an assortment of paperwork, thinking that this haphazard method of office work would never have been allowed at Stone & Son. At Stone's each carefully documented sales docket, delivery note or till receipt had its own special spike which nightly was taken through to Mrs Onions in the office. And if they did not match your sales records book, woe betide you.

Jenny turned and looked across at the kettle which wasn't even beginning to sing yet. She looked back at the desk, then across at the rickety filing cabinets. There must be years of paperwork left unfiled, she thought, and wondered why Mr Wadham had allowed it to get in such a state. Suddenly her training overwhelmed her and before she knew it she was sorting it all out into assorted piles, heedless of the fact she had no right to do so.

'Oh, there you are. I thought you'd gone home, Jenny. You've bin gone ages.'

The voice startled her and she let out a shriek. Hand to her chest, she spun around. 'Oh, Herchell, you made me jump!'

'What are you doing?' he asked, advancing.

'Oh! Oh, I . . . found meself sorting out the office. It needed doing. It's in a hell of a muddle. I've only sorted the paperwork into piles.' She realised she was on shaky ground and remorse filled her. 'D'yer think Mr Wadham will be angry?' she asked worriedly.

Herchell lifted his hat and scratched his head. 'I dunno.' He stared thoughtfully around. 'You've made a lot of difference, Jenny. It's much better than it was. No, I'm sure Mr Wadham won't mind,' he said, hoping he was right. 'In fact, I t'ink he might be grateful.'

'Oh, I hope so.'

Herchell hated to see his new friend so worried over something he knew she had taken it upon herself to do with the best of intentions. 'I'm sure I am,' he said, patting her arm reassuringly. 'Mr Wadham, he a nice . . .'

'Yes, all right, Herchell,' she cut in. 'What's done is done and I'll have ter suffer the consequences. But at least you won't all risk serious disease now I've washed down the tea area.' She scanned her eyes around and a feeling of satisfaction filled her. 'Yes, I have made a difference, haven't I? And, d'yer know, I really enjoyed meself. I wish I could get really stuck in and finish it off. Mrs Onions had a filing system in her office at Stone's. She showed me once how it worked. I wish I could help Mr Wadham by setting up one for him. Still . . . How's the yard coming on?'

He nodded. 'It's comin'. I've a lorry load ready for Mr Wadham to take. Where did you say we might get money for the stuff, Jenny?'

'The scrapyard. But why wait for him? Why not go yourself and then get another load ready?' She suddenly realised she was practically telling Herchell what to do, which wasn't really her place. 'It's only an idea, Herchell, that's all,' she added hurriedly.

'A good idea, yes, but . . . well . . . you see . . .'

Jenny's ears suddenly pricked. 'Is that someone calling for Mr Wadham?' she cut in, heading for the office door.

Followed by Herchell she entered the yard to see a middle-aged man, dressed in a brown overall coated in wood shavings and dust, standing just inside the wooden doors. He was looking around in agitation.

On spotting Jenny and Herchell emerging from the office he strode purposefully across to them. He eyed Herchell dubiously before addressing Jenny. 'Mr Wadham about?'

'He's out on business.'

He looked at her then Herchell cautiously. 'I've never seen you two about before. Just who are yer?' His eyes fell on the back of the lorry filled with scrap. 'Eh, hang on a minute, just what's going on?' he accused.

Jenny's eyes suddenly widened as it struck her that this man had assumed they were burglars. Her head came up indignantly. 'Mr Williams is working for Mr Wadham and I'm . . . I'm helping out.'

'And yer expect me to believe that? Mr Wadham's not here and the lorry's loaded with scrap. You must think I wa' born yesterday.'

Annoyance boiled within Jenny and she couldn't help but retaliate. 'You can think what yer like, mister, it's the truth. Tell him, Herchell.'

Hovering just behind Jenny, he reluctantly stepped forward. 'It is the truth, sir,' he said nervously. 'Mr Wadham he took me on yesterday after his men had their accident.' He plunged his hand into his pocket and pulled out Bill's bunch of keys. 'He gave me these to lock up with when I've finished. Mr Wadham said he might get back so you could ask him yerself.'

Jenny could see from his face that the other man wasn't convinced and her annoyance increased. 'If we were robbing the place, do we look daft enough to take it away on Wadham's own lorry with its name plastered all over it?' Just then a loud whistling noise rent the air. 'And neither would we be hanging around to mash up, would we? Now, if yer don't mind, I'd better go and take the kettle off the gas before it boils dry.'

Struck dumb by her outburst the man watched Jenny as she spun on her heel and went inside the office. Seconds later she returned to find the stranger and Herchell still standing where she had left them. 'Now is there something we can do for you?' she asked the man. 'If not, we've work to be getting on with.'

He gawped at her. 'Oh, er . . .' He paused uncomfortably. 'Look . . . er . . . yer can't blame me for thinking what I did.'

Jenny's face softened. 'No, I can't. I'd probably have thought just the same in your shoes.'

'I'd better introduce meself – Archie Gates. I'm the foreman from the wood yard. Our two lorries are out and won't be back for a good while and I've an urgent order just come in that I need delivering else I'll lose it. I wondered how Mr Wadham was fixed to help me out?'

Jenny turned towards Herchell. 'Mr Williams is in charge. It's him you should be asking.'

'Oh! But he's . . .'

'Yes, in charge,' cut in Jenny.

Blushing in embarrassment, Archie turned his attention to Herchell. He cleared his throat, uncomfortably. 'Can yer, then?'

Herchell stared at him blankly.

Jenny gave him a nudge. He turned and looked at her helplessly.

She realised that unless she took charge there was a danger of losing the work, and grabbed Herchell's arm. 'Excuse us a moment, Mr Gates,' she said, pulling Herchell out of earshot. 'You want to make a good impression on Mr Wadham, don't yer, Herchell? Well, you won't if he finds out yer've turned this work away. All you've got to do is get that stuff down the scrappy and then you could do the delivery. Simple, ain't it?'

'But . . .'

'What do we charge?'

He shrugged his shoulders. 'I dunno.'

'Oh, well, they can always sort that out later,' she said matter-of-factly. 'Now, look as though you know what you're doing, Herchell.' She moved back towards Archie, dragging Herchell along with her. 'We just have to get the lorry emptied down the scrapyard and then Mr Williams could do your delivery for you. About an hour's time, is that all right for you?'

He nodded. 'That'd suit me fine.'

'Good. About payment – you'll have to sort that out with Mr Wadham later.'

He nodded again. 'Fine.'

'Mr Williams will bring the lorry around in about an hour, then.'

As Archie departed, Jenny rubbed her hands together. 'Mr Wadham will be pleased, I bet yer. Now you'd better get off down the scrappy. While yer away I'll keep an eye on this place. I'll keep meself occupied doing some more tidying up in the office. I've already started so I might as well be hung for a sheep as a lamb. As me mam would say, in for a penny . . . Go on, off yer go,' she ordered.

Herchell hesitated, looking utterly dumbstruck at the lorry, then back at Jenny.

'What's wrong?' she asked.

'I . . . er . . . I ain't never driven a lorry before.'

Her jaw dropped. 'You ain't? Have yer never driven anything before?'

'Only an old jeep a couple of times back home. A friend of me father sort of took possession of it after the Americans left after the war. He used it to run a taxi service for the locals.'

She sighed loudly, relieved. 'Oh, God, you had me worried for a minute. Driving a lorry can't be that different,' she said reassuringly, although she hadn't a clue herself. 'Just take yer time and keep to the left. Oh, I've just thought, yer won't know where yer going and we ain't the time to be loitering.' She made a hurried decision. 'I'd better come with yer.'

Just after two o'clock the lorry jerked and spluttered its way back to the yard. As it jolted to a halt, Herchell, just managing by luck more than skill to stop it from hitting the corner of the office building, the door to the passenger side shot open and Jenny clambered out. 'Yer were right, Herchell, yer can't drive a lorry, can yer? I think you ought to get Mr Wadham to give you some lessons.' Rubbing her backside, she exhaled loudly. 'My bum feels as if it's been battered senseless. That lorry is a right old bone shaker, ain't it? Still, we got the job done and that's the main thing.' She looked at Herchell as he joined her. 'D'yer think we might get that cuppa now? I think we've earned it, don't you?'

Twenty minutes later, sipping on a welcome mug of black tea because there was no milk, and biting into cheese cobs Herchell had treated them both to from the corner shop, a thought struck Jenny and she eyed him speculatively. 'I wish I could work here,' she said. 'I've really enjoyed meself this morning. I thought I enjoyed me job at Stone's but now I can see I didn't really, I just didn't know any better. Yer don't reckon Mr Wadham has a vacancy for someone like me, do yer? I mean, there must be lots I could do. It's obvious to me he needs someone around here. What do you think, Herchell? Do you think I've a chance if I ask him?'

Just then the door opened and Bill walked in.

Jenny jumped up, sloshing tea down her front which she hurriedly wiped off. 'Mr Wadham!' she exclaimed. 'I was just . . . I was only . . . I came to bring Herchell his hat back,' she blurted out.

Bill stared at her in surprise. 'Oh, it's you, Jenny. Do sit down and finish your tea. I just popped back to see how you were getting on, Herchell,' he said.

As Jenny sank back down on to her chair Bill's drawn

expression was not lost on her. Herchell was right. Although Bill Wadham was doing his best to appear normal he could not hide the fact he was deeply upset about something, and she wondered what it was.

'From what I noticed in the yard,' he continued, 'it's coming on a treat. You're doing well. Just one thing: what have you done with all the stuff you've cleared? I couldn't see it anywhere.' He suddenly became aware of the transformation in the office. 'Someone's been busy in here, too,' he said in great surprise. 'Have you done this, Herchell?'

Jenny gulped. 'No, that was me, Mr Wadham.' She eyed him nervously. Now she was faced with Bill she wasn't sure she'd been right to act as she had. She took a deep breath. 'There's . . . er . . . a couple of things we'd . . . I'd better tell you.'

A while later Bill rubbed his chin thoughtfully. 'So, because your mother chucked you out this morning, you decided to come and run my business for me, is that right, Jenny? And you, Herchell, you just went along with it all.' He took a deep breath. 'If the police had stopped you driving the lorry we'd all have been in serious trouble, didn't you both realise that?' At the downcast expressions on their faces he couldn't help but laugh. 'Stop looking so worried, the pair of your! The police never stopped you so we'll forget about that. It's my fault. When I took you on, Herchell, I never gave a thought to whether you'd passed your driving test or not. I'll arrange to get that done.'

He eyed them both in turn. 'I don't know what to say, really. Just, thanks. The money you've earned me from the scrap and the delivery for the wood yard is a Godsend, I can't deny. And, Jenny, despite the fact you shouldn't have done it, I'm grateful for what you've achieved in here too. You must let me give you something . . .'

'I didn't do this to be paid, Mr Wadham,' she cut in, hurt. 'I just did it 'cos I'd n'ote better to do.' She suddenly realised an opportunity was presenting itself and before she could give the matter further thought blurted: 'You could let me finish off what I started by giving me a job, Mr Wadham?'

He looked at her, taken aback, then shook his head. 'This is a removals business, Jenny. No place for a woman in it. I am very impressed with what you've done, but it's strong men I need.'

As Bill turned his attention to Herchell a surge of disappointment filled her. 'Yes, of course,' she muttered, thinking she'd been stupid even to hope there could be a place for her here. A memory of her interview on Monday morning for a job in Lea's china department struck her then. In all probability, due to her dismissal without a reference from Stone's, she wouldn't get it. But then, she just might and although she'd enjoy handling the nice goods there, like at Stone's, she'd be stifled, governed by the company's rigid rules, spending years as a subordinate to her stodgy superiors in the hope of a promotion she might never get. The thought was suddenly terribly depressing.

Working for the likes of Bill Wadham would be very different, she knew. She only had to see the way he treated Herchell to know that. Jenny pursed her lips, thoughts racing. There *was* a need for her here. Bill had been wrong to dismiss her just because she was a woman. She could hump furniture – not the really heavy stuff admittedly, but the lighter bits she could. And she could learn to drive the lorry. Other women did; they had driven buses and ambulances during the war very successfully. And she could learn to do all the paperwork from start to finish. There was no end to the possibilities of her usefulness here. She just had to convince Bill Wadham. She'd grovel if necessary. She'd nothing to lose.

Putting down her half-eaten cob and now tepid mug of tea, she clasped her hands tightly and, heart hammering, took a deep calming breath. 'Mr Wadham, I know it ain't my place to tell you how to run your business but it seems to me you'd be daft to turn me away.'

He turned his head and eyed her, bemused. 'I would?'

'Yes. Admittedly I can't do all the things a strong man could but there's other things I can do.'

'Well, yes, I agree but . . .'

'I could take care of yer office. I could learn to do all yer paperwork. I'm a quick learner, honest.'

'Yes, but . . .'

'I could answer the telephone. You must lose lots of business when no one's here.'

'Yes, granted, but I haven't even got a telephone.'

'Oh! Well, you should get one then.' Jenny knew she was clutching at straws but regardless she couldn't stop herself, her desire to work here overriding all else. 'I'd keep the yard straight. I'd mash tea. I'm good at unpacking china and glass without breaking it.'

'We move ready packed stuff, Jenny, and we don't unpack it.'

'Well, you could offer to then, couldn't you? Another service you could provide,' she ventured.

Bill eyed her in surprise, realising she had a valid point which hadn't occurred to him before. Offering to pack and unpack for people was certainly something to think about for the future. 'Jenny,' he said, a warning tone in his voice, 'you've made your point and I appreciate what you're saying but I can't afford another wage at the moment.'

'Oh!' she exclaimed.

Her acute disappointment was so apparent that Bill felt sorry for this pretty young girl pleading her case. 'Look, I'll tell you what I'll do – I'll think on it, all right?' As the words left his mouth he knew he shouldn't have built up her hopes but it was too late to retract his offer without making matters worse.

'Oh, will you? Really, Mr Wadham? If you take me on, I won't let you down, honest.'

'Jenny,' he said, his hand raised in warning. 'I said, I'll think on it.'

A sudden fear that she'd made a complete and utter fool of herself engulfed her. What must Bill think of her? She'd practically begged him for a job. 'Thank you, Mr Wadham,' she muttered. Hurriedly she downed the last of her tea and jumped up. 'I'd better go and leave yer to it.' She held out her hand which Bill accepted. 'Goodbye,' she said. 'Tarra, Herchell,' she called as she fled from the office.

Bill stared thoughtfully after her for a moment before dismissing his conjectures as futile and turning back to face Herchell. 'Come on, man,' he said, rising. 'You've done enough for one day. The pub will be open soon. How do you fancy me taking you for a pint?'

# Chapter Twelve

A thoroughly fed up Jenny dawdled slowly home. She was in no rush to get there. In no mood to deal with May's sudden confusing change of personality or to discover the reason why she had thrown her daughter out for the day. Jenny had her own problems to deal with and they were taking up all her energy at the moment. Her life had changed dramatically in the last two days and she couldn't at this moment bring herself to believe the change was in any way for the better. And to add to her misery was the thought that if she couldn't persuade the owner of a backstreet firm to give her a job, what chance had she anywhere else?

She knew she was being unfair to Bill Wadham. He'd explained the reasons why he couldn't take her on and she had no reason to disbelieve him. And he had seemed genuinely pleased with her efforts of today. So maybe, as he had said, if the situation should improve in the future, she might end up working there.

The only thing that in any way lightened these black days was the fact that she had become friends with Herchell. She was really getting to like the man and was so glad their meeting had resulted in his getting a job and somewhere to live.

She really wished she could see Janet and discuss her situation with her friend but she wasn't quite sure what to do about that. There was a strong possibility that Janet, along with her other friends at Stone's, had been threatened with the loss of her job should she dare be caught socialising with an ex-employee, especially one who had been sacked for misconduct. Until Janet and the other girls showed their hand, Jenny felt it would be unfair of her to put them at risk.

She stopped by a shop window to peer inside at the goods on display. Before she could see what lay beyond the glass her own reflection stared back at her. She inwardly cringed, the sight of herself not improving her mood.

What a mess she looked. Her blonde hair had escaped from its once neat pony tail and her clothes were grubby. There were marks on her trews she'd probably never get off, and she had a large hole in her cardigan where she had caught it on a protruding nail. Her good black coat, which she had hurriedly pulled on as she had fled Wadham's office, had white specks all over it from years of dust she herself had disturbed as she had gone about her cleaning. It would take her ages to brush it all off. So much for her good deed, she thought ruefully, it hadn't done much good for her.

'Hiya, Jenny.'

The voice made her jump and she spun around to see Sandra Budgins beside her. Jenny groaned inwardly. The last person she felt like having a conversation with was Gloria's daughter who was just as nosey and gossipy as her mother. Despite their mother's friendships, the girls had never exactly got on.

Though, Jenny grudgingly admitted to herself, Sandra did look striking today. She was wearing a full red skirt, tight white blouse, a broad black plastic belt with a large gilt buckle around her trim waist, and a little blue cardigan which had red embroidered flowers on it. High black stiletto heels completed the outfit. Her hair was backcombed beehive style at the front and French-pleated at the back. All this only emphasised Jenny's own untidiness. Of all the times, she thought miserably, to bump into Sandra. And the other girl, Jenny knew by the way she was smiling, was going to make the most of this opportunity. She braced herself for what was to come.

Sandra looked her up and down, one of her plucked eyebrows arching. 'Letting yerself go a bit, ain't yer, Jenny? Yer looks ter me like you've bin dragged through an 'edge back'ards. Anyway I ain't seen you fer ages. How yer doing?' she asked.

'Oh, all right.' Jenny spoke lightly, forcing herself to ignore Sandra's rudeness. 'And you?'

'Great. I'm doing smashing. Got meself a corker of a boyfriend. He's a Teddy Boy,' Sandra said proudly. 'Works at the Robin Hood. 'Ead cellarman 'e is.' She cocked her head to one side, eyes sparkling maliciously. 'We'll have ter go out in a foursome one night. Oh, sorry, Jenny,' she said, pretending remorse. 'You ain't got a fella, 'ave yer? So me mam sez.' She flashed a false smile. 'I could try and fix you up, if yer like? I'm sure one of Jerry's mates wouldn't mind having you tagging along for a night.'

Jenny fought to control her anger. 'I'll fix meself up, thank you, Sandra,' she said evenly.

'Doesn't seem to me you're very good at fixing yerself up, Jenny. Still, on second thoughts, Jerry's mates like gels who've got it, if yer know what I mean. And you ain't exactly, 'ave yer?' She fixed her eyes scathingly on Jenny's trews. 'I wouldn't be seen dead in them things. Went out wi' the ark.' Without giving Jenny a chance to retaliate she said, 'Well, you obviously ain't got a social life, so how's yer job going?'

Jenny knew by her tone that Sandra was well aware she had lost her job. 'I decided I needed a change so I'm in between at the moment.'

'Oh, that's not what me mam sez. She told me you'd got the sack,' Sandra said smugly. 'Never mind, Jenny, I'm sure you'll get summat,' she continued patronisingly. 'I think they're looking for a barmaid at our place. You could come and work wi' me. I'll put in a good word for yer, shall I?'

'That's very nice of you, Sandra, but pub work's not for me.' And Jenny could not help but add, 'Especially not the pub you work in.'

'And what's wrong with the pub I work in?'

'Well, *you* work there for a start, Sandra. But besides that the place is a dump and I wouldn't be seen dead in it.'

Sandra's eyes bulged. 'Why, you effin' cow!' she spat.

'Tut-tut, Sandra, what language. Mind you, what can I expect coming from someone who works in the Robin Hood? The only qualification needed to work in that place is to be as thick as two short planks so you overcharge the customers, and as brazen as a hussy to keep the navvies drinking at the bar. And you certainly fit the bill, Sandra. Tarra.'

Under normal circumstances Jenny would have found the encounter extremely humorous, especially the look on Sandra's face as Jenny had spun on her heel and stalked off. She had nearly choked on her own spittle in the effort to find words to retaliate to Jenny's tirade. But Jenny was too dispirited even to summon a giggle at the episode.

As she walked on, the muted sounds of the local Espresso Coffee Bar reached her and she slowed her pace. She, Janet and the other girls had often frequented a coffee bar on Granby Street before they had caught their respective buses home after work. To loud popular music booming from the American juke box, they would sit and chatter over the day's events, make plans for their evenings out and weigh up the boys who came in.

Jenny sighed long and loudly. Those carefree times suddenly seemed far distant, as the events of the last couple of days crowded in on her. Try as she might, she could not see her immediate future changing and her misery deepened. Suddenly a picture of her mother sprang to mind. There was a ray of hope. Maybe by the time she arrived home May would have reverted back to her usual self. The mother she knew and loved, not the bewildering creature of this morning. Now that she could cope and deal with.

But Jenny's hope was to go unanswered.

Before she had inserted the key in the lock of the front door, loud banging and crashing within greeted her. 'Oh, dear God,' she groaned.

If Wadham's yard had appeared a shambles to Jenny, what she found inside the house looked as if a herd of elephants had stampeded through the rooms. But first she had had to get inside.

She had to push and shove hard at the front door in order to force a gap wide enough for her to squeeze through, and once there to her bewilderment she found the huge iron end of her mother's bed practically filling the passageway. The little front room was packed to the ceiling with furniture from upstairs. With great difficulty Jenny climbed over and through it to reach the back room where the loud noises were coming from.

'Mam, what on earth is going on?' she exclaimed in horror.

Behind the door the dining table had been pushed right up against the wall and the four chairs stacked on top. Under the sash window, one on top of the other, stood the two old armchairs. Parts of the worn lino had been ripped away from the floor, jagged pieces left lying in a heap, and the rusting metal dustbin from outside sat amid it all piled high with the tattered magazines and other rubbish that had been stacked in the corner between the sideboard and the wall.

Kneeling on the floor, a dishevelled May, in the process of pulling out all the contents of the sideboard, turned her head as Jenny entered and smiled in relief. 'There yer are at long last. I thought yer were never coming home. Come on, you can give me a hand wi' this lot. We ain't got much time, yer know.'

171

'Much time? Mother, have you gone doolally? What on earth are you doing?'

'Gettin' things ready. Stop standing there like an idiot, Jenny. Come and give me an 'and.'

'Mam, I ain't doing nothin' 'til you tell me what's going on.'

May sighed in exasperation. 'All right,' she snapped, awkwardly standing up. 'Oh, me leg's gone dead,' she groaned, giving it a vigorous rub. 'I've got ter get all this lot cleared out to mek way for the new furniture that's being delivered about six o'clock,' she said, straightening up. 'Took a lot of doing that, yer know, but the chap in the shop said he'd arrange it being's it was for me. He fancied me, yer see. I might 'ave took him up on his offer yesterday, but this is today.'

Her mother's blabbering was lost on Jenny. The words 'new furniture' were echoing in her brain. 'New furniture! Mother, what have you done?'

'Done? I'll tell you what I've done, Jenny,' she said proudly. 'Started us on our way to bettering ourselves, that's what. From now on this is me new regime. Out with the old, in with the new.'

A great sense of foreboding filled Jenny. 'How did you pay for this new furniture?'

'It doesn't matter,' said her mother dismissively.

'Yes, it does. How?'

'I didn't. Got it on the never-never. Everybody buys their new stuff that way these days, Jenny.'

'But it's still got to be paid for, and we can't, Mam.'

May's eyes narrowed warningly. 'Don't you go telling me what I can and can't do, young lady. It'll be paid for. I got it all for thirty bob a week.'

'Thirty bob? Mam, that's half me wage, which I'll remind you I'm not even earning at the moment. And how long have yer got to be paying it? Years and years, I bet. We'll never get it cleared up.'

172

'Oh, stop being a misery guts, Jennifer Jeffries. I thought you'd be pleased. With all our new furniture, you won't be ashamed to bring anyone home, will yer?'

'I wasn't before, Mam.'

'Ah, but you can ask a better class of person now, can't yer? Same as I can. Oh, stop looking so worried. Didn't yer listen to Herchell last night? That man got off his arse and went after summat better, and I decided that's what I must do for us, Jenny. I took a long look at meself and didn't like what I saw. So I'm gonna try and change meself.'

'But there's nothing wrong with you, Mam.'

'Oh, there is, Jenny. I'm . . .' May was loath to voice the word 'common' in connection with herself. 'I've let meself get like this lot round 'ere. I never used to be like it. Well . . . not as bad, I don't think. And I swear like a bleddy trooper. So I'm gonna curb me bloody language and stop drinking so much an' all. And I'm gonna dress better too. And you're going to help me.'

'Yeah, okay, I'd be happy to. But you enjoy going for a drink, Mam.'

'Yes, I do, but a proper lady doesn't go down the working men's club to play tombola. Be honest, Jenny, they don't, do they? They don't have ter because they've got decent men taking care of them who take them to nice places – places where you don't risk getting yer block knocked off in a fight at the end of the night. I thought giving this place a good clear out and a bit of spit and polish would make a lot of difference to it, but it won't, Jenny. Yer can't mek any of this old stuff look halfway decent, however much yer try. So I decided to get new. And why not, eh? Anyway, this'll cheer yer, I got you an interview for a job.'

'Eh? Doing what?'

'At the furniture shop. I'll give yer all the details later.'

'Mother . . .'

'Oh, stop going on, Jenny. You need a job, don't yer? And this one's in a shop like yer wanted. They'll take you on, I know they will. Anyway, I ain't got time for arguments. I need to get this lot cleared before the new stuff arrives and we ain't got long.'

Jenny stared at her mother aghast, trying to take in all May had thrown at her. She shook her head. Despite a terrible feeling that this was all going to end in tears, in more ways than one, it was no good trying to talk any sense into her mother. May's mind was made up and it was too late now for Jenny to do anything about it. This place was in ruins and the new furniture was on its way.

'All right, Mam, where do you want me to start?'

May beamed. 'That's my girl. I want this lot in the yard. Every last bit of it. We'll see about getting it shifted later. You'll see, it'll be all great by the time I've finished. Eh, and when I've got me new clobber sorted out, it's your turn. Me and you, we're gonna show the world what we're really made of. Okay?'

Jenny smiled. 'Okay, Mam.'

Just then Gloria's head popped around the door. She looked bewildered. 'What's 'appenin', May? It sounded like yer were knocking the house down, all the noise you were meking. I can see now that you are.'

'Wondered how long it'd be afore you showed yer face,' May said matter-of-factly. 'Well, yer can mek yerself useful and help us get this lot outside. And if yer behave yourself, Mrs Budgins,' she added, a mischievous twinkle in her eye, 'I'll let you help me arrange me new furniture.'

Gloria's mouth dropped open, eyes bulging. 'New furniture?' she mouthed in astonishment. 'A' you havin' me on?' She turned and looked at Jenny, shaking her head. 'Your mother's finally gone barmy.'

'My mother is far from barmy, Mrs Budgins,' Jenny said

protectively. 'She's as sane as she ever was. Isn't that right, Mam?'

'That's right, Jenny love. It's a new me yer gonna be seeing in future, Gloria, and if yer can't cope, yer know what you can do. But before you do, help us with this lot, there's a mate. And fetch your Cyril too to give us a hand with the heavy stuff. That's if he's not already gone down the pub.'

An hour later May appraised the back room, now devoid of its furniture, the floorboards stripped of the old linoleum. 'Where's that bleddy furniture van? I wa' told it would be here by six thirty.'

'You swore, Mam,' accused Jenny. 'I thought you said you were going to curb your language?'

'That'll be the day,' quipped Gloria.

May pursed her lips. 'Bleddy's not swearing. Anyway I'm worried about me new furniture not being delivered so I'm entitled to swear. And they've gotta go,' she suddenly blurted, pointing a chipped fingernail towards the window.

'What has?' said Jenny, looking in that direction.

'Those plastic tulips I got free wi' Daz.' May grabbed the milk bottle that was holding them. 'I never liked 'em anyway. Dust catchers, that's all they are. Free offers indeed! Free offers don't help mek the sheets any whiter, do they? I'd sooner have the money off. Here,' she said, thrusting the bottle of plastic flowers at Jenny. 'Dustbin.'

'Mam, I would go but I can't get to the dustbin under all that lot in the yard. I'll leave them in the kitchen 'til I can.'

Just then there was a loud knocking at the front door.

'Oh!' screeched an excited May. 'It's me furniture! It's come, it's come. You go, Jenny. I can't, I'm nearly wetting meself wi' excitement. I ain't never had n'ote new before.' She spun round to face Gloria. 'You going or staying?'

'I'm staying,' she snorted, folding her fleshy arms under her ample bosom. 'Yer didn't think I'd help to hump and heave all

175

that old stuff into the yard and then miss the finale, did yer?'

'Well, just mek sure you behave yerself, Gloria Budgins.'
May spun round to face Jenny. 'Fer God's sake, go and answer
that door afore they think there's no one in.'

'Those for me? That's very kind of yer,' a middle-aged man
said to Jenny jocularly as she opened the door.

'What? Oh,' she laughed, realising she was still holding the
milk bottle containing the plastic flowers. 'You can have them
if you want them, with pleasure.'

'Me wife's got a vase full, ta, me duck. Dust catchers, that's
all they are. You Mrs Jeffries?'

'Me mother is.'

'Sid Brown, pleased ter meet yer. So, let's get cracking then.
We're on overtime, yer know. Usually I don't mind a bit of
overtime but I ain't keen on a Sat'day night.' He turned from
Jenny and shouted towards the brown van blocking the road at
the back of him. 'Right place, Mr Alan, so let's get to it.'

The door to the passenger side of the van opened and a
young man jumped out. Jenny's mouth fell open and for the
second time that day she inwardly cringed. He was the most
handsome man she'd seen in a long time and here she was
looking like . . . well, God only knew. Nothing like her best at
any rate. Alan, she mused thoughtfully. That was a nice name.
Manly-sounding. His long brown overall did nothing to hide
the lithe body that lay beneath it. He was tall, at least six foot.
Jenny liked tall men, felt they had a kind of protective quality
about them.

As he came abreast of her, making his way towards the back
of the van, he gave her a smile of greeting. 'Hello,' he said
politely.

Cradling the bottle of flowers to her chest, she smiled back.
'Hello,' she muttered, wishing the ground would open and
swallow her up. Her eyes followed him as he walked towards
the back of the van. She suddenly realised there was something

176

about him that was familiar but how that could be she did not know as she had never met him before. She would certainly remember if she had.

She suddenly realised the older man was talking to her in a hushed tone. 'Yer'll 'ave ter excuse Mr Alan, miss, if he seems a bit off like.'

Jenny eyed him, bemused. 'Off? He didn't seem off to me. But why?'

'He's had a bereavement in the family but insisted on working. Said it'll help keep his mind occupied.'

'Oh, poor man,' she said sincerely.

'*Is* it me furniture?' a voice demanded.

'What? Oh, yes, Mam,' Jenny answered, going back inside. 'It's come in a big enough van, it's blocking the street.'

'And I suppose all the neighbours are gawping out of the windows?'

Jenny hadn't noticed, her attention having been completely fixed on Alan. 'I didn't see,' she said. 'But I bet they are.'

'There's no betting about it,' huffed Gloria. 'Eyes on stalks, I shouldn't wonder. Let's face it, no one around here has ever had a furniture van calling before, unless it's bin sent by the landlord to evict 'em. Oh, I say, May, is that a chair to yer new suite?' she exclaimed in awe. She gestured to Alan. 'Over here, young man, by the fireplace.'

'Hold on a minute, Gloria,' May snapped. 'I ain't decided where I'm arranging it all yet. Put it in the corner, there's a duck,' she said to Alan. 'That can go upstairs,' she ordered the older man as he struggled in carrying the headboard to her new bed. She turned to Jenny. 'Put the kettle on. The least we can do is mash these men a cuppa. Have you got any sugar, Gloria?'

A good while later, having brought in the last item on the van, the older man addressed May. 'Well, that's it all, Mrs.'

She beamed in pleasure. 'Thanks a lot. Er . . .' She turned to

Jenny who was standing at the side of her. ''Ave yer got any change for a tip?' she whispered.

'You know I ain't, Mam.'

'Oh, er . . .' She turned to the man again. 'Thanks a lot then. Jenny'll see yer out.' She nudged her daughter. 'Go on.'

Jenny gave her mother a scathing look as she showed the men to the door.

'Thank you for what you've done,' she said, mortally embarrassed at the fact that the Jeffries' financial predicament meant she couldn't reward them for their efforts. They had both worked hard, there was no denying that.

'Come on then, Bert, let's be off,' said Alan, slamming shut the van's loading doors. He smiled at her and Jenny immediately knew he realised her predicament. 'It's been our pleasure, Miss Jeffries. Thanks for all the tea. Tarra.'

Jenny watched as they both climbed into the van and its engine roared into life, thinking it a shame she hadn't met Alan under different circumstances. Then she might have stood a chance with him. Still, she thought as she made her way back to her mother and Gloria, a good-looking man like him, and nice with it too, would probably be spoken for by an equally attractive woman. As she walked down the passage, a thought suddenly struck her as odd. The older man had addressed Alan when they had first spoken as 'Mr'. Strange that, she thought, and she wondered why.

It was nearing twelve when May, Jenny and Gloria flopped exhaustedly down on May's new suite.

'God, I'm knackered,' Gloria grumbled. 'I'll give yer yer due, May, when yer buys new furniture yer certainly go to town, don't yer? I hopes yer can afford it all.'

'My financial state is none of your business, Gloria Budgins.'

'It is when yer come borrowing sugar and such like off me.'

May snorted, 'I'm only gettin' back what was mine in the first place.'

'Anyone want tea?' Jenny asked, jumping up, worried that trouble was simmering.

'Ain't yer n'ote stronger?'

'No, sorry, Mrs Budgins.'

'Then I'm off home. I can get tea in me own 'ouse.' Gloria struggled to raise her hefty body from May's new sofa. 'This ain't so comfy as yer old one, but then neither has it got springs prodding yer bum so I s'pose it's an improvement. See yer termorrow, May.'

She hadn't the energy to retaliate to Gloria's comments on her past and present settees. She just gave a weary wave of her hand. 'Yeah. Tarra, gel, and thanks for yer 'elp. Yer'd better go out the front 'cos yer won't get out the back.'

'Oh, yeah, I forget. Like the rag and bone yard out there, ain't it?' Gloria quipped. 'Oh, and being's I ain't getting n'ote by way of payment for me labours, I'll have those plaggy flowers yer were gonna chuck away,' she said, snatching them off the window ledge as she headed for the door. 'Look a treat on my mantel they will. Tarra.'

'Do you want a cuppa, Mam?' Jenny asked after Gloria had gone.

'No, thanks, lovey, I'm too tired. Going to bed I am. I'm looking forward to trying out me new bed, ain't you? Be a damned sight more comfortable than our last ones.'

'Yes, I am. Mam?'

'Mmm?'

Jenny took a deep breath. 'Are you sure we *can* afford all this? I mean, furnishing a whole house ain't cheap, is it?'

'No, I grant yer, it's not. But for the love of God, will yer stop worrying?' May's eyes ranged around the newly furnished room. 'It looks a treat, don't it, and the rest of the house too? I like this pattern of lino, goes well with the black vinyl suite. It was nice of the men to lay it, 'cos they didn't have ter do that, did they?' She eyed Jenny knowingly. 'I think that young chap had a fancy for you meself.'

'Mother, he did not. Anyway, how could he with me looking like the wreck of the Hesperus?'

'The wreck of the what? Oh, never mind.' She looked Jenny over. 'Yes, yer right. No man in his right mind 'ud fancy you looking like that.' May let out a guffaw of laughter. 'Oh, tek that stricken look off yer face – I'm only jokin'. You, my darlin', are prettier than any of the gels round here and that young man could do a lot worse than you. Sandra Budgins for a start. And talking of the Budginses, I was so worried Gloria's weight would break the legs off that settee. They don't look all that strong. But I never so much as heard a creak when she plonked herself down, thank the Lord. Eh, and what d'yer think of the record player cabinet? Posh, in't it? We can play records now, can't we?'

'We haven't got any, Mam.'

'Well, we can get some. And I want a proper cloth for the table, no more oilcloth in this 'ouse. Though we'd better use it in the meantime.'

'You chucked it away, Mam.'

'Did I? Oh! Well, we'd better use newspaper then. Don't want to risk marking me new walnut.'

'Walnut! Mother, I'm far from an expert but even I know that that table's made from oak.'

'I know it's oak but walnut sounds better. And, more to the point, I convinced Gloria it was walnut and she'll blabber to all the neighbours.' May suddenly paused and sighed as she looked at the walls. 'Only problem now is the new furniture shows up our tatty paintwork and wallpaper. That paper was on the walls when we first arrived here, so God knows how old it is. I should have decorated first, shouldn't I?'

'Mam, I think you've spent enough for one day, don't you?'

May smiled secretively. 'Ah, but I could have spent more.'

'Could you?' Jenny asked, flabbergasted. 'I don't see how.'

The corners of May's mouth twitched mischievously. 'I'd better tell you 'cos I can see you're in danger of not getting any sleep tonight.'

'Tell me what?' Jenny suddenly stared, horrified, as a terrible thought struck her. 'Mother, you ain't bought anything else and not told me, have you?'

'No. Oh, you are a whittle,' she scolded. 'The furniture didn't cost me as much as I expect you thought it did, that's all.'

'It didn't?'

'No. It's all repossessed.'

'Re what?'

May laughed. 'That's just what I said to the bloke in the shop. He explained it's all stuff people have bought then haven't met the payments on it. It's second-hand but new second-hand, if yer understands me. Got it a lot cheaper than new and no one will know. I certainly don't want Gloria knowing,' she warned.

'She won't hear it from me, Mam. I'm just relieved. Well, a bit. It's still all got to be paid for, ain't it? New or rewhatever it is.'

'Well, that won't be too much of a problem now you've practically got a job.'

'Ah, I wanted to talk to you about that, Mam . . .'

'Yeah, well, not tonight, I'm too tired.' May rose, yawning. 'I'll see yer in the morning. Night, night.'

As she departed Jenny shook her head. As much as she loved her mother, sometimes she despaired of her. Still, the arrival of the new furniture had made her very happy and Jenny had to admit that the little two up, two down terrace house had been completely transformed by it.

She rose and stretched herself. In the future, she thought, there'd be plenty of times she'd be worried over the weekly payments but for now, just like her mother, she would take pleasure in just having it.

# Chapter Thirteen

Across town Bill sat staring absently into space.

'I said, goodnight, Mr Wadham.'

'Pardon? Oh, sorry, Herchell. Goodnight.'

Herchell hesitated by the door. He knew that whatever had upset Bill the previous day was still doing so but would swear there was something else now and this bothered him. Despite having no reason to he automatically thought it must have something to do with himself and assumed he knew what it was. 'Mr Wadham, them rooms we saw – I will take one of them. I could move in tomorrow.'

Bill sat bolt upright. 'Herchell, you will not! They were so poky in all honesty I wouldn't allow a dog to stay there, let alone you. Now stop worrying. I've already told you, it's no problem you being here. In fact, I'm enjoying the company. Anyway, it's an excuse to cook a meal in the evening.'

A relieved grin split Herchell's face. 'You mean that, Mr Wadham?'

'How many times do I have to tell you? In fact, why don't you just stay here for a few weeks and give yourself a breathing space? Put some money by to get somewhere decent for when your wife . . . Blossom, isn't it? . . . comes over.'

Herchell looked stunned. 'You mean that, Mr Wadham?'

Despite his problems Bill could not help but laugh. 'I'm sorry, Herchell. I'm not laughing at you, it's just the look on your face. Yes, I do mean it. And, for goodness' sake, will you stop calling me Mr Wadham? Owen always calls me "boss", and so does Trevor. I'd like you to do the same.'

'Oh, right then, boss,' a delighted Herchell agreed. Then slowly his face grew troubled. 'Tin't my place to speak, boss, but you sure no'ting be bothering you? You have me worried, see. I know a worried man when I sees one. And you is worried.'

Bill sighed loudly. And you'd be right, Herchell, he thought. But he wasn't about to spill out his worries to anyone. They were his and his alone. But there was something he could discuss with Herchell, get the man's opinion before he acted. 'Sit down a minute, there is something I would like to talk over with you. It's about Jenny.'

Herchell perched on the armchair opposite Bill and clasped his hands. 'Jenny?' he queried.

Bill took a deep breath. 'I think I was a bit hasty in dismissing her offer to work for me so quickly. I've been sitting here thinking about it. I like her, Herchell. She's a nice girl. Very bright and willing, which is refreshing.'

'Oh, she is, boss. Nice, very nice. I likes her very much.'

'I know, I've lost count of the number of times you've told me.' And he added good-humouredly, 'Especially this evening with a couple of pints inside you. Anyway, I've been thinking. I might be a fool *not* to take her on.'

'To work for you? You mean it, boss? Oh, yes, you would be a fool not to.' Herchell suddenly realised just what he had said and his dark brown skin glistened with beads of embarrassment. 'Oh, I don't mean you *is* a fool . . .'

Bill grinned. 'It's all right, man, I know exactly what you were trying to say. Trouble is, I can't really afford to take her on at the moment. But then, I can't afford not to.' He shrugged his shoulders. 'By the time I can afford her wage a girl like Jenny will more than likely have gone somewhere else and I might not find someone with her keenness again. She gave me some damned good ideas. She's right, I do need a telephone. Now I think about it, I don't know how I've managed without one.' He gave a thoughtful smile. 'It would be good to have a woman about the place. I know Owen would like her. And Trevor . . . well, Jenny is a very pretty girl but I can't see her standing any cheek from him.'

He paused and took a deep breath. 'I really want to have a good stab at making this business grow and Jenny, like you, is just the type of person I need alongside me to do it. I've been sitting here thinking of all that she did today off her own bat. In my experience not many youngsters these days would do that, Herchell. And I must admit I was very impressed with the way she pleaded her case. I just wish I'd been a bit nicer to her.' He leaned back and ran his fingers through his hair, making it stick up wildly. 'What a dilemma, eh?'

'Mmm,' Herchell agreed.

'So what do you think I should do, Herchell?'

Herchell's large brown eyes widened. 'You askin' me, boss?'

'Well, your name is Herchell, isn't it?'

For once he wished it wasn't. He wasn't used to being asked his opinion by his superiors. And how would he himself feel if Bill took his advice and it should prove wrong? But then Bill had asked his views, which to Herchell was an honour, and the very least he could do was answer plainly. He looked Bill straight in the eye. 'We Jamaicans like to take a gamble.'

Bill frowned. 'What are you saying to me, Herchell? That I should let you throw a dice or cut the cards and decide that way?'

He shook his head. 'No, sir. I learned that the hard way. In my time I've lost more than enough good money trustin' others. You might win a bit but in the long run you lose more than you make. Bettin' is a mug's game. Too many cheatin'

185

hands around. Not that I would ever cheat anyone,' he said with conviction. 'I ain't made that way. My mother, she's a wise woman, boss, she always tell me to trust me own gut feelin'. Listen to what it be tellin' me then take a gamble on it. If you is wrong you only have yourself to blame. And she's right, my mother. Usually I find me gut feelins to be good ones.'

Bill smiled. 'Oh, I see. My mother was a very wise woman too, Herchell. I miss her badly in more ways than one. Mmm.' He leaned forward and clasped his hands. 'Well, I'll take your advice. My gut instincts tell me to take Jenny on so that's what I'll do. I'll pop around and see her tomorrow. I just hope she still wants to work for me.' And he thought to himself, let's just hope I don't fall flat on my face in the process and we all end up out of work. 'Thanks, Herchell. Now get yourself off to bed, man, I'll not be long behind you.'

After Herchell had gone, Bill leaned back in his armchair, clasped his hands behind his head and allowed his thoughts to return to his major problem, the one he'd been painfully mulling over since his conversation with the doctor the previous day and which hadn't given him a moment's peace since.

Should he go to Ernest Collier's funeral?

He felt it right to pay his last respects to a man he had once loved like a father, and admired greatly as a boss. Before that terrible incident had happened over twenty years ago, Ernest had been more than happy to have Bill marry his beloved daughter, even talked of making him a partner in his own business as a wedding present to the happy couple.

A vision of Ernest Collier rose before him. He had been a big bull of a man, his black bushy beard giving him a menacing appearance. But his appearance had belied the reality. Ernest was in fact a kind, considerate and a very humorous man. His customers loved his straight, no-nonsense approach and once he had a customer, he kept them for life.

The same with his employees. If you treated him fairly, he looked after you more than fairly in return and to be employed by Collier's Carriers was a coveted position.

Bill's mind flew back over twenty years, to relive the last time he had seen Ernest Collier alive. A scrupulously honest man himself, Ernest was looking at Bill in bewilderment, having difficulty believing what the facts were telling him.

He smashed one large fist down on the desk. 'I can't believe it, Bill. Not you of all people. If you needed money that badly, why didn't you ask me? Yer knows I would have done what I could for yer. Christ, lad, I look on you as me son. You know I was going to mek you a partner in the business when you and our Val wed. Why did you do it, Bill? Why?'

Reeling from shock himself, Bill looked him straight in the eye. 'I keep telling you, Mr Collier, I didn't.'

'But the money was in your pocket.'

'Well, I don't know how it got there.'

'It doesn't make sense. Why would someone else steal the weekly takings and put it all in your pocket? Over a hundred pounds, Bill. Why?'

He helplessly shrugged his shoulders. 'And why would I take the risk of stealing the money then hiding it where it could so easily be found, Mr Collier?'

Ernest exhaled loudly. 'I dunno, son. None of it meks sense to me.' He clamped his hands to his ruddy cheeks as he sank down on his chair. 'This whole situation is dreadful. I can see you're as shocked about all this as I am, but the fact still remains the takings were found in your possession, every penny of them, and I did find you in my office.'

'And I've told you, Mr Collier, I'd only just arrived through the side door.'

'Yes, I know what yer told me, lad, but there was no sign of anyone else. Not a soul.' He looked at Bill for several long moments before very reluctantly he said, 'I've no choice, have I?'

Bill shook his head. 'No, sir, I don't see as you do.'

'I'll have to ask you to leave immediately. Oh, Bill, this is such a sad day.' Ernest heaved a mournful sigh. 'I'll not take matters further. I don't want Val's name dragging into all this. It's a small city is Leicester. People love a scandal and their memories are long. You're going to suffer enough as it is. But I trust you'll do the honourable thing.'

'And what's that, Mr Collier?' Bill asked. He was already doing the honourable thing, wasn't he? Leaving without a fuss even though this incident had nothing to do with him.

'You'll not see my daughter again.'

Bill's heart hammered painfully. 'But, Mr Collier, why? I can't prove it but I'm innocent . . .'

'I know you are, lad, but others won't see it like that. This is a business I'm running. I've other men working for me. I can't appear to be turning a blind eye to such a serious matter, despite me own feelings. Facts are facts. And I can't have my daughter go through the rest of her life being branded the wife of a thief. If you love her as much as you say you do then you won't want her to either. I'm sorry, lad.'

And so as much as it had grieved him to do so, Bill had done the honourable thing. He had walked away from that office and out of Valerie Collier's life. The shame and the repercussions of what had happened had hit him so badly he couldn't even face his mother, or brother or the scandalised whispers and stares of neighbours and friends. Hurrying home, he had stuffed his belongings into a worn haversack, scribbled a brief note to his mother explaining what had happened, and then walked away from the city of his birth.

Three months he had stayed away, long terrible months of trudging from place to place, working when he could, sleeping in lodgings when he could afford them or rough when he couldn't. Finally he could stand it no longer. He had to return home, find out if the real culprit had been caught, beg his mother and brother's forgiveness for the pain he must have caused them. But most importantly he had to see Val. As much as he loved his family, as much as he felt he had been cruelly mistreated and needed to clear his name, Val was more important to him.

That terrible time on the road had taught him he could not live without the woman he adored. His every waking minute and his nights of fretful sleep had been filled with memories of her and the pain of her loss. He couldn't stay away from her any longer. Now he was thinking more clearly he realised that the Val he knew and loved would realise he was innocent. He also knew that she loved him enough to stand by him. And with Val by his side, Bill knew he could face anything or anyone.

But on his return home his hopes were to be dealt a bitter blow.

His mother had wept with joy when he arrived on her doorstep one bitterly cold night, wet, cold and ravenously hungry. She had thrown her arms around her son and hugged him fiercely to her. Then she had scolded him severely.

'Why did you go off like that? I knows you'd never steal from anyone. You ain't got it in yer.'

'I wasn't thinking straight, Mam. All I knew was I couldn't face you or Daniel. It was wrong of me, I know.'

'They all thought you was guilty from the way you slunk away. I told 'em all though. I held me head up and shouted on the doorstep that if you'd as much as laid one finger on that money, let God strike me dead. I'm still here, ain't I?'

He had wept then, hugging her to him. 'Oh, Mam, I've been so stupid.'

'Yes, yer have. And yer put me through purgatory. How could you, our Billy? I didn't know whether you was alive or dead. I thought the pain of losing yer dad was bad enough, but you going . . . well, just let me tell you, it was worse. Don't you dare ever do that ter me again.'

He pulled away from her, wiping his eyes on his shirt cuff. 'I won't, Mam, I promise. Did Mr Collier find out who really took the money?'

'No, son. And to my knowledge nothing has happened like it again. Strange state of affairs, if yer ask me. But I think whoever did it was disturbed in the act and yours was the nearest pocket handy.'

Bill smiled wanly. 'That's the only thing I can come up with, too.' He sighed forlornly. 'What about Daniel? I don't expect it's been easy on him, especially with him working at Collier's. I bet he went through it, too. Will he ever forgive me, Mam?'

Her face turned ashen and she moved away from him, pretending to busy herself. 'I'll get yer a cuppa and summat to eat. Yer must be starving.'

Bill knew then there was something dreadfully wrong by her whole manner. 'Mam, what is it? It's Daniel, isn't it? What's happened to him, Mam?'

She turned and looked at him for several long moments. 'Oh, son, there's no easy way of telling yer this but . . .' She took a deep breath. 'Yer brother's got himself married.'

'Married! But he wasn't even courting when I left. Wasn't even seeing anyone to my knowledge. Who to, Mam?'

The answer was a long time coming. Finally she said: 'Val.'

Bill stared at her, stunned, feeling his life's blood drain from him. 'Val? My Val?'

'Not your Val any longer, son. She's Daniel's Val now. And,' she added emotionally, her voice lowered to barely a whisper, 'there's a baby on the way.'

'Baby? No! No, Mam, I don't believe it.'

She moved across to him and put her work-worn hands on

his shoulders. 'It was as much of a shock to me as it is to you. Daniel never so much as breathed a word of any of this 'til he told me he was married – and I'm his mother. I don't know all the ins and outs, son, just that about a month after you left he comes home one night and tells me he's wed and has come to collect his stuff. He told me to tell you if ever you came home that he and Val had been secretly seeing each other for months. They both wanted to come clean about it all but couldn't bring themselves to do it. He said they didn't want to hurt yer, son.'

Bill stared at her, mortified. 'Hurt me, Mam? What do they think I'm feeling now? Let me tell you, hurt isn't a strong enough word for how I feel. Is there a word that describes having your guts ripped out?' He shook his head, bewildered. 'I can't take all this in, I just can't. Val and me were so close. We really loved each other. I'd have known if there was someone else, especially my own brother. This can't be true.'

'Why would I lie to yer, son? I'm only telling yer what I was told and it came from Daniel himself. It grieves me to be telling yer this as much as it does you to 'ear it, but I'd sooner you 'eard it from me than anyone else.'

'I'm going to go and see them.'

She grabbed his arm. 'What's the point? Besides, we ain't welcome. Neither of us.'

'What! What do you mean, we're not welcome? Whatever has happened we're still Daniel's family.'

'Not any more we ain't. He made that very clear. He said that despite feeling guilty about himself and Val, he had to live down the fact of you being a thief and the only way to do that was to have nothing to do with us any more.'

'Daniel said that? I can't believe it. And he thinks I'm guilty? My own brother thinks that?'

Hetty Wadham's eyes filled with sadness. 'It seems Val does too. She wants nothing to do with you or me ever again. They both just want to get on with their own lives.' She wrung her hands, distraught. 'Oh, Bill, you think you know someone and then you realise yer don't know 'em at all. I'd never seen your brother like that before. He was so cold, like we were nothing to him. And we were always so close, the three of us. Or so I thought. Daniel was always the quiet one, always following you around just like yer shadow, no matter how much you tried to get him ter do things fer 'imself. He would only work for Collier's 'cos you worked there. You got him set on, remember?' Hetty eyed him beseechingly. 'What went wrong, Bill? Why is 'e acting like this? I can't understand it!'

'I don't know, Mam. I thought I knew my brother inside out. I obviously didn't.' A dreadful thought suddenly struck Bill and he eyed her, horrified. 'How long had it been going on? Daniel and Val, I mean?'

'I don't know, son. Obviously long enough for them to get married almost as soon as you'd gone. Look, Bill,' she pleaded, 'you can't put yerself through it. You're not the first this has happened to. It couldn't have been easy for Daniel or Val, her being betrothed to you when all the time it was Daniel she . . . Look, son, how do yer think you would feel if you'd gone ahead and got married to her not knowing how she truly felt because she didn't want to hurt yer, and this had all come out later? 'Cos it would, yer know. People can't keep their feelings hidden forever. Best it happened now, eh? As for the theft . . . well, it just brought it all out in the open. A blessing in disguise in a funny sort of way.'

She eyed him beseechingly. 'Look, all this is hard fer me too. Daniel's my son and his wife is carrying my grandchild – and because of all this she doesn't want me to see it, or you its uncle. And that's their right, Bill. We can't force 'em, it wouldn't be fair. We have ter let 'em get on with their lives and you must get on with yours. Put the past behind yer and move on. We can always hope that things may change in the future.'

Bill knew his mother talked sense but the shock of it was

overwhelming. 'That's easier said than done, Mam. At the moment I don't care what people think of me. If they want to believe I took that money, then let them. I know I'm innocent, so do you, and deep down so does Mr Collier. That's what's most important to me. But I can't stay . . .' His voice faltered. 'I can't stay around here knowing I might bump into Daniel and Val.'

'They live the other side of town, Bill, the chances would be slim.'

'Even so, I can't risk it. I don't know if I could handle it, seeing them together, happy as a family.'

'But yer can't go away again, Bill. Yer belongs here. Yer can't let this ruin yer life. Yer twenty-four. You'll live down yer name being blackened given time. Other men have lived down worse and are still around to tell the tale. And you'll meet someone else you'll love just as much as Val, believe me yer will. Please don't go, Bill.' His mother's eyes filled with tears. 'I'll miss yer.'

Bill stared at her, fighting his conscience. He desperately wanted to get away but he was trapped and he knew it. He loved his mother dearly. She'd been the best mother a man could ever wish for. Without a word of complaint she had raised her two sons alone after their father had died when Bill himself had been hardly four years old, Daniel a year younger. She had worked her fingers to the bone in the process.

After all she had done for him out of pure motherly love, he couldn't leave her to fend for herself. And now she was having to endure all this. Her elder son branded a thief and her family divided over the love of a woman. But one thing she was wrong about: Bill knew he would never meet a woman he would love as much as Val, despite what had happened to part them.

The next three years passed in a daze for Bill, despite doing his best to come to terms with what had befallen him. The arrival of the war, despite its horrors, came as a Godsend to him. He could get away from his painful memories and hopefully learn to live with them once and for all, return with a more positive outlook for his future and at the same time still provide for his mother by way of his army allowance.

Bill's war, though, was far from the escape and chance to rebuild his life he had hoped it would be. He saw atrocities that sickened his stomach, humans doing unspeakable things to other human beings and showing no remorse. He lost friends, witnessed them blown away before his eyes. Coming on top of everything else this could have been the end of him. In fact what it did was make him view his own situation in a very different light.

When he thankfully returned the horrors of war had dulled people's memories, given them other things to think about, and his once being branded a thief was forgotten as he was hailed as a hero along with all the other men who had escaped with their lives. That problem at least had been dealt with. But his love for Val, he knew, would never leave him. He must, however, stop wallowing in self-pity.

The war had brought home forcefully to him that life was very fragile and it was selfish of him to begrudge his brother and Val their happiness. People had suffered far worse than he and lived with the consequences. That's what he must do. He must look to the future, be thankful he had one.

To his mother's joy and encouragement, with his demob payment he bought himself an old lorry and, with Owen alongside him, set himself up carrying out the only business he knew: removals. For a long time things were slow and sometimes at the end of the week he had made hardly enough to pay the bills, but Bill was happy enough with this state of affairs and plodded along.

All was fine until another blow struck him. Three years after the war ended, in 1948, his mother passed away.

Bill was distraught. She had been the woman who had given birth to him, cared for him and loved him despite everything. She had also been his rock and without her wisdom and encouragement he would never have come through such a terrible period in his life. Now she was gone and he would miss her dreadfully.

As he had sat by her coffin the night before her burial it had come to him that maybe her death could bring some good. Maybe he could put matters right with his brother. At least make peace with him. After all, Daniel's only crime was to fall in love with a woman. Bill knew their mother would not have wanted him to pass up this opportunity of trying for a reconciliation.

To his utter dismay he did not get his chance to make amends. Daniel never came to their mother's funeral. He just sent a wreath offering condolences from himself and his family. The words on the card were sharp and cold, no emotion in them at all. Bill was dumbstruck that his own brother could act so callously. But as hard as it was to understand, if this was what Daniel wanted he would have to accept it.

As Bill buried his mother, he buried his past, promising himself never to think of those dreadful times again. And he had kept his promise to himself until the death of Ernest Collier had forced him to revisit it all.

Face lined with grief, he unclasped his hands from behind his head, rose from his chair and stood before the table. He leaned over and laid his hands flat on top. The question tormented him again. Should he or should he not go to Ernest Collier's funeral?

He stood for several moments deep in contemplation, going over and over the reasons for and against, and as he did so an ironic thought struck him. He realised that his dreadful dilemma was all down to Owen. If he had not been so lost in his own thoughts that fateful morning the chances were the accident wouldn't have happened and consequently Bill would not have been at the hospital to see Val and learn of Ernest's death. By the time he had heard the news through the grapevine the funeral would probably have been over and he would not now be faced with such a terrible decision.

Then another thought struck him. If Owen hadn't lost his concentration that morning neither would Bill have had to go to the warehouse so late that night to replace Mrs Cudbull's wardrobe and come across Herchell and Jenny. So Owen's lapse and its repercussions had brought some good as well.

His thoughts returned to his problem. The beginnings of an idea began to form. He thought it out then nodded, satisfied. There was a way he could say his goodbyes to Ernest and not cause any trouble to his already deeply grieved family at such a time. At the cemetery there were several stands of trees. He would conceal himself behind one and pay his respects from a distance.

When Ernest Collier had been laid to rest Bill would once again close the door on the past and get on with his future.

# Chapter Fourteen

'Who are you looking for?'

'Pardon?' Valerie Wadham looked up at her husband, bewildered. 'I'm not looking for anyone.'

'Then why do you keep staring towards those trees?'

'Do I? Oh, I didn't realise I was, Daniel.' She shuddered. 'I just feel . . .'

'What?'

She sighed. 'Sounds silly, but a presence maybe.'

He cupped his wife's elbow. 'You're distraught. It's understandable. Come on, the others have all gone. We'd best get back to the house to welcome the mourners. It won't look right if we aren't there.'

Val smiled faintly. She wished they'd all just go to their own homes. She hadn't the heart to face a wake. But that wouldn't be fair. Her father had been a popular man, people were shocked by his sudden death and needed to stand around armed with their plates of food and glasses of beer or spirits and talk about him to ease their grief. For herself, she would rather be alone. But that would come later, when everyone had gone. 'Yes, you're right. Where's Alan?'

'He went on ahead. He knew you needed a few minutes by yourself.'

'Then we'd best hurry. It wouldn't be fair to leave our son to greet people alone.'

Several hours later Daniel handed his wife a cup of tea. 'Sure you don't want anything stronger?'

She shook her head. 'No, thank you. I'm going to drink this then go upstairs and try and get some sleep.'

'In that case I might pop out for a walk. Get some fresh air. Do you mind?'

She looked at him for a moment. The passing years had not been kind to Daniel. His once thick head of mousy hair had receded to a few fine strands on top of his pate and lanky slimness had given way to middle-aged portliness. He was in his way, though, quite handsome still and would be even more if he chose to smile more often. If only, she thought guiltily, she could love him like a wife should love her husband. If only the past didn't keep getting in the way.

At the thought of the past the memory of that strange feeling that had overcome her while standing at her father's graveside flooded vividly back. Why had she turned and stared across at the clump of trees? *Had* she sensed someone's presence? *Had* someone been watching them? Dare she let herself think it could possibly have been Bill?

Oh, Bill, she thought sadly. Despite everything, what she would give just to see his face again. But more importantly to hear for herself him telling her that he hadn't truly loved her, that all his words of endearment had been lies said so as not to hurt her. Even over twenty years later she couldn't believe that he had been able to lie so convincingly. Maybe if she could look into his eyes and hear the words from his own lips, finally she could put his memory to rest.

'Are you all right, my dear?'

She mentally shook herself. 'Pardon? Oh, I'm just tired. It's been a long day.' She eyed him worriedly. 'Daniel, are you upset by Pops leaving the business to Alan?'

'No, should I be? It was his business and he was quite entitled to leave it to whoever he wanted. Besides, I don't expect my son will turf me out as soon as he takes over the reins in six months' time.'

'Oh, Daniel, of course he wouldn't.'

'Then I've nothing to worry about, have I?' He laid a hand on her arm. 'I love you, Val. You know that, don't you? Now go to bed and get some sleep. I shan't be long.'

She watched him depart, staring blankly at the door he closed behind him, her heart filled with sadness. Had Daniel ever suspected she did not return his feelings, had never loved him the way she felt a wife should? Not the sort of love that made your heart dance wildly, like her love for Bill had done.

Having loved as deeply as she once had, Val knew the love she felt for Daniel was the kind you would feel for a brother. She had married him on the rebound. Been swept along by his pursuit of her after his brother had disappeared, leaving a note for her in Daniel's care. It was short and blunt. Bill had confessed he had tried to take the money so he could get away from Leicester and from her. He told her he did not love her any more, hadn't for a long time but couldn't bring himself to tell her. In the circumstances he felt it best they have nothing to do with each other ever again, and those were his mother's wishes too.

Val had been distracted with grief and shock.

She sighed, tears pricking her eyes as the pain of the past returned.

She had been so confused and bewildered by Bill's admission of guilt and his callous rejection of her she had unwittingly allowed herself to become overwhelmed by Daniel's persistent attentions. And, in her youthful innocence, being close to him in a strange way made her feel she still had a link with Bill. Only weeks later, with Daniel's surprise production of a special marriage licence, while she herself was still pining for the man she had lost, they had secretly married. Daniel had convinced Val it was what she wanted and made it sound exciting, like an adventure. She had gone to the register office like a lamb to the slaughter.

Very soon after, only a matter of days, it struck her with terrible force just what she had committed herself to. But it was all too late. Daniel and she were tied for life and almost immediately Alan was on the way. She had no choice but to get on with it. And she could not deny that despite the fact her life with Daniel had been a disappointment, he had been a good husband to her, a good father to Alan, and in return she felt she had been a dutiful wife.

Despite her endeavours to put Bill's memory behind her, her son's startling resemblance to his uncle was a constant reminder of what might have been. If Daniel had ever noticed his son's resemblance to his estranged brother then he hadn't commented on it and neither had her father or anyone else close to them. For that Val was thankful.

Over twenty years later she could still vividly picture her father when she had nervously broken her news of her marriage. His large fierce-looking face had creased in shock, eyes overflowing with tears. 'Oh, Val, my baby,' he had choked. 'What have you done?' And she knew he had been wondering how she could marry a man while she was still grieving for his brother. But, despite his obvious devastation he had thrown his great bear-like arms around her and pulled his daughter close. 'If this is what you want, my darlin', then I wish you the best and of course I'll welcome Daniel into the family.'

And because of his deep love for her, her father had treated Daniel very fairly and in return he had worked hard to gain Ernest's trust and become his right-hand man. Her father had started out in business with a horse and cart bought with a small legacy left him by an old maiden aunt, and Val had always been so proud of him. It had provided them all with a decent living, which she hoped would continue for Alan and eventually his family when he chose to settle down.

'You all right, Mum?'

Val jumped, to see her son standing before her. 'Oh, hello, love. I didn't hear you come in.'

'You were too deep in thought. What were you dreaming about?'

She smiled. 'Your grandpa, and how much I'll miss him.'

Alan sat down beside her. 'Me too, Mum. You know how much I loved the old bugger.'

'Alan really,' she scolded.

'A term of endearment, Mum. He would have laughed to hear me speak of him like that.'

'Yes, he would.'

'Where's Dad, Mum?'

'He's out. He says he's gone for a walk, but I know he's gone for a drink.'

'Oh, I needed to talk to him.'

'What about?'

'Grandad's will. It's not right he left the business solely to me. He should have left it to Father.'

'But that's what he wanted to do, Alan. To be truthful, your grandfather didn't expect to die so young. I expect that when he made his will he thought that by the time he did pass on, your father would be wanting to be taking things easy. Anyway, it was Pops's way of showing how much he loved and trusted you. That business was his pride and joy. And so, Alan, were you.'

Her son sniffed away tears. 'I loved him very much, Mum.'

'Pops knew you did. He said you reminded him of himself when he was young. Full of energy and purpose. My father knew what he was doing when he left Collier's Carriers to you.'

'But what about Dad? He must be upset. He must have thought Grandad would automatically leave it to him. To you both, for that matter.'

'Well, if he is upset he hasn't said anything. You're his son, Alan, it's not like your grandfather left the business to strangers. He knew you'd see your father and me all right. Your dad knows your grandfather had no ulterior motive and it's like Daniel said: you'll not turf him out when you do take over.'

Alan shook his head. 'As if I would, Mum. In fact I've been thinking when Collier's does become legally mine in six months' time I could make Dad a partner. We'd run it together then. It would be like my twenty-first birthday present to him. What do you think, Mum?'

'Oh, Alan, I think that's a wonderful idea.'

'Then that's what I'll do. It seems only right after all the work Dad has done over the years. And . . . don't tell him, Mum. I want to surprise him. I'll have all the paperwork ready to give him on my birthday.'

She threw her arms around him and hugged him tightly. 'Oh, Alan, he'll be delighted. I can't wait for your birthday to come so I can see his face.'

'I'm glad that's all settled. I feel better. Now, Mum, there is something else I wanted to ask you. Who's Uncle Bill?'

She stared at her son, shocked. Her obvious distress worried him greatly. 'Mum, what is it?'

'Oh, er . . . nothing. Who . . . who told you about him, Alan?'

'Well, you know how people talk at funerals, Mum. They love to reminisce. More to the point, why haven't you or Dad ever told me about him before?'

'It's a long story. He's your father's brother. They were estranged years ago over something that happened. At the time your Uncle Bill made it very clear he wanted nothing to do with us and he hasn't changed his mind so there didn't seem any point in our telling you about him.'

Alan's mouth set grimly. 'Did he not want anything to do with his family because he was embarrassed about trying to steal from Grandad?'

202

'You know about that!'

'Just what I overheard. That the weekly takings were found in his pocket and so Grandad sacked him. Do you think he took the money, Mam?'

'I don't know, Alan. He did admit it but . . .'

'You don't think he did?'

Before she could stop herself Val blurted, 'The Bill I knew would never have done something like that. Anyway it's all past history, best forgotten. Let's talk of something else.'

Alan stared at her, shocked. There was something here he didn't understand, something in his mother's tone that implied there was more to this business than the fact that his father's brother, who had once worked for the family business, had been caught trying to steal the takings. His curiosity was aroused, but he felt it would be unwise to probe any further at this moment.

'So,' his mother was saying, 'when are you going to get yourself a nice girlfriend? You seemed to be getting on well with Angela though I notice you haven't mentioned her for a while.'

'Mother,' he said warningly.

'I'm only showing a proper interest, Alan. I don't want to force you to settle down until you're ready. I know many men of twenty are these days but you've plenty of time for all that.' She smiled and patted his knee affectionately. 'I want to be your mother for a while longer before another woman takes over. It's just nice for me to think of you having a girl to accompany you instead of always going out drinking with your mates.'

'We don't always go out drinking, Mum. You know well enough we go dancing or to the jazz club or take it in turns at one of the lads' houses to play records.' Alan smiled. 'It's funny, though, that you should ask me if I'd met any nice girls recently. As a matter of fact I did when we helped out the furniture shop by doing that delivery for them because they hadn't a van big enough. She was very pretty.'

Val eyed her son keenly. 'So what's her name then? When are you seeing her?'

'Mum,' he scolded, 'I only said I'd met her. She was the daughter of a customer called Mrs Jeffries. A right character. She and her neighbour had us in stitches with their antics. In other circumstances I might have asked Jenny out but it didn't seem right just when Grandad had died.'

'You should have, Alan. Your grandfather would never have seen that as being in any way disrespectful to him. You know that as well as I do, son. Still, you obviously liked this girl enough to remember her name. I hope you meet up with her again.'

Alan decided to change the subject. 'Can I get you anything? A cup of tea?'

'No, thanks, dear, I'm full up with tea. Must have drunk a hundred pots of it today,' she exaggerated. 'Why don't you go and join your father for a drink?'

He shook his head. 'I'm not leaving you on your own tonight.'

'Don't be silly, Alan. I'm not ill, just in grief, which will ease with time. I'm going to bed anyway. So go on, join your father.'

'All right, I will.' He bent and kissed her cheek. 'See you in the morning, Mum.'

Daniel took a sip of his drink then put his glass down on the table before him. He was not a happy man. In fact he was livid. This turn of events was not the way he'd expected things to be at all. The business should have come to him, not his son. In reality his position was no more than that of caretaker. It wasn't fair. He'd worked hard all these years, kept his head down, played the doting husband and father, the dutiful son-in-law. And for what? For his son to reap the benefits. Well, not if *he* could help it.

Daniel pictured his son. A good-looking lad he and Val had produced. He was a nice boy too, an intelligent one. But Alan had one big flaw in Daniel's eyes: he was almost the image of Bill. It was like constantly having his brother alongside him, to remind him of what he had done.

Not that Daniel had ever had any regrets. Why should he? All his life he'd had to live in Bill's shadow. Finally he had seized his opportunity and turned events in his own favour. And as far as Daniel was aware Bill had done all right for himself. But then, Daniel had always known he would. Everything Bill had ever done made good.

For as long as he could remember Daniel had envied his elder brother. Of the two of them Bill had been blessed with the looks, blond and broad against Daniel's own mousy thinness. Even their own mother had looked on Bill as the man of the house after their father passed on. Daniel was never quite able to achieve the standards Bill set at school and got tired of teachers constantly comparing them. And he was fully aware that he only received special attention from girls as a means of their getting closer to Bill. He only got set on at Collier's as a labourer because Bill had vouched for him. Then, to top it all, the boss's daughter fell in love with Bill and Daniel's envy turned to insane jealousy.

Why couldn't it have been him? He wanted what Bill had, desperately so, but while his brother was around he would always be second best and there didn't seem to be anything he could do about it.

Daniel hadn't planned to take the money. He had entered the office by the side door just to check if Ernest Collier was still around, and if not to collect his wages from Mr Skinner the clerk and hopefully slip home early undetected. The office was empty as he'd hoped and he was just about to move on when he spotted the weekly takings piled in the middle of Ernest's desk.

Daniel stood and stared at it all, mesmerised. He'd never seen so much money before. He felt an urge to touch it, feel what it was like to hold so much in his hand, experience the power it would bring. Daniel's palms sweated profusely. The money was there for the taking.

Suddenly he saw this as his chance of escape. Bill had Val and all that came with her. What had he got? Just the promise that, as his brother, Bill would look after him. Well, this money would change all that. It would free him from Bill's shadow, afford him the chance to do something for himself. Get away, start a new life.

Before Daniel could stop himself he had stepped across and snatched it up. Then a sound reached him: the rumble of the cistern. Ernest was obviously in the cloakroom and was coming back.

Shock set in then, and blind panic at the possible repercussions. His panic was so great it didn't occur to Daniel to put the money back or leave the same way he had entered. He just spun on his heel and dashed down the corridor past the cloakroom Ernest was about to emerge from. Further on he saw the line of pegs where his fellow workers' outdoor jackets were hanging.

Bill's jacket . . . Daniel's eyes glinted darkly. He'd wished for a way to be rid of his brother and here it was. Without further ado he stashed the money inside Bill's jacket then fled unseen into the yard where he hid behind a wall to catch his breath. He then returned to the outbuilding he had come from, thankful he hadn't been observed, and pretended to busy himself until home time.

He acted as shocked as all the others to hear his brother had been sacked for theft and kept it up on arriving home to find his mother distraught, Bill's scribbled note clutched in her hand.

And then everything had fallen into place far more easily than he had dared to hope.

In her devastated state of mind after reading the letter he had so carefully forged in Bill's handwriting, Val had readily accepted Daniel's shoulder to cry on, his listening ear, such genuine sympathy, then his advances which grew in intensity. Before she knew what was happening to her Daniel had convinced her it was he she wanted and taken her to the register office. Daniel did not love Val and the fact she still harboured feelings for Bill was of no consequence to him. He could live with that knowledge when there were compensations to be had in return.

Ernest had had no choice but to accept the situation and offer to Daniel all he had been going to give to Bill. Daniel was jubilant.

Only it didn't take him long to realise that what he'd achieved was not quite all he had anticipated.

The business was not as lucrative as he'd always thought it to be. The big house and the fast car, all the trappings he felt a person of his status should have, did not materialise. True, he was elevated to Ernest's right-hand man. But it was not the soft office-bound job he had envisaged but a shirt-sleeves, turning-his-hand-to-anything-that-needed-doing existence, spent organising the men, loading and offloading, maintaining the vans, visiting customers . . . In fact little better than he had done previously but with a lot more responsibility and longer hours. No more clocking on and off at precise times, no more sloping off early when the boss wasn't looking. And for all of this Daniel considered he was paid a paltry wage, just enough to keep his wife and son comfortably in the small semi-detached house Ernest had bought for them after their marriage.

As the uneventful years slowly passed and his situation did not improve the only thought that kept Daniel going was that one day, when Ernest either retired or passed on, it would all become his. Then he could do exactly what he liked, live the kind of life he felt he should have.

When Ernest's will had been read, how Daniel had managed to contain his outrage he would never know. After all his hard work, how dare his father-in-law leave the business solely to Alan? His son was young, had his whole life in front of him to do with as he wished. Daniel was middle-aged, too old to start again, and why should he when he had laboured hard and sacrificed so much already? It was not fair.

A memory of earlier that day flashed to mind. He'd seen his wife looking continuously towards that clump of trees in the cemetery. Was she too stupid to realise that he knew who she was looking for? Bill. Val still cared for his brother after all these years and it irked Daniel deeply. Fuck you, Bill Wadham, he thought maliciously.

He lifted his glass and took a sip of his drink as a plan took shape. He knew exactly what he was going to do. What he had originally planned all those years ago when he had first clapped eyes on the mound of money sitting on Ernest Collier's desk. But no snap decision faced Daniel this time. He could take his time. He had six months until Alan was twenty-one and legally able to assume his place at the helm. Ample time for what Daniel intended to do.

A smile twitched at the corners of his lips. Caretaker, indeed. Oh, he'd caretake all right. Take great care to take all he could.

A satisfied glint sparkling in his eyes, he looked at his watch. It was eight-forty-five. Time to go home to his nice boring little wife waiting for him in his nice comfortable house in a nice part of town. He smiled, eyes narrowing. Not for much longer.

Downing the rest of his drink, he rose and departed.

Alan arrived only minutes after Daniel had left. 'Has my father been in?' he asked the landlord.

He nodded. 'Just left.'

Alan was disappointed. Despite his deep affection for his father, he had never considered them to be close exactly. There always seemed to be a gulf between them and despite Alan's continued efforts over the years, that gap remained. As a boy he could never understand this, envied the closeness between his friends and their fathers, but now he was older he had learned to accept Daniel's ways. Regardless he still harboured a desire that one day things might change between them. He had been looking forward to having a drink in the pub with him, had hoped their joint bereavement might have been a trigger to start the process. Obviously not. Setting aside his disappointment he smiled at the landlord. 'A pint of your best, please, Jim.'

Armed with his glass of beer, Alan found a vacant seat in a quiet corner and sat down. He wasn't really in the mood for company and had purposely ignored a group of people he knew gathered at the other side of the large room, hoping they didn't ask him to join them. As he sipped his beer his thoughts centred on the snippet of conversation he had overheard at the funeral and on the one he'd had with his mother.

Alan had had no idea he had a living relative on his father's side. The existence of an uncle had come as a total shock. Uncle Bill. It had a nice ring to it. Especially since he had no other uncles, that he knew of. Pity this uncle had alienated himself from his family. Despite the fact he was supposed to have been a thief, Alan would like to have known him. *I wonder if he did take the money?* he thought. But he supposed that in the circumstances that would always remain a mystery. Then a thought struck him. This mysterious uncle's surname was obviously Wadham as he was his father's brother. Bill Wadham, he mused. William Wadham. Now where had he heard that name before? It was familiar somehow but at the moment he could not work out why.

209

His thoughts were interrupted by a voice addressing him.

'You coming to join us, Alan? We're off down the Six Twenty Club soon. It's skiffle on a Monday night. Robbie Dawes is playing. I've heard he's great.'

Alan raised his head to see a woman of his own age standing on the other side of the table. She was nice, was Eileen, and an attractive girl. Alan knew she had a fancy for him, but Eileen didn't appeal to him in any other way than as a passing acquaintance so he had never pursued her obvious advances.

'If you don't mind I'll pass tonight, thanks, Eileen.'

'Oh, yeah, of course, you buried your grandad today, didn't you? Not the best way to start a week. I was sorry to hear of your loss, Alan.'

'Thanks.'

She hovered for a moment. 'Some other time then?'

'Pardon?'

'You'll join us down the skiffle club.'

'Yes, next time you all go.'

She smiled winningly. 'See you then. Tarra.'

Talking to Eileen made Alan suddenly think of Jenny. She had been of a similar height and build to Eileen but there was something different about her. What had it been? He couldn't think of anything in particular. Just something about her that had struck something within him and made him take notice of her.

He smiled to himself. She had looked a sight when they had met and she had obviously been embarrassed about it. I bet she looks very good when she dresses up, he mused. I wonder if Jenny likes skiffle? Or jazz, or the new American craze, rock and roll? Maybe after a decent interval he'd go round and ask her out. Then a thought struck him. Alan was no coward, not the sort of young man to shy away from a challenge, but to his mind a girl like Jenny would most certainly have a boyfriend, maybe even a couple on the go. She was probably engaged to be married. He didn't want to cause her the embarrassment of turning him down. So he decided against it.

His thoughts returned to his grandfather. The big man had been a huge part of Alan's life since the minute he'd been born and Alan would miss him dreadfully. There had been many good things about his grandfather but the best thing Alan felt was his wonderful legacy. It had nothing to do with money or possessions. His grandfather had taught him fairness and honesty, the best attributes any man could have to get him through life. Alan raised his glass. 'Here's to you, Grandad, wherever you are.' Downing the last of his drink, he rose and waved a cheery goodnight to the people at the other end of the room then made his way home.

Just after six on the same Monday Alan buried his beloved grandfather, Jenny bounded into the little house on Slater Street and threw her coat on the back of a new dining chair.

'Yer can bleddy pick that up and hang it where it belongs,' scolded May sharply. 'Me new regime, remember.'

Jenny snatched up her coat. 'Sorry, Mam,' she said, going to the cupboard under the stairs and hanging it on a nail behind the door.

'I can see you enjoyed yerself today,' said May, pouring her a mug of tea. 'I hope yer ain't gonna be this late every night, leaving me to cook the dinner.' Holding up a cracked mug, she grimaced at it. 'These don't look right on me new oak . . . walnut. I shall have ter see about gettin' a proper dinner service. I've never had a matching set before. The market have some nice ones. When I can afford it,' she added, noticing the look on Jenny's face. 'So you gonna tell me what happened today then or what?' she demanded.

'I was waiting to get a word in, Mam.' She took a quick sup of tea. 'Oh, I had a wonderful day. No comparison to working in some crummy furniture shop.'

May eyed her sharply. 'Hey! You'd have been grateful for that job if Mr Wadham hadn't got in first.'

'I know, I didn't mean to sound ungrateful. Anyway, I finished tidying the office, mashed tea, went out for the cobs for dinner, then helped Herchell do some more clearing up in the yard. We took another two loads down the scrapyard.'

'I thought Wadham's did removals?'

'They do, but we hadn't any lined up for today and Mr Wadham was only in for a short time early this morning. He had to go out on business and left me and Herchell to it. It's really nice to think he trusts us to keep ourselves busy. Mr Wadham's business must have been important because he was all dressed up in a black suit. He looked ever so smart.'

'He's a good-looking bloke is Mr Wadham,' said May thoughtfully. 'Nice manners too. A proper gentleman.'

Jenny looked horrified. 'Oh, no, Mam. Don't tell me you fancy my new boss? Please, Mam.'

May sniffed haughtily. 'Can't a woman say she appreciates a fine-looking man when she sees one wi'out her daughter jumping to conclusions?'

'If I have I'm sorry, but just promise me, Mam, you won't set your cap at Mr Wadham? I couldn't stand it, not with him being me boss. I don't want anything to spoil this job for me.'

'I promise yer,' May snapped, 'I wouldn't do that to you, Jenny. Anyway, Mr Wadham has probably got a woman of his own. Well, he would have, a man like him.'

Jenny sighed with relief. Despite her mother's promise she would still keep her eye on things just in case, especially when May had a drink inside her. Then she flirted with anyone whether she fancied them or not. Come to think of it though, Jenny thought, she couldn't envisage her mother and Mr Wadham in a social situation so the threat really didn't exist.

She folded her arms and leaned on the table. 'I'm going with Herchell to help with a removal tomorrow. I asked Mr

Wadham if I could. I could see he was stuck as he has some quotes to go and sort out and Herchell can't do the removal all by himself.'

'That's man's work, Jenny.'

'It might be, but I'm going to have a go. Anyway, it's no different from when we were humping all that furniture outside on Saturday. Only this time I'll be being paid for it.'

May nodded. 'Well, when yer puts it like that.'

'How did your day go?' Jenny asked her.

'Same as usual. From the minute I went in 'til the minute I came out I never saw daylight. It's only Gloria's antics that keep me goin'.' May started to laugh. 'We had a new girl start alongside us today and Gloria sent her off to the stores to get some invisible cotton for the gels on mending – in tartan! The right colour tartan, mind, Gloria warned her. And don't let Alfie the storeman palm yer off with striped.'

Jenny laughed too. 'The poor girl never fell for that, did she?'

'She did. Was beside herself when she came back and said Alfie had told her they'd run out of tartan and they'd only got sky blue pink wi' black dots on.'

' "Sky blue pink wi' black dots?" yells Gloria. "What good is that colour green to me?" ' May guffawed loudly. 'The poor gel's eyes nearly popped out. She thought she was going mad. "Oh, never mind, yer can go and get the order from the cob shop instead," Gloria instructs her, and sends her off wi' a list as long as yer arm and the poor gel was so flustered she got half of it wrong. I asked for potted meat and ended up wi' cheese and pickle. Still, she can machine a straight enough line and that's the main thing.'

'You lot in that factory are terrible to the apprentices, Mam.'

'Yeah,' she readily agreed. 'But it's good fun.'

'Are you going down the pub tonight?'

She shook her head. 'No. Me new regime, remember. I'm determined to stick to it.' She grinned. 'I had a date on Sat'day night with Ron Bates. In the excitement of getting the new furniture I forgot all about it. This new regime must be working, 'cos before I'd 'ave been mad at meself for missing a date – but d'yer know summat, our Jenny, I don't care a jot. And with the money I've saved on not drinking I'm going to get meself some material. Will you give me a hand next Sat'day aft'noon making a start on me new wardrobe?'

'Yes, 'course I will, Mam. What first? A dress?'

May nodded. 'Apparently there's a couple of nice pubs in town. A cut above yer sawdust and spittoon. I thought, dressed in me new dress, I might give 'em a try.'

'What, on yer own?'

'I don't see why not. And don't go mentioning anything to Gloria. I don't want her tagging along. She's enough to put any man off his dinner and I won't get far on me new regime with her hanging on me arm.'

'That's not nice, Mam. Gloria's been a good friend to you.'

'I don't know about good, but I agree she has had her moments, bless her. She ain't a bad old stick really though she's a gob on her like a navvy. It's no good me trying to improve meself then the likes of her letting me down, is it? I've got to be firm, our Jenny. Start as I mean to go on.'

She smiled admiringly. At least her mother was trying to do something with herself. 'Yes, I see your point and you know I'll do all I can to help you. You never know, Mam, some of your new regime might rub off on me, eh?'

'There's no need, Jenny. You're all right as you are. Although a little bit more refinement wouldn't do you any 'arm. I read an article in the *Woman's Weekly* on etti-something. I couldn't pronounce it. Teaches you how to act at the table and whatnot. You want to flip through it too, Jenny, in case you gets taken out for a nice meal sometime by a lad.' She looked at her daughter knowingly. 'Like that one who helped with the furniture. What was his name . . . Ah, yes, Alan.'

'Mam, stop it.'

'I was only going to say I wouldn't mind the likes of him as a son-in-law, that was all.'

Jenny sighed and decided it was time for a change of subject. She raised her chin in the air and took a big sniff. 'Did you say you'd cooked dinner, only it smells like it's burning.'

'Oh, damn and blast!' groaned May, jumping up. 'I've made a shepherd's pie in honour of your first day at your new job. Cost me two bob for best mince,' she grumbled, disappearing into the kitchen. 'I hope yer likes it well cooked,' she called. Jenny heard the oven door opening and seconds later a tremendous crash rent the air. All was silent for a moment then May called, 'D'yer fancy egg and chips, Jenny?'

# Chapter Fifteen

The next few weeks passed pleasantly and rapidly for the two women who lived in the crumbling two-up-two-down on Slater Street, and before they knew it Christmas Eve was upon them.

'So what you gonna be doing with yerself ternight?' May asked Jenny. 'Any plans?'

Jenny pushed her empty plate away and shrugged her shoulders. 'No plans to do anything, Mam. You can't do much without any friends, can you?'

'But it's Christmas Eve. Surely yer gonna be doing summat? I dunno, our Jenny.' Tutting, May shook her head. 'What's that saying: "All dressed up and nowhere to go"? In your case it's "Money in yer pocket and no one to spend it with". Why don't yer go around and see Janet?' she coaxed. 'You two were such good friends, and so were you and the other gels from Stone's as well. Look, yer want to ignore what that old sod said. He can't rule what his workers get up to outside work despite what he thinks.' She clicked her tongue disdainfully. 'They wanna get the Union on to it.'

'The girls wouldn't dare. We all paid the Shop Workers' Union dues but woe betide anyone who asked them about anything. Mr Stone just made sure they were sacked for something the Union couldn't argue with. Anyway, Mam, can we drop it? I've made me decision and I think it's best I let

Janet and the gels decide what they want to do. I've more than enough to be getting on with tonight.'

Jenny took a moment to gaze around the room. In the corner that used to be piled with old magazines and boxes of rubbish, the new standard lamp had been moved aside to make way for a Christmas tree. It was only a small one, held upright in a bucket of sand, but Jenny had decorated it colourfully with anything she could lay her hands on, either homemade or ornaments bought cheaply from the market. Around the walls hung twisted lengths of colourful crêpe paper and intermittent bunches of balloons. On a length of string across the back wall, secured by drawing pins, hung a dozen or so Christmas cards from neighbours and workmates. Jenny had had great fun decorating the room and thought it all looked very festive.

Her eyes lit up as she turned her attention back to her mother. 'I want the dinner tomorrow to be really special being's Herchell is coming. He's really missing his wife and family just now and with the money he's sent home towards Blossom's fare he can't afford much himself.'

'We'll give 'im a good time, stop worrying. We did the last time 'e came, din't we?'

Jenny laughed. 'Yes, we did, Mam. In fact he's still talking about it. I'm glad Mr Wadham helped him get those rooms in Belgrave Road. The landlady is a right little gem. Got no side to her. She told me she thinks Herchell's a right nice gentleman. A cut above some of the riff-raff she's had staying over the years. Mr Wadham let Herchell choose a couple of bits from his warehouse to help make the place look homely and I'm going to run up some curtains for him.'

'Sounds ter me like Herchell has got 'alf of Leicester runnin' around after 'im,' May said good-naturedly.

'Meks a change from how he was treated before. He just needs his wife to arrive now and he'll really be settled.'

'When's she getting 'ere?'

218

'End of January the boat docks. About the same time the baby is due. Herchell just hopes she can hang on to give birth 'til she gets settled in Leicester.'

'What's Mr Wadham doing?'

'Doing?'

'For Christmas?'

'Well, it's funny that 'cos I did ask him and he said he goes to family for the day. Only . . .'

'Only what?'

'Well, Herchell thinks he ain't got none. Family, I mean. Well, none visited in all the time Herchell stayed with him and he didn't seem to visit any. The only visiting he did was to the hospital to see Mr Ford. That's the man I told yer about who injured himself badly trying to shift that wardrobe off the stairs with Trevor.'

May giggled. 'I think that's really funny meself. Like something from the old Keystone Kops films.'

'Mother!' Jenny scolded.

'Well, they should 'ave bin more careful. Serves 'em right, landing up in 'ospital like they did. Anyway, some families ain't the visiting type. Maybe Mr Wadham's family don't live roundabouts.'

'Mmm, I never thought on that. It was on me mind to ask him to join us, just out of politeness being's we'd asked Herchell. But, well, he's me boss, ain't he? It didn't seem proper, so I never.'

'Well, I'm glad yer never. Yer can't expect a man like Mr Wadham to eat off chipped plates. I'm gonna get that dinner service after Christmas, I've decided, then Royalty can come for dinner for all I care.'

'Mam, yer said you were going to get the dinner service when yer could afford it. Er . . . you have paid the dues on the furniture, ain't yer, Mam?'

'Yes,' she snapped.

'Kept the payments up to date?'

'Oi, don't you go questioning me, our Jenny. I said I have, ain't I?'

'Yes, but what you say you've done and what you actually do are two different matters. You've spent a lot of money just lately on things for yerself. Your new handbag and shoes to go with the clothes we made and the material for them. And your new coat. I know that was second-hand but it weren't cheap. Not that I begrudge yer, Mam, you deserve it. But I wondered how you could afford it all and pay all our bills.' A terrible thought suddenly struck Jenny. 'Mam, you did go shopping on yer way home like yer said you would and got the chicken with the money I gave yer from me Christmas box?'

May eyed her innocently. 'Chicken? Shopping? Was I supposed ter? I thought the money was for me ter treat meself.'

'Mam, tell me yer joking?'

May laughed. ''Course I am, yer daft sod! It's hanging up in the pantry ready to be plucked.'

'Plucked! Oh, no,' cried Jenny, horrified at the thought. 'I can't do it, Mam. I'd sooner starve.'

May laughed even louder. 'Oh, this is better than the panto. You can peel yerself off the ceiling, Jenny. I got the butcher ter do the honours. Only it ain't a chicken, me darlin', it's a bloody great turkey all ready to be shoved in the oven. I thought, why shouldn't we have turkey for once being's I had the money? The butcher did me proud. It's a beauty and as clean as a baby's bum, not a feather to be seen. Even its giblets are wrapped up nicely in brown paper all ready to mek the gravy. So there's n'ote else to do tomorrow but peel the spuds and clean the Brussels.'

Jenny sighed. She had been hoping May would have change out of her Christmas box for her to buy something for herself in the New Year sales. She should have known better than to give her mother it all to do the shopping but she'd had no choice as she'd had to work right up to the last minute due to Wadham's commitments, whereas her mother's factory closed at lunchtime for the holiday period. Still, never mind, she thought, it was Christmas after all and having the money to buy a turkey had obviously given her mother a great deal of pleasure.

What an unexpected surprise receiving that Christmas box had been. Bill had gathered Jenny and Herchell around his desk at four the previous afternoon and as well as giving them a glass of sherry to toast the festive season, had handed them an envelope containing their festive gift. 'I thought money would be more beneficial to you both,' he had said. 'And it would be better to give it to you early so you could buy any Christmas extras you might need. Enjoy it, you've both earned it.'

Jenny had felt guilty because she had not bought Bill a present. Despite wanting to, she'd felt it would be far too forward of her. For Herchell she had knitted a colourful striped woollen hat, hoping it would replace the worn grey thing he wore for work. The hat was all wrapped up now sitting under the Christmas tree ready to give him. She just hoped he liked it.

'What about the pud?' she asked May. 'I've still to make that. We should have made it weeks ago but we never had the extra money to get the fruit and stuff. It'll be better than nothing though. Did you get the ingredients?'

She shook her head. 'No, I didn't. Couldn't be bothered with the palaver of it all. I bought a Peak Frean ready made and a packet of brandy custard. So all you've got to do tonight, Jenny love, is wrap my present. You have got me a present?' she asked.

'I might have,' said Jenny cagily.

'Give us a clue what it is?'

'No.'

'Oh, go on, spoilsport. I don't like surprises,' said May sulkily.

'Well, I do. I'm not telling you so you might as well give up asking. Anyway, what are you doing tonight? Going to go down that place in town again you said you liked? What was it called?'

'The White Hart on Humberstone Gate.'

'Yes, that's the one. You enjoyed yourself there. Well, you said you did.'

'Yes, I did. The people were friendly enough. But I didn't meet the kind I was hoping to. They weren't that much better than the lot who go down the North Bridge.' May sighed wistfully. 'I only want a nice man, Jenny, am I asking too much?'

'You'll meet one, Mam. It just takes time, that's all. So are you going to get yourself dolled up and go off into town?'

May shrugged her shoulders. 'Christmas Eve is a night for goin' out wi' friends and celebrating, ain't it?' she mumbled. 'I sometimes wish I'd never started on this new regime then I could have gone down the club wi' Gloria. I bet they'll all 'ave a right old time like they 'ave every other year. In for a penny, in for a pound that lot. They'll be drinking the place dry and dancing on the tables come closing time.'

'You still can, Mam,' said Jenny. 'You can always go back to your new regime after the New Year.'

May eyed her daughter keenly. 'D'yer reckon?'

She nodded. 'Go and enjoy yourself. Just promise me you won't get lumbered with someone you might regret.'

May hurriedly scraped back her chair. She didn't need any further coaxing. 'I will then.'

'Just a minute, Mam,' said Jenny, rising.

May stopped abruptly by the door and turned. 'What is it now? I'm in a 'urry.'

Jenny went over to the armchair near the Christmas tree and delved behind it. She pulled out a parcel wrapped in cheap

Christmas paper and held it out towards her mother. 'You might as well have this now as you're going out.'

'Oh, me present! What is it?' May asked excitedly as she took it.

'Why don't you open it and find out.'

She tore the wrapping in her haste. 'Oh, Jenny love! Oh, it's beautiful,' she cried, holding up the pale blue satin costume. It had a full skirt and the jacket fitted at the waist, flaring out to cover the hips. 'Did yer make this yerself?'

Jenny smiled. 'Every last stitch. Mr Wadham let me use his mother's old treadle when I told him what I wanted to do and didn't know how I'd manage without you finding out. He brought the treadle into the office for me. Said his mother would be glad to know her machine was being put to good use instead of gathering dust. I did it all in my dinner breaks. That was so nice of Mr Wadham, wasn't it?'

May threw her arms around Jenny and hugged her tightly. 'It certainly was. I wish I had a boss like him. Oh, I can't wait ter try it on. It looks like it'll fit me perfect. Oh, thanks, Jenny. Thanks. It's too bloody posh fer the club, though.' She released Jenny and looked at her, a mischievous twinkle sparkling in her eyes. 'But why not, eh? Why not let 'em all see me poshed up? Let 'em all see what May Jeffries is really made of.'

'Why not, Mam?' Jenny agreed, smiling happily.

Just then the letter box on the front door clattered loudly. 'Who the bloody 'ell can that be?' grumbled May.

'Only one way to find out.'

'If it's do-gooders collecting, tell 'em whatever they're collectin' for we need some ourselves.'

Jenny grinned. 'Mam, go and get yourself ready else yer'll never get out.'

As May ran up the stairs, Jenny went to open the front door. She was shocked when she recognised the girl standing on the cobbles outside. 'Janet!' she exclaimed.

'Hiya, Jenny. You gonna let me in? It's bloomin' parky standing out 'ere.

'So,' Janet said a while later, 'I thought, sod you, Mr Stone. Yer might pay me wage but yer don't own me. Who I have for me friend is me own business. If he sacks me just for being friends with you, I couldn't give a toss. I can always get a job at Lewis's. Since you left Stone's, Jenny, it ain't bin the same. The other gels are all right, but it's no fun any more. It used to mek me day, having a natter wi' you on the stairs or in the canteen. Anyway, enough of this. A'yer coming out with us ternight or what? I said we'd meet the others in the Stag and Pheasant at eight and they won't hang around for us, not tonight they won't. Then we're going on to the Hippodrome. Well, yer 'ave ter go dancing' on Christmas Eve, don't yer?'

Jenny smiled delightedly and threw her arms around her friend, hugging her tightly. 'Oh, Janet, I've missed yer so much. And I've so much to tell yer about me new job and . . .'

'Yeah, well, yer can while we're out,' Janet cut in. 'We ain't got time now. And,' she added, flashing her eyes, 'I wanna know how yer mam got the money to buy all this new furniture. My, it does look posh in here, Jenny. Did she have a win on the pools or summat?' She gave Jenny a friendly shove. 'Fer God's sake, go and get yerself ready.'

An hour later, feeling like a glamorous film star in the surprise new outfit that her daughter had made her for Christmas, May tottered happily down the road on her way to the club. Her mind was filled with what everyone would say. She knew she'd be the talk of the evening. Well, she was bound to be, looking like this. So preoccupied was she that the person heading towards her didn't register on May until she was almost upon her.

On recognising the woman facing her, May stopped abruptly, a great surge of panic gripping her. Then panic turned to rage and she roughly grabbed her arm. 'You!' she spat. 'And just where d'yer think you're goin'? I told yer before, yer ain't welcome around 'ere. Now, scarper,' she hissed, turning the woman around forcefully and giving her a hefty push in the direction she came from. 'And if yer ever come back again, I'll do what I threatened last time.'

The woman stumbled, regained her balance and spun back round to face May 'Stop it, please,' she begged. 'Can't yer see I'm ill? I gotta see 'er. I beg yer, May, just once before I die.'

May hurriedly scanned her. It was only a matter of weeks since she'd darkened her door for the first time in over twenty years and in those few weeks she had certainly grown thinner. Her skin now had a greyish tinge and she was slightly hunched over. But then May knew this woman of old and doubted very much she'd changed. Her appearance now could be down to the amount of drink she'd consumed, the cigarettes she'd smoked and the kind of life-style May knew she had lived over the years. Plus this woman was a first-class actress and could very easily be playing a part just to get what she wanted. Well, May was having none of it. There was too much at stake.

'No,' she cried. 'I can't allow it. She knows nothin'. The shock of you 'ud . . . well, she wouldn't be able to take it. She thinks I'm her mother. Me,' she said, stabbing herself in her chest. 'And that's the way it's goin' ter stay.'

'I can't, May. I can't leave it. I need ter see 'er before . . .'

'You, you, you! That's all yer bleddy thought of all those years ago and yer ain't changed, 'ave yer? Think of yer daughter just fer once and what you turning up and us having to explain everything would do to her. You shouldn't 'ave left it so long. For Christ's sake, yer shouldn't have left 'er at all. If yer've a decent bone in yer body, leave well alone. Yer made yer decision years ago. Do the decent thing and keep to it.'

The woman's whole body sagged in defeat. She raised her strained face to May. 'Yer right, I'm bein' selfish. And what good would it do, raking it all up? She might 'ate me, mightn't she, and I couldn't bear that. Yer won't 'ear from me again, I promise.'

May exhaled loudly in relief. 'I don't wish to hurt yer, yer have ter believe that. I'm not thinking of us, it's her I'm thinking of. I can't bear the thought of what all this would do to 'er.'

'Yes, I know. I do really.' The other woman made to turn, then stopped, leaned forward and unexpectedly kissed May on her cheek. 'Thanks for all yer've done, May. Thanks fer raising me daughter for me.'

She turned and walked away, her outline soon fading into the darkness of the night.

Long after she had gone May stared blindly after her. Finally she shook her head sadly. What she had just had to do had been hard, but she knew in her heart it was all for the best, in more ways than one. By God, she thought, if ever I needed a drink it's now. And not just one, several.

The pushing and shoving was getting on Jenny's nerves. 'Two . . . of, sod it!' she exclaimed as the barman once again ignored her and began to serve someone next to her.

'I think the lady was before me.'

Surprised, Jenny turned to see who was standing next to her. She gasped with recognition and her heart raced. The man standing beside her was the last one she had expected to see. 'Hello, Alan,' she said.

He looked at her fully. Although she was familiar, he couldn't quite place her. And he should have remembered such a pretty woman. 'I'm sorry, have we met before?' he asked as he lurched forward against the bar, having been shoved from behind by an impatient reveller wanting to be served.

'You . . .' Jenny raised her voice to be heard over the crowd. 'You delivered me mother's furniture a few weeks ago. Slater Street.'

'Oh, yes. It's Jenny, isn't it?' He openly appraised her. Dressed up she looked nothing like the dishevelled woman he'd first encountered. And he had been right in his assumption. She looked lovely in her full pink skirt and pretty red top, a black coat folded over her arm. Her blonde hair was most becomingly styled in a French pleat.

As he stood looking at her all that was going through Jenny's mind was the fact that he had remembered her name.

'Let me get you a drink,' he offered.

She smiled. 'Thanks, but it's okay, I'm buying a round for me mates.' She inclined her head. 'That's if they've not all died of thirst.'

He laughed. 'Well, you've missed your chance with the barman again. He got fed up with waiting for you to tell him what you wanted.'

'Oh,' Jenny groaned, trying to catch his attention once again.

'Give me your order,' Alan offered again. 'It's Christmas and I'm sure I can stretch to buying you and your mates a drink too. I'll bring them over for you.' A thought struck him and he added, 'Your boyfriend won't mind, will he?'

'I haven't got one at the moment.' Was it her imagination or did he look pleased at that news? She decided to fish herself. 'What about you? Won't your girlfriend mind you buying strange girls drinks, even if it is Christmas Eve?'

'I haven't got one at the moment.'

Jenny hope she hadn't betrayed her delight at this news. 'Oh, well, in that case bring your friends over to join us. I'm sure my friends won't mind.' She felt sure they wouldn't if Alan's friends were anywhere near as good-looking as him.

'Bloody 'ell, Jenny, were d'yer get him from?' asked an impressed Janet when Jenny went back to join her friends huddled in a corner by the door – the pub being so packed they were lucky to get a place to stand at all – and told them what was happening.

227

'Yes, he's nice, ain't he?' she said, eyes sparkling in anticipation. 'Just keep your eyes off, Janet,' she warned. 'His mates are all yours, but this one's mine.' She suddenly frowned. There was something about Alan, what was it? Then it struck her. He reminded her of someone but she still couldn't think who.

'What yer looking like that for, Jenny?' Janet asked, giving her friend a dig in the ribs.

'Eh? Oh, Alan reminds me of someone and I can't for the life of me think who it is.'

Janet appraised him as best she could through the crowd. 'Billy Fury or Adam Faith.'

'Oh, yes, could be. They're both blond and good-looking. Only Alan is at least a foot taller than both of them.'

They giggled.

'Shh,' mouthed Jenny. 'Here he comes with the drinks. Oh, I say, his mates ain't bad either from what I can see.'

A few hours later Alan was walking her home. 'That was a great night, Jenny, thanks for letting us join you.'

'Yes, it was a good evening,' she agreed. In fact the best Christmas Eve she could ever remember having and it was all down to having Alan with her. 'My friend Janet seemed to get on well with your friend Gavin.'

'He's taking her out on Tuesday.'

A jubilant Janet had already told this news to Jenny as they had collected their coats from the cloakroom, but she decided to act surprised. 'Is he? Oh, that's nice.'

'How . . . er . . . do you fancy making up a foursome?'

Her heart thumped wildly. Alan was asking to see her again. She couldn't quite believe it. She wanted to jump with joy and cry out her excitement for all to hear. But that wouldn't do. Instead she said casually, 'I'd love to. I don't think I'm doing anything on Tuesday.'

He grinned, pleased. 'We'll call it a date then. I'll meet you at Lea's corner about eight?'

228

'I'll look forward to it,' she said happily.

A while later she was sitting at the table nursing a mug of tea, her eyes dreamy. Who'd have thought several hours ago that her evening would end like this? Not only was she on good terms with Janet and the other girls again but she had also become reacquainted with Alan. Her first impressions of him had been correct. He was different from the type she normally came across.

Shivers ran up her spine as she contemplated her date with him on the following Tuesday night. Albeit they were going on their first date in a foursome, Jenny didn't care. He had asked to see her again and that was all that mattered. She decided it would be best to keep Alan a secret from her mother for the time being, not wanting to risk May's inevitable grilling about him and demands he should come around so she could interrogate him herself. It would be bound to put Alan off. Time for that later, when and if they became a proper item. Jenny sincerely hoped that happened.

She herself had gleaned as much about Alan on the way home as she felt she needed to know at this stage of their relationship. She hadn't wanted to delve any further in case he thought she was getting too familiar too soon. She already knew he worked for a furniture company delivering goods so they hadn't broached that subject. She had briefly told him she herself worked for a small company near where she lived, mostly office work, but didn't elaborate further on how she helped sometimes with the heavy work in case he thought it unfeminine. Time for more in-depth personal details, she thought, when she knew him better.

They chatted mostly about what they liked to do out of work, what kind of music they both enjoyed, what sort of films they went to see at the cinema and such like. To Jenny's delight they appeared to have similar tastes. And Alan was quite sporty which she thought a change from the kind of men she had been out with before who preferred to spend all their leisure time lounging in pubs or coffee bars. Alan had had girlfriends in the past but nothing serious, he said. That bit had interested her the most.

She smiled to herself. How odd, she thought, that if her mother hadn't decided to improve herself, she would not have bought all that furniture and then Jenny would never have met Alan. It was funny the way other people's decisions could affect your life. Still, on this one she wasn't complaining.

Just then the banging of the front door bouncing off the passage wall abruptly cut into her thoughts.

'I'm 'ome, Jen,' her mother shouted. 'And you, don't drop yer ash on me clean floor.'

Putting down her cup, Jenny groaned. Her mother was drunk, very drunk by the sound of it, and obviously had company with her.

A swaying May appeared in the doorway. Her new blue suit had a beer stain down the front of it, her hair was dishevelled, bag wide open and in danger of spilling, and she was hobbling lopsidedly, the heel of one of her shoes having snapped off.

"Ello, me darlin','' she cried on spotting Jenny. "Ad a good night, did yer? I did. Come in, Arnie, and meet me daughter,' she shouted, kicking off her shoes to clatter across the lino and land against the hearth. 'I met Arnie down the club. 'E's new to the area. Got lodgings down the road. 'E's come back for a cuppa,' she slurred.

Here we go again, Jenny thought. She looked at the man who'd entered and her heart sank. He was a mirror image of Antonio Brunio and looked as shifty too. After all her mother's endeavours towards self-improvement, one night down the club and a few too many drinks inside her had undone all the good. Well, not if I can help it, Jenny decided.

'One cuppa then he has to go,' she said. 'We've a big day tomorrow, Mam. It's Christmas, remember.'

'I ain't so drunk I forgot that, Jenny. Just get the kettle on, there's a love. You,' she said, beckoning Arnie, 'park yer arse on the settee. I won't be a minute,' she said, heading out the back towards the privy down the yard. 'I've just gorra pay a visit. All those gins,' she giggled.

As he plonked himself heavily on the sofa Arnie gazed around him, sizing it up. 'Nice place yer've got 'ere,' he said, impressed.

I know what you're up to, Jenny thought. In your mind you've got your bags packed all ready. She had better quash those thoughts good and proper before her mother came back.

'Yes, it is. Me mam's bloke thinks so, too. Well, he should do, he paid for it all. I'd better go and mash that tea. Milk and sugar?'

Arnie's beady eyes narrowed. 'Bloke? May never mentioned anything about havin' a bloke.'

'Me mam's forgetful when she's had a drink. She's been livin' with . . . Big Harry for years.' Big Harry thought Jenny. Where had she pulled that name from? Then it came to her. Big Harry was one of the characters in an American gangster film she'd seen a while ago at the cinema with Janet. James Stewart had played the lead and James Cagney had been the baddy. 'Big Harry should be back soon,' she continued, quite proud of the way the lies were tripping off her tongue, but then she was May's daughter. 'He went off to deliver some Christmas presents to his mother's and attend to some business. Said he'd meet me mam down the club but he obviously got waylaid. I expect he was planning some sort of job with Slippery Jack down the Pineapple. But then that's Harry. If there's money to be made, no matter how, he's in the thick of it.' She smiled sweetly. 'He's got a temper on him but you'll like Harry, I'm sure.'

Arnie was paling rapidly as she spoke. 'Oh, er . . .' he cried, hauling himself up. 'Is that the time? I've gorra go. Tell May I'll see her sometime.'

With that he shot out of the door.

From outside a loud crash resounded followed by a string of colourful expletives then silence. Jenny shook her head. On her way back from the privy her mother had obviously fallen over something then passed out which she did frequently. As she ran off to investigate Jenny thought at least this saved her from explaining Arnie's hurried departure.

# Chapter Sixteen

Bill couldn't believe he'd walked down this ward weekly for over two months. The time had gone so quickly – though he doubted Owen would agree with him.

'How are you getting on, Owen?' he asked. As he sat down he appraised him. Owen certainly looked cheerier than the last time they had spoken.

'Doctor sez I'm well on the mend, might even get home in a couple of weeks. I get the casts off me arms tomorrow. I can't bleddy wait! Nine weeks I've been holed up in here. I can't believe it's the end of January. Can't wait ter get out. Mind you, I s'pose it ain't bin that bad. Christmas were all right. Might book meself in here every year. I had you to visit me, then the nurses made a fuss of all the patients and the dinners was just grand. Turkey and all the trimmings. Yeah,' he mused, 'seems a daft thing ter say but I enjoyed meself.'

Christmas, Bill thought as he listened to Owen, had been the same as all the others for him since his mother died. Apart from visiting Owen, his day had been spent alone. He had envied Herchell going off to spend the day with Jenny and her mother. From what Herchell had told him on his return they had obviously enjoyed themselves. Bill had not liked telling the lie about having dinner with his family but had done so in order to quash any feeling of obligation Jenny might have to invite him along, which wouldn't be fair just because she worked for him. He had cooked himself a pork chop and vegetables for his dinner and then spent the rest of the day by the fire listening to the BBC Light Programme on the wireless and reading old papers, catching up with the news.

'A'you listening ter me, boss?'

'Sorry, yes, Owen. You were saying you enjoyed Christmas?'

'I knew you wasn't listenin',' he grumbled. 'I'd moved on from that to tell you the doc will only let me out providing me landlady will help fetch and carry for me 'til I get the strength back in me legs.'

'Do you think she will?'

'If I pay her extra, I dare say.'

'I take it then Mrs Daily is definitely out of the picture? I didn't like to ask before in case you thought I was prying.'

'Yes, I finally did the deed. It took me long enough to build up the courage to tell Muriel. I didn't like having to do it but I took your advice and put her right. It was only fair. She weren't happy about it though.'

'I don't expect she was.'

'So how's the business going, boss?'

'Very well, considering you aren't around to oversee things when I'm otherwise occupied. Jenny's proving a Godsend. I did right in taking her on. One of my good decisions. The office has never been so clean and tidy and she's taken to doing the books like a duck to water, which leaves me free to chase after work. She has made some mistakes but she's quick to spot them and keen to learn how to put them right.' Bill laughed. 'Mind you, I'm not exactly the best of teachers. There's much about book work I could learn myself, but we're muddling through between us. And I know I've told you before but you'll certainly get on well with Herchell, Owen. The man is so willing and capable, and apart from the first time I took him with me on a job we've not really had any problems with the customers. They're taken aback at first but no one's passed comment about him being black.'

'And so they shouldn't,' Owen said tartly. 'Bigots some people. The Irish and Scots have the same problem. The Irish are supposed to be thick and the Scots all alcoholics. Let me tell you, the Irish I know have made me feel stupid on more than one occasion, and I know of several Scots who don't touch a drop of the hard stuff. Anyway, have yer any more business coming in?'

'Ticking over as usual, thanks, Owen. Still managing to keep the bailiffs at bay. But if things go according to plan, by the time you come back I'll have more than enough to keep you busy.'

'Oh?'

'I've had a telephone installed,' Bill announced proudly.

'A telephone! My God, Wadham's is going up in the world. I don't have ter speak into it, do I?' Owen asked worriedly.

'No, that's Jenny's domain. And I can't really take the credit for the idea of having it installed. That was all down to her too.' Bill laughed. 'She's not finding the telephone easy, though. She keeps trying to put on a posh voice. It's really funny to hear her. Mind you, we've not had that many calls yet, but I hope we get to the stage where the telephone never stops ringing. I've put an advertisement in the *Leicester Mercury* about our services. I hope that might bring some results. The first one goes in on Friday.'

Owen eyed him, impressed. 'I'll keep me fingers crossed that it does do summat. When I get me casts off, 'course. Crossing me fingers wi' these on is a little bit difficult as you can imagine, boss.'

They both laughed.

Bill turned his head and looked at the large clock on the wall at the bottom of the ward. 'I can't stay the full hour tonight,

Owen. I've got to go around and see Trevor and then I've some catching up with housework to do when I get home. I've been to see your landlady, by the way, and paid your dues.' He put his hand in his pocket and pulled out a small brown packet. 'Here's the rest of your wage.'

Owen hesitated about taking it. 'Look, I really don't need what's in here, not while I'm in 'ospital anyway. I keep telling you that, boss, but yer don't listen ter me. It must be cripplin' yer doing this for me and Trevor when we ain't earning it.'

'I'm managing. Stop worrying, Owen. Now take it, for goodness' sake.'

He leaned over and slipped the packet into his bedside cabinet. 'I appreciate it, boss, yer know that.' He settled himself back on his pillows. 'Talking of Trevor, I can't understand why he's taking so long to mend. I mean, he only cracked his ankle. I think he's stringing you along meself, just too lazy to come back to work. And why should he, eh? When he's being paid to stay off.'

Bill sighed, mouth setting grimly. 'I wouldn't like to think he was up to anything like that, Owen, and if he was how could I prove it? The doctor is signing him off so he must be genuine.'

Owen grimaced. 'I bet he manages to hobble out with his mates, though, on a Friday night.'

Bill decided to ignore Owen's jibe. 'Is there anything you need? Soap?'

'Still got a bar of Lifebuoy left from the last lot you bought me and I can't think of 'ote else, boss. Ta for askin'.'

Bill rose. 'Right, I'll be off then. See you Monday night.'

He made his way out of the hospital, then caught the bus across town to Narborough Road. Trevor lived on a side street off it. His mother smiled happily when she opened the door of her dismal terraced house and found her son's boss on the doorstep.

236

''Evenin', Mr Wadham. Come with our Trev's wages, 'ave yer?' she said, holding out her hand.

The stench of overcooked cabbage and other foul odours that sailed past the filthy woman as she opened the door nearly knocked Bill sideways as always. He took a step back, forcing a smile to his face. 'Yes, I have, Mrs O'Neil.' He handed her the packet. 'Is it possible to see Trevor?'

'He's in bed asleep,' she said in a low voice as though she feared to wake her son up. A farcical statement considering the bedlam that was coming from within. 'Ankle's pained 'im summat terrible all day, poor lad. I got 'old of some sleepin' stuff and gave him a good dollop. He won't wake 'til mornin'. I'll tell him you were askin' after 'im, Mr Wadham.'

'Yes, please do. You haven't any idea when he'll be back at work, have you?'

Pushing a stray strand of greasy hair behind her ear, she folded her arms under her skinny chest. 'Bit of a stupid question to be askin', Mr Wadham, seein's my Trev's still in such pain. I reckons the 'orsepital got it wrong and 'e did much more damage than they were sayin'. They do mek mistakes, yer know.'

'Well, in that case, he should get a second opinion.'

'Yes, 'e's thinkin' on it.'

'Ask him not to think too long, please, Mrs O'Neil. I expected Trevor back at work weeks ago. I need him.'

'I'll tek 'im back to the doc's meself, Mr Wadham. Let you know next Friday what 'e's sayin'.'

'I'd appreciate that, Mrs O'Neil. If Trevor is going to be off for much longer, I'm going to have to review the situation.'

'Eh? Wadda yer mean?' she asked, worried.

'Well, it's like this, Mrs O'Neil. When I agreed to pay Trevor's wages during his absence I didn't expect him to be off for this long with just a cracked ankle. I can't afford to keep doing it. My business is only small.'

Her eyes narrowed, mouth tightening. 'I'll remind you, Mr Wadham, that my boy did 'imself damage working for you.'

'I am well aware of that. I wasn't trying to say otherwise. But I don't have to pay his wage, Mrs O'Neil. I do it because I feel partly responsible for what happened to him. My business can't support a wage that's not being earned for much longer. Maybe Trevor should enquire about claiming sick pay.'

A loud wail erupted inside the house. Mrs O'Neil turned her head and bellowed, 'Shurrup, you lot 'fore I tek the slipper ter yer! And yer dad'll be back from the pub soon, 'e'll soon sort yer out.' She turned her attention back to Bill. 'Sick pay? That pittance! That ain't gonna buy much coal, is it?'

Bill sighed. 'We'll review the situation once he's seen the doctor again. You will take him like you said?'

'I said I would, didn't I, Mr Wadham? I'm a woman of my word, I'll have you know. Now, if you'll excuse me, I've dinner ter dish up.'

With that she stepped back inside the house and slammed shut the door.

What a rude woman, Bill thought as he retraced his steps down the street. He arrived on the main Narborough Road just as his bus sailed past him. 'Oh, hell,' he muttered to himself. He drew back his jacket sleeve and glanced at his watch. It was well past eight and the buses ran every half an hour at this time of night. Be quicker to walk home, he thought. Though by the time he did get home he couldn't see himself getting through the amount of housework he had planned.

As he strode off down the long shop-lined street he wondered how Herchell and Jenny were getting on, putting the finishing touches to Herchell's rooms in readiness for the arrival of his wife Blossom in just over a week's time. Herchell

238

was so excited. Bill had given him the day off to meet her off the train and get her settled in her new home.

He smiled to himself. Herchell was like a man who had been given a million pounds and told to do exactly what he liked with it and when that million was spent another million was waiting for him. He was glad Herchell had found such good accommodation. The landlady was a dear sweet old biddy who, unlike others, hadn't seemed to notice the colour of Herchell's skin and was more concerned that her spotless rooms were to his liking. Herchell had been living there a week now and Bill sorely missed the other man's company but knew he'd have to get used to living on his own again.

The smell of fish and chips assailed him from a shop he was approaching. He sniffed appreciatively, realising he was ravenous, the last time he'd eaten being a cheese cob Jenny had fetched at lunchtime hours ago. The thought of cooking for himself didn't appeal; besides he hadn't really got anything in his larder that he fancied. Without further ado he stepped into the shop and placed his order.

'Just waiting fer chips,' the jolly woman behind the counter told him, stirring a huge metal spatula in a vat of seething fat.

Bill stood against the counter and waited.

'Bag o' chips and some scratchings, Nelly,' a voice behind him bellowed. 'I've just finished helpin' out on the buildin' site and I've money in me pocket. I'm starved and I bet me mam ain't saved me no dinner.'

The woman behind the counter scowled. 'Yer'll 'ave ter wait yer turn like this chap. Gerrin' the queue,' she ordered. 'And I'll give yer Nelly, yer cheeky sod. I might be yer auntie but when I'm workin' it's Mrs O'Neil ter you. I've told yer that before.'

Recognising the name, Bill automatically turned his head and looked behind him. Standing there was Trevor. Workman's haversack slung over his shoulder, he was dressed in a dirty pair of overalls and his face, hands and hair were covered in dust.

Trevor gawped back at him, horrified. He gulped, ''Ello, Mr Wadham. Didn't realise it wa' you.' His eyes blinked rapidly. 'Er . . . I'm just . . . er . . . It's not what yer think, 'onest.'

'And what am I thinking, Trevor?' Bill asked him coldly. 'Shall I tell you to save your lies? Your mother's given me enough of those for one day. I'm thinking an employee of mine couldn't possibly be taking money off me falsely pretending to be practically crippled. Couldn't possibly be moonlighting for someone else. I'm just annoyed with myself for not realising sooner something was going on. Well, lad, all I can say is, I hope your new employers pay you and treat you better than I did.'

'You ain't sackin' me, Mr Wadham?' Trevor blurted. 'It . . . it . . . it . . .' he stammered, fighting to find a good enough excuse '. . . were only a day's work I done, 'onest. It were just a favour to 'elp a mate out.'

'Well, let's hope today stands you in good stead and your mate can fix you up permanently. I'll send your cards in the post.' Bill turned to the woman behind the counter. 'Cancel my order, please, I've just lost my appetite.'

Leaving them both staring after him open-mouthed, Bill strode from the shop.

He couldn't believe how stupid he had been to let a young lad and his mother fool him so easily. How long had this been going on? he angrily wondered as he made his way home. For a while now Owen had been hinting something was going on and Bill had chosen to ignore it. He was struggling to run a business, trying his hardest to make it more profitable, he hadn't the resources to allow this kind of thing to happen and dreaded to think how much money it had cost him. And all because he'd wanted to be fair. Thank goodness his other staff were trustworthy and reliable.

240

A warm glow filled him as he thought of them all: Owen, Herchell, Jenny. What a team. Between them they would make Wadham's Removals a big success, he just knew they would. Provided he learned from this lesson, took his time to pick new staff correctly and never risked this kind of thing happening again.

# Chapter Seventeen

Daniel leaned back in his deceased father-in-law's comfortable old leather chair, put his feet on the desk and excitedly leafed through a booklet he had picked up from a garage that morning. He stopped at one page, eyes sparkling keenly. A Humber Sedan. It was a very nice-looking car. Leather seats, walnut dash . . . in fact all the trimmings a man of his status should have. His eyes glinted. And just what a man of his status was *going* to have in the not too distant future.

His deceased father-in-law's business was going to provide him with a car and as much money as he could amass before his son took over. Then Daniel would get right away from Leicester and start a business entirely his own. In the meantime it wouldn't hurt to take the Humber for a test run.

His eyes lingered on the photograph of the woman draped provocatively over the bonnet, dressed in a swimsuit, her ample chest spilling out of it. She was stunning, he thought. He wouldn't mind the likes of her gracing the seat next to his when he bought the new car.

His eyes stayed fixed on the woman. Just what he needed to bring some excitement into his mundane life. He was fooling himself, though, if he thought he could get anyone like her. But just the thought of having another woman stirred something within him. He gave a secret smile. All in good time, he thought.

Taking his feet off the desk he leaned forward, pulled the black-bound ledger book towards him and fixed his eyes on the balance. Just over six hundred pounds in the firm's account. Nowhere near the figure he had wanted to see. Out of that, the cheques Mr Skinner had brought through for signing would be paid and the wages bill and other incidentals. Collier's Carriers was far from the profitable firm Daniel had always thought it to be. He rubbed his hands over his chin. Time was of the essence and if he didn't do something about this his own plan was in danger of failing. Daniel couldn't allow that. This was his chance to break free, his last chance.

He sat back in his chair and raised his eyes to the ceiling. He would have to make some cost cuts. For a start, at least two of the men could be got rid of. The others would just have to work harder. And he would reduce their hourly rate by sixpence. Ernest had paid them far too much for what they did. He could also make a saving on the quality of packing materials they used. Cheaper crates for a start. People didn't care about the quality of the stuff their possessions were packed in, just the fact that they all arrived in one piece. And there was another saving he would make. Let the men be responsible for their breakages out of their own wages instead of the firm shouldering the cost. He would announce the new rules in the morning and if they didn't like it, then they knew what they could do. Plenty more where they came from.

Daniel tightened his lips grimly. His ideas were a start but still wouldn't be enough for what he wanted. But enough for one day. Leaning over, he picked up the telephone receiver and dialled a number from the catalogue. Moments later he replaced the receiver, leaned back in his chair and put his feet back on the desk.

Just then a tap sounded on the door and the elderly clerk entered.

Daniel whipped his feet off the desk, sitting bolt upright, the booklet disappearing inside the top drawer of his desk. 'What is it, Mr Skinner?' he barked, annoyed at being disturbed.

Albert Skinner coughed nervously as he advanced towards the desk. 'The jobs for next week, Mr Wadham.'

'My son takes care of all that. Give them to him,' Daniel barked.

'Yes, I know he does, Mr Wadham, but Mr Alan is so busy. And with due respect, as the boss I thought you'd like to cast yer eyes over them.'

'Yes, I am the boss, and can't you see *I'm* busy?' he snapped irritably, desperate to get back to looking through the booklet. 'Is there anything else?'

'Just the cheques to be signed.'

Albert Skinner put a sheaf of papers in front of Daniel.

He pushed them aside, wanting time to go through them to see what could be avoided. 'I'll do them tomorrow.'

'But . . .'

'Tomorrow, I said.'

Mr Skinner nodded. 'As you wish, Mr Wadham.'

Albert made his way back to the small office he shared with the wages clerk, a middle-aged woman named Violet Cummings, and wearily sat down at his desk.

Violet looked across at him. 'Did yer get the cheques signed?'

He shook his head. 'Said he'll do them tomorrow.'

'We need to get them in the post tonight. Mr Ernest always signed the cheques promptly.'

'Mr Daniel ain't Mr Ernest.'

Violet grimaced. 'And don't we know it? He always has been a miserable devil but since Mr Ernest died, well, he's starting to act like he's God or summat.' She sniffed disdainfully. 'Mr Ernest 'ud turn in his grave if he could see the way Mr Daniel is acting all above himself now he's in charge. He

245

never gets his hands dirty any more helping in the yard or out on removals, and he hardly goes out looking for business. Just sits in that office all day, ringing through to us to bring things to him. If this is the way it's going to be, roll on Mr Alan taking over, that's all I can say. What's up with Mr Daniel, d'yer reckon, Mr Skinner?'

The elderly man shrugged his shoulders. 'I don't know, Mrs Cummings. Probably just grieving, though it's my guess that the fact that Mr Ernest left the business lock, stock and barrel to young Alan hasn't gone down too well.'

Violet grimaced, shaking her head. 'No, I don't suppose it has. But then it's not like it's gone out of the family so I can't see the problem. Anyway, you'd 'ave thought Mr Daniel 'ud be pleased in a way. He can sit back soon, can't he, and let Alan do all the worrying. He's young, and from what I know of him he's more than capable of running this lot.'

'My sentiments exactly, Mrs Cummings.'

'I get the impression though, Mr Skinner, that you've never liked Mr Daniel?'

'No, I ain't and that's a fact.'

'But why?'

'Why?' Albert stared at her. 'Not that it's any of your business but it was summat that happened years ago.'

'Oh?'

He tutted. 'Well, if yer must know, I wasn't happy with the way Mr Daniel forced his attentions on Miss Val immediately his brother was accused of trying to steal the takings. Then, before yer knew it, they was married. 'Twasn't right in my book.'

Her eyes sparkled keenly. 'Oh, I din't know about that. I remember 'earing years ago, not long after I started, that an employee had tried ter rob Mr Collier but I didn't realise it were Mr Wadham's own brother.'

'Well, it's summat not spoken about outta respect. And we

shouldn't be now. Walls have ears, don't they? And I don't know about you, Mrs Cummings, but I wanna keep me job. Haven't you any work to do?'

She muttered something under her breath and immediately the rhythmical clattering of the keys on her Imperial typewriter filled the air.

The telephone rang. Albert picked it up. 'Good afternoon, Collier's Carriers. How may I help you?' He listened for a moment. 'Hold the line, please, I'll put you through.'

Five minutes later Daniel stormed into the office. 'Is my son around?' he demanded.

Albert shook his head. 'He hasn't come back in yet, Mr Wadham, and with the job he had on I doubt he will for a good while yet. Can I be of any help at all?'

'Er . . . yes, as a matter of fact you can. That was the owner of the Bell Hotel. They've had some renovations done to some of their rooms and want a price for removing the old furniture before the new lot arrives. The owner wants someone to go now. I can't because . . . er . . . I have an appointment elsewhere which I can't cancel.' To test drive a car. He was itching to get behind the wheel and that overrode anything else in Daniel's mind. 'You could go and sort out a price, Mr Skinner.'

'Me, Mr Wadham?'

'Why not?'

'With due respect, Mr Wadham, Mr Collier prided himself on the personal touch, as you know, and the likes of the owner of the Bell Hotel would be expecting the owner of Colliers to call personally, not a lowly clerk.'

Daniel inwardly fumed. Mr Skinner was right. He had no option but to go himself and price the job. He wasn't happy about having to rearrange his appointment with the garage, though. Without another word he marched back to his office and grabbed his coat.

'Well,' said Violet after Daniel had gone, 'I've never seen him in such a temper before.'

'No, me neither,' Albert Skinner muttered under his breath. And if this is the way things are going to be in future, like Mrs Cummings said, roll on Mr Alan taking over, he thought.

# Chapter Eighteen

May took a sip of her drink and looked around, from under her lashes, wondering what on earth had possessed her to come in here in the first place. It had been on a whim. As she had tottered past the Bell Hotel on her way to the White Hart, preoccupied with thoughts of whether this would be her lucky night or not, a man entering by the revolving door had caught her eye. He was tall and smart with a handsome profile, just the type she had dreamed of meeting. Well, in for a penny, she had thought as she had followed him through the doors and into the plush interior.

She found herself inside a large foyer teeming with people. Women of all ages were wearing low-cut, floor-length evening gowns in vibrant silks and satins, fur stoles draped around their shoulders. Men in expensive black evening dress, starched white shirts and bowties stood gathered in groups, smoking cigars and guffawing loudly at jokes. Nearby a woman had her arm tucked beneath a man's and they were talking intimately. She was young and beautiful and the man she was with was the one May had followed.

She suddenly became dreadfully conscious of her own appearance, realising she looked cheap in her red satin dress run up on the old treadle with material from the market, pennies knocked off because the fabric was from the end of a roll. She might look like a glamorous film star to the people who frequented the likes of the working men's club, passable to those at the White Hart Hotel, but here she knew the ladies surrounding her saw her for exactly what she was: a middle-aged woman from the back streets, failing miserably in her attempt to elevate her station. She felt every eye in the foyer was on her.

Oh, May Jeffries, she inwardly scolded herself. What were you thinking of? What possessed you to try and be something you'll never be? She wanted to get out of this place as fast as she could. She made to turn and retrace her steps then stopped. Why should I? she thought. What makes these people think they're better than me just because they have money and I don't? In fact, what makes *me* think these people are better than me? *I'm* as good as anybody.

'Oi, you, where's the bar?' she demanded of a passing bell boy.

'Through there, madam,' he said, pointing.

'Ta very much.' With her head held high she walked as sedately as she could on her three-inch-heels through to the bar area.

'Gin and it,' she told the liveried barman, then nearly choked when he asked for one shilling and sixpence in return.

She couldn't afford to stay the evening in this place even if she wanted. How did they get away with the prices they charged? A gin and it at the club was only sixpence. Well, she had paid an extortionate amount of money for her drink so she might as well enjoy it. Finding the only seat vacant she sat down, crossing her shapely legs and giving a haughty stare at two women who dared look askance at her.

In the reception area Daniel was furious. 'What do you mean, Mr Hargraves is sorry to keep me waiting? He asked me to come. Six-thirty sharp he said. It's a quarter to eight. I gave up an important appointment to come here.'

'I'm sorry, sir, but there's been a hitch in the kitchen and we

250

have two hundred guests expecting to eat at eight.'

'Hitch! I don't care if World War Three has broken out. Tell Mr Hargraves he either comes now or he can get someone else to quote for shifting his furniture.' How dare the man keep me waiting? Daniel inwardly fumed. Me, the head of Collier's Carriers. How dare he?

The receptionist eyed him pompously. 'I'm sure he won't be much longer, sir. Would you care to wait in the lounge? Maybe you'd like a drink?'

Daniel glared at him. 'Complimentary, I hope. Get me a brandy.'

The man clicked his fingers and miraculously a bell boy appeared. 'Would you take Mr Wadham through to the lounge? Make sure he's comfortable and get him a drink.'

'A brandy,' Daniel reaffirmed. 'A large one.'

The receptionist flashed him a scathing look then nodded at the bell boy.

The only vacant seat the bell boy could find was opposite May. 'Would yer mind if this gentleman sits 'ere, madam?' he addressed her.

She raised her eyes and looked up at Daniel. Her heart leaped. Before her stood a distinguished man of about her own age. He wasn't exactly good-looking, balding and turning to fat, in fact. But he must be affluent judging from the cut of his suit. Would she mind? What a stupid question. She did her best not to appear too eager. 'Be my guest,' she said casually.

The bell boy pulled out the chair and Daniel sat down. He flashed his companion a glance. She was a bit over the hill was his immediate thought. The woman smiled at him and he nodded a greeting back. Then he looked more closely at her. For her age he supposed she wasn't bad-looking. She reminded him of a much older version of Diana Dors. But what really caught Daniel's attention was the woman's cleavage. He couldn't take his eyes off it.

251

It looked so inviting, spilling out of the top of her cheap red dress, and for some inexplicable reason he had to fight an urge to lean over and release her breasts from their restraints. He felt a stirring in his groin, a surge of excitement building inside him. While he was executing his plan, why shouldn't he have some fun, a little distraction? And maybe this woman was the one to give it to him.

He had been loyal to his wife, never strayed once in all their married life, and all the time she had been hankering after another man, his own brother. Daniel had had to live with that knowledge so what did he owe Val? Nothing as far as he was concerned. And besides, what she didn't know couldn't hurt her. He licked his lips as all thoughts of what he was actually doing in the Bell left him.

Leaning over, he looked May in the eye, holding out his hand. 'Da—' He suddenly realised that to give his real name would be stupid. He would have to learn to be very careful if he was going to proceed with this dalliance. 'Paul Smith, pleased to meet you.'

May put down her glass and leaned across to accept his hand. 'May Jeffries. Likewise, I'm sure.'

'Look . . . er . . . it's very crowded in here. How do you fancy finding somewhere quieter for a drink?'

May smiled winningly. 'I wouldn't mind in the least. But won't your wife mind?'

'Wife?' Daniel shook his head. 'I'm not married.'

Just around the corner from the Bell Hotel, in the Stamford Arms on Charles Street, Jenny was feeling very happy with herself. She stole a glance at Alan from under her lashes as he arrived back at the table with their drinks. They had been seeing each other for nearly a month now and for Jenny it felt as if she'd known Alan forever. She was in love. Desperately so. He was the man of her dreams. Not only was he good-looking, he

252

was kind, considerate, and most important of all seemed to Jenny to like her as much as she did him.

As he put the drinks on the table and sat down next to her she started fantasising. Had she met her future husband? Was Alan the one? Mrs . . .? She suddenly realised that during their conversations they had not actually got around to divulging intimate details about each other. Before now it hadn't seemed important to Jenny. But she couldn't fantasise about being his wife without knowing his surname, could she? At the first opportunity she would ask him.

'So what would you like to do, Jenny?' he was saying.

She smiled at him happily. 'I really don't mind.'

'Well, in that case, we could go down the skiffle club, if you like? I'm not sure who's playing, though.'

Jenny didn't care a jot who was playing. She was with Alan, that was all that mattered to her. 'I'd like that.' As she took a sip of her drink she realised he was staring at her. 'What's the matter? Why are you looking at me like that?'

He mentally shook himself. 'Was I? Oh.' He had been thinking how lovely she looked in her floppy pink jumper and straight dark trousers, and how happy he always felt in her company. It didn't matter where they were. In a pub, at the dance hall with a crowd of others, or just strolling along hand in hand, chatting. Alan had known almost from the start that Jenny was special and now he knew without a doubt he had met the woman with whom he wanted to share his life. But he felt it was too soon even to hint at his intentions. He wasn't quite sure of her feelings towards him yet and the last thing he wanted to do was frighten her off. Nice and gradual would be best, he felt. 'I was just thinking how pretty you looked.'

Jenny beamed happily. 'Were you? Oh, thanks. I knitted this jumper meself. I could knit you one, if you like?'

His mother knitted all his pullovers but regardless he said, 'That'd be nice. I could do with a blue V neck. Come on, drink up and let's go so we can get a seat. The club gets packed after nine-thirty.'

On their way to the club they were ambling contentedly down the Humberstone Gate when a man bursting out of the doors of the Bell Hotel to run down the three steps to the pavement collided with them.

'I'm sorry,' he began. 'Oh, Jenny! Well, I'll be blowed, I was just thinking of you.'

'You were?'

'You'll never guess what's happened,' Bill Wadham blurted excitedly, grabbing her arm. 'I was just leaving the yard tonight when the phone rang. It was the Bell wanting me to price the removal of some furniture. The manager saw our advert in the *Mercury* and decided to give us a try. He had asked another company but he had to keep them waiting and . . . well, they didn't. Their loss but our gain, eh? Oh, Jenny, I feel this is the start of better things.' He suddenly stopped, realising she had someone with her. 'I'm sorry, how rude of me. You must think me a madman going on like that.'

'He *is* mad,' Jenny laughed. 'He had to be, taking me on. Alan, this is my boss.'

Bill held out his hand in greeting. 'Wadham. Bill Wadham. Pleased to meet you.'

Frozen rigid by the name, Alan mechanically accepted his hand and shook it.

'And you are?' Bill asked.

Alan's mind was whirling frantically. He couldn't believe this was happening to him. It was like a nightmare. This man was his uncle. A man he'd only learned of a few weeks ago. And a man others maintained was a thief. Although he'd just met him, it seemed to Alan this man had far too open and honest an air about him to be anything of the sort. Thieves had a shifty look, didn't they? But more worrying was the fact that the woman he loved was working for this man and it was obvious from the way Jenny was acting, that she thought very highly of him. She had often spoken of her boss but Alan had had no idea who he was. He himself had only to give his name now and the obvious questions would be asked. What a dilemma. What did he do? He realised Jenny and Bill were eyeing him expectantly. He decided to play for time until he'd decided how best to deal with this worrying state of affairs and forced a smile to his face. 'Alan. Pleased to meet you too.'

Jenny fought to control her disappointment. Was she ever going to find out his surname without blatantly asking him?

'Look, I don't want to impose myself upon you both, but you don't fancy coming for a celebration drink? Just a quick one,' Bill asked.

Jenny turned to her companion. 'Alan?'

It was the last thing he wanted but he couldn't very well refuse without questions being asked by Jenny. Alan ran his fingers through his hair, took a deep breath and nodded.

At his action Jenny suddenly exclaimed, 'Oh!'

The two men looked at her.

She grinned. 'I'm sorry, it's just that both of you have always reminded me of someone and until now I hadn't a clue who. Now I know. You remind me of each other. If I didn't know better, I'd say you were father and son.' Without waiting for a response, she linked her arm through Alan's. 'Come on, then, let's go and have this celebration drink.'

Much later that evening Jenny alighted from the bus and began to walk the short distance to her house. She was humming happily to herself. She'd had a wonderful evening and was seeing Alan again on Sunday, going to watch him play football for the local Sunday team.

The only blight on the evening was that she had noticed he seemed unusually quiet during the short time they had been in Bill Wadham's company. But then in fairness her boss was a stranger and knowing Alan like she did, he was probably just showing his respect for an elder. She was so pleased for her boss, though. Hopefully this was the break he had been hoping for that would lead to bigger things.

As she turned the corner of Slater Street a blast of icy January wind whipped around her and for a moment the imminent arrival of Herchell's wife Blossom crossed her mind. That poor woman, she thought, was going to wonder what had possessed her coming to a climate that for certain months of the year was so hostile. Then Jenny smiled to herself. Until Blossom was used to it she would probably do what her husband did to combat the cold and that was dress in several layers of outdoor clothing. Jenny herself couldn't wait to meet Blossom and welcome her to England. She sounded a lovely woman from what Herchell had told her. And then there was all the excitement of the new baby. Jenny wondered what they would call it. Something exotic, she hoped, in keeping with its origins.

As Jenny neared her house she quickened her pace, wanting to get home, hoping the fire still had enough life about it to warm her cold bones before she went to bed. She knew her mother wouldn't be home yet. May had gone down the town again in her continued effort to improve her life. She so hoped her mother met someone nice soon, someone worthy of her, or Jenny worried there was a danger May would return to her old way of life and she didn't relish that prospect. At least since she had embarked on this quest the house had been kept cleaner and their resources seemed to be stretching a little farther since they no longer had to keep May's 'guests' provided for.

Voices suddenly reached her ears. 'There she is!' she heard someone shout.

Next thing Jenny realised Gloria was running towards her, the nightdress under her open coat billowing, holey slippers flapping on the damp cobbles. She halted, confused.

'Oh, me duck, me duck!' Gloria cried, reaching her and grabbing her arm.

'What's the matter, Mrs Budgins?' she asked then spotted the policeman accompanying her. Panic took hold. 'What's going on? What's happened?' she urgently demanded, eyes darting from one to the other.

'It's yer mam,' Gloria blurted.

'Me mam? What about her?'

'She's in the hospital, miss,' the policeman said. 'I've been asked to fetch you. You are the young lady from number twelve?'

Jenny nodded. 'What's happened to me mam? Has she had an accident or what?'

'I'm not sure, miss. My station had a call from the hospital to fetch the young lady from number twelve urgently. All I know is it's very serious.' He cupped her elbow. 'We'd better go. I've a car here.'

Fear gripped Jenny and then she started to shake. This was a nightmare, it wasn't happening. Any minute now she'd wake up.

'Go with the copper, Jenny love,' Gloria urged, giving her a gentle push towards the car. 'I'll get dressed and follow you down.'

'Best you stay here,' the policeman whispered, leaning towards her. 'Have you a key to her house?'

Gloria nodded. 'Yeah, I've the spare one like they 'ave mine in case of emergencies.'

'Then I suggest you get the house warm and the kettle on,' he said kindly. 'I've a feeling this young lady is going to need your support when I bring her back.'

Gloria clapped her hand to her mouth, eyes filling with horror. 'Oh!'

She watched dumbstruck as the burly policeman guided an ashen-faced Jenny towards the black Wolseley parked nearby. Seconds later, blue siren wailing and flashing, it sped away.

# Chapter Nineteen

Gloria gave the fire a prod and watched distractedly as the sparks from the coke flew up the chimney. She wearily straightened up and raised her eyes to the tin clock ticking merrily on the mantel. It seemed out of place amongst May's smart new furniture. Gloria sighed. Only half an hour had passed since she had watched Jenny being taken to the hospital by the kindly policeman but to Gloria it seemed like hours. She gave another sad sigh and put the poker back against the fireplace, plonking her heavy body back down in the armchair and extending her cold feet to rest them on the warm hearth.

'Any news, Mother?'

Gloria raised her head to see her husband Cyril standing just inside the door. She shook her head. 'Not yet. Poor Jenny. I don't know how's she gonna tek this, I'm sure.' Tears filled her eyes and she sniffed. 'I'll miss 'er, I will. I know we 'ad our up and downs but she weren't a bad old stick, weren't May.'

'Ah, come on, love,' Cyril said, advancing towards her. 'You've got the woman dead already and it might not be as bad as that.'

''Course it is, yer daft sod. Coppers ain't summoned to fetch folks for nothin'. She's dead or just about, I knows she is. I wonder what 'appened? Accident, I expect. Knowing May like I do, I should think she was as drunk as a lord and stepped in front of a bus. Summat like that. Mind you, I knew n'ote 'ud

259

come of this new regime lark. She was getting right above herself. New furniture, new clothes. Even I weren't good enough for the likes of 'er no more.'

Cyril took a deep breath and hooked his thumbs through his braces. 'Ah, come on, me duck, yer can't 'old a grudge against yer friend fer wantin' ter better 'erself.'

'Better 'erself, my foot! In my book yer can't change the 'abits of a lifetime. She mighta looked different on the outside but underneath she wa' still the same old May. And look where it's got 'er – under the wheel of a number twenty-six.'

'Yer don't know that, old gel.'

'Well, what else can it be? She was as right as rain at work today.'

'No, I meant the number of the bus. It coulda bin a fourteen for all you know.'

Gloria's face reddened in annoyance at her husband's inappropriate remark but before she had chance to scold him she heard the key turning in the lock.

Her eyes flashed at him warningly. 'You get yerself off 'ome. This is women's business.'

He nodded thankfully and hurried away.

Gloria heaved her hefty body out of the chair, preparing herself to comfort an extremely distressed girl, and suddenly frowned, confused. Was that humming she could hear? The clacking of heels echoed down the short corridor and then the back-room door burst open and Gloria gasped at the sight of May teetering on the threshold.

'Oi, Jenny!' she bellowed. 'Yer'll never guess what's happened . . .' She stopped, mouth wide in astonishment, as she suddenly realised it was her neighbour she was facing, not her daughter. 'What are you doing 'ere?' she demanded.

'More ter the point, warra you?' Gloria cried, stunned. 'You're dead, ain't yer?'

Bewildered, May flashed a glance down over herself and

patted her chest. 'I don't think so.' She raised her eyes back to Gloria. 'What a'you bin drinking, yer daft cow?'

'N'ote, I'm as sober as a judge. But . . . but the coppers fetched Jenny. Said it were serious. Her mother, he said, asking fer 'er at the 'ospital. They had to 'urry, the copper said, afore it was too late.'

May grimaced scornfully. 'As yer can see, they've got it wrong. I'm as much alive as I was when I left here. Bloody coppers get nothin' right, do they? No wonder this country's in such a state.' Then a terrible thought suddenly struck May and her face paled. 'Gloria, yer did say Jenny's *mother* was askin' fer 'er?'

Mystified, she nodded.

'Oh, my God!'

Gloria stepped across to her and grabbed her arm. 'What is it, May?'

'Eh? N'ote. Nothin'. I've got ter get meself down the 'ospital. You get off 'ome.'

'No, I'll stay . . .'

'Get off 'ome, I said. Look, thanks fer all you've done. I'll . . . I'll speak ter yer termorrer.'

With that May turned and fled into the night.

At the hospital a kindly nurse handed Jenny a cup of tea. 'You say you didn't know Iris Linney? Very strange. She seemed to know you.'

Thankful that it wasn't her mother after all, but still upset from the aftermath of the shock she had received, Jenny slowly shook her head. 'I've never seen her before.'

The nurse grimaced as she sat in the chair next to Jenny. 'We get some funny things happen in the hospital but this is most peculiar. Iris has been with us for nearly a month. I'm surprised she's lasted this long really.' She shook her head sadly. 'When she came in we knew it was only a matter of time. She had no visitors, poor soul. She talked a lot about you, though. Was so proud of her daughter. And just before the end she begged us to fetch you. I was surprised that you'd never visited her before.' The kindly nurse eyed her quizzically. 'But then, if you've never seen her it couldn't have been you she was talking about, could it?'

Mystified, Jenny shook her head again.

The nurse tightened her lips. 'But I don't know of another Slater Street in Leicester and she was so clear about the address. Still, I suppose we'll never know the truth now. It's a shame she died before you got here.'

Jenny sighed despondently, finding the whole situation confusing.

'Oh, I've just remembered something the police might be interested in,' said the nurse suddenly as a memory returned. 'I was making Iris comfortable last night and she was rambling a bit. People nearing their end do, you know, and she suddenly mentioned a sister. "I've got a sister, yer know, nurse. She's been good to me she 'as. Brought my girl up for me." ' The nurse frowned thoughtfully. 'Now what did she say her sister's name was? Maybe it might help the police trace her proper relatives. Er . . .' She sat for a moment deep in contemplation then suddenly said, 'April, yes, that's it. But she said the sister now called herself by her second name of May.'

Jenny gawped. '*May*, you said?'

'Why, yes, dear. Does the name mean something to you?'

Just then a commotion resounded from outside the office and the nurse jumped up. 'What on earth . . .'

The door flew open and a dishevelled May stood there, panting heavily.

Jenny jumped up also. 'Mam, what's . . .'

May's hand was raised in warning. 'Jenny love, just believe me, I never meant this to happen. Go home. I'll explain everythin' later.' She turned to the nurse. 'It's Iris, isn't it? Please, can I see her?'

'Mother . . .'

'Not now, Jenny. Go home like I said. Please, lovey,' she pleaded. 'Let me deal with this first.'

Though Jenny didn't want to, she knew by the tone of May's voice that she'd better obey.

By the time May arrived home over an hour later a distraught and extremely confused Jenny had nearly worn a trench in the new lino with all her pacing. As she heard the key turn in the lock she stopped and pounced on May as soon as she entered.

'What's going on? Was that woman my mother?' she demanded.

Face etched with grief, wearily May wrenched off her coat, letting it slip to the floor. She shook her head sadly as she went to the armchair and sat down. She held her frozen hands out towards the glowing cinders and rubbed them vigorously. 'She thought she was, lovey, but she wasn't. I'm yer mother.' She exhaled forlornly and looked down at herself. 'Look at me bleddy new dress,' she grumbled, holding the skirt out wide. 'Ruined, ain't it?'

'Mother?'

May raised her head and looked at her apologetically. 'I'm sorry, Jenny, you deserve an explanation. I'm just in shock, that's all. I thought she was lying ter me, yer see.' She gave a deep sigh. 'Sit yerself down.' May waited a moment as Jenny did as she was told. Before beginning her story, she took a deep calming breath. 'Jenny, the woman in the hospital was me sister, Iris.' She saw the girl's face pale, heard the gasp of shock she gave out, but continued regardless. 'She was always a bit of a gel, if yer understand what I mean. Headstrong, a law unto 'erself was Iris. I've not exactly been the Virgin Mary meself, but compared to me sister I'd say I was a saint. I'm just

263

glad my old mam never lived to see the way she turned out.

'Me mother died, Jenny, when I was seventeen and Iris was sixteen. Thankfully I was working and able to take over the rent on the house. We lived in Cossington Street. A two up, two down, a bit like this place only it were dripping with damp and the bugs ... I had a constant battle with those little blighters. Life weren't easy, I wasn't on much of a wage but I did me best to manage. I did me best also to keep me eye on our Iris, keep her on the straight and narrow, but what with me workin' and courting yer dad quite strong, it was nigh on impossible.

'It was the final straw for me when I caught my sister up the back entry one night with a bloke even Scabby Nell the local bag lady wouldn't pass the time of day with, and I knew Iris was taking money from him.' She shook her head grimly. 'It's awful for me to 'ave to admit to you that yer own auntie, my sister, was nothing more than a prostitute, but it's no good me flowering it up, she was what she was. Anyway, I lost me temper and chucked her out. Told her that until she could act decent I didn't want her to darken me door again. I thought it might finally knock some sense into her, Jenny. I should 'ave known better, though.' She paused and eyed her daughter worriedly. 'I'm shocking yer, lovey, ain't I?'

Shock wasn't a strong enough word to describe how Jenny was feeling. 'Just go on, Mam,' she urged.

May took a deep breath and clasped her hands tightly. 'I never heard a word from Iris for nearly a year. I can't say that I didn't think about her or worry about her but I hadn't a clue where she was so I just got on with me life and hoped she was doing all right for 'erself. I'd just got home from work one night when she walks in as bold as brass. She ...' May stopped abruptly, fighting hard against the lump of distress that was forming in her throat. 'She ... had a baby in 'er arms.' Her eyes misted over as painful memories returned and she wrung her hands tightly. 'Right scrawny little thing it was,' she continued, her voice thick with emotion. 'But by Christ could it yell. "I've come back," Iris announces without a by your leave. She wouldn't give no details about the baby's father or anything. It's my guess she hadn't a clue. All she said was, "I want to raise me child proper."

'I was dumbstruck by this change in her, but then, yer know yer mother, Jenny,' she said, eyeing her. 'I've never been one for keeping me gob shut. I let rip. Told her in no uncertain terms that it was about time she got to grips with herself now she had the responsibility of a child. She promised me she wouldn't let me down if I let her stay. She told me that the baby had made her see sense at last. I believed her, Jenny. I thought the arrival of the child would do that. I welcomed her back gladly and promised I'd help her all I could.' May sadly shook her head. 'What a fool I was. Iris had been back just over a week when one night she asked me if I would look after the child while she went out on an errand.'

'What was her name, Mam?' Jenny asked.

'Whose?'

'The child?'

'Oh.' May smiled distantly. 'Iris hadn't given her a name. Said she wanted to wait 'til she thought of something really nice. I just called her "cherub" in the meantime. I must say I'd got quite attached to her by then. She was a sickly little thing. Couldn't keep her milk down. Cried all the time. But she had the face of an angel and a smile that broke my heart. I found meself rushing home at lunchtime and in the evening to help take care of her.'

May realised she was upsetting herself unnecessarily and shook herself. 'Anyway, to get back to me story, Iris said she had business to sort out that night and would I watch her? Said she was going to see the father of the child to get some money. Well, as it was me that was paying for everything and I was beginning to find it quite a struggle, I thought that seemed sensible. Even if the father only coughed up enough for the baby's milk it'd be a help. I told 'er not to be too long, though, as I was going out meself that night to . . .' Her voice trailed off.

'Mam?' Jenny urged.

May looked at her. She took a deep breath. 'I was going to see your father, Jenny. I had something of me own to tell him.' Look, yer might as well know, I was pregnant meself with you and had steeled meself to break the news to him. But Iris never came back.'

'What do you mean, she never came back? That night, you mean?'

'She never came back at all, Jenny, and when I checked her bedroom all her clothes were gone.'

Jenny's mouth fell open, her brow furrowed deeply. 'She just abandoned her baby?'

May nodded. 'That's what she did all right. And I never saw 'er again 'til a few weeks ago when she knocked on my door out of the blue demanding to see her daughter. Said she was dying and wanted to make amends before it was too late.' She gave a sad sigh. 'You can understand now why I didn't believe her, Jenny. I thought she was just making it up to get her foot in the door again.'

'Oh!' Jenny exclaimed as a memory struck. 'It makes sense now.'

'What does?'

'You acting really strange one night, asking me if I'd seen a woman hanging about.'

'Well, I was worried, see. I never told you before because there didn't seem to be any point as it all happened before you were born, and I wanted to forget all about it. You can understand that. But Iris suddenly turning up out of the blue was like a bolt. If she got to you and convinced you she was your mother then I'd have had to explain the whole terrible story to the pair of you, and to be honest I couldn't face it all coming out and the hurt it would cause. And I didn't know what you'd think of me.'

Jenny sighed sadly. 'Oh, Mam, how could you think I'd think the worst of you? But this is all so awful. That poor baby.' She eyed her mother questioningly. 'What happened to her? Did she land up in a home?'

'No. I couldn't have put that poor little thing in one of them places. That child didn't ask ter be born. I was prepared to raise her meself but . . .' May paused, sighing forlornly, wringing her hands. 'Only two weeks later she died, bless her.'

'Died!'

'Caught a cold, that was all, and it killed the poor little mite. The doctors said she had a weak heart and it was a wonder she had lasted as long as she had.' She choked back a sob. 'I know I'd only had her for a short time but I'd grown to love that child, Jenny. I had her christened Angela and buried her as though she was me own. I was angry, Jenny. I was bloody incensed if yer want the truth. That little girl had died and was buried without her proper mother being with her. I hated Iris then. I would have killed 'er for sure if she'd shown her face. Thank God she didn't. That's when I moved. I just upped and went and left no forwarding address and started to call meself May Jeffries, which was me mother's maiden name. Me proper name's April May. I never liked April so that was no hardship.'

'I thought Jeffries was your married name, Mam?'

'Eh! Oh, I'm getting meself confused with all this coming out. I called meself . . . Brown, that was me mother's maiden name. Then I married yer dad, of course, and changed it to Jeffries. Then he died, and you know the rest of it. Anyway when Iris turned up outta the blue a few weeks ago, as much as I wanted to smack her face for how she'd treated that baby and me, how could I tell her her child had died only a week or so after she'd left? For twenty years, Jenny, she had thought her child was alive and well and was now a grown woman. As much as I hated me sister I couldn't tell her. When it came down to it I couldn't hurt her. I let Iris believe you was her baby to save her the heartache. I know it was wrong of me but, yer see, I never thought you'd find out. I suppose in the light of everything I'm glad Iris didn't.'

Jenny eyed her mother tenderly. 'Oh, Mam. What you did was a wonderful thing.'

May sniffed disdainfully. 'Was it? I dunno, Jenny. Maybe I should 'ave told Iris the truth. Let her suffer like I did over the loss of her child. Still that's all in the past. Iris has gone and she'll do no more harm now.'

'Oh, Mam,' Jenny exclaimed, horrified.

'Don't "*oh, Mam*" me like that, our Jenny,' May said, hurt. 'You may think I sound hard, like I've got no feelings, but I lost everything through Iris.'

'What do you mean, Mam?'

'I mean . . .' She stared at Jenny, horrified, her mind racing frantically as she fought to find a plausible explanation for what she had just said. Not the truth. That was not on the agenda, now or ever. 'I mean, I just ain't told you the 'alf about me sister. In all honesty I've made her sound like an angel. She used ter steal off me and all sorts, and me with not two 'alfpennies to rub together trying to keep her and that baby . . . Anyway, I'm glad it's all out in the open. It just remains for me to bury Iris now and Lord knows where the money's coming from to do that.'

'We'll find it somehow, Mam, and I'll come to the funeral with you.'

'You will?'

''Course I will. You'll need my support. And after all, she was my auntie.'

'Some auntie. But thanks, lovey, I do appreciate it.' May sighed despondently. 'I've got ter think of a good story to tell

Gloria 'cos one thing's fer sure, I ain't telling 'er the truth. Be all round the street before the last word was out me mouth.'

'You'll come up with something, Mam.'

'I'm sure I will. Mek us a cuppa, will yer, please, gel. Although to be 'onest I could murder a gin.'

While Jenny busied herself mashing a pot of tea, May sat deep in thought. She was genuinely sorry that her sister was dead; sorry also that a secret she had kept from Jenny all these years had had to be divulged in such an awful way, and for the terrible shock her daughter must have suffered thinking it was May herself that was dead. But she could not change that. She sighed. At least there was part of the story she had still managed to keep secret. She had nearly let it slip but thankfully had covered up quickly enough not to arouse her daughter's suspicions. What would Jenny's reaction be if she learned that? thought May worriedly. Well, she never would.

'Here you go, Mam,' said Jenny moments later, handing her a mug of steaming tea.

May gave a loud yawn. 'Thanks, me darlin'. I've just realised I've got work in the morning and it's almost three. Thank God it's Sat'day and I only have to work until twelve. I'll just drink this and then I'd better get some shut eye.'

Jenny looked at the clock. 'Yes, I'd better get to bed too. We've a lot on tomorrow. I bumped into Mr Wadham tonight. He was just coming out of the Bell Hotel. He was ever so excited 'cos he's just landed a job shifting furniture for them. Me and Alan went for a celebration drink with him,' she said proudly.

At the mention of the Bell Hotel May's face was suddenly wreathed in excitement. 'Oh, that reminds me,' she blurted out. 'I ain't told yer me good news.'

'Good news? There is some in all this?'

May scowled. 'Life goes on, Jenny. I'm upset me sister's dead but don't ask me to mourn a woman who didn't give a jot about me.'

Jenny tightened her lips. 'I'm sorry, Mam. So what is your good news then?'

'I've met a bloke. Oh, he's lovely, Jenny! Lives out of Leicester but comes in once a week on business. We got on ever so well. I'm sure you'll like him. And let me tell you, he's nothing like all the other lot. This man's a gentleman,' she said proudly. 'He's a widower and at the moment lives with his old mother. She's ill. In a wheelchair. Paul Smith his name is, and I'm meeting him next Wednesday. He's taking me for a meal. Fancy that, eh? No man's ever taken me for a meal. He must have money to afford that.'

Jenny smiled warmly. 'I'm pleased for you, Mam.'

'I'm pleased for meself. Keep yer fingers crossed. This is the one, I feel he is.' She narrowed her eyes questioningly. 'And when am I goin' ter meet this young chap of yours? It's getting serious, I can tell.'

'If it ever does get serious, Mam, you'll get to meet him. At the moment we're just friends.'

'Are you ashamed of me?' asked May.

'No, Mam, far from it. But you'll frighten him off, you know you will, with all the questions you'll ask. And if you don't, Gloria's bound to.'

May sniffed haughtily. 'I suppose,' she admitted grudgingly. 'But you introduced him to your boss?' she accused.

'That was by way of an accident, Mam. Anyway, Mr Wadham didn't give him a grilling like you would have done. Now you'll meet him, Mam, all in good time.'

'Well, you'll meet my new bloke quicker than you think. On Wednesday I'm gonna invite him to 'ave a meal with us some time. I bet he doesn't get much in the way of looking after being's he's on the road so much, and when he's at 'ome it's obviously him that cares for his mam, her being an invalid. Will yer 'elp me with the cooking? I want to make a good impression.'

Jenny smiled. ''Course I will, Mam. Shall we do that recipe we did for Herchell the first night he came round? That fishy thing,' she said, trying to control her laughter. 'I bet Mr Smith'll definitely want to marry you if you make him that.'

May flapped her hand. 'Get ter bed with yer and less of yer cheek! Just be thankful you're too old for me to scalp yer arse.'

Jenny threw her arms around her mother and gave her a kiss on her cheek. 'Oh, Mam, I do love you. I don't know what I'd do without you.' Her voice was harsh with emotion. 'I can't tell you how upset I was when I thought it was you that was dead.'

'Yeah, well, remember how yer felt the next time you get mad with me,' May said good-humouredly.

As it was, when Daniel and May next met he politely refused her invitation to dinner, convincing her that it was a lot of trouble for her to go to when he never knew when he could be called home urgently due to his mother's ill health. He didn't want to spoil the occasion. He felt it wasn't fair.

Despite his convincing refusal it was nevertheless a disappointed May who told Jenny she wouldn't, this time, be needing her help in preparing the meal.

# Chapter Twenty

Alan tiptoed quietly down the stairs, along the passage and into the spacious kitchen. Shutting the door, he switched on the light and blinked his eyes rapidly, accustoming them to the brightness which seemed to bounce off the cream-painted walls to blind him momentarily. He didn't look at the clock on the wall, he already knew the time from the alarm clock on the dresser in his bedroom. It was just coming up to one o'clock. Going over to the stove, he picked up the shiny kettle and lit the gas.

Leaning back in his chair, he rubbed his gritty eyes and gave a mournful sigh. What a dreadful state of affairs to find himself in, bad enough to stop him from dropping off to sleep. What were the odds, he thought, of discovering that an uncle you had only found out about a matter of weeks ago, a man who according to others had tried to steal a substantial amount of money off his own employer, turns out to be the boss of the woman you love?

Alan shook his head. And it got worse. This uncle had made it very clear, according to Alan's own mother, that he wanted nothing whatsoever to do with his family. What would Bill Wadham's reaction have been if I'd announced my name tonight over our celebration drink in the pub? Alan asked himself worriedly. What would the reaction of my mother and father be if I tell them of this turn of events? And Jenny?

Whatever action he took it seemed to Alan someone would be hurt. But then to keep his own counsel on every count amounted to deception. Whatever he did Alan knew he could not win.

Just then the kitchen door opened and he saw his mother entering. She looked tired and it was obvious from her face that something was bothering her.

'Mum, what on earth are you doing up at this time of night?'

She smiled at him wanly. 'I could ask the same of you. I couldn't sleep. What's your excuse?' The kettle started to whistle and she stepped across to the stove to pour boiling water from the kettle into the teapot. 'Well?' she urged Alan.

He looked at her. Despite her tousled hair and tired face his mother was a striking woman who could easily pass for someone much younger than her forty-four years. She was beautiful, he thought. He remembered her walking him to school when he was very young, his small hand clasped proudly in hers. He could still picture how the other mothers had looked on enviously. Val was wearing a blue cotton summer dress, her naturally wavy blonde hair pinned becomingly in a roll around the back of her neck. The other children swarmed around them, drawn by her warm, sunny nature but probably more so by the bag of home-made toffee she always carried, mostly for the unfortunate children whose mothers were too poor to give their offspring treats. A warm feeling filled him. She had been the best mother he could ever wish for. How lucky he was, he thought.

He pictured his father and for the first time it struck him that had he not known his mother and father were married he would not have put them together. But how odd he should suddenly think that. He supposed he was likening his parents' relationship to his and Jenny's. How they were always chatting and laughing together, at ease in each other's company. That could not be said of his own parents, nothing like it. They could sit for hours of an evening, his mother quietly knitting or reading, his father in the chair opposite, head buried in the newspaper or watching a programme on the television, hardly saying a word to each other. They barely went out on any social events, even for a night at the pictures or a walk in the park. And now he was thinking about it Alan realised how few displays of affection they showed towards each other apart from the customary peck on the cheek. Still, they had been married for over twenty years and living together obviously suited them both.

Alan took a deep breath. He desperately wanted to answer his mother's question truthfully, but how did you suddenly announce you'd been socialising with your estranged scoundrel of an uncle who just happens to be your girlfriend's boss? Not casually over a cup of tea at this late hour. He needed time to sort out his thoughts on this emotive situation before he said anything. 'Why couldn't you sleep?' he asked.

Val looked at her son. Her motherly instincts told her he was worried about something but whatever it was he wasn't going to divulge it easily. She hoped he hadn't had a falling out with Jenny. Not that Val had had the privilege of meeting her son's new girlfriend as yet, but she could tell from the snippets Alan had divulged about her, and from the way his face lit up when he did, that this girl was special. Val couldn't wait to meet the woman who had made such an impression on him.

She took a deep breath. 'Your father was late home tonight. He arrived just before you and woke me up. I couldn't get back off so eventually, like you it seems, I decided a nice cuppa might do the trick.'

'Father was out on business that late?' he queried.

'Mmm. Something to do with the Bell Hotel. Daniel didn't go into all the details. He just said he'd been requested late this afternoon to give them a price for removing some furniture from rooms they'd had renovated and the owner kept him waiting for hours thanks to some problem or other he was having to deal with. Your father wasn't very pleased. In the end he was offered a meal by way of apology, which I thought was rather nice myself. Daniel said that if it hadn't been so late he would have telephoned me to join him.'

Val sighed. It was a pity her husband hadn't taken the trouble to telephone her and inform her what was going on then she wouldn't have got his meal ready, which she had had to throw away, nor would she have sat worrying, thinking something dreadful could have happened to him.

Alan frowned, puzzled. Bill Wadham had been celebrating his luck on landing a job at the Bell, the same job that his mother had just described. He and Jenny had met up with Bill just after eight-thirty. Something wasn't right somewhere. Or maybe his mother had got the name of the hotel wrong, which wasn't like her as she was usually very accurate with any information she imparted. And if she had it seemed to Alan a coincidence that two hotels should be requesting prices on the same sort of job at the same time.

'What's wrong, dear? You look very concerned about something.'

'Pardon? Oh, I'm just tired, Mum. Is that tea mashed yet?'

'How are things down at the yard?' she asked as she took the muslin cover off the jug and poured milk into the cups.

'Fine. Not quite as busy as we usually are but then that gives us chance to give the vans a good overhaul and catch up with other things. There's nothing worse than a van breaking down on a job.'

'I know,' Val agreed, picking up the teapot. 'Did your grandfather ever tell you the story about the wheel that came off a lorry?'

Alan laughed. 'Yes, several times. The wheel nuts hadn't been tightened properly and the van had to be unloaded so it could be jacked up and then reloaded again. Grandad said he couldn't believe it when he just happened to be passing and saw two of the men had set out a table and chairs on the pavement and were sitting having a cup of tea that one of the women from the houses had given them while the other had gone back to the yard to get a wheel brace.'

They both laughed at the memory.

'Your grandad said that taught him a valuable lesson and since that time he made sure any man who worked for him had a good grounding in vehicle maintenance.'

'He was full of stories of things that happened during the early days of the business,' said Alan wistfully.

Val sighed and smiled wanly. 'Yes, it hasn't all been plain sailing. We've had men fall off ladders, deliveries going to wrong addresses, accidents with furniture – but nothing your grandad could not sort out to keep the good name of the firm intact. And that'll carry on, Alan, won't it, under your father and yourself?'

He leaned over and patted her hand affectionately. 'You don't doubt that, Mum, do you?'

She shook her head. 'No. I know it's in good hands with you.'

'And Father, don't forget.'

She stared at him. What had made her say that? 'Yes, of course,' she said hurriedly. 'I meant both of you. It's just that . . .'

'What, Mum? What's worrying you?'

Wearily she rubbed her face with her hands. She would have liked nothing more than to talk to her son. But what was the point in worrying him over something she wasn't sure of? Since Ernest's death a change had come over Daniel. Quite what, she couldn't exactly pinpoint. It was just there. He had never been a talkative man. In truth, despite her efforts over the years she actually knew very little of what went on in his mind, but he was definitely keeping something back at the moment, was very preoccupied about something and becoming increasingly less approachable.

Val was worried that her husband was finding the responsibility of running the business too much and that it would make him ill. Daniel was not the sort of man to admit to defeat and ask for help, that she did know about him.

She had tried to approach him about her concerns, to offer her help even if it was only by way of someone to talk to, but her careful probing had led to nothing. She was probably worrying unnecessarily. There was bound to be an unsettled period while everyone got over Ernest's death. Now she was giving the matter proper consideration she felt sure time was all her husband needed. And he had come home in a cheery mood tonight, despite his obvious annoyance at the deplorable way in which the owner of the Bell had treated him.

Val smiled warmly at her son. 'I'm just being wifely and motherly, that's all. We women worry about things that are really nothing at all. It's our job, Alan.'

'You're not making sense, Mum.'

'No, I know I'm not. Take no notice of me.' Val decided it would be best to change the subject. 'I do hope the firm gets that job at the Bell. I would hate to think your father's evening had been totally wasted. Daniel seemed to be positive he would get it.'

'Not that particular job he won't,' Alan said without thinking.

Val eyed her son quizzically. 'How could you know that?'

His mind raced frantically. What on earth had possessed him to blurt that out without thinking? But what was most glaring was the fact that his father had obviously lied to his mother. Why not just tell her that he had left the hotel without pricing the job because he had got fed up with the owner keeping him waiting and then gone off down the pub, which was obviously what he'd done. Why had his father lied?

278

Alan turned from her and picked up the teapot. 'Oh, I was thinking about something else, Mum, just forget what I said. I'm tired, that's all. More tea?'

She knew by his manner that her son had lied to her. Why? 'Just a drop for me,' she said. 'Alan, everything is all right, isn't it?'

'Yes. Why do you ask?' he casually replied.

Picking up her cup, Val took a sip of tea. 'Just taking an interest, that's all. Did you have a nice evening tonight? You went out with Jenny, didn't you?'

'Yes, I did. And yes, I did have a nice time, thanks, Mum.'

His answer had come just a little too hurriedly for her liking. Her son was definitely bothered about something, she just knew he was.

He rose, yawning. 'I'm going to bed now,' he announced.

He leaned over and gave her a kiss on her cheek.

'Yes, I'm just going to finish this and I'm going up myself,' she said, responding warmly to his gesture. She grabbed his arm and looked at him.

'Mum, what is it?'

'Oh, Alan, you're a grown man now. Too big for me to gather on my knee and cuddle. I just wanted to tell you I love you,' she said softly. 'And I'm always here for you. You know that, don't you?'

His eyes filled with tenderness. 'I know that, Mum, and the same goes for me too. You know that, don't you?'

She nodded. 'I do. I'll see you in the morning. Good night, darling.'

# Chapter Twenty-One

Jenny gazed in awe at the woman standing before her. Blossom Williams was beautiful. To Jenny it was hardly credible that she had given birth to a baby only a matter of days ago in what sounded like terrible conditions on board a ship nearing the end of an arduous month-long journey, with only her female travelling companions to aid the birth. The tiny cabin she had shared with these women and their several offspring had been cramped, dingy, dripping with water and extremely noisy, it being close to the engine room in the rusting bowels of the ship. A place hardly fitting for humans to live in, let alone one in which to bring forth a new life.

Herchell dwarfed his wife, she being barely five foot tall and underneath the several layers of clothing she was wearing to ward off the cold, as Jenny's mother would say, as slender as a clothes prop. Springing from the top of her well-shaped head was a mop of jet black wiry curls. Above high cheekbones were wide brown eyes, sparkling with life, edged by a row of dense black eyelashes. As she looked up at her husband before turning her attention to Jenny, the love she held for him was clear for all to see.

'It's so lovely to meet you at last,' Blossom said. 'My husband he been tellin' me how good you and your mother have been to him. And Boss too. I want to t'ank you.'

Jenny smiled warmly. 'It's been a pleasure. How are you

settling in? Do you like your rooms?'

'Oh, very much, yes. I t'ink I'll be very happy here. Herchell he tell me you helped to make it all so nice for my comin'. And Boss gave us some furniture. I don't know how to t'ank you both.'

'There's no need for thanks, I enjoyed every minute and I know Mr Wadham was very glad to help too. Of course, if yer not keen on the curtains I can easily run you up some more. Herchell wasn't sure what colour or pattern you'd like so we took a chance.'

'Oh, I love dem, really, they are so pretty. You made a good choice.'

Jenny stepped over and peered down into the wicker crib. 'She's so lovely,' she said wistfully. 'What are you going to call her?'

Blossom looked up at her husband. 'Have you not told her yet?'

He shook his head. 'I thought you'd like to do that?'

A delighted smile spread over Blossom's face. 'We going to be callin' her Billy Jenny, after Boss and you.'

Jenny's mouth dropped open in shock. 'Oh!'

Herchell's face fell. 'You not pleased, Jenny?'

'Oh, yes,' she cried. 'I'm just . . . overwhelmed. I can't tell you how honoured I feel.'

Blossom linked her arm through her husband's. 'We very honoured too. I honoured to be in your country and have you as a friend. The only thing I don't like is that it's so cold but Herchell he say I'll get used to it. You will stay for dinner, Jenny, please? I brought some salt fish and peas, plantain and yams over from Jamaica, and best of all Wray & Nephew white rum. I cook you a proper West Indian meal, yes?'

Jenny smiled in delight, despite being unsure whether she'd like it. 'You must let me help,' she offered.

Before she went to join Blossom in the kitchen area she took a moment to take another peek into the crib. The baby stirred and a smile caused by wind twitched the corners of her mouth. Motherly instincts raced through Jenny and a longing for a family of her own, to be as happy as Herchell and Blossom obviously were, filled her very being. She sincerely hoped such happiness lay with Alan. It was still early days yet, they being new to their relationship, but Jenny knew without a doubt he was definitely the man she wanted to spend the rest of her life with. She only hoped he felt the same about her. If he didn't she was going to be terribly disappointed.

'You all right, Jenny?'

She raised her eyes to Herchell. 'I'm fine, thank you. And you?'

'I'm a very happy man. I miss me mother and father, and me brothers and sisters and all the rest of me family. I miss the sun on me skin, Jenny. But I got everyt'ing else a man could ever want right here. I lucky, ain't I?'

Jenny looked at Blossom busying herself by the stove, unearthing strange-looking vegetables from a bag, then down at the baby, then back to Herchell. 'You are,' she heartily agreed.

# Chapter Twenty-Two

The day was surprisingly warm for the end of January. It could have been mistaken for spring. The two women standing by the grave felt uncomfortably warm in their layers of thick clothing in the seemingly deserted cemetery.

'You gave her a good send off, Mam,' Jenny said softly.

Huddled close to her daughter, their arms linked, May wiped a tear from her eye. She looked down into the open grave holding her sister's coffin. The brass-plated plaque bearing Iris's name seemed to glint back at her, like an eye winking. She shuddered. 'I did the best I could,' she uttered. 'But it don't seem right, just us two seeing her off. When I put the notice in the paper I thought some friends of hers must see it. I'm wondering now if she had any.' She shook her head sadly. 'Or anyone that loved her for that matter.'

'Some people don't read the paper, Mam, especially the deaths column, it makes them depressed, so they might not have seen it.'

'Yes, I suppose. But I still wish just a few had turned up. Still, we came and that's the main thing.'

'It was a lovely service and the flowers are beautiful.'

'Yeah, but the dead can't appreciate them, can they? Iris won't know she had a decent send off, will she?'

'But *you* know yer gave yer sister the best you could and that's what matters, Mam. You didn't have to, not after the way

285

she treated you. Without you, Auntie Iris would have had a pauper's funeral.'

May sighed forlornly again. 'I couldn't allow that, Jenny. She was me sister when all's said and done. I couldn't turn me back on her like she did on me. Two wrongs don't mek a right, do they? I ain't a religious woman, seen too much hurt to believe there's a guardian guiding our lives, but I do hope her soul is at peace,' she muttered, sniffing away more tears that threatened to fall. 'I feel strange.'

'Strange?'

'Yes. Like Iris's going is a chapter of me own life closing. The business I told yer about has always haunted me. At the back of me mind I always lived with the dread that one day she'd somehow find out her baby had died and accuse me . . .'

'Of what, Mam?'

May patted her daughter's hand. 'Oh, I dunno, love. Just accuse me of lying to her, not trying hard enough to find her when Angela died so she could be there to bury her.'

'That was a terrible time for you, Mam, and you did yer best to find her. I admire what you did and I think you should be proud of yerself to know that should little Angela not have died you'd have raised her as yer own. Auntie Iris must have known you'd take care of her else she'd never have left her baby with you.'

'The trouble was Iris knew me too well,' May blurted out. 'Anyway, it's all past history now.' Taking a deep breath, she turned her head and looked her daughter full in the face. 'Life goes on, gel, I've told yer that often enough. We've both gorra get back to work this afternoon and I've a date with Paul tonight. What about you?'

'After work I'm seeing Janet. We're having a girlie night at her house.'

'Good, then we've both summat to look forward to. Oh, talking of girlie nights reminds me I need me roots touching up,' she said, patting her hair. 'I must speak to Gloria about doin' 'em.'

'Mam?'

'What?'

Was now the time, Jenny thought, to ask her mother how she had found the money to pay for the funeral? Something that had been bothering Jenny since May had announced that, despite everything that had gone on between them, it was only right she buried her sister properly.

'Well, spit it out,' she prompted.

'It's just that I wondered how you'd paid for all this, that's all?'

'I paid fer it, that's all that matters.' May breathed in deeply, then sighed noisily. 'If yer must know I got a deal on the coffin. It might look like good oak but it's polished box wood, and the vicar said in the circumstances he'd do the service for free. I got the flowers really reasonable from Vickers on the Braunstone Gate. He made the wreath from flowers he couldn't sell.'

Jenny frowned. If indeed the coffin was box wood it was the most excellent imitation of oak she had ever come across and the flowers making up the wreath looked as fresh as if they'd just been cut. Regardless of her doubts as to the accuracy of her mother's words, she said, 'Oh, I see. I'm sorry I asked, Mam.'

'That's all right, darlin'. Funerals don't come cheap and yer've a right to ask. I was quoted ten quid from them lot on the Fosse Road. Ten quid! That's bloody daylight robbery. I told 'em so an' all. Prey on the bereaved, that's what some of them lot do. And call 'emselves caring! So I shopped around and came up with what I did. Anyway, enough of this. I could do with a nice cuppa tea. How about you?'

'Sounds good to me, Mam.'

May stared for a moment down into the grave. 'Well, tarra, Iris,' she said.

Then, arm in arm, she and Jenny walked slowly down the path and out of the cemetery.

# Chapter Twenty-Three

The door of Daniel's office burst open and a grim-faced Alan came through.

'Dad, what have you done?' he demanded.

Daniel leaned back in his chair, eyes narrowing darkly. 'In three months' time this business will be all yours and you can do what the hell you like with it but in the meantime, until you're of age, I run it. Is that clear? Don't you ever burst in here like that again. Now, I take it you're referring to the three men I let go?'

'Let go? You sacked them, Dad. Sid Brown, Wally Hammond and Bert Smith have all been working here since they left school. They're good men, Dad. They know the business inside out. What reason did you have to get rid of them?'

'What I did was to try and make sure you had a business to take over when you turn twenty-one. We can't afford their wages, it's as simple as that. Business has been slacking off just lately.'

'Not enough to let three of our best men go, surely, Dad? I know we're not exactly run off our feet at the moment but we've still plenty of work to see us through. Apart from everything else he did, Sid was our best mechanic, have you forgotten that, Dad? With him gone we'll have to get a proper garage mechanic to come in to do any of the big repairs. That won't come cheap.'

'Rubbish. Young Gordon knows enough to get by and all the other men know the rudiments. Christ, even you can fix a gasket come to that, so what's your problem? Anyway, those three men are all approaching retirement age. If work does pick up we can always hire younger, stronger men and on a lot less money. Your grandpa paid them far too much.'

Alan looked aghast. 'Dad, he didn't. Those men earn every penny of their money as you well know. Anyway Sid Brown might be nearing retirement age but the other two are only in their early-fifties.'

'Too old then to be shifting heavy furniture around,' Daniel snapped dismissively. 'Now if you don't mind I've work to do,' he said, pulling several sheets of paper in front of him and pretending to study them.

Alan clenched his fists in an effort to control his anger. Despite his father's excuses he still felt the sackings were unjustified. In the short term Alan could see wages being saved but in the long term it could cost them dearly in training up new recruits, not to mention whether they would show the firm the same commitment as the three men his father had just sacked. 'Grandad wouldn't like this, Dad. He said good workmen are the backbone of a business. When things are bad, he said, the last thing to do is get rid of good men.'

Daniel raised his head, eyes cold. 'Your grandad is dead in case you've forgotten. And I'll remind you I was working with him before you were born. You have a long way to go yet before you know as much as I do about running this business. I decided the men had to go and that's that. And you might as well know I'll be making some more cuts. I'm dropping all the men's wages by sixpence an hour and I'm putting the office clerks on part-time. And your grandfather's practice of supplying the men with their tea is going to stop. The firm's milk bill alone comes to nearly ten shillings a week. They can buy their own in future.'

Alan couldn't believe his ears. 'What? Business can't be so bad that we have to resort to this sort of penny pinching.'

'Not quite yet. But the writing's on the wall. I'm planning ahead.'

'Dad,' he pleaded, 'before you acted, you could have talked to me first. There's a lot we could have done before this.'

'Like what? Conjure work out of thin air? Magician now, are you, Alan?'

'There's no need to be sarcastic, Dad. This is only temporary. All firms have their slack periods. Grandad was always on the lookout for work. At times like you say we're heading for, he used to try extra hard. And he usually succeeded.'

'And what do you think I've been doing?'

What indeed? Alan thought. Whatever it was it never seemed to produce any positive results. His father barely left the office during the day and his late nights out twice a week, when he said he was entertaining prospective clients, didn't seem to have done much by way of generating any work.

Alan suddenly wished his own responsibilities left him time to explore new business propositions for the firm. His grandfather, he knew, had been quite happy with the small profit margin the business had brought in, his only concern being that it kept his family and employees housed and fed. And it had. The work coming in now was generated by loyal regulars of long years' standing, plus new work brought in through word of mouth. Alan had long ago realised that this was far too risky a way to ensure the company's future existence but he was far too respectful of his grandfather ever to voice his opinions aloud.

He had ideas, good ones which he knew would transform the company into a much larger concern, make its future more secure and profitable. Should his plans materialise, not only could he reward the workers well but his own father would be able to take it easier, spend more time with his wife, be able to do things with her previously denied them through lack of finance. More importantly, he would not have to toil such long arduous hours and risk going to an early grave like Ernest had. And Alan himself could marry Jenny and provide well for her. He wanted so much to do all that.

Grabbing a chair, he pulled it up in front of the desk and sat down. 'Dad, listen to me. I have plans for expansion. We . . .'

Daniel's head jerked. '*You* have plans for expansion?' he cut in with a hint of mockery. 'Barely out of nappies and you think you know it all!'

'Dad, listen to me. My plans could make this company very profitable. I know they could.'

At the word 'profitable' Daniel's eyes glinted. 'Oh,' he said, sitting back in his chair and clasping his hands. 'And what are these wonderful ideas of yours then?'

'Expand our services. As you know, Dad, there are firms that need their goods transporting but not often enough to warrant investing in their own lorries. We already offer that service to some extent like our work for the furniture shop but those jobs are few and far between. I was thinking more of factories with urgent deliveries to make who need transport in a hurry. If we could have several firms like that on our books we could keep at least one man and a lorry occupied ten hours a day, possibly two or three vans and men if all went well. And that's just to start. And we can charge more for what we call our "emergency" services. Times are changing, Dad. More and more people are moving to different cities. Instead of us just handling loads around Leicester and the shires, we could do longer hauls up and down the country and bring loads back. It wouldn't have to be furniture on the return journey either. Those are just a couple of my ideas.'

Daniel stared at his son. Stupid boy, he thought. Expansion cost money before any benefits were reaped, which would take an age to materialise. Daniel didn't have the time. He needed ideas that would generate a substantial amount immediately, not in years to come.

'These ideas of yours are all well and good but how do you propose we finance the initial outlay for vans and such like?'

'From the bank?'

Daniel's eyes widened. 'Bank?'

'Yes.'

Daniel stared at him. Of course, he thought. A loan from a bank. Damn, why hadn't he thought of that? His mind whirled frantically. In his innocence Alan had handed him the answer he was seeking. Now he could raise all the money he needed to start his new life. He felt overjoyed. So excited, he wanted to jump with joy.

'How much do you think the bank will give us?'

'Depends, Dad. We'd have to present the manager with our ideas and costings, and if he saw it as good business sense we'd get what we asked for. The fact that Collier's is a firm in good standing should go in our favour.'

Daniel was seeing pound notes, hundreds of them, flashing before his eyes. 'All right, Alan.'

'You're agreeing to expansion?'

'In principle,' Daniel said cagily. 'And being's it's your idea, you can do the outline to put to the bank.'

Alan looked at him eagerly. 'It'll probably take me a couple of weeks to get all the information together and cost it all out.'

'Two weeks it is then. I'll look forward to going over it with you.'

Yes, he'd look forward to seeing it very much, Daniel thought, as a vision rose before him of the new lifestyle he could finance, with money raised from Collier's, in a town or city far away from Leicester. He realised Alan was still talking to him. 'What?' he snapped irritably, wanting nothing more than to be left alone with his thoughts.

'The men, Dad. When we expand we'll need men like them

working for us. Surely we can afford to keep them on in the meantime? They'd be hard to replace, and I can't help worrying they have families to keep.'

Daniel's eyes narrowed. Those men were paid five pounds a week, money he'd prefer in his pocket, not theirs. Money raided from the bank was still just a prospect which might not materialise and until it did he was not prepared to risk losing what money he could. 'We're not a charity, Alan,' he said dismissively. Standing up, he placed his hands flat on the desk and looked at his son, his face hard. 'If and when we do expand, I'll consider their reinstatement. Until then this business is just ticking over, and we need to cut costs. There's no room for sentiment when a business is at stake, Alan. If you're going to make a success of running it then you'll have to learn that. Now, haven't you got work to do or are you giving me good reason to get rid of another man as you seem to have plenty of time to waste here?'

Open-mouthed Alan stared at his father. He couldn't believe Daniel was acting so callously. This was a side to him Alan had never witnessed before. He sighed in resignation. Maybe his father was right. He was being too sentimental. If the business was only just breaking even then to keep the men on could jeopardise the rest of the workforce, including themselves. It was a pity, though, that he couldn't demand to see the account books, see exactly how matters lay, and also if there weren't other ways savings could be made instead of having to resort to these sackings. But to do that would be to undermine his father and he couldn't do it.

'I'll see you at home tonight, Dad.'

Daniel sat down in his chair. 'Not tonight you won't. I'll be home late. Tell your mother not to save any dinner for me. I've a business appointment and I don't know how long it'll last.'

A vision of May rose before Daniel and the corners of his mouth twitched. He was having a good time with her. She was coarse, greatly lacking in social graces, but she certainly made up for her shortcomings in the way she treated a man. She was gullible, too. Believed every lie he told her. In fact she was the perfect woman to have as a mistress. The funny part was May didn't actually have any idea she was a mistress, was under the mistaken illusion she was the only woman in his life apart, of course, from the poor invalid mother who relied so heavily on 'Paul', thus making it impossible for him to travel to Leicester to see May more often.

He had been seeing her now for coming up to two months and she had certainly made a difference to his life, greatly relieved his boredom while he executed his plans. He loved the intrigue of it all, the illicit nature of an affair. It surprised him though to realise that he would miss May when the time came for them to part. But in the meantime, his fixed intention was to enjoy himself.

He realised Alan was talking again. 'What?'

'I asked, Father, who you were meeting on business tonight?'

Daniel's eyes narrowed. 'Interrogation, is it, Alan?'

'No, Dad, I was just interested to know who we might be getting some work from, that was all,' he said, wondering why Daniel was being so evasive.

'The name of the company slips my mind at this precise moment, but rest assured you'll know if the work comes our way because your job is to organise the workforce. Shut the door on your way out. I have some quotes to check over and I like peace and quiet while I do it.'

Alan left the office full of enthusiasm for his task of planning the firm's future but his heart was heavy too, saddened by his failure to convince his father to reinstate the men. Outside the icy February air hit him full blast and he shivered. Across the yard he saw the men in question huddled together by one of the large brown vans. It was obvious what they were discussing. Sid Brown spotted him, said something to the others and came over to Alan, steel-capped boots echoing on the frozen cobbles.

'Mr Alan, did yer manage to speak to yer dad?'

He took a deep breath and nodded. 'Yes, I did, but no joy, I'm afraid, Sid. My father wasn't happy with what he had to do but things are getting tight here and he had no choice. I'm so sorry.'

Sid's weather-beaten face fell in dismay. 'Not as sorry as me, Wally and Bert, Mr Alan. I dunno how I'm gonna tell me wife. And Bert's daughter's getting married next week. Some wedding present for 'er, eh?'

Alan looked helplessly at him, finding no words to make the situation any better.

Sid made to walk away then stopped, spinning back round to face Alan, his expression grim. 'Mr Daniel never gave us a chance to say a word on our own behalf. Well, I'd like to say my piece and I'm sorry it has to be to you. I think what yer dad's done is disgusting after all we've done for this firm. Your grandad, God rest his soul, would be turning in 'is grave if he knew. I've worked for Collier's straight from school at thirteen and seen it through some very lean periods. There was many times in the early days I know yer grandad took no money home at the end of the week, but by God he seen 'is men were paid all right. And it didn't matter how tight things got, it never crossed 'is mind to save money by sackings.'

Sid shook his head. 'With due respect, Mr Alan, we ain't stupid. Things might be a bit slow at the minute, but not enough to justify this.' He paused and took a deep breath, face filling with shame. 'I've maybe said too much, I'll tek me leave. I do wish *you* all the best. Yer a good lad, like yer grandad in more ways than one. It's just a pity the old man passed on before you came of age to take over the reins, that's all I can say. Goodbye then. Please give yer mother me best.'

He made to walk away but Alan caught his arm. 'Sid . . . look, if you should need a reference . . . anything . . . I'll be only too glad to do what I can. And if you're struggling for money . . .'

Lips clamped, sticking out his chin, Sid raised one hand in refusal. 'I don't tek charity, Mr Alan, thanks all the same.'

'I'm sorry, I didn't mean to suggest anything of the kind, I was just . . .'

Sid patted his arm. 'I know, lad, I know. You were just trying to help.'

With mixed emotions Alan watched as Sid strode back across the yard to join the other men.

'Alan, are you all right?' Jenny asked that evening as they sat together in the Cricketers' Arms on Church Gate. 'Only I'm sure you're not listening to a word I'm saying. Alan?'

'Pardon? Oh.' He gave a deep sigh. 'I'm sorry, Jenny, I've a lot on my mind.'

She frowned, worried for a moment whether this was something to do with her. 'Do you want to talk about it?' she asked hesitantly.

He shrugged his shoulders. 'Not much to talk about, really. It's just that we had to let three men go today and I feel very bad about it.'

'Oh,' Jenny said, quite relieved that Alan's unusually sombre mood was nothing to do with her, but not liking to hear of men losing their jobs. 'Is the furniture not selling very well at the moment, then?'

'Pardon?' He eyed her quizzically. What on earth was she going on about selling furniture for? 'I've no idea whether it is or not.'

'Oh!' she exclaimed, puzzled. Considering he worked for a furniture shop, delivering their wares, she thought this odd but decided not to comment further. 'I'm glad to say that

Wadham's situation is just the opposite. Mr Wadham reckons he'll need more men soon if business continues to come in like it is. Ever so busy we are. The telephone never stops ringing with people wanting jobs priced and more often than not we land the job. Mr Wadham's very pleased and he's told us if this continues, he's going to put our pay up. Isn't that good of him?'

Alan was staring at her. Unaware of the connection between Bill Wadham and him, Jenny was continually singing his uncle's praises and the more she did the more confused Alan became. And now here she was telling him that as the business was doing so well Bill was going to reward the contribution of his staff by raising their wages. It didn't make sense to Alan. These actions were hardly those of a man driven by selfish greed. But he couldn't cope with thinking about this now, hadn't the capacity to try to figure it all out, not while concentrating so much time and effort on securing the future of Collier's Carriers with his proposals to the bank, properly handling his own day job plus spending time with Jenny.

'Look, Jenny, I'm sorry, would you mind if I saw you to your bus?' he said now. 'It's nothing to do with you, just that I'm not very good company tonight.' Not that he wanted to leave her, but he did want to get home and start putting his thoughts down on paper.

'Oh, no, of course I don't mind,' she said, hiding her dismay.

He took her hand and closed his own around it affectionately. 'I'll make it up to you Friday, all right? We'll make up a foursome, if you like, with Janet and Gavin. Or we could just go out on our own, if you'd prefer? A meal or something? Go somewhere nice.'

She beamed happily. As long as she was with Alan anything sounded good to her. 'I don't mind what we do, I'll leave you to decide.' She picked up her glass and downed the remains of her shandy. Then, gathering up her coat and handbag, she stood up. 'Come on,' she said, taking his hand. 'I could do with an early night myself,' she said lightly, hoping she was not betraying the disappointment she was feeling at the end of her evening. 'My mother's out with her . . .' She hesitated, wanting to be careful how she expressed what she was about to say, not wanting to make her mother sound terrible. 'Her man friend. I'll have the house to myself for a change, to catch up with the ironing and maybe read some more of my book.'

They said their goodbyes at the bus station, ending with a lingering kiss before Alan saw Jenny onto her bus, waving as it pulled out of St Margaret's bus station.

A while later Jenny let herself into the house. It was freezing cold and she shivered, glad to be home. As she pushed open the door to the back room, raising her hand to the light switch, movement from within startled her and she froze momentarily.

In the light cast by the fire she saw a shadowy figure jump up from the settee. 'Oh, 'ello, Jenny love,' said a flustered May, straightening her clothes. 'I didn't expect yer so early. Thought you'd gone out with yer young man?'

Switching on the light, Jenny advanced into the room. 'You gave me a start, Mam. He had things to do, so we made it an early night. I'd thought you'd gone out yerself with . . .'

'Paul, this is me daughter, Jenny,' May cut in before Jenny could say any more and possibly embarrass her.

Jenny's eyes flashed to the man seated on the settee whom she hadn't noticed before. As he rose and stepped towards her, hand outstretched in greeting, she hurriedly appraised him and was pleased to note he did not seem anything like her mother's usual type. May had been accurate in her description of this man. He was very smart, clean-shaven, his hair tidily brushed, and he certainly had manners which was more than she could say for any of the others her mother had introduced her to.

Jenny shook his hand. 'Pleased to meet you. My mother's told me so much about you. I'm sorry you couldn't manage to come and have a meal with us, I know she was looking forward to it, but I understand your own mother is very ill and you often get called home?'

'Yes, she is and I do,' he matter-of-factly replied.

'Well, maybe . . .'

'That's enough, our Jenny,' May cut in. 'Don't want to frighten Mr Smith off, do we?' she said jocularly. But knowing her as she did, Jenny knew she had just received a warning to watch her mouth.

As they shook hands Daniel gave Jenny the once over. A good-looking daughter May had, he thought. A girl he'd never had any intention of meeting though, and he wasn't happy about this situation one little bit, May having told him they had the house to themselves until at least eleven o'clock. But what was annoying him the most about Jenny's unexpected appearance was that he and May had just been about to go upstairs. His libido, aroused to fever pitch by May, was screaming at him but was obviously not going to be fulfilled – not tonight at any rate. Oh, well, he thought, he would have to make do with Val. If she was asleep, he'd wake her.

Withdrawing his hand, he turned to May. 'I'd better be off.'

'Oh, yer don't need to go,' she responded, disappointed. 'At least 'ave a cuppa. Jenny, put the kettle on.'

'No, really, May, don't bother for me. I've an early start in the morning. I really need to get home. There's a train at eleven o'clock and I'd like to catch it. My mother's had one of her turns,' he blatantly lied. 'I'm worried about her.'

'Oh, I see. Well, I hope yer mam's okay, poor soul. She does seem ter suffer greatly, from what yer've told me. I'll see yer soon, though?'

'I'll be in Leicester next Wednesday as usual.' He turned to Jenny. 'Nice to meet you.'

'Yes, you too,' she replied.

At the front door Daniel took May's hand and said in hushed

tones, 'Look, don't take this wrong, but while my mother's as she is I can't make firm plans and I felt . . . well . . . awkward meeting your daughter. I don't want her to get the wrong impression of me, you see. That's really why I refused your invitation to dinner that time. I didn't feel it was right. My intentions towards you are honourable, May. You know that, don't you?'

She smiled, love radiating from her eyes. 'Yes, Paul, 'course I do.'

'Good, because I'd hate you to think otherwise. So, I was thinking, to avoid your daughter getting the wrong end of the stick and making it difficult for you, I'd better not come back here until my mother . . . Well, to be blunt, May, she's not long for this world. It's only a matter of time. If she wasn't in such ill health I'd like nothing more than to introduce you to her, but she can be very cantankerous and quite nasty and I don't want to subject you to any unpleasantness. It wouldn't be fair on you. It's just a case of us both having a bit of patience.'

May was glowing inside. In his way, Paul was asking her to wait for him. He wanted to marry her. Patience was not one of her virtues but she'd find it from somewhere if it meant having him. She just hoped his mother didn't linger for too long – then hoped she hadn't condemned her own soul to hell for having such terrible thoughts.

'Next Wednesday,' he was saying. 'We could have a meal. Then how would you feel if I got us a room?'

She frowned, eyes narrowing. Prostitutes went with men to hotel rooms and charged them for the privilege. Was Paul . . .? No, she must have it wrong. Or had she? A wave of hurt and humiliation swept through her. However much she cared for him, how dare he proposition her like this? Her temper rose. 'A room?' she hissed. 'You think I'm *that* kind of woman?'

'What? Oh, for goodness' sake, no, May. If I made you think that I'm very sorry. I just want to be alone with you, that's all, without being disturbed. We don't have much time together, and what we have I just wanted to make the most of. I thought you would too. It's only a suggestion. We can always just go for a drink. Wait to be alone together until after my mother passes on. However long that may be.'

May's face fell. Her and her big mouth, she thought, annoyed with herself. Why didn't she think before she spoke? Now she had upset Paul. 'I'm sorry,' she said. 'I'd love it if you got us a room. We've no other chance 'ave we, to 'ave some privacy. And yer right, dear, when yer mam . . . er . . . well, yer know, calls it a day, then'll be the time to introduce yer properly to me daughter and for you two to get to know each other.'

He kissed her cheek. 'You're a wonderful woman, May Jeffries. And I'm a lucky man to have someone so understanding.' He opened the door. 'Until Wednesday then,' he said, patting her backside. 'Same time, usual place.'

She nodded happily and watched, eyes tender, until he had disappeared from view around the corner of the street.

'So what did yer think to him then?' she asked Jenny when she returned to the back room.

Toasting her cold feet on the fender, Jenny turned her head and glanced across at her mother. 'He seems nice, Mam. I'm happy for you.'

'I'm happy for meself,' said May, sitting down. She looked round the room. 'I'm so glad I took the plunge and smartened this place up. I'd never 'ave brought a man like Paul back here the way it was before.' And unable to stop herself, she blurted out excitedly: 'He's asked me to marry him. Wadda yer think about that, eh?'

Jenny gasped, eyes wide. 'Really, Mam?' She was just as excited. 'Oh, I'm delighted. When . . .'

'Hang on a minute,' May cut in, realising the implications of what she had just announced. 'I . . . er . . . well, it's not exactly a proposal.'

Jenny grimaced. 'What do you mean? Either he has asked you or he hasn't?'

May sniffed haughtily, folding her arms. 'Well, it's difficult, if yer know what I mean.'

Her grimace deepening, Jenny said, 'No, I don't see what you mean.'

'Oh, Jenny, fer God's sake,' May snapped irritably. 'He's got an old bugger of a mother and can't commit himself to marriage 'til she kicks the bucket. I can't put it plainer than that, can I?'

'Oh, I see.'

'So, we're engaged but we ain't. I've just got to be patient.'

Which was one quality Jenny knew her mother did not possess. 'Can you be, Mam?'

'I've got no choice, 'ave I? Unless you know someone who's willing ter bump an old lady off. Painless, like. I wouldn't want 'er to suffer.'

'Mother!'

May grinned wickedly. 'I didn't mean it, yer daft sod! One thing I ain't and that's a murderer. Paul's mother, though, she doesn't sound very nice, so if she was done in I don't think it'd be much of a loss to him. And don't look like that – I told yer, I'm just 'aving fun.' She sighed deeply. 'I s'pose I'll have ter find the patience somewhere. Pity yer can't buy a patience pill over the counter at Boot's.'

Jenny laughed. 'Oh, Mam, you are funny.'

May laughed too. 'Yeah, I 'ave me moments, don't I?' She gave a wistful sigh. 'Oh, I do like 'im, Jenny. Paul's such a gent. Knows how ter treat a woman. He opens doors for me and pulls chairs out before I sit down. Pays for me drinks an' all. I ain't put me 'and in me purse once since I've known 'im. He's definitely the one, Jenny. Mrs Paul Smith . . . I like it. It's got a certain ring, don't yer think?'

Jenny nodded. 'It has. But in all honesty, Mam, I couldn't

care what his name is. He treats you well and that's all that matters to me.' She looked at her mother for long moments. 'You love him, don't yer?'

May stared at her thoughtfully before replying. 'I dunno about love, ducky, but I like being with 'im, feel good in 'is company, and I miss 'im when I don't see 'im, so I suppose I do as near as dammit. But as for true love, the kind that makes yer feel dizzy, the kind where you feel that should the other person be in danger you'd lay down yer own life . . . well, I've only ever felt like that once before and that was fer yer father.'

Lips pressed tight, Jenny stared at her. 'Oh, Mam,' she said emotionally. 'Why did me dad have to go and die, eh? Do yer still miss him?'

'Yes,' she said without hesitation. 'I think about him all the time.'

'You do? After twenty odd years?'

May nodded. 'Heartache fades given time, gel, but memories last forever. Hard as you try, they pop up when yer least expect and you have no choice but to relive certain moments. Some nice, some not so nice. Depends what triggered them.'

'But your memories of me dad are nice ones, Mam, ain't they?'

'Oh, yeah,' she said, reaching over for the poker to give the fire a prod. 'Mostly.' The fire crackled and spluttered and black ash from smouldering household waste flew up the chimney. May sighed distractedly as she replaced the poker and relaxed in her chair. 'Yeah, mostly nice,' she repeated absently. She looked over at Jenny and gave a sudden smile. 'But as I've said before, life goes on. Yer dad's gone and Paul's come along and I don't intend to lose this one, not if I can help it.' Just then the front door knocker sounded. 'Who the 'ell's that at this time o' night?' snapped May, annoyed. 'You get it, Jenny. I've just got meself comfy. Gloria's right. These new chairs might be modern but they ain't nowhere near as comfortable as me old ones used ter be.'

'Yer mam in, me duck?' Gloria asked as Jenny opened the front door. 'Only I fancy a bit of company. As usual Cyril's snoring 'is 'ead off in the chair and his bloody great size elevens are blocking the fire. Kelvin and Sandra are out. When are they ever in is more the point. I wa' feeling a bit lonely. I don't see much of yer mam these days, ever since she started her revamp lark. The new 'er,' Gloria said mockingly. 'She is in, ain't she?'

Jenny nodded. 'Come through, Mrs Budgins.'

'Eh up, May,' Gloria greeted her friend as she barged into the room. 'Oh, good, yer've got a fire blazing. Ours is about snuffed it and I've just about ran out of coal. Can't afford no more 'til pay day. You ain't got any spare, 'ave yer, May?'

'No.'

Gloria pulled a face. 'What, not even a bucket of slack?'

'I might stretch ter that. Jenny'll check and see when yer on yer way out.'

'Ta, May, you're a gem.'

'Idiot more like.'

'Eh, you've 'ad enough off me over the years, May Jeffries. Helped you out of a few 'oles, I have, so don't you go begrudging me a bucket of slack,' snapped Gloria, plonking herself down in the armchair Jenny had just vacated to answer the door. 'By the way, May, d'yer know yer back door's locked? That's why I had to come around the front. Nearly did meself a damage feeling me way down the entry. It ain't 'arf dark out ternight.'

'Yeah,' May replied. 'It would be locked.'

'Why would it be locked? I've never know yer lock it afore.'

'I did ternight ter stop nosey beggars like you charging in unannounced.'

'Oh,' Gloria mouthed knowingly, holding out her hands to the fire to warm them. ''Ad a visitor, did yer?'

'Might 'ave,' May replied cagily. 'But that's fer me to know and you ter wonder about. Anyhow, I'm glad you've come in. I need me roots doing, and by the looks on it so do you.'

'Cheeky sod,' Gloria snorted. 'They ain't that bad.'

'They are. At least an inch. And you ain't 'alf going grey.' Fighting hard to keep her face straight, she added, 'You'd better let me do 'em before anyone realises you ain't a natural blonde. How about termorrer night?'

'One of these days, May Jeffries,' Gloria warned, wagging a podgy finger, 'that gob of yours is gonna get you in serious trouble. It's a good job I know yer only joking. I ain't got n'ote better on termorrer night. I'll bring a bottle of sherry wi' me – it'll help dull the pain of you yanking me hair out. Mind you, I say I'm free termorrer night but there's always the chance Clark Gable'll knock on me door, and ask me out.'

May let out a bellow of mirth. 'Some hope you've got, gel. Same hope as I 'ave. So termorrer it is then. Come round about seven. Cuppa?'

'Thought yer'd never ask.'

'Put the kettle on, Jenny.'

She sighed. So much for her peaceful early night.

# Chapter Twenty-Four

'It's very dark up here, Jenny.'

'Shall I see if I can get a candle from the missus?'

'Would you? I ain't goin' to be able to clear this place out if I can't see what I'm doing.'

Herchell did have a point, she thought. 'Don't move, I won't be a minute.'

He had no intention of moving an inch until he could see exactly what he was facing in the dark confines around him. Perched precariously on the edge of the attic hatch, he peered around. Shadowy shapes loomed before him and he wished with all his heart Jenny would hurry up with the candle so he could at least make out what the eerie outlines were. For the most part he loved his job but this part of it he didn't. It wasn't the first attic he'd had to volunteer to empty for some elderly spinster lady or widow woman who had employed Wadham's services, and he knew it wouldn't be the last, but each time the same feeling would overcome him as he pushed back the hatch and popped through his head.

No matter what time of day it was, how bright the sun outside, attics were always places of dread for Herchell. They were dark, stale rooms filled with decaying relics of bygone times, every discarded object caked in layers of dust. He hated the cobwebs which drifted up as the rush of air from the hatch wafted past. He shuddered as he waited.

It seemed like hours to him before Jenny finally returned.

'Sorry I took so long,' she called breathlessly, beginning to climb up the rotting, flimsy ladder towards him. 'Mrs Withers couldn't remember where she'd put them. I'm not surprised, considering the chaos downstairs. And up here for that matter. Yer know,' she said, reaching up to pass him the candle, 'people on the move never cease to amaze me. You'd think they'd start packing weeks before, not start on the day they're gonna leave.'

'Matches?'

'Eh?'

'Did you get matches to light the candle with, Jenny?'

'Oh! No, I never thought. Stay there, I won't be a minute.'

It seemed another age to him before she returned again. 'I had to go to the corner shop. Can you believe it, Mrs Withers hadn't a match in the house. Not one.' She passed the box of Swan Vestas to him and waited while he lit the candle. 'Right, I'll leave you to it. I'm helping the old dear pack her good china. If you need a hand with anything, give me a shout.'

Peering into the gloom in front of him, Herchell said, 'Will do.' Then reluctantly hauled himself through the small hatch.

Downstairs Jenny carefully placed a newspaper-wrapped piece of china in a half-full crate. 'You have some lovely things, Mrs Withers.'

The old lady beamed in pleasure. 'Yes, I do, don't I? All inherited from my family. My daughter who I'm going to live with will inherit them from me. I do appreciate your help, my dear. I did try to tackle it all but . . .'

'It's quite all right, Mrs Withers, all part of our service.' But having said that, all the extra work she and Herchell were having to do in order to get this old lady out of her house and settled across town with her daughter had come as a shock, and it had not been priced in the original quote. It was also taking much longer to do than the estimated three hours and they had another job to tackle later that afternoon. Thank goodness Mr

Ford was returning to work soon. They certainly needed him. 'Now,' Jenny said, looking around, 'that's all the china safely packed and there's nothing left to do in here except load the furniture on the van which we'll do when Mr Williams is finished in the attic. What next? Is your linen packed?'

'Oh, yes, I've done all that, dear. Mrs Jordan from next door helped me with it yesterday. It was just the china that was bothering me, really. I was afraid of dropping it. My arthritis is worse some days than others and today seemed to arrive so quickly and . . .'

Jenny laid a comforting hand on the flustered old lady's arm. 'Stop worrying yerself, Mrs Withers. It's all done now and that's what counts.'

Her aged face was transformed by relief. 'You're such a nice girl, my dear. I have to admit, I had a shock when you and the bla— Mr . . . er . . .'

'Williams.'

'Yes, Mr Williams turned up this morning. Well, in all honesty, dear, this isn't the usual kind of occupation for a young lady. But you're a natural at it, aren't you? Mr Wadham assured me when I accepted his quote that he had the best staff to do the work and he was right. He's a nice man, is Mr Wadham. My son-in-law is in the throes of moving business premises. He's doing ever so well, you know, expanding. I could suggest Wadham's to him. Do you do that sort of work?'

'We do anything on the removals front, Mrs Withers, if it's within our limits. Mr Wadham would be most happy to quote him a price.'

'Then I shall recommend him, my dear. Happy to.'

'That's very good of you. Now, I suggest next we tackle the . . .' Just then a piercing scream of terror rent the air, to be followed moments later by the noise of scrambling across the ceiling, then the dull thud of a large heavy object crashing down on something solid.

'Oh, my God,' Jenny cried. 'What was that?'

Spinning on her heel, she raced from the room and up the stairs to find a quaking Herchell in a heap at the bottom of the attic ladder, the snuffed out candle still clutched in his hand.

Bewildered, Jenny dropped down by the side of him, grabbed his arm and shook him. 'What on earth happened, Herchell? Did you fall through the hatch or what? Are you hurt?'

Face contorted in terror, eyes wide, he slowly turned his head and looked at her. With a shaking hand he pointed one finger upwards.

'What?' Jenny urged. 'What is it, Herchell? For God's sake, will you tell me?'

'Up . . . up . . . there,' he stammered.

Jenny looked at the gaping entrance to the attic, then back to Herchell. 'What is?'

'D . . . d . . . dead body.'

Her mouth dropped open. 'What! Herchell, you did say "dead body"?'

Still pointing, he nodded. 'Up there.'

Jenny froze.

'What has happened?' a breathless voice asked.

She turned her head to see Mrs Withers nearing the top of the stairs.

'In your attic,' Jenny uttered, still reeling in shock from Herchell's announcement.

'What is?' Mrs Withers asked, her face bewildered.

Jenny gathered her wits and took a deep breath. 'A dead body in your attic.'

Mrs Withers arrived next to her. 'A dead body!' she exclaimed in horror. 'In my attic? Well, I've never heard the like. And me moving as well. Who put it there?' she demanded, peeved.

Jenny shook her head. 'I've no idea.' She turned back to Herchell. 'Did you actually see it, a dead body? You are sure?'

'I . . . I saw the coffin.'

'Coffin!' Jenny exclaimed, her own sense of horror accelerating rapidly.

'Coffin?' echoed the old lady. 'Oh . . . the coffin.'

They both looked at her.

She grinned sheepishly. 'It's mine. There's no body in it, though. Well, at least, I hope not.'

'The coffin is yours?' Jenny queried.

'Yes. I'd forgotten all about it. My husband bought one for each of us many years ago, you see. Thought it would save money. Actually he was right. When he died several years ago the price of a burial had gone up something terrible and not having to pay for a coffin saved quite a bit of money. He was like that, my husband, very thoughtful.' She looked at Herchell, ashamed. 'I'm so sorry, Mr Williams, that it gave you such a fright.'

Taking several deep breaths, he forced a smile to his face. 'No damage done, Mrs Withers,' he said with a great effort. 'But are you quite sure there's not'ing inside the coffin?'

'Positive,' she said. 'Oh, maybe just a few odds and ends. They make very good storage boxes do coffins. Right, had we better get on?'


Bill was laughing. He was laughing so hard his ribs ached and tears of mirth were rolling down his face. 'Oh, I just wish I'd been there!'

'It wasn't funny, boss.'

Bill fought to control his amusement. 'No, Herchell, I'm sure it wasn't.'

'It's funny now,' said Jenny. 'But I have to agree it wasn't at the time. I just wish I could've got a photograph of Herchell's face when Mrs Withers told us the coffin was hers. It was . . . well . . . a picture.'

Herchell scowled. 'I just hope, Jenny, not'ing like that ever happens to you.'

'Oh, so do I,' she heartily agreed. 'I tell you something, though – if ever it should, I'd scream louder than you did. Anyway, Mr Wadham, Mrs Withers is happily settled at her daughter's and very happy with the job we did. She's going to recommend you to her son-in-law who's moving business premises.'

Bill eyed her, impressed. 'That's good news. Right, time's wearing on. Are you sure you're all right to go with Herchell again this afternoon? I am grateful, Jenny, but in truth your main job is here.'

'Stop worrying, Mr Wadham. As my mam would say, in for a penny in for a pound. And that applies to my job as far as I'm concerned. I love doing my office work but I also like helping out with the shifting. And work here is easy caught up with. I just worry about the telephone not being answered, that's all, 'cos I know you've got to go out too and quote for some jobs. But anyone who doesn't get an answer will ring back, I'm sure.'

'Thanks, Jenny, I appreciate all you're doing,' he said. 'It shouldn't be so bad from Monday as Mr Ford is returning then. And I'd better let you both know I'm going to see about taking on a couple more men now I'm confident business is moving in the right direction, as well as seeing about a decent van. Two, in fact.'

'Really?' said Jenny, impressed.

He nodded. 'Not before time, is it? I'm amazed my old lorry has kept going as long as she has. Well, it's time to put her out to pasture. While she's still running we can use her, of course, but just on small jobs. I'm going to see the bank manager next week about loaning us some money. I must admit, the thought of being in debt frightens me a bit but for the business to move forward I have to do this. I only want to borrow enough for second-hand vehicles, I'm not in a position to buy new yet. But we're definitely on the way up and I've you two to thank for that.'

Jenny and Herchell both blushed scarlet at the compliment.

'We're only too glad to be part of it, ain't we, Herchell?'

He nodded. 'Jenny's right, boss. Blossom was only sayin' to me last night how lucky I am to be workin' for you. In fact, she sez it to me every night. Oh, and she asked me to ask you when you were comin' around fer dinner again? And you, Jenny. I've still some rum left in the bottle, boss.'

Bill groaned. 'And my head still remembers the morning after the last time we opened it. Tell Blossom next week sometime. Now you two can show me how much you like working for me by getting yourselves off to do the other job for this afternoon before they ring up and cancel. But have a cuppa before you both go.'

Across town Alan was eyeing his father hesitantly. 'So what do you think then, Dad?'

Daniel raised his head to look at him, face devoid of any expression. In truth, his heart was pounding, pulses racing as excitement flowed within him, but he couldn't let his son see that. 'Seems a lot of money we're talking about, Alan. You sure your calculations are correct?'

'Positive. I've checked everything several times to make sure. In between jobs I managed to fit in quite a few appointments with firms who could be interested in what we'd be offering, and they seemed very keen. Of course we don't have to buy new vans, second-hand would do just as well, but I was thinking long term and the costs of possible breakdowns with second-hand vehicles. At least with new vans you have a year's warranty. Then, of course, we needn't expand into next door, we could manage here with a squeeze, but I thought as the premises were becoming vacant in two months' time we

313

should go for it. They might not become free again for a long time, if ever, and if we do get too big for this place finding suitable premises and doing renovations could prove very expensive.'

Daniel hadn't a clue that the firm next door was moving out but didn't let his son know that. Neither did he tell Alan how impressed he had been with all the work he had done coming up with these figures. He hadn't realised before that his son possessed such an astute business brain. It made him feel inadequate. He could never have done this.

'It's still a lot of money, Alan. Are you sure the bank will be willing to lend this kind of sum?' he asked matter-of-factly.

'I think they will when we put all this to them. I'm positive, in fact.'

Ten thousand pounds, Daniel mused. More than he had ever envisaged having. It was a small fortune. What he could do with it all! Buy a decent car, a grand house, start his own business, and still have change . . .

He picked up the report, pulled open a drawer in his desk, slipped the report inside, and locked it up. 'I'll think on it,' he said.

'But, Dad . . .'

Daniel raised one hand in warning. 'I said, I'll think on it. This is a big decision, Alan. Don't forget, in several weeks this firm will become all yours. If we go ahead then it's a big responsibility that'll land on your shoulders. Be a different matter altogether if I was solely responsible for the business, me being far more experienced than you, or you were going to become a junior partner and me still at the helm, but your grandfather saw fit to decide otherwise. I sometimes wonder if he was sound in his mind when he made his will. Still . . . give me a couple of weeks to mull it over.'

Alan bit his tongue, desperate to tell his father about his plan to make them equal partners, to be announced on his birthday in six weeks' time. The paperwork was being drawn up right now by a solicitor under strict orders of secrecy so as not to spoil the surprise. And there was something else he wanted to announce at his birthday party, but for that he had to ask Jenny a question first and of course the announcement depended on her answer.

A sudden great urge to see her filled him. During this last two weeks, as he had laboured hard to complete his task, he'd not managed to see much of her. He had missed her greatly, their time apart only serving to bring home to him just how much he loved her. What would years of courting prove? he thought. He knew now he loved Jenny enough to want to spend the rest of his life with her. Waiting a sensible period of time to ask her to marry him, as society expected, seemed pointless to him when he knew his mind now.

He knew Jenny loved him. He'd be a fool not to know that. She probably had no idea how obviously she showed it. It was in her every action. The way her eyes sparkled tenderly when she looked at him; the way she held his hand tightly; the way she let him kiss her and her eager response. But it was more than that. It was how she listened attentively to him when he was telling her something; how she offered her opinions but allowed for the fact he had his own, too; her appreciation of the small things he did for her, but how she never took him for granted. How he felt lonely without her at his side. In fact, it was everything about her that Alan loved.

All sense and reason suddenly left him as an urgent desire to settle matters between himself and Jenny filled him. He was going to ask her to marry him, but first he'd arrange for her to meet his parents. Over a meal, that would be best.

He looked at his father. 'All right, Dad, I'll leave it with you. Er . . . are you free on Saturday night?'

Daniel frowned. 'Why?'

'I'd like you and Mum to meet Jenny.' As the words left his

mouth he hoped he wasn't taking her acceptance for granted. He should have asked her first. Then he suddenly realised there was also the business of being related to Bill Wadham. He really should tell her, explain it all. But he didn't know how to without divulging the reasons for his family's estrangement. What a mess it all was.

He realised his father was talking to him. 'Pardon, Dad?'

'I asked who this Jenny was?' Daniel repeated, annoyed.

'My girlfriend, Dad,' Alan said, hurt he hadn't remembered. 'I've spoken of her often enough.'

'Yes, yes, but I've had so much on my mind with running this place. Well, if I must meet her, I suppose Saturday's as good a day as any,' his father said dismissively, wanting to return to his own affairs. Who Alan married was of no real interest to him, not now. 'Just tell me when and where.'

'Oh . . . er . . . somewhere like the Bell Hotel.'

'The Bell?' Daniel nearly choked. That was the last place he wanted to dine with his family. There was just the chance someone had seen him there with May the night they had first met and might pass remarks. And what if May herself just happened to be there? 'Not the Bell, Alan. It's . . . er . . . well, I wasn't particularly impressed with the food when I ate there that night the manager kept me waiting.'

'Oh,' Alan said, disappointed. He quite liked the atmosphere in the Bell Hotel, thought the setting just right for the occasion he had in mind. A memory suddenly struck him. 'Did we get that job you went to price, Dad? Only you've never mentioned it since.'

'No,' said Daniel in such an abrupt tone it stunned Alan for a moment. 'What about the Grand?'

'Pardon?'

'The Grand for a meal on Saturday. What's the matter with you, Alan, gone deaf or something?'

'No, Dad, I was just thinking about something. Yes, the

Grand Hotel would be perfect. Thanks for suggesting it.' He just hoped he could afford it, the Grand Hotel was very expensive.

'Right, I'll leave you to it then, Dad.'

Daniel eyed him blankly. 'I wish you would.'

# Chapter Twenty-Five

'Janet, I can't go, I've nothing suitable to wear. I mean, what *do* you wear to meet your boyfriend's parents for the first time? And at the Grand Hotel of all places. It's so posh. The nearest place I've ever eaten in to that is Kingman's Café in the Market Place.' Jenny's bottom lip trembled worriedly. 'I'll do something stupid, Janet, I know I will. Knock the waiter flying. Fall off me chair. I'll show Alan up, you see if I don't. Oh, God, I can't go. I'll have to make some excuse. That I've come down with something really horrible . . .'

Seated on Jenny's bed, Janet began to laugh. 'If you could see yerself, Jenny. If I didn't know you better I'd say you want locking up, ranting and raving like a madwoman! Just shurrup and listen. You're being stupid. You ain't gonna do anything daft and neither will yer show Alan up. For Christ's sake, he loves yer, woman. Get that through yer thick head. Why else would he want yer to meet his parents? It's a big thing is that. I wish it was Gavin taking me to see his. And I know for a fact, 'cos me and Gavin have been out with you both often enough, that you could walk naked through the market on the Saturday before Christmas with a bunch of bananas on yer head and Alan'd not turn a hair.'

'No, but she'd be bloody freezin'', May remarked matter-of-factly as she stood framed in the bedroom doorway.

'Evenin'', Mrs Jeffries,' Janet said, smiling a greeting. 'Excitin' in't it, all this?'

Leaning on the doorframe May sniffed haughtily, folding her arms under her bosom. 'You might think so. I ain't even met this *Alan* yet. Hardly know 'ote about him in fact. His first name and that's about it. Kept real quiet 'as our Jenny. She's ashamed of me, yer know, Janet. 'Tain't right, is it, bein' ashamed of yer own mother?'

'Mam, stop it,' Jenny cried, annoyed. 'I'm not ashamed of you and you know it. I never told you much about Alan before because . . . because . . . well, you know you'd only have frightened him off. Please don't be angry with me, Mam. I knew he was going to be special to me nearly as soon as we met and I didn't want to jeopardise anything.'

'And introducing him ter me would 'ave, is that what yer saying?' May demanded.

'No. Yes. Oh, Mother, you are *so* annoying sometimes. If I'd let you within a mile of Alan you'd have put him through the mincer, yer know yer would. Go on, admit it.'

May sniffed haughtily again and eyed her innocently. 'Only 'cos I 'ave yer best interests at heart.'

Jenny smiled, her eyes tender. 'I know that, Mam. But I know your ways as well. Alan doesn't.'

'And what's that supposed ter mean? Just what *ways* yer referring to?'

'Mam, stop it. You know exactly what I'm talking about. If I'd brought him round here, within minutes he'd have shot out the door, thankful for what a lucky escape he'd had, and I'd never have seen him again.'

Her mother's head was back, eyes narrowed darkly, and Janet gasped. Trouble was obviously brewing. She eyed the door, wondering how quickly she could make her own escape. In the past she had witnessed several of May's outbursts and didn't fancy seeing another one.

Jenny was staring at her mother, horrified, realising she had gone too far. 'Mam, I'm sorry, I shouldn't have . . .'

May's hand came up in warning. 'Too late, yer've said it,' she barked. Then, unexpectedly, her face relaxed and she grinned. 'Fer once I agree with yer, gel. That poor lad wouldn'ta known what had hit him. I wouldn't just 'ave put him through the mincer, I'd 'ave added carrots and onions and stewed him in the oven! But as I've already told yer, it's only 'cos I love yer, Jenny, and don't want yer to mek the same mistakes as I have.' Her eyes flashed enquiringly. 'So when am I gonna meet this chappie of yours then?'

Jenny went over to May, threw her arms around her and hugged her tightly. 'Soon, Mam. What about Sunday? I'll have to check with Alan first, of course.'

'That'll do, I suppose. Better than at the church on yer wedding day. Ask him for dinner. I'll see if I can stretch to buying a joint. You can cook it as you're better than me. Don't want to put him off, do we, eh?'

'Oh, Mam,' Jenny soothed her. 'I'm sorry if I hurt you. I never meant to. It's just that Alan means so much to me.'

'And you obviously do to him if he's teking yer to meet his parents.'

Jenny pulled away from her mother and eyed her questioningly. 'Do you think he's serious about me then, Mam? Do you really?'

Janet guffawed. 'God, is your daughter something else or what, Mrs J? Is he serious?' she said mockingly. 'No, Jenny, he's taking you to meet his folks 'cos he's n'ote better to do. She's a daft 'a'porth, ain't she?'

'Brainless, I'd say. 'Course he's serious, Jenny. Men don't tek just any gel to meet their folks. Only intended ones.'

'Oh!' Jenny exclaimed, her eyes wide. 'I do hope you're both right.'

'I hope I am,' said May matter-of-factly. 'I've been wanting rid of yer for years.'

'Mother!'

'Well, I have,' she said, tongue in cheek. 'Bloody nuisance you are, have bin since the minute you were born. Oh, fer God's sake, tek that stricken look off yer face, I'm only joking. You were the most perfect baby and you're the best daughter any mother could want. Well, for the most part,' she added, a twinkle in her eye. 'Now, what yer gonna wear on Sat'day? You'd better hurry up and decide – I can't stand the tension. Pity it's too late to run summat up on the treadle, in't it?'

Jenny turned and scanned her eyes across the pile of clothes on her bed, none of which seemed suitable for the occasion. Her heart sank. 'It's no good, there's nothing I can wear to the Grand,' she wailed despairingly. 'And I really want to make a good impression.'

'You'll make a good impression whatever yer wearing, Jenny,' May said with conviction. She glanced at the assortment of clothes strewn across her daughter's bed. Jenny was right. There was nothing amongst the mainly home-made skirts and jumpers, trews and blouses, that would put together a suitable outfit for the Grand Hotel. Nor were the three dresses Jenny possessed decent enough either. She wanted her daughter to look nice.

Then a thought suddenly crossed her mind. How was it that Alan's parents could afford to treat the couple to a meal at the Grand? It wasn't cheap there. But that wasn't the issue right this minute. Making sure her daughter looked good was. And it was in May's power to make sure she did. 'Just hang on a minute,' she called, disappearing from the room.

'Where's she gone?' asked Janet.

Jenny shrugged her shoulders. 'I don't know.'

May reappeared, holding out her hand towards Jenny. ''Ere,' she said.

'What is it?'

'Why don't yer tek it and find out?'

Jenny did then gasped. 'Three pounds, Mam?'

'I'm well aware of that. You're ter go up town on Sat'day and get yerself rigged out. You shouldn't 'ave any trouble getting summat really nice with three quid. C & A might be yer best bet. Or they 'ave some nice costumes and dresses in Paige's on Gallowtree Gate. Marshall and Snelgrove's and Lewis's tend to be pricey, and besides they don't really cater for you young 'uns. If yer lucky you might have enough to get yerself a pair of shoes in Freeman, Hardy & Willis.'

Jenny was staring at her, overwhelmed. 'But you can't spare this, Mam. We've rent to pay and we've no coal and . . .' She stopped abruptly, face grave. 'And anyway, how did you get it? It ain't pay day 'til tomorrow.'

'Oi, you listen to me, gel. That's none of your business. I hope you ain't accusing me of stealing?'

'Don't be daft, Mam. But three quid. Well, it's a week's wage.'

'Oh, fer God's sake, Jenny, will yer give yer mouth a rest? That three quid is a gift from yer mother. Accept it and shurrup, will yer?' May smiled. 'It's given with my love.'

Jenny threw her arms around her again, hugging her fiercely. 'Oh, Mam. Thanks. Thanks so much.'

'Yer welcome. And yer can thank me best by popping down the offy and getting me a bottle of beer.'

'I'll do that, Mam, 'course I will. Eh, but what about your new regime? I thought . . .'

'I didn't say I'd cut out drinking altogether, just said I'd cut down. And that's what I've done. I don't get half so sozzled as I used ter, and not nearly so often.'

'Yes, that's very true, Mam. I never thought you'd stick to your new regime lark, you know. You've really amazed me,' Jenny said proudly.

May grinned. 'Neither did I. Just shows what the love of a good man can do for yer.'

'For both of us, Mam. Will you come with me and Janet to

323

choose something? We could go straight after we both finish work at twelve. You are coming too, ain't you, Janet?' she asked, looking across at her friend still perched on the edge of her bed.

'You try and stop me,' she replied.

'You really want me to come?' May asked.

'Yes, why shouldn't I? I'd value your opinion.'

'Then I will,' she said, delighted. 'Between the three of us we'll have you looking good enough to knock Alan's socks off. You see if we don't.'

# Chapter Twenty-Six

Alan's eyes lit up on spotting Jenny waiting for him at the front of Timothy White's opposite the clock tower. He hurried across to her, in his haste just avoiding a collision with a car. 'You look beautiful,' he said, drinking in the sight of her, eyes shining. He kissed her lightly on her lips, then took hold of her hand.

Jenny beamed at the compliment. It had taken the three of them all afternoon to choose her outfit of a silver and grey flecked lightweight satin material. Its full skirt ended mid-calf; the jacket was boned but had been softened so that it kept its fitted shape while flaring out just below her waist. A white blouse with a pretty Peter Pan collar completed the outfit. Jenny's blonde hair was pinned up becomingly in a French pleat.

The suit had been her first choice, in the first shop they had gone into, Paige's Fashions. On trying it on she had gazed at her reflection in the mirror and fallen in love with it, thinking it perfect, an outfit she could wear many times over. The price had been right, too, leaving her enough for a pair of grey suede high-heeled court shoes, but both Janet and her mother had insisted they should look around before making a final decision.

And look around they had. Practically every shop in Leicester had been visited, most of them far too expensive for Jenny's pocket. Smart evening dresses as well as costumes, skirts and blouses had been tried on before they had returned to purchase her original choice. By the time they had arrived home on the six o'clock bus, Jenny had hardly time to get herself ready before she'd had to rush out again to meet Alan.

'You really do think I look all right?' she reiterated.

He stepped back and looked her up and down. 'Well, I have to say you look a little better than the first time I saw you.'

She was horrified. 'Only a little?' she exclaimed. 'Oh . . .'

Laughing, he pulled her to him and kissed her again. 'I'm teasing you, Jenny. You look absolutely ravishing.'

She sighed with relief. 'I wanted to look nice for you. And you look so smart,' she said, appraising his dark blue suit and crisp white shirt.

'And I wanted to look nice for you. I'm glad you think I do,' he replied, smiling. 'Now come on, I don't want to keep my parents waiting.'

They hurried all the way up Gallowtree Gate, dodging other pedestrians making their way to various evening destinations. By the time they arrived at the elaborate frontage of the Grand Hotel, halfway up Granby Street, Jenny was quite breathless.

'Good evening, sir, madam,' a doorman greeted them, running up the entrance steps to open one of the wide glass entrance doors for them.

The foyer was imposing and as her new shoes sank into the plush red carpet, Jenny tried to quell the swirl of anxiety in her stomach. People in evening dress were milling around, having an aperitif before they went in to dinner. Never having been in such an environment before, she suddenly felt out of her depth.

Alan felt her hand tighten on his. Sensing her fears, he turned to her and whispered in her ear, 'Don't be nervous, darling. If it's any consolation, you're not as nervous as I'll be tomorrow when I come to meet your mother.'

Her heart thumped painfully. Alan had called her 'darling'. Suddenly her nervousness vanished. She was with Alan. He loved her. Everything would be all right, she just knew it would be. She would love his parents, and they her, and the evening would be a great success.

'Ah, the restaurant is this way,' said Alan, guiding her across.

The maître d' greeted them. 'Good evening, sir. What name?' he asked, consulting his reservations book.

Alan suddenly froze, heart hammering, mind whirling frantically, realising what an idiot he had been. He had forgotten he would have to give the name the table was booked under and Jenny would immediately ask questions when he announced it. He had done this all the wrong way round. In the urgency to firm up his relationship with Jenny it hadn't occurred to him that questions would inevitably be asked. But it was too late now. He grabbed her hand and pulled her aside. 'Jenny, please don't ask me any questions. I know this is going to seem . . .'

She was looking at him, bewildered. 'Seem what, Alan? What's going on?'

He squeezed her hand tightly, acutely conscious the maître d' and other guests were staring at them. 'There isn't time to explain now. Please just trust me. But whatever you do, Jenny, don't mention it to my parents . . . I won't be a moment,' he said to the waiting man.

'Mention what, Alan?' she asked, bewildered.

'That . . .'

'Is there anything wrong, sir?' the maître d' interrupted, joining them. 'Only I have other people waiting.'

'Er . . . no, nothing.'

'So the name the table's booked in, sir?'

'Er . . .' Alan's eyes flashed worriedly to Jenny, then back to the maître d' and around the restaurant. 'Oh,' he exclaimed thankfully. 'There are my parents over there.'

'Oh, you're with the Wa—'

'Yes, that's right,' Alan cut in sharply.

The man eyed him a moment before clicking his fingers to summon a waiter who immediately appeared at the side of them. 'This way, please.'

Feeling he was about to step into a lion's den, he followed the waiter. Several paces behind Alan trailed Jenny, totally bemused by his puzzling behaviour. Skirting tables, they weaved their way through the busy restaurant towards the back of the room. The waiter arrived at a table where a man and a woman were already sitting, their backs to them. He proceeded to pull out one of the two vacant chairs. As Alan arrived several feet in front of Jenny, the man seated at the table scraped back his chair and stood up. He turned full face to greet Alan, and Jenny stopped abruptly, mouth dropping open in surprise. The man, obviously Alan's father, was none other than 'Paul Smith', her mother's boyfriend.

Oh, God, she thought. This could not be happening. It couldn't be true. This situation was dreadful, a nightmare. Instinctively she took several steps back. What was she going to do? She couldn't be introduced to Alan's father, couldn't pretend she didn't know him. And what would Paul Smith – or whatever his name really was – do when he recognised her?

But mixed with this was a great urge to step up to this cheating man and beat him with her fists. Her beloved mother had fallen in love with him, believed his lies about his invalid mother. He had fooled May into thinking he was going to marry her. May thought this man was her saviour, her future and all her hopes and dreams were pinned entirely on him. This man, Alan's father, was nothing more than a liar and a cheat.

A great feeling of foreboding flooded through Jenny. Any second now Alan would wonder why she wasn't at his side and fetch her over. She knew what she had to do. Spinning on her heel, she fled from the restaurant, nearly colliding with several waiters and guests en route, then left the hotel.

# Chapter Twenty-Seven

'Please, Mrs Jeffries – please let me see Jenny.'

The plea was that of a desperate man but as far as May was concerned he was the cause of her beloved daughter's misery and she remained obdurate. 'No,' she cried. 'Besides, Jenny won't even talk ter me. She flew into the house, leaving the front door wide open, and now she's barricaded herself in 'er bedroom and refuses to come out. She's bawlin' her eyes out.' May, her own face thunderous, folded her arms and took up a firm stance, blocking the way with her body in case Alan should try to force his way in. 'I wanna know what yer've done to my daughter!'

He raked his fingers through his hair, bewildered. 'Nothing, Mrs Jeffries. We were in the restaurant at the Grand, I thought she was behind me, and when I turned to introduce her to my parents, she was gone. I don't understand it. She was fine. Nervous about meeting them, that was all. I don't know why she's acting like this.'

He seemed so sincere May actually believed him but the evidence was telling her otherwise. 'And do I look like I were born yesterday?' she erupted. 'Tek me for a fool, d'yer? My daughter left this 'ouse full of the joys of spring and now she's sobbing her heart out, so don't you stand on my front doorstep, young man, and expect me ter believe that cock and bull.'

'But it's true, Mrs Jeffries . . .'

'Look, I ain't got time fer this,' May erupted, unfolding her arms and stepping back into the passageway. 'I've an upset daughter I need to deal with. I'll get to the bottom of this, believe me I will. You get yerself off home. If Jenny does want ter see yer, she'll contact yer, I'm sure.'

It suddenly struck him that she did not know his exact address. Thrusting his hand in his inside jacket pocket, Alan pulled out a small notebook and pen, suddenly glad it was something he always carried. He scribbled on a sheet of notepaper then thrust it at May. 'My address. You will give it to her, won't you, Mrs Jeffries?'

May took it and looked at it. She grimaced. 'Oh, that's where yer live, is it? Bit posh is Groby Road. For the likes of a van driver.'

With that she shut the door.

As he stared openmouthed at the door which had just been slammed in his face a thought struck Alan and he groaned. In his haste to make sure Jenny knew exactly where he could be contacted he had forgotten to add his telephone number. It was too late now. At least she had his address.

He suddenly became aware that curtains in adjoining houses were twitching. Thrusting his hands into his pockets, shoulders hunched, he turned and walked slowly back down the street.

'Alan!' Val cried, jumping up to greet him as he walked into his own house. 'Your father's in bed but I was so worried, I had to wait up for you. Did you see Jenny?'

'No.'

'Oh. Come on through to the kitchen and I'll make you a cuppa. You're wet, Alan, take your coat off.'

'Please stop fussing, Mum, I'm all right. But I could do with a cuppa, thanks.'

For several minutes Val silently busied herself preparing the tea, greatly distressed to see her beloved son in such a dreadful state. Unable to contain herself any longer she turned to face him, sitting at the table, head cradled in his hands, and asked, 'Have you any idea why she ran off? Any idea at all?'

Face strained, he raised his eyes to her and sighed despairingly. 'No. I told Jenny's mother the same but she didn't believe me.'

'Oh, Alan,' Val said, putting her arm gently around his shoulders in a motherly gesture. 'I can only tell you that whatever caused Jenny to act this way, she'll tell you when she's ready.'

'But I want to know why now, Mum, so I can put whatever it is right,' he whispered, choked. 'What did Dad say about what happened?'

'Nothing much. We left just after you did. We couldn't eat after what happened.' She did not say Daniel had been very displeased by the incident and had stormed out of the restaurant, leaving Val herself to offer an apology and an explanation. On returning home Daniel had gone straight upstairs, hardly saying a word to her. 'Well, all I can advise you is to leave it a couple of days until Jenny has calmed down, then go and see her again.'

'Yes, maybe you're right.' Then a thought suddenly struck him. 'I wonder if . . .' He stopped abruptly, suddenly realising he was about to voice aloud his concern that somehow Jenny had found out or realised their connection to her employer. But that was impossible. Whatever had caused her to bolt was beyond his reasoning.

'I wonder what, Alan?' his mother was asking him. 'Have you remembered something?'

'Pardon? No . . . er . . . well, something did strike me. But that couldn't be possible.'

'You're not making sense, Alan. What couldn't be possible?'

He stared at her, horrified, and she looked back at him, waiting for his answer. Wringing his hands, he sighed. The time had come to tell his mother about Bill Wadham. Not to would only make matters worse in the long run when it eventually did come out. 'Mother, sit down. I've something to tell you.'

By the tone of her son's voice, whatever he was about to tell her Val knew it was something serious, something that deeply disturbed him. Her whole body filling with fear of what was to come, she sat down in the chair next to his. 'What is it?'

He took a deep breath, and clasped his hands.

A while later, Val rose from her chair and walked across the room, wringing her hands, face still white with the shock of what she had been told. It was several long moments before she turned back to her son. 'Alan, I thought we'd always been honest with each other. Why didn't you tell me you'd met your Uncle Bill before now? Did you not realise what a terrible situation you put us all in tonight?'

'By the time I realised, it was too late. I just wanted you and Dad to meet Jenny and her you, that's all I could think of. After I met Uncle Bill I wasn't sure how to approach you and Dad about it. I didn't know what your reaction would be. You told me he was a thief, that he didn't want anything to do with us. I was in an awful situation and, to be honest, if this hadn't happened tonight I don't think I'd be telling you just now.'

'And Bill doesn't know who you are either?'

He shook his head.

Val sighed loudly. 'And you've never told Jenny your surname in case she asked questions and you had to tell her all about our family skeletons?'

He shook his head again. 'It just hadn't really come up before. When I realised who Jenny worked for, I avoided it.' He shrugged his shoulders helplessly. 'Of course, I was going to once I'd spoken to you and Dad. Only I never spoke to you, did I? I was wrong not to, I know that now. I was confused. I'd only just found out that Uncle Bill existed and to meet him so soon afterwards, in the way that I did, shocked me. He's nothing like I expected. He's okay, Mum. I like him. Jenny always speaks so highly of him and what I'd been told about him didn't make sense. I was all mixed up. I wanted to get to know my uncle, yet at the same time I felt disloyal to you and Dad, but especially to Grandad. After all, he was the person Uncle Bill supposedly tried to steal that money off, yet after meeting him I can't imagine him doing it. Do you understand what I'm saying, Mum?'

She smiled wanly and nodded. 'Yes, I understand. Oh, Alan, what a mess.'

He eyed her, ashamed. 'I know, Mum. I'm so sorry.'

She walked across to him and laid a reassuring hand on his shoulder. 'This is none of your doing. What are the chances of all this happening? Of your meeting Jenny, falling in love, and then finding out the man she works for is your estranged uncle? But it has happened and so we have to deal with it.'

'You don't expect me to stop seeing her then?'

'No, of course I don't. Why should I just because Bill is her boss?'

'What about my uncle?'

Val contemplated his question for several long moments. 'You're old enough to make your own mind up, Alan. I can't stop you and I wouldn't want to. Bill is your own flesh and blood. But, Alan, I don't want you to get hurt. I don't know how Bill will react when he finds out who you are. According to your father, Bill was adamant he wanted nothing whatsoever to do with us and as he's never tried to get in touch that situation probably hasn't changed.' Her face softened tenderly. 'Just be careful, that's all I ask. Don't expect too much. And, Alan, until I speak to your father about this, please don't say anything to him. I have to pick my moment to broach this particular subject.'

'I won't, Mum. I've not made up my mind what to do yet

regarding Uncle Bill. Actually I can't think of anything at the moment except Jenny.'

Val smiled tightly. 'That's understandable. Love does that to you, Alan. You can't think of anything but the other person and how much you want to be with them. I'm sure what caused Jenny to run is something and nothing. She'll come around, just give her time.'

'Do you think so, Mum?' he asked hopefully.

'If she's the girl you've told me she is, and she loves you as much as you obviously do her, yes, she will. I think she suddenly had an attack of nerves at the prospect of meeting me and your father, especially in a place like the Grand. Well, that's enough to overwhelm any young girl, isn't it? I suspect she now feels foolish and can't face you, that's all. Like I said, give her a couple of days to calm down and then go and see her. It'll all be fine, you'll see.'

'I hope you're right, Mum. I can't bear the thought of losing her.'

'Stop thinking like that. Go to bed and get a good night's sleep. It'll all seem better in the morning. As for telling your father . . . I'll have to wait for the right moment to approach him. I'll let you know when I have.' In fact Daniel and she hardly talked since her father had died. The physical side of their marriage she could never have described as passionate, nowhere near it, but now even token pecks on the cheek were almost non-existent. The stress of running the business, she thought, was telling strongly on her husband.

Maybe once Alan came of age in a few weeks' time and the problems associated with running the business were shared between them, Daniel would revert to his old self. She would wait until then, Val decided. Though how her husband would react to their son meeting up with and wanting to get to know the brother who had wanted nothing to do with him or his family for over twenty years, she had no idea.

She returned her son's show of affection, with a kiss on the cheek and watched sadly as he left the kitchen to make his way to bed. As the kitchen door was pulled to, despite her deep concern for her son and the dreadful situation they were in, she sighed, staring blindly into space as a vision of the only man she had ever truly loved rose before her. 'Oh, Bill,' she said aloud.

# Chapter Twenty-Eight

'Well, here goes,' Bill said, picking up the account books. 'Will I need anything else, do you think? I've never been to see a bank manager before but Mr Willaby comes highly recommended. Apparently he's very approachable, not like some of them who make you feel they're doing you a great favour just letting you into their inner sanctum. Well, so Mr Cross, the owner of the wood yard, said when I asked him who he used for his business. I hope he's right. Shan't be long, Jenny. My appointment's for eleven. Wish me luck. Jenny, are you listening to me?'

'Oh,' she mouthed, mentally shaking herself. 'Er . . . yes. Good luck, Mr Wadham.' She forced a smile to her face. 'You'll be fine, I'm sure,' she said with forced brightness.

He paused by the door, eyeing the employee of whom he had grown very fond. 'Jenny, I know I keep asking you, but are you sure nothing's wrong? You're not yourself at all.' 'Not herself' was an understatement, he thought. Jenny was obviously deeply upset about something. It wasn't just her distracted manner that was betraying this. It was her whole appearance.

Jenny's clothes might not be the best quality but she always turned up for work looking neat and clean, even when she was going out on a dirty removal. Not so today. Her clothes were crumpled and obviously pulled on hurriedly. Her cardigan was inside out. But besides that, one look at her pale, pain-filled face would tell anyone she had not slept last night and by her swollen, red-ringed eyes had spent most of it crying. He wondered if this had anything to do with Alan. Jenny had told him she was to meet his parents for the first time on Saturday evening. Had been really excited about it. Maybe something had gone wrong, maybe that was what was upsetting her?

'I'm fine, Mr Wadham, I keep telling you that. I think I've a cold coming.'

She was lying but regardless he said, 'Well, you just take care of yourself. I'll be off then. Don't want to keep the bank manager waiting, do I? That wouldn't look very good, me trying to convince him I'm a good business risk and then expecting him to believe me when I'm late for my appointment.'

When Bill's light-hearted effort to make Jenny smile fell flat he walked out and shut the door behind him.

Moments after he had gone, Owen walked in. 'Oh, boss gone, has he?'

Jenny raised her head from her work. 'Eh? Oh, yes, Mr Ford. About ten minutes ago. He'll be about an hour, I should think.'

'Oh, never mind.' Owen ambled slowly up to her desk. 'I'm at a loose end 'til he comes back. With all that was on 'is mind, he didn't tell me what to do next. N'ote to do in the yard 'cos you and Herchell have cleaned it up. It looks much better, I 'ave to say. Got quite a bit for the scrap, so boss told me.' He sat down in the chair at the front of her desk. 'I could quite easily 'ave gone out on that job with Herchell this morning,' he mused. 'I keep telling boss I'm fit enough now. Me bones 'ave healed nicely, bit of shifting won't hurt me none, but he won't listen. I've got to ease in gradually, so he sez. I 'ope Herchell's copin' all right on his own. I do like him.'

Owen laughed. 'I can hardly understand a word he sez 'cos of that foreign accent of 'is, but he does make me laugh, trying to get to grips with our lingo. He's certainly built for this kinda job. "Brick shit 'ouse" best describes him. I couldn't believe me eyes this morning when I watched him single-handedly shift that old mangle from one side of the yard to the other, as easy as if he wa' pushing a pram. I like him, look forward to working alongside 'im.' He looked at Jenny, head bent over the invoices she was preparing, who didn't appear to have heard a word. 'I said, he's a nice man is Herchell,' Owen repeated, loudly.

Her head jerked. 'Pardon? Oh, yes, Mr Ford, he is,' she said distractedly.

Owen frowned. Bill had described Jenny as a pretty young girl, full of life, always chattering and laughing. This girl was nothing like that. Although he had to admit that despite her obvious distress she was indeed very pretty. He gazed at her for a moment, puzzled. He'd only met her for the very first time a few hours ago when they'd all arrived for work, but regardless there was something about her, something he couldn't fathom, just something that was making him feel he'd known her all her life. He was being stupid, he knew. Put it down to the fact he'd been incarcerated in his sick bed for too long removed from the real world, denied proper conversation apart from the times Bill had visited.

'Fancy a cuppa?' he asked.

'Eh? Oh, I wouldn't mind,' Jenny replied. 'I'll mash it,' she offered, attempting to rise.

'Stay where you are, gel. I'll do it. Boss might feel I ain't fit enough yet ter help with the heavy lifting but I can stretch to lifting a kettle,' said Owen, standing up and making his way to the tea area. 'Milk and sugar?' he called. 'Oi, Jenny, milk and sugar?'

Head bent over her work again, she said, 'Yes, please.'

'And a good dollop of arsenic?'

'Yes, two spoons.'

Walking back to stand in front of her desk, Owen squared his legs, folded his arms and looked at her intently. 'Look, 'tain't none of my business but what's wrong, gel? You look like the Grim Reaper's about to pay you a visit. Surely whatever it is, can't be that bad?'

Jenny raised her head and looked at him. Mr Wadham had done nothing all morning but ask her what the matter was. Herchell too had quizzed her unsuccessfully before he had gone out to do a job. Why couldn't they just leave her alone? She suddenly felt guilty for having these feelings. Mr Wadham, Herchell and now Mr Ford were only showing kindness and consideration towards her. They knew she was upset about something and were only trying to offer their help. She sighed miserably. In truth she didn't really want to be here, didn't want to be at home either. Didn't know where she wanted to be. But what she did want was to be left in peace with her misery and the awful problem of what to do regarding her mother.

The remainder of the weekend had been dreadful. When she had finally emerged from her room, only because she was desperate for the toilet and a drink, at every opportunity May had broached the subject of what had happened until Jenny had shouted at her to stop and then felt terrible afterwards for addressing her mother in such a way. Yet it was the only way to get her to give up going on about it. She knew she should tell May the truth about Alan's dad but realising the pain that would cause her mother, she couldn't bring herself to. But the longer she left it, the worse it would become. If only she could run away and hide and forget everything, pretend it hadn't happened. But it had, and she had to face it, without the strength or the will.

At the forefront of her mind was the miserable knowledge that she must never see Alan again. Her love for him meant she could not face him, knowing what she did, for fear of letting something slip in an unguarded moment. Then the rest would have to come out. Alan would never learn the truth about his father, not from her. If that meant the terrible pain of never seeing him again, then that was what she must suffer.

Jenny took a deep breath and raised her chin. 'Mr Ford, I told Mr Wadham and Herchell, I've just got a cold coming, that's all.'

'Some cold, gel, ter affect you like this. Why don't yer go home then? Yer might feel better termorrer.'

'I'm all right, really.' Her voice was sharp. 'Besides, I have to get these invoices prepared and in the post tonight or we won't get the money in.'

'Forgive me fer askin',' Owen said, insulted.

Jenny sighed. 'I'm sorry, Mr Ford, I didn't mean to speak to you in that tone.'

'It's okay, gel,' he said good-naturedly. 'Yer quite within yer rights to tell me to mind me own business. It's my fault fer being so bloody nosey. You carry on with yer invoices. I'll mash that tea.'

Thoughtfully Jenny watched him as he busied himself. Mr Wadham had been right. Owen Ford really was very nice. She considered that for a man of his age he was quite attractive. As far as she knew, from the snippets she had gleaned from Bill Wadham, Owen wasn't married, never had been, and lived in a shabby room with a misery of a landlady. She found herself feeling sorry for him and wondering why a nice man like him did not have an equally nice woman by his side and a horde of children, just like she had hoped to have with Alan. At that thought a great surge of grief for her own dire situation flooded through her. With a great effort she shoved away all thoughts of anything other than the work she was concentrating on and resumed her task.

Just as the kettle started to boil Bill bounded in, his face wreathed in delight. 'Well, that wasn't anywhere near as bad as I thought it was going to be. Mr Willaby is a very friendly man. He was interested in what I had to say. Seemed quite positive the bank would be able to help me. He's just to put the facts and figures to the board. Says he'll be able to give me a firm decision by the end of the week and all being well I should have the cheque the following week.'

Bill didn't add that now he had gone ahead with his expansion plan he was a worried man. Whether the business prospered or not, bank loans accrued high interest that had to be paid back and it was solely his responsibility to make sure this happened. The consequences of failure could include bankruptcy. That prospect he would not burden his workforce with. 'Jenny,' he said, 'are you listening to me? This is a momentous day for Wadham's.'

'I'm listenin', boss,' Owen piped up. 'Proud of yer, I am, and I know I speak for all of us when I say we're behind yer.'

Bill smiled. 'Thanks, Owen. It's only having all of you on board that's given me the push to go ahead with this. Even Mr Willaby agreed a firm is only as good as its employees.' He turned to face Jenny. 'So what do you think?'

'Pardon? Did you ask me something, Mr Wadham?'

Bill gave a loud groan. 'For goodness' sake, Jenny, are you in the same room as us or what?' He knew her well enough to know that normally this news would have had her jumping up and down in excitement. 'Right, that's it. You're making me feel miserable. You've upset Herchell, and I'm sure Owen's getting the wrong impression of you. Look, my dear, why don't you go home? In fact, I'm telling you. Go home.'

'But it's only one o'clock . . .'

'I know exactly what the time is. Jenny, love, it's not that I don't want you here but this cold you say you're coming down with is obviously telling a lot more on you than you're letting on.' He walked over to the back of the door and unhooked her coat. 'Leave that lot. It'll wait. Get this on and get off. That's an order. And I don't want to see you in the morning unless you're fully recovered.'

Meekly Jenny rose. She knew she couldn't carry on like this.

Her mood was affecting everyone and that wasn't fair. She needed to sit quietly and decide how to break to her mother what she had discovered. All she had to cope with then was her heartache over Alan. She tried to convince herself time would heal that hurt.

Daunted by what faced her, she donned her coat and left.

'Yer did the right thing, boss,' Owen said, placing a mug of tea on Bill's desk. 'Summat serious is up with that girl, believe me. I tried to get 'er to open up ter me, but I got nowhere. Home's the best place for 'er. Now look here, boss, I don't care what you think but I am fit enough to help with the shifting. The doctor obviously thought so too or he wouldn'ta signed me off fit for work. He knew what kinda work I did. I'm wandering round this place bored silly so I'm gonna go and see how Herchell is getting on, and if he needs a hand.'

'Owen . . .' Bill began, then sighed in defeat. 'All right, but just promise me you won't do anything daft and risk setting yourself back?'

'I promise. See yer later.'

Not long after Owen had left there was a tap at the door.

Concentrating on sorting out jobs for the following week, a distracted Bill lifted his head. He stared in surprise to see a middle-aged man standing just inside the door, nervously clutching his cap.

'Can I help you?' he began then stopped, a smile of recognition on his face. 'Why, bless my soul, it's Sid, isn't it? Sid Brown?'

He nodded. 'I didn't think you'd remember me, Mr Wadham.'

'Remember you? How could I forget?' he said, rising and walking round his desk, holding out his hand in greeting. 'You're the man who sent me to pack a crate of fresh air on my first day at Collier's. You had me flummoxed for ages, trying to fathom how to do it.'

345

'That was just a laugh, and believe me mild to what we could 'ave got yer doing, but we men took a shine ter yer and didn't want to put you off,' Sid laughed, accepting Bill's hand and shaking it vigorously.

'I'd have known you anywhere, Sid. You haven't changed a bit in . . . what is it? . . . must be over twenty years. Sit down and rest your legs. Is this a social visit?'

Sid shook his head. 'Well, not exactly, Mr Wadham. Look . . . er . . . can I say first I never thought you'd done it? Never in a million years would you do summat like that. You was a good lad. Probably the best we ever 'ad. All the others agreed, Mr Wadham. We all said it musta bin some outsider that somehow snuck in wi'out being seen and then got scared by summat and that's how it landed in your pocket.'

Bill sighed as he walked back around his desk and sat down. Leaning on his desk, he looked Sid straight in the eye. 'I take it you're talking about the money?'

Sid shifted uncomfortably. 'I am, Mr Wadham, yes. I knew Mr Collier well, bin working for 'im since I left school, and I knew he thought you was innocent. But he couldn't do n'ote about it.'

Bill sighed again. 'It's good to hear this, Sid. I never tried to take that money. But it's no good harping on about the past. My only regret in all this sorry business is that the real culprit wasn't unearthed somehow. Anyway, it's nice to see you. So, to what do I owe the pleasure?'

'Work, Mr Wadham.'

'Work? But . . .'

'Mr Daniel's let three of us go. Me, Wally and Bert. Said he'd not got enough jobs to keep us all busy. Two weeks ago it was.'

'Really? But according to the grapevine Collier's hasn't suffered unduly from Ernest's death. I must admit I've picked up some work myself which might otherwise have gone to

346

them, but even so I wouldn't have thought it would affect the business much.' Bill grimaced. 'Whatever can my brother be thinking of? You three are his best men.'

'He's changed just lately, Mr Wadham. I've never . . .' Sid's voice trailed off, realising that he was talking about Bill's brother when all was said and done, and what he was about to say about Daniel's attitude towards the workers was perhaps better left unsaid. 'Well . . . as a youngster he was an amiable enough fellow though he never actually pulled his weight, always sloping off somewhere or other. Lucky never ter be caught. Not like you, Mr Wadham. You were a totally different kettle of fish. When Mr Daniel married Miss Val . . . well, he . . . let's put it this way . . . He's not bin the easiest boss to get along with, but since Mr Ernest died he's got worse. We hardly see him, in fact. Installed himself in Mr Ernest's old office and never seems to leave it. What he does all day in there is anyone's guess. Mr Skinner and Mrs Cummings do most of the office work. Mind you, I heard he's put them on part-time, so maybe he's doing the rest of the work himself now,' Sid mused. 'But one of the lads reckons every time he passes the window, Mr Daniel is sitting wi' his feet on the desk flicking through car catalogues.

'Mr Alan deals with anything to do with the actual removals. In fact, apart from the money side of things he does practically everything. Nice lad is young Mr Alan. Got his head screwed on. Knows how to get the best out of the men. In lots of ways he's like his grandad. He's right cut up about our sackings, Mr Alan is.'

Bill sighed as Sid talked. He suddenly felt cheated of getting to know his nephew, never having clapped eyes on him in fact. Val and Daniel's son, he thought, should have been his own and Val's if things had been different. He wondered, and not for the first time, what Alan looked like. But as matters stood, he knew he would never know. A sad shame, he thought.

Despite what had happened in the past, Alan and he were family. He suddenly wondered if the lad had ever actually been told of his existence?

Bill realised Sid was asking him a question. 'I'm sorry, what did you say?'

'I asked how you were fixed then?'

'Fixed?'

'For work. I have ter be 'onest, Mr Wadham, I was a bit worried about coming ter see yer. Didn't know how you'd react to me in the circumstances. But I've tried everywhere else, see, and I'm getting desperate.'

Bill smiled at him. 'Well, Sid, as a matter of fact I think I might be able to help you, and there's a good possibility I could do something for Wally and Bert too. Actually you three could be the answer to my prayers. Let's talk.'

A few streets away Daniel trotted down three worn stone steps, rubbing his hands gleefully. Well, that had gone far better than he had dared hope. It was a stab in the dark using this bank, but it couldn't be the bank Collier's usually used for obvious reasons and a better choice he couldn't have made. Mr Willaby seemed a thoroughly decent type to be a bank manager and from what he had led Daniel to believe, the money was practically his. Willaby had been very impressed by Alan's costing and meticulous plans for Collier's expansion.

Not that Daniel had told the man his son had done all the work, just let him believe Daniel himself was responsible and taken the praise. All that remained was for Mr Willaby to pay a visit to the yard and check matters for himself. Just a formality, he had told Daniel, then he would put his recommendations to the board. He had no doubt they would agree the loan. Collier's was a firm of long standing locally with an excellent reputation. Even though the loan was a substantial one, it would be considered a low risk by the bank.

As he strode off down the street, hands in his trouser pockets, macintosh billowing behind him, trilby hat set at a jaunty angle on his head, a smile of utter delight spread across Daniel's face. In not much over a couple of weeks, he would have enough money in his pocket to get right away from Leicester, away from a life he had grown mortally tired of, to begin afresh elsewhere, run things and do things exactly the way he wanted. And he was going to be able to afford it all thanks to his clever son.

As his father was congratulating himself outside the bank, a miserable and utterly confused Alan was trying with all his might to concentrate on the job in hand, to no avail. That morning his mind was elsewhere. He had given wrong instructions to the men resulting in two different-sized vans and crews turning up at each other's addresses, and to make matters worse at the wrong time, to be received by outraged customers. Plus on a removal he was present at Alan had dropped a valuable walnut occasional table and broken three of the ornate spindles decorating the carved lip edging the top. To restore it was going to cost dearly and he was dreading telling his father.

No matter how much he went over and over that evening he still couldn't fathom what could possibly have happened to cause Jenny to react like that. Finally he could stand it no longer. He had to see her and clear up whatever misunderstanding it was that had caused her bewildering behaviour. He obviously wasn't going to be able to see her at home, not with her mother standing guard, so his only option was to catch her at work. Wadham's yard was the last place he wanted to go, but he had no choice. Without another thought for what he was actually doing or the resulting repercussions, he slammed shut the van doors and called across to the two men he was working with, chattering and bantering as they emerged from the house expecting to collect the next load. 'Explain to Mr and Mrs

Dawson I've got to pop out somewhere. I don't know how long I'll be. We'll finish their move when I get back. In the meantime get yourselves a cuppa or something.'

The men looked on astonished as, without giving them chance to respond, Alan ran around the side of the van, jumped into the driver's seat and drove off.

A while later, leaning against the side wall of Wadham's yard, Alan pulled back the cuff of his shirt sleeve and looked at his watch. It was coming up to four-thirty. He had been pacing up and down the cobbled lane for over an hour and not one glimpse had he caught of Jenny. Dispirited he looked up at the sky. Black clouds were rolling in. Just then it started to rain, getting heavier by the second. Typical March weather, he thought. Rain, wind, more rain and wind. The whole of March had been like this, not the best kind of weather to be carrying out removals. Customers complained when their precious furniture got wet, blaming the removal company as though they were responsible for conditions. Still, at this moment the weather was the last thing on his mind.

Stepping sideways, he peered through the narrow gap between the end of the wall and the warped frame holding in place the wooden doors that secured the yard. There was no sign of Jenny at all. He resumed his previous position. She would have to come out eventually even if he waited until it was time for her to go home. One thing he did know and that was he didn't care how wet he became or how cold, he wasn't budging from this place until he did see her.

Just then muffled voices reached his ears and he strained to hear, hoping one of them was Jenny's.

Inside the yard, Sid was shaking Bill's hand vigorously. 'Well, thanks a lot then, Mr Wadham. I'll see yer Monday and I'll send Wally and Bert to see yer.'

'Yes, 'bye, Sid. Monday. Sharp at seven-thirty, mind.'

'I'll be there, clean shirt, boots black, Mr Wadham.'

Alan froze in horror as the implications of being discovered at this location by Sid Brown hit him full force. He looked around, desperate for somewhere to hide himself, but before he could move an inch Sid, his face creased happily, strode jauntily through the entrance doors and almost collided with him. Sid stopped abruptly and eyed him, astonished. 'Why, 'ello, Mr Alan.' His voice was loud and Alan cringed. 'Fancy seeing you here,' Sid continued. 'But then, why shouldn't you be here? After all Mr Wadham is yer . . .'

'Nice to see you, Sid,' he cut in hurriedly.

'Oh, yeah, nice ter see you too.' His eyes lit up excitedly. 'I've gorra job with Mr Wadham. That's good news, ain't it? Me wife won't 'alf be chuffed, I can tell yer. And that's not all. Mr Wadham's gonna see what he can do fer Wally and Bert, too. Asked me to send them to see him. Well, must dash. Nice ter see yer again.'

'Yes, and you. Goodbye, Sid.'

'Alan?'

His head jerked around and he saw Bill Wadham staring at him, the expression on his face a mixture of surprise and embarrassment.

'Hello,' said Bill. 'Sorry, I was being nosey, wondering who Sid was talking to.' He raked his hand through his hair. 'I take it you've come to see Jenny? She was . . . er . . . not feeling herself, so I sent her home.' Alan's appearance immediately struck Bill. He looked drawn and ashen, as though he hadn't slept for a week. His disappointment at not finding Jenny here was apparent. But there was something else bothering Alan. Something Bill couldn't put his finger on. He could only ascribe the young man's manner to Bill's being the last person he wanted to see. But he must be wrong there, he thought. He hardly knew Alan personally and had done nothing to upset him. Bill decided the lad's behaviour must be to do with what was going on between Jenny and himself.

Suddenly all Bill's thwarted fatherly instincts surfaced, and worry for Jenny and now this young man filled his being. How he wished he could help the young couple overcome whatever had caused the obvious estrangement between them. He decided to see if he could get Alan to talk. He suspected that whatever lay behind this was something and nothing that had been blown out of proportion. Maybe it just needed a little hand from someone like himself to help sort it out. First, though, he had to get Alan inside. 'Look, come in and have a cuppa until this rain goes off. You're shivering, lad,' he said.

That was the last thing Alan wanted to do. Anxiously, mind racing for a plausible excuse, he raked his hand through his hair. 'Oh, er . . . I . . . don't want to intrude on your time, Mr Wadham. If you would just tell Jenny I called? Please say I would like to see her.'

Bill pressed his lips together. Apart from dragging Alan bodily into his office and forcing him to talk there wasn't much else he could do. But at least he had tried. 'As you wish, Alan. I'll give Jenny your message. See you soon then, I hope.' Bill made to run back inside out of the rain when a thought suddenly struck him and he stopped and called after Alan who was hurrying towards his van, parked further down the lane. 'Just a minute.'

Blinking rain out of his eyes, Alan stopped and turned. 'Yes, Mr Wadham?'

Bill came up to him. 'I'm just interested to hear how you know Sid Brown? And, more to the point, why he addressed you as Mr Alan. It strikes me as odd.'

Alan froze and stared at Bill for several long seconds. Then his whole body sagged and he exhaled loudly. He was in a dilemma which, being the upright person he was, had only one outcome. The time had come for his second confession.

A long time later Bill rose from his chair and walked towards the window. He stood there for several minutes, staring blindly out before he turned back to face Alan and smiled wanly at him. 'Well . . . what a turn of events, isn't it? The very last thing I expected you to tell me.'

Alan nodded. 'I'm sorry Uncle Bill, I hope you don't mind my calling you that, but you are, aren't you? I didn't mean to lie to you when we first met. Well, I didn't lie exactly, just never came clean on who I was. But I was so shocked at the time. You were the very last person I expected to meet. When Jenny introduced us, I didn't know what to do. So I played it safe.'

'Yes, I expect you were shocked, coming face to face with me out of the blue like that. Just as I am now. Shocked . . . no, I'm reeling.' Bill took a deep breath. 'I expect when you were first told of me you pictured . . .' He put his hands in his trouser pockets, rocking backwards and forwards on his heels. 'Well, what do thieves look like, Alan? Unshaven, eye patch, striped jumper, carrying a swag bag over their shoulder? Shifty-looking? I hope I'm not a bit like that.' He eyed the young man intently. 'As I told you earlier, whoever tried to take that money it wasn't me. It's important to me that you believe that.'

'I believe you, Uncle Bill. Jenny thinks the world of you and her opinion is good enough for me.'

Bill smiled, greatly relieved. 'Thank you,' he said gratefully. He took his hands out of his trouser pockets and walked back to his chair. He gazed at his nephew fondly. 'I've often wondered about you. What you were like as a person, who you took after.' He grinned. 'You look like me, don't you? Actually, it's quite unnerving, as if I'm looking in a mirror and seeing myself as a young man. Jenny remarked on the likeness the night we first met and I took no notice, too excited about the job I'd just landed to give anyone else much attention.' He gave a sad sigh. 'I feel cheated, not being allowed to know you, not seeing you grow. Your being here is like a miracle. Something I never dreamed would happen.'

'Really, Uncle Bill?'

He nodded. 'I suppose in a way I can understand your mother not wanting to have anything to do with me. It wasn't just the fact I was branded a thief. More, I suspect, to do with the fact that we were engaged to be married and her guilt that she loved someone else – and that someone else my brother, which I presume only made her guilt worse. She couldn't face me. I don't blame her for that, Alan.'

The young man was gawping at him. Something Bill was saying wasn't ringing true. He could have sworn his mother had told him that it was his uncle himself who had wanted nothing to do with them. But, regardless, something else Bill had said overrode that fact and blasted it from his mind. 'Engaged? You and my mother?'

Bill nodded, then eyed him worriedly. 'You didn't know that, Alan?'

He shook his head.

'Then I'm sorry I blurted it out. I thought you knew. Val and I were engaged before she married my brother. I loved her very much, Alan, but it appears she didn't return my feelings. I was obviously blind to what was going on behind my back. Anyway, it hurt me dreadfully that she wouldn't even let me tell her my side of things after the attempted robbery, but after a while, when I had come to terms with things enough to reason them out, I learned to understand why she acted as she did. I've never held a grudge against her, Alan. After all, we can't help our feelings, can we?

'I wish I could say the same about your father. I don't hold a grudge against him for falling in love with Val, but what I can't understand is why in God's name he cut me and our mother off without a by your leave. That I'll never come to terms with. We were his family, Alan. Daniel must know I would never have tried to steal that money, yet he seemed readily to accept that I did and told my mother – his mother – in no uncertain terms that he never wanted to see either me or her again. I can understand him wanting himself and Val to be left in peace to get on with their lives, but surely he could have kept in touch with his mother? And especially when you came along.

'Your grandmother would have given her eye teeth to have held you in her arms. You would have liked her, Alan. She was a lovely lady. Still, there's no point in going over old ground, raking up hurt, asking questions that won't be answered. What's done is done.' He looked Alan straight in the eye. 'We can't pretend we've not met or forget this has happened. What are we going to do about it, Alan? What do *you* want to do? I'll respect your wishes whatever you decide. I'm a reasonable man.'

Alan could see that. He sighed. 'When I told my mother about meeting you, she said I was old enough to make my own decisions and she wouldn't try to stop me. She just asked me to be careful what I said in front of my father until she had talked to him. But I want you to know, Uncle Bill, I'm so glad we've met.'

Bill smiled warmly. 'So am I,' he said with conviction. 'I'd like to get to know you, Alan. Like the chance to be a proper uncle to you. Your mother seems all right about it, but I wouldn't like this to cause any trouble between you and your father.'

'I hope it won't. I'm not sure how he'll react when my mother tells him. He's very distracted by work. He's . . . he's not himself at the moment.'

'Oh,' Bill cut in worriedly. 'He is all right, though?'

'Oh, yes, in good health, if that's what you mean. I expect he's just worried about the business, that's all. All that responsibility must have been a lot for him to take on when Grandad died. I can't wait until I come of age and it legally becomes mine, then I can take some of the burden off him.'

'Ernest left the business to you, Alan?'

He nodded. 'Grandad always told me the business would be mine but I took it with a pinch of salt, expecting him to outlive both of us. I was so shocked when the will was read out. My mother explained to me that what Grandad did was nothing against my father. He did it because he thought by the time he died I would be much older and my dad ready to take things easy. Grandad knew me well and realised I'd look after my parents financially.'

Bill smiled. 'Your grandad was a shrewd man, Alan. He obviously trusted you very much. I know his business meant everything to him and he'd want to know it was in good hands when he was ready to pass it on.'

'Well, I'm worried about it at the moment. Dad says we're in trouble. I think he's got it into his head we'll go bankrupt and that's why he sacked the men. I've tried to tell him not to worry, that all firms suffer lean periods, but he won't listen to me. I've given him suggestions for expansion. Done a plan and costed it out. I know it's the way forward, something we must do. He's mulling it over, but I don't think he's too keen because it means we'd have to borrow quite a lot of money.' Alan stopped abruptly, frowning and bothered. Bill noticed and realised instinctively what was troubling him.

'Don't worry, Alan, you haven't been disloyal in telling me about your firm's situation. If it makes you feel better, I'll let you into my secret. I'm expanding, too. Nothing on the scale you're proposing. Just a couple of second-hand vans and three more men, but it's expansion all the same. I can appreciate why Daniel is reluctant to. Bank loans have to be paid back whatever happens and that's a big worry. I have the same worries too. Anyway, it's good to hear of any firm making plans to expand especially one that's run by my own family. Despite what's happened between us we *are* family and I want to hear you're doing well. Collier's is an excellent firm with a good reputation. I'm all for competition, wherever it comes from.'

'My sentiments exactly, Uncle Bill. As well as looking alike, we think alike too. I only hope my father sees things in the same way.' Alan eyed Bill excitedly. 'It would be great if somehow we could all get back together, wouldn't it? Then we'd all become a proper family again.'

'One step at a time, Alan,' Bill gently warned. 'I'd be grateful myself for the opportunity to be on speaking terms with Daniel again. Anything else would be a bonus as far as I am concerned.'

'Yes, you're right, Uncle Bill. One step at a time. My mother will do her best to convince my father to make amends to you, I know she will. I've been so lucky to have her as my mother. She's a lovely woman.'

Bill lowered his head and studied his hands. 'Yes,' he said quietly. 'I know she is.' He raised his head and looked directly at Alan. 'How is she?'

He still loves her, Alan thought. And the knowledge came as a shock to him. 'She's fine.'

There were so many questions Bill was desperate to ask about Val but if he did, he realised, Alan would soon work out that his questions had more behind them than just general enquiries. 'Good,' he said hurriedly, feeling it best to change the subject. 'Now this business with Jenny. I can't understand it myself but women are strange creatures. Get upset about things we men don't understand, and I don't suppose we ever will. I can only tell you she was very excited about meeting your parents. She talked about you often, but since you asked her to meet your parents it was all she talked about. She was worried she had nothing suitable to wear and had got it into her head she would somehow show you up. To be honest, she went on so much about it that Herchell told her to shut up. If he hadn't, I would have. Now, all I can tell you is that she's deeply upset about something. What I've no idea. I can only think myself she must have had an attack of nerves and before she could reason with herself she bolted. Now she's too embarrassed to face you. That's all. Give her a couple of days to calm down.'

'That's what my mother suggested.'

'Well, both of us can't be wrong, can we?'

'I hope not. Jenny means so much to me, I can't concentrate on anything but making it up with her.'

Bill eyed him for several long moments. 'You'll have to tell her about the connection between me and you. If you don't tell her soon, she's bound to guess. Jenny is very bright.'

Alan nodded. 'I know she is. I'll tell her as soon as we get things straight between us.'

'Good. Well, son, why don't you take yourself off home, get some hot food inside you and have a good night's sleep? When I see Jenny tomorrow, I'll tell her you called and to contact you. She will, I'm sure.'

'I hope you're right, Uncle Bill.'

# Chapter Twenty-Nine

In the back room of the little house in Slater Street, curled up in the armchair, a miserable Jenny stared up at the clock on the mantel. It was coming up to five. In an hour or so her mother would be home. For the last few hours she had wrestled with her conscience, trying to come up with the right words to use to break the terrible news she had to impart. But nothing had come to her. No words she could think of were going to soften the blow May was about to receive and Jenny knew without a doubt that her mother was going to be devastated.

She sniffed back fresh tears and wiped her wet eyes with an already sodden handkerchief, then shivered with cold. With neither the strength nor the inclination to light the fire, the room was decidedly chilly. She stared into the empty grate. It mirrored her life, she thought. Cold, grey and empty. Alan had brought so much into her life. With him she had found completeness. A man she trusted, felt comfortable and secure with. Most importantly she had experienced true love. The kind that comes from deep within because you know someone, care for them, worry for their well-being, only feel whole when you are with them. She had felt all that with Alan and knew without a doubt that his feelings for her mirrored her own.

A vision of him rose before her. He would be utterly bewildered now and terribly hurt by her actions. The thought of his suffering pained her greatly. But she had no choice. Alan would get over her in time, her memory fading into the past as someone else he'd grown to love replaced it, but the pain of finding out his father's true character would never fade, wounds caused by such deceit never heal. However hurtful to him Jenny's actions were, surely they must be kinder on him than having to live with that knowledge for the rest of his life?

A loud hammering on the door made her jump. Normally she and her mother were at work at this time so no one who knew them could possibly be calling, and that included Alan himself who would still be at work. She couldn't face any strangers, she decided. She would ignore it. The hammering came again, this time more of a determined thump on the door. Whoever it was was hell-bent on getting an answer.

'All right, all right,' she called, worried that if this carried on the next blow threatened to knock the door right off its hinges. Giving her face a wipe, she reluctantly rose to answer it.

She opened the door to find three men standing on the cobbles: an official-looking type dressed in a shabby brown suit, a worn trilby hat covering his mop of greasy greying hair, and two other men hovering behind him dressed in long brown overalls over their worn clothes, the same brown coats removal men wore. It was then she noticed the huge van parked in the road. It was a furniture van, there was no mistaking it.

Her eyes flashed back to the official-looking man. 'Yes?' she asked, frowning.

'Mrs Jeffries?' he demanded.

'I'm Miss Jeffries. Mrs Jeffries is my mother. She's at work. Why . . .'

'That's by the by,' he said. With the flat of his hand he pushed Jenny back inside the passage and stepped inside the house. 'Come on, men,' he said, beckoning the other two forward. 'You know what to do.'

'What is this?' Jenny cried, bewildered. 'What's going on? What are you doing here?'

'It's obvious, isn't it?' he said mockingly. 'Collecting the furniture. No payments, no furniture. Fair, wouldn't you say?'

'No payments . . . Look, mister, there must be some misunderstanding. My mother's paid, I know she has.'

'She hasn't. Not for four weeks. She's been sent a written warning. She's had her chance to pay up and has chosen to ignore it. Just tell her she still owes the back payments and someone will be along next week to collect the money. Now, if I were you, I'd stand aside.'

All her problems suddenly flew away as Jenny's temper rose. 'I won't! I won't let you do this. At least wait until my mother comes home. Give her the chance to clear up this misunderstanding.'

The man's face darkened. 'I've told yer, there's no misunderstanding, miss. Now, if yer don't want to get hurt, I'd stand out of the way.'

The man's tone frightened Jenny witless. He meant business, there was no doubt about that. Flattening herself against the wall, she watched helplessly as the men proceeded to empty the house of her mother's new furniture.

It took the two burly workmen, with the official supervising, no time at all. Before she knew it the house was empty, the van and the men gone.

Rigid with shock, Jenny stood for an age in the cold empty house. All she could think of was what effect this would have on her mother when she came home. Suddenly she became conscious that any time now May would walk through the door. This coming on top of everything else Jenny couldn't face, couldn't cope with. It was all too much. As tears of distress poured down her face, she grabbed her coat from the back of the door and fled.

On and on she ran until she stopped abruptly at the end of a lane. It was pitch dark. Through her tear-filled eyes she hurriedly looked around her, trying to get her bearings. It was with shock she realised where she was. Outside Wadham's yard. She looked through the gates and across the cobbles. A light was shining from under the ill-fitting office door. Mr Wadham was obviously still working. She felt a great desire to run into the warmth and unburden herself of all her troubles to the man she was fond of and deeply respected. But in her low state she couldn't face even him. She was just about to turn and hurry away when the office door opened and Bill appeared.

'Who's there?' he called sternly. 'I know someone is so show yourself before I call the police.'

Jenny gulped, hardly daring to breathe.

Bill called again, 'I know someone's there. I'll give you one last chance to show yourself.'

She had no choice but to speak up. 'It's . . . it's only me, Mr Wadham,' she called with forced lightness.

Frowning he walked out of the office, peering hard into the gloom. 'Jenny? Is that you?'

Hurriedly wiping her face, she cleared her throat. 'Yes,' she called. 'I er . . . was just taking a walk, I'm sorry if I startled you.'

'Walk?' Bill queried, heading across the yard towards her. 'It was running I heard. What were you running from, Jenny?' Next thing she knew he was before her. 'Why, you're crying!' he exclaimed, and stared at her worriedly. He had sent Jenny home this afternoon deeply upset; now she looked completely and utterly devastated. Deep concern for her rose within him. Something else had happened to her between his sending her home and now. Instinctively he knew it was something dreadful that she was trying to cover up. He took her arm. 'Come inside and talk to me, Jenny,' he coaxed. 'It's all right, everyone else has gone home. I'll make you a cuppa.'

'No, really, Mr Wadham, I should be off. It's just this dratted cold. A good night's sleep will do me the world of good.'

Bill wasn't going to be fobbed off so easily. 'I wasn't born yesterday, Jenny. You've no more got a cold than I have. Now what has upset you badly enough to send you hurtling down this lane?'

'Nothing,' she said innocently. 'I'm fine, Mr Wadham. Why don't you believe me?'

'I don't believe you, Jenny, because you're not telling me the truth. I'm concerned for you, my dear. I'm not just your employer, I hope I'm your friend too.'

Nerves stretched to breaking point, Jenny looked up at him, saw genuine concern for her beaming from his eyes. She broke down then, not able to contain herself any longer. The tears came, gushing down her cheeks like a tap full on. 'Oh, Mr Wadham,' she wailed. 'It's not my mam's fault . . .'

'What, Jenny love?' he coaxed. 'What's not your mother's fault?'

She froze, realising with horror she had just been about to divulge the shocking story of her mother's innocent affair with Alan's father. She couldn't tell anyone about that. It was just too awful. They would brand her mother an adulteress, think her a terrible woman. Jenny couldn't bear that.

'Jenny?' he urged. 'What wasn't your mother's fault?'

'Eh? Oh . . . the . . . the furniture, Mr Wadham.'

'Furniture? What furniture?'

'Ours. They took it all, Mr Wadham. Every last stick. It's not my mother's fault, I know it's not. They said she hadn't paid but I know it's a mistake 'cos she promised me she had. I think me mam's in a hell of a mess, Mr Wadham, and I don't know how I'm going ter find the money to get her out of it.' Jenny gave a violent shudder. 'And she's going to be ever so upset when she finds the house empty. She'll not know what's happened. She'll think we've been robbed. She was so proud of that furniture. Oh, Mr Wadham, what am I going to do?'

Her distress was pitiful. Gently he pulled her into his arms and smoothed his hand over the top of her head. 'Now, now, stop worrying, Jenny. I'll tell you what we're going to do. We're going to get the van and go around to the warehouse and load it with furniture, and then we're going to take it round to your house. It might not be the best stuff but it'll do your mother for now.'

She gave a loud sniff and eyed him, shocked. 'I can't expect yer to do that, Mr Wadham.'

'You didn't expect me to. I'm offering.'

'But . . . but we can't pay you.'

'I never asked for any payment, did I? Actually you'd be doing me a favour.'

She sniffed again, wiping her tear-streaked face on the sleeve of her coat. 'I can't see how.'

'No, neither can I at the moment. But I'll think of something. Now, while we're at it, are you going to tell me what's happened between you and Alan? Something has, hasn't it? That's why you were so upset today. Had a lovers' tiff, have you?'

She gulped, casting her eyes down for several long moments before raising her head to look him in the eye. 'I made a mistake, Mr Wadham,' she said, with such conviction she almost believed it herself. 'Alan's not for me.'

He looked at her sadly. 'Are you sure, Jenny? If he's not for you, why is this affecting you so badly?'

'Because . . . because I don't like the thought of hurting him, that's all. Now I appreciate your trying to help, Mr Wadham, but I don't really want to talk about this any more.'

Bill knew she was lying but it was obvious by her tone she wasn't going to divulge the real reason for such final actions. 'It's a shame. I thought you made a lovely couple. Still, maybe, given time . . .'

'Nothing will change, Mr Wadham,' she cut in. 'Alan and I are finished and that's that.'

'If you say so, Jenny. But I don't think he will give up so easily.'

She stared at him thoughtfully. 'I suspect you're right. He won't get past me mother at our house, that's for sure. But if he should come round to the yard, would yer please tell him I don't want to see him?'

He looked at her, astonished, then shook his head. 'No.'

'No?'

Bill shook his head again. 'I'm sorry, Jenny, but that is something you'll have to do yourself.'

She nodded. 'Yes, you're right. It's not fair to ask yer, I'm sorry.'

He smiled kindly at her. 'That's all right, Jenny, I haven't taken offence. I must tell you, though, Alan was here this afternoon and asked me to ask you to contact him. Well, begged, Jenny. If I were you I would think very carefully before you do something so final. He's very upset.'

So am I, she thought. And the thought of seeing Alan face to face she did not relish. 'I'll send him a letter,' she said, then realised that despite the length of time they had been courting she didn't know his actual address. 'Oh, but I don't know where he lives.'

'I can help you with that,' Bill said without thinking.

'Oh?' She frowned. 'How do you know Alan's address, Mr Wadham?'

His mind leaped into action. 'He . . . er . . . left it. Yes, that's what he did. For you to contact him. He wrote it down. I put it somewhere. If I can't find the piece of paper I can remember it, so don't worry. Now let's go and get the van loaded and sort out some nice bits for your mother.'

'That was so good of Mr Wadham, Jenny, wasn't it?' May said after Bill had left. 'He's such a nice man.' Her eyes flashed. 'Doesn't look so grand now, but this stuff's better than n'ote, I

365

suppose.' She patted the arm of a chair. 'Same style I got rid of – it's like having me old bits back again.' She sighed. 'Oh, well, it were nice while it lasted. At least I know what it feels like ter be posh. Some don't get the chance, do they? I didn't know what ter think when I got home and found the place empty save for our own bits and pieces. I thought we'd bin robbed. Mind you,' she said scornfully, 'it did look like the place had been robbed, the way all our private stuff was tipped around. What a mess! They'd yanked all me clothes out the wardrobe and chucked 'em on the floor. I've a good mind to complain.'

'You can hardly do that in the circumstances, Mam.'

May sniffed haughtily. 'I expect yer right. I bet the neighbours had a good laugh. What's the betting any minute Gloria'll be around for a nosey?'

'The neighbours are the least of our worries, Mam.' Perched in the shabby moquette armchair opposite, Jenny folded her arms and eyed her mother knowingly. 'Mam, why didn't you call the police when you got home and thought we'd had burglars?'

'Eh? Well . . . I . . . I . . . was just about ter when the van pulled up with you and Mr Wadham in it.'

Jenny tilted her head, mouth set grimly. 'You knew what had happened, didn't you, Mam? You knew the men were coming to collect the furniture?'

May eyed her sheepishly. 'Yes, I did. I'm just sorry it happened when you were here, that's all. For that matter, why were you here when you should have bin at work?'

'I wasn't feeling well so Mr Wadham sent me home. But that's not important just now, Mam. I want to know why you hadn't made the payments like you told me you had.'

May's eyes flashed as her temper rose. 'Who are you ter be questioning me? Why d'yer bleddy think I hadn't made the payments? 'Cos I hadn't got the bloody money, that's why.'

366

'Oh, Mam,' Jenny sighed despairingly. 'You said we could afford to keep them up.'

'And so we could.'

'Well, if we could why didn't yer? You spent the money, didn't you, Mam?'

'No, I didn't,' May snapped. 'Look, this is none of your business . . .'

'It is,' Jenny erupted. 'When I get threatened by three huge men it is.' She exhaled loudly, her face softening. 'Mam, of course it's my business, I'm your daughter. You should have told me you were getting into trouble. I could have tried to help.'

'How? You give me half yer wage as it is. Anyway, I didn't think they'd do what they threatened so soon. I thought I could catch up. Only I ain't 'ad so much overtime these last few weeks and I just got further and further behind.' She rubbed her hand backwards and forwards over her forehead. 'I never thought she'd be so bleddy nasty. Sweet little old lady, my arse!'

Jenny grimaced questioningly. 'What on earth are you going on about?'

'Eh? Oh, never mind me, me duck, I was just rambling.'

'Cooee, May, you in?'

'Oh, thank God,' she cried, relieved. 'It's Gloria. Come in, me duck,' she called.

'Oh, no Mam. You ain't fobbing me off that easy.' Jenny shot up from her chair and ran to the kitchen just as Gloria waddled through the back door.

She beamed on spotting Jenny. ''Ello, lovey. What a carryin' on ternight, eh? Better than a bleddy pantomime. Our Cyril sez it's all they're talking of down the pub.'

Jenny's face reddened angrily. 'Oh, and just what are folk gossiping about down the pub, Mrs Budgins?'

'Why, May's new furniture being seized by the bailiffs, as if you didn't know,' Gloria guffawed. She slapped Jenny on her arm. 'Oh, you are a card! Getting nearly as bad as yer mam, Jenny. Anyway, then you 'ad another lot delivered. By your boss, if I ain't mistaken. I've gotta say, though, it don't look anywhere near as good as the last lot. Still, if yer can't pay, yer can't be choosy, can yer?' Her eyes sparkled with an 'I told you so' gleam. 'I 'ope May's learned 'er lesson. It doesn't pay to get above yerself. I knew she wouldn't be able to afford the payments. I knew she'd come a cropper. I was right, wasn't I?'

'No, yer not, Mrs Budgins.'

Gloria gawped. 'I ain't?'

'For your information – and you can tell the rest of the street as well – my mother didn't like the new furniture so she sent it back,' Jenny lied. 'Those men you saw weren't bailiffs, they were removal men. The stuff you saw Mr Wadham delivering was paid for in cash me mam had saved. And she'll tell you the same when next you see her. Now, if you'll excuse me, Mrs Budgins, it's not convenient for you to visit tonight.'

'Eh?'

'I said, we're busy.'

Gloria gawped at Jenny indignantly. 'A'you telling me ter sling me hook, is that it?'

'If you want to put it like that, yes,' she said. 'But please don't take offence, Mrs Budgins. Me and me mam are just having a personal discussion. Private like.'

'Oh,' Gloria mouthed knowingly. 'Private, I see. When's it due then?'

'Pardon?'

'The baby?'

Jenny sighed in exasperation. 'Mrs Budgins, please shut the door on your way out.'

'Shut the . . . Well!' she snorted. 'Like that, is it? And me yer mother's bestest friend. Well, yer needn't think I'm gonna be doing any knittin' for the poor little tyke if that's yer attitude,

Jennifer Jeffries. Yer can tell May that I'll see 'er termorrer. That's if I'm still good enough, like.'

With that she stormed out of the door, slamming it behind her.

'I could 'ave done me own lying, thanks, Jenny,' May snapped when she returned. 'And yer shouldn't 'ave sent Gloria away, she'll 'ave the right arse with me now she will.'

'That's nothing unusual, Mam. She'll get over it. You two will be as thick as thieves by tomorrow night. Now, I want to know who this nasty lady is?'

May eyed her innocently. 'What nasty lady?'

'Mother, stop it. You're covering something up and I won't stop until you tell me the truth. I'm getting really worried something awful is going on. Please, Mam, tell me?'

May opened her mouth, then snapped it shut. She gave a loud sigh. 'I suppose I'd better tell yer. I . . . I 'ad to tek a loan from Mrs Chivers.'

Jenny eyed her blankly. 'Loan? Whatever for, Mam?' Then she exclaimed, 'Oh, Mam, you didn't borrow money from Snakey Lil? Even the kids know she charges extortionate interest. Borrow a penny from her and she wants a shilling back. And why in God's name did yer need to borrow anyway?'

'To pay for yer Aunt Iris's funeral, that's why,' May blurted. 'Now a'yer satisfied?'

'Oh, Mam. But you told me . . .'

'I know what I told yer, but I lied. Iris's funeral cost me a bloody fortune. But I had to bury her decent, Jenny, she was me sister when all's said and done. The only way I could get the money was to borrow it from Snakey Lil. Oh, she jumped at it she did. I was too upset at the time to think straight. It didn't really register with me until after the funeral just what I'd have ter pay back each week but it was too late then. If I hadn't 'ave 'ad the payments on the furniture I could just about 'ave managed but I couldn't manage both. So now yer know. I don't regret what I done, Jenny. Furniture is furniture. Me sister was me sister.'

'I don't blame you, Mam,' she said softly. 'And that three quid yer gave me for my outfit?' she asked, already knowing the answer.

'A pound each for Lil and the furniture shop to keep 'em sweet 'til I could catch up with the back payments, and a pound off the rent arrears.' May looked Jenny straight in the eye. 'But you needed a new outfit. You deserved to look nice and that three quid made sure yer did. Anyway, what can they do ter me, eh? If I ain't got it, they can't 'ave it, can they?'

'No, but the owner of the furniture shop can get you slung in jail and Snakey Lil will send her sons around to force it out of yer, one way or another. That ain't going to happen, Mam, not while I'm living and breathing.'

'Oh, and you can magic up money, can yer? In that case I'll have twenty quid.'

'Stop being sarky, Mam. We're in a right pickle and this ain't the time for jokes.'

'Me not we,' May erupted, poking herself in her chest with her finger. 'This is my fault, Jenny, not yours. I'll sort it out.'

'How?'

She shrugged her shoulders. 'A bit each week is better than n'ote.'

'Mam, neither Lil nor the owner of the furniture shop is going to settle for that and neither will the landlord eventually. If we carry on like this we'll end up on the streets with nothing but still up to our eyes in hock. And you surely can't think I'd pretend I know nothing about this and leave you with all the worry?' Jenny's eyes softened tenderly. 'Oh, Mam, what you did was a lovely thing, for Aunt Iris and for me.'

May sniffed. 'Stupid, more like.'

'Don't, Mam. What you did wasn't stupid. You did it 'cos you loved us. I'm just sorry it's got you into so much bother.

370

Right, let's make plans. How much do you owe altogether, Mam? I know you owe the furniture shop four weeks.' She quickly did a calculation in her head. 'At thirty bob a week, that's six pounds. How much do you owe Snakey Lil?'

May grabbed her packet of cigarettes, pulled one out and lit it, drawing deeply. 'I ain't in the mood fer this. I've told yer before, Jenny, and I'll tell yer again, this is my business and I'll sort it.'

'And I'm telling you, you can't, Mam,' Jenny cried angrily. 'You're just getting in deeper and deeper. You'll pay one week then something'll happen and you'll forget a week and end up worse off than you are now. It might not bother you to open the door and face threatening men demanding money but it terrifies the life out of me. I can't live like that and I ain't going to, so stop treating me like a kid, Mam. Let me help with this and see if we can work something out to get us straight. Now, how much?'

May blew out her cheeks then sighed in resignation. 'All right. I borrowed fifteen quid.'

Jenny gawped. 'Fifteen . . . Oh, Mam. And?'

'And what?'

'How much does she want back?'

May mumbled something inaudible under her breath.

'Speak up, Mam!' Jenny snapped. 'I can't try and get us out of this mess if you don't come clean with me. Now how much does she want back altogether?'

'Thirty quid.'

'What! That's daylight robbery. That's one hundred percent interest. She wants stringing up, does Snakey Lil. Oh, dear God,' Jenny groaned. 'That's thirty-six pounds we owe. We'll be paying this off when we're pensioners. And you still haven't told me how much we're behind with the rent yet. Well, for a start I can get a part-time job. Sandra Budgins told me a few weeks ago that the Robin Hood needs barmaids.'

'I ain't 'aving you working in a place like that.'

'Mam, we're in no position to be choosy. Barmaids earn seven and six a night. If I can earn at least thirty bob extra a week, that'll go a long way towards paying all this off. We'll have to cut back on other things, too.'

'I don't know how,' May grumbled.

'No, neither do I, but we'll have to.'

'Well, me overtime should pick up again soon. That'll help, won't it?' May offered.

Jenny smiled. 'That's the spirit, Mam.'

'But what about Alan?'

Jenny stiffened. 'What about him?'

'I don't think he'll like you barmaiding.'

'What I do is none of Alan's business. We're finished.'

'Finished?' May's eyes were questioning. 'Did he try and force you into doing summat . . .'

'No, Mam,' Jenny erupted. 'He did no such thing. Please don't think of him like that,' she cried.

'Well, he must 'ave done summat bad for you to act like this. So what happened?' May demanded. 'I know summat did. Now I've told yer my secret, you tell me yours.'

Jenny took a deep breath, her eyes icy. 'Why did something have to happen, Mam? Can't it just be that we weren't suited?' Her tone was firm. 'And that's what I realised that night, that we weren't suited. We're finished for good and that's the end of it.'

May looked at her, knew her daughter was lying, but also knew that whatever had caused her to act this way was going to remain a secret so there was no point in pursuing the matter. 'Suit yerself,' she said, and gave a sudden smile. 'Thanks fer 'elping me with all this money business. It's a weight lifted, you knowing. Right,' she said, looking up at the clock. 'Look at the time. I'd better get a move on.'

Jenny looked up at her, bewildered. 'But we haven't finished sorting this business out yet, not properly. Anyway, where are you going, Mam?'

'Out. It's Wednesday. I've a date with Paul ternight and if I don't hurry I'll keep him waiting. Can't do that to the man I'm gonna marry, can I?' said May, her eyes sparkling happily.

Jenny froze. That terrible problem had momentarily slipped her mind. Now it came back full force. Jumping up, she went over to her mother and grabbed her arms, gripping them tightly. 'Mam . . .'

'What?' May cried, shocked. 'Get off,' she shouted, wrenching her arms free and giving them a rub. 'What's got into you, gel? Look what yer've done, you've bruised me.'

'I didn't mean to, Mam, I'm sorry. It's just that I need to talk to you. It's about . . . about . . .'

'About what?' May demanded.

Jenny stared at her.

'Well?'

'Er . . .' She stopped abruptly and gulped, fighting for the right words. 'Er . . .'

'You sound like a stuck record, Jenny. Fer God's sake, spit it out. I ain't got all night.'

Jenny stepped backwards, clasped her hands tightly and took a deep breath. 'It's about Pa—'

Just then the letter box on the front door rattled.

Jenny jumped.

'A'you expecting anyone?' May asked.

She shook her head.

'Well, I ain't. Anyway what were yer about ter tell me that was so important?'

'About . . .'

The letter box rattled again.

'Oh, fer God's sake, go and answer the door, Jenny. If it's anyone fer me, tell 'em I ain't receiving visitors.'

'Mother, please stay there, I really do need to talk to you.'

Jenny ran down the passageway, fully intent on getting rid of whoever it was so she could resume her painful conversation with her mother. She couldn't bear the thought of Alan's father making a fool of her mother any longer. She had made up her mind to get the dreadful deed over with tonight.

She was taken aback to see a beaming Herchell and Blossom standing before her. Blossom had Billy Jenny cradled in her arms while Herchell was carrying a covered enamel dish on one hand and a brown carrier bag in the other.

'Oh!' Jenny exclaimed.

Herchell's face fell. 'We called at the wrong time, Jenny?' he asked, noting the preoccupied expression on her face.

'Oh, no, Herchell, not at all. It's lovely to see you both.'

He sighed, relieved. 'Mr Wadham told us he sent you home 'cos of your cold, Jenny, so Blossom and me bring things to help make you better.'

'I made ackee and butter bean soup,' Blossom said proudly. 'I've never made soup before. I made up the recipe myself. It'll warm you. Take the chill off your chest.'

'Oh, that's very good of you,' Jenny said sincerely.

'And I brought me rum,' said Herchell. 'You got milk, Jenny?'

She frowned, puzzled. 'Milk? Yes, I think we've some left.'

'Good. Rum and milk and a good stirrin' a sugar'll help you sleep. It's an old Jamaican remedy.'

'Is it?' Blossom asked her husband, her beautiful dark face serious. 'I knows all dem recipes and I never heard that one. I happen ter think it's a good excuse for you to join Jenny in a glass.'

Herchell laughed. 'Can't fool my Blossom none, can I? Er . . . can we come in then, Jenny?'

'Pardon? Oh! I'm so sorry,' she said, standing aside, realising her talk with her mother was not going to happen tonight. Part of her was relieved that she hadn't to face it, the other part annoyed, wanting to get it over with. 'I'm forgetting myself. Please come in. Here, let me take Billy Jenny for you,' she said, holding out her arms.

May greeted them warmly as they all arrived in the back room. 'Ah, she's gettin' a right bonny gel, ain't she, Blossom?' she said, admiring the baby Jenny was rocking in her arms. 'Just look at them eyelashes. Give me eye teeth for them, I would. It's hell trying to get mascara on my sparse offerings.'

'You've lovely eyelashes, Mam,' Jenny said.

'Oh, not bad, I s'pose, but not compared to those I ain't,' she said enviously. 'Anyway, I'm glad you've all come, be nice company for Jenny. You'll not mind me, will yer, but I'm off out. Got a date wi' me future husband,' she said excitedly. 'You all 'ave a nice evening and don't wait up fer me, Jenny,' she said, disappearing from the room.

Jenny sighed in despair.

'Anyt'ing wrong?' Blossom asked her, gently. 'Only your pretty face is all screwed up. My mammy used to tell me pulling faces like that frightened our guiding spirits away.' She smiled kindly at Jenny. 'If what Herchell tells me is true and you and your boyfriend had a fallin' out, then you'll need all your guiding spirits to love and support you through the pain. That's better. Now you want to talk about it, Jenny? I'm a good listener.'

Jenny looked at the woman she was becoming firm friends with. If only she could unburden herself. 'Thanks for your kindness, Blossom, but there's nothing to talk about. Now you take the baby and I'll mash you a nice cup of tea. Then you can tell me all that's been happening since I saw you last week.'

Daniel stopped dead in front of the showroom window and gazed longingly at the Humber Saloon inside. Over the last few weeks he had test driven several makes and models but this car was the one that had taken his fancy. He'd set his heart on it. The salesman had been very disappointed not to make the sale. He wasn't to know Daniel hadn't actually got the money, despite leading the man into believing he had. But soon he would.

He rubbed his hands gleefully. Mr Willaby had called that morning to have a look around. Most impressed he had been. Daniel smiled. How clever of him to time the visit for when none of the staff was on the premises. It hadn't been easy but he'd managed it. The men were all out on jobs, overseen by Alan so that hadn't been a problem; Mr Skinner he had dispatched on a wild goose chase across town, looking for a firm that didn't exist, saying he had heard they were manufacturing a new padded type of packing crate he wanted checking out. Daniel would value Mr Skinner's opinion. The clerk had returned most apologetically after scouring the area Daniel had told him, having been unable to find the company. Daniel had told him that obviously, if he wanted a job doing, the only way was to do it himself. How he had stopped himself from laughing at the old man's horrified expression he would never know. Violet Cummings had been sent home ill even though the woman had insisted she was in perfect health.

Daniel had had one narrow escape. Just as he was seeing Mr Willaby off the premises, Alan had returned to collect some extra packing cases needed for a job they were doing.

'Who was that?' he had asked after Mr Willaby had gone.

Daniel had told him the truth. Well, partly.

'The bank manager. Look, son, I've pursued your plan for expansion but the bank isn't willing to take the risk. It's known that you'll be taking over shortly, and your inexperience worries them. They thought your plan was good but want to wait until you've been at the helm for a while, proving yourself. You can't blame them.' He placed a fatherly arm around Alan's shoulders. 'He said he'll reconsider again in six to nine months' time, if you still want to go ahead. I'm sorry, son, but that's the way it is. I was going to tell you tonight at home.'

Daniel hadn't even the grace to blush at the look of acute disappointment on his son's face or his reply. 'That plan was solid and the bank would have got every penny of their money back. Grandad used them for years, was very friendly with Mr Cox. He knows Grandad taught me well so how could he say he's worried about my inexperience? Anyway, that man wasn't Mr Cox.'

'He's retired,' Daniel said without hesitating. 'That's the new chap who's taken over. I thought he was a decent type. Seemed to know what he was talking about, and I've no doubt in six months he'll give you what you ask for. Have patience, son. Now, I've some work to be getting on with.'

And he had. Looking over some details of premises he had been sent, private and confidential, from an agent in Leeds. The premises looked ideal for his new business. Daniel's only problem was whether to buy the yard outright for the sum of four thousand pounds, or just rent, leaving him with more money in his pocket to buy himself luxuries. Pity he had this problem, he thought. Ideally he would have liked to have reaped enough from Collier's not to have to work at all. But he mustn't grumble. What he was going to get was better than being beholden to his son for the rest of his life.

A noise from across the road made him turn and he watched as, laughing and joking, three men tumbled out of the public house across the road. The aroma of best bitter wafted up Daniel's nostrils and he sniffed appreciatively. He pulled his cuff up and glanced at his watch. He was late for meeting May. Suddenly the allure she held for him started to evaporate. He felt he couldn't be bothered with her any more. Having an affair held no more excitement for him. Contemplating his new future and all it entailed did. He couldn't do that with May

377

whining on about the day when they could be together.

God, that woman was thick to think a man like him would really settle for someone like her. Why she had never questioned the seedy places he had taken her to or the dark corners where they had sat was beyond him. Daniel had had a good time, though. But now she had served her purpose. She had seen him through a period of limbo while his plans had been made. Now it was time for them to part and tonight was as good a time as any.

Without another thought for May, he squared his shoulders, walked across the street and into the pub.

Jenny raised her head and listened as the front door unexpectedly opened and shut and May's heels pattered across the worn passageway linoleum.

'Excuse me a minute,' she said to Blossom and Herchell as she got up from her chair.

'Mam,' she said, meeting her mother halfway down the passage. 'Why are you home so early?' She knew by May's manner that something was wrong.

'He din't come,' she said brokenly.

Jenny's heart leaped. 'Maybe it's over and he didn't want to tell you?'

'Why d'yer say that?' May cried, hurt. 'His mother must be ill and he was called 'ome, that's why he didn't show. Never got time to get a message to me. He will, you'll see.'

It was then Jenny noticed the tears of disappointment glistening in her eyes and despite desperately wanting this relationship to be over, to save her the awful task of telling her mother the truth about the man she had fallen in love with and pinned all her future dreams on, she hated to see May so upset and her heart went out to her. 'Oh, Mam,' she said tenderly. 'These things happen, don't they?' And although she prayed he wouldn't, she said, 'I expect he'll be in touch soon. Come and join us. Herchell's brought his bottle of rum.' She hoped this news would cheer her mother up.

But it didn't. May sniffed and shook her head. 'I'm going ter bed, Jenny. Tell Blossom and Herchell I've a headache or summat. I'll see you in the morning.' She pecked Jenny on the cheek. 'Good night, lovey.'

She watched sadly as her mother plodded dispiritedly up the stairs. Then a great surge of anger against 'Paul Smith' filled her being. Blast you, she inwardly screamed. I hope wherever you are something terrible happens to you for the misery you've caused my mother. And Alan and me too. And his poor unsuspecting mother.

# Chapter Thirty

Four nights later Sandra Budgins looked at the new barmaid gloatingly. 'Well, how the mighty have fallen,' she said, smirking wickedly. 'Weren't so long back, Jennifer Jeffries, you said you'd never be seen dead in the Robin Hood. I dunno, the poor Jeffries family seem to be havin' their fair share of troubles just lately. First yer gets the bailiffs calling. Now I suspect you've lost yer job again and had ter lower yerself to working 'ere. And me mam told me your fella's given you the push, and your mam's has too by all accounts. Don't 'ave much luck, the pair of yer, do yer? Tut-tut, whatever next?'

In her effort to control her anger at Sandra's sniping, Jenny bit her tongue. She felt a sharp sting from the gash and grimaced at the taste of her own blood. But it wouldn't do to retaliate, which was exactly what Sandra was aiming for. Jenny knew without a doubt the other girl didn't want her here, felt mortally threatened by her since her position as the pretty young barmaid all the men lusted after was in grave danger now Jenny was around. But she needed this job to help get the Jeffries out of the financial trouble they were in and she wasn't about to lose it by being baited by a neighbour's spiteful daughter.

Jenny forced a sweet smile on to her face as the landlord appeared.

'All right, girls?' he asked.

Still smiling, she nodded. 'Yes, thank you. Sandra's doing a great job of showing me the ropes, aren't you, Sandra? But I have to admit she's so good I doubt I'll ever come close to her. Let me assure you, though, I'll do my best, Mr Coleman.' She turned and looked Sandra straight in the eye. 'You were telling me about the different beers, I believe.'

How Jenny stopped herself from laughing at the look of complete and utter hatred on Sandra's face, she would never know.

# Chapter Thirty-One

'Hello, Alan. What a nice surprise. I was wondering when I'd see you. Come in and sit yourself down. I'll make you a cuppa.'

'I'm not disturbing you, am I, Uncle Bill?'

'Not at all, son,' he said, rising from his chair. 'To be honest, I'd welcome your company. I've been sitting here worrying.'

'Oh?'

'Just about what I've taken on. Hoping I've not bitten off more than I can chew, so to speak. I've never borrowed money in my life and this loan means I'll be in debt to the tune of nearly eight hundred pounds. I've only borrowed five but you can't forget the interest, can you? Still, I've done it now. Mr Willaby contacted me this morning and said the loan had been agreed and I can expect the draft about Thursday next week. To be honest, I didn't know whether to jump for joy or cry with the burden.' Bill's face lit up excitedly. 'Mind you, everything looks very promising.

'As soon as Mr Willaby gave me the news I confirmed our purchase of two new vans. Well, second-hand they are, but new to me. I take delivery as soon as I hand over the money. And I asked the garage to book my old lorry in for a good overhaul, get her as much up to scratch as I can afford. Then I made definite commitments to take on Wally and Bert. So that's my workforce at full strength. Two men to each vehicle and the lorry spare for such things as trips to the scrapyard. Then I signed the contracts I'd been sitting on until I knew the bank's decision, to deliver urgent orders for two big hosiery concerns whenever and wherever they want, and I've placed a new advert in the *Leicester Mercury* informing possible customers of our new operations, namely that Wadham's are no longer just a little local company but a country-wide outfit. We'll go any distance. And as soon as I can afford it I'm going to see about renting some better premises, lift the image of the company.

'So you see why I'm worried, Alan. Not only is all this going to take meticulous planning when the jobs come in, I have to make sure my costings are spot on to be competitive yet still make enough profit to keep it all going.' He paused and drew breath. 'And I shouldn't be telling you all this, being's we're rivals.'

'But you trust me, Uncle Bill, don't you? We're talking as uncle and nephew and what's said between us does not go beyond these walls.'

Bill smiled warmly at him. 'My sentiments exactly.' He tilted his head and looked at Alan closely. 'You know, it's strange but I feel I've known you all your life. We get on well, don't we?' He slapped Alan affectionately on the shoulder. 'You're a good lad, I know your father must be proud of you. Now, any news on your plans? Has your father made a decision yet on whether to go ahead or not?'

Alan shook his head and proceeded to tell Bill what Daniel had told him. 'I was very disappointed but, as Dad says, what's six months? I've just got to be patient. I know people think I'm young but my plans are sound and it's the way forward for Collier's.'

'I've no doubt you're right. But you can't blame the bank for being cautious. How are things with the business? Has the financial situation improved any since I saw you last week?'

'Father keeps those things very much to himself. I could be wrong but I get the feeling he still thinks of me as a youngster not up to handling that side of things. But I am. Right from when I could walk I spent a lot of time with my grandad. Over the years he taught me all the ins and outs. There's not much I don't know about the removals business. I know as much about the financial side as I do the actual labour. So there's a lot I could help Dad with, if only he would let me. Things will change, I'm sure, when I surprise him with a partnership on my birthday. I'll be able to take some of the burden off him then. I hope he'll be pleased.'

'I'm sure he will be, Alan. He'll be absolutely delighted, I feel positive he will. I know I would.'

Alan smiled. 'I was on the verge of telling him when he passed on the verdict of the bank. I feel sure their decision would have been different if they'd known he was still going to have a hand in running things, but I just didn't want to spoil my surprise. I suppose it was a bit bad of me to let Dad believe I was upset at having to wait six months to begin our expansion, but I hope once our partnership is known to him he'll approach the bank again.' He sighed. 'I must admit, Uncle Bill, that Dad's worries about the business confuse me. We seem to be as busy as we've ever been and sorely miss Sid, Bert and Wally. I'm having a hell of a job juggling the jobs so we can cope with the work. But, to be honest, I'm glad it's taking so much of my energies. It stops me from thinking so much about Jenny.'

Bill had wondered when she was going to be brought into the conversation.

'How . . . how is she?' Alan tentatively asked.

Bill shrugged his shoulders. 'I have to say, she appears her usual self.'

'Oh! Has . . . er . . . she mentioned me at all?'

'No. I'm sorry, Alan.'

'Oh, well, I was hoping things might have altered but she spelled out very clearly to me in her letter that I wasn't for her. Just what she meant by that I still don't understand, but I have to accept we're finished and that's that. I'll always love her though, Uncle Bill. I'll never find another like her.'

Bill knew exactly what he meant. Alan's own mother was his own only true love. No matter who came along afterwards, they never quite compared. Unfortunately history seemed to be repeating itself to a certain extent. Uncle and nephew had lost the love of their lives, due to circumstances beyond their control, and both would have to live with the aftermath. Although Bill did hope that Alan's situation might have a happy ending, given time.

'I didn't come here to pump you about Jenny, Uncle Bill,' he was saying. 'I purposely timed my visit for when I knew she'd have gone home. I came to see *you*. I never meant to bring her into our conversation, it just sort of happened. I couldn't help myself, I'm sorry. I shan't do it again.'

'No apology necessary. I understand. Anyway, how do you fancy joining your old uncle for a drink?'

Alan appraised him for a moment. How fortunate he was that he had found his uncle. Their relationship was still very new, there was much they still had to learn about each other, but Alan already felt his uncle was playing an important role in his life. He suddenly realised he wished his own father was more like his brother in nature. Bill was everything his father was not. Then guilt rose within him for having these feelings. Alan loved his father and it wasn't right he should be wishing he was like someone else. But wouldn't it be great, he thought, if somehow he could bring his parents and Bill together, get them to put the past behind them and be a family again? But that was for the future. As his Uncle Bill had said the night Alan had revealed his identity, one step at a time.

# Chapter Thirty-Two

Mr Willaby replaced the telephone receiver back in its cradle and sighed in exasperation. That man was becoming the bane of his life. For the last week, since he had confirmed the bank's agreement to make the loan, Daniel Wadham had called at least twice a day to see how matters were progressing and demanded to know precisely when he would have the bank draft in his hands. Each time Mr Willaby had very patiently told his caller that all was progressing smoothly, that banks had their age-old rules and regulations which had to be adhered to. Today he had added that all he was waiting for now was the return of the legal documents endorsed by head office, which he expected today, then he could authorise his clerk to make out the bank draft and it would be dispatched by messenger first thing in the morning.

He pressed an intercom switch on his desk and summoned his chief clerk, a Mr Randall.

'Ah, Randall, I've just had Mr Wadham on the telephone again, can you believe? Has the documentation in respect of his loan been received back from head office yet?'

Mr Randall nodded. 'I've just opened the post, Mr Willaby, and yes, it's here.'

'Thank goodness for that. I'll be glad to see the back of that man, he's becoming a nuisance. Get his draft made out and I'll sign it. And, Mr Randall, make doubly sure Harold delivers it before he does any other errands in the morning.'

'I will, Mr Willaby. Oh, and the documents have also been returned for the other Mr Wadham's loan. It's all in order, too.'

'Good. Then get that bank draft made out to him and it can be delivered tomorrow. Strange that, don't you think, Mr Randall? That the bank should have requests at the same time for loans from two people with the same name and, interestingly, both in the removals business? I wonder if they're related by any chance? Not that it matters. Oh, by the way, how's the new junior shaping up?'

Mr Randall grimaced. 'She's not, Mr Willaby. I'm most concerned that she never seems to have her mind fully on the job. It took her all of yesterday afternoon to type a simple two-line letter and then it was full of mistakes. She's been with us two weeks now and hasn't even got to grips with the tea-making, let alone much else.'

Mr Willaby tutted. 'Youngsters today, I don't know. Heads stuffed with boys, I shouldn't wonder. And her mother such a nice woman. Keep your eye on her, Mr Randall. Don't give her anything more taxing to do than stamping the post and putting letters in envelopes. I'll have a talk to her, see if I can get her to buck her ideas up, that might do the trick. If she doesn't improve, well, I see no other option but to inform her that a bank really isn't the place for her to be earning her living. Shame. If she'd just apply herself she could have a good future with us.'

Later that afternoon Mr Randall placed two letters on the office junior's desk. Pinned to each was a bank draft, plus an addressed envelope. 'Miss Gates, please pay attention. After you've finished stamping the normal post, put these letters and bank drafts in their envelopes and place them in Harold's pigeon hole. Is that clear, Miss Gates?'

Sally Gates was gazing up at Mr Randall who at thirty-five years of age seemed ancient to her, wondering what he would look like sporting a 'DA' hairstyle just like her boyfriend Ronald wore, instead of his close-cropped short back and sides.

'Miss Gates,' he was saying. 'Are you paying attention to me?'

'Eh? Yeah, yeah,' she said. 'Yer want them putting in 'Arold's tray. I'm not daft you know.'

Taking a deep breath, Mr Randall turned and walked away. He sat down at his desk and immersed himself in his work.

At the other end of the room, having moved on from thoughts of whether a 'DA' would suit Mr Randall, Sally Gates was humming 'Blue Suede Shoes' loudly to herself, her mind filled with visions of the latest heart throb to have all the women swooning: Elvis the Pelvis. He was singing the song just for her. As she yanked the paper clips from both letters and separated them from their envelopes, just as Mr Randall had instructed, she arrived at the part in the song she could never remember the correct words to. *Why don't you . . . Why don't you . . .* Oh, damn, what comes next? she thought, annoyed with herself. Then it came to her. Of course . . . *Put on yer blue suede shoes.*

Still humming, she absently picked up a letter attached to which was a bank draft for five hundred pounds. It was made out to a Mr Wadham. She fingered the envelope. 'Mr Wadham' was the name typed on it above the address. She folded the letter and bank draft into three, slipped them into the envelope, ran the adhesive edge over a wetted piece of sponge and sealed it. She then repeated the process with the other letter and bank draft and duly placed them, as instructed, in the messenger's tray, thoroughly pleased with herself for carrying out Mr Randall's instructions.

# Chapter Thirty-Three

In his eagerness Daniel snatched the envelope out of the messenger's hand. 'About time,' he snapped abruptly. 'I thought you were supposed to be here first thing? I suppose you want me to sign for this?'

'Yes, please, sir. If you would, just there,' Harold the messenger lad said, politely indicating the correct place on his paperwork. In truth he'd have liked to have given this extremely rude man a piece of his mind for this most unwarranted attitude but it was more than his job was worth. Most visits he made resulted in a small remuneration – it was a perk of the job to which the bank turned a blind eye, but Harold could see he'd be stupid to hope for anything out of this man.

Without further ado he made a hurried exit, hoping his next port of call received him more genially.

After Harold had gone, clutching another letter in his hand, Daniel walked slowly round his desk and sat down. Holding the envelope in front of him, he stared at it for several moments. Inside it was the finance he needed to start his new life. He savoured the moment. Then, a smile twitching at the corners of his mouth, he picked up the paper knife and slit open the top.

Several moments later a loud cry of outrage had Mr Skinner running in.

'What's the matter, Mr Daniel?' he asked, deeply worried.

Eyes ablaze in fury settled on him. 'Get out!' Daniel spat.

Back in the outer office Violet Cummings asked Mr Skinner, 'What on earth was that all about?'

He shrugged his shoulders. 'I dunno but something's upset him.' He noticed a red indicator light on the office switchboard. 'Oh, he's on the telephone to someone. I wonder who?' he mused.

The atmosphere in the office of Wadham's Removals was tense.

For the third time that morning Bill popped his head around the door and asked, 'Has he been yet, Jenny?'

She shook her head. 'No, Mr Wadham. When Mr Randall from the bank rang yesterday afternoon, he said their messenger would be calling early but he didn't give an exact time.'

'Oh, I see. I'm just in the yard then, Jenny. When he comes, you'll give me a call?'

'Yes, Mr Wadham.' She looked at him. 'You've already asked me three times to do that. I know how important this is. I won't forget, I promise.'

He smiled sheepishly. 'I'm acting like an infant. I apologise, Jenny. It's just that as soon as the messenger's been, I can start to organise things. I can't tell you how excited I am about it. Right, er . . . I'll be out in the yard then.'

Not long after Bill had left, Owen walked in. 'Boss is driving me nuts. I wish that bloody messenger would hurry up and make his appearance and put us all out of our misery.' He walked over to Jenny's desk, pulled out a chair and sat down. 'So, what's new with you then?' he asked. He looked closely at her. 'I 'ave ter say, you look tired, gel. Not sleeping properly?' He eyed her knowingly. 'Still brooding over that young man?'

Jenny decided that if Mr Ford wanted to believe that, then let him. To tell him the true reason for her fatigue would mean divulging family problems and that she wouldn't do.

Jenny wasn't in the least bit surprised she looked tired because she was. Dead on her feet, if the truth be known. Four nights a week working at the Robin Hood as well as holding down her own day job, plus coping with her misery over Alan and her mother's moping due to the man she knew as Paul Smith's sudden disappearance, was beginning to tell on her. She had known working behind a bar wasn't easy, but until she had actually done it, she hadn't realised how hard it actually was. From the moment she walked behind the bar at seven o'clock sharp at the start of her shift, until nearly midnight after they had cleared up, she did not stop.

The pub was a busy one, its clientele rough working men plus a few shady characters. And the women who drank there were no shrinking violets either. All their language was peppered with expletives and demands for drinks came thick and fast, service expected instantly or all hell broke loose. It happened often enough as it was and a bloody punch up, several sometimes, was a nightly occurrence. But Jenny turned a blind eye to it all because at the end of the week, for her four nights' hard labour, she received thirty shillings, every last penny of which went straight into the pocket of Snakey Lil to reduce their debt. Jenny had calculated that at this rate, and bearing in mind her mother's sporadic contributions to the debt, overtime permitting, it would take them just over two years to get all their debts paid off. That was, of course, not allowing for any major drains on their resources in the meantime.

When Jenny nodded her agreement to his suggestion that she was having sleepless nights because of her estrangement from her young man, Owen looked hard at the young woman sitting on the other side of the desk. She was a lovely girl, there was no denying it, and an asset to the firm. All the men, including himself, thought the world of her. She mothered them all, worried for their welfare, and did all she could to make their working environment a pleasant and happy one.

It pained him greatly to see the sadness in her eyes and an overwhelming desire to give her some fatherly advice, to try and do something for her, like she did for them, filled him.

He leaned forward, resting his arms on the desk, face filled with concern. 'Oh, Jenny love, I hate to see a pretty young gel like you grieving so badly. I know yer try to hide it, but you're not being very successful. Tek some advice from an older person, lovey. Don't let pride stand in your way. Do summat about it before it's too late.'

She gave a wan smile. 'It *is* too late, Mr Ford.'

'No, Jenny, but if yer leave it much longer it . . .'

'Please, Mr Ford,' she cut in. 'I appreciate your concern, but it's over between Alan and me. Sometimes the kindest thing is to walk away. It puts a stop to unnecessary pain.'

At her words, past memories flooded back to Owen, and his eyes glazed over. Hadn't he done that, walked away, and what had he achieved? Years of loneliness, pining after a woman he'd pushed away through his own stupidity. He hadn't a clue what had gone on between Jenny and her young man, but it was obvious to all of them that what she had done was something she hadn't wanted to or why was she suffering so much? It suddenly became important to him to try and make Jenny see the error of her ways. If she counted this as interference then he'd suffer her displeasure sooner than walk away, as he'd done in the past. Rather than live with regret that he hadn't tried to help her.

He clasped his hands and looked her straight in the eye. 'Jenny love, I'm gonna tell you summat I ain't never told a living soul before. I don't care if yer don't want to hear it, but if what I have ter say meks yer see reason, then that's all to the good.'

'Mr Ford . . .'

'No, Jenny, let me have me say. I've had me fair share of women, had lots of chances to settle, but I never have because

394

I was always comparing them, see. I've always compared them to the only woman I've ever really loved.' He gave a distant smile. 'She was everything I've ever wanted. A real looker. She turned heads she did. A tongue on her that could cut glass and have a grown man quivering when her temper was up. But she had a softness to her, too, a real kind side which not many people were privileged to see.

'We were engaged to be married, saving as much as we could for the wedding. I'll not go into details but summat happened involving her family which was none of her doing but she wanted badly to do something about it. It was a very kind thing she wanted to do, summat only someone decent like her would consider. I never even took time to think about what she was suggesting. I flatly refused to go along with it. Gave her an ultimatum. I was young, Jenny, full of me own importance, thought she should go along with my wishes, never acknowledged she had a right to her own. I stubbornly saw her actions as a threat to me manhood, stupidly thought that what she wanted to do would come between us. She stood her ground. I walked away. By the time I came to me senses, put me male pride aside, it was too late. She'd gone. I never saw her again, never got the chance to try and make amends, and I've lived with me regrets ever since.

'I'm a lonely man, Jenny. I live in lodgings with a misery of a landlady who wouldn't care tuppence whether I was livin' or dead so long as she got her rent. Me only saving grace is I've got a job I enjoy. I could have been very happy, Jenny. Had it all. I let it go by walking away.

'Now my story might not mek sense, might not seem to have anything to do with what's happened to you. All I'm trying to get across is . . .' He shrugged his shoulders. 'I dunno really what I'm trying to say. I just had a notion my story might have some bearing. Thought it might be stubborn pride getting in the way of sorting things out with your young man. If it ain't you, maybe he's the stubborn one.'

Jenny's eyes were riveted on Owen as she listened to his tale. If only, she thought, it was just stubborn pride that was standing between her and Alan. But it was something far greater – the loss to Alan of his respect and love for the man who had fathered him and, should his mother find out, the damage to her this knowledge would cause.

Jenny appreciated very much, though, the fact that Owen Ford had bared his soul to her, something she was well aware it must have taken courage to do. It wasn't easy admitting to a mistake. She knew he had taken the risk of belittling himself in her eyes, all for the sake of trying to help her.

What a lovely man he was, she thought. Just the kind of man she would have liked for a father. Pity her mother couldn't meet a man like him. If circumstances were different – Owen pining and comparing every woman he met to his long-lost love; her mother never quite having got over her father's death and leaping from one doomed relationship to another – maybe she could have introduced them.

A thought suddenly struck Jenny. There was something she could do which she felt sure Mr Ford would appreciate: offer him a home-cooked meal. By the way he had spoken she suspected his landlady wasn't up to much in that department.

'Mr Ford, I appreciate what you've told me and I'll bear in mind what you've said. It's just a thought, but would you fancy coming round for dinner one night? I can't promise what we'll have but it'll be hot and filling. Your company might just cheer my mother up. She's a bit down at the moment.'

Owen's face lit up. The last time he'd eaten decently was the day he'd left hospital. He had a gas ring in his room which was grossly inadequate. He lived mostly off tins of soup or things that could be cooked in one pan which usually ended up a sloppy mess. 'Why, thank you. I'd love to. About seven then.'

Jenny realised with horror he thought she meant tonight. At

least it wasn't a pub night, but the house was a mess, her mother having lapsed back into her slovenly ways and Jenny being so tired from her work regime and miserable herself only making token efforts at cleaning up; there was no food in the house with which to make a meal suitable for a guest, but above all she was terribly tired and had been looking forward to an early night. Regardless she planted a smile on her face. 'Seven would be fine, Mr Ford.'

He rubbed his hands. 'I'll look forward to it. Does yer mam like a bottle of beer? I could bring a couple.'

'She does and I'm sure she'd appreciate it.'

'He's still not been then?'

Both of them turned and looked across the room. Bill was standing just inside the door, wiping his hands on an oily rag.

'It's not yet nine o'clock, Mr Wadham. It's still early,' said Jenny.

'Oh, I thought it was later than that.' He turned his full attention to Owen. 'Do you remember the old generator that old man forced on us years ago when we did his move? Well, trying to keep myself occupied while I waited for the messenger to come, I started to tinker with it. Anyway I think I've got it working.'

Owen stood up and walked over to him. 'Have yer, boss?' he said, impressed. 'God almighty, I thought that old thing were only fit for the knacker's yard.'

'Well, if we can get it running smoothly someone might be glad of it, pay us a couple of quid. Only I need some engine oil before I can test it. Can you pop down to Tibby's garage on Belgrave Gate and get me some? A couple of pints should do.' With a twinkle in his eye he added, 'Well, I can see you ain't exactly busy at the moment if you've time to chat to Jenny.'

Owen grinned sheepishly. 'We were just putting the world ter rights, weren't we, Jenny?'

She smiled.

397

'Anyway, boss,' he continued, 'I offered to go and help Herchell and Sid on that move but you said you needed me here.'

'And I do. As soon as I get that money banked there's errands I'll need you to do for me.'

Owen eyed him knowingly. 'Oh. It's not what I was thinking then, that you still don't think I'm fit enough to be humping and carrying?'

Bill actually didn't but wouldn't upset Owen by saying so. He cared about the welfare of all his workers very much and didn't want Owen having a setback because he'd jumped in the deep end just a little too soon. 'Not at all, man. Just giving you an easy time of it before we go full fettle, all guns blazing. Which I hope will be any minute now,' he said, turning and looking across the yard in the hope of seeing the messenger arriving. 'Just a small can of oil, Owen,' he said, turning back. 'Jenny will give you the money out of petty cash. Oh, Jenny, I know you're busy tallying the books but would you run over to the shop and get me something to eat, please? I'm starving. In my excitement I forgot to have any breakfast this morning and my stomach's rumbling.'

She nodded, smiling. ''Course I will. Sausage and tomato cobs do you?'

'Smashing. Get me two, please. And whatever you want, Jenny. Owen?'

'Cheese and beetroot. No point having anything hot – it'll be cold by the time I get back,' he grumbled.

His staff departed on their respective errands, Bill walked over and sat down in his chair behind his desk. It was an old chair and not very comfortable. He placed his hands on his shoulders and gave them a rub. He was stiff with tension, in a state of anxiety, worried that at the very last minute something would go wrong and put a stop to all his plans. Deep down he knew his worry was unnecessary. The bank had no reason to retract their offer at this late stage.

'Mr Wadham?'

Bill's head jerked up to see a young man standing just inside the door. He was holding a long brown official-looking envelope and a clipboard.

Bill stood up. 'You're the messenger from the bank?' he said hopefully.

'Yes, sir. Bit late on me rounds this morning. After me first call me bike had a puncture and I'd no patches so I had to find a bike shop. Then I couldn't get the tyre off as I'd no levers. Had to borrow two spoons to do the job.' He grinned. 'Woman I borrowed 'em off weren't pleased 'cos I bent the handles.' He held out the envelope towards Bill. 'If you'll excuse me being in a hurry, would yer just sign here?'

Bill had never been so happy to sign his name in all his life. The precious envelope in his hands, he took a shilling from his pocket. 'This'll help pay for your puncture outfit.'

Harold's whole face lit up. 'Ta, Mr Wadham. Much appreciated, I'm sure.'

Alone again, Bill walked slowly around his desk and sat down. Holding the envelope out in front of him he looked at it for several long moments. Inside, on a single piece of paper, was all the finance he needed to move the firm of Wadham's Removals to a higher status and secure not only the future of his workers but his own as well.

With the tip of his thumb nail he slit the envelope open and pulled out the contents. His eyes immediately settled on the figure payable in the box at the bottom. His mouth fell open in shock. Ten thousand pounds! It was a fortune. There was some mistake. Then he noticed the name of the bearer. It wasn't his own. Ah, he thought. Somehow the bank had made a mix up and given him another firm's draft. Then the name registered full force. Collier's Carriers.

He frowned. Why would the bank be giving such a substantial amount to Collier's? His mind went blank for several long moments. Then, slowly, snippets of the conversation he'd had with Alan came back.

Suddenly the telephone shrilled and he jumped.

Going over to Jenny's desk, he picked it up. 'Wadham's Removals, can I help you?'

Bill heard a sigh of relief. 'Ah, Mr Wadham,' a voice on the other end said. 'It's Willaby here from the bank. Er . . . have you by any chance received a bank draft made out to Collier's Carriers?'

'I have,' replied Bill.

Another sigh of relief. 'Then I owe you an apology. I've just had another client of ours, coincidentally with the same surname as yourself, on the telephone and it appears he is in possession of the draft meant for you.' Mr Willaby declined to mention that his other client had bellowed his anger at the bank's mistake, demanding it be rectified immediately. 'We have delivered them wrongly, I'm afraid. I'll despatch our messenger straight away. I'm sorry for any inconvenience, Mr Wadham, and hope this little mishap will not deter you from continuing our business relationship.'

'Not at all,' said Bill. 'These things happen. Er . . . just as a matter of interest, this draft for Collier's, is it to be used for their expansion plan?'

'I'm not at liberty to discuss confidential matters, Mr Wadham.'

'I understand,' Bill said. 'It was wrong of me to ask.'

As he replaced the receiver he stared thoughtfully into space. Alan had told him his father had said the bank had refused them a loan at this particular time. That refusal had apparently been made due to Alan's taking over shortly and the elders of the bank being concerned about his lack of managerial experience, which they saw as a risk they were not prepared to take. Daniel had told his son the firm was in financial trouble and had made drastic cuts to compensate, much to the young man's bewilderment as the work coming in wasn't much less, not enough to warrant drastic actions anyway. And, Bill thought, Alan should know as he distributed the work amongst the crews. Why was Daniel acting so oddly?

But one question sprang out more clearly than the others. If it was true and the firm was nearly bankrupt, then how come the bank was lending it such a large amount of money? Banks didn't lend money to struggling firms. Besides, repayments on a loan that size would be enormous. It didn't make sense.

Then the only reason for all of this slowly began to dawn on him. Bill didn't like what he was thinking one bit. Couldn't believe it was true. But there was no other explanation for what he was holding in his hand. How did he find out whether his suspicions were correct? There was only one way. It was something he didn't relish, but something he had to face. If Daniel were doing what he suspected, Bill couldn't stand by and let him get away with it. He felt he owed it to Alan and also to Val to intervene.

As he picked up the telephone to inform the bank that he would personally arrange to exchange the drafts he muttered to himself, 'Dear God, I hope I am wrong.'

# Chapter Thirty-Four

Daniel's nerves were stretched to breaking point. Having lived on pure adrenaline since the bank had agreed to the loan, terrified a last-minute hitch could put an end to his plans, learning of the mix up of his draft with another customer's had almost caused him a seizure. Realising the other customer was none other than his brother had for several long moments induced panic. But then he talked sense to himself. It was just a coincidence. Pure chance that both brothers had used the same bank at the same time. Once the exchange of drafts was made his plan would be back on track.

And then he had fumed. Why banks went to all the time and trouble to raise drafts in the first place was beyond him. Why not just put the money straight into the account without all this antiquated palaver? It was just a pure waste of time in Daniel's opinion, something to keep lowly clerks occupied when they weren't making mistakes. He paced the office, waiting for the messenger to reappear. And wouldn't Daniel give him hell for the worry he had put him through when he did! Whether it was his fault what had happened or not. He'd better hurry. It had taken Daniel a lot of planning to ensure he was the only one in the office when the messenger called, making sure even at this last minute no questions were asked or suspicions raised until he was in the clear. Skinner and Violet Cummings would be back soon. And Daniel had a train to catch which, due to the bank's disgraceful conduct, he'd probably miss. And he had to visit the bank en route to the station to deposit the draft. Once deposited Daniel could have asked to withdraw the cash immediately, but he had thought better of that. The bank could be suspicious as to why he wanted the money all at once. So he proposed to do it in several small amounts using different branches in another town he'd chosen far away from Leicester, just to play safe.

He was so proud of his plan. In his suitcase, out of sight under his desk amongst a few clothes he'd secretly packed ready for his departure, was the firm's cheque book. Withdrawing the money could be done in any of the bank's branches in any town and he proposed to do it in Birmingham, a place far from his final destination of Leeds. Birmingham was a place large enough to keep the authorities searching for weeks but they'd find no other trace of him except for bank records of five separate two-thousand-pound withdrawals. Seedy backstreet bed and breakfast places didn't bother checking their guests' identities. And he proposed to change his name once he arrived in Leeds. Daniel Wadham would no longer exist.

Daniel was well aware the firm's staff thought he hardly did a stroke of work all day. He did work, all right, but on matters concerning his own future, not Collier's.

But then the bank called again to inform him that Mr Wadham would be calling personally to swap the drafts, and wasn't that kind of him? Daniel froze rigid at the news. When working out his meticulous plans he hadn't bargained for a visit from his estranged brother, nor for that brother to be clutching the financial means for Daniel's escape in his hand.

How he managed to contain his outrage as Bill walked calmly into his office he'd never know. Seated behind his desk, face stony, he said, 'You have something of mine, I believe.' And held out his hand towards Bill.

'I had expected a slightly warmer reception after all these years, Daniel.'

'Well, you expected wrong.'

'I *am* your brother.'

'A brother who's a thief.'

'Oh, Daniel, I never tried to take that money and I would have thought you of all people would have known that.'

'I made my feelings plain twenty years ago and they haven't changed. Now can we get this business over with? Just give me what's mine and go.'

'Yours? Collier's surely, Daniel?'

'Collier's then. That was just a figure of speech. Are you going to hand it over?'

Bill's eyes narrowed. 'What's your hurry, Daniel?'

'I want you out of here. I've got nothing to say.'

Bill slowly walked the rest of the way across the office and stood before the desk. 'Haven't you? Well, I have. Why did you cut us off, Daniel? I'm not so concerned about me, I can understand why you wanted to do that. You must have felt guilty about carrying on with Val behind my back. But Mother didn't deserve to be rejected by you and especially being refused the chance to get to know her grandson. How could you? You hurt her so badly.'

Daniel felt his temper rising. He hadn't time for this. 'Mother's dead so what does it matter?'

'It matters to me, Daniel. I want to know why you acted like you did and I'm not leaving until I do.'

Daniel pushed back his chair and stood up, his temper rising. 'All right, if you must know I was fed up, that's why.'

'Fed up?' Bill queried. 'I don't understand. With what?'

'Being second best to you.' His brother's face hardened, eyes glinting coldly. 'Everywhere I turned it was Bill this, Bill that. I followed in your shadow, from cradle to school to work. You got everything. The blue-eyed boy. People didn't notice

405

me when you were around. Can you imagine what that was like for me? I was always second. Even down to your cast off-clothes and cast-off women. I only got the job at Collier's in the first place because *you* got it for me. I didn't want to work here, but you saw to it I did.' Daniel was off now and could not stop himself from spewing out the years of pent-up grudges he'd harboured against his brother. 'You only wanted me working at Collier's so you could lord it over me. And gloat,' he spat.

Bill was staring at his brother in disbelief. 'Gloat? What do you mean, Daniel?' he asked.

He was losing control now, his rage fuelled by seeing the brother he despised. 'About *her* and all you'd get when you married her,' he shouted. 'Only you didn't get to marry her, I did,' he said, jabbing himself in the chest. 'One in the eye for you that was, wasn't it? Mind you, what you ever saw in her defeats me. She's a cold fish. I never loved her and I'm damned sure she's never loved me. But I didn't care. I'd finally won something over you, Bill, finally got what you should have had. The only problem was I left your shadow for Ernest's. I had to do what he said, live on the pittance he paid me, live in a house he provided. And I was expected to work my fingers to the bone for the privilege. But I was clever, you see. I knew if I played the dutiful son-in-law one day it'd all be mine and I'd get what I deserve.'

Daniel's voice rose to near hysteria. 'Only I was fucking wrong. This business should have been mine when Ernest died, but what did he do? Left it to my damned son, lock, stock and barrel, and not even a thank you to me for all the years of loyalty I gave him. Well, I'm not going to live in Alan's shadow for the rest of my life, reliant on him for every last penny he decides to pay me. And what makes it worse is that he damned well looks like *you*. It's like having you right beside me all over again.'

406

His eyes hardened maliciously. 'I was stopped from getting away once with the means to better myself. Well, no one's going to stop me this time. Hand that fucking draft over before I take it from you.'

Bill was staring at him, stunned. He couldn't believe the pent-up venom that was spewing from his brother's mouth. And how he was controlling his anger after the dreadful lies Daniel had told about Val was beyond him. The girl he had known had been loving and giving. But above all that something else Daniel had blurted out had hit Bill full force and a horrible suspicion was forming.

'Daniel, just what do you mean when you said you were stopped once from getting away? What did you mean by that?'

He smirked. 'You mean, you've never guessed, big brother? And you the clever one. Go on, work it out,' he mockingly challenged.

Bill's face turned ashen. 'It was you, wasn't it?'

Daniel laughed. 'So what if it was? You never suffered. I knew you wouldn't. The fuss soon died down. You've done all right for yourself, so what's your problem?'

'But you let me take the blame for something you did and let others believe you thought I was guilty, which only made it worse. If your own brother doesn't believe in you, then who will? I lost everything through you, Daniel. My job. My reputation. And the woman I loved. How could you?' Bill's face tightened grimly as it struck him that his suspicions regarding the draft were correct. 'The bank loan . . . it isn't for the firm. It's for you, isn't it?'

Daniel grinned wickedly. 'Well, how clever, dear brother. Yes. All for me. It's what I should have got by rights when Ernest died.'

'But it's *not* yours by rights. He left the firm to Alan. You're supposed to be protecting your son's interests until he's legally able to take over. You're stealing from your own son, Daniel.

How could you do that to him? I'm not letting you get away with this. I'll see you in hell first.'

Daniel smiled, eyeing him cockily. 'And how are you going to stop me? You can't prove anything.'

Bill stared at him, stunned. Daniel was right. He had no proof of his brother's intentions, only suspicions. The authorities did not act on suspicions, only facts. Bill's mind whirled frantically. He couldn't let Daniel do this to Val and Alan, he just couldn't. Then a solution struck him. 'I can stop you.'

Daniel laughed mockingly. 'You can't. The money's as good as in my pocket. By the time anyone finds out what I've done, I'll be long gone.'

'I can.'

Daniel's smirk faded. 'How?'

'I'm no great business authority but I know enough to understand that on Alan's birthday, when Ernest's bequest comes into effect, your entitlement to sign company cheques ceases automatically. Whatever authority Alan decides to give you when he's the firm's legal owner, every cheque you make out will need his counter signature. Even if he should make you a partner. That's the law, Daniel, even you can't get round that.'

His face was darkening thunderously. 'You think you're so fucking clever, don't you? I *know* all this. Why do you think I secured the loan before Alan took over? You still can't stop me. You can rip up the draft, burn it, eat it for all I care. I'll tell the bank you didn't appear, they'll put a stop on that draft and raise another. See, you're not so clever, Bill.'

'But the bank wouldn't stop that draft or raise another if I tell them I've given it to your son. That I couldn't find you and that he's in possession of it.'

Daniel froze. 'What?'

Bill smiled. 'Now you're not so clever, Daniel. I'm well ahead of you. And when I make sure Alan gets it, it will have a

408

letter accompanying it which you're going to write, Daniel. You're going to tell your son that you secretly arranged the bank loan as your gift to him on his twenty-first birthday, emphasising it's not to be banked until then. He's bound to ask questions about why you don't want it banked before his birthday but a good son never goes against his father. This way at least I'll know the draft will be safe in Alan's hands, not yours.'

Daniel glared at him. 'You can't make me do that,' he sneered.

'No, I can't. But if you don't, I'll personally go to see Alan and Val and tell them what you are up to. If they don't believe me all they have to do is ring the bank who'll confirm the loan. If nothing else, it will arouse Alan and Val's suspicions and they'll be watching you like a hawk. If you don't write the letter, I'll do that, you have my word. Concede defeat, Daniel. You are not going to get your hands on that money. And are you prepared to risk losing everything if your family discovers what you tried to do? They'll find out just how wicked you are then. They'll never forgive you, and Alan will let you have no part in the business. Stop this now, Daniel, and what you tried to do will remain between us, you have my word. I'm satisfied you won't be able to do anything in the future, not without full control.'

Daniel knew he was beaten. Clenching his fists, he snarled, 'You bastard.'

Turning away from Bill he stalked towards the window, staring blindly out, his mind whirling frantically, thinking of a possible way he could still try and salvage the situation. But Bill had him and there was nothing he could do about it. Then an idea came to him. This plan might have failed but that would not stop him from trying something else in the future. He was good at biding his time. He could do that again. With the bank loan, his son was going to build up this company and by waiting a while Daniel's reward could be far greater than a paltry ten thousand pounds. He could make sacrifices until then while he watched and waited and planned his next move. But he wasn't going to let Bill see he had won so easily. If his brother was expecting him to make such huge sacrifices then Daniel would make sure Bill did so too, by way of recompense.

He turned to face Bill, eyes glinting wickedly. 'You seem to be very concerned to protect my family's good name. Why? Do you think I'm stupid? You still love her, don't you, Bill? What's really important to you is protecting Val.' He sneered. 'All right, let's protect her. I'll write your letter on one condition.' He pulled Bill's bank draft out of his jacket pocket and waved it towards him. 'You give me this. If you don't, you have my blessing to go ahead and tell her. But that's what you're trying to avoid, isn't it, Bill? Because you know it will crucify Val to learn that the father of her son tried to rob them blind. And think what it'll do to the firm's good name when it leaks out.

'And it will, Bill, because I'll make sure it does. People will think if the father's a thief, maybe the son is too. Business will dry up and then where will your precious Val and her son be? Don't think I won't do this because I will. I've already got money out of the firm I made from my cutbacks. It's safe. Only I can touch it. It's nothing like the amount I'd hoped to get but enough to start me off somewhere else.

'But I can put up with my miserable life with that money topped up with five hundred pounds. I can buy the car I've had my eye on. That should help compensate me for having to endure purgatory with Val.'

And, he thought, he could pick up with May again until he found someone better. That should do much to relieve his boredom in the meantime.

'Val will continue to live with her nice husband. Alan will

have his honest father. Their and the firm's good names remain intact. The choice is yours, Bill. I think my proposal is fair considering what you're expecting me to give up, don't you?'

Bill couldn't speak.

'Well, brother?' Daniel mocked. 'What's it to be? Do I go with you to the bank to cash your draft and we all live happily ever after, or do you tell my family their father is a crook and let them suffer the consequences? Hurry up, I haven't all day.'

Bill raked his hand through his hair. Such a terrible dilemma. It was a small sum to some but so much depended on that five hundred pounds. And there was the terrible worry that without the work that money would have brought in he would still have to find the funds to pay back the loan. His loyalties were painfully divided. Without the money to fund his expansion, his employees – his friends – and those about to join him would suffer. If he refused Daniel's ultimatum it would be his beloved nephew and his mother, the woman Bill adored, who suffered. To his own bleak future he gave no thought.

His mind raced frantically, trying to fathom another solution, but there was nothing. He had no choice. His family came first. He sighed despairingly, hoping his friends would understand. But then, how could they when he could never tell them any of this? They would just think he had let them down. But he'd have to suffer that in order to save his family.

He raised his eyes to Daniel. 'Get paper and a pen,' he said, his voice flat. 'Then we'll visit the bank.'

# Chapter Thirty-Five

'What's up wi' your face?'

'Eh? Oh, hello, Mam. Sorry, I didn't see you. I was thinking about Mr Wadham.'

'What about 'im?'

'Just disappointed that he never came back to the yard today after getting the draft from the bank. It arrived while I was out fetching the cobs. I know it did because the empty envelope from the bank was on his desk. We were all so excited, and we'd all put together to buy a bottle of sherry for a toast to the firm's new future. We'll have to wait 'til tomorrow now.'

'Key?'

Jenny looked at her mother, puzzled. 'Pardon?'

'Have you your key for the door or are we gonna stand 'ere all night?'

'Oh, sorry,' said Jenny, fumbling in her bag. 'I thought you'd got yours out.'

'Yer know what thought did. Hurry up, Jenny, I'm desperate for a cuppa. What's in the bag?' asked May, noticing she was carrying a brown carrier.

'Oh, faggots and potatoes. Mam, I hope you don't mind but I've asked Mr Ford for dinner tonight.'

'Eh? Oh, Jenny, I ain't in the mood for visitors.'

'Come on, Mam, Mr Ford's ever so nice. Bit of company will do you good. He's going to bring a couple of bottles.'

'Port?'

'No, beer.'

'Oh,' May mouthed, disappointed. She sniffed disparagingly. 'I s'pose beer is better than n'ote. What's he like then, this Mr Ford?'

'He's nice, I told yer. He's the one who was in hospital for quite a while after having an argument with a wardrobe. You remember, I told you all about it. Mr Ford lives in lodgings and I don't think his landlady is very nice from what he's told me.'

'And you thought you'd give him some home comforts?'

'Doesn't hurt to be charitable, does it, Mam? Just be nice to him, that's all I ask. I have to work with him, remember.'

'I'll do me best but I can't promise,' said May, grudgingly. 'I knew a Mr Ford once,' she mused distractedly. 'He wa' nice too.'

'What, Mam?'

'Eh?'

Jenny tutted. 'Oh, it doesn't matter.' She suddenly wished she could somehow cancel the evening but it was too late now. 'Will you help me tidy up? I don't want Mr Ford knowing we live in a pig sty. Ah, here it is,' she said, finally unearthing the key.

'About time,' May grumbled.

'So, will you?' Jenny asked, inserting the key into the lock.

'Will I what?'

'Help me tidy up.'

'I suppose,' May reluctantly agreed.

Jenny looked at her, eyes tender. 'Mam, you've got to get yourself out of this mood. He's gone, whatever his reasons, and you can't brood forever.' She turned the key and pushed open the door. 'Get yourself out and find someone else.'

'Don't want to. I can't be bothered. Besides, I'm finished with men.'

Jenny shook her head, standing aside to let her mother through before closing the door. It still saddened her to witness

414

her mother's misery but better that than the truth coming out. As she closed the door Jenny noticed a note sticking out of the letterbox. She pulled it out, glancing at it as she followed May down the passage. 'There's a letter for you, Mam.'

'Who from?' she asked, arriving in the back room.

'How should I know?' Jenny said, putting the carrier bag and her handbag on the floor, the letter on the table. She sighed despondently as she gazed around. The table was still stacked with last night's pots, May hadn't bothered to clear after Jenny had rushed off to the pub. The grate was still filled with yesterday's cold ashes and the floor needed a sweep. And that was just this room. She'd better get cracking unless she wanted to be mortally embarrassed when Mr Ford arrived in just over an hour's time.

May snatched the letter up from the table. She looked at the envelope with just her name on it. 'Probably a bill for summat or other,' she grumbled, ripping it open and pulling the contents out. 'Oh,' she exclaimed.

Hands filled with dirty pots, Jenny looked at her. 'What is it?'

Shining eyes met hers. 'It's from Paul. He wants me to meet 'im ternight at eight outside the Stag and Pheasant. Said he's sorry he ain't been in touch but his mam's been ill.'

Jenny gasped and there was a loud crash made by the pots she had been holding. Before she could stop herself, she cried: 'Oh, God, no, Mam! You can't meet him. You can't, you just can't.'

May stared at her in astonishment. 'Why not?' she demanded.

'Because . . .' The fear of God flooded through Jenny. She had to tell her mother the truth. She couldn't just stand by and witness this terrible man make a fool of her again. 'Because . . . oh, Mam, I was hoping not to have to tell you this. But I have to.'

'Tell me what? Have you gone doolally or what?'

'Mam, listen to me. This Paul . . . Only he's not Paul . . . he's . . . Mam, he's . . .' Jenny's face screwed up painfully. 'He's Alan's dad, Mam.'

May was looking at her, stupefied. 'Don't be daft. Paul ain't married.'

'But he is, Mam.'

'What? You're lying. You've got ter be.'

'It's Paul who's been lying to you. He's married, Mam. There never was a mother, he was never going to marry you. He used yer, Mam.'

Stunned, May backed towards an armchair and sank into it. 'He's Alan's dad?' she uttered. 'No, I don't believe it. He seemed so honest.' She raised her eyes to Jenny, her face contorted in pain. 'I ain't a fool, Jenny. I can spot a liar a mile off. I'd 'ave known if Paul was lying ter me. You've made a mistake.'

'I haven't, Mam, believe me. Do you think I'd be putting you through this if I wasn't sure? I saw him with his wife. It was at the Grand. That's why I bolted. I didn't know what to do, Mam. I couldn't tell you because of what it would do to you. I was so relieved when I thought he'd gone off. I thought you'd never have to find out about him. I hated seeing yer so miserable but I thought it was kinder than you knowing the truth. And I couldn't tell Alan that his dad was a cheating liar. So I finished it between us. I had no other choice.'

May raised tear-filled eyes to her daughter. 'Oh, Jenny, what an idiot I've bin!'

'No, Mam,' she cried, kneeling in front of her mother. She took May's hands gently in hers. 'You're not an idiot.'

Her mother's eyes hardened. 'No, I ain't,' she spat venomously. 'But the likes of Alan's dad is, for messing wi' May Jeffries. And what's worse, that man has ruined your life too, Jenny, and I ain't having that. Excuse me,' she said, pushing her daughter out of the way. At the unexpected movement Jenny lost her balance and toppled over.

May jumped up, stepped over her prostrate daughter and retrieved her coat off the back of the settee.

'Where are you going?' Jenny cried, pulling herself upright.

'Never you mind,' her mother hissed, disappearing out of the door.

# Chapter Thirty-Six

Val walked into the bedroom and stood for a moment watching her husband pull a comb through his sparse hair. She took a breath and clasped her hands together. 'Daniel, do you really have to go out tonight? I was hoping we could talk.'

He turned his head to look at her. 'Talk? What about?' he asked disinterestedly.

'Just talk, Daniel. We never talk,' she said, walking towards him. She lifted her hand to flick a white speck off his dark jacket and smiled up at him. 'I thought it might help you too. You seem so preoccupied these days. I know I don't understand much about the firm's business but I'm a good listener.'

'Oh, for goodness' sake, Val. I have enough of the firm's problems during working hours. The last thing I want to do when I come home is talk about them. I've told you, I've got to go out. It's not much fun sitting in a gentleman's club listening to boring ex-military types going on about their experiences in the war, but it helps make good contacts. And, by God, Collier's needs some decent contacts, the way it's going. If I have to suffer for a few hours a couple of nights a week to make sure Alan's inheritance is worth having, then you of all people should be more supportive. Now where's my wallet?'

She sighed. 'On the bedside cabinet. Daniel, we do need to discuss Alan's birthday. It's next week, remember.'

As if he could forget. Retrieving his wallet, he turned to her. 'What about it? You're better arranging things. What do you need to discuss with me?'

She said, 'I just thought you'd like to know what I've arranged, that's all. I'll tell you when you're less busy. Oh, by the way, Father's solicitor called today. He tried you at the office but you weren't there. He needs to make an appointment with you and Alan to formalise matters.' Val was being very careful what she said, not wanting her husband to have the slightest inkling of the surprise Alan was going to spring on his father regarding the partnership.

Daniel's lips tightened grimly. 'Yes, that. Well, he'll have to keep trying until he gets me. I am a busy man. By the way, I'm buying a car.'

Val stared at him. 'A car! Can we afford one?'

'We can't afford not to have a car. It's embarrassing, a man of my status, having to turn up for business meetings on the bus.'

'Can we afford the repayments?'

'Val,' he snapped angrily, 'I give you your housekeeping. What I do with what's left is my business.'

Her mouth tightened in humiliation.

Daniel glanced at the clock. He'd need to hurry if he wasn't to keep May waiting. He had some making up to do to get matters back on an even footing between himself and her, until he found a woman to take her place. After the day he'd had, the huge disappointment he'd suffered, he felt he deserved at the very least an evening in bed and had booked a cheap room in readiness. Keeping a woman like May hanging around while he chit-chatted with his wife was not going to help his cause.

The doorbell chimed loudly.

'Are you going to answer that?' he asked matter-of-factly, wanting Val out of the way so he could splash on after-shave. The doorbell pealed again, longer this time. 'Val, are you going to get that or what? It's probably one of your WI women come to discuss jam making or jumble sales, I expect.'

'Oh, yes, I expect it is,' she said, disappointed that once again Daniel had dismissed her efforts to get him to talk to her about what was bothering him. He always made her feel that his life outside these walls was none of her business. As she made her way down the stairs it suddenly occurred to her that she was little more than a housekeeper to Daniel. Hopefully that would change when Alan took a larger share in the responsibilities and the pressure eased on his father. It had to, she didn't know how much longer she could go on living like this.

As Daniel descended the stairs the sound of voices reached him. Val and her visitor were obviously well into their discussions. It was on his mind just to leave without saying goodbye but then he thought better of it. He had to live with Val for the foreseeable future, no point in causing unnecessary antagonism. He pushed open the living-room door. 'I'm off then . . .' The words froze in his throat, eyes bulging in horrified recognition of the person sitting in the armchair opposite his wife.

'Hello, Paul,' said May, smiling sweetly at him. 'I'm glad ter see yer mother's recovered from whatever it was that was ailing her. She looks in damned good health ter me! Mind you, you did her an injustice. She ain't anywhere near as old as you led me to believe.'

Daniel's heart was thumping painfully, his mouth opening and closing fish-like.

Just then Alan walked in behind his father. 'Hello, Mum.' He spotted May and his mouth fell open in surprise. 'Mrs Jeffries!' he exclaimed. 'What are you doing here?' A great fear suddenly filled him. 'Is it about Jenny? She's all right, isn't she?' he demanded.

'No, she ain't all right. She's broken-hearted over you.

421

That's why I'm here. I think yer should know the reason,' May said evenly. She brought her eyes to rest on Daniel. 'Yer see, Paul, or whatever yer real name is, *I* can take being had for a mug but where me daughter's concerned, it's a different matter altogether.'

A fear so great exploded through Daniel that he shrank back against the wall, pressing his body right into it. He saw all his dreams, hopes, his hard labours of the last twenty years, crashing down around him.

'Don't believe her!' he screamed at Val. 'She's a liar . . . She's . . .'

May jumped up, her face contorted furiously. 'Liar, am I? I'm a baby in that respect compared to you. I don't think your wife will think I'm a liar, nor your son by the time I've finished. But you . . . oh, boy . . . they'll know all about you. You'll live ter regret the day you messed wi' May Jeffries.'

# Chapter Thirty-Seven

'Is there anything wrong, Jenny?' Owen asked in concern. 'Only yer seem a bit on edge.'

'No, I'm fine, Mr Ford. Just . . . er . . . disappointed Mr Wadham didn't come back before we all left. I was desperate to hear his news. And that we never got to give him our surprise.'

'Ah, I expect he was out and about sorting things, desperate to get started. That's boss for yer. I know I keep saying it but I'm so chuffed for 'im about all this. He deserves everything he gets, does Bill Wadham. Better bloke I couldn't be working for.'

Jenny smiled. 'Yes, me too. Another faggot, Mr Ford? You might as well, it looks like me mother's going to be longer than I thought.' Wherever she's rushed off to, Jenny thought worriedly.

'No, I'm full, thanks, lovey. That meal were grand, best I've had in ages. I couldn't eat another mouthful. I wouldn't mind another cuppa, though.'

'Yes, of course,' she said distractedly. She was desperate for her mother to return. May had been gone two hours now and in the mood she had left the house in, Jenny feared she had gone down the pub and was in the process of drinking herself silly. When she did that there was no telling what would happen. If only Mr Ford wasn't here, Jenny could go looking for her.

'I'm sorry I might not get to meet your mam, Jenny. Some other time, eh? Do you mind if I smoke?'

'No, not at all. Me mam smokes like a chimney.'

Owen sat back and contentedly lit up. It was strange, he thought. He'd never set foot in this house before but he felt so at home here.

Jenny looked anxiously at the clock. Just then she heard the key inserted into the lock and leaped up. 'Oh, it's me mam,' she cried in relief. 'Excuse me a minute, Mr Ford,' she said, rushing from the room.

She met May just as she stepped over the threshold. 'Mam, where've you been?' she demanded. 'I've been worried sick.'

May patted her hand. 'Putting wrongs right, me darlin'. Now I'll tell yer it all later. Get yer coat, you've a visitor.'

'A visitor?' Jenny said, bemused.

'That's what I said. He's waiting outside. So get yer coat.'

'Mam, our visitor is already here. Mr Ford's . . .'

'Don't worry about 'im,' said May, flapping her hand. 'I'll keep him occupied. Just do as I tell yer. In fact, yer don't need yer coat, it ain't that cold. Now go on, hurry, don't keep him waiting.'

With that she shoved Jenny out of the door and shut it after her.

Out on the pavement she stood for a moment, dazed, thinking her mother had gone mad. She felt a presence by her side and turned her head. She gasped. The man beside her was the very last person she'd expected to see.

'Alan,' she uttered. 'But . . .'

He took her hand. 'Come with me, Jenny. We need to talk.'

Mind whirling, she allowed him to lead her to the end of Slater Street where the River Soar ran by. Sitting her down on the grassy bank, Alan took his jacket off and laid it around her shoulders. He looked at her, his face grave. 'I have so much to tell you, Jenny, but first I want you to know how much I love you.'

'Oh, Alan . . .'

'No, hear me out. Please don't say a word until I've finished. It's not very nice, I'm still in shock from what I've learned myself.'

'Oh, God,' she groaned despairingly as the horrible truth dawned upon her. 'You know about your father. My mother's been to see you, hasn't she? Oh, Alan, I'm so sorry. I never meant for you to find out, really I didn't.'

'I'm sorry, too, Jenny and so is my mother. But we know now and we have to deal with it.'

'Your poor mother. Oh, Alan, how is she?'

'It's odd really but she's very composed about it all. I expect she's in shock. I have to get back to her but she sent me to speak to you, to sort things out between us.'

'She did?'

Alan smiled wanly. 'She's a lovely woman, Jenny. I know you'll like her. She can't wait to meet you.'

'So . . . what happened then?' she asked.

Alan sighed. 'I think it's best I start at the very beginning. Tell you everything.'

A long time later Jenny rubbed her forehead, confused. 'I can't take all this in. Mr Wadham's your uncle?'

Alan eyed her worriedly. 'I didn't purposely keep any of that from you, Jenny, or the fact I wasn't just a van driver for a furniture company. To be honest, I didn't realise you thought that at first but I can see how you made that assumption. We never really discussed my work, did we?'

'No.' She smiled distantly. 'We had too much else to talk about. I'm happy you found your uncle, Alan. Mr Wadham's a lovely man.'

'Yes. And it was all through you. If I hadn't met you I probably would never have got the chance to know him. Strange how things happen, isn't it?'

She nodded. 'I can't get over your mother being engaged

to Mr Wadham before she settled for your father. That story about the mix up over the money is awful, Alan. Fancy Mr Wadham being branded a thief. It's a mistake,' she said with conviction. 'He wouldn't take a penny from anyone, I know he wouldn't.'

'I know that too. Whoever was responsible for it will remain a mystery. But that's how my mother and dad got together. My father was a fool to do what he did. He's lost everything now.'

'Will your mother not forgive him?'

'She might have. But when my father realised he was losing the battle, he said things I know she will never get over.'

'What things?' Jenny asked.

Alan sighed. 'He said what did it matter if he'd had a fling with your mother? She had meant nothing to him, he was just having fun. He said my mother had never loved him anyway, only married him on the rebound when she found out Bill had tried to take that money. He'd turned a blind eye to that all these years so he saw no reason why they couldn't just carry on as if nothing had happened.'

'Oh!' Jenny cried. 'How awful! What did your mother say back?'

'She never got the chance to say anything. Your mother flew at him then.'

'Oh, no.'

'If it wasn't so serious, Jenny, I could see the funny side. She punched him on the jaw, bellowing at him that it was one thing treating her like she was a nobody but how dare he treat his wife and son with such disrespect? Or words to that effect, Jenny. Your mother's language was quite colourful.'

Her jaw dropped, mortified, finding no words that could excuse her mother's behaviour. 'Where's your father now?'

Alan shrugged his shoulders. 'Who knows? To be honest, at this moment I never want to see him again.'

She sighed. 'I can understand that.'

He took her hand in his and gazed at her tenderly. 'Now you know all this, Jenny, you'll still marry me, won't you?'

'Oh, Alan . . .'

'Shush,' he said. 'Just say yes, Jenny?'

'Oh, Alan, yes,' she cried, throwing her arms around his neck. 'I thought I'd lost you for good. I can't believe this.'

'Believe it, my darling,' he said, kissing her passionately.

After several long minutes she pulled back from him, breathless. 'I feel guilty for being so happy, Alan, when your mother must be suffering so much. And my mother too. I hate to say this but she really liked your father.'

'Between us both we'll help them get over him. Us together, eh?'

Jenny beamed.

Back at her front door he took her in his arms. 'I'll see you tomorrow then, my darling. You sure you don't want me to come in with you?'

'No, you need to get back to your mother. She'll be needing you, Alan, like mine will me.'

He kissed her again, made to depart then stopped. 'Oh, before I go. No more working down the pub.'

'You know about that?'

He nodded. 'I know, Jenny. When you love someone you find things out because you care for them regardless of whether you're together or not. Uncle Bill told me about your money problems. Between you and me he's going to approach you and see what help he can give you when he's sorted his own finances out in respect to his expansion, seen how his money situation is. Meantime I've been racking my brains as to how I could help you without your knowing. Well, now I can do it openly. We'll talk about it tomorrow. Good night, darling.'

She stared after him, watching until he disappeared around the corner, her heart filled with utter joy.

Not having her key on her, she walked down the entry and around the back. As she arrived at the door she took a deep breath, preparing herself to spend the rest of the evening comforting her mother. She expected Mr Ford had left by now. She'd apologise for her absence as soon as she saw him in the morning and hoped he would understand. She did hope her mother had been welcoming towards their guest.

Making straight for the back room, Jenny pushed open the door. 'Mo—' Her voice trailed off, eyes filled with astonishment at the sight that met them.

Standing in front of the fire, May and Owen had their arms wrapped around each other. They were kissing passionately.

Jenny couldn't believe what she was seeing. How could her mother do this to her? It was unforgivable.

'Mother!' she cried crossly.

They sprang apart.

'Oh, 'ello, Jenny lovey,' May said, straightening her clothes.

'Don't *Jenny lovey* me, Mam. How could you do this to me, Mother? Mr Ford and I work together. I'm so sorry, Mr Ford,' she said. 'What must you be thinking? I . . .'

'Oh, shut up, Jenny,' May interjected. 'If yer'd stop going on maybe I could get a word in. Look, there's no easy way of telling yer this but me and Owen are getting married. Ain't that right, Owen?'

Beaming, he nodded. 'Summat we shoulda done years ago – that right, May? – if I hadn't been so pig-headed?'

'Yeah, well, I hope ter God yer've grown out of that,' she said, chuckling. 'The only pigs heads we allow in this 'ouse go in the pan ter make brawn.'

A stunned Jenny was staring open-mouthed from one to the other.

'You . . . you . . . know each other?' she stammered.

'Bit more than just know each other,' May confirmed. 'And, Jenny lovey, there's summat . . .'

'Let me, May. Let me tell her?' Owen begged.

'Oh, go on then,' she agreed, smiling adoringly into his eyes.

'Tell me what?' Jenny cried. 'Surely there can't be anything else? I can't stand any more tonight.'

Owen's arms were held out towards her, his face wreathed in smiles. 'Oh, just come here, Jenny,' he ordered. 'Come and give yer father a hug.'

As Jenny's face filled with a look of astounded shock May suddenly realised that in her excitement at being reunited with the only man she had ever loved she had forgotten that her daughter had no idea who Owen really was. She leapt over and grabbed Jenny's arms.

'Oh, Jenny love, I'm so sorry,' she cried. 'But it is true, Owen is yer dad.' Her face filled with shame. 'I told yer he wa' dead 'cos it seemed simpler that way. Yer see, Owen never knew about you. I never told him. I thought, yer see . . .'

Owen joined them, standing in front of Jenny, clasping his hands together tightly, his eyes shameful. 'It was my fault, Jenny. I was so bloody incensed over the fact that May was proposing to raise Iris's kiddy as our own I never gave her the chance to tell me about you.'

'Yes, and I thought that if this was his reaction to raising someone else's baby, then what would he say when I told him I was expecting ours!'

Jenny was staring at them both. 'So . . . so who is Jim Jeffries?' she uttered.

May shook her head. 'He never existed, Jenny love. I know it was wrong of me but in the circumstances I just thought it was better for you to think that yer dad wa' dead, less painful for yer than growing up thinking . . . thinking . . . Oh Jenny love, can yer ever forgive me?' she cried, throwing her arms around her daughter and hugging her until she could barely breathe. 'I only tried to do what I thought was best.'

'Oh Mam,' Jenny whispered, 'I know you did.' She pulled away from May's grasp and looked at Owen, her eyes tender. 'We have a lot of catching up to do. But can I give you that hug first?' she asked, opening out her arms.

# Chapter Thirty-Eight

Wearily Bill unlocked the door to his office, flicking on the light switch as he walked in. His eyes immediately went to the bottle of sherry and mugs on his desk and with a heavy heart he knew what they were for. His friends had clubbed together, finding the money from their own meagre resources to toast his future success. They had done such a thing because they all cared for him, were happy for him, trusted him implicitly. How on earth was he going to tell them that none of it was going to happen, that there was a grave possibility he would have to let Jenny and Herchell go, and maybe Owen too?

He couldn't lie to them about the bank draft's non-arrival. Jenny would know it had come as he had left the empty envelope on his desk. He rubbed his hand despairingly over his chin. This situation was dreadful. What on earth was he going to tell them that they would believe without divulging the truth? He wanted to weep.

Suddenly another thought struck him. In his depressed state he had not remembered to despatch the letter and draft to Alan. He would have to arrange that in the morning or he himself could be charged with theft should Daniel choose to do so. With everything else, that he didn't need.

Face grave, he stared around him. A few hours ago what a bright future they'd all had. Now his employees' futures were in jeopardy until they all found new jobs, and he was faced with ruin. But, regardless, he still felt it was better than Val and Alan learning the truth about Daniel. He just prayed his brother had learned his lesson and would never, ever try anything like this again. There was one thing Bill knew for certain. Should he ever hear, through Alan or anyone else, Daniel's name connected with anything remotely suspicious he would be straight onto him and wouldn't be so lenient in his handling of the matter.

The creaking of the door slowly opening caught his attention. Eyes riveted on it, he slowly rose, thinking he was about to be visited by a burglar.

As he recognised the figure appearing through the door Bill gasped in disbelief. 'Val?' he whispered, thinking he was imagining her.

He could see she was greatly distressed, had been crying. 'Val, what is it?'

A beautiful face etched with grief looked up at him. 'Oh, Bill, I'm so sorry,' she uttered. 'I didn't know where to turn. And Alan spoke so well of you. I just hoped . . . just thought . . .'

All worries of his own flying from him, he protectively took her arm. 'Come and sit down,' he gently coaxed.

'No, Bill, I'm sorry, I shouldn't be here. I just felt a terrible urge to see you and before I knew it I was coming through your door. Please forgive me,' she said, turning away from him.

'No, Val, please don't go,' he begged. 'At least let me get you a drink.' Suddenly a terrible thought struck him. 'Whatever's upset you? Has it anything to do with Daniel?'

She turned back to face him, her expression bemused. 'Everything,' she said, confused. 'But you ask me as if you know already. Did you know that he was seeing Jenny's mother? Did you, Bill? But if you did, how could you? Of course, Jenny must have told you.'

Face grave, reeling from this latest revelation about Daniel, Bill shook his head. 'No, she didn't tell me. I didn't know about that, Val.'

'Oh? Then I just think it odd you should think I was upset over something to do with Daniel when it could have been anything. Oh, look, I'm sorry,' she said in distress. 'This isn't fair to you. You made it very plain all those years ago that you never, ever wanted to see me again. I shouldn't have come.'

'Val, don't go. Please.' Bill looked mystified. 'Er . . . what do you mean, I made it plain I didn't want to see you? You're confused, Val. It was you who made it plain you didn't want to see *me*. Daniel left your letter with my mother. She gave it to me.'

She eyed him, confused. 'No, you wrote to me,' she insisted. 'Daniel gave me *your* letter. Oh!' she exclaimed as the horrible truth struck her. 'Oh, no. No, he didn't do that to us both . . . Oh, Bill, I can't bear it. I've thought all these years you tried to take that money in order to get away from me. That's what the letter said. You didn't write it, did you, Bill?'

He shook his head. 'No, Val, not me. Daniel must have, like he did the one I received from you.'

She looked at him hopefully. 'So you did love me, Bill. It wasn't like Daniel said?'

'I loved you. The last thing I would ever have done was try to take money to get away from you. I was trying to earn money for us to get married.' He opened his arms to her. 'I still do love you, Val. Always have and always will do.'

She stared up at him for several long moments before she fell into his arms.

# Chapter Thirty-Nine

'Here they come! Here they come!' Jenny shrieked excitedly as four brand-new twelve-ton box vans drove slowly into the yard.

Hearing her daughter's yelps of delight, May ran out of the office to join her.

'Oh, I say. They ain't 'alf posh vans, ain't they?'

'Only the best for us, Mam.'

'Where's my 'usband?' May cried, scanning each of the four driver's cabs in turn. 'Oh, there 'e is,' she said, grinning on spotting him alighting from the lead van. 'Oi, Owen,' she shouted. 'Yer've 'ad yer fun. Come on, hurry up, we've gorra shop to open. Bleddy customers'll be queuing down the road for their second-'and bits and we're not there to serve 'em.' She turned to Jenny. 'And if I know Gloria she'll be first in the queue 'cos I told 'er we've a nice wardrobe just come in. I said she could 'ave it a bit cheaper, being's she's me friend.'

'Mother,' Jenny playfully scolded. 'You'll never make a profit on the second-hand furniture shop if you go giving everything away.'

'Oh, I ain't givin' it away, just knocking a couple o' bob off, that's all. Trying ter make up for all those cups of sugar I borrowed off 'er over the years. Come ter think of it, she probably owes me more than I owe her, so I'll add a couple of bob on.'

'Oh, Mam,' Jenny said, laughing. 'Just give the wardrobe to Gloria. We can afford it. We're doing so well.'

'Yeah,' May mused thoughtfully. 'Who'd 'a' believed it, eh? Two years ago there was me and you, both manless and penniless. Now look at us. Both married to our fellas and a nice house each with regular money coming in, enough to live on and a bit more besides. Who'd 'a' believed it, eh?'

Jenny beamed happily at her mother. 'Yes, who would have believed it?'

Owen came across to them. He kissed Jenny affectionately on the cheek, then put his arm around May, giving her a loving squeeze. 'Proud of yer old man, then a'yer May?' he said. 'Boss let me drive lead. Grand vans they are. Can't compare the old jalopy me and boss used for years to these monsters. And the load they can hold! Whole house in one go. Pity I . . .'

'Oi,' cut in May. 'We've bin through all that, Owen Ford. All the humping and shifting you're going to be doing in future is what's needed at the shop. Leave the youngsters to the removal lark. I don't mind yer helping out now and again when things are busy. But that's all.'

'Bossy, ain't she, yer mother?' he said to Jenny, a twinkle in his eye. 'All right then, Mrs Ford. Let's get off to the shop. See yer later, Jenny?'

'Yes, tarra, Mam, Dad. Oh, don't forget the new vans' celebration dinner Blossom is cooking us tonight. She's expecting us all at eight o'clock sharp,' Jenny called after them as, arms linked, they made their way out of the yard.

Bill came up to join her. 'Grand, aren't they, Jenny?' he said, gazing proudly across at the vans. 'Who'd have thought it? Me in partnership with Alan and the business thriving so much we've been able to clear the original bank loan and raise another to expand our fleet and take on more men.' He paused for a moment and wondered, not for the first time, what

Daniel had spent his five hundred pounds on. Used it to build himself a future or, as threatened, wasted it on a car? He pushed the thought away. It belonged in the past. 'And all in a couple of years.'

'It's only what you and Alan deserve, Bill. You've both worked so hard.'

'We've all worked hard. None of this could have happened without everyone here.'

'Yes, we all played our parts,' Jenny agreed. 'I can't wait for Saturday,' she said, smiling.

Bill's face lit up excitedly. 'You can't. *I* can't, Jenny. I've waited over twenty years for this day to come. I never thought it would. Val my wife, eh? Who'd have thought it?'

Jenny playfully nudged her future father-in-law in the ribs. 'I've seen the dress. She's going to look beautiful.'

'If she looks anywhere near as beautiful as you did on your and Alan's wedding day, then I'll be bursting with pride.'

Jenny smiled happily at his compliment.

Herchell ran across to them. 'Boss, I off then with Sid and Wally to do that removal. Van's great,' he enthused. 'And I never stalled it once on the drive back to the yard. Wait 'til I writes and tells me folks back in Jamaica about drivin' a brand-new van. They won't believe it.'

Bill laughed. 'We'll make a driver of you yet.'

'Oh, Blossom she told me to remind you about tonight. She bin cookin' all week getting everyt'ing ready to celebrate our new vans.'

'We'll all be there. Looking forward to it, aren't we, Jenny? And especially if you're going to promise to produce that famous rum of yours.'

'It's a promise, boss.'

'Oh, no,' groaned Jenny. 'Please watch how much me mam has of the rum, Herchell. You know what she's like when she's had a drink.'

437

'Yeah, she's funny,' he said, laughing. 'See yer later then. Oh, hello, boss,' he addressed Alan. 'I just off, see yer later.'

'Yes, see you later,' Alan replied. 'And tell Blossom I'm looking forward to it. I hope she's got ackee and boiled calaloo on the menu. I'm getting quite a taste for them.' He kissed his wife on the cheek and smiled at his uncle. 'Who would have thought it, eh, Uncle Bill? Nearly two years in partnership and look at us.'

'You've no regrets then?' Bill asked.

'None. I've never seen Mum happier. You deserve each other, Uncle Bill. You more than have my blessing. I don't wish my father ill. I hope whatever he's doing and wherever he is, he's happy. But he's only himself to blame for losing his family and his share in the business. I do feel guilty for not being able to thank him for arranging that loan for my birthday but at the time I was too angry about what he did to Mum. But . . . well . . . that's in the past.'

Yes, thought Bill, and much more than you know has been left in the past, too. Things about Daniel that Val and Alan need never know.

'I couldn't be happier with how things are, Uncle Bill,' Alan was saying to him. 'What about you?'

Bill smiled. 'Me too, Alan. Right, I've got potential customers to visit. I'll leave you to it.'

Mr Skinner popped his head out of the office doorway. 'Mrs Wadham, there's a Mr Coates on the telephone. Wants someone to price him for a regular weekly load to Sheffield and back. Oh, and Mrs Cummings told me ter tell you the tea's mashed.'

'Just coming,' called Jenny. She smiled up at her husband. 'Well, Mr Wadham, work beckons. Can't stand here chatting to you all day. Even if you are joint boss. And you've crews to organise.'

'Just a minute,' he said, pulling her into his arms. 'You are happy, aren't you Jenny?'

She looked her beloved husband straight in the eye. 'As me mam would say, I've landed the pound.' She smiled happily. 'Look around you, my darling. I've all this, all of our friends, but more importantly than all that, I've got you. What more could a girl wish for?'

# Out With The Old

## Lynda Page

Her daughter's wedding day should have been one of the happiest for Vinnie Deakin, but instead it ends in devastation when Vinnie's husband calmly announces that he is leaving her.

Vinnie tries to hide the truth from her workmates, but Betty Trubshaw isn't a fool. She's heard the rumours about Tommy Deakin and, when events take a dramatic turn, Betty's friendship gives Vinnie the strength to carry on. Betty's not the only one who cares about Vinnie – her neighbour, Noreen Adler, though brash and outspoken, surely means well; and her boss, Mr Hamlin, has always had a soft spot for her.

But sometimes people are not what they seem, and Vinnie must face some shocking revelations before she can trust again . . .

Don't miss Lynda Page's other sagas, also available from Headline.

'A welcome read for fans of Cookson and Cox' *Daily Express*

'Full of lively characters' *Best*

'It's a story to grip you from the first page to the last' *Coventry Evening Telegraph*

'It keeps the reader enthralled from start to finish' *Hull Daily Mail*

0 7553 0110 2

**headline**

# A Cut Above

## Lynda Page

For Kacie Cooper, life in Leicester in 1959 is almost perfect. Jobs are plentiful, shops are filled with the latest fashions and dance halls are packed with people jiving to rock 'n' roll hits. Kacie is the top stylist in a reputable hair salon and her machine-mechanic husband Dennis is dreaming of the big time with his band, Vernon and the Vipers. Only one thing mars her happiness: her parents' constant disapproval that she doesn't have a 'proper' job or a more respectable husband, like her sister Caroline.

But when Caroline turns up on Kacie's doorstep, asking to stay for a while, it's clear that her sister's marriage has been far from idyllic. It is a revelation that plunges Kacie's own life into chaos and threatens everything that matters . . .

Don't miss Lynda Page's other sagas, also available from Headline.

'Cookson/Cox aficionados who've missed her should grab this. Romantic and gripping' *Peterborough Evening Telegraph*

'It keeps the reader enthralled from start to finish' *Hull Daily Mail*

'It's a story to grip you from the first page to the last' *Coventry Evening Telegraph*

'Full of lively characters' *Best*

0 7472 6674 3

**headline**

# All or Nothing

## Lynda Page

Francine Champion and Stella Simpson have been best friends since school. Now, in 1950, the two girls – though different in many ways – are as close as ever. Frankie works as a car mechanic at her uncle's garage and is hoping to marry her childhood sweetheart Ian. Meanwhile, Stella has an office job in Leicester and is engaged to Ian's friend Roger. The future seems bright for the happy foursome.

But none of them bargains on Eddie Taylor entering their lives. His selfish ambition is about to change everything. His devilish charm and scheming lies will break one heart after another, destroying trust, friendship and love. With Eddie around, can Frankie or Stella ever hope to regain the happiness they once knew?

Don't miss Lynda Page's other sagas, also available from Headline.

'You'll be hooked from page one' *Woman's Realm*

'Filled with lively characters and compelling action' *Books*

'Cookson/Cox aficionados who've missed her should grab this. Romantic and gripping' *Peterborough Evening Telegraph*

'Full of lively characters' *Best*

0 7472 6669 7

**headline**

Now you can buy any of these other bestselling books by **Lynda Page** from your bookshop or *direct from her publisher*.

## FREE P&P AND UK DELIVERY
(Overseas and Ireland £3.50 per book)